THE LOST W...

B...

MW01129044

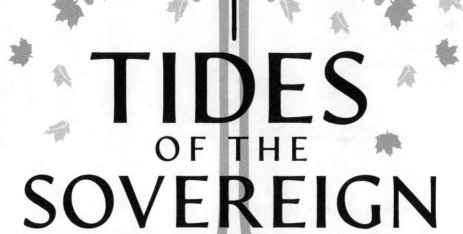

TIDES
OF THE
SOVEREIGN

KATE GATELEY

FriesenPress

One Printers Way
Altona, MB R0G 0B0,
Canada

www.friesenpress.com

Author photo by Ashley Marston Photography

Cover Design by Covet Design

ISBN
978-1-03-912658-9 (Hardcover)
978-1-03-912657-2 (Paperback)
978-1-03-912659-6 (eBook)

1. FICTION, FANTASY, CONTEMPORARY

Distributed to the trade by The Ingram Book Company

For Pierce and Noel,
May you always find strength in your intuition.

PROLOGUE

168 AD.

The entrance to the cave was located high above, within the Apennine Mountains, difficult to scale and impossible to find without exact directions. After a climb like that, Cassius had at least expected a ceremonial stone or epitaph to signal the terminus of his ascent. But there was nothing. Not even a sign to ward off approaching foes. Instead, all he found scattered at the gap between the here-and-now and the abyss beyond were handfuls of dried oak leaves. They crunched loudly under his sandaled feet, a stark contrast to the deafening silence that emanated from within the chamber.

However, he could still feel the place and its guardian. In the same way she could feel him. He *was* the enemy, but she would already know that; no need to mark the occasion. It was said the Oracle had perished ages ago, leaving behind her many scrolls to be interpreted by the bloated and thankless modern-day Romans. But he knew different.

He loathed them all, the men and women below. Their pompous impropriety and greed were pitiful excuses for *real power*. The stations they occupied were scarcely earned, and instead inherited each generation through flagrant nepotism. As a *true* Child of Rome, he had fought tooth-and-nail every step along the way for his survival and was well acquainted with his own mortality.

Yet, he was dying. They all were. The new plague rumoured from the Near East was making swift work of the Empire, decimating whole cities, their populations decreasing by the thousands every day. What set Cassius apart from their weakness and imminent death was that he knew about *magic*.

He had stumbled upon its existence years ago while fighting for scraps on the streets of Rome when a young boy, no older than ten, had stolen a meagre lump of bread from his fingertips. Hungry and outraged, Cassius had swiftly killed him. Strangely, however, he had committed the act without actually laying a hand on the boy. It felt like he'd gathered an invisible force in his palms and pushed it forcefully outward to snuff out his life. And it had felt *good*. That was when he first discovered that he was special. Different and gifted.

And now it all stood in the balance, but *she* held the answers.

There were many supposed entrances to the chambers of the Prophetess, rumoured to lead towards *truth* and *hell*. In future, he would come to equate the two as one and the same. Passing through the cool dark, he felt goosebumps spread across his sweaty forearms as he descended the tunnel towards the innermost chamber. The summer heat had reached its pinnacle across Rome, signalling doom amongst the masses as the plague swept through the legions. And so, this was his moment to strike. While the masses lay afraid, hidden and dying, he would rise to the top of the mysterious mountain and press the Sibyl for her truths.

It was immortality that he craved above all else.

Sifting through the endless gossip and propaganda of the state, it had taken him decades to gather enough information to locate this particular place. And even then, the entrance wouldn't show itself to just anyone; the place was enchanted, and only those with gifts like *his* were granted access.

At last, he had sought the advice of a purported Soothsayer who was in the midst of dying from the pestilence. Cassius had known immediately that the man held no *real* magic. Yet, in his final breaths, the man had uttered the directions needed for his ascent. He also offered a dire warning about the consequences of angering the Prophetess, outlining the importance of asking the *right questions*. At this, Cassius had plunged his tarnished dagger harshly into the man's side and left him to die. The man had outlived his usefulness, and no one could know his mission.

Travelling now through the Oracle's grotto, Cassius watched as unseen torches sparked to life while he delved deeper into the earth. The dense air grew more oppressive with each step, and weakened further yet by his burgeoning illness, his hunger for eternal life was the only thing left spurring him onward. Cassius breathed heavily through his teeth and wiped dried blood from his cracked lips; the tang of iron and bile was nothing compared to the taste of magic in the air. She was close.

After several more minutes of painstaking descent, he passed at last through a narrow archway into an almost womblike chamber. That was when he finally saw her.

Wrapped in filthy rags, the milky-eyed Sibyl was beyond ancient, practically withering away atop a circular stone perch. Flickering light emanating from a low fire shone impossibly through her as Cassius's heart pounded violently into his chest; she really *was* immortal.

The Prophetess gaped at him wildly in a toothless grimace. "You've come."

She slowly laid back onto what he now realized was a bed and opened her legs to him. Cassius felt a familiar hatred burn violently within. "You will give me the answers I seek, Oracle! No games!"

"Will I?" she said, her echoing laugh bouncing off the stone walls like a shrill chorus of her many voices throughout the ages. "You'll need to lie with me for that. It's been *so* long."

"I will do no such thing, filth!" he spat at her. "I demand the secret to your immortality!"

Face exploding with primeval anger, she transformed from woman to wolf before his very eyes, grizzled and horrendous in stature. He blinked several times, unable to distinguish between illusion and reality. "Enough with your tricks!" he roared.

Then, the ghostly she-wolf began to howl.

The sound was deafening, forcing Cassius to his knees in excruciating pain. He threw his hands up to protect his ears, but it was futile. "Stop at once!" Cassius cried.

But she did not. The sound grew more thunderous with each passing moment, and soon he knew there was only one way out; he must lie with the Prophetess and take her immortality for himself. At his advance, she transformed back into the Crone, emaciated and hollow. He felt bile scorch the back of his throat and swore to himself that, when he finished the task, he would dispatch of her for good.

During the ritual, she transformed once more, the blossoming curves of her body reminding him darkly of the *meretrices* from the brothels of his childhood. She was suddenly warm and succulent, a stark contrast to his dehydrated and disease-ridden mortal form. When his body shuddered to her surrender at last, he could scarcely hold back his own disgust.

But then, to his surprise, he felt his body healing as her essence slowly seeped into his core. She spoke intimately into his ear, the words tickling him with a voice that reminded him appallingly of his own *mater*.

With the death of the mother, a wayward ship never built to sail,
Will come the birth of another, a soul-forged gift of the Sun and Moon.

As the World Ruler reigns in his summer house, so the hourglass begins.
When the Sovereign accepts her destiny, midsummer bells will toll the end.

The Child of Rome has but one true enemy, borne of Crone and Celt,
Darkness walks a path destined to fail, should the hourglass run out.

And then the Prophetess began to laugh. The abrupt and maniacal sound pierced his ears like a flock of vengeful crows, mocking him viciously as he stood up, sweating and exposed above her.

"Fool!" she screeched, cackling in further delight.

"What is the meaning of this?" he said, fresh ire scorching within; the whore had tricked him.

"It is my final prophecy," she said, shunting the words straight into the heart of him. "At long last . . . I can die."

Cassius's wrath exploded violently outward as he tossed her to the floor. "Witch!"

All around, the room began to shake. He could hear the sound of cascading, rattling bones, and suddenly feared he would be buried alive. Somehow, she had barred the door with her trickery, creating an illusion to make it impossible for Cassius to discern which way was out. Panic rose in his chest, and he swallowed hard, noticing that his throat no longer burned with illness. He took several more steadying breaths as he continued to search the writhing room for an exit.

"Let me out of here, woman!"

He looked down in anger at the Prophetess' discarded form, only to discover she had transformed for a final time. Laying broken beside a small opening on the floor, she wore the face of a maiden girl, with her tattered rags now wrapped around her like gossamer. The hole revealed itself to be a hidden well-spring, trickling quietly and enveloping her in light. He watched in silent rage as she passed to the Otherworld, an innocent smile etched forever across her timeless lips.

The room stood still once more. Looking up as he wiped his brow, Cassius could now see the exit quite plainly before him as he took several more moments to calm his inner chaos. He could feel her stolen magic surging, almost pulsating within him, but knew it wouldn't last. True immortality wasn't hers to give, only a glimpse of it, a mere spark in the long dark ahead.

CHAPTER 1

I t was impossible to know when exactly in time my story would truly begin, or even worse, when it would end. That was the thing about divining, you could never depend on it when you needed it most.

Even my everyday magic had been nothing short of unpredictable as of late. In fact, if not for having to navigate the low-slung rafters and swaying stacks of mildewed boxes in my grandmother's attic, I might have missed sensing the enchanted quilt altogether.

I had already spent the bulk of a gruelling, hot August afternoon attempting to diagnose the source of last winter's leak. My back was sore, and my head throbbed painfully. Traversing through my grandma Gertie's clutter, I had managed to hit my head not only once but *twice* on the same cedar beam, knocking over an ornate floor-height lamp in the process and shattering glass across the dusty floor.

I was frustrated now. "For *fuck's* sake!"

Pushing the largest shards aside with my sneakered foot, I stood in the now-dry attic and rubbed my raw scalp resentfully while surveying the teetering landscape before me. I pulled my thick auburn hair into a loose knot at the base of my neck before continuing onward. Regardless of any irritation, the task at hand still bore significance to me.

Gertie had been adamant even on her deathbed that I needed to see to the roof repair before the rains returned over the darkening months ahead. During the final days of her illness, she had wandered erratically in and out of consciousness. Cancer, of course, took no pity on the old. Her speech had bordered on incoherent by the end, but about this, she had been perfectly lucid.

"Julia! Dearest, you *really* should see to that damned leak at the cottage, and before winter too, please!" she announced loudly and without warning early one morning, after a particularly rough night in the hospital.

I startled dramatically out of the awkward guest chair at the shrill cry of my name, having only just dozed off at my bedside vigil. I toppled over my half-full Styrofoam cup of cold coffee, knocking several foil-wrapped chocolate eggs onto the floor for good measure. Despite a splatter of pallid liquid across the only clean t-shirt I had with me, I burst into a fit of laughter at her absurd proclamation; I was overtired and perhaps a touch loopy myself.

"Alright, Gertie, I will. I promise," I said with a wistful smile as I took her withered hand into my own.

"Brilliant!" she exclaimed, before drifting back to sleep. Her British accent and eccentricity had grown more pronounced throughout her dying days, perhaps because she meandered through childhood memories during her increased spans of absence from this plane. She passed away shortly thereafter. But, somehow, in a delightful homage to her character, the roof repair seemed like her final dying wish.

Rubbing several aggressive dust bunnies out of my eyes, I strained my neck further, looking ever upward for the leak. I was beginning to doubt my resolve to find it within the next forty-eight hours. My only other choice was to abandon the house until Christmas break, inviting another winter of slow hydro-seepage and elaborate mould cultivation. While home repair was never exactly my strong suit, I had taught myself enough to get by when my late mother neglected the essentials, or when Gertie needed my help during one of my cherished visits on Salt Spring Island.

I was going to have to give it my best shot.

Still, I couldn't shake the feeling that things would be infinitely easier if I could access even a hint of magic right now. It had of course been *far* worse when my mother died; that was when my grandmother feared I had lost the gift altogether. No smoke, no fire. Nothing. This time around, the grief I carried seemed to snuff out any spark of magic I tried to conjure, regardless of whether I was trying to source it from within myself or access it from the outside world.

But at least there was a spark. Even if I couldn't call upon it now, my Bearer's fire still sputtered.

There was a great distinction in the world of magic between *Bearers*, more commonly referred to throughout history as Witches, and *Wielders*. Bearers were born with the inherent ability to carry and source their own inner magic. Wielders, while able to gather magic, technically never produced it from within.

Gertie used to sing a rather convoluted verse differentiating the two:

> *All Bearers are Witches, and all Witches are Wielders,*
> *but Wielders may be neither Witches nor Bearers.*

Speaking the words aloud, I was reminded of how complex the verse really was. In the simplest terms, Bearing was innate and Wielding was harnessed. The more complicated bit was that Witches could actually do *both*.

And *I* was a Witch.

I knew very little about Wielders, which apparently included sects like the Druids, but I had always trusted Gertie's word on their existence. What we did share in common, however, was that we all lived in secrecy. This fact made for a rather lonely existence for someone like me, who had just lost her last real connection to the magical world to cancer.

I recited Gertie's words under my breath several more times as I continued my lonely search. The verse reminded me strongly of the games-theory section on a long-since-discarded law-school admission test. I could see the abandoned stack of workbooks sitting in the corner of the attic by the door, their contents and my ambitions for law school all but abandoned when Gertie had first fallen ill in the new year.

Since then, nothing had felt right, like I was constantly wearing shoes two sizes too small, never entirely sure which direction my pained feet should take me. I was reluctant to commit to anything beyond the next several months that lay before me, and even that was a struggle. Indeed, both my inner and outer worlds seemed woefully fragmented.

Releasing a long sigh, I stretched my arms above my head as best I could in the over-encumbered space and dismissed the burden from my mind to carry on with my search.

That was when I saw it: *the quilt.*

Peeking out from a faded and slumping hat box was a slip of blood-red velvet fabric. It was marked with what looked like delicate white hand stitching, and was curiously untouched by the dust and mildew that plagued the rest of the dim attic space. I was instantly intrigued.

The container housing it was fairly unremarkable at first glance, blending in with the other water-stained boxes that brimmed with outdated recipe books, cross-stitch patterns, and kitschy Canadian home and garden manuals from the 1960s and '70s. A neighbouring box contained a glut of random newspaper clippings and greeting cards from long before I was born. Another bore an ominously foul smell and was marked in Gertie's curly handwriting: *"Cannot be disposed of by conventional means."* I stepped warily around *that* one.

My grandmother had considered herself an "Earth Witch," a rooted caretaker of the land. This of course was an uncomplicated way of saying that she followed her own magical path, bonded to the world through natural exploration, all the while amassing physical relics along the way. It also explained why her attic crawl space had become the chaotic refuge that it was.

I tried to ignore the gnawing fact that Gertie's vast collection of things was now *my* problem as I tiptoed across the attic, box in hand. My heel landed hard as I hopped over the last stack of boxes towards one of the few free spaces at the centre of the room. The sensation caused my head to throb painfully in response. I sank down gingerly to inspect my findings.

Beneath years of wear, the box had once been thoughtfully hand painted with forget-me-nots, repeating the same pattern over and over in yellow and light-blue clusters of three, five, and nine across its sage-green surface; I had always preferred the balance of odd number groupings in design. My fleeting appreciation of this artist's particular rendition, however, was quickly stifled by the vengeful dust specters floating through the late afternoon light and directly into my lungs.

I coughed dramatically for a solid ten seconds before standing up and surveying my surroundings once more. The attic was dim and the air brutally stagnant; I needed fresh air. A small, mock Tudor-style window lay just beyond another stack of boxes, a discarded television, and a theatrically leaning mannequin wearing a bowler hat. I tucked the unopened box under my arm and smiled at the absurdity of it all.

Growing up, I had absolutely relished Gertie's doting attention whenever we were together. She often said that we were kindred spirits, and although gifted in our own unique ways, we "sisters of the moon" had to stick together. The fact that I had demonstrated signs of inherent magical ability from an early age had positively delighted her, and absolutely appalled my mother. She, in whom magic seemed as fleeting as the whiff of smoke after a candle is snuffed, believed that there was no place for any magic in the modern world.

And so, their lifelong dispute over the nature of my magical education was born.

Through Gertie's early teachings, I had been warned against relying too heavily on my untamed inner magic. Bearing magic, she claimed, "was really more of an offensive skill anyway, and not overly useful in a practical, civilized society." Apparently, true Bearing magic was complicated and immensely difficult to master. Examples included intricately woven protection spells, speaking into someone's mind without verbal utterance, or enchanting objects to hold certain properties over an extended period time. It also included the Sight. *Big potatoes*. And with my limited knowledge and experience, it might as well have been the stuff of legend.

Wielding magic, at least for Witches, was distinctly more practical. It embodied daily tasks like lighting fires, keeping drafts out, or mixing healing balms. Passed down through the generations, this knowledge was often held within a family grimoire or recipe book, and usually involved intentional rituals or cultivating ceremonial space.

Both branches of magic took dedication and practice. However, due to the secrecy we upheld, it came as no surprise that modern Witches tended towards the more discreet and less complex Wielding magic over its older, wilder counterpart. Gertie maintained that it was far safer to "rely on the consistent subtleties of well Wielded earth magic, rather than the rambunctious magics of a Bearer unhinged." Wielding magic was always easily accessed in small, mindful doses. It had been made sufficiently clear to me from an early age that frugality and magic went hand in hand. It was as sturdy of a method of being as she was as a woman. Dependable Gertie.

And now, she was gone.

My lungs tightened as I fought back a sudden wave of grief. My resolve was rapidly weakening in the over-encumbered space; why I thought I could find the breach during a drought remained a mystery, but determination knows no bounds for a procrastinator when the clock approaches nuclear midnight.

Naturally, I found myself grateful for a new excuse to break from leak hunting as I performed a final set of hurtles towards the window. Placing the box atop a sturdy desk wedged into the angled roof before tugging on the slight brass latch, I was pleasantly surprised when it popped open without resistance, swinging wide but inviting in only a slight breeze. I wiped my sticky hands on my denim overall shorts, but the moisture stubbornly remained.

It was just *so damn hot.*

With sweaty palms, I at last removed the stiffened cardboard lid and freed the enchanted quilt from its hiding place. My first reaction was that it was a very unusual-looking collage, a muddled patchwork of different fabrics that had been sewn together with what seemed like a random mix of fibres and stitch types. Then I felt my heartrate quicken, excitement rising as my breath slowed. My inner magic was stirring, almost crackling within me, centering on what seemed to be an uncommonly rare artifact. I sat down in a rickety chair and unfolded it across my legs to take a closer look, careful not to drag it through the dust moats that surrounded me. I lightly traced my fingers along the varied patches, which were oddly cool to the touch.

It was what my grandma Gertie would have called "lap sized," yet it didn't lack in weight, despite its smaller composition. I had spent many hours peacefully sewing side-by-side with her as a girl and had long since learned my way around a sewing needle.

However, the second thing I noted was how intricate and intentional each individual stitch and chosen fabric seemed to be, with the majority of the techniques used falling well beyond my skill set. Turning it over in my hands, I couldn't imagine using it on a bed. Perhaps it was meant to be put on display? In fact, the more I explored it, the more it began to positively burst with detail, shimmering delightfully in the thin stream of sunlight pouring in through the tiny window.

I stood once more and held the quilt in front of me while swinging to the side, this time aptly dodging the low-slung cedar beam above. I was completely perplexed now. If I didn't know better, I would say the quilt was attempting to tell me a story. Or perhaps more accurately, since it seemed that many hands had forged its existence, it was in fact spinning more than one yarn simultaneously. This would certainly explain the surrounding frenetic energy; it was positively vibrating in my fingertips.

Between a small scrap of cream-coloured linen and a swatch of crisp blue and white seersucker print, I noticed a sweetly intricate row of Irish crochet, its spidery threads holding the two pieces together with surprising firmness. In other areas, heavier fabrics like denim and tweed weighed the quilt down considerably. Strangely, it contained several crocheted, rainbow granny squares intermixed with a loose blanket stitch. Some patches were so tightly woven together that they threw the tension off, while others were only loosely gathered and bordered on dangling from the larger piece. What at first had looked like a completely chaotic design, conversely, somehow felt completely balanced. It was utterly bizarre.

The light was fading quickly now, making it more difficult to see the detail with each passing moment. Peering over my shoulder, I eyed the dodgy lamp that I had manhandled earlier, but thought better of it. There were no overhead lights up here, which was probably for the best considering the attic's proclivity for moisture collection.

I yanked my phone out of my pocket to check the time, but it was unsurprisingly defunct. Something about the magic that surrounded Gertie's cottage, particularly up here in the crawl space, sent any electronics into a tailspin; it ebbed and flowed from the place like a king tide.

My stomach gave way to the hour, though, growling audibly in protest to the extended time in the heat of the attic. I had skipped lunch in my preoccupied wander through the house, and judging by the angle of the sun and the displeasure of my gut, it was high-time for supper.

Clearly my stint in the attic had expired, so I threw caution to the wind. More important than the leak, I needed to find out what secrets the enchanted quilt was hiding! I closed my eyes in a weak attempt at divining the stories it so clearly wanted to tell, but was quickly met with a wall of solid, impenetrable magic. I tried again. I dug deep into my inner hearth and envisioned pulling the magic *through* myself and into the cryptic quilt. Nope, nothing. The only finding was a stinging reminder of the great gap in my own knowledge and skill.

I had gleaned from an early age that I was different than most other magic Bearers, although initially no one told me outright *why*. When the nightmares began around puberty, they were followed by spontaneous visions that left me incapacitated for hours at a time. My mother had outwardly dismissed them as migraines, but I could remember her phoning Gertie in complete panic, unaware that I was watching from a secret hiding spot in the hallway.

"What's wrong with her? What can be done?"

She wrung her hands repeatedly as she spoke, an all too familiar manic look spreading recklessly across her face. From where I sat, I could almost hear Gertie's muffled voice as it uttered something from the other end of the line.

My mother had gasped audibly. "The Sight? That's impossible!" she said, and loudly hung up the receiver. I cowered, unsure what any of this meant.

I would learn that I had inherited this unique ability from some great ancestor of mine. Records of her name had been lost long ago, allegedly burned in a house fire with the original family grimoire. Ultimately, as neither Gertie nor my mother possessed this unique trait, I was left incomplete in what felt like a rather critical area of my personal development.

My grandmother attempted to placate my worries of my undeveloped power with the hard truth that it was exceptionally dangerous to be a Bearer, let alone one with exceptional gifts. Sure, it was good to rely on your inner magic to keep yourself safe, but its very existence painted a target on your back. Countless Witches over the past several centuries had been hunted down for their rare and unique gifts, and by extension, their seemingly infinite access to raw power. The fact was that magic wasn't always used for good; dark Sorcery had maintained strongholds throughout the ages, its powerful draw always seeking new recruits.

"Imagine what *they* would do to you if you were taken," Gertie had exclaimed.

I never knew exactly who "they" were, but this was a common truth in our community. We were a hunted people and had been for centuries. In Gertie's opinion, I was safer to drown in my own confused magic than to shine too brightly and be used for someone's more sinister purpose.

Returning my thoughts to the quilt in front of me, I scrunched my face up in one final push of determination and made my final attempt at divination. But it was futile. My neck and back were completely drenched in sweat, and I was starving; it was time to move on.

I exhaled heavily as I threw my head back.

Then, clear as day, I saw the source of the roof leak directly above me. I must have checked that section of ceiling at least three times in the span of the afternoon. How could I have missed what now looked like a flashing neon sign screaming, "Fix me!"

I gently folded up the quilt and placed it back in its original box on the desk before retrieving my selected tools to seal the leak, which included a modest chunk of plywood and a hearty tub of roofing tar. It smelled terrible, but in the end, the patch took little time at all. I was honestly surprised at how much water had managed to seep in through such a small crack in the cottage's defences.

Immense relief washed over me to have completed the task at last, almost as if it were the end of a long chapter in Gertie's story that had finally reached its conclusion. I smiled, grateful for her memory. I had been so frustrated with her all afternoon while traversing the claustrophobic crawl space that it was nice to feel warmth about her again. Still, I made a mental note to stop shoving things I didn't want to deal with into the attic as well.

I cast my gaze across the space one last time before pushing my now unbound hair back from my damp face. With a final deep breath, I readied myself to climb through the half-size attic door back into the cottage at large.

And then I paused; the window was still open.

Thankfully, my frustration had subsided considerably since patching the leak. I closed the window latch tightly before scooping up the almost forgotten quilt box. I managed the trek once more with considerably fewer incidents, knocking over only a small pack of holiday ornaments in the process. Pulling the attic door shut behind me, I placed my plunder just outside of the hidden attic entrance, which (by Gertie's design) was cleverly located through a larger and rather non-descript upstairs hall closet. No one would find it there, and this way it would also be protected from any more possible leaks.

Just in case.

CHAPTER 2

This summer had been unseasonably warm; the heat brought with it a wretched dearth that threatened the honeybees, along with any fruits and vegetables in the region. To make matters worse, the orange haze of forest-fire smoke from Washington state left you feeling forcibly pressed and suffocated against the parched earth below.

August on the coast reminded me unpleasantly of brown, wilted death.

I always thought of the 'dog days of summer,' a time the Greeks and Romans believed could cause disaster from the heat. It was signalled by the arrival of Sirius the Dog Star just before sunrise. Although I hadn't noticed any special stars seated on the horizon today, the ancients weren't wrong about the heat bringing potential catastrophe; I felt sure I would faint any moment.

The mid-morning sun was already painfully scorching the back of my neck as I tended to the cottage garden. My back-breaking work was interrupted by a rather unpleasant rendezvous with a garden slug, the result being that my fingers were now completely covered in slime. I wasn't even sure how I had managed to touch it, slugs being decidedly *not* the sun-bathing type. I hastily rubbed my hands across the brittle grass lining the garden bed, but it only made matters worse; dry bits of crumbling turf and sun-baked earth clung to the viscous mass like shredded tissue paper to white glue.

I pushed myself up from the arid landscape of Gertie's garden and wandered to the corroded hose bib protruding from the back of the white-stucco cottage. After some difficulty turning it on, I ran my fingers under the cool water in another vain attempt to clear my fingertips of the implacable adhesive. The fact that I had failed to locate my well-worn garden gloves earlier that morning was not lost on me.

Several pairs of Gertie's gloves sat neatly stowed away in the potting shed, but there was no way my long fingers would slide into her considerably more stoutly sets. This came as no surprise, however; I looked nothing like Gertie, or my mother for that matter. Both women were low and sturdy, with my mother only slightly narrower in the shoulders than Gertie had been. But ultimately, they were cut from the same cloth.

In addition to my notable height difference, my bold red-brown hair drew considerable attention my way. Yet another reason I had felt like a perpetual outsider, both within my own family and out of it.

As a child, I had often asked my mother about my father's family, but it turned out she had never *actually* met them. I fantasized that my paternal lineage was a regal-looking bunch, tall and fair skinned, with thick auburn hair and big grins just like mine. Some days it was almost as if I *could* remember them, but that was a common confusion of having the Sight; it was difficult to determine what was real and what was merely the fruit of an exceptional childhood imagination.

There had never been any pictures of my father to be found, save for the single Polaroid from his marriage to my mother. But she had burned it long ago, the distinct odour of plastic and chemicals emanating from my mother's bathroom singed into my memory. We had only been living on Vancouver Island for a few months at that time, and while I had managed to make fast friends at my new school, she had been flailing. Looking back, perhaps more ghosts had followed her to the coast than I could comprehend.

I found her standing before the deep bathroom windowsill of our basement rental suite, having set up an impromptu alter. The ledge was lined with freshly lit votive candles, a few new-to-my-eyes polished stones, and one small, unassuming metal bowl placed in the centre that held their wedding portrait. This would serve as my first and last observation of my mother performing any kind of magic ritual. I would never forget how her grimace had been a twisted mirror of the vacant expression on her face in the melting photograph.

"Mommy . . . what are you doing?"

"Julia!" she shrieked. "Get out of here, now!" She chased me from the room, shouting wildly that I would never ask about my father *ever* again if I knew what was best for me. The scene that unfolded before me in the dim bathroom had naturally generated more questions than answers for me, a relentlessly curious child.

One drizzly afternoon while visiting Gertie on Salt Spring, I had mustered the courage to ask her about my father's family. We had been enjoying a peaceful lunch together, just the two of us, seated at her kitchen table, a familiar and open space I was well-accustomed to.

She too dismissed my inquiry with the same brand of wounded precision.

"Oh, for crying in the soup, child! I only met the man once, but I don't recall him having any red in his hair. He had a ridiculous hat on anyway, but quite frankly, I was too busy noticing his outright belligerence to notice anything else!" I was startled by the outburst and learned quickly thereafter that she had absolutely no interest in 'filling the air' with conversation about him. End of story.

She had patted my hand gently, and witnessing the frightened look on my face, swiftly re-directed the conversation to more suitable topics, such as what trouble her seven Nigerian Dwarf goats had been up to since my last visit, or whether or not the winter Brussels sprout harvest was coming along.

Today, Gertie's cottage still brimmed with just as many ritual spaces and ceremonial epitaphs as it had when I was a girl. I could remember spending hours wandering around her home on my regular weekend visits. Every nook and cranny housed some secret shining trinket or charmed item, and I was utterly enchanted with the magic that percolated from every adorned ledge.

Now, however, it simply looked like an unsurmountable mountain of work that lay ahead of me. Wisely, or so I thought, I decided to leave the cottage *as is* until I returned over the Christmas holidays, intending to sort out then what would go into storage and what I would part with before selling the house. I was dreading the process wholeheartedly.

Turning my attention outdoors instead, I spent the better part of the Sunday morning before my departure pulling the last surplus of summer squash and doing my best to clean up the wilted tomato and cucumber plants, their vines brittle and tangled on their cages and climbing frames.

Gertie's garden had always fared somewhat better than the rest, no doubt because she had imparted her own earthen magic deep into the dirt. I had tenderly weeded around what she dubbed 'Witches herbs,' most of which had little purpose since I'd assumed the role of caretaker-in-chief. Some of my favourite plants growing up had names like Moonwort, Feverfew, Knitbone, and Bloodroot, their unique titles stirring imaginings of fantastic landscapes or more sinister adventures in a world of my own invention. Believing them to be early visions, I envisaged a tall golden prince striding towards Gertie's cottage to rescue me from some unforeseen, menacing foe. Pulling me deftly onto his horse, we would ride off together, boldly setting after our next epic quest.

I eventually outgrew the idea that I needed saving; that was the stuff of childhood fairy tales.

I peered over the low white picket fence towards Gertie's wilted garden and lamented the redundancy of all that remained planted there. Behind stood the empty chicken coop, the sun beating down relentlessly on its pale cedar shakes. I had relocated Gertie's remaining heritage chickens immediately after her passing. The hens deserved better than what I was able to offer, and I didn't know how long I would be staying at the cottage anyways. A neighbour eager to expand their flock happily took them, and soon six fluffy feathered bums happily waltzed towards their new home without a single glance back. *Ungrateful shits.* But that's chickens for you.

Gertie always allowed her birds their natural seasonal cycle. She had explained how important it was for the hens to have a break to moult and re-set in the winter for the coming spring. Once the hens began to lay again, it was time to begin tilling the garden and sprouting seeds. Gertie's cottage had always served as a steadfast reminder of the intentional cycles of nature and of the importance of connection to place. Now that sole sense of place felt irrevocably shaken, shrouded in thickly veiled grief as I traversed the inner and outer aspects of the home.

I dumped the final stems and cuttings into a tidy pile atop the compost heap and wiped my brow; it was good enough. I looked up at the cottage and smiled ruefully. While I was tremendously relieved to have sorted the leaky roof at long last, I was equally anxious to return to Vancouver and complete my long overdue Linguistics undergraduate degree at UBC.

When Gertie had first fallen ill, I had immediately dropped out of my final semester of classes without more than a second thought, despite her loud protests.

"You're so close to the finish line, don't stop on account of an old woman like me!"

I had been lucky enough to leave my classes before the drop-out deadline near the end of January. That was at least one windfall. But the truth was, I had felt unsettled about my final leg of school, somehow unable to complete any essay before its deadline or focus on the simplest assignments.

My days had been steeped in the feeling that I was perpetually in the wrong place at the wrong time. Almost as if I were homesick. I had initially chalked it up to the Sight, but it felt far more significant than any past premonitions. So, when Gertie called to inform me that she was terminally ill, I blindly took this as the explanation for why I had felt so displaced. But after she passed away less than three months later, the feeling failed to lift.

If anything, it intensified.

I spent the months following her death numbing my pain with what was arguably alcohol abuse tied in with an unhealthy dose of reckless adventure. A handful of old work friends were on their way to camp, surf, and party into oblivion along the sandy shorelines of Tofino, and I eagerly jumped at the chance to tag along. It had been a good distraction for a time. I even found fleeting romance with an old flame.

Soon though, the feeling of displacement became too overwhelming as it began suffocating my waking thoughts and infiltrating my already torrid nightmares. When the panic finally led me to lose feeling in my hands entirely, I knew then it was time to return home.

I made my excuses and returned to Gertie's cottage, spiralling as my thirtieth birthday fast approached. It forced me to confront my worsening tailspin. What the hell I was doing with my life? The best solution I could arrive at, and the one that returned the most feeling to my fingertips, was to place one gruelling foot in front of the other until my degree was complete.

So, there I sat on the Sunday afternoon of the September long weekend, my truck lightly loaded and the cottage closed up tight for the next several months. I snagged one of the last boxes of Gertie's preserves from the previous fall, which contained several bright jars of pickled beets, pressure-canned salsa, and sweet jelly. The low crate sat on the passenger-side floor, a plastic bag of excess summer squash shoved begrudgingly beside it. I tipped my invisible hat once in farewell and ground the gears into reverse before backing carefully down the drive.

Apart from the hours of waiting painfully in queue for the ferry, what I dreaded most about the return to the mainland was the frenzied energy once my wheels hit land. The tacky bumper stickers seen on the Gulf Islands that read, "Slow Down, This Isn't the Mainland!" were a joke amongst tourists, but their sentiment wasn't far off.

Thankfully, the ferry traffic was much quieter than anticipated for a long weekend. When I finally put my truck into park on the lower vehicle deck of the *Queen of Cowichan,* pulling the emergency break with considerable effort, I breathed an audible sigh of relief that my first leg was complete.

I had received two texts from my roommate, Virginia Jones, as I sat in the ferry line:

> *When are you getting your butt back to the city? We have been*
> *re-arranging the shelter – it's been a complete nightmare! Could*
> *really use some volunteer help with clothing donations.*
> *Oh, and obviously I'm excited to see you!*

She worked at a downtown women's shelter and was a true gem of a human. Justice was in her bones, and if I was honest, sometimes she made me feel ashamed of my lack of effort in *any* community, even if it wasn't her intention.

Since the lease was solely in her name, our third roommate was her cousin Ben. He was notably younger than we were, awkward, and extremely private. Virginia had done her aunt a favour by putting him up while he got settled into his job at a tech start up, though I rarely saw him. Still, he was polite, tidy, and cut my rent down considerably.

Neither Virginia nor Ben were magic users, so it was far safer for all involved that they didn't know the truth about me. It was challenging to connect with others on a deeper level, but I had become surprisingly adept at bending the truth around the eccentricities of my existence, and so far, it seemed to work for us.

My phoned pinged loudly as I settled into a vacant window seat in the cafeteria berth of the vessel. All around, it smelled overwhelmingly like French fries and chemical cleaner, like some disgusting rendition of fish and chips. I gagged slightly as I quickly toggled my phone's volume to silent; I was glad at least to see that it was again reliable. With an audible sigh, I plunked my soft-sided leather satchel unceremoniously onto the floor in front of me, and since the coffee I had just purchased was still far too hot to drink, I opted to check the notification.

It was an email:

> *Greetings Julia,*
> *I wanted to personally extend my most sincere welcome*
> *to Linguistics 447G, A Sociolinguistic Exploration of*
> *Colloquialism in the Modern Era.*
> *Your peers were advised to purchase their reading packages in*
> *advance, but as you joined our roster late, I have attached the*
> *first several readings to this email in hopes that you will find*
> *them useful until you can obtain the package in full.*
> *Students are expected to complete the weekly readings in*
> *advance of attending the seminar; those who haven't will be*
> *asked not to participate in that week's lesson. As such, I have*
> *also attached this semester's syllabus.*
> *Looking forward to meeting everyone on Wednesday!*
> *Kindly,*
> *Prof. D. O'Brien*

Fucking great.

I'd had a feeling this seminar was too good to be true, and now I knew it, already landed with homework, and I hadn't even gotten off the boat. Due to my late decision to re-enrol, I had been struggling to gather enough credits to complete my degree by the end of the calendar year. Then, seemingly out of the blue, a chance spot opened up in one section of the required seminar, and with technology shockingly cooperative for once, I'd registered for the course immediately.

I groaned as I opened the attached documents: seventy scanned pages of reading for the first week, and a hundred for the next. To top it off, the font was miniscule and somewhat blurry.

Wait. How could he know that I hadn't purchased the package yet?

Borne from a sudden, overpowering curiosity, I entered a quick search on my phone for Professor D. O'Brien, but discovered surprisingly little about his endeavours, academic or otherwise. I could see that he was a visiting professor from N.U.I. Galway in Ireland. Apparently, he specialised in the courses he was teaching this semester: Intro to Sociolinguistics, Irish Language, and of course, our seminar. The UBC website also said his interests were tied specifically to something called, "Adaptive Ethnography," whatever that meant.

I supposed that a 'good student' would begin their readings now, but I opted for a cat nap instead after yawning into my sleeve. Curling my knees up under my chin, it felt like a safe bet to close my eyes; my magic had been so stifled lately that there was a small chance of waking up thrashing my way through a nightmare.

A trio of bracing bell-tones were followed by a jarring voice from overhead: "For those passengers in vehicles, please return to the vehicle deck. Walk on passengers will exit through the front . . ."

I jumped in my seat.

I must have slept for a deceptive chunk of time judging by the drool smeared on my cheek. Wiping my face with slight embarrassment, I scooped up my bag and headed towards my still-sleeping truck, stepping carefully over the raised nautical doorways as I joined the queue of tourists and commuters on the slow descent to the decks below.

The drive between the ferry terminal and my apartment was as stressful as anticipated, so it came with great relief when I finally ground the gear shift into 'park.' Rush-hour traffic and my beat-up old truck went together about as well as library books and ketchup chips. That is to say, not well at all.

Throwing my sixty-litre hiking backpack over my shoulder, I noted several floors of rickety scaffolding had been erected up the north side of the house. The owners seemed chronically strapped for cash, with everything taking a lifetime to fix. The word 'ramshackle' came to mind, but it was certainly good enough for one last semester.

It was sweltering on the first-floor hall landing, the August heat having not yet given way to cooler fall days. However, as I rounded the corner towards the second floor, I was met with an entirely different feeling. I faced the battered yellow door bearing a brassy letter 'B' and was filled with a sudden and immense feeling of dread. The air felt thick and slow on the landing, like cold maple syrup. Goosebumps prickled across my arms as my body adjusted to the sudden change in atmosphere.

"What the—"

And then, as if by magic, the feeling was gone as quickly as it had arrived, the late-summer stifle hastily pressing in again. I wasn't entirely sure if it *had* been an act of magic; perhaps I was simply about to lose feeling in my hands once more, the displacement returning with a cold vengeance. Something about the situation had piqued my Witch's intuition, however.

I looked around cautiously before reaching deep into the pockets of my sun-bleached denim shorts for my keys. The lock was sticky—yet another thing the landlords had failed to fix over the past several years. There was more resistance in the lock than usual though, *almost* as if it were enchanted. I wriggled the keys with more vigour, and the lock finally sprung open. My back was aching, and there was nothing I wanted more than a cold beer on our tiny second-floor balcony.

"Hello?" I said, unsettled by the notable silence within the apartment.

I set my bags down by the door and went to poke my head into Virginia's bedroom. "Hey girl! I'm back!"

Still nothing. Very strange.

Her room was tidy as usual, and it appeared she had been there recently since her computer screen was still on. Ginny, as I preferred to call her, typically spent her Sundays at home getting ready for the week ahead, pre-portioning her lunches and cleaning house. She was a creature of habit, and I had come to appreciate her stability in our shared accommodations. However, I hadn't *actually* heard from her since the text in the ferry line, and so was unsure if plans had changed.

Ben's door was closed. With some hesitation, I knocked on it. Better to avoid startling him with my arrival and bear an uncomfortable conversation;

he had always been a bit jumpy. I heard several loud scrapes across the floor, followed by the sound of dresser drawers being slammed shut. Following a few more muffled thumps, and what I thought sounded like several curse words under his breath, at last there was a heavy hand on the latch.

He opened his door a crack before it stopped abruptly; he had installed a chain lock across the top between the gap. Ben's room was now fortified, it would seem.

"Hey, Ben." I lingered on the first part of the greeting. "Just wanted to let you know I'm back."

"I see that," he said, his pale face protruding from the dim room, eyes red-rimmed from what I assumed was lack of sleep. Ben was no stranger to late nights.

I shrugged and pursed my lips into a short smile. If I was honest, he was creeping me out.

"Do you know where your cousin is?" I asked, trying to keep the energy light. Unfortunately, I didn't think it was working for either of us.

"No." He was staring at me like a cornered feral cat, barely blinking.

"Alright. Well . . . I'm going to unpack my things. See you later."

I must have been a bit whale-eyed myself during the encounter, and rightfully so. He looked like he was about to reach out and scratch me in warning. That or slam the door in my face. Thankfully he chose the latter, closing his door with a snap that made me lurch on the spot.

"Julia!" came Virginia's sing-song voice suddenly from the hallway. "You're back!"

Jumping for a second time, I realized I hadn't shut the door behind me. With my heart still fluttering, we embraced in an awkward but friendly hug; she was holding a paper bag in one arm and a thick black plastic bag with clinking bottles in the other.

"I popped down to the store to get some welcome-home drinks and nibbles for supper! I'm so sorry I wasn't here!"

"Amazing!"

She ushered me towards the kitchen before turning back to close and lock the apartment door. I noticed her toss an unusual glance towards Ben's bedroom, the strain across her brows resembling something between fear and anxiety.

"Hey so . . . Ben's changed a bit," I said casually, digging around in the cutlery drawer for a bottle opener. "Is he doing alright?"

She waved her hand dismissively, retrieving the 'church key' from the ceramic fruit bowl on the counter and popping open two sweating bottles of beer. "He's just been working a lot, that's all. He's a bit stressed too, maybe . . ."

I wasn't convinced but decided to let it slide. He was her cousin after all, she would know better. And really, it was none of my business anyway.

"Excellent! Cheers then!"

"Cheers!"

Precariously balancing our drinks and a mixed plate of hummus, crackers, and snap peas, we climbed through an open window onto a questionable excuse for a balcony, settling into the comfortable conversation I had come to adore.

Admittedly, I had neglected our friendship as of late. She had become one of my closest friends over the past several years, so I looked forward to a proper catch up. Naturally, she understood the reason for my absence, but I sensed she was deeply grateful that I had returned.

"It's been lonely without you here, Jules. Ben and I have both been working a lot. It's sort of felt like two ships passing in the night, you know? This place needs some *life* breathed back into it, and some dinner parties!"

I nodded in agreement, filling with gratitude. "Yeah! This semester is looking brutal though. I think I'll be spending a lot of it reading and writing papers."

"Hey, at least you'll be outside of your room and say hi to me. Unlike that meatball," she said, gesturing towards Ben's room. She seemed much more lighthearted now about him, and I wondered if perhaps I had misread the whole situation entirely.

The 'balcony' only had room for two metal lawn chairs and a wooden crate we had turned upside down to use as a table. Several potted plants sat precariously along the rail-less edge, dried out and dead in the late summer sun.

"The plants didn't stand a chance!" she said happily, pointing towards the shrivelled greenery. "We did manage a few bowlfuls of grape tomatoes back in July though!" The evening air smelled of exhaust and residual heat from city streets. Every so often, a slight breeze would brush by, both of us pretending we could smell the distant ocean air moving in through the concrete maze of the cityscape.

"The garden at Gertie's was similar. I had such good intentions in the spring, thinking it was therapeutic and all that," I said with a shrug, "but by the middle of August, I just ran out of steam and let the damn thing cook."

I laughed deeply, as did she. I was surprised at how glad I was to be back in the realm of the living; I had spent so much of the last few months grieving and had wondered if I even remembered how to connect with others after the ordeal.

As it turned out, I did.

CHAPTER 3

There had always been a *natural magic* that shrouded the back-to-school experience for me. Nostalgic sights and smells normally beckoned me back into the halls of learning, the scent of loose-leaf and newly polished floors, or even the dull acidic smell of wet brown paper towel in the washrooms delivered welcome reminiscence. In fact, it *usually* brought about a sense of excited anticipation and renewed energy.

However, this year felt like a greater adjustment than ever as I attempted to settle into academic life. I could only assume this was due to the distinctly looming, almost foreboding end to the final chapter of my post-secondary education. Big changes were on my horizon, but the vision around the direction of my fate was not yet clear, particularly with my divining still cloudy as ever.

Despite my reservations, the first day of classes had consisted of the predictable rigmarole of syllabus distribution, outlining the rhythm of the semester ahead, and early dismissal for what I assumed were faculty socials. As much as I felt like this could have been more efficiently handled over email, I was grateful for the prosaic pattern of events.

I had somehow managed to weight my schedule more heavily on Tuesdays and Thursdays, which left the other weekdays open for reading, studying, and rest. What I hadn't considered, however, was that my cleverly planned back-to-back classes were located on completely opposite ends of campus. It left me with ten minutes to traverse what was realistically a twenty-five-minute walk, one way, *if* I was moving briskly. And that was without consideration of the construction zones that popped up like wild mushrooms throughout the grounds. Lucky for me, I did this in the return direction as well.

I was grateful to have enough money in savings to negate the need for employment, far preferring to deplete my funds than take on short-term work. In any case, I also had the sale of Gertie's house to look forward to in the springtime, which would not only allow me some financial freedom but would also provide me time and space while I sorted out where my path might *truly* lie.

The second day of classes dawned far too early after what had been a particularly restless night. My dreams had been disturbing, plagued with images of missing girls, bodies ripped apart in violent chaos, and blood spattered from floor to ceiling in dim motel rooms. While I was used to recurring nightmares, these felt more like dark visions—vivid events that were happening in real time, which made them altogether more upsetting. I chalked up the terrifying imaginings to the discussion Virginia and I had shared over dinner the night before.

She was facing challenges at work around the increase in missing women in the greater Vancouver area. She had been lamenting the lack of funding, staff, and volunteers at the shelter. Despite a successful run of impromptu youth groups held at Dude Chilling Park, her enthusiasm was wearing thin.

She grimaced while an icy finger dragged down my spine. "Ginny, what is it?"

"Well, they're afraid, mostly. You've seen the reports over the last few months, you know, all of the bodies . . ."

I shook my head; I hadn't really, having effectively shut myself off from the world for the bulk of the summer.

Her sharp intake of breath in reply indicated that the issue had clearly become a heavy burden. "No one seems to know *why* they've been targeted. A few of them have been sex workers, which naturally the police fail to take seriously enough. One girl was in the foster system, so that drew a bit of attention . . . but it's mostly been the ones who slip through the cracks." She shifted uncomfortably in her chair.

I genuinely furrowed my brow in an effort to prompt her.

"We're trying our best to help out with any information we can offer, but it almost seems as if . . . okay this is going to sound nuts." She looked at me nervously. "It feels like another fucked-up person is gaming the system . . . like intentionally hiding their murders behind a massive gap in justice that's already there, you know?"

I let out a low whistle through my teeth as the dark images clouded my mind. With her anxiety clearly rising and my heart sinking into the bottom of my chest, we opted to spend the remainder of the meal chatting lightly about what TV shows she had binged over the summer.

That morning, the front door slammed twice as both Virginia and Ben left for work in quick succession. I finally dragged myself out of bed an hour later, tossing my feet unceremoniously onto the cool floor. Following a shower so long that I ran out of hot water, I padded quietly into the kitchen in my favourite thin grey waffle robe, desperate for a cup of coffee. Virginia always made a full pot in the morning, so there was usually at least one gulp left when I woke up; she knew all too well that I suffered from nightmares. I gratefully poured the last dark remnants from the stained coffee pot into a glazed clay mug. Closing my eyes, I drank it in . . . the scent of the bean water a tonic in itself. And then I looked at the clock.

Shit.

My overly long shower meant I would have to start my day in a rush, not that this was anything new. I knew I had nine or ten minutes to get dressed and outside to catch the last possible *B-Line* to campus, catch the transfer, and then walk hurriedly to my morning class on time. The route shuttled me directly between my house in South Main towards the UBC Campus, perhaps a little *too* efficiently for someone like me who had a proclivity to leave as late as humanly possible.

I hustled into my tiny bedroom, which contained only a modest double bed, a small desk, and a four-drawer dresser. They'd come with the suite but were more than enough to meet my needs, and as a bonus, I wouldn't have to deal with furniture when I moved out in December. I hadn't bothered to unpack yet and was kicking myself for leaving a heap of crumpled clothes to choose from for the day. Shoving through the disorganized pile, I made a mental note to deal with the mess when I returned later that evening, vowing to keep the promise to myself from only days earlier.

Despite it being early September, the mornings were already crisp but still followed with resounding afternoon heat. It made for a wardrobe conundrum; perhaps this was why parents always fussed so much about "back to school" clothes for their smaller children.

I found what I was looking for at the bottom of my hiking backpack, my favourite high-waisted black jeans and a flattering, albeit slightly wrinkled, jewel green t-shirt. I eyed the combination in the mirror with satisfaction. The shirt highlighted the deep red tones in my hastily towel-dried auburn hair, which fell easily past my shoulders in heavy waves. My personal style was that of comfort and ease, with plenty of room for the changing weather.

After a quick application of tinted moisturiser and mascara, I slid on my leather sandals, shoved my raincoat into my satchel, and hurtled out the front door.

Transit to campus had been fairly uneventful, but my mind had been preoccupied. I found myself checking my phone at regular intervals for new emails and felt a strange compulsion to re-visit the email from "Prof. D. O'Brien." It only dawned on me with embarrassment, as I arrived at my destination, that I had failed to *actually* formulate a reply. However, it was too late now. I had no idea why it had piqued my interest anyway. I knew absolutely nothing about the man but concluded he would be much like any other linguistics professor I had encountered; intelligently dry-witted, if not a little bland. And yet, I detected something vaguely familiar in the tone of his message.

Following another quick syllabus discussion in my morning class, Pragmatics, I wandered around gratefully outside. I eventually dropped my bag carelessly onto the grass under a gnarled and well-aged oak tree, taking extra care not to spill my freshly acquired coffee. I was exhausted, but somehow didn't get the impression from his email that this afternoon's seminar would have the same laid-back pace as my other classes. Thankfully, I had two hours to kill. I rubbed my eyes drowsily, hopeful that I might catch a few winks in the shade.

I was suddenly overcome with the most extraordinary feeling.

At first it reminded me of what the touch of a water skeeter might feel like as it skated along the surface of a pond. Instead, the impression was across my own flesh, the resulting sensation forming a barely tangible skiff over my slightly perspiring face and arms. And while it was warm out, there was notably no breeze. This was *magic*.

I sank down at the base of the tree and closed my eyes for a moment, attempting with what little practice I had to draw more of this mysterious force towards myself. Growing up, Gertie had called these sites of natural respite *"thin places,"* and I soon had the overwhelming sense that I was exactly where I needed to be.

She had explained that the existence of thin places and communication with the mother Goddess was originally a Celtic belief but had been co-opted by the Christian Church to signify a closeness to their monotheistic male God. The fact remained, however, that closeness to nature was *always* soothing for Bearers and natural Wielders alike, regardless of their spiritual beliefs. Perhaps this served as a direct explanation as to why Gertie had peacefully holed up on the mountainside and why I felt so unsettled walking amongst the concrete pillars of the vast cityscape. Lucky for me, UBC boasted an abundance of greenery, and the magic that exuded from this particular tree was ancient and profound, much like the unceded territory it grew upon.

I sat reposed under the shade of the oak for as long as possible, gently tapping into the fluid magic of the earth by visualizing the deep connection between myself and the natural world. Gertie would have been proud of me for embracing such a space, and soon the pain of her loss rang loudly from my heart. I missed her desperately.

When it at last came time to relocate, I wandered ethereally towards the first seminar of the semester, practically floating as I approached the entrance to Totem Field Studios. The air felt lighter than it had in months, the magic that surrounded me now resembling tiny butterflies touching down and taking off across my exposed skin. My limbs swam through each stride as I glided forward.

As I rounded the corner into the smallest main-floor classroom, my airy thoughts were soon brought heartily back to earth with a sharp jolt. I'm not entirely sure who I had been expecting to meet in that space, but Professor O'Brien was quintessentially *not* him.

Standing well over six feet tall, he looked like he was much more suited to a football stadium than a classroom. Clearly, the man spent regular time in the gym, based on the tight stretch of his light-brown khakis across his thighs. No one was that fit without putting in the work. I snorted in spite of myself. He was definitely not what one conjures to mind when they think of a visiting Linguistics professor specializing in "Adaptive Ethnography."

And holy hell, he was absolutely *gorgeous.*

He grinned broadly as he leaned forward casually at the head of the shared seminar table, arms open wide and broad palms outstretched on its surface. It was a considerably narrow space to accommodate both the elongated table and the dozen or so students around it, and I watched cautiously as my peers struggled to seat themselves between apologetic looks at their scraping chairs.

I seated myself in the last remaining chair, smack at the centre of the table, and looked around. I immediately recognized my friends Rebecca and Dave from last year, who were seated on the opposite end and had waved enthusiastically upon my arrival. There were also a handful of new faces; my delayed final semester meant that a whole new wave of students would also be graduating with me. While I had thought a self-proclaimed "mature-student status" bore wisdom like a fine Cabernet Sauvignon, it felt like it actually resembled a carboy of suspect home-brew wine in an undergraduate's bathtub. A bit *ripe*, perhaps.

Alas, only three and a half more months to go.

The other students seemed incredibly eager, having studiously placed this week's readings out in front of them. They sat straight and looked expectantly at our commander in chief. I had also completed the work, but instead waited for the class to begin, spinning my pen in my fingers.

"Excellent! Welcome, welcome!"

His accent was definitely Irish, which came as no surprise. What *was* surprising was his age. He couldn't be more than five or six years older than me, ten at the most. His eyes crinkled pleasantly at the edges when he smiled, but upon relaxing, only the beginning signs of crow's feet remained. Definitely under forty.

"Now, please grab the first assigned article, and we'll begin!" he said, eyebrows raised expectantly in the direction of the collective.

No introduction, and definitely no pre-amble about the syllabus. I watched as my peers shuffled their white papers in a flurry, like a flock of seagulls after a discarded half-eaten ham sandwich on the beach. It would seem he was a bit of a drill sergeant, even if he wore the most beatific smile on his face as he prepared to begin.

Meanwhile, I relaxed into my seat, poised only with a pen in hand and an empty sheet of loose-leaf before me. I purposely left the articles safely tucked into the plastic side pocket of my mustard-yellow clipboard. I already had the distinct impression that he was the kind of professor who was more interested in what you could glean from the articles than what you could regurgitate back at him.

He cracked on enthusiastically through the readings and their associated discussion points. It was obvious that he genuinely enjoyed teaching, his natural gravitas drawing in even the most subdued participant. He also held the group at a very high level of expectation, aptly demonstrated by the precision of his questions and the pace at which he drove the class onward.

He spoke with his hands when he was excited, long fingers equally as expressive as his lively face. Indeed, it was positively delightful the way he smiled and nodded his head enthusiastically when someone was on the right track; his low murmurs of approval reminded me of the gratified purr of a self-satisfied cat as they escaped his throat. To my surprise, I found it almost impossible to keep from admiring his perfectly groomed, thick, sandy-brown beard, my gaze tracing perhaps too intimately the lines of his full lips, and—

"It's Julia, right? What did you think about Bridge's point regarding the efficacy of our comparatively *short* modern attention spans for accumulating new turns of phrase?" he asked, a tiny smirk lingering in the corner of his mouth.

Shoving my ill-timed daydreams aside, all eyes were on me as I scrambled to gather my bearings around the arguably more pressing subject matter. "Well, I guess I didn't agree, because she doesn't take into account the medium used," I said, aligning my shoulders to face him. "There is still such a generational gap between *how* technology is approached. Wouldn't this have had a greater influence on the natural acquisition of the terms, rather than the terms themselves?"

He nodded, evidently impressed, but not willing to concede his side so easily. "Sure, but the data suggests that, when set across an equal playing field, all four generations in the study shifted in how they *perceived* the new terms relative to the subject matter."

I sat up taller yet, heat rising. "But you've just proved my point! Instead of considering only the generations, she needed to also consider the delivery itself, because there is clearly a disparity in the data there, if you ask me."

I leaned back now, cheeks flushed. I wasn't embarrassed, yet often my body's physical response betrayed my inner thoughts—remnants of a childhood spent fighting to be heard, no doubt.

Professor O'Brien smiled appreciatively and moved on swiftly to the last of his discussion points. Nearing the end of the seminar, he was visibly exhausted and exhilarated in equal measure. Sensing the end was near, everyone was organizing their papers and packing up to leave, equally drained and ready for relief.

All at once, the late-afternoon sun shifted its position just enough to shine through the west-facing window, highlighting the intricate waves of gold woven throughout his light-brown locks. I had already noted the several generous inches of length to his hair during the occasions when he pushed it back from his face as he pondered a discussion topic. And so, with an unexpected return to my daydreams, the effect of the dappled sun on his face became positively *kingly*.

Without warning, I was overcome by the smell of sea salt, warm sand, and glowing sunshine, reminding me with nostalgia of the carefree summers spent at the beach with my grandmother as a child. Gold and blue light engulfed the sensation; I realised that it was the first time in months that I had truly seen the *colour* behind one of my visions.

The moment was fleeting. I looked around nervously, fearful that someone had spotted the unusual expression that had more than likely adorned my face, but they were already pushing their chairs back loudly and filing from the room.

"Oh!" Professor O'Brien boomed over the din. "If you like rugby, the Faculty of Arts is hosting a scrimmage next Friday night against the medical students. Pop over to that fancy new pitch and have a pint to cheer us on! It's for charity!"

Aha! He *did* look like a rugby player, now that I came to think of it, not that I knew anything about rugby. My peers nodded enthusiastically in support. However, I doubted many of them would attend on Friday; he was perhaps preaching to the wrong choir. To my own surprise, I was unexpectedly and heartily tempted, and hoped selfishly that Rebecca or Dave might like to join me as well. The three of us had been in classes together off and on since the beginning of my degree studies and had sort of become classroom companions. They could likely be convinced if beer was involved.

As if by instinct, I looked back towards Professor O'Brien as I was exiting the classroom. I caught his gaze resting rather intently on me for just a moment before he shifted his eyes back to his papers. Was that a slight flush to his cheeks?

No, I must have been imagining it. At any rate, it was warm in the room.

Having successfully convinced Rebecca and Dave to join me at the match, we found ourselves walking across campus towards the new rugby pavilion, chatting heartily about our classes and workloads for the coming semester. Phonology had apparently been particularly egregious, and I was grateful I had signed up for Morphology instead.

Rebecca knew the fundamentals of rugby since she had briefly played for her high school team long ago. "I quit though because I always felt too small." She laughed her signature "ha-ha!" following the statement. Her laughter was one of my favourite things about her. "Some of those girls were so intense! And *really*, I preferred theatre anyways."

Her knowledge would be an invaluable base in understanding what was going on during the match, but in truth, my personal interest was driven by other forces. What was it about Professor O'Brien that was spurring on such an uncharacteristic surge of fascination from me? He had even joined the pandemonium of my dreams ever since the first night after our seminar, and I sensed that he wouldn't be vacating the space any time soon. He and I were both in for a wild ride if that were to be the case.

My friends and I made our way through admissions, which was essentially a plastic folding table with a dented black metal cash box. The makeshift counter was manned by several intelligent-looking women who were clearly medical students, and one out-of-place man I could only assume was the arts student representative for this particular shift.

"What's in it for you?" I asked him jokingly under my breath, nodding my head at the banner that clearly stated this was a medical school fundraiser.

He proffered an *"Isn't it obvious?"* look, raising his eyebrows and grinning nervously, casting an almost imperceptible glance at his co-volunteers.

Entering the lounge, Dave waved us off momentarily as he recognized some of his friends from his geology elective gathered at the bar counter and headed towards them.

"Does he seriously know *everyone*?" Rebecca asked. "This is a *massive* campus."

I called out to his back, "You'll get the first round then?"

He waved back in acknowledgement, already halfway into a one-armed embrace with a friend of his and launching into some boisterous anecdote.

What was it about sporting events that brought out our need for primal sparring? It reminded me of male plumage in birds and how competitive the animal kingdom could be when trying to capture the eyes of a mate.

Rebecca and I settled ourselves into the second-lowest row of outdoor seating, the day still pleasantly warm from the lingering early fall sun. I was grateful for my sunglasses with our south-facing vantage point and leaned back coolly to view the pitch. I had the distinct sense that *someone* could be eying me at any moment, and much to my chagrin, I felt the instinct to put my own plumage on display.

Good grief, I really was a woman "on the bleachers," an irony that wasn't lost on me.

Dave joined us shortly before the players jogged onto the pitch in their clustered teams, three brimming cups of frosty beer precariously clutched in his triangulated grasp. Slick condensation had gathered on the clear plastic, causing Dave to almost drop the lot of them before settling into his own seat.

"Oops! That was close," he said, but was soon leaning in conspiratorially. "Apparently, this match basically comes down to a rivalry between Professor O'Brien and one of the medical faculty. They're both Irish, I guess, and total berserkers on the pitch. It started out as a bet and then morphed into a fundraiser."

"How practical," Rebecca said with a grin.

I smiled back, further intrigue dawning around the ways and means of a certain linguistics professor. While Dave also knew next to nothing about rugby, he was extremely reliable when it came to relaying any decent gossip or story of interest, so I trusted his word.

The players organized themselves on the field, with the medical team aligning to take the first kick.

"Okay, so," Rebecca explained, "you know that the ball can only be passed backwards, right?"

"Yes. But the players move forward," I said.

"Correct! And it's illegal to drop the ball forward too; that's called a knock-on."

"I know some random words, like 'scrum' and 'ruck.'" I laughed. I had grown up with rugby being played at my own schools but clearly had never taken much of an interest in it other than the words.

"I'm partial to 'grubber' and 'Garryowen' myself," Rebecca said.

Apparently, both were the outcomes of kicks, the first one where the ball bounced on the ground, and the latter when it was kicked high into the air. It all seemed completely random to me, but I nodded in an honest attempt at understanding.

We continued on in the collegial frivolity only awarded to the first weeks of school, and I took surprising pleasure in drinking my beer and casually watching the match. It was easy to spot Professor O'Brien, who was a forward, according to my rugby translator. He was big and powerful, responsible for pushing and scrambling on the front line to retrieve the ball.

I was wholly impressed at his ferocity as he leaned in for each scrum or thrashed his legs around in a ruck. He wore the standard rugby shorts, which easily showed off his robust thighs. I marvelled at his agility in spite of his tall, broad frame. The brute force between the opposing teams was palpable, even for a charity match. Quite frankly, I wasn't surprised in the least to learn how much brawling went on at or around these matches throughout the sport's history.

"But the players still have to follow the laws on the pitch," Rebecca said.

"I like how it's 'laws' in rugby, not rules," I said.

Dave chuckled. "Sounds very official, laws. I'm partial to the idea of Australian rules myself. It sounds like some kind of epic lawless wasteland! *Mad Max* style."

"Hardly," Rebecca said, characteristic mirth spilling over.

However, we had also just witnessed one player in the scrum 'rake' another on the back with their cleated foot, and it certainly hadn't been called as a foul of any sort.

Dave had grown up playing hockey apparently but didn't seem to have any difficulty getting into the spirit of the game. For my own part, I was trying to shake this overpowering feeling of familiarity around the battle, or match, unfolding before me. Besides the obvious similarities between modern-day sports and ancient warfare, there was something else about the gameplay that felt almost like déjà vu. Chalking it up to more flaky intuition on my part, I hopped up to buy the next round of beer.

"Be right back!" I said, wanting to beat the halftime hustle, which was apparently only five minutes but always a mad dash for people to top their drinks.

Standing at a slightly higher vantage point, I experienced only a mildly different view of the match as it proceeded just before they whistled for half-time. Much like the stadium beer, I was beginning to feel pleasantly quaffable myself, and was giggling when the teams arranged themselves into what was apparently called a 'line out.' It reminded me of synchronised swimming, but with the players suspended awkwardly in the air on dry land.

Suddenly then, in a most unwelcome rush, my vision went shockingly red. I could smell the distinctive iron tang of blood paired with the sour repugnance of vomit. Choking back my own bile, I did my absolute best to shake the vision while clutching blindly at the nearest thing I could find, which was (most unfortunately) a half-full garbage can.

My stomach lurched as I eyed the varied waste contents of the bin, and I hastily closed my eyes, slowly counting backwards from ten. The vison had been distressingly specific. And while I was used to my own brand of unpre-dictable magic, this was a whole new ball game.

Returning to Rebecca and Dave, notably without beer in hand, I did my best to disguise my momentary lapse.

"Are you alright, girl?" Rebecca asked. "You don't look too hot."

"Oh yeah, just having a bit of reflux . . . didn't eat enough before maybe," I lied.

While I was gone, the two had apparently deduced that our cunning professor's rival was likely a 'back' on the opposing team. The first piece of evidence was that the two were clearly the heart of their teams, the second being the escalating goading and catcalling going on between the two of them, although from our location, it was hard to hear exactly what words were exchanged.

I nodded in feigned interest and continued to watch the second half of the game, but my attention was split. At its completion, the medical team was victorious due only to a single penalty, much to Professor O'Brien's very visible indignation. I made my apologies for leaving so abruptly and staggered towards the bus stop on autopilot. Only really significant visions could derail me as such, almost like a magically induced bender, which I knew all too well would be followed by a debilitating hangover.

And this one I desperately needed to sleep off.

CHAPTER 4

I f my final semester of university was to have a theme, it would be "hurry up and wait." The days dragged by with a multitude of quizzes and paper submissions each week, on top of the already extensive readings provided by one professor in particular.

"Have you had a chance to start your essay for O'Brien's class?" Dave asked. We had met in the library to study for the upcoming quiz in Advanced Semantics.

"Yeah . . . well, sort of." I paused. "Okay, no. Not yet."

He laughed. "Me neither. I feel like he's going to be a total ass about the first grades he hands out anyways, so I'm not sure whether I should just brush it off because it's not worth very much, or if I should bust my balls on it and see what shakes out. I kind of feel like I don't want to disappoint him."

I smiled in embarrassed agreement. Our weekly seminars had continued on much like the first, with an overabundance of information over too short a time. For my part, the hour together was also fuelled by playful sparring and not-so-lightly veiled tension. My peers found the seminar equally gruelling, but none of them shared the same additional friction as I did.

True to my discussion with Dave, I completed my first paper for Professor O'Brien at three a.m. on Tuesday night, exhausted and sweaty on my top half, but with comparatively frozen feet and hands. I was surprised, when I finally hit the print button, at how nervous I was to share my writing and ideas with him. My chosen topic felt extremely personal, and much to my own irritation, I too felt a strong urge to impress the man.

Our first assignments were to be submitted in person on Wednesday before the October long weekend. Professor O'Brien was the old-school sort, who apparently intended to mark each page diligently by hand, rather than use a tablet or even a laptop. His excuse was that he couldn't be bothered to log on to a computer and sort each essay out, but I had the distinct sense he was a bit of a technophobe in spite of his age.

Throughout the semester, I had wondered how difficult it would be to leave this all behind at the end of term; it wasn't the class I was going to miss. Something about Professor O'Brien was positively spellbinding for me, almost like he was some sort of magical conduit. Sure, he was obviously handsome and charming, but the way my Witch's fire stoked almost ferociously in his presence was impossible to ignore.

To the casual observer, this undeniable connection had already become quite the topic of delighted gossip.

"He loves to pick on you though, doesn't he?" Rebecca had said the previous Thursday afternoon in Historical Linguistics. It was exceedingly dry work, and so we often found ourselves chatting quietly as we broke down the assigned language trees. I was working through an obscure limb of the Proto-Indo-European line, while Rebecca was unpacking a far more interesting looking Proto-Salishan branch.

"Oh, I don't know. I wouldn't say that . . ." I looked up and grinned. "Okay, maybe a little bit. But I kind of like to egg him on, so I suppose it's a bit of my own fault. He's so . . . provocative."

"That's one word for it," she had said with a wink, her low chuckle a dead give-away that she figured I was doomed.

It was becoming more of an egg-on-face situation, with my peers audibly bemoaning our verbal spars as class ran over the time limit. I was way too old for this type of thing, and yet I couldn't seem to help myself. Even so, it felt completely ludicrous for me to even consider dating a professor, especially when the direction of my life was headed far away from the world of academia. That much I *knew* to be true.

Still, I couldn't fight the impulse to be near him.

When it finally came time to hand in my essay to Professor O'Brien, I thought to stagger my exit from my peers by dropping my favourite pen on the floor. Unfortunately, my brilliant stalling tactic resulted in smacking my head abruptly on the bottom of the dated Formica desk. I groaned audibly as my peers stacked their stapled essays above me into a faded brown file folder and quickly shuffled out of the room.

"Are you alright under there?" he asked, bewitching smile on full beam. He didn't bother to hide the fact that he was laughing at me, but it didn't lack for kindness.

"Yeah, I'm good. Just dropped my pen," I said, waggling the offending blue stick at him. I straightened myself up and pulled my paper from the side pocket of my clipboard.

Julia Harrison
Linguistics 447G
Modern Implications of Patriarchal Structure on Gendered
Language Acquisition

I placed my crumpled essay, which at the very least was free of coffee stains, onto the stack. Our hands brushed together just slightly as he reached out to collect the remainder of the work. I felt a surge of raw electricity pass through my body, followed by an unexpected, and almost unbearable, feeling of homesickness.

My eyes shot up towards him, only to be met by his much more pensive gaze. His smile had faded slightly, expressing a brief moment of anguish from which he seemed to struggle to regain control.

"Thanks very much Julia," he said simply, running his hand through his hair and looking towards the exit. My gaze lingered on his fingers. I felt my entire face bloom bright pink, my breath unexpectedly caught in my throat. This was my moment and already it felt like it was slipping away.

I panicked.

"Well . . . I hope you have a good long weekend," I said as I turned towards the door. I paused and spun to face him again, perhaps a little too quickly. "Don't have too much fun marking all those papers." And then I *winked* at him. Winked! What on the Goddess' good green earth had gotten into me?

"I will. *Thanks*, Julia," he said, and closed his faded leather briefcase with a quick snap before launching himself into the hallway. I leaned out of his way as he strode purposefully in the direction of his office without looking back, almost as if he couldn't get away fast enough.

I let out a long sigh; I was disappointed to not have had my advances returned, even if they were decidedly awkward. Without intending to, I wandered out of the building and towards the large oak tree, its brown leaves and acorns now cast askew at its roots like confetti. Autumn on the coast was the most spectacular time. While many plants move into dormancy, winter foliage would come to life, almost blindly ambitious with its greenery on even the dullest of days.

I usually looked forward to the arrival of cooler temperatures, but this year I was worried about the effect the darker winter days might have on my mental health. Apart from when I was distracted by schoolwork or sitting in class, I still felt painfully displaced, like I was going through the motions without forming any memories or appreciable connections. Well, that wasn't entirely true. I *had* felt a strong connection between myself and Professor O'Brien, but it seemed like that too was destined to fizzle out. Still, that didn't explain why my Bearing magic went positively primal any time I was near him.

That night, I had the most horrific dream.

I was riding on horseback across an expanse of deadened grass while being chased at great speed by riders on dark stallions, their black cloaks billowing behind them as they screamed out my name. Or at least, I thought it was my name, but it sounded strange. It was clearly another time, or another place, but I had no sense of any bearings.

What with the timing of dreams always being slightly askew, I approached the distant mountain pass I had apparently been aiming for and quietly slipped through a great stone archway atop my chestnut mare. I spoke to her then, congratulating her on reaching our destination. Instead of relaxing, she whinnied, stamping her hooves nervously and looking around. Her coat was glossy from exertion, and I hastily slid off to try to calm her nerves.

Suddenly, a golden-haired man appeared from behind one of the recesses, brandishing a great long sword in one hand and a shorter dagger in the other. Clearly a warrior, he braced himself while looking through the narrow space between the stones and towards the open field. His face remained hidden, but he reminded me strongly of the prince from my childhood imaginings.

Time passed once more, this time in a flurry of black cloaks, arching and colliding steel blades, and the red tang of freshly spilled blood. The fair warrior had been slain, and my horse all but disappeared. A horrible dark laughter filled my ears, and I thought my heart might just rip from my body in anguish.

When I awoke, I was drenched in sweat and shaking uncontrollably as the malevolent cackle still permeated my thoughts. I rolled over to check the time. Three a.m. I ran my fingers though my damp, unbound hair and sat up, completely unnerved and perplexed. While I had enjoyed many experiences in my life, I had in fact never ridden a horse, so this was a strange dream indeed. Moreover, who *was* the golden man? And why were we being hunted to the death?

Initially, I chalked my disturbed sleep up to the uncomfortable exchange the afternoon before, having gone to bed with the residual feelings of disappointment still heavy in my heart. But the dream felt strangely contrary to all of that, only serving to deepen the sense of intuitive knowing forming within my unconscious. Finding no easy answers, I rolled over and chased tumultuous sleep for the remainder of the night.

The rest of the week dragged on. My nightmares were only slightly improved by the addition of an evening cup of peppermint and chamomile tea before tucking into my lumpy subletted bed. I had never garnered much success with any of the 'formal' sleep aids on the market, nor had I had any success with the more illicit ones either.

Gertie, master of herbal remedies, had once taken my sleep woes on as a special project, but she too had been at a loss for the right combination of plants and elixirs to help my cause. I had my suspicions that it was my divining magic interacting negatively with the expected effects of exhaustion, so had long given up on my fruitless search for sleep support. Thankfully, apart from a few outliers, my sleep patterns *had* been gradually improving since my arrival back in the city.

When I was child, my mother had called me, 'hypersensitive,' dismissing my fatigue as attention-seeking behaviour or unwanted neediness. Her regular state of personal crisis was always far more important than my childish demands. Soon, I learned it was far simpler to wage my nighttime battles with silence by forging onward through the darkness alone.

I could remember several of my elementary teachers sharing genuine concern with my mother, during chance encounters with her after school, about how lethargic and unfocused I was. She would shrug it off and say that she couldn't imagine why, since I stayed in my room all night. "Well, she goes to bed around nine p.m., and usually I have to wake her up several times in the morning before she *actually* gets out of bed and ready for school. It's *quite* the production." My teachers would usually nod skeptically but accept her explanation without further inquiry, since I would reactively redouble my efforts to hide my exhaustion, effectively quelling their concerns until the next teacher came along.

As an adult, I began to piece together that my disturbed sleep was largely due to my untrained magic—in particular the influences of the Sight—rather than any diagnosable sleep disorder. Indeed, the recurring visions of the past and present, and even the rare divinations of the future, combined recklessly into the confused effluvium that would haunt me though each circadian struggle.

I would eventually learn that my mother too shared my sleep troubles, right up until the day she died. I surmised it was more than likely due to the complete suppression of her magic, rather than a lack of training. I didn't often reminisce over the final days, months, or even years of my mother's existence, as those were some of the darkest times of my young life. However, with Gertie's recent passing, I had found myself stewing on how the grief had overtaken me so completely at that time.

My mother had died when I was in my final year of high school. At just seventeen years old, I felt like the abundant future hopes that I was supposed to share with the rest of my peers had been completely dashed away without any consideration for my wants and dreams. I was angry, confused, and utterly shattered. And as far as I was concerned, I was also an orphan.

Gertie had moved over from Salt Spring to live with me while I completed school. While my friends were applying for university, I spent my evenings wandering the familiar streets of my Victoria neighbourhood, staring endlessly at the skies, trying to plot myself in the churning tides of the universe, to avail. My feet would often lead me to the oceanside, where I would stare hopelessly into the darkness and wish this life away for an easier one. Some nights, I would be so desperate for respite from my pain that I would wade into the surf, offering myself to the Goddess so that I could at least have some kind of purpose, rather than these lost days navigating a map with no compass.

I was perhaps a touch theatrical then. But at the time, my wound was so raw and open that, most of the time, I felt like screaming into the abyss.

An even bleaker consequence during this time was the absolute disappearance of my magic. A loneliness crept in then that was infinite in comparison to the loss of my mother. She had abandoned me spiritually long ago, but my magic had long served as a defining comfort as I grew up, largely because it was what set me apart from her dark past. And now, I had lost it all.

Gertie, deciding enough was enough, sent me to the Prairies for the summer to work as an apprentice on a honey farm. She had long since said that my magic had always been sweet and mysteriously powerful, and she felt sure that the bees would serve well to rekindle my fire. She herself had kept a small apiary at the cottage for a time, so I took her word for it. Not to mention, I was keen to get as far away as possible from my mother's ghosts. I skipped my grade-twelve graduation ceremony, hopped onto a Greyhound bus, and headed east towards the Land of the Living Skies.

And it was exactly what I needed: pure magic.

The farm was owned by some distant second or third cousin of hers, Cam Sawchuk. Immediately upon our meeting, I discovered that he was about as stubborn as they came, yet generous and kind to those who put in an honest day's work. He was also delightfully quick-witted, which made for a dynamic first meeting.

Picking me up at the bus stop, I found Cam leaning back onto his well-tended but aged Chevy pickup. I guessed he was likely in his late fifties. Though he was easily several inches shorter than me, I could tell immediately that this did nothing to diminish the stature of his mind, as he too took the measure of me.

"Welcome, Julia! I've got to say, I was quite surprised when Gertie called me up and asked if I needed some extra help on the farm this summer. But . . . here you are!"

He removed his flat-brimmed cap and scratched his scalp thoughtfully before replacing it atop his sunburnt head. I nodded shyly and looked down to my scrawny arms, wondering if we all had made a huge miscalculation in my ability to take this on.

"Don't mistake my meaning, I'm sure you'll do great! It's just that those Stephenson girls never took much of a liking to our Prairie lifestyle." He chuckled to himself. "Come on, let's get rolling."

Cam was surprisingly easy company as we drove down the roughly paved highway. He had apparently been a Philosophy major with his hopes set towards law school. But when his father had passed away suddenly in his final semester, his path had been forcibly laid out before him. He regaled me with his university adventures with fondness, but never pressed me on what my plans were for the coming year.

"Of course, that dream completely *bought the farm*, if you take my meaning," he said, pulling his cap off once more. "But you know what? I've made the best of it."

We drove on in silence for a while as the road turned to gravel. I had the distinct sense there was much more behind the meaning of the story than what was on the surface; yet, Cam didn't need to tell me another word.

It had been a hot and gruelling summer. I soon came to enjoy the solitary moments among the hives, working through the frames and collecting honey as the different mono-crops bloomed across the fields. This was quite a different experience than I had witnessed on the West Coast. Still, I revelled in both the scale and challenge. The smell of smoke and propolis soon became my signature scent, and to this day, the smell of beehives reminds me of the time I found my magic, and myself, once more.

I discovered there was something almost otherworldly about honeybees. Driven by the pheromone of the queen and the overall health of the colony, they work tirelessly day-in and day-out to collect enough pollen and nectar for their winter stores, tending to the various stages of young bees, developing a healthy comb, all in devotion to the queen and hive health. Every female bee in the colony has a job, a worker role, which morphs along with them throughout their development cycle. Meanwhile the drones, or male bees, serve a singular albeit relevant reproductive purpose. The queen is only as important as her ability to ensure the passage of healthy genetics, producing eggs and creating cohesion within the colony. Her laying ebbs and flows intuitively each season in parallel to the summer solstice, the longest day of the year.

If this wasn't magic, I didn't know what was. However, even she could be replaced if necessary for the sake of colony survival. It was all rather brutally Utilitarian yet beautifully spiritual all at once.

One unexpected delight of the summer had come in the form of a young man named Jake Enns. He was several years older than me, fun loving, and perfectly sun-kissed from the hot Prairie summer. He was Cam's nephew and had joined us to help with the honey harvest during the latter half of the season. He would return to university in the fall to complete his finance degree, and had presented himself as the perfect distraction before I returned to the Coast.

We spent several hot-and-heavy weeks balancing life between working the hives. Sticky with honey and warm with sweat, we enjoyed each other well into the long summer evenings. Together, we would sneak off behind the storage shed at regular intervals, with Jake lifting me all too easily onto the work bench as we tore off our white bee suits in fits of young, lustful passion.

I celebrated my eighteenth birthday among the hives. My transition into legal adulthood felt somewhat adorned by the abundant supply of sweet honey and propolis, which never seemed to wash fully from clothes or body. Being born on the eighth of August, also known as the Lion's Gate, my birthdate had long been thought to hail increased energy flow between the physical and spiritual realm. If I had ever been unsure of its truth before, I had certainly witnessed its exceptional power first-hand that summer, both in myself and in the harvest.

I felt the wings of freedom for the first time in a lifetime, or at least since I had been a very small child. Finally sensing a balance between my inner and outer magics, the resulting alignment had left a permanent and lasting impression that I would not soon forget.

Sadly, however, by the end of summer, things fell awkward between Jake and I.

"Julia, I think I'm falling in love with you," he'd said one night as we lay with our backs on the grass, faces surrendered towards the stars.

"No, you're not," I answered playfully, keenly wishing to shrug off the sudden intensity.

It had been a magical summer together; there was no doubt about it. But I had learned early on in my life that all good things must come to an end, and I had no interest in tying myself to anyone, or *anywhere* for that matter. Not to mention that I had zero interest in over-wintering myself in the Prairies.

"I'm serious. I've never felt this way about anyone before. You're so . . . different than anyone I've ever been with."

Pursing my lips, I exhaled forcefully through both nostrils. I *was* different. I was a Witch, a magic Bearer. My power had awoken spectacularly during the long days working on the farm, and I was finally starting to feel well and truly alive. No wonder he was so drawn to me; it was hard for ordinary people *not* to notice raw magic as it bubbled over and spilled out, influencing absolutely everything it touched. Magic in this form was even known to leave a distinctive mark behind if you knew what you were looking for.

I knew in my heart that the reason behind this year's bountiful harvest was partly due to my manual manipulation of the hives. None of it had been intentional, of course. I convinced myself not to feel too guilty for influencing nature as such. What I did feel guilty for, however, was the evident effect I'd had on poor Jake.

In that moment, to ease the imminent heartbreak to come, I convinced myself that it had likely been an accidental glamour I had placed on him. It was time to cut the cord and not look back.

"I'm sorry, Jake, I just . . . don't feel the same way. It's been a wonderful summer, but . . . this is where we'll have to leave it."

Immediately, his eyes filled with pain, darting back and forth frantically to look anywhere but at my face. Soon, his anguish was replaced with a haunted look of anger and shame as it spread violently across his brow. That was the first time I had ever witnessed someone's heart literally break in front of me, and I swore in that moment, as I watched him walk away, shoulders lifting in silent sobs, that I would never do it again.

The truth was, I would have to send men away several more times just like this during my twenties, and it never got any easier. Eventually, I began to believe that I was better suited to a life of singledom, much like my Gran, which I was slowly coming to terms with; I had learned long ago how to fend for myself and be the solution to my own problems for better or for worse.

However, there was a hidden part of me curiously open to that one person who might change my mind. Magic worked in mysterious ways after all, so who was I to argue with the design of destiny

CHAPTER 5

I planned to stay in the city for the October long weekend. There was no reason to run back to the cottage for only a few nights when I still had several papers to write and readings to catch up on. I would miss Gertie this year to be sure but had no interest in sitting in the empty cottage without her either.

Virginia and I were invited to dinner with some of her friends who had also found themselves without family connection over the holiday. I had attempted to back-out of the invite at the last minute, not really craving company, but Virginia's loud protests convinced me otherwise.

"Please, Julia? You've been a hermit for weeks. You're starting to remind me of Ben!"

I shot her a look, but I knew she didn't mean it, not entirely anyways. I *had* been more of a loner than she was accustomed to this semester, but it was with good reason.

"Fine," I said, "but I don't want to stay super late."

"Deal!" she said, clapping her hands together loudly before scooping up her bean dip, grabbing her car keys, and heading for the door without another word.

We drove over to Virginia's friend Nathan's place in her well-loved Honda Civic, even though it was only several long city-blocks from our place. I re-routed us once along the way to stop for a bag of corn chips to go with the dip. My quick and unenthusiastic contribution to the meal matched my feelings about the whole situation. I struggled to feel a sense of attachment to almost anyone these days, but at least this group was welcoming and happy to have any contributions brought forth to the table. And what a presentation it was.

A smattering of colourful vegetarian entrees consisting of bright-orange sweet potatoes and a hearty mix of root vegetables were thoughtfully laid out in thrifted pottery atop several conjoined tables. Complementing the warmer dishes, of course, was the standard oversupply of decorated kale salads, their ever-creative adornments of scattered nuts, seeds, and dried fruits blinking up blissfully.

An assortment of pickles was tucked into a series of oblong false-crystal dishes that reminded me warmly of my grandma Gertie. Sitting down on a retro vinyl stacking stool, which also felt familiar, I puzzled at a proffered bowl of purple mashed potatoes; somehow, they just didn't look as appetizing as the regular kind.

A fellow named Robin and his partner brought a painstakingly prepared "turducken," which, for some, was the crowning jewel of the meal. Virginia had eaten plant-based for the better part of the last decade, and happily heaped extra helpings of the savoury veggies onto her plate as I tucked into the random bits of turkey, duck, and chicken. Craft beers, ciders, and richly coloured wines were shared generously, leading to a close and congenial atmosphere.

I was perched atop my stool at the edge of the group, enjoying a wild fermented wine from somewhere in the Okanagan valley, its unusual notes of honey and yeast reminding me fondly of my summer at the apiary. Conversation ranged between rants or raves about the latest trendy restaurants to the political climate south of the border. Naturally, the increasing number of missing-person cases was most notable, with several of the group's women expressing explicit apprehension around the statistics leaning so negatively in their direction.

"It all just seems so blatantly targeted, but then at the same time, why does it seem like nothing is being done about it?" one person said, articulating the shocking regularity with which the bodies turned up.

"Do they think it's a serial killer? Or like, a syndicate or something?" voiced one true-crime-loving member of the party, though not altogether insensitively.

"Whoever the perpetrator is, they seem to have taken a special interest in homeless and addicted youth, as if they don't experience enough violence as it is," Virginia piped in, informing the others of what she knew, or more accurately, what she was allowed to share. I knew that she had been actively involved in several police investigations over the past months; the strain was starting to visibly wear on her.

I unfortunately had my own growing suspicions on the matter. Both the seemingly ritualistic aspect of the killings as well as the horrific evidence playing out in my recurring nightmares led me to believe some aspect of Sorcery was involved. But since I was the only magic user in the room this evening, I kept my more supernaturally inclined opinions to myself.

Well warmed from the food, drink, and pleasant company, Virginia and I left shortly after ten on foot. "Let's just walk home," I had suggested, the clear, cool air of the evening welcome after the humidity of the stuffy house.

"Agreed! I shouldn't drive right now anyways."

While I appreciated her responsible choice, I was somewhat surprised at her lack of resistance. She was usually quite vocal in her wariness around being out alone at night as a woman, regardless of the neighbourhood. And she wasn't wrong, if our earlier conversation was anything to go by. Still, she was apparently satisfied that our pairing would be more than safe enough, as she was already happily striding down the street with her eyes to the stars before I had even registered her decision.

"I was *so* impressed with the little apple pies that Leigh made," she called back with glee.

"Mm, me too!" I said, jogging briefly to keep up. I had eaten one entirely to myself and felt it now.

We continued to walk along the concrete sidewalk, gradually making our way uphill towards our home neighbourhood. The network of streets and medians had been quite confusing to me when I'd first moved into the area, but Virginia had grown up in Vancouver and navigated the area with ease, even when inebriated.

The air had grown chillier, even since leaving Nathan's, making our walk seem much longer than it should have. Soon, a deep sense of unease began to unfurl in my stomach, like the coils of a giant sleeping snake.

"Ginny, haven't we already walked down this street?"

"What? No!" she said, staunch in her navigational prowess.

We continued on for another few minutes, the snake lifting its head curiously as we rounded yet another corner, only to encounter the exact same fenced-in tear-down sandwiched between two larger heritage homes.

"I could swear we've been here already," I said. Something definitely wasn't right.

"Maybe you had more to drink tonight than you thought, Jul-ee-a!" she said, lingering on the middle of my name with a grin, but I definitely had not. I also sure as shit knew a magical disturbance when I felt it, even with my weakened defences. We seemed to be stuck in some kind of bewildering glamour or enchantment; Virginia, however, was completely and woefully unaware.

I dug my hands frantically into my coat pockets, sorting past my housekeys and palm-sized wallet to yank out my cellphone. I aggressively poked at the screen.

"Fuck!"

While not in the best shape, it usually performed its basic duties in the city, if the conditions were right. However, much like every cell I had owned since my very first flip phone at sixteen, it was thrown into a complete fit of malfunction at the slightest magical interruption. Frankly, the reliability of *any* technology that sent or received signals had always been greatly influenced by unpredictable magical disturbances where I was concerned, but for some reason, cellphones were the worst.

I needed to gather my wits about me.

Pausing, I bore deep into my centre to hopefully get a sense of where the magic was originating from. I closed my eyes while taking several measured breaths and finally sensed it, but just barely. Regardless of the fact that I was in a particularly rusty time of life, magically speaking, I knew it wasn't a strong force surrounding us. My best guess was that it was coming from a Wielder, since its power didn't seem to be rooted anywhere specifically.

Gertie had called this "free-Wielding" magic, which was her play on "free-wheeling." It was charged and unpredictable, but also didn't boast an indefinite timestamp. Magic like this usually originated from an outside source, so there were often cracks between the user, the intended target, and the force being applied. When a Bearer conducted magic nearby, you could almost feel it pulsing through the earth, the effect being altogether more intense—solid and unyielding, you could say, woven *through* the magic user, rather than *from*.

Confidence growing, I turned to walk in what felt like the wrong direction, much to Virginia's displeasure and borderline panic. "Julia! You're going the wrong way!"

I didn't respond, as I was far too focused on pushing back on the wall of free-Wielding magic that surrounded us. There was something languid about it, the sickly-sweet smell around us reminding me of someone's breath when they are coming down with an illness. I recoiled, but there was no escaping it yet.

"Where are you going?" she asked again, sobering with each exasperated word. I was taking measured steps against the direction that felt correct, when Virginia caught up to me and grabbed my arm. "It's not safe for us to be wandering around aimlessly like this. We need to go home!"

She was right, but clearly not experiencing the same depth of enchantment as I was; glamours like these affected non-magic users differently. I mumbled something about dropping my keys as she stood anxiously behind me. I braced myself and leaned into the barrier once more, and then with a slight vibration, the disorientating magic ceased entirely.

The way home was suddenly completely clear, like a camera lens falling into focus. Much to our collective shock, we were actually standing only about thirty meters from the front door of our rental property.

"What was in that *wine*?" Virginia asked, pushing her palms into her eye sockets briefly. She shook her head in an attempt to release the residual confusion and strode towards the old house, looking over her shoulder only briefly to make sure I was keeping up.

"Indeed," I said quietly, and followed in her wake, cautiously looking over my own shoulder for signs of *who* had cast the mysterious spell.

I had the strangest feeling we had just brushed rather close to fate.

Dom O'Brien was hardly the first Celt to use the *Glasgow Kiss* as a means of delivering a clear message to an adversary, but he wasn't in the mood for originality today. Truthfully, he was about as Irish as they came, but in this very moment, a Celt was a Celt; a little modern Scottish flare would serve him just fine. Not to mention that the little gobshite more than deserved it. The utter nonsense spilling from the boy's mouth for the past ten minutes was starting to get under his skin, and he had woken up in a horrendous mood to begin with.

"Get up, or I'll knock your head into this wall! We'll see how much you like talking then, shall we?"

"Christ, man, he's hardly going to be able to string a sentence together, let alone stay conscious, if you bash his face in anymore," Ronan said, leaning casually against the brick-and-mortar wall of St. Paul's hospital. He clearly wasn't fussed at Dom's actions toward the little bastard, but felt a duty to offer a warning because of the oath he'd sworn.

Even on the poorly lit side street, the boy in question clearly had a bad dose of it, his skin pallid and face severely gaunt. He hadn't looked particularly well after Dom pulled him from the trunk of his car either, but he'd had to bring him to Ronan somehow; the borrowed compass only got him so far.

Regardless of how sickly he was, he currently had two *very* healthy streams of blood running down his face from both nostrils. He spat the blood pooling in his mouth onto Dom's feet, finding one last resolve to challenge the formidable man standing above him.

"Fuck you!" he said thickly through the collection of viscous substances in his mouth.

Dom pulled his lips back into a snarl. One more move like *that* and this would be the boy's last chance at leaving the confrontation with his head attached to his body.

"Try that again. I dare you." He had no patience for these "weaker men." There was no room for spinelessness where he came from; you either survived, or you perished, and your allegiances could make or break your fate in an instant. His father had taught him that much, at the very least.

Still the boy said nothing. Dom's restraint sat poised on the edge of a knife.

"Give us what we need, and we'll let you go quietly. We know you've been earwigging into the police business at the women's shelter, so there's no use denying it now. Who are you working for, and what have they promised in return?" he asked as he grabbed the boy by his hair and yanked him to his feet. Dom then slammed him into the wall for good measure as he inched his powerful fingers menacingly towards his throat.

Ronan stood slightly straighter but continued to look just as bored, "Dom . . ."

Being that Dom had no magic ability of his own, he had often resorted to his raw physical strength and aloof hardiness in these instances, rather than the *much* tidier actions of his friends and allies. He wasn't always proud of it, but there he stood.

"Talk!" he commanded. The boy was turning a funny grey colour underneath all of the blood, but the great Celt released his grip only slightly.

Ben Masters stood at a mere five-foot-seven and greatly resembled a drowned sewer rat. He was fine boned and had a short pointy nose, appropriately separating his sunken, beady brown eyes.

"I . . . have a condition," he said finally, "and they said they had a cure."

"Who's *they?*" Dom asked. Ronan strode several steps closer, listening intently.

"I don't know what they're called. I found them online . . . some sort of dark-web group who have access to more than just medical research. They said . . ." he paused, peering around nervously. "They said that if I gave them information about what Virg—what my cousin was telling the police at the shelter, they would give me access to a cure."

"You're not honestly that thick, are you?" Dom scoffed.

It was the wrong thing to say, and the boy was soon thrashing underneath Dom's strong grasp, trying to escape once more, the resultant struggle turning his lips a deep shade of purple.

"Listen, I can probably help," Ronan piped in, showing Ben his ID.

Dr. Ronan Gallagher
Clinician-Researcher UBC
Department of Emergency Medicine.

52

"There is a much safer way to go about this. But you'll need to answer several more questions before I can help you."

Dom released the boy from the wall, jerking him towards Ronan with zero consideration for his ability to walk.

"Help him then," Dom said, eyeing Ronan skeptically before turning his dark gaze towards Ben once more. "But if I find out you've been feeding information to those filthy Wraiths, I won't be so kind next time."

Ronan gave Dom a slow nod, then turned his attention towards the boy to assess his injuries. Ronan wouldn't tell the boy he was a Druid; that was far too risky, and besides, the *true* Druidic order was an impeccably contained secret, even amongst other magical folks.

"We know that you were attempting to Wield magic tonight. Did you get it from *them*?"

"What's it to you?"

"It's extremely foolish to meddle with dangerous things you don't understand, Ben. Especially when it comes to dark magic." Ronan now spoke with the clear, objective tone of a physician.

Alarm now rose in Ben's voice. "I can't *Wield* anything. I don't even know what you're talking about, or what Wraiths are. They just gave me a small pouch full of black sand and said the contents would delay anyone coming close, so I had time to gather information, and—" He looked nervously again towards Dom, who had just cracked his knuckles into a tight fist before tossing the apprehended pouch at Ronan's feet, now empty of its contents. "—and to use it sparingly, because I wasn't getting any more," Ben finished hastily.

Ronan kept his composure but exhaled quietly through both nostrils. He was flummoxed that the Wraiths would entrust such a meek creature with their magic, however primitive it was. "And you believed them?"

"They probably didn't intend for him to survive the ordeal," Dom said, reading Ronan's mind. "He's clearly weak, and those fuckers just take whatever they need and cast away the remains."

"True. I mean, he doesn't even know why they want the intel. It's clearly Cassius."

Dom silenced Ronan with a look.

Ben looked between the foreboding men in confusion, their conversation having moved to a plane he no longer understood. In turn, they gave him dark looks of pity mixed with disgust but made no effort to include him in their discussion any longer.

"Would it explain why we hadn't been able to track Ben down?" Dom said.

Ronan shook his head. "There wouldn't have been enough magic in that pouch to do that; he must have had some other kind of enchantment placed around him."

Dom nodded slowly, pondering their current situation. They would have to relocate the boy, of course, perhaps citing the upcoming medical treatments as an excuse; there was no way the little bastard would be going back to finish the job. Ronan and the others would see to that though as he had never liked to dabble in the fussy bits once the action was over.

"You'll take care of it?" Dom asked rhetorically.

"Of course," Ronan said simply, then took Ben by the elbow towards the side entrance to the hospital.

Dom let out a low sigh before turning in the opposite direction. Something about how elusive Ben had been throughout their tracking of him made Dom uneasy. He didn't know magic, but somehow the boy had concealed himself like he had it, almost like he was hiding a bigger secret, even though he knew so little. Ronan seemed appeased enough at this point though, so he let it slide.

Unlocking his car door, Dom could feel the boiling rage inside him start to simmer, making way for more challenging emotions. He wished he could drag Ronan from work to go out on the tear; the other feelings were the ones he truly needed distraction from, and a night of drink would serve as a welcome Band-Aid. Instead, he had essays to mark, and Ronan was obviously needed at the hospital.

Dom yawned loudly as he shifted the car into drive. Ever since finally meeting Julia at the university, he had barely been able to cobble more than three hours of sleep together at any one time, waking frequently in a cold sweat, the nightmares and flashbacks his all too regular bed companions. And then there was the longing. Indeed, he was not looking forward to another night spent alone, especially when he knew she was somewhere *just* out of his reach.

CHAPTER 6

We awoke to discover that Ben had moved out silently in the night. Naturally, Virginia was mortified. He left behind only a hastily scribbled note stating that his plans had suddenly changed with work, and that he would be relocating to San Francisco, posthaste. There was "nothing to worry about," and he would be getting in touch when he could.

We'd both failed to notice whether or not Ben had already been gone when we'd gotten home the night before, having gone directly to bed after our ordeal with the disorientation spell. Virginia spent the better part of the holiday Monday morning sharing panicked phone conversations with her aunt and family, who knew about as much as she did.

Virginia's questions rang through the air in anxious ramblings. "I just don't understand how he could up and move away without saying goodbye. I mean, I know he's seemed a bit off for the past while, but who does that?"

Unbeknownst to me, Ben had an extremely rare genetic condition, which Virginia had explicitly promised *not* to tell me about. It had allegedly been causing him some issues with his sleep and daily function as of late, which explained a few things. He had also been having some difficulties at work with bullies, which Virginia surmised was likely another important piece of the puzzle.

In the end, it looked like what he had said was true, and he had gone to California.

"Sometimes you just need a fresh start," I offered, feeling unexpectedly sympathetic towards his plight. I knew it was often easier to just duck out than talk in circles with someone who isn't able to see your perspective.

When I was only five years old, my mother had uprooted us from our small town in the heart of the Prairies, transplanting us to what her neighbours would (behind her back) nastily refer to as *Lotusland*.

"That Cheryl, she's always been running away from her own shadow!" one particularly outspoken woman in the Shop Easy checkout line had said as we gathered the last of our groceries before leaving town. I remembered vividly the dirty look my mother had shot her as I was pulled through the swinging automatic doors and out of the store by the wrist.

"Julia, this is going to be exactly *what we need! We can spend more time with your gran, and you can maybe go to one of those fancy private schools everyone talks about! This was never our hometown anyways. You're a West Coast girl, through and through, just like me!"* She had proclaimed this loudly as we'd stuffed the last of our things into the back of her rusted powder-blue Oldsmobile, clearly hoping one of our neighbours might hear.

I would never learn *what* exactly she had been running from that day, or why she chose that particular timeframe to dismantle our entire life and head west. Her explanation at the time was that we needed a fresh start. But the truth, or at least my best guess at it, was that she was escaping the oppressive reminders of my abusive late father. After years of prodding for information, and despite the expected and regular rebuffs, I managed to gather a few more concrete facts.

When they'd met, it had been a whirlwind romance. He was a businessman from somewhere outside of Toronto, their paths crossing serendipitously one hot summer as she visited friends out East. Young and free, everyone told her she was moving too fast and that there was plenty of time for marriage later, but she'd ignored the dire warnings and married him anyway.

"He was sweet once," she'd said. But he had quickly turned bitter and eventually downright cruel when his business failed and he'd been forced to liquidate all that they owned. They had then packed up and moved to an isolated border town in Southern Alberta, where he had inherited a dilapidated farmhouse from a distant and deceased uncle. From then on, my mother was forced into isolation for the sake of her marriage. Her magic was all but

absent in these years, conscious or subconscious suppression of powers obviously at work. I don't think he knew she was a Witch at all.

He'd stuck around long enough to acknowledge my birth on a hot August night. A neighbour apparently delivered me in the twilight hours when it became clear there was no way my mother would make it to the hospital in time. My father had flat out refused to listen to her incessant moaning and had driven himself into town to drink instead.

She said I had been beautiful, a true gift, with my reddish hair already sweetly shining atop my squished pink face. She had prayed that the miracle of my arrival would bring his heart back to her, but it was a fool's hope. He'd left her the following month once I had survived the first weeks of infanthood, abandoning her to raise me through the upcoming fall and bitter Prairie winter alone.

Her shadows had crept in as surely as the winter frost, pushing any community away and determined to do it on her own. By the time we emerged in the spring, she was a wholly changed woman, no longer able to bloom fully under the sun's warming rays. We stuck around for five long years, my mother cycling through the seasons of time without concern or consequence. I don't think I was neglected during this time; however, we didn't have a lot, and it began to wear on her.

My grandmother, for her part, had tried her best to raise a daughter who could stand on her own two feet, but she too had faced challenges as a mother.

Gertie had only just arrived from England before hastily marrying an American draft-dodger hiding out on Salt Spring Island during the middle years of the Vietnam War, just as displaced as she was. Despite the early passion, they weren't a love match. He retreated to the U.S. after several years of struggle, abandoning Gertie to raise my mother alone.

Our cross-country trek to Gertie's had been arduous for me and my mother, so the joy when we arrived was indescribable. In my heart, I'd desperately craved to be nearer my grandmother and her magic, so much so that in grade four I had even begged my mother to allow me to move in with Gertie full time. The look of sadness that spread across her face then kept me from ever asking again. So, I'd settled for my "summers on Salty," as I affectionately called them, and spent the school year with my mother in Victoria.

I had always attributed my mother's dismissal of spiritual connection as mere jealousy, but as I grew older, I realized how much more complicated it all was. The threat of being a woman in your full power, let alone a magical one standing to your full stature, was immensely frightening to her, particularly having been raised in a society that was built on the oppression and commodification of women's worth, intuitive abilities, and agency at every turn. Indeed, the immense danger of exposing our true selves was a persistent truth for everyone in the magical community. We had lost much of our own culture, shared history, and celebrations as Witches, blending in and adopting the contemporary holidays and ceremonies, and it was a damn shame.

Both Gertie and my mother had wandered through my thoughts more than anticipated this fall, so I found myself pining for the presence of other magical beings, particularly as Samhain approached. It had been a long while since I had connected with any other Witches, Gertie being one of the only Bearers I actually knew in person.

One of the perks of the current Pagan revival and call to the Divine Feminine was that gatherings could be held more publicly. This allowed those of us who were true magic holders to meet seemingly out in the open. They were peculiar things, magical gatherings. You would run into the whole mix, both true Wielders and wildly enthusiastic but plainly ordinary folks. And if you were really lucky, perhaps a handful of Bearers as well.

I was tempted to seek out a Samhain gathering at the end of the month, if only to ask any local Witch if they knew more about the missing girls. My instinct, and horrific nightmares, had now firmed into a belief that the disappearances were not only targeted but magically motivated.

Another reason for attending a gathering, which I was less inclined to admit to myself, was that I had been lonelier than anticipated this fall, even with the distractions of school and Professor O'Brien occupying my thoughts. After our awkward interaction several weeks previous—the one where I winked at the bastard—things had slid back to normal with an almost irritating ease. What was worse, I had developed a rather irresistible proclivity for explicit daydreams when I wasn't being called upon.

The furnace system in Totem Field Studios operated well within the range of normal, but Professor O'Brien seemed to run hot, and would hastily discard his outer jacket or wool sweater approximately halfway through each seminar. So far, his wardrobe underneath had consisted of three different linen-blend dress shirts, one each in sage green, off-white, and a gorgeous sky blue. He clearly hadn't bought into the cultural trends of "fast fashion" common in the last several decades, and I appreciated his tidy capsule. The man knew what worked for him, and he went for it.

Already vigorously engaged in discussion by that point, he would nimbly remove the garment mid-sentence, hardly losing stride as he continued to press on with his selected materials. Charging on, his shoulders would first flex and then settle underneath the fabric as it pulled slightly across his chest with each intake of breath. I found myself wondering how difficult it would be to remove his shirt with haste, careful not to ruin the buttons, of course.

My own chest consistently tightened at the thought.

Strangely, he never turned his back to us while discharging his shell, which seemed instinctually to make more sense. But I wasn't really complaining. If I was really lucky, from where I sat halfway down the table, sometimes I could visually trace the lean muscle of his lower abdomen, its firm surface imparted with golden hair that looked both soft and inviting. And holy hell what I would like to do with—

"Julia?"

I attempted to pull myself together quickly, but I knew my cheeks were well and fully flushed. Thankfully, the room *was* warm today, but the look on his face told me he wasn't buying it.

"Hmm?" I gulped.

"I think we will leave it there for now and end a few minutes early. The others don't have any objection . . . Do you?"

"Oh. No, of course not."

I cut my finger on the corner of a crumpled piece of paper as I scrambled to slam my notes into my clipboard. Sucking on my painful finger, I blushed further as I noticed half of the seminar group had already pushed in their chairs and were exiting the room. Rebecca was giggling at me from behind her always-over-loaded backpack, shaking her head. I shrugged in admittance.

Professor O'Brien too had a slight smirk on his face, but there was something else lingering behind his gaze. He seemed to be a man of dualities; while his aura was of pure golden sunshine, I also sensed a lurking darkness within him that I found challenging to deny. It reminded me of a forest at night—deep, restful, and full of unexpected possibility.

Curiosity couldn't begin to describe how it made me feel.

"Any plans for Samhain?" he asked as he gathered up his soft leather briefcase. I noticed that it was empty but for today's notes.

"Samhain?" I asked, giving away my surprise.

Did he suspect something? Why else would he ask about a Pagan celebration? I knew he wasn't a Bearer; that much was clear. It was almost impossible to miss other Bearers in such a tightly shared space, their own force of magic pushing with surety against your own. Perhaps he was a Wielder? I always had a hard time detecting them unless they were fully in the act of magic, but he definitely had some sort of strong presence about him, almost like an ancient, motivated gravity.

I thought again of the rugby match last month and the vision of the battle that had overflowed so aggressively into my psyche; he definitely gave off the distinct energy of a warrior.

"Sorry, Halloween," he said as if the two were indistinguishable.

"Nothing concrete yet."

"Well, be careful out there. You never know which ghoulies or hobgoblins might be lurking about," he said. It was his turn to offer me a wink, but his eyes were piercing.

The room had cleared out, and as usual, it was just us two bringing up the rear.

"What about you?" I asked, feeling suddenly brave about any potential shared weekend prospects.

"Oh, you *really* weren't listening earlier, were you?" he said, eyebrows raised and accent drawn out slightly to make his meaning plain, but I could tell he wasn't angry. "I'm headed to the airport here shortly. Have to take a quick trip south over the next few days. I won't be back until early next week."

"Oh . . ." I said, not bothering to disclose my disappointment. It seemed impossible not to wear my heart on my sleeve around him anyway.

Admittedly, I had long considered this to be one of my weaker traits while navigating polite conversation, speaking my mind perhaps a bit too freely without considering the consequences. But with him, it felt like an utter betrayal to hide my true self. This was new territory for me.

"Well, I hope you have a safe trip," I said, offering up what I thought was a carefree smile.

"Thanks. Have a great weekend, Julia."

I turned from the room, the broad Irishman treading audibly in my wake as he closed the door loudly behind us. He bid me adieu once more, and with a nod and a curt smile, he turned to the right down the hallway towards the faculty offices on the second floor. I veered left.

The previous week, I had actually been obliged to make the same ascent to his office. However, the journey fell sadly short of any of my more recent fantasies. My printer had failed in what felt like planned obsolescence but had more likely been caused by my own magical interference. Thus, I was forced to print my second essay in the closest library. Brimming with anticipation, and prepared to cite both transit delay and printer malfunction, I practically sprinted down the hallway before arriving in his doorway, panting heavily but eager to see him.

To my disappointment, the Linguistics faculty head had popped in as well, and they were sharing strident conversation about language revitalization, discussing the effect of colonisation on what were now endangered Indigenous languages in Canada, and the near loss of the Irish language throughout its own history. I had backtracked quickly after a few polite turns of phrase and shoved my essay awkwardly into his outstretched hand. I didn't linger.

However, I had been struck with just how barren his office really was. Apart from a tired-looking office chair and standard-issue desk, the only other items were his rugby duffel bag heaped in a crumpled pile under a coat hook and a select few file folders stacked neatly on the adjacent shelves. His computer sat in shutdown mode, seemingly untouched. How long was he intending to stick around?

With my mind still lingering on the past, I barely noticed the oak tree before almost colliding headlong into it. Not for the first time this month, my feet had led me to the special thin place amidst the institution's concrete walls.

It was late in the day now, but the October sun was delivering the most delightful show of fall colour. Dark clouds often hung close from the sky during this time of year, but every so often, the sun would sneak out, generously gracing everyone who was lucky enough to bask in its light. It was the kind of radiance that formed long, warm strands of light across the ground, almost as though someone was shining a giant flashlight on the still-falling orange leaves and startlingly deep-green conifers against the backdrop of deep grey sky.

The effect was not lost on other students, who revelled in the natural magic. Many of them paused to gratefully soak up the sun's sweet and unexpected gift. I stood for several minutes, closing my eyes in surrender as the low rays briefly caressed my face. Moments like this always reminded me of when I was beekeeping in the Prairies, when the sun would finally begin to set after a long day among the hives. The air even smelled enchanted in those moments, leaving me with no doubt that *anyone* could be made a believer in magic during the golden hour.

Only when my face cooled, as the sun retreated behind the clouds once more, did I open my eyes and witness the back side of Professor O'Brien as he rode away on his ten-speed bike, the strap of his rugby bag slung casually over his shoulder. He was peddling extremely hard, an impressive image to be sure. My heart was suddenly racing. I had the distinct feeling that he had been watching me during my brief moment in the sun and wondered what he had made of it.

I convinced Virginia to drive me to a Samhain gathering in Burnaby; after all, I *had* joined her at the potluck earlier in the month. Some of her coworkers had recently begun showing interest in what she called "witchy things," and so it was an easy sell for her to come along, friends in tow. I suspected she was skeptical but curious. She had always been open to the different ways women chose to connect.

"Do you think they actually think it's real? Magic? Or is it just another way for women to find their way out from under the thumb of the oppressor? A bridge to lost feminine spirituality or what not."

"Does it matter?" I asked, surprised at the hint of defensiveness in my tone.

She passively waved her hand through the air. "Of course not. I like it, and I'm glad we are getting time to hang out before you go." Virginia had recently begun exploring her own heritage through bead weaving, so I knew she too understood the deep need to reconnect with the spirit of ancestral memory.

We had found few opportunities to connect since Ben had left; her work occupied the majority of her time, and my evenings were filled to the brim with reading and studying. She had received a promotion at work, which, while very exciting, had drastically increased the demands placed upon her. She was going to be away off and on for several weekends leading up to the Christmas holidays for conferences, and so this night out would likely be our last chance to connect outside of home before I left for good.

"I'm going to be away for a *whole* week at the beginning of December, which means I'll be gone when you move out!"

She had been grumbling for weeks about how much work she would miss for this particular trip, but it was an extremely important gathering of some of the foremost non-profits on the West Coast. There was no way she would be missing *that*.

"I'm really sorry to leave you with no roommates, Ginny, with Ben fucking off like that. I didn't expect you would be hung out to dry like this."

She banged her hands on the steering wheel, suddenly excited. "Oh! I didn't tell you! I actually found two roommates for January! They are sisters, and get this, they play in a band. Should be fun, right?"

Relief rushed through me, and she seemed so genuinely pleased with the situation that was forming that I couldn't help but laugh. Apparently, they were related to one of her co-workers and would come into the situation quite well-vetted.

She paused in sharing her good news. "I'll really miss you though."

I knew she meant it. "Of course!" I said and patted her shoulder affectionately. "But this is great. See? All things work out in the end!"

If only I felt so sure about my own fate.

After parking in a well-lit spot on a side street, we met up with Virginia's friends Lisa and Shonny just outside the community-centre doors, both shivering in the cold, their red noses begging desperately to be somewhere warmer. While the weather had been mild so far this fall, tonight was exceptionally cold and blustery. I was grateful they had chosen to relocate the gathering indoors, even if foregoing the bonfire was a disappointment. There was always next year.

This particular celebration was a lighthearted one, put together by some local, more Celtic-leaning Pagans. It meant there would indeed be a wide-array of folks, including Wiccans and members of the Druidic order alike. As expected, it worked exceptionally well to cloak the actual Bearers and Wielders in with the believers, as well as the curious bystanders who wanted to learn more about this particular way of living. The goal of these events was always clear, however: an inclusive expression of truth and an informative challenge against negative perception.

We shuffled between the several rows of splintered wooden tables surrounded by newer-looking chairs that were neatly arranged. There was a group of women sitting in a circle, knitting and spinning their own yarns. In the corner, a Celtic band was playing a delightful reel amongst some small children who were dancing around, holding hands in a tiny, adorable circle.

I loved the ritual of it all and the sense of connection to a shared history. So often I had yearned for the connection of community and would find myself almost weeping when a particular wise woman or man would speak from their hearts and souls, or if a moving story was told. It usually felt like a homecoming, even if I had to keep the truth of my real magic a secret.

Also, the food was usually incredible.

Once the first portions were set aside as offerings to the dead, the attendees lined up buffet style, hungrily heaping scoops of colourful bean salad, baked eggs with leafy greens and mushrooms, and apple and berry crumbles onto their plates. Several colourfully decorated focaccia breads were set out, the warm images of flowery gardens created atop them using sliced grape tomatoes, rosemary sprigs, and black olives, making for a visually powerful display. The tabletop itself was adorned with candles of varying heights and colours, along with pomegranates and apples intermixed between the dishes. It was impossible not to appreciate the language and magic of shared food offerings, especially in these particular settings.

After loading our own plates with a variety of delicious morsels, we settled back at the long table to eat. The others were soon talking excitedly about the goings-on at work, complaining about one co-worker in particular who always forgot their lunch in the staff-room fridge.

"I mean, come on, just take the container home, right? So gross," Virginia commented.

"And I feel so bad throwing out perfectly fine recyclables, but it's just way too disgusting to clean them out. Not my job," Lisa said as Shonny nodded vigorously.

I smiled in reply but wasn't really interested in chatting about the ins-and-outs of office life tonight. What I *really* wanted was to track down an actual Witch, or even a Druid, who could perhaps offer me some information about the evidently occult murders that had been occurring all around us. While the police had initially withheld the information, they had elaborated more recently on the clearly ritualistic elements of the deaths, presumably in the hope of gathering more public insight. What it had done instead, however, was only further reinforce the already harboured prejudices in our society against Pagan beliefs.

However, it had affirmed my conviction to discover the truth.

I could feel the hum of several Bearer's magical forces coming from all sides, but as there was so much activity going on, it would be hard to nail down any one person without actually touching them, or better yet, having them reveal themselves to me.

"I'm going to have a look around," I said, kindly deflecting the others' apologies for ignoring me and gabbing about work. I moved to the side of the room opposite the buffet table and stood quietly, scanning around for anyone who actually looked like a real Witch, but was hard pressed to find one. The room was filled with all sorts of men and women, any of whom could have been magic users.

"It's never a good idea to judge a book by its cover or a Witch by their jacket," Gertie used to always say, and she wasn't wrong. Indeed, there was really no way to visually single out another magic user, unless of course they wanted to be found. I grinned fondly at the *Gertie-ism* and decided that I should perhaps pause my search and return to the table with Virginia and her friends. After all, the whole reason I was here in the first place was to find connection with other humans.

Just as I started to consider a second helping of food, I felt a peculiar sensation pushing against me, much harder than the rest. It would seem someone else was looking to make a magical connection this evening. But it wasn't at all who I had anticipated. A small girl, maybe four or five years old, sat in the corner holding onto what looked like a hand-made stuffed dog. She too had red hair, and although hers was much brighter than mine, I felt a sure kinship there.

"Oh, hi there," I said, taking caution not to frighten her as I approached and searched the room for her attached parents. "What's your name?"

She wore a colourful yellow, pink, and tangerine vest, which clashed violently with her hair. It was neatly adorned with hand-carved wooden buttons.

"My mom made this for me. I got to pick out the yarn all by myself at the store!" she said proudly.

"Did you? Wow it's so . . . colourful. I really like it."

Soon, a red-haired woman approached, beaming proudly at her young daughter while juggling a small pink-cheeked boy on her hip, who was very clearly teething. "Addie, it's time to go home; your little brother needs to sleep."

The young girl hopped up and took her mother's hand. "Bye then!"

I smiled back, thinking wistfully about what life would have been like had I grown up immersed in a community such as this while watching the loving family struggle with the logistics of jackets, hats, and a diaper bag before exiting the hall.

Just then, I was knocked from my warm present reality with a short, harsh vision. A shrouded figure stood with his back to the light in an executive office fully outfitted with westward-facing windows. Palm trees waved happily in the distance, but there was no joy found here. A man knelt before him, his balding head and liver spots giving away his advancing age.

"Is there a reason you felt the need to share company business with your family?" the ominous voice asked. "I would hate to think that your grandchildren might be put in danger."

The man didn't reply; he was shaking too violently to utter even a single syllable.

"Redundancy is a real shame, you know. I hate to do it, but . . . business is business."

With a slash of a charred blade, the kneeling man was slain right then and there on the office's polished floor, his blood slowly running towards an incongruous sewer drain in the centre of the room.

When I came to, I had slumped down into the corner where the small girl had been seated only moments previously. Thankfully, no one seemed to notice my brief departure from this realm. I straightened myself up, head throbbing wildly. I had no idea what the vision meant, but what I *did* know was that it was definitely time to go home.

CHAPTER 7

The month of November dragged on with the determination of a banana slug in the rain—implausibly slow but brimming with conviction. Plodding onward across the saturated grass towards my final week of classes at UBC, I cursed the inclement weather and the expected grueling week ahead. Multiple times on Monday morning, I had barely resisted the urge to turn heel and head straight back home to curl up under my covers until the sun finally emerged again.

Perhaps my final exams could write themselves. Or maybe I could skip them altogether? There had to be some kind of practical magic solution, but my grandmother's voice was back before I could let the thought blossom any further.

"Keep yourself queenright in the ordinary world, my dear."

She had often tied her advice for me to bee magic, and it had the rare effect of making me feel that she spoke in my heart's true language. Many moons ago, she had explained that the cost of magic was much like the collection of honey at summer's end. Sure, we could take all the delicious stores of sweet liquid for ourselves, but if none was left for the bees, they would never survive the winter. This was precisely how our magic worked too. It always came with a cost, and as such, you were well advised to consider the long-term effects of its use.

In any case, my grades were high enough that it was quite literally impossible for me to fail, so there was very little to worry about. What remained a concern was my honour's thesis, due for submission on Friday afternoon. Assuming I completed it without significant human or technological error, I would be in the clear to finally complete the never-ending undergraduate degree of Julia Harrison.

Well, not quite.

Due to circumstance, a handful of us were completing our honours program midway through the year. While not technically unusual, what set this semester apart was that Professor O'Brien, along with S.A.L.S.A. (the *Speech and Linguistics Student Association*) had the brilliant idea of hosting "mini honours presentations" before the traditional pre-Christmas wine and cheese social. It was completely optional, of course, but since Rebecca was particularly invested in this pilot project, being heavily involved with the student executive herself, I had begrudgingly agreed.

"Oh, come on, Julia. Your topic is so interesting! Don't you want to share it?"

"Not at all, actually," I said with a wry smile.

She smiled a little too wholesomely in reply. "Professor O'Brien will be there . . ."

I groaned. If I had only completed my degree in the spring as intended, I could have avoided the scenario entirely. It certainly wasn't the norm to have to present your undergraduate thesis in this program. It also wasn't the norm to extend writing it over two school years either; perhaps I was just prone to academic abnormality.

"Fine," I said. She looked pleased.

I probably would have skipped the wine and cheese event altogether if not for my commitment to the presentation. Even though it had a reputation of being a delightful evening, the reality was that I was extremely anxious to get moving.

Following Friday's events, and during what was likely to be a weak attempt at studying over the weekend, I would pack up my room at Virginia's. Since the furniture would be staying behind, I was counting on easily loading my possessions into my pickup and taking off as soon as possible after my exams the following week. Unfortunately, I would have to spend the bulk of December and January on Salt Spring, packing up more of Grandma Gertie's house.

Fortuitously though, I had been invited on a trip to California for the remainder of the winter with Alice, my old friend from high school. I had committed perhaps a bit impulsively, but it had provided something to look forward to. I found it almost impossible to resist the notion of sunshine and surf over the perpetually grey skies I was currently witnessing. The current plan was to meet up in Big Sur in early February. She was heading there regardless of my acceptance of her invitation, and she was just so enthusiastic that I couldn't help but feel swept up in the energy. Following our antici-pated beach fest, we would then attend a month-long yoga, meditation, and writing retreat.

I was slightly hesitant, unsure where my gift would factor into the medi-tative process. The last thing I needed was to drift into deep memory or vision during a routine Savasana, but I felt like Grandma Gertie would have encouraged me to explore my dreams in such a supportive environment.

With my mind on sunshine, I darkened at the thought of spending any extended time in that rainy old house without my grandmother's warmth to keep me company. I had still resolved to sell the place the coming spring, even if it was sure to be a royal pain in the ass.

It was encouraging that Joe Linder would help me navigate the sale, his dry humour an expected and tranquilising comfort. He had been steadfast when arranging Grandma Gertie's Will. She had transferred the house's title to me long before her decline, which was a blessing. A Witch's gift for intu-ition was helpful when you wanted to avoid taxes and sitting in probate for too long.

Still, I felt repelled by the harsh memories of loss, and hoped the cottage would pass on to someone who could truly appreciate its peace and tranquil-ity atop the mountain road. I *also* hoped the damned leak hadn't returned. My thoughts invariably wandered briefly towards that strange quilt I had rescued. A puzzle for later.

Wednesday dawned with an irritating level of anxiety. As it was my last seminar with Professor O'Brien, I knew I would likely be pressed on whether or not I was ready for my looming presentation on Friday. I was someone who thrived on the last-minute panic that was ritual to procrastinators, but he always had a way of making me feel like I need to show my accountability up front. His energy was perplexing . . . positively beguiling, really.

There was now so much unreleased tension between us that I felt like we might just explode during the seminar at any given moment. It had continued to build steadily throughout November. But as of late, the feelings had started to confuse themselves in my throat, caught somewhere between tears and passion. They usually resulted in an embarrassingly heated argument about his stubborn opinion on the topic of the day, when really I just desperately wanted to jump his bones.

And yet for his part, he fought and kept control like it was his last bastion in the world, his low voice forcibly calm, waiting with perfectly calculated timing to pounce on the flaws in my argument. I wondered if the other students made wagers about when one of us would finally crack as they leaned back in their seats to watch the show; we had long since surpassed what was generally deemed academically appropriate conduct.

There was no question that Professor O'Brien shared the turmoil over the electrical storm brewing between us, and I wondered for the hundredth time why he might be so averse to the thought of me as anything other than a pupil. He wore no ring, nor had he ever mentioned a wife or partner, but I supposed I couldn't rule that out. And if it *was* an age thing, there was no arguing the fact that I was much closer to his age than the majority of my peers. Still, he had an ancient quality about him that left me feeling rather unfledged whenever we spoke, mounting pressure notwithstanding.

I was late for my Wednesday morning class, but thankfully it was just a prep-hour for our final exam the following week. By the sheer grace of the Goddess, my exams had strangely all lined up in the first week of December. This was unheard of with UBC's over-accommodating system, which always scheduled final exams as far apart as possible.

At the end of the hour, I looked down at my phone and noticed a mass email had arrived from Professor O'Brien. My heart sunk, and not just because I had been up past midnight completing his final term paper.

> *Greetings all,*
> *Due to an unforeseen staffing dilemma, I will unfortunately*
> *have to cancel our final seminar for the year. I realize this is*

terribly short notice, so please accept my apologies for complicat-
ing what is already a chaotic season.
You may submit your final papers electronically instead,
by midnight tonight – hopefully this brief extension is to
your benefit.
Please do not hesitate to contact me with any questions
or concerns.
For any of you who are participating in the honours presenta-
tions, I look forward to seeing you on Friday at the social.
Kindly,
Professor D. O'Brien

Disappointed, but also exhausted, I went straight home and napped for the entire afternoon.

Thursday morning, I was in a haze. Now that my seminar paper was sub-mitted, I could turn my attention towards completing my thesis. Thankfully, but for a bit of polishing and pulling together its associated presentation, it was nearly complete. Still, I was feeling oddly derailed by yesterday's cancelled seminar. It looked like Friday was likely to be my final chance to see Professor O'Brien before term ended. Or ever really. I did my best to concentrate on my final coursework throughout the evening, but my thoughts were con-stantly meandering to what it would be like to share a meal with him, or visit somewhere exciting just us two, or better yet, to spend the night together.

Focus, Julia.

Despite my distraction, a part of me had revelled in coming up with clever "Cockney Rhyming Slang" examples for my presentation, procuring some vivid quotes and stories that were sure to make my peers and professors chuckle as I wove in the less-interesting details. I had a good feeling that sociolinguistics was a much finer end-of-term wine-and-cheese topic than what I expected from my more technically minded peers.

The *short* presentations would take place at four o'clock, with the wine and cheese social following immediately thereafter in the same space. Typical to academic life, drinking at happy hour on Friday was a given. I was grateful that I would at least have a beer in hand as I deflected, for the hundredth time, questions about why I hadn't applied for my master's in Linguistics or

Speech Therapy at the university. Or even law school for that matter, ambitions of which I had only shared with my closest peers. Frankly, I was sick and tired of fielding curious questions, no matter how well-intentioned.

Skipping my Friday morning class in favour of sleep, I rolled out of bed late and took my time preparing for the day. I carefully selected my outfit, pulling on my best black jeans followed by an understated soft-denim button-down shirt. I pulled my thick hair into a mature ponytail midway on my head—classic and confident. Finishing the look, I clasped a brushed-silver pendant with a compass rose on it around my neck. Something about the necklace had always felt like a bit of a talisman to me, helping me believe in my direction, regardless of whether or not I actually knew where I was going.

Unfortunately, the rain seemed determined to reach "atmospheric river" levels by mid-afternoon, so I donned my obnoxiously large black raincoat over the ensemble, pulled on my freshly cleaned leather, Chelsea-style boots and strode out the door.

Cautious not to arrive too early, I found myself quietly wandering the corridors of the Buchanan building before diving in at last to the hum of people and conversation. Although it boasted a wet bar and a handful of relaxed-looking couches, the rented student space still smelled vaguely like floor wax and photocopier toner. I wondered absently if I would *actually* miss the smell of academia once I left it all behind.

Several dozen chairs had been arranged in a semi-circle around a short podium at the far end of the hall, evidently to give the impression of inclusion. It felt awkward, this being the first honours presentation and the space being designed for more casual gatherings. But I had no doubt that, once the wine started flowing, the furniture would migrate into a much more appeasing pattern around the room.

I was slated to speak second, and definitely felt grateful that someone would be breaking the ice before me. On the other hand, it wasn't so late in the line-up that people were at peak boredom. Noticing Rebecca furiously reading her presentation notes across the room, I dug into my satchel for my own scribbled set, not that I would really use them. I was far more of a shoot-from-the-hip kind of presenter. That, and it was really only supposed to be five minutes long. How much was there to say?

Casually glancing around the room, I immediately spotted Professor O'Brien as he plunked himself down onto a purple and blue couch. He stuck out like a sore thumb as usual, formidable rugby shoulders punctuated by the stretched seams on his brown tweed jacket. His hair was slightly tussled, but it did look like he had run a comb through it.

He smiled merrily about at his students before diving into what looked to be a spirited story to some of the other faculty. They were clearly quite taken by his presence, laughing along with him appreciably as he waved his hands around during the tale. His charm was palpable even from here; my nerves lit up at the thought that soon I would be smack dab in front of him, open once more for intense scrutiny.

Soon it was time for the presentations to begin. A slight bit of panic grew in my belly as the first presenter stood up. Where was my divining magic when I needed it? I wanted some kind of assurance that today's path would be clear of rocks. Instead, I was drawing a complete blank as the opening presentation drove onwards. I took a deep breath as the light applause petered out.

As it drew to a close, I stood and approached the podium for my turn. I hated standing formally while I presented, far preferring to walk back and forth while I spoke. Diving in at last, I deliberately avoided eye contact with Professor O'Brien as I meandered from side to side. Much to my delight, my jokes landed with precision, and overall, I was able to convey myself quickly and without clumsiness. I migrated to a table near to the podium and leaned back gracefully as I finished up, beaming out dazzlingly towards the room. The faculty and students clapped heartily at the end of my presentation, and I strode away from the podium with glee, sweat dripping down my back and sweet relief chiming in my ears.

Unexpectedly, my gut wrenched when I saw that Professor O'Brien was no longer seated on the couch. Had he left in the middle of my presentation? I searched the room with more distress than I cared to admit, and finally spotted him at the back of the hall speaking quietly, albeit rather aggressively, to a man I had never seen before. They seemed to be arguing about something, and the charming linguistics professor's face looked nothing short of formidable. The other man then backed quickly from the hall, door closing with a bang behind him.

I settled back into my seat, completely perplexed at what I had just witnessed. The next presenter had already begun, with no one taking notice of the events. But who was that man, and why was he so important that he'd needed to see him out with such force? With more questions than answers, I stared forward but took in little of what was said. As a result, the remaining presentations flew by. Soon enough, I was in the steadily gathering queue at the bar, smiling brightly at my peers and craving fresh air in earnest.

"Fantastic work, Julia, that was one of the most delightful presentations I have seen in years!" one eccentric professor exclaimed.

"Are you sure you don't want to continue on with this next year?" another said. "You've established a wonderful foundation for further research!"

I smiled gratefully and vaguely explained that I had some family threads to tie up, and then I would consider my next steps. I even found myself mumbling something about law school, which I knew was an outright lie.

"Well, don't wait for too long, Harrison. Someone might snatch this research up while you're away!" Dave said with mock innocence.

"Sure, buddy, help yourself," I said, laughing with a wink. His teasing was harmless, as his interests lay in a completely unrelated discipline.

Waiting in the slow-moving line, I scrutinized the room for Professor O'Brien once more. The end of the scheduled program was signalled by a brief toast from the student association, and I felt real regret building within me that my fantasies had never come to fruition. So, I threw one final wish out to the universe that perhaps we would connect at last.

Shockingly, I then felt his presence, even before I could see him. My heart began to pound with abrupt ferocity. For as long as I could remember, I had been able to pick up on the exceptional energies of the magic users around me, but whether or not I could locate them was another question. The magical dampening of the past several months had all but stifled my fire, yes, but if the events in October had showed me anything, it was that I hadn't lost the skill altogether.

This, however, was something entirely different.

I was more than certain he wasn't a magic user, and yet I felt inexplicably alerted to his presence in the room tonight. I looked purposefully around the cramped room, but he was nowhere to be seen. Very odd. But then again, in the past, he had always been exactly where I expected him to be, either in our seminar, his office, or the rugby pitch. I had never actually *felt* for his presence; instead, it was more like I had predicted it. After all, I was somewhat hyper-focused on the man.

Someone dared to begin another toast, against the rising volume of cross-talking from the attendees. It was stifling in the room, and I shook my head, clearing my senses as best I could. What was with the thermostat? I was starting to feel panicky. Holy hell, I *desperately* needed a beer.

After finally arriving at the front of the queue, and successfully getting a beer in hand, I was lowering my lips to the overfull ale when a firm hand grasped my elbow out of the abyss. I spun around a little bit too quickly to be called graceful, frothy beer slopping onto my boots. Suddenly, I was face to face with *the* Professor D. O'Brien himself.

"Julia, your presentation was absolutely *magical!*" He practically sang his praise to me in a spritely tone that I had never heard from him before.

I flushed. Standing closer than ever, I could smell something delightfully earthy and spiced coming from his person. Cologne or beard oil, perhaps? His eyes were sparkling and focused entirely on me. He had obviously slipped away to change into one of his thick woolen sweaters, which was much more accommodating to his powerful frame than the tweed jacket he had donned earlier.

"Well, I wouldn't call it magical, but I did enjoy myself more than I expected," I said, pausing, my eyes now meeting his with intensity. "Were you able to hear the whole thing?"

I was trying not to sound accusatory, but something about the look on his face as he'd ushered the leering man out of the room had ignited my curiosity, and also made me feel surprisingly nervous.

One sandy eyebrow raised. "You saw that did you?"

Finally taking a sip of the remaining beer that wasn't already splattered onto my boots, I set down my glass and waited patiently for further explanation.

"It was just an old colleague looking to cause trouble with the faculty is all," he said dismissively, but his face showed the spark of the same anger I had seen from across the room. "I took care of it."

"I saw that. Same staffing dilemma from earlier in the week?" It had just begun to dawn on me how odd it was for a visiting professor to have a grudge with a previous faculty member.

"Something like that," he said, turning his body away briefly, making it clear that the discussion regarding the interloper was over. He rolled his shoulders back several times, and then, with another swift move, faced me squarely once more before bracing my shoulders with his powerful hands. He was seriously going to give me whiplash before the conversation was through, and I was grateful I had at least put my beer down this time.

While I was undoubtedly a tall woman, his height was notably greater as I looked up to his raw stature. I stood stone still as he slowly lowered his hands down the sides of my arms before finally letting go. My heart was absolutely pounding, and I wondered absently if anyone was watching us, and then realized that I didn't actually care if they were.

"I really don't enjoy these gatherings very much, contrary to what you might think," he said, eyes crinkling as a naughty smile spread across mouth.

I grinned back. "Honestly, I was only going to stay for a few drinks and then head home to pack . . ." I said, silently acknowledging this as my last hope towards the warmth of the moment leading to alternative plans between us. I looked awkwardly down at my soggy boots. Sighing audibly, I lifted each heel one at a time and unstuck myself from the polished concrete flooring.

He let out a low "Hmm" before stepping closer yet. I could feel the wool of his sweater just barely pulling at my shirt. I drew my eyes back up towards his. His scent was positively intoxicating now in its proximity.

"I only have two finals next week, and I've already submitted all of my final papers for everything else," I continued with a wave of my hand. "I'll be leaving Vancouver next weekend." My breath caught in my throat at the thought.

He cocked his head in reply, an impish grin intensifying on his lips. "Well, my dear, I'm absolutely famished. I think you had better escort us for a bite to eat and a pint!" he announced loudly, altogether ignoring my ramblings.

I surprised myself with a snorting giggle and was soon frogmarched out the door.

CHAPTER 8

"Oh, that's much better!" Professor O'Brien said following a deep breath as we stepped outside the stuffy social hall. We were met with a brief and welcome respite from the day's relentless deluge as we made our way across the grounds.

I had bussed to campus, so it looked like he would be providing transport to the aforementioned venue. Following his lead, we walked merrily down the sidewalk towards one of the faculty parking lots. Impulsively, I wanted to ask him if this was, in fact, a date. I thought better of myself, however, not wishing to jinx the magic of the moment that had finally arrived at long last.

I discovered quickly that he was remarkably easy company outside of the classroom. "It's a lot like Ireland in the winter, really. Well . . . maybe a bit gloomier, but still," he said, casually gesturing towards the stormy skies. After a pause, he said, "I'm going home in January, you know."

I didn't.

I'd assumed he was on a short contract for his position based on the naked state of his office, but I couldn't imagine why the university would bring him in to work for only one term. "I had no idea they offered such short research stints," I replied with interest after a slight pause.

"Well, they don't usually, but I was covering an unexpected medical leave. Plus, I was able to find what I needed *much* more quickly than I had anticipated."

"Oh, well that's too bad. You probably haven't even had much of a chance to explore the area." I was shocked to realize that I was angling to invite him over to the cottage.

"It's true, but I'm needed back in Galway soon anyway," he said with a chuckle. "If you can imagine, I think they've been lost without me!" He was so wonderfully lighthearted, and it was uplifting to feel the words flow so freely between us. In fact, he was positively gleeful, and it made my heart sing.

"Will you be staying in Vancouver for the holidays?" I pivoted, prodding for details of his short-term plans. I wondered if I might alternatively find an excuse to delay my trip back to the cottage altogether. "I suppose you have a lot of marking to do . . ."

He laughed a deep sing-song laugh, "You could say so, sure."

I noticed that he was being rather non-committal in his replies, but perhaps he was simply being polite. The conversation turned towards the weather once more, as these things do when you're settling into comfort-ability. He scoffed when I explained that this particular weather system was referred to as a "Pineapple Express."

"You're joking!"

"Nope, I'm not. It's fun, hey?"

He shook his head in amazement as we arrived at his car, a cobalt-blue Toyota Corolla that he was quick to inform me was leased. It positively oozed with new-car smell the moment I opened the door.

"Wow, you don't drive this thing much, do you?" I said, scrunching my nose. I knew he usually biked to work, but he must have brought his car in today due to the torrential rain.

"Not really," he said with a smile. "It's a bit more practical than my usual taste. Oh—and don't open the trunk—I spilled some groceries in there last week, and it smells terrible."

I beamed as I climbed into the passenger seat and waited for him to round the vehicle and join me inside. I had pulled my hair out of its tight ponytail as we walked and was delighting in running my fingers through my heavy locks, sighing with relief as I rubbed my tender scalp.

"You know, you do have the loveliest hair . . ." he said shyly, though I detected a hint of mischief. "In the right light, it almost shimmers with strands of orange and gold. I noticed it especially tonight during the presentation."

My system flooded with apprehension.

Twice now this evening he had commented on the somewhat super-natural effects of my presentation. It seemed like such an innocent and endearing compliment though, flirty and light, so I stifled any hopefully misplaced suspicions.

"Oh, thanks," I replied a little awkwardly. "My grandma Gertie always said it had a mind of its own, and she wasn't wrong." I gathered up my unruly mane into my fist, waggling it around in mock demonstration of its wild nature before pulling it back into a messy knot at the nape of my neck. "She passed away this past spring actually."

"I bet you miss her dreadfully," he said sympathetically.

"I do," I replied. I was biting my lip and fighting back unexpected tears, so I turned my head to look out the window as he backed up the vehicle. How was he able to take my guard down with such ease?

We drove in silence for several long minutes, but it wasn't unpleasant. I relished in the fact that he drove stick with the adept skills of a man well used to navigating the Irish countryside. The one-way streets and awkward on-ramps of Vancouver seemed second nature to him. I'll admit, watching a man who looked like *that* drive a manual transmission was an extreme turn on.

"Where are we headed?" I asked casually.

"Oh! Sorry. To my neighbourhood in the West End. I hope that's alright. I thought we would go to the pub or something," he said, awkwardly realizing he hadn't actually disclosed our destination.

I nodded in agreement. "Sounds perfect!" I wasn't picky on dates. It was the intricacies of conversation I wanted to explore, rather than those of a pretentious menu at a quiet, overpriced restaurant.

We arrived on a smoother stretch of road as he reached his agile fingers to the console to turn on the radio. Immediately, a top-forty-style pop song was blasting through the speakers at full volume, and he shook his head indig-nantly before abruptly turning it down.

"Utter rubbish," he mumbled, but the look on his face had me wonder-ing if he had in fact been caught in the act of intentionally listening to that station at volume. I raised my eyebrows, grinning. He shot me a playful *"don't you dare"* kind of look before turning the dial deliberately towards another frequency, landing on a muffled oldies station broadcasting from Bellingham. I instantly recognized "Oh, Pretty Woman" by Roy Orbison.

"Oh, good enough then," he remarked. Then, throwing his head back, he dove headlong into crooning to me with a hilarious grin, followed by the song's infamous low growl.

Fireworks exploded deep within my belly. Who *was* this man sitting beside me? I had seen hints of his magnetic vitality during our seminar, but this was something else altogether. My jaw literally hurt from smiling.

Suddenly, he enthusiastically threw the car into park, and said, "Pick your poison, love."

We arrived onto Davie Street far quicker than anticipated, likely due to this evening's unexpected entertainment. Somehow, yet not altogether unsurprisingly, he had scored a parking spot on the main road. Lucky bastard. With a quick yank on the e-brake, he hopped out of the car with gusto and skirted around to my side. I was amazed at how agile he was, especially considering his broad frame.

"My place isn't far from here," he said, opening the door for me and extending his hand in a chivalric gesture. "And so, as you can imagine, I've tried most of the restaurants *at least* once. What would suit you?" His accent seemed to be building in strength to match his enthusiasm. I accepted his outstretched hand while tolerating what felt like an outdated act of courtliness, simply because his joy was vibrating at such a frequency.

"You're the one who's *famished*, remember?" I said, leaning into him with a playful shove. "You decide!"

"Fine, but no complaining if it's not to your taste!"

We walked hand in hand for several blocks, chatting happily. My hands were chronically cold, so his firm grasp quickly proved a much more pleasant residence than the worn pockets of my raincoat, which contained several bunches of Kleenex, my faulty cellphone, and a pair of tangled earbuds. Not to mention that it felt completely natural. Without warning, I was redirected smoothly into a long and narrow pub, sandwiched between an overstuffed consignment store and a trendy barber shop. I was disappointed to let go of his hand when we reached our tableside.

"If I'm *completely* honest," he said, sliding a chair out for me, "I've wanted to take you out for a pint since I first set my eyes upon you."

I widened my eyes, my disbelief probably a little too obvious.

He scoffed at my reaction. "Oh, come now! Don't look so surprised! It's true!"

The man was as charming as a kingly lion, but I wasn't ready to be played with like a ball of yarn just yet; two could play at this game. "Oh, *really*?" I said, raising my eyebrows and grabbing the opposite chair for myself instead. "I never would have guessed by the way you spoke to me in class. Positively combative some days, *in fact.*" I teased his accent slightly and moved my queen into position. *Check.*

"Well, I had to maintain some level of professionalism, didn't I?" he offered, his Irish lilt still singing to me through each word.

"Oh-ho! I think we passed the realm of academic integrity months ago!" I said, laughing. Professionalism was one word for it, but I could think of a whole different lexicon of terms that were far less appropriate, yet still applied.

"Okay, okay! I'm sorry," he said, raising his hands in surrender and sheepishly admitting his defeat. "I had a bit too much fun keeping the discourse . . . interesting for you."

Checkmate.

"Thank you for admitting that," I said, squinting with mock skepticism.

Once we had settled into our wooden seats following our joust, he proceeded to order us both overfull pints of beer, putting it on his tab with a nod to the server, with whom he was obviously on a first-name basis. "No problem, Dom!"

I realized that I hadn't really considered him by his first name, and silently tried it on for size in my mouth, slowly rolling around and shaping the word several times when he wasn't looking. My thoughts quickly wandered in a rather filthy direction, and I snorted loudly again, blushing heartily in spite of myself.

"Are you alright, Julia?" he asked, confusion briefly dawning on his face.

I also liked how he said my name, and gulped. "Yep, I'm fine. Sorry. Tell me more about Ireland!"

Ignoring my blooming awkwardness, he quickly regaled me on the merits of the pubs over in the UK and Ireland, stating that the West Coast knockoffs were never quite as authentic or comfortable, no matter how hard they tried.

"Maybe there just isn't enough beer soaked into the carpets yet," I teased. "They haven't had enough time to *really* permeate that authentic pub smell."

"Oh ho! It's true, this country is practically a baby compared to Ireland!" he said, folding his long fingers under his bearded chin and gazing at me affectionately.

"Well, as a settler nation, sure, but we *are* sitting on traditional territories, right? So—"

"Yes, yes, of course."

I started adjusting my posture, habitually ready to debate him in earnest.

He continued. "You're right. I just meant the architecture," he said, gesturing around the room and clearly not wishing to spar with me tonight. I gave him a passive smile and looked up, searching hopefully for deliverance in the form of a cold glass of beer.

After several minutes, my drink arrived, brimming with a chocolatey brew made over in Victoria that was a special favourite of mine. Thick, frothy, and perfect. His was a malty red ale I hadn't heard of from some obscure craft brewery down the road; he really was quite adept at acting the local.

"Are you going to let me try a taste of that? It looks thick as a pudding!" he asked, eyeing my pint with hungry eyes. I obliged, my thoughts lingering on his sweet lips as he drank. His sandy whiskers collected some of the heady malt from the top of the glass, and I felt my pelvic floor flex responsively. I reasonably assumed at this point that my cheeks would be bright red for the entirety of the evening.

He grinned at me then like a cat licking his lips after an especially thick bowl of cream. "Well, that *is* delightful!" he said and slid the pint back to me across the table. Our hands touched slightly, resulting in the now-expected jolt of electricity.

His smile never faltered as the conversation flowed freely between us. Interestingly, he had quite a proclivity for turning questions back towards me whenever I tried to ask for more about him; I wasn't used to being on a date with a man who preferred to learn more about me than boast about himself.

And it was indeed a date.

That point had made been quite plain when he reached across the table and gently stroked my hand for the third or fourth time in about fifteen minutes. Below the table, a hearty game of "footsie" was also serving as a barometer, as far as these things were concerned anyways. I felt like a teenager all over again.

It turned out we were closer in age than I had expected, with slightly less than four and a half years separating my thirty to his thirty-four. He would turn thirty-five just before Christmas. To some extent, I was a bit embarrassed that he already boasted a tidy doctoral degree, while I was still absently floundering in the annals of undergraduate misery. I reminded myself that I had long divined that my destiny didn't include a lifetime of academia. That much *was* clear. The rest remained hazy and unknown, darker than the bottom of my almost-empty pint glass.

Dom ordered us each another drink, as well as a formidable amount of food to share between us. I was impassive on my preference once more, and he rolled his eyes in playful annoyance.

"You really are impossible when it comes to choosing what to eat," he said, as if he had been sharing meals with me all his life.

"No, I'm just really not very picky," I said resolutely. It was true, but there again was that unnerving familiarity about him tonight, like he could anticipate my every need. Perhaps he was exceptionally intuitive, or maybe just skillfully adept at taking women out on dates; with a face and personality like his, he surely had no trouble making plans on a Friday night.

Speaking of which, the pub was growing more cramped by the moment. The weekend crowd gradually transitioned from chatty huddles around the small wooden tables to more boisterous groups who shuffled their tables together haphazardly, the occupants now several pitchers deep in beer.

I excused myself to use the washroom to break from the narrowing atmosphere. I didn't want this night to end, and fervently hoped that the evening's travels might lead us towards a more intimate setting. So far, it had all felt too good to be true, but I was cautiously optimistic.

Tipsy and happily at ease, having just relieved a *very* full bladder, I mindlessly fussed with my hair in the low-hanging bathroom mirror. Pulling it loose from its ponytail, I tucked the stray strands of hair behind my reddened ears but was quickly reminded of my seventh-grade class photo. I grimaced. Thinking better of it, I instead tousled my hair deliberately, rearranging it to the opposite side of my natural part, giving in fully to its untamed nature.

A sudden anticipation washed over me then, like the excitement that rises just before arriving at your intended destination. The physicality of the bathroom ebbed and swirled before me, and I was rocked with a shockingly bright vision.

I stood on an impossibly high stone precipice. My hair was whipping wildly across my face in a storm-driven wind as I outstretched my arms in full surrender to the sky. Moments later, I stepped out, only to fall abruptly towards the earth. Only it didn't feel like falling in the truest sense, where the bottom plummets violently out of your stomach. Instead, starting from my feet and slowly climbing all the way up my legs, through my torso, and towards my head, I felt strangely like my body had actually locked back into place.

Precipitously returning to my own reality, the vision had admittedly been frightening. However, I was also bewildered at the immense sense of peace and knowing that I now held clutched tightly to my heart. It wasn't uncommon for the visual interpretation to be slightly mismatched with the residual feelings when it came to the Sight, but this contrast was exceptional. The vivid clarity of the dream now settled as warmth within my ribcage, almost like a homecoming.

Turning my gaze inward, it was clear that my Witch's fire was indeed blazing keenly, crackling away comfortably and warming the hearth deeply rooted between my ribs. I took this to be a good sign and exited the bathroom, ready to take the plunge.

Dom greeted me with a brilliant, white-toothed smile upon my return, giving me the distinct sense that he liked what he saw. I sat back down, eying each of the plates of food on the table before us. He had made a considerable dent in them during my short absence.

"Were you planning to save some for me?" I teased.

He dropped his jaw in sudden embarrassment. "Oh no, I'm so sorry. I tend to eat a lot, especially when I'm nervous."

"Nervous?" I said, unable to hide my surprise.

He blushed deeply. "You're . . . a special woman. Unlike anyone I've ever met, actually."

I'll admit, I was taken aback by his sudden romantics, my own proclivity being to become rather awkward in such instances. "Don't worry, I ate earlier," I lied, nodding encouragingly. "Go ahead!"

Veering towards more light-hearted conversation, we continued on for a while with more common pleasantries. I'd taken pity on the abashed look on his face about the food and helped him polish off the plate of hot wings with rapt enthusiasm. Soon enough, I needed the washroom once more.

"That's what I get for breaking the seal," I said awkwardly as I hopped up from the table and scooted off. Dom laughed at me, clearly confused. I was feeling the drink much more than I had been during my last trip to the toilet. It was a good thing I had helped finish the wings.

When I returned from what, this time, had been an uneventful voyage, Dom had already paid our bill. He dutifully held out my oversized raincoat while gesturing cordially towards the door. Soon he placed his capable arm around my waist, deftly navigating us both through the thronging crowd of increasingly younger-looking pub-goers. In any other situation, his protective masculinity would have raised red flags, but with Dom, there was something different in his care. It was as if he was greeting the world by my side rather than commanding my direction.

We stepped outside together onto the concrete sidewalk where the rain had returned with a redoubled effort. Holding hands once more, we ran down the street, slopping through the puddles in the opposite direction of his car. My heart was soaring, and I was overwhelmed with a hunger to know him more deeply still.

"Well, I obviously can't drive you home like this," he said finally, mid-sprint. "I think you better come back to my place, and I can sober up with some toast," he said matter-of-factly.

Smooth.

"I was wondering where you were dragging me off to next!" I said, rubbing the rain and crumbling mascara away from under my eyes. "I can just take the bus home though, it's totally fine."

"Oh ho! Don't tell me you're not coming along willingly!" He was as playful as a puppy. "Shall I convince you, then?" he said, planting his feet abruptly and drawing me in close. Just when I couldn't believe it was possible to charm me any further, here we were.

"You might just have to," I said breathily, already surrendering to his gaze.

He leaned in close. Even in the deluge, I could smell his alluring masculine scent, and I breathed it in deep. My heart pounded a dramatic tattoo against my ribs as he ran his fingers through the rain-soaked hair at the nape of my neck. He then glanced his thumb along my chin, effectively kicking my Witch's fire to bonfire-level before brushing his lips against mine for a delicate kiss; the continued precision of his actions was swiftly turning my legs to jelly.

"Okay," I said, swaying slightly. "I think I'm convinced—"

Suddenly, he leaned back to take the measure of me.

"You're completely drenched! We'd best get you dried off!" A playful grin spread across his face. "And lucky for you, my place *is* just around the corner."

"How convenient," I murmured, almost speechless.

Before I knew it, I was being led down a side street towards a charming three-story walk up with a rather ornate entrance lobby. I could see his bike locked to a gilded silver railing off to the side and mentally commended his bravery, or stupidity, for leaving it as fodder to the thieves in this city. Once inside the threshold, I could immediately smell the powdered soap from a communal laundry on the main floor mingled with the lingering scent of someone's late-night dinner.

"Why didn't you stay in the visiting-faculty housing on campus?" I asked, honestly confused at his choice of rental for such a short time in the city.

"Oh, I prefer to be closer to the culture of a city . . . and the food," he said, as if it was completely obvious that someone with his worldliness would prefer the finer aspects of the downtown Vancouver rental market.

He led me down a wide hallway towards the front-corner apartment, its dark wood door boasting a silver number "205." The building bore the distinct neighbourhood charm of the West End and surely cost a pretty penny to rent.

Dom dug around for his keys but was struggling slightly to reach them, his muscular thighs having greatly diminished the functionality of his front pockets. When he deftly unlocked the door at last, he rested his hand gently on my back as he guided us both in.

"Welcome home!"

CHAPTER 9

For the third time within the hour, I found myself alone in a strange bathroom. Happily, it was once again a vision free experience.

Dom's washroom was small but tidy, with only a few travel-size body products set out in the shower caddy, a simple beige bar of soap on the ledge, and a neat box of tissues set on the back of the toilet. Its starkness reminded me of a hotel, and mirrored his similarly bare office. I resisted the urge to peek into his medicine cabinet, responsibly assuming that it only contained a tube of toothpaste, a razor, and other bathroom basics common to someone who isn't planning to stay long.

Three fluffy grey towels were neatly rolled up in an alcove behind the bathroom door. I snatched one with my bone-chilled fingers and enthusiastically dried my sopping hair, enjoying the fresh scent of his laundry soap.

Then I realized something and cringed, swearing under my breath. "Fuck!"

I hadn't worn my best underwear today. Though, since I owned very little fancy lingerie, "best" really wasn't saying much. However, it hadn't crossed my mind this morning, as I'd prepared the final aspects of my presentation, that I might need to remove my pants in front of another human being before the day was out. Or perhaps I had simply been in protective denial.

Standing here now, the presentation felt like a lifetime ago. In fact, the evening so far had been completely spellbinding. I shook my head resolutely, smiling in earnest at my predicament; at least this pair of underwear didn't have any holes in them, and thanks to my overlong raincoat, my pants were dry enough to wear without discomfort.

Maybe he would lend me one of his cozy Irish sweaters to snuggle into while we chatted well into the evening about our favourite books and movies, letting our guards down further through flirtatious stories that might then lead to more playful touching. And then? Well, I had always imagined him as a whisky drinker at home, fantasizing about the peaty warmth on his breath in a more intimate setting.

I ran my fingers through my tangled locks once more before deciding resolutely that he really didn't seem like the kind of man who cared about traditional beauty anyways. In fact, I felt like he could almost see right through me, beyond all of the bullshit and ridiculous societal expectations. It was high time for me to let my guard down. He had opened up more to me over the span of this evening than he had all semester. I hoped fervently that he would continue to share more of himself, both mentally and physically, as the hours chimed on.

When I finally entered his living room, I could still smell the dampness of the winter rains. He must have cracked opened a window, despite the coolness of the late November evening.

I froze.

He was standing with his back to me, arms stretched wide, grasping white-knuckled onto the edges of the window frame like some kind of fierce bird of prey.

Dom had removed his sodden sweater while I was in the bathroom, but I could still smell the sour damp of authentic wool somewhere in the room. What remained draped over his impressive frame resembled a soft white-linen tunic, now completely untucked from his fitted green khaki pants. It stuck to his damp body in ways that shouldn't be legal in the light of day. I could see the shadowed outlines of a large tattoo across the canvas of his back. Looks like this were truly criminal.

"You have—" my voice caught in my throat, but he didn't notice.

"There's something I need to tell you, Julia," his voice sounded gravelly but still within his usual calm control. All hints of earlier laugher, however, were long gone.

"It's the reason I'm here . . ." he continued slowly, ". . . the reason we're both here, actually."

His accent was coming in thicker now, laced with intensity.

I moved a few more steps towards him, but something deep behind my navel warned me to shelter in place while he grappled with whatever ferocious thing was fighting its way out. I thought of the deeper parts of him, the ones that I had silently detected in our past encounters, full of the unknown beasts that wandered the forest during long nights.

We both knew why we were here in Vancouver at the university: me to finally finish my bloody undergraduate degree, and him to complete his doctoral research. I wasn't sure this was anything to be fretting over, not after how wonderfully the evening had gone. The thought of his smiling eyes focused so intently on me over dinner made me weak in the knees, anticipatory warmth and a hopeful feeling blossoming powerfully within.

Still facing away from me, he reached up and ran his exquisite fingers through his damp sandy hair, creating more waves and soft swirls throughout. Mouth now completely dry, my eyes followed the lines of his body, up his side and around his gracefully arced shoulder. It had been several hours since we'd snuck out into the night together, but I still felt so inexplicably nervous to be close to him, all alone. As I visually traced the line from his elbow down his perfect forearms, ready to greedily feed my eyes on the hands I had already studied for hours during seminar, he reached back and grasped the neck of his shirt, ripping it over his head in one swift tug.

Holy. Hell.

Muscles still twitching from the abrupt movement, he had revealed nothing short of a masterpiece. Across his powerful shoulders ran the lines of countless delicately crossed branches, perfectly intertwined across his kingly frame. The branches stemmed from a great oak tree, its blackish-blue ink hardening into a solid base in the center of his back. Below, the tree's roots were woven into intricate Celtic knots that reached up to encircle the tree, never quite meeting the hanging branches above. It was a remarkable rendition of the Celtic Tree of Life. And it was *full* of magic.

"It hasn't been easy keeping it from you," he said, followed by a forced exhale through his pursed lips. "I wish there was another way."

I noticed his breathing had changed from hesitant to heavy, his chest and shoulders now straining with each focused respiration. Even from across the room, I could see the gooseflesh raising on his body in a visible chill.

Meanwhile, my face had flushed entirely. I felt heat rising from every corner of my being, leaving behind zero trace of the evening's cool bite in my bones.

"I'm sorry but—" My breath hitched in what now felt like forbidden longing. "Keeping *what* from me?"

He continued, almost unhearing. "It's a story. Well, sort of . . . It's . . . It'll explain our story to you, to remind you . . . that this isn't our first lifetime—"

"What?" I asked, cutting him off. "What are you talking about?" I sensed that, somehow, I already knew what he was going to say.

"We . . . you and I, that is . . . we're stuck in a cycle. We die, we're reborn, and we meet again . . ."

I shook my head, not wanting to accept any of this. Wouldn't I know this already? Surely, I would know.

He let out a low sob. "You used to remember every time. But after so many cycles—"

"So many? How many?" I demanded.

"More than I can count."

Mouth agape, I hastily licked my lips before attempting to speak again. It didn't work, and an awkward gagging sound burst from my throat. "Excuse me, but . . . *What the actual fuck?*" I felt suddenly defensive. He didn't flinch. Confidence entirely shaken, I was confused, painfully embarrassed, and a tinge fearful. I began to panic, my hands going numb as the words *"too good to be true"* echoed ominously in my mind.

I had to regain my composure and fast. Frantically, I searched the floor for my discarded bag and cellphone. Where the hell were they? I blinked slowly, failing to hold back hurt tears.

"Julia, I'm telling the truth. Please don't go."

Practically frozen in time, I turned myself cautiously towards the stone-still man and stared breathlessly at the canvas before me. Nothing in his posture, or his sombre tone, indicated this was a joke. After several painful moments and long breaths, I tried again.

"You're not making any sense. What are you playing at here, Dom?"

91

It felt strange to say his name in this way.

Grasping a simple cedar sofa table beside me, it took all of my effort to keep my tone from being accusatory. I felt like a dog whose deceptively delicious treat had been taken away from her without a moment's notice, met instead with scarcity. I was struggling to keep the sense of injustice and anger from rising within me.

The evening's conversation had been accentuated by lively, bountiful laughter flowing between us like a freshwater spring. And the building sexual tension had been palpable. My soul had danced in his presence with the pulsing drums of my own intuition, banging on in a way I had never experienced, or even dreamed of happening in this lifetime. Bathroom vision notwithstanding, a low throb of anticipation had permeated deep into my core throughout the evening, an almost indescribable yearning taking over all conscious thought. Our time together had been nothing short of magic in its purest form. And now, we were landed in complete contradiction, words passing between us as thick as mud.

Failing to sense my imminent internal collapse, he continued on.

"You'll have to touch it. Use your *gift*. I am not sure there is any other way to explain it to you," he said, resolute.

"My gift?" I was aghast. How did he know? Blood rushed to my head. It was all too much and the room swam before me. Where were my housekeys?

"Yes, Julia, your gift of the Sight. I know all about it . . . or at least, parts of it. Please don't panic," he said with soft sadness, lilt heavier than ever.

My grandmother's voice was suddenly ringing in my ears: *"Be careful who you share your magic with, Julia. There are many who would seek to exploit your powers for their own gain as they have done for centuries. Beware the ones who take without giving back. Those are the ones who are most dangerous of all."*

My impulse was to argue with him, but something in his tone gave me further pause. He wasn't accusing me of anything but was rather simply stating what he believed to be fact. He didn't seem dangerous, not towards me anyways. He had no intention of taking anything from me. I somehow knew that this was *entirely* an act of sharing.

"I know you're a Witch. A magic Bearer. I know a lot more than that . . . but . . . Christ, Julia, just use magic, and you'll understand!" he shouted, though his frustration was only momentary. "And . . . and then you can decide for yourself."

Failing to collect my erratically scattered thoughts, I watched in shocked sympathy as his shoulders slumped. He seemed to be simultaneously releasing and gaining a great burden. Helplessly hoping.

Sorry, Gertie.

Stepping forward in three long strides, I met him beside the window. My body heat was dizzying, having gone from arousal, to anger, to panic far too quickly for it to adjust gracefully. He spun around intuitively to catch me in my stupor, and I felt grateful for his immovable frame. Looking up, I saw that his eyes were full of desperate pleading, and some kind of deep and ancient longing that felt altogether too familiar.

I dropped my gaze and steadied myself with some effort; now wasn't the time to faint. This also wasn't how I had imagined crashing against his body for the first time, and almost childlike, the "maiden" within me frowned.

"I'm so sorry, Julia. Please, you have to understand. I never wanted any of this to happen to us . . . not like this." His voice was now openly desperate, bordering on begging. "Please. Just . . . use your magic and . . . then you can decide."

I closed my eyes and waited.

It all felt like a twisted lucid dream that I was patiently waiting to wake up from. When I didn't wake up after several moments of effort, I swore under my breath and accepted that there was nothing left to do but let the fates decide.

Leaning back slowly, I braced my hands on his cool shoulders, avoiding his eyes for fear I might lose my resolve. My hands passed over his soft chest hair as I gently nudged him to turn away from me. He still smelled of sunshine and sea salt, and even in this moment, I was overwhelmed by his utter perfection.

I took several slow breaths and simultaneously hoped for the best, trying in vain to digest all he had just said. He knew about my gift, and that I would be able to access the enchantment locked within the expansive back-piece. For my part, however, I had absolutely *no clue* how I would go about doing it.

"You never said anything about having a tattoo," I remarked, a feigned attempt at casual conversation. I was stalling.

He replied through clenched teeth. "I guess it just never came up."

I could sense he was drawing on all of his energy to maintain composure. This evening had taken such an unexpected direction, I couldn't blame him for taking a turn at holding on for dear life.

"It's beautiful," I said, mustering my courage, but my voice still shook. "There's magic in it. Lots of it. Ancient . . ." I had no idea how I knew this, but it felt so true as I spoke it that I had zero doubt.

"Well, you *did* create it," he said flatly, affirming my knowing. "It regenerates with me each time."

Mesmerized, I stared thoughtfully at the image. I tilted my head slowly from left to right, as if that would change my perception somehow. It was altogether complete, the spell, yet I had the distinct sense that everything was about to come wildly unwound. There really *was* something about it that was old beyond recognition, yet Dom's flesh and bone were of a man in his mid-thirties.

Throwing all caution and my grandmother's warnings to the wind, I reached forward and began to delicately trace the lines around and down his back. The intimacy of the act was arresting, and he shuddered. I removed my hands momentarily. What was he so afraid of?

But, in truth, I felt it too. We were standing together on a precipice, waiting to dive into something far beyond our control. There was so little veiled between us now; it was time to step off the ledge.

I continued again with my soft tracing, but this time with slightly more intention. To my surprise, both the magic and the intricately inked lines of the tattoo began to lift. A shimmering golden light emerged from the intertwined branches and knots, reaching out and beckoning me closer as it pulsed at my fingertips. I already knew his essence was golden; I had sensed it the very first time we met. But the magic embedded in the tattoo was singularly more powerful than any spell I had ever encountered, brilliant and flickering as it rose from the surface of his skin.

After a moment that felt like a lifetime, Dom's back was breathtakingly bare.

Slowly at first, I could feel the enchantment as it moved through me, throbbing deliberately up my arms and towards my chest. I *knew* this magic, almost as if it were returning home at last. Before I could explore the sensation further, a pressure in my chest grew so exponentially that I could barely feel my heartbeat at all; my inner hearth-fire was now uncontrollably ablaze. I could feel the physical energies gathering around me too, senses sharpening as I crossed over into the otherworldly realm.

My nostrils flared at the smell, and my eyes rolled back violently.

Peat, I was right, and something that reminded me of old stone, earth, and acrid smoke. It was all too familiar, yet completely unknown. That was the thing about the Sight, it had the power to knock you off your feet.

And it would seem that *now* was a perfect time to faint.

The vision arrived like a patchwork of thoughts.

No, that wasn't quite it.

It was like threads in the warp and weft of a woolen weaving being pulled simultaneously both taut and coming unbound all at once. The gathering colours that swirled around me soon resembled a hex quilt, painstakingly connected one inch at a time, each stich as important as the one before, or the one that followed.

A voice called out, vaguely distant, and incredibly ancient to my young ears.

> *With the death of the mother, a wayward ship never built to sail,*
> *Will come the birth of another, a soul-forged gift of the Sun and Moon.*
>
> *As the World Ruler reigns in his summer house, so the hourglass begins.*
> *When the Sovereign accepts her destiny, midsummer bells will toll the end.*
>
> *The Child of Rome has but one true enemy, borne of Crone and Celt,*
> *Darkness walks a path destined to fail, should the hourglass run out.*

Next, I was yanked by my magical bindings towards a completely different era altogether. This was indeed a complex spell woven painstakingly through the annals of time, and my intuition practically screamed that these messages were clearly intended for *me*.

I arrived in a room so strikingly different than the one I inhabited in my present-day body that I had no doubt this was the most ancient vision I had ever encountered. The vison came abruptly into focus, walls literally encircling me as I sat slightly hunched on a low stool at the edge of a completely round dwelling. The timber-and-wattle structure with its thatched roof was perhaps the first giveaway of this being a completely different time. In the centre, a great black cauldron was propped over a low-burning peat fire, its heat surprisingly powerful in the small, dim space. There was no chimney, but the smoke seemed to be escaping easily through the thatch.

Around me, I could smell various dried roots and herbs, hanging above, and was that the lingering scent of roast chicken? Something was strikingly familiar about the space. I had been there before and knew the owner of the hut well.

Through the cracks of a low wood-frame door, which stood maybe only a metre and a half tall, I could see that the sun was now resting low in the sky. Based on the startlingly cool air rushing in through the recesses, I sensed it must have been late in the afternoon in midwinter.

Was I keeping watch for something?

"Girl!" someone called out to me, or at least I think it was to me. I jumped.

Gertie? No, not quite.

An aged woman was standing over the charred cauldron, grizzled waist-length grey hair completely askew and clearly unkept from the gruelling task at hand.

She was short and stout, resembling something rather akin to a teapot if I was honest. She dipped and poured different liquids and powders into the steaming vessel. A leather-bound book with burnt and stained pages lay open at her feet, but I couldn't discern its contents from where I stooped. It seemed strange to me that she didn't have it propped on the low table where there was clearly a perfectly reasonable spot for it between the various bunches of plants and a worn basin-shaped stone clearly used for grinding grains and herbs. I quickly realized the location of the book was a result of the urgency and intensity with which she worked.

What was also clear was that it was a magical book: a grimoire.

"This is dark magic. I don't like it. Not one bit. Nasty stuff. Evil."

She looked almost afraid to touch the book, muttering on about imminent danger and darkness as she turned to the next page with her calloused toe.

I looked down at my hands and realized they were indeed my own, slender fingers and long thumbs, although my nails seemed much more brittle and absolutely filthy.

"You did well in collecting the belladonna. Those roots aren't easy to find, dear one. Very lucky." Her words filled the air weakly, like when someone discusses the weather after an extremely serious emotional blow has been dealt. Fluff and nonsense.

Glancing out the window at regular intervals, I knew something was coming but couldn't quite put my finger on it. My head was swimming with the intensity of the vision, but I felt the apprehension clearly in the alert, taught muscles of my ancient body. I watched her diligently work in silence as she carefully chopped and ground the roots, using a short silver knife she pulled from her leather belt, one of the two she kept tucked there.

Moments later, she pulled out the second knife and sliced off a great lock of her own hair, promptly dropping it into the cauldron. I gasped, but I wasn't entirely sure why. Time passed at a strange pace as the contents of the cauldron bubbled and smoked menacingly, causing us both to jump when a loud knock came at the door.

"Grianne, let me in!" the voice hollered, but it didn't sound dangerous. Just spitting mad.

The older woman's eyes lingered on me then, pouring out a deep sadness that spoke of the tales of the ancient ones, the ones who were here before . . . the ones who walked in the halls of destiny and knew something the others did not. A look of knowing.

She shook her head, recalibrating to the present situation. "A moment!"

Shoving the dark book under the shadow of the well-worn table, she shuffled to the heavy wooden door, cursing under her breath as she pulled it open.

"What is it?"

I nervously gathered the blue wool of my skirt into my hands, its textures raw against my already shredded fingertips. The visitor pushed in from behind the door, breezing past the elder woman with little care to her station, and stared at me head-on.

"Come at once. This Prophecy, it's madness!"

I sat frozen in front of the open door, a cool breeze flowing off my neck. I noticed then that, if not for their age differences, the two women were practically identical with their hands on their hips, poised to boil over like two overfilled kettles.

The older of the two let out an exasperated sigh as she dropped her hands to her skirt front. "It's not that simple. She's been marked! By *him*. We have to get her out of here."

"And how do you suppose we do that, *Mother?* Cart her off, hidden under one of the covered grain wagons headed east? That's not going to stop *him* from finding her."

"I don't mean on *this* plane." With that, Grianne pulled the filthy book out from under the table with her blackened heel, and the younger of the two gasped.

Her voice was hoarse as she spoke with an oddly familiar terseness. "Where did you get that?"

The older woman shook her head ruefully. "It doesn't matter. What matters is that we have to give her a fighting chance to *defeat him*. For all our sakes."

The other woman laughed manically, mouth agape and eyes frantic, clearly at a loss for words.

"Excuse me—" I tried to interject, but the pair silenced me with their identical icy glares. The apple didn't fall far from the tree between these two, although the younger seemed decidedly less magically inclined and more fit to anger.

The vision blurred violently then, jarring me painfully as threads and stitches pushed and pulled around me, tightening harshly around my waist and wrists, binding my body and driving it forward through what felt like an all-too-familiar timeline.

Next, I was standing in the same room, but it was dusk.

Again, that wasn't quite it.

I rubbed my eyes; it was almost dawn.

The air smelled foul, heavily laden with dark magics and the dull haze of smoke that filled the familiar, low-ceilinged hut. I stood barefoot beside the now-spilled cauldron, holding the light silver knife clenched in my white-knuckled hand.

Looking down, I noticed fresh blood spattered down the front of my light apron, leading ominously to an aged, lifeless body spread out at my feet on the dirt floor. Panic set in as I took in the grizzly scene.

Why can't I remember what happened?

I peered towards the door, heart pounding, and noticed the other woman lying in a heap beside the closed door, Grianne's second, darker knife wedged forcefully into the small of her back.

What had I done?

I suddenly smelled the unmistakable meatiness of burning parchment; the ancient grimoire had been cast into to the low-burning peat fire. Grappling for the wrought-iron poker from beside the cauldron, I tried to fish out the damaged book. As if provoked, the leather volume burst into angry, untameable flames at my touch, and soon, livid hot tendrils were lapping up towards the thatched roof.

I had to get out of there, book be damned.

Shoving the silver knife into the band of my apron, I hiked up my heavily bloodied skirts as best I could and moved to leave when suddenly, a man stepped into the doorway.

Tall, broad, and incredibly familiar.

I cried out, "I don't know what happened!"

I was already choking on the smoke, dizzily attempting to round the room as the flames reached aggressively for the damp wool of my hem. In a nearly supernatural feat, he leapt deftly over the dead body of the woman I could only assume was my mother, and pulled me from the flames.

Sputtering, the powerful Celt dragged me a safe distance from the thatched cottage to where his sweaty horse was hobbled, only moments before the entire structure went up in brilliant orange and white flames, clearly ignited by the magic contained within the dark grimoire.

He turned towards me. "My love . . ."

But the vision was already fading, fear spreading across his face like the rogue flames behind us, and soon, I could remember no more.

CHAPTER 10

S ince I had spent much of my childhood struggling to find sleep, the
dim early morning light following a torrid night almost always arrived
as a cocoon of safety, a sure sign that I had survived yet another cycle of
confused and damaging nightmares that made no sense to a seven, nine, or
even twelve-year-old brain.

When I opened my eyes in Dom's bedroom, my thirty-year-old-brain
was greeted with a much brighter than anticipated sunbeam, its light shining
boldly through a thin crack between two faded-blue polyester curtains. Sun
already well established in the sky, I wondered absently how long I had
actually been asleep. Terrible dreams and tumultuous visions had consumed
my entire consciousness after the initial impact of the spell, and I couldn't
recall exactly *how* I had made it to the bedroom, but no doubt Dom had
assisted me.

Squinting painfully, I could barely stitch together the medley of thoughts
I had gathered overnight. But several things were clear. I was me, in this time
and on this plane, but my body and soul had been on an ancient journey for
centuries. Something, or someone, was hunting me, and the danger was so
great that it had been worth the risk of repeatedly sending me through time.
The only constant along that journey was Dom, his devotion and bravery
bending our paths together through each cycle of rebirth.

Indeed, since that first telling in the woman Grianne's cottage, I had been undoubtedly adrift, lost in grief, pain, joy, and some kind of ageless sorrow, no doubt thrashing and crying out, absent from the plane of normal human consciousness.

And then there was the *Prophecy*.

I shuddered. But at least I now knew why Dom had spoken with such pain and fear the night before. I held onto residual hazy images of Dom's face, his eyes searching and wracked with worry as I navigated the planes of the Sight, transmuting deep into the Otherworld.

With my swollen eyes now fully functional in the ordinary world, I looked over to find him leaning forward with his elbows on his strong thighs, careful fingers entwined through his sandy-blond hair and clasped tightly behind his head. Perhaps he had fallen asleep in the long wait for my return? He reminded me of a slumbering granite statue. Solid and unmoving.

Meanwhile, my head was throbbing, and my mouth tasted like a sewer. I needed water.

As I slowly pushed the covers back from myself, he jolted at the slight movement, eyes red-rimmed with secret tears that had long-since dried.

"Julia! You're awake. Oh, thank God!"

His relief was palpable.

I nodded slowly, noticing that he had changed into a soft cotton t-shirt and sweatpants at some point, likely once I had drifted off into a more settled, dreamless slumber. He didn't look comfortable at all though, stooped awkwardly in the corner on a small wooden chair beside a black metal waste-paper basket.

"I'm going to have to take you home. To your island," he said, rubbing his eyes and standing up abruptly.

I startled in response, and the world around me spun violently. I proceeded then to dry heave over the edge of the bed, hoping to miss his clean bedding. He shoved the garbage can towards me, but nothing came up.

"I don't think there's much left in there, love," he said, helping me turn onto my side, his hand gently caressing my arm as he seated himself on the edge of the mattress. My head was splitting, the light of day raking harshly at my eyes.

Completely spent, this was infinitely worse than a normal hangover.

I lay still for a while, eyes shut tight and safely tucked in underneath the dark-grey duvet of his double bed. When the room finally stopped spinning, I reached down and noticed that I was no longer wearing any pants. Some crazed part of me laughed internally at the fact that my plain underwear had made an untimely appearance after all. Unfortunately, it was likely because I had thrown up all over my jeans.

Seeing my expression, and clearly worried I suspected more sinister motives, he spoke up then. "I didn't—"

"Of course, you didn't."

My necklace was missing too, but I assumed that it had also been damaged in the fray. I smiled weakly, still surprised at my voice, heavy with an unexpected and ancient love. We sat in silence again for some time while my stomach threatened menacingly to heave once more. After a time, I dug my knuckles firmly into my temples, desperate to relieve some of the tension. The visions had washed over me without reprieve; the weight of our story— our repeated, rolling, prophetic dream of a story—had left me feeling sure that I would drown.

And then something dawned on me with a crushing awareness.

He had lived it all . . . over and over *and over* again. Never escaping the pain of our continuous struggle for survival. Never forgetting. Never free. Meanwhile, my memories were shattered and disjointed. I felt the uncomfortably familiar feeling of having more questions than answers.

How many times had he needed to explain it all to me, or failed to find me altogether, spending a lifetime searching before our time ran out? How many times had we actually been reborn over the past centuries? Or worse, how many times had we died?

Most importantly, perhaps, why hadn't he told me this as soon as he'd found me?

"It's never been *this* bad before," he said, reading my mind.

My heart filled with a grief I could scarcely comprehend. The notion of Dom having to endure these repeated, arduous trials in order to complete the call of the Prophecy was inexplicably painful.

I closed my eyes, still hoping this was all a dream. It wasn't.

"How many times? I can't—"

The look on his face made the words catch in my throat. He moved slowly to lie down, facing me, on the bed, the mattress straining beneath his solid weight. He clasped my hands gently within his own warm palms.

"I'm so sorry," he said as tears welled in his eyes, bottomless with grief.

I resolutely choked back scorching bile as hot tears filled my eyes.

"I used to remember . . . more?"

He nodded, but in that moment, there was nothing to say. Not because I didn't have a thousand questions, of course, but because in that very moment, everything between us had been said. My memories might not have been completely clear, but the song in my heart was as loud and sure as it had ever been. He had always been mine. And we had fought for this life, *our life*, over and over again for the better part of the past millennium.

Looking back over the past year in particular though, it honestly explained a lot. It was now abundantly clear that fate had been pushing—or rather *forcing*—us together with an ever-increasing gusto. I had never felt quite right walking through this world, and now I knew why.

Silent thoughts passed between us like electrical currents, eyes locked together as we held on for dear life to this infinitely fragile thread in time where we were safe, and whole, and together.

Finally.

I knew in the depths of my soul that this was all that mattered, to live in the here and now with this man who had dedicated countless lifetimes to my safety.

And then he broke the connection.

"We should probably get you cleaned up. I didn't think it would be safe to move you again while you were in that state," he said thoughtfully.

What *had* my body endured as the spell overtook me? Mortified, I took a deep sniff of my shirt and then hair, realizing that I smelled distinctly of vomit.

"Ugh. I'm sorry."

He chuckled. "It's no matter."

Carefully lifting me to my feet by the elbow, he wrapped his arm around my back and helped me slowly walk toward his cool bathroom. I stepped gingerly into his bathtub, unbuttoning my ruined shirt before sitting straight down with my bra and underwear still on. I drew my knees to my chin and wrapped my arms protectively around my legs. He cranked on the tap, checking the temperature with his sure fingers. I was grateful for the pleasantly warm stream now running down my back—chilly since leaving the safe haven of the bed.

After a time, I could feel my muscles starting to relax and slowly stretched my arms above my head. My ribs ached from the magical implosion I had endured, and I wanted to sleep for a week.

My rational brain thought about all I had to do this week, including writing two finals and packing my room. It all seemed so mundane and unimportant now. There was no way I could fathom going forward, not without leaving all of this behind.

Once I had at last raised myself to standing in the shower, and he was sure I wasn't going to faint on the spot, Dom exited the room to find some clean clothes for me to change into. He returned as quickly as he had left, setting a pair of soft grey sweatpants with a rugby logo and a black band t-shirt down onto the edge of the sink.

"It's not much, but it will have to do for now. I don't have a lot with me," he said through the shower curtain. "And, well, I think your clothes are probably ruined."

He let out a soft chuckle.

I poked my head out shyly. "Probably. But I'm alright now, honestly. I don't think I'm going to keel over any time soon."

"Alright then," he said, taking the hint that I needed a moment to collect myself, but I could sense the hesitation in his voice. "I'll be right outside the door if you need me."

After washing with a travel-size bar of soap and relishing in the heat for a few more moments, the exhaustion from standing was soon almost unbearable. I slowly climbed out of the shower and towelled off my tender body. My soggy undergarments now lay in a sad heap beside the drain. Perhaps they would end up in the garbage too; at this pace, I couldn't imagine having the energy to worry about things like laundry anymore.

Gingerly tugging on Dom's roomy sweatpants, I cinched up the waist slightly and unfolded the black t-shirt. It smelled just like him, warm and earthen, much like the late-day sunshine twinkling through the trees after a long day sitting by the seaside. It was a comfort to have his familiar smell close to my naked skin. My nipples bloomed with bold enthusiasm through the thin shirt, and I crossed my arms protectively. I wasn't sure why I felt so shy when he had clearly known me intimately for over a thousand years.

It was all so confusing.

While I had now witnessed the magically implanted visions and heard the Prophecy, none of the meanings were entirely clear. All of those memories, my memories, still slipped too easily between my fingertips. I felt disjointed, as if suddenly my words were not my own. Why couldn't the memories just stay put? And what made matters worse was that none of my magic was any surer now than it had been before I traced the intricate lines of Dom's tattoo.

Another fascination of the experience was that I could apparently translate language through my own memories. It reminded me of some kind of *TARDIS* effect, and I wondered absently whether, if I gave learning Irish a real crack, it would come with ease.

Gertie's words arrived right on cue: *"One thing at a time, Julia."*

And so, taking a slow, steadying breath, I reached for the doorhandle, enacting my life-long ritual of simply putting one foot in front of the other. Dom was standing just outside the door, and immediately reached for my arm before guiding me tenderly towards his bedroom.

"I think you had better lay down again," he said, obviously still concerned I might pass out at any moment. "And then how about I make us some coffee? Maybe a bite to eat as well?"

I wasn't remotely hungry, but the idea of even smelling coffee sounded like it would be soothing and hopefully take the edge off my lingering headache.

"Funny, I always pictured you as a tea drinker," I said, slight grin on my face.

He rolled his eyes playfully and mumbled something about mixing up stereotypes before heading towards his small kitchen. I was relieved to see that some of his brightness had returned, despite his evident exhaustion.

It felt peaceful to embrace normalcy for few moments as I sat back down on his bed and absently checked my phone, but there were no new messages—though I *had* sent Virginia a text from the pub bathroom that I was finally on a date with "my hunky professor," to which she had instantly and enthusiastically replied:

Get it, girl!

I chuckled and set my phone aside; she was on her way to her conference now, so I wouldn't have been missed at home this morning anyways. I could hear Dom filling the kettle with water, loudly banging around cups from the pile of dried dishes beside the sink.

Destiny. Divining. Witches. Princes. Druids.

These were all things that had haunted my bones for centuries. Just because I couldn't remember them with clarity didn't decrease their considerable burden within me. I wondered if it was a luxury or a curse to be able to forget. Dom bore the pain of remembering, and true to his character, I knew he would be able to help me unpack the memories one thought at a time.

The man himself interrupted my wandering thoughts, approaching with two full cups of hot coffee in hand. Carefully handing me my cup, he deftly settled once again beside me on the bed.

"This bed is too small for you," I remarked, thumbing the green floral pattern that was etched across the small glass coffee cup. It reminded me of something from a church basement garage sale.

"I know; it's terrible. But none of this stuff is mine, so beggars can't be choosers," he said as he took a cautious sip of his coffee.

I found it hard to believe that he couldn't have sourced more appropriately sized furniture for himself, but knowing what I did now, it made a lot more sense. The irony of my own lack of furniture wasn't lost on me either. His substantial presence was unbelievably grounding, and I let out a long sigh. Both the scent of the coffee and of him were tranquilizing.

After a few moments, he announced, "I really don't think you should write your exams this week."

"I wish," I replied flatly.

"Oh, come on, smarty pants. You and I both know you don't need to write them. Plus, I'm sure we could get you a doctor's note if you're that worried about it," he said, feigning optimism.

I almost spat out my coffee. "You're joking right?"

He raised his eyebrows and turned towards me, making it quite plain that he meant no jest. "Why not?"

"A doctor's note," I continued. "What would it say? Julia is a flaky Witch at best, and she had a bit of a run in with an unexpected magical tidal wave and will be unable to write her end-of-term exams because she can't stop throwing up and has lost her pants?" I shook my head and took a hearty gulp of my coffee, not that I needed it. I still had a lot of adrenaline in my system, clearly. My stomach winced at the arrival of the acidic liquid.

"What? I do have a good friend who just so happens to be a doctor!" he said, obviously failing to grasp the absurdity of his suggestion.

"Oh, I know you do. I saw him beat you at rugby, remember? Or did you not notice me watching the match?" I was surprised at how flirty I still felt around him.

"I didn't. Definitely did *not*."

He tapped the side of his nose twice, grinning broadly.

We glanced at each other out of the corner of our eyes for a brief moment before bursting out in fits of relieved laughter, months of tension continuing to slowly melt away.

Eventually we settled back into a comfortable silence as he polished off some cold Korean BBQ from his fridge. He claimed it was leftovers, but it was clear he had ordered himself an entire extra meal to take home. Without a doubt, the man had an appetite more than equal to his stature.

Satiated at last, Dom shared more of our story. "Well, I won't go too much into the specifics now; you need to rest and there's plenty of time for that ahead. But in the beginning, you could remember almost everything from the previous attempts."

"Attempts?"

"On your life. You see, as long as there's been the Prophecy, *you've* been hunted."

It sounded so fantastical. Hardly possible to consider it real.

"By . . . *him?*"

He nodded solemnly. "By Cassius, correct."

The words of the Prophecy, from the night before, rang loudly through my ears, and I felt all-too-familiar chills run down my spine. The meaning of it all, however, was still so completely jumbled in my mind, so I had to take his word for it at this point.

On top of being hunted by Cassius, we had also apparently long been haunted by the mystery of whatever occult magic had been in that grimoire, which had all too conveniently burned with the cottage on that fortuitous night all those years ago.

"In the beginning, like clockwork, your cycle of the curse would activate when you were approximately eighteen years old, and was always linked to the death of your birth mother. She would die, I would be reborn, and things would be set into motion once more. Apart from that, we've honestly never been able to figure out how it all works. But you're always reborn as 'yourself,' for all intents and purposes.

"Over the first few cycles, the memories returned then too, coinciding with the activation of your curse. I would be reborn remembering it all during the next winter solstice, then you would find me shortly thereafter. We would then have six months—until the height of the summer solstice—to try to defeat Cassius."

I nodded, keeping up for now.

"Over time, your memories began to fade, and we had to make . . . adjustments," he said, suddenly hesitating. "For a while there, when the memories first started to fade, you would recall everything as soon as you saw me, sort of like . . . I would jog your memory at first glance."

He smiled wistfully at some distant memory.

"I definitely felt something powerful when I first saw you," I offered. "To be honest, it felt much closer to love at first sight than I cared to admit at the time."

He blushed. "Well, that's good to know. But what you still needed was the vision hidden in the tattoo, so you could know the truth before we . . ."

"Took things any further. I understand."

He was honourable practically to a fault, and I wondered what it must have been like for him, holding back his longing for me all these months, when he alone knew the truth. And then I recalled how bloody combative he had been, the rousing energy passing between us impossibly charged. He had obviously been trying to find as many ways as possible to brush up against me without *crossing the line*, whatever form that took.

"We didn't always need the tattoo, but it was one of your cleverer ideas, to be sure," he said, scarcely hiding his pride.

"So . . . why did you wait so long to show me?"

He set his empty plate on the bedside table and pondered his response, running his fingers through his hair several times before speaking again. I realized now that this was one of his tells, manifesting when he was grappling with complicated thoughts.

"Honestly? You just seemed so happy on your own. Brilliant, really. Positively thriving. You didn't need me dragging you into this mess and I . . . well, I was afraid I would ruin your life."

"What?"

Not for the first time within twenty-four hours, I was well and truly shocked.

This time, however, I was damn sure to keep up. I turned my body abruptly towards him on the bed, and taking his hands into my own, pleaded for him to see reason.

"How could you possibly think that?"

"Please don't look at me like that, Julia. I'm not a monster. The Prophecy, our curses . . . it all comes at a such a perilous price. I just . . . I can't help but feel like, with each regeneration, I've become the deliverer of your death," he said, grief taking over the reins. "I wondered . . . What if I left you in peace? Then maybe you would be free of it all, at long last. But then I realized they would come for you no matter what."

He looked away, ashamed.

I dropped my eyes and slowly traced my thumbs across the tops of his beautiful hands, pondering how best to offer him comfort when I knew so little of our past and had no point of reference other than the deep feeling of *knowing* burning ferociously at my core.

"Look, I obviously don't have the answers . . . not yet at least. But what I do know is that destiny has always had her own plans for me, and obviously for you too," I said, demanding now that he meet my eyes. "And what I do remember, or know, is that we are meant to be together, Dom."

He started at the use of his name.

"I've never been so sure of anything. And despite what you think you saw in me *before*, I've never felt right in this life. The truth is, I've always felt completely out of step, with literally every single thing. Until I saw you."

I wasn't usually so brazen in my romantic proclamations, but this was spoken through my heart, and forged deep within my soul. He pressed his forehead into mine as his entire body shuddered in release, pushing his palms into my thighs as if to ground himself.

"It feels like, each time, it's exponentially harder on you," he said quietly. "And each time you remember even less. Like you've lost even more of yourself to the past. It . . . it breaks my heart."

After a time, we began to shift into a more comfortable position, and I stifled a yawn apologetically, embarrassed at how quickly I was losing the battle with the relentless weight of my eyelids.

"But . . . what about you?"

"I remember everything," he said simply.

We lay back together on the bed, my heart sinking through the mattress with the weight of his words. Placing my head tentatively onto his shoulder, I breathed in his presence and tried to steady myself. While my mind was burning with more questions, my heart told me there was no safer place in the world than here, right now, with him. What we both needed now was rest.

"I have one more question," I said.

"Hmm?"

"Do you think the curse is fading? Or what does it mean?"

He took a deep breath, studying his broad palms out in front of him. Then closing his eyes and fists simultaneously, he spoke to me in barely a whisper.

"It means, I think, that we are running out of time."

We slept off and on for the rest of the day. Instinctively, I had curled onto my right side, forming a protective ball around my pained chest. Meanwhile, Dom lay flat on his back, arms resting across his own expansive chest, a perfect stone king atop an ancient tomb.

Awake at one point, I found myself staring at him in pained curiosity. Was he truly asleep, or was his mind placidly rocking on a solitary boat, lost in a sea of memory? Closing my eyes once more, I drifted off into an uncharacteristically dreamless sleep.

When I awoke several hours later, spectre-like fingers of late-day winter shadows were reaching menacingly into the apartment. Dusk was fast approaching, and I knew soon we would have to make a move towards whatever future our destiny held in store.

Dom had lovingly encircled my body with his own from behind, having finally arrived into his own restful slumber. The rise and fall of his chest and steady breath against my back served as a calming metronome against the chaotic song still dancing through my heart. His long arm was heavy and grounding where it rested on my waist, and I wondered how many times we had shared this pose, so familiar to him that he did it in his sleep.

To my surprise, I could also feel his erection pressing hard against my borrowed sweatpants, and I smiled at this simplistic aspect of spooning with a sleeping man. While I was tempted to roll over and wake him, I guiltily realized that he probably hadn't slept a wink all night; he had long since passed the brink of exhaustion as I'd been in the throes of my visions. Even with the newly acquired knowledge of our eternal bond, I knew with surety that I still had time to explore him for the first time . . . again. I would leave him to sleep longer.

I had spent so much of my early life learning to fend for myself or managing the feelings and climate of those around me that I had forgotten what it felt like to feel safe and protected. Or, perhaps, I had never really known it in the first place. Not in this life at any rate.

My mother used to shout in anger about my "daddy-abandonment issues" if I expressed any sort of need for safety or security. In hindsight, this felt like more of a reflection of herself that she was attempting to deflect onto me, rather than the issues of a small child. As an adult, however, I had definitely struggled to allow others to take care of me.

Dom had demonstrated such a natural sense of attunement towards me since the events of the night before that his gentle protectiveness arrived as an almost foreign entity.

This level of care was certainly going to take some getting used to.

He stirred in his sleep, and I rolled onto my back to greet him as he woke. He started at first, looking around the room frantically, searching for that same foe that still remained a secret between us. He relaxed when he saw that I was exactly where he had left me, and slowly closed his eyes again, blinking away the residue of sleep.

"Hello, my love," he said instinctively, breathing in the scent of my hair as he roused.

My love.

"Hello," I said as I rolled to my side to nuzzle into his warm chest. I was still in disbelief that he was—and had always been—mine.

"I'm so sorry I drifted off," he said, breathing through his nose in a deep sigh. "I honestly don't remember the last time I slept *so* soundly."

His Irish accent lingered on the "so" rather deliciously.

"Me either," I said and reached my arm over his side to cautiously trace my hands along the curve of his back once more. Both the tattoo and the spell were gone, any hints of magic long since dispersed into the coastal air. All that remained was his robust and powerful body. He was a marvel, a man like no other.

"Does this change things then?" he asked, unexpectedly serious, looking deeply into my bedroom eyes. I pondered his question for a moment, still gently discerning the intricacies of his body as he quivered at my touch.

"Oh, Dom. I think this . . . it changes *everything.*"

He buried his face into my hair once again and began kissing my neck in earnest. "You have no idea what you mean to me."

His voice was muffled, and I could feel his heat rising. I moved to meet him, raw and open to whatever came next.

Zzzzz. Zzz. Zzz.

Zzz. Zzz. Zzz.

For all his natural grace, the vibrate setting on his phone was positively obnoxious. It went on aggressively for several minutes in the attempt, with whoever was trying to contact him avoiding his voicemail and then starting all over again. Dom continued to ignore the attempted correspondence for another few minutes, moving between moments of kissing me with ever-increasing gusto, and then pausing to trace my lips with his thumb, looking deeply into my eyes.

He knew *exactly* what he was doing.

"There was a day when you stood under the trees, after class," he said between yet another handful of kisses. "When the sunlight hit you. You were . . . well . . . your hair was illuminated like fire from the sun, and you stood there like the queen of my waking daydreams."

Another kiss. And then a few more. He lingered a moment, relishing in the memory held fondly in his mind's eye. "I almost rushed over and told you everything right then and there."

I chuckled. "I'm not sure how well *that* would have gone."

"You're probably right," he said, smiling in earnest.

"Okay, wait though . . . Are you *actually* a professor?" I asked, pausing the play.

He grinned cheekily, raising an eyebrow. "Do you want me to be?"

I smacked him playfully in the chest with my open palm, revelling in the sensation that followed as his low baritone laugh purred through his body, transforming into a still deeper sound of longing. I responded in turn with my own deep inner hum, magical and feminine fires fully ablaze.

He was so completely in love with me, with the depths of his devotion revealed across his face with bursts of mingled disbelief and unadulterated joy. The song of his body, on the other hand, was singing surer and more vigorously with each passing moment. Indeed, there was no disbelief in his commanding physical presence; he would finally claim what had been long lost, and I was more than willing to let him.

Pressing me gently onto my back, he pulled my legs up to wrap around him in one swift movement. He leaned back then, and his eyes lingered on my chest; I still wore his thin band t-shirt, but my shyness from earlier had completely evaporated. He wore a devilish smile on his face.

Zzzzz. Zzz. Zzz.

Zzz. Zzz. Zzz.

He jerked his head back and glared at the hallway. "Oh! Come on!"

"Are you going to answer that?" I asked, raising my eyebrows.

"This is positively rude. I am *so* sorry, Julia!" he said, hopping out of bed and scrambling towards the hall table.

I waited peacefully where he'd left me, delicious anticipation building for the man who would soon be returning. While I knew a fair bit about magic, all things considered, this was a magic like I had never encountered before. Exiting the room, he had been fully cocked and ready to meet my eager willingness. I heard a loud "Fuck" from the hallway, and when he quickly returned, he was full of alarm and utterly formidable.

"I don't believe it," he growled under his breath.

I sat up, pulling the covers to my chest protectively.

He was moving with forceful exasperation as he slammed around the room, searching for a pair of jeans. "I wish I could explain, but it can't wait."

I moved my feet to the floor and made to gather my things.

"No!" he said firmly. "You're staying here."

I snapped, my own confusion and fear rising. "No way in hell—"

"Julia, you don't understand the intricacies of our position just yet," he said, his eyes rapidly changing from anger to anguish. "I absolutely *have* to keep you safe."

What occurred in the following five minutes would teach me infinitely more about Dom O'Brien than a lifetime of memories could supply.

Whiplash, indeed.

CHAPTER 11

“I can't believe this!” Dom growled again.

His phone vibrated obnoxiously once more as I scrambled to collect my things. I located my bag, sitting atop my still-damp boots by the door, and hastily shoved my cellphone and keys unceremoniously onto my crumpled presentation notes at the bottom. While I was still understandably shaken from the effects of the tattoo magic, he was absolutely delusional if he thought I would be parting from his side any time soon.

Still in the bedroom, I could hear him digging around in the bottom of his closet, swearing colourfully as he tossed out the rejected items that had the audacity to impede his desperate search. A loud bang came from somewhere outside the suite, followed by several gruff voices hollering out.

“Fuck!” Dom roared. “They're already here! Julia, gather your things. It looks like we are going to have to fight our way out.”

Shoving my bare feet into my moist boots, I nabbed a grey wool sweater from a hook by the door and quickly yanked it over my head as armour against whatever came next. Dom moved at a dizzying pace as he tossed a duffel bag at my feet, simultaneously shoving what seemed to be a sheathed dagger into the waistband of his jeans and slamming his feet into his leather boots, but there was no time to tie them.

“What—”

Cut-off by the mingled look of rage and terror in his eyes, I took his prof-fered hand without another word.

Opening the door with a crash, we left it ajar behind us as Dom led me forcefully down the hallway towards the back fire-escape. Smashing open the outer window with the small axe encased beside an aged fire hose, he helped me climb through the jagged opening and onto a rickety metal ladder that led down to the courtyard behind his apartment.

My sweater caught at first, and Dom swore loudly as he freed me, tossing the duffel bag down to the ground below.

"Thank God I answered my phone!" he said.

No sooner had Dom slid down the ladder behind me, landing with his legs braced wide and ready for impact, than we heard the crash of hurried footsteps echo down the hallway above. He marshalled the bag in one hand and my own hand in the other, hastily leading me forward, a half-step behind him as we rounded the east side of the building. His gait was slightly lowered, ready to spring into action at any moment.

With a solid abruptness, Dom halted as we approached a narrow concrete staircase that separated the lower courtyard at the back of the apartment from the street above. Not expecting the pause, I ran full bore into his broad form.

"Shit!"

He took little notice of our collision, placing the bulk of his attention onto our surroundings.

Peering around him, I noticed the tops of the stone banisters boasted what must have once been an ornate pair of carved gryphons, both of which stared down at us, their scrutinizing faces melding ominously with the black mould and slow mosses of time. The width of the stairs they guarded would be barely enough for two people to pass at a time, and if I didn't know better, I would say that we were thoroughly pigeonholed.

Dom sniffed the air like a menacing dog on the hunt, and I wouldn't have been surprised if he let out a low snapping growl next. The duffel bag clattered to the ground at my feet, mysterious contents jostling ominously within. Bracing himself further yet, he spread himself wide as he unsheathed the concealed dagger at his waist with his free hand, the other still holding tightly onto mine.

All at once, the air reeked of sulfur and wood ash, causing my eyes to burn terribly as my still tender stomach rolled over several times from the stench. I silently pleaded with my internal organs to behave. The last thing we needed right now was a fit of dry heaving.

"Fucking Wraiths," Dom said under his breath.

Before I had a chance to ask what they were, a leering voice called out in answer.

"Well, well, well. What we have we here?" The voice came from a figure in a dark hooded cloak at the top of the staircase. "He said you had likely found her again. Thanks for that."

The voice oozed mocking gratitude, the tone causing my arm hair to raise in alarm.

"Do you honestly think I'm going to give her up?" Dom asked, his own voice low and formidable. "Or that you'll even live through the night?"

Two more of what he had called *Wraiths* appeared in a swirl of black cloaks at the top of the stairs, flanking the first. As if choreographed, their leader simultaneously reached both hands down and theatrically spread open his cloak in response to Dom's challenge, showing off its armaments. If not for the fact that these weren't mere costumes or toy weapons, I might have found the scene oddly comical.

However, the wicked and gleaming silver sickle that hung from its waist, as well as some sort of shorter jewel-hilted sword sheathed at its side, were hardly humorous. They looked immensely dangerous, as did their owner.

Attached to the Wraith's waist belt were also several small bags, which I could only assume were the magical source of the heavy putrefaction hanging in the air. I could immediately sense that these men were Wielders of some sort, but it looked like they didn't adhere willingly to the laws of nature. It *also* looked like they meant us serious harm.

This was dark magic.

The other two men were clearly his underlings, clutching smaller flat-black sickles in their fists. The weapons looked almost raw from the blacksmith, but that didn't diminish their threat by any measure.

"Give her to us, and we'll consider a clean death for you, *Domhnall Mac Brien,*" the centre Wraith said, openly lying through his shrouded teeth.

Dizzy, and still overwhelmed by the rancid scent of the dark magics, I wondered stupidly what had ever happened to good old fisticuffs when fighting over a girl? This was utterly ridiculous, and I shook my head in a vain attempt to wipe away this reality; ancient weaponry and dark magic had no place on city streets among normal citizens.

And to make matters worse, it was clear we were at a disadvantage in terms of both position and weaponry. I knew my magic would be of no use under this amount of pressure, and internally cursed my ineptitudes as a spellcaster in duress. Since I had never actually learned to use my Bearing magic offensively, I was once again made painfully aware of how ill-prepared I had been in my magical upbringing, at least in this lifetime, with these memories.

The peril of our situation continued to sink in further.

"Go to hell," Dom said with a surprising lack of emotion, considering what followed.

Cloak billowing, the left-stationed Wraith jumped the length of the stairs, knees tucked to his chest and darkened sickle raised in attack.

Dom ducked forward deftly in response, lowering himself just enough to drive his broad shoulder into his airborne adversary, sending the hooded figure sideways into the wall of the apartment with a muffled thud.

I dove out of the way behind a low hedge that ran along the length of the sidewalk, but by the time I had righted myself, the second flanking Wraith was already charging down the stairs on foot, with Dom roaring forward to meet him.

With his dagger in his right hand, Dom's full force collided with the sickle-handed wrist, slicing through the tendons and small bones with unexpected ease. Shockingly, in the same motion, he drove his powerful left fist into the folds of the Wraith's cloak, followed by a distinct *"whoosh"* as the air was knocked from its body.

The first attacker was on his feet again and charging Dom from behind, but I couldn't scream out a warning. My throat and lungs had completely seized up from the dark sulphurous air, almost as though my mouth had filled with coarse sand. Clasping at my throat, I was struggling to take anything more than a shallow breath without panicking. Perhaps that was one of the dark casting's ill intents, to inhibit the spellcaster's ability to speak? Not that it mattered in my case; I didn't even know where to begin.

Meanwhile, the Celtic warrior before me spun with the controlled fury of a man who had fought for his life far too many times to count. He drove his dagger deep into the side of an enemy, then offered him a swift head-butt to the face for good measure.

I could see now why he enjoyed the power and strength behind rugby; he truly was a brawler in the best and worst sense of the word. The word *"berserker"* came to mind when I took in the sheer rage in his eyes, and it frightened me somewhat, but he was similarly spectacular in his raw-edged power and grace.

This must have been where he found his magic and connection to his Gods. The way he commanded his body to do his bidding was nothing short of otherworldly, and I wondered what it must be like for him to find himself in modern times, where wars were fought with highly refined technology or across the great realms of the internet. Where did a warrior of that calibre fit in this world?

Well, evidently his brand of trouble still had a way of finding him . . . or finding *us*.

The Wraith slunk to the ground with the dagger still embedded in his ribs, and Dom turned his attention back towards the winded Wraith who was no longer slumped on the stairs but rather staggering forward on the offensive once more, this time with only one functional arm.

In one swift movement, Dom ducked behind his enemy, and bracing his all too capable hands around the Wraith's head, broke his neck cleanly with a dull *pop!* The speed of battle was so staggering that I had almost lost track of the lead Wraith, who had hung back from the fray.

"I see you haven't lost any of your skill, *Dalcassian* ... but you forget, this is not our first encounter." The voice was dripping with malice.

"I have no fear of you, nor any of your damned kin," Dom replied.

If he had ever known the Wraith's true name, he was flatly refusing to use it. I was in awe of the controlled coolness coming from his voice as his shoulders heaved conversely from exertion.

Were these so-called Wraiths the decedents of ancient Wielders who were rumoured to have taken the paths of darkness all those years ago? I knew practically nothing about the lost lore of the original Druids, but the stories that were told claimed they had split several millennia ago. It was all so secretive that it had never registered as remotely real to me, simply a clever design to scare young magic users onto the path of the straight and narrow. However, hidden truths seemed to be the benchmark of any magical sect, and from where I stood, I was beginning to wonder if the fantastical tales were, indeed, entirely factual.

Judging by his stature and delayed entry to the fray, I guessed the lead Wraith was high up in the ranks of darkness, whatever those happened to be. He was clearly powerful though, or at least was boasting to be, and my heart soon felt like it was trying to crawl out of my throat.

How could Dom, a man touched by magic but not a user himself, take on someone who had overwhelming access to the black arts? Sure, he had used the stairs to his physical advantage thus far, but this was a whole different level of combat. On top of that, the Wraith seemed to be emitting some kind of acrid smoke that prevented Dom from reaching him, the result being a distinct advantage for an offensive attack from his side.

"Your time is up," the Wraith called. "She's ours."

Dom seemingly ignored the Wraith, and looked to be pondering some unknown entity, his head tilted and looking to the sky. Soon, a new voice sounded on the air from beyond the dark spellcaster—a light voice, but one that also chimed with magic, speaking a spell of some sort, which I couldn't make out. Almost instantly, I detected the scent of summer dandelion and freshly mown grass permeating the putrid smoke, opening my lungs fully again as the Wraith shifted his attention, obviously thrown by this newly arrived opponent.

"Took you long enough, Ronan!" Dom yelled scornfully, and in that split second of distraction, he leaped the final stairs, grabbed the third Wraith by the skull, and smashed his head clean into the stone gryphon, sending shards of weathered concrete cascading down the staircase.

The Wraith pushed himself to his knees, wildly slashing his silver sickle towards Dom's flexed thigh, but Ronan had arrived on foot at last, speaking another enchantment with his palms raised towards the Wraith, momentarily freezing him in place.

"*Haigh, a Dhomhnaill!*" Ronan shouted casually in greeting, in what I assumed was Irish.

This act had shifted matters just long enough to allow Dom to deliver one powerful blow of his knee to the Wraith's nose, or where I assumed his nose would be under his dark hood. The blow emitted an awful crunching sound as dark-red blood spattered out, covering the lower portion of Dom's light jeans.

The spell broke, and the Wraith staggered back up to his feet, taking off at a run, but not before tossing one of his belt pouches behind him, its contents exploding with dark-purple smoke. Soon, it smelled of rotting flesh, forcibly stopping the two men in their tracks and inhibiting any immediate pursuit.

He was gone. Both men peered into the night, hacking and retching intermittently. Wiping his mouth, Dom turned to grasp his friend's shoulders.

"Thank you, Ronan. As usual, I am forever in your debt."

"Add it to the pile," said Ronan with a wry laugh, his own Irish brogue clearer now that he wasn't hurling incantations.

He shook his head in disgust at the bodies of the two wraiths on the ground.

"This bloody bastard thought he would try to evoke some kind of *night shade* on you. Good thing he's a pitiful excuse for a Wraith."

Dom was already on his way back down the stairs towards me, kicking a piece of the stone gryphon out of his way as he rushed to my side.

"I didn't expect so many of them," he panted. "I am so sorry I wasn't more prepared; all I had was that shitty dagger." He gestured passively at the tarnished blade wedged neatly into the Wraith's side. I was getting the distinct impression the two men didn't think highly of the escaped Wraith, in moral standing *or* magical station.

"You . . . killed them?" I gasped.

I could barely speak, having once more purged the contents of my stomach into the bushes, the final putrid blow of the Wraith's dark alchemy pushing my tender belly beyond its breaking point. Spending time with Dom seemed to include an unusual amount of nausea, and in this moment, I wasn't particularly enthusiastic about it.

"Sort of . . . It's kind of hard to kill something that's already technically dead," he said.

Ronan spoke from the top of the stairs, "We can't talk about it here, man. What if someone overhears? Or worse, they rally and come back?"

Dom shrugged and gathered me up into his arms, face full of relief. "Are you alright?"

His eyes, honed with the cool rage of battle only moments before, were now overcome with concern as he brushed stands of hair away from my pallid face. I'm sure I looked a real treat, covered in cold sweat from fear and vomiting. Not to mention that I was standing there sockless, braless, and wearing his pants, with my head still positively spinning from the abruptness of the battle.

My turn to shrug. "I'll survive."

Dom, for his part, looked positively brazen, face keenly alight with the fire of battle. Every bit the victorious Celtic prince.

And he really *was* an ancient Celtic prince, though I was struggling to recall the specifics. When the Wraith had spoken his name, however, it was as if another memory had been unlocked within me. I saw him then, all those years ago, standing beside his father and many brothers as I watched from afar during some sort of formal presentation in a great hall with not one but *two* hearths. I was every bit the peasant class Witch, and he was *very* much the son of Brian Boru, the High King of Ireland. What had I gotten myself into all those years ago?

Better question: What the hell had I gotten myself into now?

Ronan was moving rhythmically at the top of the stairs, busying himself with some kind of incantation, which I assumed was to remove any trace of our presence. As he flowed through the motions of what was clearly Druidic Wielding magic, I noticed that, while he was slighter than Dom, he was still formidable in stature. There was a mysterious rawness to the magic that surrounded him; he certainly wasn't someone to be trifled with.

My thoughts were finally beginning to catch up to me, and I had questions. *Lots* of questions.

"Okay, wait. So why . . . how did they know where to find us?" I asked Dom.

Dom sighed. "I should have warned you this might happen once we invoked this part of the curse; that kind of magical energy is hard to miss—"

"Dom, we need to move!" Ronan called anxiously from above.

"Where are we going to go?" I asked as I was abruptly ushered up the staircase towards the lights of the street. No doubt the crumpled bodies of the

Wraiths would be retrieved by those in league with them before the night was out, and I sensed from the Irishmen's behaviour that our window for escape was narrowing.

"I'll explain more once we're somewhere safe," Dom said hastily as we crossed the wet lawn in front of his apartment. I could see out of the corner of my eye that we had left the apartment lights on, and laughed with slight hysterics at our apparent lack of care.

My hands were shaking violently, but happily, I still retained some feeling in them. I forced myself to take long deep breaths as we approached an army-green Range Rover SUV parked haphazardly on the grassy boulevard.

A group of girls on their way home from the bar were giggling at the park job, but as soon as they saw Dom and Ronan, their body language changed immediately from silly to seductive. What was it about men who looked like they'd just come off the rugby pitch that drove women mad? Even with blood splattered down his pant leg, Dom looked positively ravishing.

Ronan offered a charming smile to the tittering girls before hopping into the driver's seat with his own brand of self-assured coolness. I noticed that he was younger than I had initially assumed, maybe around forty or forty-five? He had the beginnings of salt and pepper hair at his temples, but for the most part, it was a glossy dark-chestnut brown, almost bordering on black. Overall, he had a very handsome face; his eyes were icy blue and framed by dark brows, while his aquiline nose boasted a distinctly Roman flare.

Dom ignored the women altogether and helped me into the backseat.

The car smelled of new leather, and some other herbal remnants, but was also *impeccably* clean. I thought of my truck, with its wide, sun-faded grey, upholstered bench seat, always smelling a little bit like motor oil, soil, and on occasion, cannabis. I bristled defensively at this sterile excuse for transport.

Dom ran quickly behind the back of the SUV and soon settled into the seat opposite me, dropping his duffel bag onto the ground between us with a soft *thunk*.

"You're going to need to leave the city for a while, Dom. We're going to need time to get rid of your trail. Is there somewhere you can lay low for a while?" Ronan asked as he ground through the gears of the sleek SUV, rocketing us onto a main road headed southwest.

"Take us to the ferry. We're going to Julia's grandmother's cottage," Dom replied, resolutely.

"What? No! I have to go—"

"Julia, please don't tell me, after what you have seen tonight, that you still want to write your exams," Dom said, turning towards me in disbelief.

"No, no," I said waving my hand through the darkness. "I'm fine to skip those. But what about all of my stuff? And my truck?"

I felt somewhat foolish worrying about trivial things like my laptop and rainboots, but it felt anchoring in that moment to tie myself to the ordinary world somehow. And I really *did* like my truck.

"Don't worry, Julia, all will be taken care of. We just need to get you and Dom out of this godforsaken city while we come up with a plan." Ronan's Irish accent was less pronounced than Dom's, though his tone was bordering on condescension. "And if it makes you feel any better, I can write you a doctor's note or something to get you out of your undergraduate exams."

Yup, condescending. I looked at Dom, eyes wide, and soon started to laugh again in earnest, the notes of hysteria not yet having left my system.

"You really weren't kidding about the doctor's note, were you?" I said, reaching my now chilled hand out to him.

The shock of the night's events was sinking in, and I was shaking considerably now.

He reached out, the response instinctual and nurturing, and gently stroked my hand with his thumb. Immediately at his touch, I felt the peace of safety and warmth, and we sat in silence for several minutes as the traffic and streetlights pulsed rhythmically into the dim back seat. My body was practically begging me to nod off for a bit, which was likely the effect of repeated magical onslaughts over a twenty-four-hour period, but new questions continued to explode in my mind, urging me to stay wide awake.

"Okay wait, what did that . . . um . . . *Wraith* call you? And him?" I asked, gesturing towards Ronan and breaking the steadying lull.

"Oh, Domhnall. That's my name. It's Irish," he said, pronouncing it *"Donal."* "It's Anglicised form is closer to Donald, or even Daniel, which would be more familiar to you."

"Hmm," I said, brows furrowed trying to picture the word. Why was I having to struggle so much to grasp the names and language that I had fluently spoken in the past. More so, why couldn't I even recall his full name? "How is it spelled?"

"D-O-M-H-N-A-L-L," he said slowly. "So, I suppose I really should go by Don, but most people over here are so perplexed by the existence of the 'M' that it's been easier to opt for Dom and call it a day."

"Call it a day," I said, stifling a yawn with my only slightly warmer hand.

"And don't call him 'Donny.' He won't thank you for that," Ronan barked out from the front seat, his laughter, albeit rough, was much more welcoming than his aloof exterior.

Dom rolled his eyes, and we sat back into silence once more.

"I know you have a lot of questions, Julia, and I promise I'll answer them. But for now, you should rest."

He wasn't wrong, exhaustion finally overcoming me as the streetlights continued to flash by. I closed my eyes for what only felt like a moment.

When I awoke, we were boarding the final ferry of the evening, sailing towards Grandma Gertie's and into the night.

CHAPTER 12

The gravel crunched familiarly beneath Ronan's tires as we approached the mock Tudor-style cottage, its charming facade peacefully asleep as it sat nestled quietly into the mountainside. Gertie had it built as a special commission back in the seventies, a cheeky modern replica of her childhood home in England; it was equal parts quirky and delightful, and so quintessentially *Gertie*.

My heart leapt unexpectedly at the sight of the false dark wood shutters and aged casement windows, which stood in bold contrast to the white stucco as the Range Rover's LED lights flashed with loud modernity onto the front of the cottage.

Ronan put the SUV into park and shut off the engine with a quiet shudder.

As the vehicle's interior lights turned on, I noticed for the first time a medical parking tag hanging from his rear-view mirror, labelled the UBC Department of Medicine. It came as no surprise that Ronan was currently a practicing physician in Vancouver, however this wasn't where the pair of Celts had first met. I'd spent most of the ferry ride listening to increasingly raucous stories about their days spent at the University of Cork, where Ronan was completing his residency and Dom was working his way through yet another research avenue. Dom had hopped into the front seat with Ronan to allow me to stretch out and sleep during the nautical voyage, but it was nearly impossible to doze with their lively banter.

Piecing my way through their increasingly thick brogue, I gathered that, through their shared friendship, it had accidentally been discovered that Ronan was a Druid, sealing the bond between the two men as best friends and allies.

"Well, I was starting to suspect there was something off with the man," Dom said, "and obviously the Druidic order is a sworn secret. But unbeknownst to him, I'm practically an honorary Druid by association. I've been working with the Druids for centuries—so long that you could even say I have a Druid sixth sense."

He laughed at his own joke, and Ronan scoffed.

"You don't have a Druid sixth sense, *mar dhea!*" Ronan said sarcastically before turning back to me. "The bastard got me ripping drunk one night and just flat out asked me. I couldn't believe the pair on him."

"But I was right, wasn't I?" Dom smiled innocently while Ronan rolled his eyes in resignation.

Fate had clearly had a hand in their meeting as well, it would seem. I had tried to catch some sleep then, but it wasn't restful.

My mind had wandered aimlessly down different paths as they spoke: some light, others frighteningly dark. Usual worries around practical things like exams and roommates drifted through my mind, dogged by dark images of Wraiths who wished to kill my lover and then capture me for some evil purpose I hadn't yet divined with any clarity.

About twenty minutes before we arrived on Salt Spring Island, Dom called back to me, assuming I was asleep.

"Julia, are you up? We're going to need your help here soon, I think."

I shook away the insidious thoughts, knowing there would be plenty of time to discuss them when the sun rose. That left me with the more practical worries, and I wasn't in the mood to fuss over domestic logistics either. However, the ferry had slowed to a troll; allegedly some of the navigation equipment was on the fritz.

"It's your magic," Ronan said as if it were the most obvious thing in the world.

"What are you talking about? I come and go from here all the time."

Dom thought for a moment, obviously hoping to explain it to me in a way that made magical sense. Thinking better of it, he unfortunately deferred, with a nod, to Ronan instead.

"You've come and gone since Gertie's passing, sure, but you've been *alone.*"

I looked at him, perplexed. How could he possibly know that?

"But *we're* with you now, and I'm thinking the enchantment is likely to bar us. Well, *me* in particular. It's probably fine with Dom."

I thought back to all the times since Gertie's passing that I had left Salt Spring, and indeed, I *had* been alone.

"You're going to need to give us, me and Ronan, directions, I think," Dom said, his logistical mind showing. "That way we can navigate our way towards the house."

"What do you mean? What enchantment? I mean . . . technology is always wonky over there, but I always assumed it was just because Gertie was such a nut and had imparted too much of her magic into the bones of the place."

"That's probably part of it. Bearing magic is hard on anything that sends or receives signals, for sure. But this is something else. We think it's why we weren't able to properly pinpoint you at the cottage, and also likely why we were never able to fully locate your place in Vancouver either. Anywhere that holds a sense of . . . of *place* for you, you seem to somehow naturally protect . . . to keep yourself from being found."

"Sense of place" had been on my mind a lot over the summer. I was surprised to discover that I had, in fact, made these important magical connections throughout the past months, when in my mind, I had felt so utterly disconnected.

Thankfully, Dom and Ronan's directional theory worked a treat, with the ferry taking off again almost immediately after I explained to them *exactly* where we were going, the magic apparently accepting this shared knowledge as a sign that it didn't need to protect me from them. Soon enough, we were disembarking from the vessel and on the road towards the cottage, unhindered by my own sentient inner protection spell.

It was pitch black on the property, and I hopped out of the car to wave my arm at the motion-sensor lights. Nothing. I must have switched them off when I'd left at the end of the summer. I pulled out my phone for the flashlight, but it was dead too. No surprise there. Resigned to the aspect of darkness, I allowed my eyes a moment to adjust to the moonlight, and eventually noticed that Bill, our neighbour up the road, had unfailingly kept his promise to keep things tidy on the property while I was away.

That was the beauty of the Gulf Islands. While isolation could allow loneliness to manifest in the darkest of ways, it also lent itself generously to the magic of community and support. I always felt that you couldn't have one without the other, and that the combination created some kind of safe haven for those who craved a different path than the mundane.

"I think I'll head back to catch the first ferry in the morning," Ronan said.

The three of us were standing awkwardly in the dark in front of my makeshift homeplace. His voice had retreated back towards formality, the barking laughter from the front seat long gone.

"That's ridiculous. Stay here with us," I offered, confidence growing now that I was in my apparent homeplace. It felt absurd that he should go sleep in his car in the ferry line up when there were several perfectly plush and welcoming beds waiting inside for any weary traveller.

"Julia is right. Stay. We can regroup and make a plan in the morning," Dom said with a hint of command that was unfamiliar.

I felt uneasy, which was likely more due to exhaustion than threat, and shivered in the cold.

"No. Thank you, though. I have some work to do while I wait," Ronan replied with a stern nod to Dom that seemed to seal some unspoken understanding. "And besides, I am still on nights. I don't think I could sleep anyways."

Watching in silence until his taillights left the driveway, I turned towards the front door, with Dom's hand tracing tentatively across my lower back. More shivers but not from the cold.

Hopping up the three steps by pure muscle memory, I quickly crouched down on the creaking deck boards in search of the spare key. Mine was sitting safely with my truck keys, back in Vancouver at the apartment. I tipped over the pots of rosemary and sage, as well as one containing a few feeble stalks of parsley and chives that had somehow survived the winter thus far. Together, their fragrance made it clear that this was a Witch's domain; make no mistake.

"Don't tell me we'll have to break into *your* house?" Dom mused with a smile, crouching down in kind to aid in the search.

"It's not my house. Not really," I said dismissively as I checked under another cracked pot. "Aha!" I said as I grasped the small gold key.

I fumbled with the lock in the dark, Dom approaching me from behind before I could fully turn the latch, arms wrapping around me in a protective embrace.

"Hi," I said with a yawn. I leaned my head back, savouring the moment of safety. Not even three hours ago we had been fleeing from imminent death, and now, here we were, completely alone, *together*.

"Hello you," he said, brushing my ratty hair back and placing a simple kiss on my neck.

I had the distinct impression he was struggling to restrain himself from a need to catch up on all the lost years of affection.

Throughout my life, I had often been confused about where *home* was, preferring to ground myself to a phase or an experience, rather than a specific building or particular person. Gertie's cottage was the closest thing to home I had found, but standing there with his broad chest firmly behind me, I felt the truest sense of coming home yet.

It was, and had always been, *him*. And I was equal parts thrilled and terrified.

"It's going to be pretty cold inside, but we should be able to warm it fast enough with the woodstove," I said instinctively as I deflected the moment of intimacy and internal panic. "Bill probably has wood stacked and ready outside."

I had always been the kind of lover who preferred laughter in the bedroom over seriousness, but something about Dom's air of ancient valour was threatening to change all of that and make a true romantic of me yet.

"I don't know who Bill is, but Julia . . . if there is wood that needs splitting, I'll gladly do so." His voice was low and soothing. "However, I would *guess* that with a quilt, and holding each other close through the night . . . we should fare well enough until morning."

The quilt. I had almost, *almost,* forgotten about it. The months focusing on school and Dom—okay, mostly on Dom—had almost erased it from my thoughts. But not entirely. I knew it was tucked away upstairs in the hall closet, right where I'd left it. Despite not thinking of it, I could almost feel its presence as we'd driven up the driveway, almost in greeting. I could certainly feel its magic stirring now as we crossed the threshold into the cottage. Dom looked at me quizzically. Clearly, my thoughts had wandered in a different direction than his.

"Let's use the bedroom downstairs. It's mine anyways and has the biggest bed. Unless . . . you would prefer to sleep on your own? There are two bedrooms upstairs," I offered awkwardly as a trailing afterthought.

Yesterday afternoon's intimacy in his West-End apartment felt like a thousand years ago and miles away, especially after what had happened during our escape. I could understand if he wanted to sleep soundly on his own. Not to mention that I was an absolutely treacherous sleeper and knew all too well how disturbing I could be while partners attempted to chase their own dreams. But if I was completely honest, I was also extremely nervous to jump straight back into a place of deep intimacy with him, even if the longing to be near him was equally pressing.

He smiled at me kindly, the tiniest hint of pity in his voice for my continued abstractions of where our destiny truly lay. "Julia, the only place I will *ever* sleep soundly again is by your side."

Too exhausted to argue, I saw no need for further discussion, and my reply took the form of my borderline-sleepwalking body heading towards the musty downstairs bedroom, with Dom trailing along like a phantom in my wake.

That night, my dreams were riddled with images of Wraiths, warring Celtic princes, and ancient forest Druids. I grappled with the complex emotions of fear, flight, and the relief of being saved as I crafted my own dream oracle, body twitching and moving as I navigated deep into the nether realms of my own magical psyche. It was an even wilder ride than usual.

Unbeknownst to me, Dom had held me close through each rising and falling tide of my dreams, until finally we'd both settled into peaceful, dreamless sleep. Like clockwork, I awoke in the early hours of the morning, thirsty, chilled, and wide awake. Dom, who had evidently been slumbering peacefully, startled and pushed himself up onto his right arm instinctually, searching the room and checking the door. Old habits die hard.

We had passed out last night with our clothes still on, with the exception of Dom's blood-stained jeans, which lay in a crumpled heap in the corner. Pure exhaustion had overcome us almost before we could push the bedcovers back.

Assured that we were indeed safe, he settled back onto the pillow behind him, muscular arm raised up above his head. Pure Adonis.

"What magic is this, for me to hold you through yet another night, only to awake once more with you sweetly slumbering at my side," he said sleepily.

I laughed in spite of myself. "Hardly sweet and barely slumbering. And I have to pee."

Hopping out of bed, I headed for the bathroom with some urgency.

Staring into the mirror, my eyes widened at the dishevelled person standing there.

Aren't you just a picture of wellness?

Today felt a bit like waking up after a bender, only the frivolity had included a life-threatening battle and harrowing escape. I guess to people like Dom, that probably counted as a fun night out. I prodded lazily at the dark circles under my eyes. My hair resembled something far worse than a rat's nest. On the other hand, there was more colour than usual to my cheeks, and a brightness in my eyes themselves that I hadn't witnessed in a very long time, if ever. Honestly, I barely recognized myself. Basic instinct told me to shower and then sleep for the rest of my life. However, primal urges screamed otherwise, and I felt extremely anxious to be back by his side.

I padded back to the bedroom where I found Dom lying on his back, eyes closed but clearly not asleep. In the short time I had known him with any intimacy in this life, he had chosen this pose more often than not when left alone to his thoughts.

"Can I get you anything?" I asked, wishing to be a good host. "Well, the fridge is empty obviously, but can I get you some water?"

I climbed onto the edge of the bed, facing his prone figure and tilting my head in question. This had usually been my bedroom when I visited my grandmother. She preferred the smaller rooms upstairs. *"Closer to God's wonder, Julia!"* she had said.

I understood that it was more likely because those upstairs rooms were warmer in the winter, but I liked to pretend she would chatter to the birds outside her windows as they perched merrily on the fir trees behind the house.

"No, my love. Just you. All I need is *you* . . . here beside me," he said with complete absolution. This was equally as enchanting as it was bewildering. These profound declarations of love were *definitely* going to take some getting used to.

Something was still sitting uncomfortably with me though.

"Dom, can I ask you something?"

He looked at me dreamily. "Anything."

"When you fought those Wraiths last night . . . you said something about not killing something that was already dead . . . What did that mean?"

Judging by the surprise on his face, my question certainly wasn't landing within the vein of expected topics.

"Oh, that," he said, sitting up. "Well, it comes down to the difference between a mortal wound, and a mere flesh wound," he said with a wink. "Wraiths use dark magic to extend their lives . . . to around two hundred years or so, I think. They're able to heal anything that isn't too significant or damaging."

His lightheartedness was doing little to quell my concern.

"So, they weren't dead?"

"Oh, no. I killed them dead. The best way to handle Wraiths is to deal in fatality."

My eyes widened, and he backtracked frantically.

"No, Julia. It's not like that, I swear. I'm not a murderer who kills for sport. They are pure evil and would have killed each of us with far less concern if I had let them. Unlike the Druids, who are mindful of Wielding only what they need and returning the magic back to the earth in due course, the Wraiths *only* take. Sure, they have an unnaturally long life, but the cost of their magic is much worse."

I shifted slightly, my stomach wanting to revolt once more. "Worse?"

"Ronan can probably explain it better, since it's what he's *actually* studying right now; emergency medicine is just a cover," he waved his hand dismissively. "Anyways, the aspect of the *mortal wound*, in this case, is bringing them to heel. Wraiths extend their lives and heal themselves using magic taken from others. So, destroying them redirects the stolen power back to where it belongs, returning it to the earth and the beings it was taken from. They don't survive it, of course, as there is nothing else left and they are far beyond redemption. But the balance is restored."

I still didn't fully understand, but then I recalled the violent nightmare in which what I now knew to be Wraiths were chasing me on horseback, and showing absolutely no remorse in slaying the hero. I shivered, too terrified of the imagery in my head to ask Dom if the dream had, in fact, been real.

"So . . . the price for their long life is losing their souls?"

He looked almost inappropriately proud. "You catch on quickly!"

I wished I hadn't, but this aspect at least made some sense. *All* magic had a cost, and anyone who said otherwise was a fool.

"The bastards also have a completely skewed perception of mortality though. Turns them into great fighters, but they've also become rather addicted to their own power. I won't lie to you and say I don't take at least *some* pleasure in tearing them down."

Once again, he was as frightening as he was astounding. I thought back to how his body had moved during the fight, almost travelling between space and time while he cast down his foes. But then I thought, perhaps he had a skewed sense of mortality too. My heart sank.

"You must be starving," I said, my discomfort overflowing into a compulsive need to feed people in order to bring them comfort, and ultimately regain control of the environment.

On the other hand, I also knew he had an insatiable appetite.

"Always, but it can wait. I assume nothing will be open yet anyways. It's still so early. Come, cuddle me," he said, raising the soft quilts to welcome me with a cheeky grin.

There remained a damp chill to the room, even though I'd had the sense to turn on the electric heat before we'd passed out in bed. It looked like he would likely be chopping wood after all before the day was through. With that thought, I dove in, the coziness of the covers far more alluring than I could resist.

As I slid under the duvet, his arms found me. I self-consciously wished I had worn deodorant, but as the room smelled of sleep, bodies, and human desire, this was a minor detail. Not to mention that, in the past, we had very likely *literally* slept in a barn together.

"Do you think we're safe here?" I asked.

Daylight was spilling in more with each passing moment, the dawn an imposing reminder of all that could, or would, follow in our coming days. I yearned to capture this safe space and intimate moment forever.

"I do. For now, at least. In the past, you were always able to hold the protection spells for a good length of time. Now, it seems like your subconscious is doing the work for you. *Clever girl!"* he said, teasing an English accent.

His grin was bright, but my own emotions felt far less luminous.

In truth, while I could touch on the deep memory of our love and feel its weight now with surety, situated comfortably within the space that had always felt so barren, I still had to learn *how* to know and love him again. Clearly his memory didn't work the same as mine with each regeneration, and that meant he was arriving fully loaded with adoration, whereas I had to grow into my love once more. Not that I didn't feel a burning passion towards the man, of course.

To his credit, he had been respectfully restrained. However, looking back on our short time together through a new lens, I could already see the challenge it posed for him. I longed so deeply to know him again, truly, with all of my five senses, my body, and my soul. But I was also afraid, and not only because of all that stood to be lost.

"Julia, I don't want you to feel like you have to rush anything," he said with unexpected seriousness, and some sadness. "I know that I hold the bulk of our memories together. It must feel so strange . . ."

I sighed. He was reading my mind again.

"Honestly, Dom, there is nothing I want more than to know you . . . like I used to. Or like I will? I don't know. I guess I just want to find you again. But I'm also . . ." After a moment, I shrugged, not holding back but unsure of how to articulate what I was trying to say.

Taking advantage of our intimate blanket nest, I was honestly shocked at how comfortably I was voicing my vulnerability, but then again, I had always felt like expressing my authentic self around him.

"I know, it's a lot," he said.

I felt such surprising safety in the cottage, especially considering the mood with which I had departed at the end of the summer. However, bringing Dom into the space felt different. Throughout all the turmoil of the centuries, had *he* in fact become my homeplace? It felt like a bit of a gamble, based on our history, but right now, I felt safe and whole.

I felt his powerful legs against mine as a surprising rush burned from within me; I was suddenly *very* short of breath. Now thoroughly tucked under the covers with him, I dragged my fingertips along his powerful thighs towards his hips, where he was wearing simple black boxer-briefs.

"Those scrubs Ronan offered me barely fit over my butt," he said playfully, inching closer yet towards me. "He's got a skinny little arse; there's no way I would have fit."

I reached behind him and gripped his powerful glutes. "I hadn't noticed."

He laughed and gave his own bottom an emphatic *smack!*

And then he kissed me. Tender, assuring, and safe. It was the sort of kiss that said he knew I had been afraid only hours, or even moments, before, but one that promised we were truly safe in the here and now. We continued like this for a few moments, gently exploring each other's mouths and delicately tracing long fingers across sensitive flesh, a giggle here, a suggestive stroke there. Clearly, we had always been as much playmates in life as we were lovers, and I felt a deep gratitude for this. It was truly an intimate act, the exploration and slow re-acquaintance, as well as the simultaneous revival of my magic, as it seemed to be wholly anchored to him.

"I feel like such a goober," I said in playful embarrassment, the lingering feeling of unfamiliarity making me suddenly self-conscious. "Seriously. Look at what I'm wearing." I pulled away and held out his thin band t-shirt in front of me.

"Well, as those are my clothes, I would think that means you're calling me a goober too!" He said, gleefully combative as he pushed my wrists gently back beside my head, moving himself into a dominant position.

He looked down, eyes wrought with barely contained desire. "Any man worth his salt would look at a woman wearing naught but his clothes, after a bloody harrowing escape, and feel an overwhelming lust," he said, flirtatious danger clouding his eyes, "and lucky for me, I love you more than just *any* man."

My mouth was so parched I felt like I was wearing sweaters on my teeth. But in that moment, with his adoring gaze shining down on me, I did indeed feel like the sexiest woman alive.

He leaned in and kissed me, at first as softly as before, and then with increasing ferocity, his mouth moving with the jarring surety of his intimate knowledge of me. In that moment, I had no doubt he would be an infinitely fulfilling lover, and all I wanted to do was melt into the sheets, existence null.

But a voice from deep within me called out, halting the progress of my slow cascade towards euphoria. I was still me, in this body, and this time. He undoubtedly had an unfair advantage in his knowledge, and I would be damned if I didn't get to have a say in this chapter of our destiny.

I pushed the palms of my hands onto his expansive chest, stopping his trumpeting battle march and throbbing act of conquest momentarily in its tracks. Instead, I intended to demand he slow down and dance to the rhythmic melody of my body instead. At first, he looked concerned, followed by surprise, and then his growing grin showed what I could only describe as hopeful curiosity.

"Vixen," he said, practically purring. He leaned back to take the measure of me, eyes narrowed in feigned suspicion.

"Shirt off please. And then roll onto your stomach," I said calmly, with just a hint of command; this wasn't a point up for discussion. I wanted to see his back again, without the tattoo, and I then wanted to kiss every inch of his back from top to bottom. I would start with his neck, shoulders, back, and then hips. It was suddenly *very* important to me that I reacquaint myself with every single inch of his perfect body.

"You know, a good warrior never turns his back on his opponent," he grumbled into the pillow as he settled onto his stomach, muscular arms raised and flexed above his head.

"Good thing I'm not a threat," I said matter-of-factly. "Hmm, you *do* have a big bum!"

I wriggled onto his backside, straddling his impressive glutes between my legs.

"As if you hadn't noticed," he teased. "Honestly, Julia . . . sometimes the look on your face during seminar—"

I gave him a playful smack to the shoulder. "Quiet, you!"

He resigned himself to submission, purring with low laugher as he lifted his hands in surrender. It was time to begin my research.

I started by gently tracing my fingertips along his spine, grateful there was no remaining magic hidden within the flesh. His skin was pleasantly warm, like a summer's day, and I noticed with keen interest that there were faint freckles across his powerful shoulders, even in the wintertime. I was at once overwhelmed with the scent and sound of waves crashing against oceanside rocks and could almost hear the cry of distant gulls. I closed my eyes and felt the summer sunshine that surrounded him shining warmly on my face, his golden essence deliciously inviting.

"Is everything okay?" Dom asked, breaking me from my warm reveries.

I placed my hand on his back in reassurance. I must have gone frozen briefly as I let his pleasant aura surround me entirely, but my face felt cool again, having been brought swiftly back into the here and now.

"Of course," I said, not wanting to delve into details about the effect he was having on my awakening magic. It was a powerful force, and my instinct was to not interrupt the duality forming between the rekindling of my Witch's fire and my reacquaintance with *him*.

I continued my tracing, his body occasionally rising in response to my interrogation, his anticipation and budding impatience becoming ever more present with each gentle stroke. I enjoyed those parts perhaps more than I should have, but I supposed that was one of the true delights of really *knowing* your lover. I had always taken pride in being the kind of woman who didn't require a mate to navigate the world. My mother had taught me that, at the very least, through her many failed relationships and botched attempts at giving me a father figure. But when I was around Dom, this need to prove my independence washed away, and a stronger tide of desire and togetherness overtook me; I had long yearned for *balance*.

He groaned impatiently below me, mumbling something about "cruel and unusual punishment" into his pillow.

Ignoring his protests, I noticed that he had several faint scars barely visible in the early morning light, and a few that were significantly more pronounced. One in particular ran along the right side of his rib cage and looked like it was born of a nasty blow.

"These scars . . . they aren't from this life, are they?" I asked, unexpectedly nervous to hear the answer.

"No, not those. Most scars don't carry over during the rebirth either, which isn't altogether that different from the Wraiths I suppose. Some wounds can be healed by the magic of the rebirth, but the particularly . . . *nasty* ones seem to carry through," he said, voice trailing off as his body tensed slightly.

Death blows. That's what he meant by "particularly nasty ones carrying through."

So much still remained unspoken between us, and our newly revealed historical intimacy seemed to be leading us to as many closed doors as open ones. I realized then that, while I desperately wanted to understand his process of rebirth, it also seemed an extremely personal line of inquiry. Based on his physical response alone, it was quite plain that now wasn't the time. Not to mention that I wasn't interested in darkening the playful mood I was carefully crafting around us.

Returning my focus to more pointed work, he quickly relaxed once more into our blissful, early morning daydream.

"You always did like to tease," he said, grasping the pillows in his fists as I began to kiss down his neck and onto his spine. His back was exceptionally sensitive, and I immensely enjoyed the act of teasing out his pleasure, kiss by kiss.

When I had at last decided that I'd tortured him enough with the longing and vulnerability, I allowed him to flip onto his back as I rose up fully onto my knees. But I wasn't quite ready to relinquish control yet. In fact, the voice inside me was demanding our reunion more loudly than ever, almost hammering out the importance of cautious steps in rekindling my fire.

"I'm not done my research project yet," I said devilishly.

He grimaced impatiently but didn't argue. However, I could feel other aspects of his heavenly body putting up a resounding protest at my delaying tactics.

"Hmm . . ." I said, shifting slightly on top of him. "I've been thinking about doing this since I first laid eyes on you."

He looked up at me, the chaos of the universe dancing in his eyes.

"Oh, and what's that?" he said breathily.

"You'll see . . ."

How many times had this scene played out in our story, and how many times had he welcomed me into his world again with full knowledge of the oncoming storm.

Removing the grimy borrowed sweatpants at last, I would have completely exposed my bottom half if not for his t-shirt that draped to the very tops of my thighs.

He reached his hand out, beckoning cheekily that I hand over the remainder of his borrowed clothes. "I want my shirt back too please."

I leaned forward and ran my fingers through his fine, golden chest hair and down his broad torso, noticing that his nipples were already raised in anticipation of my touch. He jammed his thumbs into the elastic of his boxers, clearly intending to remove them with haste. With an unexpected hitch in my breath, I stopped abruptly, running my fingers over a particularly large scar just below the right side of his ribcage. Was this the entry point of the wicked scar on his back? If so, this was clearly evidence of a death blow.

Suddenly, a rush of blackness clouded my thoughts, and with a forceful push of magic all around me, I was somewhere else entirely.

At least in my mind.

CHAPTER 13

When the haze of transcendence finally cleared, I was met with an equally violent onslaught of jagged ice crystals, their slashing bite shockingly aggressive against my naked face. My eyes burned painfully, and I squinted in an attempt to gather my bearings. Some visions were certainly more jarring and realistic than others, both visually and physically.

Several long paces before me, a tall man stood with his unbound hair plastered icily against his face and neck. He was backing slowly towards the edge of a high oceanside cliff, the sea below churning hungrily amidst a north-coast winter storm. Forcing my attention further into the vision, I could see it was indeed Dom, although my heart had known this fact immediately. He was down to only linen shirt and leather breeks, wind and sleet whipping his shirttails this way and that as he slowly sunk to the ground like a sailboat taking on too much water in a gale.

Slipping haphazardly in the mud and snow, he staggered barefoot another step while still holding up a huge broadsword in his capable hands. His limbs were shaking in the struggle to remain upright, his strength visibly waning with each passing moment. A sword like that was exceptionally heavy at the best of times, but in his hands, it looked like he carried the weight of the world. I had no way of knowing when and where we were, but "the ends of the earth" came to mind.

The vision shifted slightly, and I was now witnessing his strife from above. A hooded man came into view, his dark eyes cold and infinitely menacing as his thin lips raised into a nasty hairline sneer.

"Once again, we meet at your demise, Dalcassian. It's such a shame she had to die before you could say goodbye," said a voice wrought with evil. "I would have liked to let you watch as we performed the Soothsaying ritual."

"There's nothing more you can take from me," Dom said, voice heavy with great sorrow.

His foe, a grey-cloaked man of no great height, stood somehow looming over the declining Celt in a vastly enchanted stature.

Sorcerer.

I blinked again, struggling to distinguish between his true and enchanted forms. He was holding a dagger that looked similar to the one the Wraith had carried; however, this one was much simpler in its makeup and altogether more menacing. What was worse, he was clearly only moments away from using it precisely for its intended purpose.

Sneering, the Sorcerer continued. "You are no *'World Ruler.'* Time and time again, I cast you down. When will you learn?"

Not waiting for a reply, the shadowy figure moved with terrible speed towards Dom, and with one powerful lunge, drove his enchanted dagger forcefully into his right side.

Dom dropped his sword in surrender only milliseconds before the impact, stepping backwards off the cliff as the dagger snuffed out his life. His body cascaded in a graceful arc towards the roaring ocean below, shirt billowing and body breaking tragically on the rocks just before Neptune claimed his lifeless form for his own with one great, screaming wave.

When I opened my eyes again, I was still straddling Dom, our bodies now drenched in cold sweat. Heartsore tears ran down my cheeks, a far cry from the salt water that had claimed Dom's lifeless form.

"That was one of my cleaner deaths, truth be told. If you saw what I think you did," he said, his voice echoing in my ears as if still thousands of miles away.

My hands went numb.

Fighting back the oncoming panic, I closed my eyes and focused on grounding myself in the here and now. I thought of the roots of this place, travelling deep into the mountain. I thought of the body of this home, and the welcoming arms of my grandma Gertie, and her community. The air *did* feel infinitely clearer here. Breathing deeply once more, I looked down to find that his face had gone completely blank, outer self hastily retreating behind his own inner halls of stone.

"Oh, Dom," I said, more tears falling. "How can you bear to remember it all?"

I threw myself onto his chest, the pain now almost unbearable. He remained eerily still, stealing away all emotion around his memories and sorting them neatly into place.

"Yond Cassius has a lean and hungry look," Dom said.

He automatically stroked my hair back from my neck, but there was little emotion to the gesture. I sat up then, confused and sniffling.

"What did he mean by 'World Ruler?'"

He took a deep breath. "Oh, that. It's what my name means."

"Feels like a lot of pressure for one person," I said with a sob. "Dom . . . what happens to you . . . after you die?"

His eyes were distant, but his response was level and devoid of any emotion.

"I spend some time . . . *in-between*." He paused. "I'm never really sure how long. And then I simply wake up again the next time the curse is activated. In the tomb."

"Wait. What? A tomb?"

My eyes widened at the thought of him being trapped below the earth, claustrophobic feelings kicking in forcibly.

"Well, more like ancient Druidic chamber. It's not closed or anything. At the winter solstice, the longest night followed by the birth of the day. That's when sun shines in through the chamber . . . and there I am."

This was stuff of legend, not the stories of a fully fleshed man living in the here and now. I had *so many* questions, but just as I was about to press on, he closed his eyes and set his jaw in pained resolution; evidently the discussion was over for now.

With no memory of drifting off, I was surprised to wake in my bed, alone.

I had been neatly tucked into bed, a full glass of water sitting on the bedside table beside a handwritten note, on stationary paper I recognized from my grandmother's upstairs writing desk.

Heart in my throat, I reached hastily for the note, punching the glass of water towards the floor in my haste.

"Shit!"

I shot my hand out to stop the glass mid-tumble, subconscious magic flowing through me as it landed neatly on the floor, unbroken, but completely devoid of water. Still rusty, but curiously, my abilities seemed to be slowly returning.

Silently, I unfolded the note.

Gone to find food. Stole back my track pants, sorry!
Back before nightfall.
-D

He had also sketched a small happy face at the end, but I felt only mild relief. The message was lighthearted enough I supposed, and I was glad for him that he had managed to solve his pants predicament for the time being. I definitely didn't have anything here that would have fit his frame and be appropriate for public wear, especially during the wintertime.

However, something still wasn't sitting right in my gut. He was clearly coping and maybe just hungry or needing some space to clear his head. But the truth was, I didn't know him well enough in this lifetime to even begin to guess his thought process or how best to support him through his grief. What was more, I was shocked at how I desperately I wanted to.

I had always been the kind of friend or partner to offer supportive advice when necessary, but admittedly, sometimes it wasn't warranted. I tended to speak my mind in the name of truth, though I had learned with age that not everyone wanted my opinions, or for me to pry for information that I wasn't entitled to, simply for *me* to feel more comfortable with a situation. Boundaries truly made for healthier relationships, and it was something I had to continue to work on.

It would seem I had neglected this fact with Dom already, pressing him on personal matters and experiences that he was not ready to share, no matter how contrary I felt on the subject. It was just so complicated trying to reconcile the fact that, just because we had experienced countless lifetimes intertwined together, it didn't mean we weren't still fully actualized individuals. Realistically, did I even have a right to any of the memories or experiences he held onto? Did I even want them? Well, the uncontrolled visions that had plagued me this fall seemed to have other plans, divulging terrifying truths whether we liked it or not.

Shivering now, I realized I had *also* taken for granted the warmth Dom had provided so far as a bed mate. Drawing my knees to my chest, I collected my scattered thoughts about the best move forward. With my mind decidedly foggy on the subject, I deferred to basic personal care.

I reached for my phone to check the time and found that it was actually dead this time. Groaning, I realized my charger was in Vancouver along with all of my other things. I had to have one here somewhere, likely shoved at the bottom of my closet with the many other discarded items from the past year. Alas, retrieving my possessions was yet another thing that would need dealing with. I had plenty of clothes here though. A long hot shower would be the most logical first step, followed by the task of chopping wood, and putting the house back into working order so a more solid plan could be carefully hatched over the next few weeks.

Dragging myself into the small downstairs bathroom, I noticed immediately that Dom had showered before leaving, his damp towel neatly folded on the rack and the scent of Gertie's earthy handmade soap still lingering on the chilled air. The exposed cedar wainscoting that lined the bathroom still smelled damp too, so I surmised that he must have left not long ago.

Stepping lightly into the dated pinkish-brown tub for my own turn, I relished in the slow process of washing my tangled hair and travel-worn body, residual dark memories slipping away down the drain with each frothy soap bubble. Following my shower, I loosely braided my hair before dressing in my familiar, thick, mustard-brown work overalls and a long-sleeve merino-wool shirt. Finally, pulling out a well-worn pair of socks with holes worn through in each heel, I found myself singing lightheartedly as I ran my fingers along the aged wooden surface of the dresser. How many times had I opened and closed those drawers without a second thought, when now they seemed so safe and familiar? Everything in the cottage did now, really.

Fondly, I eyed a framed photo of Grandma Gertie and I aboard *The Duchess of Persuasion*, a small fishing boat that had belonged to some of her long-time island friends. The picture had been taken several summers ago just as we'd boarded the vessel during spot prawn season, but unfortunately, the afternoon hadn't panned out as anticipated.

Setting out just before lunch to check the traps, we had looked forward to bringing our fresh catch to a potluck dinner hosted by several of our neighbours later in the day. It had been a pleasant afternoon, with our skipper having unearthed a stash of *Lucky Lager* from under one of the bench seats while the sun beamed down, its warming rays practically begging me to partake.

Our fearless captain, an older man who went by the name of Drake, had been having difficulties with the marine radio throughout the entire voyage, but assured us it was nothing to worry about. He *did* have a reputation for being extremely diligent with the care of his vessel, and had grown up on the water after all, so I thought nothing of it.

When both outboard motors died too, however, Gertie and I eyed each other with suspicion.

"I can't believe it! Both the main motor *and* the kicker are dead. This is unprecedented," Drake said, visibly flummoxed. From underneath another bench, he yanked out a red float bag with a yellow rope coiled inside, and was soon fishing around inside of it for a second radio. Much to his dismay, it too was non-functional.

For my own part, I'd been decently drunk with an empty stomach, and starting to get an angry sunburn across my shoulders. It had been entertaining enough to watch Gertie throw back several cans of beer with the rest of her retired counterparts, however.

"And can you believe it, the filthy liar ran out of the restaurant with his pants literally on fire!" she had recounted, laughing heartily over some misdeeds from long ago. Gertie's social side was something I had come to appreciate as I got older, realizing that she had indeed found her own brand of chosen family in the end.

We continued to enjoy the sunny afternoon despite the malfunctions, optimistic that another mariner would soon pass by and offer us aid. Ironically, we continued to be extremely *unlucky*, with the water being exceptionally quiet that day. We had blown our life-jacket whistles at one point in an attempt to attract some attention, but it was pointless. We were dead in the water.

With the sun starting to set, we were left at last with the only option: paddle ourselves towards land. We were all immensely thankful that at least the traps had been set relatively close to shore and could be scooped up along the way. Midway to our destination, a larger family-owned commercial fishing boat on its way home had swooped in and rescued us.

Looking back from where I stood today, I realised it was more than likely that my own subconscious protection spells had altered the course of the afternoon. I felt the hair raise on the back of my neck, mortified at the thought of Wraiths, or something worse, being nearby as we crossed the calm waters. How many more of these "dots" would I be connecting over the coming weeks? I was exhausted just thinking about it.

A nervous chill reminded me that there was little enjoyment indoors this time of year without heat, and I dug around the bottom of the front-entry closet for my old pair of steel-toe boots. They still smelled heavily of asphalt and diesel fuel from a summer spent doing road maintenance. While they would offer more protection than was perhaps necessary for chopping wood, they were the sturdiest thing I had at the cottage. Naturally, Gertie wouldn't have seen the need to dispose of them, and as they fit me well, I remained grateful.

Underneath each boot, I found two tightly folded slips of dirty white paper. I knew what *this* was immediately; an old Witch's trick to be rid of someone or something in your life that you needed respite from. Mildly curious as to who or what Gertie was trying to send away, it still felt rather prying to unfold the papers and peek into her personal life that way, even post-mortem. Not wishing to pry, I crumpled them up and threw the faded papers into the fireplace for good measure.

Opening the cottage's red, spring-loaded screen door at last, I confidently stepped into the cool early December afternoon, the door snapping loudly shut behind me. I paused a moment to fill my lungs with the invigorating clear coastal air, refreshment spreading across my cheeks and nose as I took in several more grateful breaths. I could smell the green-tinged moisture of the forest that surrounded me, as well as the distant scent of wood smoke drifting over from our neighbours' homes. It was so boldly contrasted to the suffocating dryness when I'd been here last and *instantly* grounding.

What was more, I truly looked forward to the simple manual-labour task ahead. Physical jobs like chopping wood had always helped me navigate stress with a clear head and kept any visions at bay. In fact, I had found this to be the case most of my life; if I was busy with my hands, either being productive or creative, my thoughts seemed to settle into clearer streams.

Perhaps this was why I had dragged out my degree so painfully, sensing the need for recreation between the striving pushes of each semester. A wise woman had once told me I was doing my "master's in life," and not to worry about what others thought of my path. But I still felt self-conscious about how long it took to complete anything, academically or otherwise.

Digging into my task at last, I focused on the power behind each axe stroke and the satisfaction of splitting the wood into manageable sizes. Sometimes I would come across a more challenging piece, but if that wasn't a cliché metaphor for life, I didn't know what was.

There was some truth to it though, as I had learned much as I worked countless jobs and travelled considerably throughout most of the western parts of the continent, slowly piecing together my life, much like that of a patchwork quilt.

The quilt.

My inner gaze pointed towards the upstairs hall closet once more. Something about the textile felt ominous and undeniably connected to this path of destiny. Right now, however, I just needed fucking wood to heat the place and for my attention to stop drifting from the task at hand. I thought back to my attitudes the last time I had been on this property, when grief and fear had overcome me, and I'd been prone to stillness and self-abuse through substances and poor eating. The six months prior to that visit hadn't been the finest examples of coping. Instead, I had fed the wound.

But I had felt a shift this fall, at long last. Only to have it all turned completely upside down by a certain ancient Celt and foreboding Prophecy that included none other than yours truly. Another dot connected. Obviously, *that* had been the cause of the shift.

Again, I was reminded of my pitiful training as a Bearer, particularly my inability to manage the visions that arose anytime I got close to Dom. It was said that true Bearers with the Sight could see as deeply into their pasts as the oldest, most gnarled tree roots in the ancient forests of the world, but could also sense and navigate the oncoming waves of any future threat. They were the ancient storytellers, boasting an uncanny ability to access the knowledge and wisdom from the Otherworld. Their magic was consistent, beautiful, and endlessly powerful.

My powers, on the other hand, were dismal. And since true Diviners were uncommonly rare these days, and I had also grown up in a relatively isolated community on the West Coast of Canada, I was woefully untrained.

Sometimes my prophetic magic arrived in bursts of shimmering clarity, bright as the sun across the July water in the Salish Sea, and drifted through my mind in the symphonic dance of memories of past, present, and future lives. I felt hope in these moments, like perhaps I had a greater purpose in this life than the seemingly mundane, disenfranchised, and socially prescribed trajectory to which I felt a constant pressure to adhere.

Other times, the Sight within me was as muddy as a boreal bog, black flies attacking any bare patch of my vulnerable and exposed skin, my flesh crawling unbearably at the thought of never knowing where I existed within the patchwork of time—never feeling like I belonged. Those were the times in my life that were wrought with nightmares, which was the case more often than not in my adult life.

Ultimately, I wasn't clear in the least as to what our next steps would be and hoped Dom would be returning before dark with nourishment and a plan. It was already late in the afternoon, and we were going to lose the sun soon. Not to mention the fact that I was completely starving. I had scrounged up a handful of practically fossilised almonds from the back of the pantry after my shower, but it had been a hard sell, and most had been tossed unceremoniously into the garbage.

I had just begun to make good progress on my pile for the wood stove, mind clearing with each focused swing of the axe, when I heard footsteps crunching up the drive and jumped. With momentary disappointment, I discovered it was my neighbour to the south, Bill Blake, now methodically moving towards me with what looked like a baking dish wrapped in a tea towel.

He was a mostly solitary man, who rarely said more than a handful of words at a time, but they were always relevant and wholeheartedly to the point. His wife had been ill for many years and had passed several summers ago. I was always thankful that he and Gertie had taken to checking in on one another during the long and isolating winter days.

I had planned to visit him first thing tomorrow morning to let him know that I would be home for the time being, but he had clearly beaten me to the punch.

"Julia, you're home early. All is well?" he said, voice soft, soothing, and free from alarm.

"Yes! Plans changed and I was able to complete my coursework early. I'm glad to be back," I said, a hint of surprise in my voice with the latter statement.

"Good. How long will you stay?" he asked, ignoring my skittery prose.

"I'm not one hundred percent on that yet, but I assume until sometime after the holidays. I'm still hammering out the details."

I raised my shoulders good naturedly, trying to offer a tone of assurance that I was working on a plan.

"Good. Got my niece visiting. Worried I wouldn't be able to take care of things this month," he said, gesturing to the lawn and garden. "She leaves before the new year."

Typical Bill, never divulging more information than was necessary.

"No problem. I'm on it!" I said, brandishing my axe perhaps a little over enthusiastically.

Shaky from hunger, I was covered in sweat and my braid had halfway fallen out, but he surely didn't care.

"She made some pie, more than I need. Thought you might like it," he said, holding out the tea-towelled pastry towards me.

"Oh wow! How thoughtful, thank you!" I said, genuinely grateful as my stomach practically howled at the prospect of finally being fed.

"There was a man here. You know him?" he asked, getting straight to it now.

"Yep, he's with me," I answered, taking on his guarded language style briefly, but gave myself away as my face flushed pink at the question.

"Good. Good. You take care, Julia."

Turning on his heel, he headed silently down the drive. I was thankful for his lack of reaction. Carol, the other neighbour up the road, would have had *much* more to say on the topic of my brawny visitor.

"Thanks, Bill, I'll let you know my plan once there is one!" I called out, and he raised his hand casually in response, his back still towards me as he disappeared into the growing dark. People were good like that on this island; while there was always room for exceptional local gossip, the usual old adage of "live and let live" was the much more common mantra.

I finished moving my final stack of wood beside the front door and then turned towards the pie sitting on the stoop waiting for me.

"You and I have a date with destiny," I said, eyeing it hungrily as I shuttled it towards the kitchen in search of a fork.

CHAPTER 14

Considering that dusk had been gathering thickly for thirty minutes already, I was beginning to expect that Dom wouldn't return today at all. Since there was nothing on *this* island that would have barred him from arriving by now, I assumed that he had actually travelled to the mainland to take care of more of his mysterious business; perhaps he'd misjudged the ferry schedules and was now stuck somewhere else entirely. Surely, as he had lived for centuries past, his sense of time and the importance of punctuality were likely fairly rusty. I tried not to feel resentful, but there it was.

Sitting down to the table at last, good fortune displayed delightfully in front of me in all its bumbleberry glory, I heard a soft knock on the door.

"Just a second!" I looked towards the pie with deep longing as I pushed back from Grandma Gertie's ancient and stained maple-wood table.

The knocking increased, followed by the doorbell.

"It's *me,* Julia, but my hands are full!" Dom called out. My heart instantly beat a brilliant staccato against my ribs. The hero had returned at long last! And as it turned out, I was glad after all. I shuffled merrily towards the door, wool socks sliding smoothly on the familiar hardwood, and opened the latch.

There he stood, strapping as ever, with his arms and hands completely over-encumbered with paper grocery bags and a box of something that sounded like various bottles of wine and whisky banging together merrily. This must have been what he considered modern "battle provisions."

Several other bundles of groceries lay on the ground beside him, as well as a simple black travel case on wheels. I chuckled at the sight; he was clearly the kind of man who needed to carry everything to the door in a single trip. I glanced briefly past his shoulder to see if he had left any personal detritus strewn along the driveway in his struggle, and my jaw dropped.

"My truck!"

I was shocked I had not heard the tracks on the gravel or seen the lights. My affair with the pie had obviously become wholly engrossing—that and the curtains had also been protectively closed.

"Surprise!" he said. "Ronan had it sorted for you. He had your . . . roommate help pack your things into the back of the truck first thing this morning when he got back," he said, shifting one especially heavy-looking package from one arm to the other, a look of playful desperation in his eyes.

I noticed the strange pause around the word roommate and raised my eyebrows suspiciously, just as the teetering bags in his arms began to fall towards me.

"Oof! Sorry!" I said, grabbing the topmost bundle from him before it toppled over. The bag was oddly heavy and smelled of roast chicken.

Our hands brushed slightly, that familiar spark of electricity surging predictably between us.

"Provisions," he said with a smile. I laughed heartily at the word, because I had, in fact, been correct. He wore a fresh pair of light jeans and a maroon pullover windbreaker from his rugby kit. It draped over his broad shoulders attractively, and I noticed with an internal sigh of relief how much more relaxed his entire demeanour was compared to when we'd last spoken.

We turned in unison through the threshold and into the entryway, bumping our shoulders together awkwardly.

"I still haven't started the fire. But the wood is chopped!" I said, proudly gesturing to the unseen pile outside.

He looked impressed. "Well done, you!"

We stood awkwardly for a moment, shuffling around each other with shy smiles before depositing the groceries on the kitchen counter. I pulled my phone out of my back pocket in yet another attempt to find a signal.

"Two things. First, I don't actually have your phone number." I blushed in spite of myself but brushed it off with my hand. "It doesn't matter right now."

Why did I suddenly feel like I was in high school again asking for a boy's number?

"And then, I actually tried to text Ginny this morning, but my phone's kaput. I found an old charger, but it had no signal anyways once I had it turned on. Oh, and how did Ronan manage to get into the apartment? I thought Ginny was still away until early next week."

Dom looked awkward again. "Oh, yeah. About that. Your phone I mean. We had it disconnected overnight so that you can't be traced. Sorry, I meant to tell you but—"

But you disappeared without a reasonable discussion?

"Fair enough," I said, cutting him off, not wanting to pick a fight. "But what about—"

Dom suddenly yanked the phone out of my hand and smashed it on the edge of the counter.

"Um! *Excuse me?* Barbarian!"

He looked sheepish, but there was something unexpectedly humorous about the situation. "Sorry, Lennie, a Druid who works with me, said I actually needed to disconnect it in person."

"Yeah . . . probably could have just pulled out the SIM card," I said, suddenly doubled over in a fit of laughter, hot tears running down my face as I leaned on the now-cluttered countertop.

He grinned, somewhat abashed.

"Oh. Yeah . . . sorry."

He still wasn't off the hook, but the laughter helped.

"And the apartment?" I asked, wiping the moisture off my cheeks.

Dom still looked embarrassed, but a flash of something that momentarily resembled anger crossed his brow at the mention of the apartment. He was clearly hiding something.

"Oh . . . yeah, she wasn't back yet. So . . . Ronan broke in. But he found your spare keys and locked up properly before he left. He drove your truck over himself, and I met him at the ferry on this side." He looked at me in earnest then. Maybe he just wasn't keen on Ronan breaking in? I had my doubts though.

"Hmm," I said, appeased for now at least. I would have to try to get a hold of Ginny soon. A problem for tomorrow, or later this week, I supposed. It wasn't as if my phone was remotely functional anymore anyways.

Still navigating the awkward tension, Dom turned abruptly to bring in my belongings from the truck, but I stopped him by gently grabbing his hand. As usual, it was warm and inviting, and he turned his body back towards me. He smelled positively delicious, like he had been walking through the forest before coming home, rain and wood-smoke emanating alluringly from his person.

"I'm sorry," I said, not really sure what I was apologising for, but it felt right in the moment, if not a tad compulsive.

He barked out a laugh. "For what? I'm the arse who wandered off without explanation."

"You left a note," I supplied, not altogether generously.

He shook his head and kissed me atop my brow, a gesture he was clearly used to performing on impulse.

"I'm an arse," he said, ending the discussion.

It took sparingly few trips to bring all my possessions inside; my previous reflections about the packrat experience in the attic had paid off. Once again, my mind wandered to the quilt in the upstairs hall closet, but I didn't feel like it was the moment to bring it to light just yet. Oddly enough, I felt protective of it.

"I stopped at the grocers on the way, and at the liquor store obviously." He looked somewhat perplexed. "There's not a lot open on Sundays out here, is there?" He discarded a second box full of clinking bottles on the faded beige and gold Formica countertop.

"Just wait until you try to shop on a Monday," I answered.

This was just the way it was out here in these smaller West Coast communities, but sometimes I forgot how unusual that probably was for most people.

"It's like that back home too in some places. I'm impatient when I'm hungry though."

He popped off the clear, domed lid of a black-bottomed, plastic container. It contained a shrivelled roast chicken that had clearly been cooked *much* earlier in the day. Ignoring its shrivelled appearance, he tore a leg off the bird enthusiastically and looked at me fleetingly before he took a bite, "Sorry to be rude . . . but I'm starving."

Standing in the kitchen beside the groceries and haphazardly strewn luggage around his feet, he looked so perfectly innocent in comparison to last night's dagger-brandishing hero, or the stone-walled prince of this morning.

"Hey, you don't have to apologise to me. I was about to devour a whole pie to myself before you came home."

Home.

I wondered if perhaps the gathering peace of coming home had less to do with Dom and more to do with the intuition that I was exactly where I was supposed to be at this particular moment in time. Here, at the cottage, with Dom, with this "new" future before us—or was it that our past was now ahead of us?

We enjoyed our respective meals in silence, Dom groaning with pleasure as he devoured the meagre bird with almost too much vigour. I was able to polish off half the pie before its sticky sweet contents started to give me a stomachache. Sitting back in the familiar chair, I stretched my body out, watching in amazement as he ate the entire roast chicken, as well as the second half of the pie, with my permission, of course.

"Oof, I'm stuffed! Where did this pie come from anyways?" he asked as he finished the last morsels, satiated pleasure spread wide across his face.

I ran my hands along the well-polished arms of the chair, sensory memories of childhood trickling in and out of my mind. "Bill, from down the road. His niece made it."

"Not bad," he said, patting his muscular stomach with satisfaction. How on earth this man could consume endless volumes of food and still maintain the physique of an elite athlete, or better yet, a formidable warrior prince, continued to pose a significant mystery.

"They ransacked my apartment before Ronan could get back to it with the others," he said a matter-of-factly, "But they didn't take anything of value. I had all of that in the duffel bag."

He gestured towards the bag slumped carelessly beside a tacky vintage umbrella stand beside the front door, still sitting exactly where he had left it from our initial arrival. The stand itself was dangerously close to tipping over and spilling its contents—a single cracked shoehorn and an unfamiliar wooden cane—onto the floor.

I suddenly felt self-conscious that I hadn't guarded it nearly well enough during the melee, or worse, that he hadn't trusted me with the knowledge of its importance.

"Well, it can't be that important if you haven't told me what's inside of it yet," I said, defensiveness and shame rising; I was already going against my intention to honour boundaries, and it seemed to immediately get under his skin.

He frowned as his face paled briefly, but he quickly brought a smile back to it, clearly mustering positivity, or mastering something else more sinister from within. "Well, it's not important, yet. I had kind of hoped . . . that you might ignore it for the time being."

His voice held a hint of pleading that indicated I should let this issue drop for now. Perhaps our previous verbal sparring matches had made him apprehensive of my willingness to trust his word.

"Okay then, tell me more about Ronan," I asked, changing the subject.

He looked relieved. "Ah, Ronan. Well, he's a fully-fledged Druid. And a physician. And also ex-military. Frankly, I'm not sure how he's managed all of it without some kind of magical rebirth curse of his own. But I assure you, he's only walked this one life."

"No kidding," I said, curiosity mounting as I listened with rapt attention.

He nodded. "Well, you know how we met, but he has a pretty interesting life story. You'll have to ask him about his childhood sometime, but I think it was pretty loosely ruled. A lot of freedom landed him in a big lot of trouble as a lad, and eventually he was pushed towards the military as a teenager, and then from there he went on to medical school."

Dom focused as he recounted mentally the rough timeline of Ronan's life.

"And the Druid training? Was he born into a family of Druids or taught?"

I knew a tiny bit about Druids, only what Gertie had relayed really, but not enough to understand entirely how their lineage worked. Being Wielders meant they weren't necessarily born into their power, like Bearers, but could instead learn through rigorous training to connect to the magic that surrounded them, if they had the gift. Technically a Witch could be a Druid, if that was their chosen path, but not the other way around. It was fascinating to consider such a similar, yet individual, arm of Paganism. Witches tended to stick to their own; however, I had no doubt there were *many* Druids on the West Coast too. Ronan now being one of them.

"Well," Dom said, leaning in conspiratorially, "people used to call his granddad 'the man of the forest,' because he lived alone out there and apparently had this absolutely massive beard. Rumours always swirled that he was a Druid, which was of course complete horseshit. The man was a drunk, and Ronan's gran had long since kicked him out. But Ronan . . . he found the Druids young. I think that was some of the trouble he was getting into before he was shunted into the army. Magical troubles. But of course, he never stopped being a Druid. I'm told that once you connect with the power . . ."

I nodded in agreement.

"Sounds like something from *Buffy the Vampire Slayer*."

He looked at me with confusion. "Come on, Julia. Vampires aren't real."

I chuckled to myself; our disjointed history was going to take some getting used to.

With what felt like a natural break in the conversation, I moved to collect the empty pie plate and plastic chicken container from the aged table. How many times had my grandmother and I sat here, enjoying meals and oversteeped tea, and chatting late into the night? I remembered always arriving at that table feeling like my problems held the weight of the world and leaving feeling profoundly unburdened.

This was no exception. Dom had started to share with me truths beyond the magical world I had come to understand in this lifetime. With every question answered, I felt like I had ten more, but the avenues of communication had opened between us again. I was thankful, albeit still suspicious of the number of secrets that had yet to be uncovered.

"Let me grab those. And can I get you a drink?" he asked, doting again as he dutifully cleared the table.

I put my hands up in play surrender. "Sure! But I'll light the fire!"

We'd had the old fireplace replaced by a woodstove insert about ten winters ago. Grandma Gertie was miserable about it at the time, claiming it would threaten the flow of the ancient ways and the energy of the house, but after one cool winter and a built-in electric fan that kicked in at regular intervals, she didn't complain ever again.

I grabbed a single stick from the long match holder mounted on the plaster-and-whitewash wall nearby. My grandma's voice, ever present, spoke in earnest.

"Don't waste your magic on the mundane, Julia. What will happen when you need it most?" I rolled my eyes in memory of Gertie's teaching. This wasn't some act of prestidigitation. I was simply lighting a fire. Plus, it wasn't like my magic was reliable these days anyways, so I took this moment while Dom wasn't watching to test my spontaneous magical prowess.

Crumpling up a handful of newspaper and then stacking some smaller pieces of kindling on top, I tentatively reached out my hands towards the dry timber. Then, with a quick flick of the wrist (and much to my surprise), the fire was soon dancing merrily without much more than a thought. In fact, the fire was so quickly vibrant and hot that I was able to fill the woodstove with larger logs immediately. And I still felt steady inside.

With a small prayer of gratitude to the Witches who'd come before me, I quietly tucked the unused match back into the holder before relocating onto the vintage orange, grey, and beige floral-pattered hide-a-bed couch in front of the window. Settling into my usual spot, I folded my legs to the side while simultaneously tugging an aged crocheted Afghan off the back of it and onto my lap. I had done this motion a thousand times before and found the ritual both familiar and grounding. The blanket consisted of patchwork rainbow "granny squares" on a base of black, joined by black yarn. Gertie had made it, using her scraps, as a graduation present for me before I'd left to see the bees.

"Here you are, my love. Nice fire!" Dom said as he passed me an overfull glass of slightly effervescent white wine. He certainly wasn't someone who did things in halves, and I eyed it greedily while tucking the Afghan more closely around myself with my free hand.

"My grandma made me this before I went away. After my mother died." I stroked the blanket unconsciously, surprised at myself for offering up my grief so freely.

"It's lovely," he said as he settled himself into a deep and comfy teal-green armchair across from me; I wondered then if I would ever grow tired of his *lovely* accent.

"That was Gertie's," I said, quickly gesturing for him to sit back down as he popped up in alarm that he had unknowingly crossed a line. "Sit. She would have wanted you to be comfortable here."

He wiped the beer he had slopped on his hand onto his shirt and smiled. "I don't blame her; this chair *is* comfortable." He paused, sipping his drink. "In fact, I think I'll take a good nap here tomorrow after we have a hike around the island's best trails!"

"Oh ho!" I replied, feigning inconvenience. "So now I'm a tour guide too!"

We both took long sips of our drinks and smiled at one another. The distance between us was surprisingly comfortable, and it reminded me of that early teenage love that took thrills from holding hands and slight pecks on the lips. There was a TV in the room, but we had no need of it.

"I have to call and get the Wi-Fi hooked up again. I'm assuming you will need to convene with the university before the month is out?" I asked, my question only slightly probing.

"Well, I have everyone's papers downloaded, so I can work remotely for now. And truthfully, that's something we need to talk about," he said, setting his drink down on his knee and looking towards me, semi-devoid of emotion but clearly battling nerves and needing to get a point across.

"Oh?" I offered, anxiety building.

BOOM!

A log in the fire exploded with more than the usual crack of wet wood, but the woodstove seemed intact still. I suddenly felt shaky.

"Oh, just that any cellular and internet signals we have will be watched, so it may not be a good idea to connect the internet here just yet. Lennie suggested we get you a new phone altogether too," he said, eyes lingering on the moody fire nervously.

"Oh! Oh . . . well, of course. My phone plan sucks anyways. Whatever is safest." I was staring intently into the fire, internally begging my wild magic to calm itself in this moment. To my utmost satisfaction, it listened.

He paused for a moment, a lightbulb going off. "I haven't marked your paper yet, if that's what you're worried about." I didn't know what had set off my magic, but it sure as shit wasn't due to any worries about my paper.

"Oh, I'm not worried about that. I *know* I aced it," I said cheekily.

Having navigated several complicated conversational roadblocks already, I was thankful then that were able to chat through the rest of the evening without any other barriers.

When I finally dosed off on the couch around midnight, wine glass drooping dangerously, I awoke to Dom gently scooping me up and carrying me towards our shared bed, safe and cared for. Loved, in fact. I slumbered peacefully for the majority of the night, something that only happened on the rarest of moons.

There was blood everywhere.

As usual, Desmond had failed to provide any kind of helpful assurance towards the current shape of the Prophecy, so the girl's death had *almost* been an utter waste. He would deal with the useless *Indovino* in a moment, once his own rage had subsided and the girl's magic had been successfully collected for his own.

He knew that, if he were to waste the energy needed to reach far enough back into the annals of his own memory, there had once been a time when he'd felt remorse for the dying young girls, or at least regret for the mess he left behind. Looking to more recent memory, he could also remember a time where he had felt immense pleasure in taking their magic by force and using it for his own means. Those had been better days.

Now, however, he felt an insatiable sense of necessity. And rage.

This girl had been maybe fifteen or sixteen years old, and had reminded him distinctly of *her*, red-headed and obstinate. He could smell the metallic twang of her spilled blood throughout the dim hotel room, the air still charged and crackling with her dismally released magical lifeforce.

"I'm . . . I'm sorry, Cassius. The girl c-couldn't . . . I couldn't s-see anything different," Desmond stuttered as he clamoured around the blood-stained carpet, clearly avoiding making eye contact with the strangely bent form of the girl atop the solitary queen bed as he searched for his silver-framed glasses.

"It would seem, Desmond, that your usefulness to me is fast diminishing."

"No, no, I promise. I can divine it. She just wasn't powerful enough. And I—"

Cassius silenced Desmond with a cold stare, then turned to continue the intricate work of cleaning the extraction blades. Carefully folding his crisp white handkerchief into three, he slid the fabric corner between the cool metal prongs to wipe away her dark red blood. Back and forth, and then round and round, he polished the blades until they sang, ready for his next victim at only a moment's notice; the cleaning ritual was often the only thing that kept his rage in check after yet another failed divining attempt.

Taking one final deep breath as the last of her magic reached the darkest recesses within, Cassius looked down at her discarded body. She must have been beautiful once, but the permanent scream etched onto the roundness of her mouth resembled some sort of grotesque theatrical mask. She was plenty powerful, so much so that he could still taste her magic on his lips. But the pitiful Indovino didn't need to know that detail. In fact, it was of utmost importance that no one know the full extent of his current predicament.

He stood up slowly, the intoxicating magic of the young woman pulsing through his veins like the first hit of a *very* powerful drug. It would take days for the stolen magic to settle within him, and until then, he wouldn't be able to travel discreetly.

"I need you to do something for me, Desmond."

"Yes. Yes . . . anything."

The man was practically grovelling at his feet now, and it took all his energy not to crush the dismal creature like a bug on the floor. Alas, *capable* men were hard to come by.

"I need you to go take a little trip. A reconnaissance mission, may have you. Hector failed me in Vancouver several nights ago. I need you to find out what happened and report back. I know he's lying about something."

Desmond's eyes grew wide. "Yes master, but—"

"And when you've finished, discard of his body more discretely than this disaster."

The blood had spurted spectacularly from floor to ceiling when Desmond had finally cut the girls jugular with his silver blade; he was *truly* adept at creating the best palates for reading the future, which was indeed a great quality in a Soothsayer.

Cassius tucked his wicked knife into the inside of his wool suit coat and stormed out of the hotel room without closing the door behind him, drunk on power and hellbent on having a little bit of fun for the next few days.

CHAPTER 15

Monday morning dawned rather domestically and I groaned sleepily at the cacophony of clanging pans and the whistle of a boiling kettle. I buried my head into the pillows, noticing that Dom's was cool to the touch. He was clearly an early riser.

I could hear him banging around in the kitchen while talking enthusiastically on his burner phone to whom I could only assume was Ronan, based on the intermittent expletives peppered between rounds of laughter and a sometimes commanding tone.

To my disappointment, I still didn't feel caught up on sleep after the tumultuous events of the past seventy-two hours. I stretched languorously, and eventually kicked my feet over the side of the bed. The house smelled of coffee, fried meat, and hot butter. I rounded the corner to the kitchen, sleepily rubbing my eyes while taking in the appetizing sight before me.

There was Dom, gleefully flipping fresh eggs over in a sizzling cast-iron pan, all the while balancing his phone on one shoulder, a folded tea-towel over the other. He was wearing some tantalizingly short maroon rugby shorts that I hadn't yet seen and a loose, grey cotton t-shirt. I delighted in the sight of his powerful legs and sturdy bare feet shuffling through the kitchen as he prepared breakfast. A merry fire was crackling away in the woodstove, and the open kitchen and dining area were both warm and inviting.

"Hello, love! Top o' the morning to ye!" he said, a massive grin on his face as he laughed at his own apparent levity.

"Do people actually say that?" I asked, gratefully accepting the steaming cup of coffee handed my way, eyes still adjusting to the daylight.

"Not really," he laughed. Ronan clearly said something rude from the other end of the line, and Dom let out a hearty laugh.

I closed my eyes and sniffed the piping hot drink held between my hands, steam spreading around my face in welcome tendrils. Was there anything more soothing than a fresh cup of coffee in the morning? Perhaps a big pot of tea in the late afternoon, but no one said it had to be a competition. Both, not either, as my grandma would say.

"You've been busy," I said, eyeing the full breakfast orchestration in front of me.

He had finished his phone call with a quick, *"Slán,"* and returned his focus to preparing our meal.

"Hope you're hungry. Breakfast is my absolute favourite," he said with a smile, accent lingering deliciously on the word "absolute." I *was* in fact hungry and looked forward to his interpretation of a solid Irish breakfast to start the week out with a bang. He piled my plate high with bacon, sausage, two pieces of toast, fried tomatoes and mushrooms, and a heaping pile of seasoned hash browns.

"You're lucky I'm not a vegetarian."

"I don't think that would work out well for my cooking style," he said spearing a pork sausage with his fork before sitting down at the table. When it came to food, he seemed happiest when it was woven seamlessly into his day, leaving him unburdened of the all-too-annoying pangs of hunger.

"That was Ronan on the phone," he said, swallowing a large mouthful of eggs and tomato. "He's taking care of your phone situation this morning."

I nodded enthusiastically, my own mouth full of bacon and potatoes.

"But . . . he wasn't planning to come over until the end of the week, once he's off nightshifts, if you're okay to wait for that long?" His sandy eyebrows raised in question.

"Oh yeah, I don't really have anyone to call or contact right now anyways," I said, and then thought of Ginny. "Actually, there is one thing I need to do."

"Already done, I think! I didn't realize it, but Ronan actually left a note for Ginny explaining that you had to leave early due to something with the house, that you had busted your phone when getting off the bus, and that this was the best you could manage for now. He left an enchantment on it that would leave her feeling peaceful and trusting. So that should be all buttoned up for now!"

"Oh. Okay . . ."

This meddlesome use of magic made me uneasy. Yet, I also couldn't think of another way to tell her what had happened; she had no idea I was a Witch, let alone the fact that I was *technically* about a millennium old. Shit, I had only just found *that* part out for myself.

"I might like to send her an email though, but I suppose that can wait until Friday."

He smiled. "I'm sorry, Julia. You must feel like you're being cut off from everyone you know. But it's only for a short while until we can be sure you're safe."

I shrugged. While I had few connections of consequence these days, with my lived experience as a Witch leading to a rather wobbly sense of attachment to the world, I still *deeply* craved a secure sense of community. More to the point, I was also pretty peeved about having all of my points of contact effectively taken away from me.

Pulling me from my reveries, Dom spoke. "Ronan said he might like to spend the weekend with us. That way we can hatch a plan before he heads back to his gran in Ireland before Christmas. She's getting on these days."

"I'm surprised he gets the holidays off," I said, pushing back from the table to grab a glass of water.

Dom gestured that he would like one too, mouth full of toast. I smiled at his sunny demeanour now permeating through the house, beaming lightly into every neglected dark corner. It had been a long time since the old cottage had felt so alive, and I knew in my bones that Gertie was smiling at the homey scene with pleasure.

"Well, he's a bit of a special favourite around the hospital. Came on a favour from the Dean of Medicine to teach some specific element of emergency medicine while contributing some of his research too. Honestly, it's all completely beyond me, but I know he was able to angle for what he needed when he was negotiating his contract. He's got another four years to go, but he's pretty sure they don't want to lose him early because of any inconveniences," Dom explained dismissively, as if this was just the way Ronan's world worked.

"You keep some pretty prestigious company," I said, returning to the table with two full mason jars of water, which he eyed curiously. "Gertie was a bit of a recycling nut. She used to have a decent set of glasses, years ago, but over time, she just replaced most of the broken ones with canning jars."

Since returning to the mountainside cottage, I had found myself saddled with a new appreciation of the intricacies, and eccentricities, of what was now *my* home.

"I think I like it," he said, drinking gratefully. He polished the water off in several massive gulps. *Never anything in halves,* I mused once more.

It was pleasant being around him in such a relaxed state. There was no doubt that his massive frame was more suited to the rugby pitch or battlefield. But he managed to fill out the space in the room with immense grace and moved with the honed precision of a warrior, even when being *decidedly* domestic.

"I'll get the dishes, Julia. Why don't you go hop through the shower and then you can show me around," he said, looking slightly embarrassed at his command. "That is, of course, if you didn't have other plans?"

Aware that we were still dancing cautiously around propriety, I helped him collect our empty plates and cups, and said with an easy smile, "I don't think I'll ever turn down someone else cooking or doing the dishes. Are you buttering me up or something?"

I couldn't quite put my finger on it, but things still felt slightly awkward between us, even if our breakfast together had been positively delightful. Ever since the incident yesterday morning, I had been afraid that my magical reawakening was damaging the fabric of our complex relationship. After all, he wasn't a Bearer or a Wielder; he was an ordinary man trapped in an extraordinary cycle of prophecy, death, and rebirth. The laws of nature had to disagree with his involvement to some degree.

Well, he wasn't *exactly* ordinary though, I had to admit.

As we reached the sink, he instantly started running the hot water and plugging the drain, humming quietly to himself in a beautiful baritone. A girl could get used to this kind of treatment.

I listened fondly to his melodic musings while I turned on my heels towards the bathroom. Then all at once, I found myself being whirled back around by my shoulders to face him once again. He gathered my hands into his still soapy palms, looking down at me. I noticed a scant few tears had nestled into his usually smiling eyes.

We both took a deep breath.

"Look. I think I need time to get used to it all again. I had hoped . . ." he said, his voice trailing off as he looked to the ceiling and blinked away any tears that might be attempting to fall. "I had hoped it would go back to the way it was, all those times before. But the truth is . . . each time you're farther away. And I'm more damaged. And, well . . . I am not entirely sure how I find my way back to you."

I felt such deep sorrow for the man standing before me; he had endured what no one person should have to in search of a destiny that seemed more remote with each passing cycle.

"I know. And I can't imagine the toll this has had on you," I said, allowing him to rest his forehead on mine. "I wish there was a way I could track down all of my memories, so we could share this burden together again, fully."

He stood oddly silent, which unsettled me to my core.

Was there, in fact, a way we could access my lost memories? Since unearthing the tattoo magic, I had honestly felt like I had some kind of selective magical amnesia.

"There is a way . . . or there was . . . something. But I haven't been able to locate it," he said.

"What would it be, or look like?" I said, fully believing there was no way I could have come across such an item in my travels. My life, while magical in its essence, had been mostly devoid of any *exceptional* magical circumstances.

"It's always been like a tapestry, or kind of an unusual quilt. But it's not here. It's pretty hard to miss," he said, clearly disappointed. "But it's enchanted to make you forget about it easily, so that complicates things . . ." His voice trailed off again.

"Excuse me?" I said, disbelief taking hold as I stepped back from him and collided solidly with the fridge behind me. "Hold on. How do *you* know it isn't here?"

"I'm sorry, Julia! I didn't poke around very much, really. I just did a walk-through of the house to see if it was here, laying on a bed or across an arm-chair or something. I wasn't snooping!"

"Well, it would have been nice if you'd mentioned this to me earlier," I said, anger and adrenaline rising simultaneously.

I was beginning to feel like we needed to have a *wee* conversation about the difference between privacy, healthy boundaries, and keeping potentially *dangerous secrets*.

"Do you . . . have you seen something like that?" he said, quickly shifting gears into logistical mode.

I turned and wordlessly shuffled up the winding stairs and towards the second floor, with him following behind me. At the top of the rise, we reached a narrow landing, bordered with an unassuming hall closet.

"It's not really a hall closet, more of a thoroughfare towards the small door into the attic crawl space," I said, explaining the peculiar home design out of sheer habit as I pulled the doors open. It was one of those distinctive additions my grandma Gertie had adapted from her childhood home in England and was usually considered one of the more charming and mysterious aspects of the cottage for new visitors.

He clearly wasn't listening.

"Is this it?" I said, practically yelling as I launched myself onto the floor to drag out the box. Dom stood behind me, mouth agape and an unexpected redness creeping up his neck and onto his cheeks.

Yes. This was *definitely* it.

"I found it this summer when I was looking for a leak in the attic. Gertie had been adamant on her deathbed that I repair the roof before the end of summer. I am beginning to think she had other motives . . . or maybe destiny did," I said, a few more dots hastily connecting.

"That's it, alright," he said, having regained his composure and crouching down beside me. I had pulled the lid off the box and was slowly unfolding the quilt, its weight far heavier than I remembered.

"It would have been enchanted so that only *you* could find it. Even if your granny knew about it or where it was, she would have forgotten about it right away. . . That's how it usually works anyways. Otherwise, I can't seem to recall anything about it either. I think its cursed, or enchanted, or something. All I ever remember is that it's an important tool linked to you, and that we need to find it," Dom said.

"Oof!" I said, rocking back from sitting on my knees and onto my butt, back resting against the short attic door. "And you have no idea what it does?"

"I don't," he said, eyes resting on me, waiting rather irritatingly in the wings for my reaction. "I guess I was hoping *you* did?"

I looked up, all of a sudden *very* aggravated by his stare. "What? How am I supposed to know what to do with this? Argh!"

I slammed my head down to my knees in exasperation. I thought back to my failed attempts to untangle whatever enchantments were on the quilt this summer, and I felt ashamed once more at my lack of ability.

"Julia, you don't have to know or do anything right now. But the fact that it's been located is huge. Just wait until Ronan finds out!" he replied, excitement rising as he rose to his feet.

"Seriously?"

He had to be kidding me. Of all of the moments to bring up Ronan and their mysterious cause, about which I was still woefully uninformed. I had been trying so hard to be patient with him around his part of the story, to honour his boundaries, but I was honestly starting to feel like specific aspects of *my own life* were being kept from me on purpose. Anger was quickly taking over my rational brain; evidently, he had touched on an old, perhaps ancient, wound.

I felt completely betrayed, and I didn't even fully understand why.

"You've sure been taking your *sweet-ass time* in telling me about all of this. And honestly, so far I feel like I've been deliberately left in the dark!"

"It's not like that, I promise, it's just that—"

"No, thanks." My voice was now low and menacing, like a feral cat trapped in a corner letting out a low warning growl before striking, "Either you tell me the truth, your truth, our truth, the whole *fucking* truth, or leave me alone to carry on with my life!"

I didn't mean that. Not entirely. But all the emotional exhaustion of the past several days had accumulated, and I was fast approaching a breaking point.

"Julia . . ."

He looked hurt, but I was fully activated now, heart pounding and mouth gone dry. I shoved the faded forget-me-not box and enchanted quilt into Dom's arms.

"Here. You take it! Maybe you and Ronan can figure out what it does. Obviously, I can't!"

"Oh, come on! Be reasonable," he said, his expression grappling somewhere between pleading, pain, and what look to be a rapidly rising anger of his own, his lips now thinning menacingly.

"Reasonable?" I said, triggered and feeling venomous.

I straightened to my full height and, taking several heaving breaths, realized my inner magic was suddenly running wild and close to explosive levels. While I hadn't lost control like that since I was a teenager, I also didn't fancy the idea of Dom witnessing me amidst an unexpected magical meltdown.

Charging past him, I stormed down the stairs towards the front door, the screen slamming with its usual loud snap behind me. It was absolutely pouring rain, with the deluge calling out to me to immerse myself in its grounding presence immediately.

Slipping on the oversized rubber boots that lay slumped beside the small stack of wood by the door, I trudged out into the rain, splashing and squelching as I stomped down the driveway. I felt like a toddler in full tantrum. But what was a tantrum if not an overflow of untamed and misunderstood emotion—you have to feel for the little guys.

One of the negative effects of living with untamed Bearing magic was that, while it could be temporarily snuffed out by grief or adverse circumstance, it also held the potential to be stoked into an uncontrollable blaze. I couldn't remember when my inner fire first began to burn out of control, but my best guess was probably sometime around early puberty. I had always been a strong-willed child, but I remember feeling the anger overwhelm me insurmountably as I grew into a teenager. Hot, molten, and dangerously magical.

My mother would recount stories over the phone to Gertie of when my anger would get the best of me, which included anything from causing a cereal bowl before me to crack in two, to causing an entire bank of windows to shatter at the orthodontist's office. In my defence, the hygienist that day was being exceptionally rough.

"Honestly, Julia," she would chide me during the retelling, "sometimes you are just so completely *unreasonable!*"

In reality, I had been increasingly frustrated during those years with her revolving door of boyfriends and her seeming inability to stand up for herself, entering into one co-dependent cycle after another, and *always* leaving me to fend for myself.

Sure, there was always Gertie, but what angsty teenager wanted to spend her free time alone on a small island with her aging granny? And I was *often* filled with rage in those days, soon turning to abusing myself through binge drinking mickeys of vanilla vodka on the weekends with people who claimed to be my friends and participating in increasingly risky behaviour on the regular. I'd needed to dull the pain, all the while trying to scream my existence to the universe.

Thankfully, and as anticipated, the falling rain had almost immediately doused my fire. Armed now with only a gnawing feeling of déjà vu, I wondered painfully if this had been the case in many or all of my rebirths. Breathing in deep and looking inward, I had the distinct sense that this was indeed a cycle that had been going on for many centuries. Dom's presence in my life had already brought up so many truths from deep within me, along with a mounting desire to find that place of comfortability at long last. On the other hand, I was also contending greatly with my fear and frustrations.

I was still so furious about the secrets that were beginning to emerge in spades, along with the knowledge that there was still likely much I didn't, or wouldn't ever, know about the intricacies of this story. The child within me felt like Dom carried the full knowledge of our truth like a crown, like it was his *alone* to bear. Which was utter bullshit, of course.

What I was *really* outraged with was the micromanaging that had evidently gone on during this life cycle behind my back. Did they think they knew better about how I should live my life than *I* did?

After several long moments, I heard the screen door snap once more, but no footsteps approached on the gravel drive. He was evidently waiting under the protection of the front stoop, giving me the necessary space to find composure. I found this to be instantly irritating, another unfair advantage in his knowledge around my care needs. Still somewhat steaming, I dropped my arms in further frustration and started to trudge down the drive towards the main road.

"Julia! Wait!" he called out, his voice bearing no trace of anger.

I considered ignoring him but paused in my increasing state of renewed clarity.

I had no interest in punishing him for his actions. He had simply done as he had thought was best, and he owned that right, even if I didn't agree. I knew enough from the memories and feelings locked in the tattoo's spell to know that he had never, and would never, do anything to intentionally harm me. Or us, for that matter.

I slowly turned towards him, fresh tears streaming down my face along with the rain. His shoulders fell when he saw the anguish I carried, and to my surprise, he looked ashamed.

"You don't get to decide our woven path or our shaped destiny alone, *Domhnall,*" I called out, using his true name on purpose with hope that it would cut him, like when your mother uses your entire legal name to get your attention. But in my rapidly fading anger, I regretted it immediately.

"I'm so sorry," he said. "I am going to tell you everything I can before Ronan comes. I promise. But it's a bit of a long story."

"I'm all ears," I replied as we headed inside, seeking shelter together from the rain.

Stepping into the entryway just off the kitchen, I decided to pull my sopping clothes off right then and there; the only dry part of my outfit being my socks. Dom steadied me by the elbow as I pulled my soggy pajama pants off and balled them up unceremoniously with my t-shirt.

"Here, let me take those," he offered, politely keeping his eyes on my face.

I ignored him and carried the saturated package directly to the washing machine, plunking it in with a loud slop.

"I'll need to do a load of laundry soon anyways," I said plainly, closing the washer with a bang. I would need to remember to open it later so the clothes wouldn't get mildew on them before I started the wash, but for now, I was still trying to make my mood clear, albeit rather childishly.

I felt exhausted, and it wasn't even noon, and I was now also shivering uncontrollably.

"You're absolutely frozen," he said.

"You don't say," I said, residual anger still taking its time to ebb away. It always took time once ignited.

"I'm going to hop in the shower, and then *you're* going to talk."

I wasn't willing to wait for the "right moment" any longer. I wanted to know who he was working with, how long he had been shaping our destiny without my involvement, and what was in that godforsaken duffel bag, and not in any particular order. Not a small request, but it was time.

He put his hands up in surrender. "I'm yours. I'll put on a kettle."

"Good," I said shortly, standing in the doorway to the bathroom, eyeing him scrupulously.

He looked sheepish, but the mood had already lightened significantly, and I was grateful to see that we were remembering how to come back to centre after a conflict, albeit clumsily. I noticed a tiny cheeky smile briefly cross his lips as he soldiered off to the kitchen to prepare our tea; I was totally naked after all.

Towelling off my hair in the bedroom after my quick shower, I heard his lyrical voice coming from the other room. It sounded calm and friendly, so I assumed he was on the phone with Ronan or someone else from his band of merry men. I made a mental note that I also needed to ask for more details about who the others were.

Pulling on a clean pair of leggings and a roomy plum-coloured sweatshirt, I poked my head out of the bedroom door and noticed that he was actually speaking to someone at the front door.

"Oh, there she is! Julia, a Mr. Joe Linder is here from the law office," Dom said happily.

People didn't miss a beat over here, did they?

"Hi, Joe!" I said, quickly pulling my socks on and shuffling over to greet him at the door.

"I was just passing by the area and saw that the lights were on. I wanted to chat with you about the timeline for the sale this spring and wrapping up the remaining items in probate before then. I will be away for most of January, so I am glad to have caught you!"

I had already told him I would be in touch before Christmas, so this felt a little bit more like a welfare check than a targeted pop in. He did live up on this end of the island though and *was* a genuinely helpful person, so I gave him the benefit of the doubt.

"Oh sorry, I was going to give you a call later this week," I offered.

"Not to worry. I'm a bit premature! People have already been asking about this place so I don't think you will have much of a lag once you decide to list it," he said with an enthusiastic smile. The last time we had spoken, I made it perfectly clear that I had no hard feelings towards the folks of Salt Spring Island, but that I intended to leave this place behind for a time. If I was honest with myself now though, I wasn't entirely sure I wanted to sell anymore.

"You know what, Joe, I am not one hundred percent on when I would want to list it. I had a few plans change on me, so I may hold off for a while. But we can certainly meet to clear up Gertie's remaining items before you go away," I said, trying to keep the mood light, but not offering much more in terms of my own reasons or plans.

Joe tipped his brown oilskin hat to me, and then turned his eyes towards Dom. "Let me know if you still want to grab that drink. I would love to pick your brain about your collection!"

"Absolutely! I'll be in touch. Julia has your number?"

How long had they been chatting? Or did Dom just have the gift of the gab with all middle-aged professionals?

"Of course. Take care, Julia, Dom," Joe said as he crossed back over the front porch and into the din of the rain towards his simple gold Nissan sedan.

The door clicked shut, and I shook my head with a laugh. I wondered how many more neighbours would take it upon themselves to check in on me and my mystery guest. At least Joe was a kind soul and seemed to like Dom, so he would be able to vouch for positives at the morning coffee row in the main village.

"He's a pleasant fella, that's for sure!" Dom said, his civility feeling like a weak and dissatisfying breeze after a scorching hot day.

I waved my hand instinctively through the air, like swatting away wandering smoke from a campfire. "He's a kind man, definitely."

I wasn't interested at all in small talk about the varied personalities in my current neighbourhood, and quite frankly, for our safety, it was probably best if our time here passed relatively unnoticed.

We settled into our now usual positions, with me on the weathered love-seat, and Dom in my grandmother's chair. He had laid out our tea service on a dusty and cracked wooden tray from on top of the kitchen cupboards. I breathed in deep and could smell the pleasant toasted-rice scent coming from a steaming pot of genmaicha green tea.

"Excellent choice," I said with a gesture to the tea spread. He had also placed a few packets of shortbread he must have grabbed from the grocery store. I reminded myself to take a better look in the pantry and see what was actually in there.

"Mmm! One of my favourites too," he said, leaning forward to pour each of us a large mug of hot golden liquid. He was definitely on his best behaviour now, and silence between us blossomed once more as he paused to look into his cup thoughtfully.

"I suppose I should start with what's in the duffel bag."

I remained quiet as he popped up to grab the bag from the door, slopping a splash of tea on the floor, followed by a "Fuck!" under his breath.

"Take it easy over there, Spilly Willy," I said, laughing from my belly in spite of myself.

After wiping up the warm drops with his sock on his pass back towards the living room, he plunked the duffel-bag onto the foot stool between us and opened it with the familiar screeching *ziiiip* that was trademark to sturdy bags such as this.

First, he pulled out a palm-sized black and bronze compass, which he set carefully on the table.

"This is Ronan's, but he's lent it to me for the time being. He uses it to detect Wraith magic. It's never worked quite right for me though."

I raised my eyebrows in interest. So, they were hunting Wraiths in Vancouver, were they?

"I don't have any of my usual weapons here, kind of hard to bring across the border. Plus, kind of hard to be discreet with a bloody sword in your hands."

He laughed, and I grimaced.

Sorting around in the bag more intentionally now, I noticed he had a look of concern growing on his brow. I learned forward to inquire closer, and he held up his other hand to stop me.

"Some of this stuff is very, very old. I don't know what stories they will tell you if you fall into a vision or divination," he said, his voice offering respect, not judgement. "Best we wait until I'm finished showing you everything."

I sat back and nodded in agreement as I took a small sip of my piping hot tea. This was already a bloody minefield.

First, he pulled out three smooth, palm-sized rocks. Each one was bored through with several holes in various sizes, which I recognized as being the result of water erosion.

"Hag stones!" I exclaimed, and he nodded silently before sliding them well out of my reach.

Next, he removed several small, weathered leather journals, followed by an accordion folder full of what looked like newspaper clippings and other stacks of bulldog-clipped documents. He also had an antiquated-looking black laptop that I was pretty sure was at least fifteen years old; it was as thick as a dictionary with several bulky USB keys sticking out of the side. There were several maps and guidebooks of different areas of the world, and I could make out a few specifically designed for Northern Europe, with black markings all over them. The last one he pulled from the bag was a yellow map book of Western Canada that looked like it came from a dusty truck-stop gas station along the Trans-Canada Highway.

"I picked up that Western Canadian one just outside of Saskatoon, Saskatchewan," he said, labouring over the central Prairie province's pronunciation.

I chuckled. "Yeah, looks like it. Why were you there?"

"Well, that takes me to right before we found you. I suppose that's probably the best place to begin."

CHAPTER 16

D om had been waiting in agony for several years already before tracing any known signs of Julia in this particular place and time. The past few months had been especially wracked with anxiety, as Cassius and his "front-men" had been establishing powerful strongholds throughout the West at an astounding rate. Regular intelligence was received concerning new business acquisitions, hidden subsidiaries, offshore accounts, and massive international conglomerates that seemed to be popping up like dandelions, and all connected to *his* name in one way or another.

Meanwhile, his Wraiths were wreaking equal havoc behind the scenes throughout the underground circles, essentially raping and pillaging their way through the hidden communities, stealing and commodifying *any* magic they could get their filthy hands on.

Cassius and his relentless march to gain power had dogged them for ages. But somehow, with all the advancements of technology in the last several decades, it felt even more threatening. There were so many secrets hidden in the modern capitalist regime, but thankfully, there were equally as many opportunities to have them all found out.

Dom had only been around for slightly more than a decade so far, but he already knew that this time around, things were *drastically* different.

He always returned earth-side in his twenty-three-year-old body, and in the same place each time. He likened it to the birth of an infant: cold, confusing, and altogether overwhelming. Only he didn't have a mother or a family to take him in, not in the conventional sense. It usually only took him a handful of years to acclimate himself in the current time period, but this re-incarnation had been especially jarring.

Thankfully, he still maintained several bank accounts and dedicated trusts in his name that would usually carry forward fairly simply, all things considered. He had also always owned at least one property in Ireland that served as a safe harbour. Because of this, he would consistently be reborn with assets and means. Typically, the Druids would take care of the rest, updating his knowledge, passed on through their oral tradition, of relevant happenings or advancements while he was "away."

He had arrived severely lacking in the skills necessary for modern practicalities like computers, smartphones, and countless other revolutionary developments that he had missed, but thankfully, this time around he had also been met by an exceptionally savvy group of modern Druids, who had been integral in his orientation to a *very* fast-paced world. While he had been immediately keen on things like on-demand television, on the whole, not much else had been easy.

Early on, he had been connected with a man named Lennie, who was, for all intents and purposes, a complete asshole. But he was also extremely gifted when it came to cyber-technology and hacking, which was apparently integral to their defensive position. Dom had been informed that most battles these days were taking place digitally, and it had been an extremely steep learning curve to climb, not helped in the least by Lennie's impatience with his ancient ineptitude.

"I just don't understand the need to rely on all of this fucking tech!" Dom had said in frustration when Lennie was showing him how to connect his laptop to their greater network, allowing Lennie access to any intelligence Dom would gather in his travels.

"Calm down; you remind me of my grandfather!" Lennie had snarked, which only served to piss Dom off further; it was all so bloody convoluted.

Arguably, the Druids' proclivity to rely on oral tradition had proven to be their greatest defence of all against the growing technological powers harnessed by Cassius, but that didn't mean that they wouldn't need to play the game as well. It had never sat well with Dom that while an excess of technology would make it easier to track someone or to orient oneself, it also made you a *much* easier target yourself. The old ways seemed arguably safer.

This was also why it was positively astounding that they hadn't been able to locate Julia, no matter how many different strategies were implemented. He knew she had always been clever with protection spells, yet this seemed exceptional considering how many electronic "paper trails" any one person could leave in a single day alone. By some miracle, the first sure sign of Julia's most recent location had arrived as he was sitting in a breakfast restaurant attached to a truck stop on the side of a dusty highway, smack in the middle of the Canadian Prairies.

It was midsummer, and the skies were wide, blue, and clear. He was in good spirits all things considered, spending the better part of the last few weeks tracing a magical imprint Julia had left soon after the curse had been activated over a decade ago. He had finally traced it to a remote farm that housed a large-scale honey operation.

Ronan had lent him his enchanted compass, which was more often used for tracking Wraith magic. Hoping this particular function wouldn't be needed on this mission, he had the strange feeling that it might work differently in Dom's palm than his own.

"One of the ways it works is by tying into my own need to find the magic. And since I track and hunt Wraiths, that's precisely what it does for me. But for you, I just have this strange feeling it will find something different." Dom didn't pretend to understand what he was talking about, but he did know there was indeed a deeper magical connection between himself and Julia than they had ever been able to explain, especially since he was no magic user. It was worth a shot.

And indeed, at his home in Ireland, he had placed the compass onto a large table-sized map of Canada, and the compass had started to spin and whirl uncontrollably when he moved it over the centremost Prairie province.

It was his first time visiting the region, and the people were generally friendly and helpful, sometimes almost too helpful if he was honest, but he found it endearing. He felt immense relief to finally be treading across ground that she had also shared during this lifetime. Literally one step at a time, he was moving closer towards *her*.

Indeed, as soon as he traversed the dirt treads that lead towards the farm, he could feel the sparks of her essence jutting out at every angle, his internal tie to the curse pulling inexplicably as soon as he approached the apiary proper. It had always been this way when the curse first activated, which always happened on or around the day of her mother's death. She practically oozed with it for the first several months in her grief, her magic spilling wildly every which way. She never saw it this way when asked, inevitably citing a period of a complete loss and utter lack of magic, but the clues were *always* there for him to find, if he knew where to look.

However, it was the conversation with a man named Jake Enns that really tipped him off that she had spent significant time here. He bristled at the memory.

The conflict, if you could call it that, had occurred after he had spent the better part of the afternoon schmoozing up the old farmer, Cam. Soon enough, they had settled into his back office for a nip of regionally made whisky from a green 'Special Edition' commemorative bottle. Though the drink was mediocre, the man was intelligent and had a great sense of humour, and Dom found himself enjoying this aspect of the mission rather more than he'd expected. The old farmer had such a sense of "rootedness" about him that, if Dom couldn't actually see the man's feet, he would have guessed they were firmly planted almost a foot underground; it would explain his short stature at any rate.

Shortly before his arrival, Dom had notified Lennie of the pinpointed location, but after a quick search, he'd been immensely frustrated with his inability to access anything remotely due to the farm's technologically deficient practices. As usual, Dom was baffled by the lack of patience these days when it came to gathering information, but he was also shamelessly pleased at Lennie's inherent frustration. This type of bare-bones mission fell precisely within Dom's wheelhouse, and he more than gladly accepted the challenge. Not to mention that it felt incredible to finally be *doing* something.

The diversion into Cam's office had presented the perfect opportunity to access any previous payrolls with a quick slip of the hand while plugging in a specialized USB key into their offline accounting computer. He also hoped to have a look into any old file boxes for physical copies of information, if time and circumstance allowed.

All was going to plan when the man called Jake had entered into the equation.

"Oh! Jake. This is Dom O'Brien. He's visiting from Ireland and was curious about our farm. He's a professor specialising in Environmental Sustainability and is curious about our beekeeping practices as compared to those in Ireland." This was of course a lie, not that he didn't find this all mildly interesting, but he was far from certified to be posing as anyone with any authority on the subject. Thankfully, he was an exceptional liar.

"Nice to meet you, Dom," Jake said, but he looked agitated.

Cam's eyes darkened. "What is it now?"

Jake looked between the two men, obviously hesitant to share any secrets.

"That same asshole called back, and he wants more records, dating all the way back to . . ." Jake paused.

Cam raised his eyebrows. "Back to when, Jake?"

Dom felt uneasy to be intruding on a private matter, and he tossed back the last of his drink vibrantly as he quietly slipped the USB key back into his pocket.

Jake looked like he was doing quick math in his head, still somewhat ignoring Dom.

"Twelve years. You know . . . that summer."

A deep look of understanding passed between the two men, and Dom's heart was suddenly pounding, having done the math himself long before this moment. In his excitement, he foolishly threw caution to the wind.

"You know what, I used to know someone who worked out here at an apiary," he said, feigning lighthearted vagueness. "Not entirely sure the location though. Her name was Julia."

Both men locked eyes on him, Cam mildly concerned and Jake suddenly furious.

"Who the hell are you? Are you working for them too?" he asked, eyes sparking like a livewire.

Cam stood slowly, and flexing his natural calm grace, he gently escorted Dom towards the door, filling the air with polite conversation while making it all too clear that their friendly discussion was over.

"She did work here. Broke poor Jake's heart. Her gran was a distant relative of mine, Gertie Stephenson. But that was a long time ago, not important now. I'll need to attend to this private matter. Thank you so much for taking an interest in our farm, Dom. Hope you enjoy the rest of your travels," he said. And with that, the door was effectively shut.

Dom was left standing alone outside. The muffled sound of the two men arguing was barely audible behind the closed door, their voices easily drowned out by the crickets chirping in the ditch.

Climbing into his gutless rental car, he was surprised to feel violent jealousy rising within him once more, but he bit it back just as he had always done. Obviously, she would have taken other lovers this time around; it's not like she hadn't in the past. The more her memory faded with each cycle, the more she waded into the world of romantic love without him. Hell, he had bedded plenty of women through the years in frustration and desperation on his lonely search, but they meant nothing to him. It was always, and only, *her*.

Since he was in a foul mood already, he dialed Lennie for an update as he sped off down the narrow, pot-holed highway, the sunset leaving long orange and purple streaks across the wide palate of Prairie sky before him.

He was frustrated to find out that while he was at the farm, Lennie had discovered Jake had committed minor tax fraud the year following the summer Julia had been there, due to an exceptional bumper crop of honey that he'd failed to file proper dues on. The money was paid in full eventually, and so that should have been the end of it. However, over the last ten years, he had conducted a series of further infractions when it came to remittance, and it would seem that the Canada Revenue Agency was seriously breathing down his neck.

Dom had the sense that Cam was trying to help Jake sort out his troubles, but it wasn't going well for him. He mentioned to Lennie that Julia had been there, and that Cam was a relative of her grandmother.

"I'm not surprised things went that way," Lennie said, far too smugly for Dom's liking after he recounted the rocky interaction.

"Oh yeah? Would have been nice for you to share that information with me *before* I went in there," Dom said coolly into the speaker phone as he drove down the road, staring across the seemingly endless fields.

"I can't control the speed of information, Dom. When I get it, I give it to you. That's it. I'm a busy man. Load that USB into the computer, and we can talk later." And with that, Lennie hung up.

Arse.

While uncomfortably completed, the visit had ultimately been a success. He wasn't able to access any hard copies of anything due to Jake's rude interruption, but the special USB had done the trick, albeit not in the way they had expected.

Julia's grandmother, Gertie. *She* was their clue. Dom had also taken special notice to the way Cam had referenced her, in the past tense. It would seem that her grandmother had passed away. That meant obituaries, and potentially more recent land titles and probate documents. It still didn't explain the constant nagging worry around why Julia had proven so exceptionally difficult to track down this time, but a lead was a lead, and he wasn't complaining.

Sitting in his lonely roadside hotel room that evening, Dom plugged the USB into his laptop, and Lennie took over from there in his London apartment. After some digging, Lennie was able to open an old Microsoft address book embedded on the computer's hard drive, and there she was: Gertie Stephenson. Apparently, she'd lived somewhere called Salt Spring Island on the West Coast of Canada, and that was enough for Lennie to track down any and all of the information they needed. But he needed some time.

Dom had expressed concern that the people currently pressing Jake on the matter weren't from the Canadian government at all but were rather more of Cassius's men looking for info on Julia. However, Ronan and Lennie had both assured him in separate emails that government bodies could be easily as pressing as dark-magic organizations when they wanted their money paid back in full; this was hardly suspicious behaviour.

He barely slept that night.

The following morning, while enduring the aggravating wait for further intelligence from Lennie regarding Julia's current whereabouts, he decided sustenance was the answer. Looking out the window to the truck stop beyond the small restaurant, Dom sat patiently at his assigned booth, sipping on a strong, hot coffee. As soon as he had the information he needed, he would be gone like a shot, driving through the night if that's what it took.

He had ordered himself something called a "breakfast skillet," which arrived in a cast-iron dish containing a heaping pile of deep-fried hash browns under a bed of scrambled eggs, peppers, onions, diced pork sausage, thin hollandaise sauce, and a dusting of tasteless dried parsley. It smelled extremely savoury, and likely tasted as overtly gratuitous as it looked, but his stomach was growling after having spent the past forty-eight hours on planes followed by the long drive to the farm with only pale gas station sandwiches as nourishment.

He looked down in shock at the abundant meal that had landed before him. Agreeing with the aged server to add the extra bacon was a bit over the top, even he had to admit, but he dug in gratefully.

After several minutes, she returned. "How's everything tasting here? Did you need a warm up?"

She was a petite woman, late middle age, who had clearly spent far too much time in a tanning bed, her skin leathery and worn, strikingly similar to the colour of the fried potatoes before him.

"Hmm," he said, mouth still full of the hot and heavy breakfast, and slid his bone-coloured coffee mug gratefully towards her. "Please."

She smiled kindly, eying his map book. "You heading west?"

They had already engaged in conversation about his accent and country of origin. No doubt she would now feel called to offer local hospitality.

He nodded. "Actually I am. The Coast."

"Nice time of year for it, no snow in the passes. It's not a trip you'll be wanting to make in the wintertime!" she said lamentably.

She went on to tell him a detailed story about her vehicle hitting the ditch in the snow on the Coquihalla highway and a friendly semi-truck driver finally towing her out when she thought she might freeze to death. What was unusual was that she was smiling almost as if the harrowing experience had been some sort of grand adventure. Canadians were a little bit funny about the weather.

A new set of customers arrived and interrupted her, and soon she bustled off on her way. He continued to pour over a map of Western Canada in the cramped vinyl booth, sopping up the last of the sauce with a corner of brown toast, when his phone pinged. It was an email.

> *D,*
>
> *So, it's definitely her, but she's on the move again, a bit of a nomad.*
>
> *I've attached the probate documents from public record for her grandmother's will, which confirms the house address.*

*I hacked into her lawyer's email account and found cor-
respondence between the two, plus a forwarded email from her
realtor (again, see attached). It mentions a final semester of
courses at the University of British Columbia, so that might be
useful information, especially since Ronan is already there. I've
cc'd him.*

*I'll look into her actual living situation in Vancouver when
I have more spare time, but for now she should be *roughly*
where she's supposed to be.*

Good luck with that.

L

Dom groaned at the grating tone of the email; Lennie always felt the need to make it clear that this kind of research was beneath his station, whatever station that actually was. He wasn't sure Lennie really understood the importance of finding Julia in the war against Cassius, or that any of them truly did. This burden of his rebirth had become an increasingly solitary one over time.

He rolled his shoulders back several times before slowly running his hands down his thighs in thought, tapping his fingers lightly on his knees under the table for good measure. Yet another complication, but that was nothing new; there had always been variables around Julia's aspect of their shared destiny.

In the beginning, six months was all they ever really had together at a time. He often lamented for the passion of those days, when they would reunite like gunpowder tossed onto a fire, explosive and incredibly powerful in each other's arms, but perhaps not as clear headed as they should have been.

Over time, her birthplace began to shift, and soon they struggled to find one another with the same level of immediacy. Previously, she had always been the one to find him, but without her help, he'd enlisted the Druids to acclimate him instead. This was also when his mission to find her each time was born. Unexpectedly, this lag in reunion would actually serve to extend their individual existences until they reunited. It was a lonely road at first, but both of them had always been equally desperate to find one another as quickly as humanly possible.

She had been very much in control of her powers then, building her strength with each passing cycle, fervently hoping that perhaps *this time* might be the chance where they could out-muster and out-magic Cassius.

She had access to mentors and what had seemed like easy access to her powers when she needed them. And she remembered him.

As her memories began to fade, Julia, being both clever and brave, had woven their story into the flesh of his back in the form of an intricate tattoo, where it would stay until they needed it, reappearing after each regeneration cycle. Admittedly, it had been one of her riskier ideas. The required magic was rather sinister in nature, but her confidence had been all the assurance he had needed to endure the procedure.

He wasn't sure if he was imagining it or not, but the tattoo had started itching on his back since visiting the farm yesterday, and he reached back and scratched frantically before signalling to the waitress that he would welcome a refill of his coffee.

The server, whose red nametag read *Brenda*, smiled warmly at him once more. "Is there anything else I can get you? Or just the bill?"

With a quick shake of his head, he returned to scouring his maps. He didn't mean to be rude but had decided he would head west today regardless of further intel, and wanted to be sure he knew where he was driving for the next twelve hours at least. He didn't want to have to pull over and waste time with directions or fighting with the damned GPS on his phone. A rather grating complication in the whole regeneration matter was that, with each passing lifetime, she had become increasingly more difficult to track down. Ronan's compass, while helpful initially, seemed completely free of function now, pointing due north almost mockingly.

He *used to* be able to count on her being born somewhere in Ireland, and could usually find her quickly. After one rebirth where he'd failed to locate her altogether before it was too late, she had shown up next in eastern Canada and had continued to be born throughout the massive nation ever since.

Their more recent regenerations had cost him about a decade each time, give or take several years, to learn all he needed to know about the current timeframe and to also locate her. In fact, this was the longest he had lived yet, with his upcoming thirty-fifth birthday bringing a new record, if he made it there. But that was no consolation. Regardless of how long he spent acclimating or searching, they only ever had the *maximum* possibility of three-hundred and sixty-four days together, *if* they were lucky enough to find each other and *truly* reunite immediately following a summer solstice. In that case, there would be enough time for the wheel of fortune to take one full turn through the seasons before Cassius would strike at the summer solstice that followed, demanding that they start the cycle all over again. If they reunited mid-year, then their fate would still be decided at the next summer solstice to arrive, giving them much less time together, loving and fighting for their survival.

After finishing his fourth cup of coffee, he was now positively vibrating and couldn't bear the idea of sitting still any longer. It was high time he headed west, but judging by the maps, it would appear there was no straight line through.

He found a city called Drumheller to be rather interesting, igniting his own vivid memories of learning about dinosaur fossils for the first time in the 1800s as an adult man. He had always wondered what it would have been like to grow up as a child with the knowledge of these ancient beasts; he was quite certain he would have been a *big* fan. His journey across the Rocky Mountains had been relatively uneventful, apart from the fact that he was continuously irritated with the rental car he had been saddled with, kicking himself for being so frugal and not going with a beefier vehicle. In retaliation, he'd pushed the weak beast to its absolute limit with each mountain pass. It beat riding a horse at any rate; at least he had a cupholder and climate control.

Due to his ancient origins, he had never really given in to the pressures of the modern-day consumer culture, which had developed over the past century. If he needed it, he bought it. And if he wanted it? Well, that depended on how badly. It wasn't like he had grown up without privilege and an appreciation for nice things, but when you live enough lifetimes, the material things seem to matter less and less.

He did *love* cars, however. And this one was absolute trash.

His intention was also to be as inconspicuous as possible in his travels. Cassius's spies were everywhere, and it was simply easier to travel inconspicuously by road at this time rather than hop on a plane—air travel meant more chances for identification and tracking. Alas, a common rental car was also far less likely to draw attention to him than something flashier.

Pulling off into a rest stop to use the bathroom and sleep for a few hours before the next leg, he realized that a small part of him regretted not being able to take in more of the scenery. Only a small part though, as every other inch of his body was practically screaming to be as close to her as possible, as soon as possible. Maybe someday she would take him here, but he could barely think farther ahead than the next several hours at this point. He was honed in and wholeheartedly focused on the task ahead.

Leaning back in the reclined passenger seat, he stretched out to slumber. He could sleep almost anywhere, and this shitty tin can of a car was no exception. Just as he was dozing off, however, his phone rang. *Ronan.*

Before he could even muster a groggy hello, Ronan spoke. "Dom! You're in luck."

"I am?"

"There's a faculty position open at UBC, and get this, it's in the Department of Linguistics! You'll *easily* pull that one off."

His thoughts were racing as his planning brain began to simultaneously organize his next moves at lightning speed, "Oh. Oh . . . yes. That will work just fine."

"That's not even the best part. I just got off the phone with Lennie," Ronan paused.

The bastard was leaving him hanging on purpose now.

"Get on with it, Ronan!" he growled.

"Guess who is completing her final semester of a Linguistics degree? You guessed it. Julia Harrison."

Harrison.

Her last name always changed, but somehow her first was always some iteration of Julia, or at least it had been over the past several hundred years. It was yet another quirk of the magic that they had come to accept. But he still found his heart catch in his throat at the newest version; a new name, another life lived.

"Domhnall? Did you hear me?"

He did but couldn't gather any useful words just yet. He fought back tears as he mentally thanked the powers of God and destiny for what must have been the thousandth time. "Looks like things are coming together, as they always do," he said at last, clearing his throat.

Ronan snorted. "You could say so . . . Oh, come on! Domhnall! It's incredible. And I'm already here, which is obviously fate. Lennie should be emailing you as we speak with next steps. I have to go."

"Thanks, Ronan."

He hung up and stared out the window at the towering parking-lot lights above him, their rounded plastic covers blurring in his vision as heavy tears now flowed freely down his cheeks and into his beard.

It made absolute sense to him; destiny always had a hand in their path.

"Don't you dare let me forget about you, Domhnall!" she had told him sternly during one of their more recent existences together, chin out and leaving absolutely no room for discussion on such important matters of the heart. Her words still haunted his dreams with longing but ultimately fueled the fire of his mission. Good God, he missed her.

He sat in contemplation for a long time before remembering he was expecting an email from Lennie. He sat up again momentarily and squinted at his phone.

> *D,*
> *You must literally shit horseshoes.*
> *Ronan said he wanted to tell you the news; hope you answered your phone before reading this.*
> *She's registered at UBC in September, Linguistics.*
> *You'll have to fill the empty faculty position quickly, but that shouldn't be hard to pull off. We can push where it's needed, but Ronan thinks you should be a shoe in. It's covering a short-term medical leave until the end of the year. I'm assuming that will give you enough time?*
> *I've accessed her registration info. She's not signed up for any of the courses you'd be teaching – you'll have to think of a way to mitigate that.*
> *I've attached some documents that may be of interest.*
> *L*

He leaned back once more and breathed in a deep sigh of sweet relief.

CHAPTER 17

The dusky veil of midwinter had fallen upon us almost unexpectedly, and soon we were switching on lamps. Dom's stomach growled audibly for dinner, but he pressed on.

I had listened as intently as possible as he recounted his tale, taking great pains not to pepper him with questions as he worked though the details; I feared that if I interrupted his flow, he would lose his confidence in the telling. It took a surprising amount of personal restraint, but when he finally finished, I was actually speechless.

I exhaled loudly as my hidden hands shook slightly under the crocheted blanket.

"I . . . I don't even know what to say."

I watched his comparatively still body as he stood staring absently out the window. My heart ached for him, and although I could sense cathartic relief flowing through him as he recounted the details of the weeks leading up to our meeting, he was clearly spent.

He smiled, but it didn't reach his eyes. "It's not been easy . . . to be so lonely."

It was hard to believe all he had endured to find me, painfully wondering about my journey as we aged into our adult lives without one another. It hurt to imagine him spending so many sleepless nights alone, imagining that someone else, in that very moment, was with me not only physically but emotionally too. The yearning and the jealousy, the loneliness and the waiting. He had essentially spent each of his waking days trying to be one step ahead of our enemy, while always feeling two steps behind in locating me. And the *trust* he placed in our destiny through all of it . . . well, it was utterly astonishing.

I felt a pang of guilt remembering the look in his eyes when he'd recounted the part of his story where he'd met Jake, and as if reading my mind, he addressed the matter head on.

"Julia, I've long accepted that since your memories started fading, you were going to live your adult life absent of me. I wouldn't want it any other way. You deserved . . . *deserve* happiness. In whatever life you lead."

He had paced the room for much of his retelling, sitting only briefly from time to time before popping up again when he was clearly feeling agitated, usually about Lennie. He was in Gertie's chair now, quiet and still.

"Dom. Come sit beside me," I said, pushing back my blanket and patting the space beside me in invitation. His bravery was astounding, and suddenly I wanted nothing more than to hold him.

He blinked several times and groaned slightly as he slid out of the deep-set armchair. The small couch creaked beneath him as he settled beside me, its worn foundations causing us to lean in close together in the centre.

"For what it's worth," I said, turning towards him and taking his hands in mine, "I don't think I've ever been in love in this lifetime. Not really."

Good grief, it was all so confusing, citing which life I had lived, when and where, but he took my meaning clear enough.

He leaned in and kissed me softly across my brow. "It's all in the past now."

There was a slight question in his tone, the kind that craves reassurance.

"It's all in the past," I said before kissing him tenderly in return.

I guessed this to be the most challenging aspect in the variance between our rebirths: how the curses shaped our individual journeys. He would be reborn at the same place and age, but in an altogether different time; meanwhile, I would have lived a new life leading up to our reunion, starting at birth in each particular timeline. No doubt, each time I would arrive with a totally different perspective, which must have been challenging and even heartbreaking for him.

"Have I ever been so different that you didn't recognize me?"

192

He laughed then, which came as a surprise. "Never. You're always *very much* yourself. Hard to outgrow that feisty personality of yours!"

He tickled me playfully, which ultimately resulted in me sitting across his lap. I felt like I was eighteen years old again, but in the best possible way.

"And any changes," he said, nuzzling into my neck as I leaned into him, "have honestly suited your character nicely. It's hard not to love witnessing you blossom into an even more wonderful version of yourself . . . even if sometimes you can be a bit petulant about it!"

My turn to retaliate. "Oh really? Because you *never* push my buttons or act out yourself, *do* you?"

I dug my fingers into his ribs, which resulted in a sound rather akin to a squealing pig, and he tossed me off his lap and back onto the couch beside him. We giggled like teenagers for a while, relaxing into one another with ease.

"We've always enjoyed our time together . . . that's for sure," he said, breathing heavily during a break in the play.

I snuggled into his outstretched arms as they wrapped around me from behind and began playing fondly with his fingers, stretching out each digit individually and appreciating his capable hands.

"I believe it. We have time to settle in together, right?"

If my new understanding of my subconscious protection spell around Salt Spring Island held true, we would hopefully be allowed several weeks of safety ahead to re-acquaint ourselves to one another.

"I think so. But if it's all the same to you," he said, pulling back from the embrace, "before we do anything else, I need to eat."

A deep belly laugh filled me to the core, and I was delighted to see that certain aspects of his character had remained wholly unchanged, despite the great emotional turmoil he had faced in the telling of his tale.

"Let's grab a bite in town! Pretend we're *normal* for a bit," I said.

"Normal! Good one!" he laughed, and then pulled me into an unexpected bear hug. I was used to people hugging me—it was one of those West Coast *things*—but this was wholly different; it was a lover's embrace. Relieved, grateful, and at peace.

While much of the peace and relief we had shared during our talk had remained, it was shaky in its existence. The prospect of Ronan's arrival the following weekend had put a sour taste in my mouth for the remainder of the week, although I couldn't quite put my finger on exactly why. My best assumption was that I wasn't ready to share Dom's attention with anyone else just yet; I felt suddenly greedy for his affections, having only just "got him back."

The faded memories that had been released by the tattoo's spell, along with the new truths around Dom's endurance on the road to find me, made for some confused attachment issues on my end.

On the day of Ronan's anticipated arrival, my shoulders were tense, and I couldn't seem to keep myself from clenching my jaw. I wondered absently what had ever happened to my long-lost mouth guards; teeth grinding was nothing new for me in times of unexpected or added stress. Much of the morning had been spent relocating random piles of sweaters and discarded books with no real intention, my own mood and temper matching the short- ness of the winter days. It was useless to try to use practical magic when I was this agitated, so I relied instead on the sweat equity from the tasks at hand to get the job done.

To his credit, Dom was doing his fair share in preparing Gertie's cottage for company, although he clearly thought the level of detail I expected was pointless.

"Ronan doesn't care about a clear counter, love. He'll just be glad for a break from the hospital and a hot meal set before him."

"Does he expect me to cook for him?" I asked, anger rising like bile to the back of my throat.

"Don't be foolish, Julia. Of course not," he said, shaking his head.

He had clearly been walking on eggshells all morning, although I could see the hint of frustration cross his face at this most recent comment.

"Ugh. I'm sorry," I said. "I'm just overwhelmed. And exhausted. And I don't feel ready for guests." I threw the broom handle I was holding to the floor.

Dom leaned over and picked up the abused tool. "I understand. It's a lot. But I promise you'll like him. He's the closest thing to family I've had all these years." He kissed me on the cheek, and I unclenched my jaw slightly; he was probably one of the only people I knew who truly understood the yearning for a chosen family.

I spent the afternoon in a redoubled effort to clean the cottage, scrubbing floors, washing walls, and conducting myself with general storminess at each turn. I blasted such loud music through the house that I think Dom went outside to chop wood just to get out of my deluge of emotion and heavy drumbeats.

If I was completely honest with myself, I was jealous of Ronan and Dom's closeness, and the time they had spent together in this life thus far. It *did* feel foolish, as if I had regressed into my childhood self and had been stomping around my bedroom angrily about some minor social injustice at school. But since I had craved connection and familiarity growing up, so deeply, their relationship felt like a salty sting on a very old wound.

Giving up at last on my cleaning tirade, I brushed my hair back into a sweaty ponytail before locating Dom sitting quietly outside on the front step, humming to himself tranquilly in the winter sunlight.

"Okay," I said, rubbing my sweaty palms on the fronts of my thighs.

He smiled but continued to hum wordlessly.

"I'm struggling a bit, between my previous life—Lives?—and what's happened so far in this one. It's . . . a lot."

That latter phrase seemed to be coming up with an obnoxious frequency.

I placed my hand on his woolen shoulder, and he turned his head and rubbed his beard across the top of it before planting a soft kiss on my clammy skin.

"And I am guessing Ronan's visit isn't helping with that feeling."

"No. It isn't. But it's just old wounds and what-not," I said, and plunked down heavily beside him. "Really. I'll figure it out."

His smile was kind and hiding what looked like a hint of relief. "*We* will figure it out."

And before we could discuss it further, Ronan's flashy SUV turned up the drive. Privately, I was grateful for the visual provided by our united front on the cottage step, and I waved enthusiastically alongside Dom as we welcomed our first visitor as a couple into Gertie's cottage.

Much to my chagrin, Ronan proved to be an exceptional house guest. He was tidy, courteous, and immensely helpful when called upon, and scarce when not. He brought fresh wild-caught salmon to prepare for dinner, which he cooked on cedar planks with a side of herbed rice and some local root veggies he'd picked up from the market on the way in. I had the distinct impression he had been placed on strict orders of best behaviour by Dom, but I appreciated the effort nonetheless.

After dinner, we migrated into the living room, Dom and myself squeezed together onto the hide-a-bed couch while Ronan leaned back comfortably in Gertie's chair. Ronan had, naturally, brought along the perfect wine pairings for the meal, and we were well into the fourth bottle between the three of us. I was definitely feeling its effects.

Dom had no reservations around showing his affection for me in front of Ronan, and I found myself straddling somewhere between pleasure and embarrassment. I wasn't used to someone who was so openly comfortable with publicly expressing their love towards me. He was also half-cut, so that had to count for part of it as well. Ronan didn't seem to be phased in the least, so I leaned in and soaked up the protective and adoring spell Dom was casting around me.

The conversation passed casually between the three of us, with Dom carrying the bulk of the narrative; he really was a magnificent storyteller. It was also quickly apparent that they were comfortably familiar with the rhythm of a social evening together, as no sooner had our drinks emptied than Ronan had risen to pour another round.

"Thanks a million, Ronan," Dom said, nodding gratefully. "So, Julia doesn't know a lot about Druids in the modern day, and she's . . . having a bit of hard time accessing her memories of Druids in the past . . . at the moment."

Dom looked to me cautiously, wincing slightly at his potential overshare, but I placed my hand on his arm.

"No, no. It's okay," I said. "Look, it's true. I'm missing a lot of memories. More than ever apparently. Which isn't great for our cause . . . or is it *the* cause?" I trailed off awkwardly as Ronan furrowed his brow. It didn't seem to be based around my flawed magical memory predicament, however.

"Well, I'm not actually allowed to share many of the secrets, but as you and Dom are the ones *the Prophecy* speaks of, I suppose you have a right to know as much as I can tell you."

He'd dragged out "the Prophecy" with marked skepticism, but I nodded encouragingly, far too curious to be offended.

"Much of it is still a mystery to me too, Julia," Dom said. "The bastards like their secrets."

Ronan rolled his eyes. "And that's not my fault, Domhnall. You could always learn more. We told you that you need only ask. Didn't you say something about being an 'honorary Druid' once?"

"You don't know the half of it, *a mhaicín*," Dom bristled as he sat up straight, ready for their usual brotherly sparring.

Coughing loudly, I raised my glass to my lips, "So . . . about the Druids?"

I caught Dom staring hungrily at my mouth then, and I offered a playful smile in his direction. If our seminar had taught me anything, it was that his passion for discourse resided on the same plane as his more carnal desires, as he could toggle so easily between the two, especially, it would seem, when drink was involved.

Ronan obviously sensed the same distracted ferocity brewing in Dom and forged onward with the task at hand, purposely ignoring his boisterous energy.

"Well, you obviously know about the concept of Bearers and Wielders. Druids are Wielders, but so are Wraiths. However, we have very different means of obtaining and using magic. Honestly, the designation of Wielder is a lot more complex than the title depicts."

So, we were starting from the very basics, it would seem.

He wasn't wrong, though. Not only did it include Druids and Wraiths, but also Witches, Sorcerers, and a whole host of other magically inclined beings around the world that I couldn't pretend to even begin to know anything about. The common thread among all magical beings, however, was that it *always* came with a cost.

"Yours is sourced from within. I'm told it's kind of like a magical core? Meanwhile, mine is sourced from all around me. In the rocks and trees and streams, in the people around me and animals I meet."

"Mine can also be sourced outwardly," I corrected, gesturing around the room in demonstration. "Some Witches even prefer the outer magic to their own inner workings. Gertie preferred it much of the time. I mean look around you; it's a practical treasure trove of magically charged artifacts to draw on. I also think it's why she always kept such a robust garden and all of the animals too."

I thought back to Beatrice, a particularly nasty nanny goat who'd bit me as a kid. I was never entirely sure what *her* point was, but for the most part, Gertie's familiars were friendly and helpful to her. And, certainly, a source of calm and dependable power.

"True. And do you feel the cost more significantly when taken from the outside, or when you source it from inside?"

That was a *great* question, and I was suddenly starting to find Ronan very intriguing.

Leaning forward, I focused my mind on the differences between the two sources, imagining my inner fire against the tangible presence of magic in the world all around me. Dom continued to watch and listen in uncharacteristic silence.

"No . . . they are definitely different. My inner magic, it's . . . more chaotic? But it's also . . . pure? And solid. It's hard to explain. I feel like it comes at a greater cost to truly deplete it, but it also feels like an infinitely more powerful source, for me anyways. It takes greater skill to fully harness though . . . and that needs training, which I've never really had access to."

I was rambling now, doing what felt like a rather poor job of explaining myself. Ronan nodded slowly and Dom looked between us, wondering where this was headed.

"Right, so your inner magics are *yours*. And depending on your own mental state and experience," he raised his hand gesturing towards me, "that magic *should* always be there as long as you don't deplete it to the point of losing it."

I nodded again, excited to be speaking so frankly with another magical being; it had been far too long. However, I was also sensing an underlying message woven through his tone. I wondered if Dom had told him about the loss of my mother and grandmother in this lifetime and how it had affected me, but it wasn't important right now, I was desperate to keep the conversation going.

"Yes! And it regenerates on its own. As long as I remain grounded to the world around me, there it is, burning away."

I looked down at my palms, visually tracing the life lines as I recalled the darkest of times when it had all felt so lost to me.

Ronan forged onward.

"So, for us Druids, we only Wield magic that we gather from nature, be it plants, elements, and even animals. And more often than not, it's shared and exchanged with other beings and sources. Rather than *taking* it to use for spell casting, it's borrowed. And then returned. However, when we reach a certain point in our learning, we learn to Wield the magic in a more tangible way, through practical alchemy and ritual. But this skill is only obtained after a significant amount of time, and always with a considerable nod towards consequence."

"Do no harm," Dom said, and Ronan nodded somberly.

"You'll see why being a doctor was such an intuitive fit for me. The military . . . not so much." Ronan chuckled, brightening the mood. "But we need Druids in all facets, whether natural, technological, combat, or peace-keeping. Cassius certainly hasn't shied away from the use of technology. And that's where many of the world's battles are taking place these days, anyways."

I didn't know much yet about our one true enemy, other than the blurred glimpses of him I had faced in my most recent visions and nightmares, or what Dom had told me so far, but I had been assured that this would all be covered over Ronan's visit, and I wasn't particularly anxious to unpack the full reality of our threat tonight.

"Anyways, it's all about sustainability, whatever path we take. And *if* we take, we have to give back. That's how we maintain the sacred circle. There are rules that we have to follow."

"You certainly like to break the rules though, don't you? At least from time to time," Dom baited with a wink.

Ronan shook his head innocently. "Sometimes you have to make discretionary calls. But in the Druidic order, we are also always responsible for any consequences. So, what goes around comes around, as they say. And it's nothing compared to what the Wraiths do. They *only* take and consume. No giving back. And you've seen first-hand now what *that* looks like."

I thought of the wretched smell and sickly presence of the Wraiths and gagged slightly at the memory before attempting another sip of wine to wash it away. Unfortunately, my glass was empty. I had to pee anyways though, so I offered to grab the next round. Admittedly, I was pretty tipsy, and ended up opting for a cool glass of water instead, nibbling on the end of a bun from the corner basket in the kitchen before returning to join the group.

My return to the living room went unnoticed as the two men had poured themselves each a whisky and were now brightly discussing Ronan's trip back to Vancouver earlier in the week. I leaned on the thick cedar beam that ran from floor to ceiling, dividing the dining and living rooms respectively.

"I thought her truck was going to die on me right as I drove on the ferry." Ronan laughed, and I suddenly felt personally attacked, and cleared my throat.

"Oh, sorry, Julia!" Dom said, hopping up awkwardly from the couch to greet me.

I furrowed my brows and was suddenly feeling very aggravated and tired; apparently the drink was hitting me harder than I had expected.

"How did it go at the apartment anyways, Ronan? Dom was pretty vague on the details."

I noticed Dom clench his fist, but I was pissed now and wanted answers.

"Oh. Well," Ronan looked to Dom, whose eyes were wide as if to tell him to drop it, but Ronan was far too straightforward for that. "It was a bit of a surprise, as we had no idea Ben was your roommate. Kind of answered a few questions for us though."

He chuckled darkly as the tone of the room took a similar swing.

Dom let out a low growl. "Ronan . . ."

Questions exploded out of my mouth as I looked rapidly between the two Irishmen now standing formidably shoulder to shoulder in my living room.

"I'm sorry, hold on? How do you know Ben? I *knew* something was off when I came back this year. What did you do to him? Is he okay?"

Ronan spoke first, Dom still attempting in vain to regain his own composure. His lips were so thin they had disappeared entirely between his mustache and beard.

"He's fine actually. Really fine. We are helping him get the treatment he needs," Ronan said. His voice held compassion in it, so I held my tongue long enough for him to finish his thought. "He was manipulated by Wraiths to gather information about what his cousin Virginia was up to. They even gave him spellcasting bags, which was *unbelievably* dangerous. He could have killed himself with that much raw magic. We knew he was up to something, but we couldn't trace him properly. We assumed it was because of some of the magic they gave him—"

"But it was because of you," Dom said, voice so low it was barely audible.

"Sorry, what?" I was flabbergasted now. "What are you implying?"

Ronan stepped in, sensing correctly that his friend was about to blow. "Long story short, Julia. Your magic doesn't allow us to track you using technology; that's why Dom had to sign up to be your professor, so that we could find you."

"I know that, but—"

"*But* we missed a very important piece to the puzzle. That . . . that little shite was *living* with you. In the same house. He could have so easily given you over to . . . *him.*"

My heart sunk. I had known there was something off about Ben this fall, but I had no idea he was capable of such potential destruction. And by the sounds of it, I wasn't entirely sure Ben had been aware of it either.

"Is that why you left the morning after we arrived?" I turned to interrogate Dom next.

He nodded. "Ronan had messaged me about who your other roommate had been, and I . . ." He gritted his teeth, unable to continue.

"I think that if Dom had known you were living with Ben, he might have killed him outright when we interrogated him on Thanksgiving. So perhaps it was all for the best."

Dom let out a forceful snort, and I sunk down onto Gertie's armchair. Were they normally this nonchalant about someone else's life?

I racked my memory about the October long weekend, but my thoughts were clashing together like one of Gertie's bad plaid pantsuits from the seventies in the upstairs closet. That was the night Virginia and I had walked through the disorienting magic on our way home. It *must* have been Ben trying to lose their trail. Did we just miss Dom or Ronan on their hunt? Or had our imminent return drawn Ben out of the apartment, inadvertently springing his own trap?

I gathered up what clues I knew to be true.

"My name wasn't on the lease. Only Virginia's. But I don't think Ben's name was on it either. So . . . you couldn't have found either of us out that way. And I didn't have any mail sent to the city this fall, only to Gertie's because I was going to be there such a short while. But obviously you found Ben, I presume by tracing his mail? Or . . . were you following him?"

I looked between the two, expectant. Their silence answered my question.

"Okay. Then why didn't you just follow me home too?"

Ronan raised his eyebrows at Dom; evidently the choice *not* to follow me had been a bone of contention.

"Well . . . I'm not a stalker," Dom answered, though he was facing Ronan. He then turned to face me. "You know I wanted to give you space to come around to me. You deserved that, at the very least. It also just felt like the timing wasn't right yet for fate. But unfortunately, it almost cost us every-thing." He hardened his gaze back at Ronan, almost daring his friend to press the issue further.

No wonder Dom was having such a hard time managing his emotions when we'd arrived here. He'd made a serious miscalculation, but the whole issue was far more complicated than that.

"It's not your fault entirely," I said, trying to help. "I should have detected the dark magic too. I mean I did a bit, but my Witch's intuition wasn't exactly functional this fall. So . . . I missed it, somehow."

Ronan still said nothing, but instead took a deep breath, exhaled rapidly through his nostrils, and looked towards Dom. I now understood their vol-leyed glances with a renewed meaning; they signalled a much deeper dis-agreement about my safety and agency. So I was grateful when Dom stepped in and put an end to the conversation.

"Don't, Ronan. Not tonight. You've done enough."

Ronan ran his tongue across his teeth under his front lip, which now had shades of a five o'clock shadow, and readied for battle. However, considering the look on Dom's face, he seemed to think better of himself and turned silently to climb the stairs towards Gertie's old bedroom for the night.

Dom mumbled something about going for a walk and turned for the door. Instead of following, I dragged myself wordlessly to the bedroom. I was exhausted and certainly not sober enough for further discussion. Dom followed me to bed about twenty minutes after I had settled in, but within moments, he was sound asleep, snoring ever so slightly as he lay flat on his back. I wasn't sure what I had been expecting with his return, but I was grateful he'd still found his way back to me after such an unexpected turn of events.

Over-encumbered by worry, I lay awake for several hours, despite my crushing fatigue. I rolled around in my thoughts all I that had learned over the past week about the way things *were* and felt such a distinct juxtaposition to how my instinct was telling me they *should be*. One thing I knew for sure though was that I was done allowing others to influence my path in such an indirect manner. It was time for me to be included in the details, and thankfully, when we awoke the next morning, Dom shared a similar sentiment.

"Julia," he said, when I at last stirred in my sleep. He had evidently been awake for some time, our sleep schedules still quite staggered.

"Mm?" I said groggily as he kissed me softly on my shoulder, brushing my tangled hair away from my face.

He took a deep breath and rolled onto his side, placing his head in his hand. Even in this moment, he was utterly spectacular to behold, with sandy tousled hair and his warm physical presence filling my entire field of vision. I wanted to burrow into his soft chest hair and go back to sleep, pretending last night's conversation hadn't so jaggedly relayed the darkness of our more recent history to me.

"I should have told you about Ben," he said.

"I know. You should have. But . . . I haven't exactly told you about my own worries about what's been going on either. Ever since I returned to school this fall, something just hasn't felt right . . . what with the missing women and just this . . . *ominous* feeling. I thought it was because my magic has been so unreliable, like a faulty antenna . . . but I think I was confusing my intuition with my own fragility."

His smiled, but there was a sadness to it. "You have always been so forgiving of my mistakes. I don't deserve it."

I snuggled in close, and he gently stroked the centre of my back.

"And," he added, "you're *anything* but fragile."

"I don't know, Dom. You heard how Ronan hinted at how unreliable my magic could be. Does he have something against Witches?"

"Ronan? No, no, of course not. He's just such a pragmatist that he has a hard time truly believing in the Prophecy. Even though I was *literally* born into a stone tomb as a fully-grown man, it's not enough proof for him that we should put all our eggs into one basket, as they say."

"Am I the basket or the eggs in this scenario?"

He chuckled, a deep pleasurable sound that was instantly grounding.

"He doesn't know the depths of our story. Of your story. Nor does he know the strength you carry inside." He poked me squarely in the chest.

"Well, I can see his point in that regard; it's not like I know the depths of my own story either."

Dom shook his head. "You don't. Not yet. But you will." He seemed so sure, and I latched onto his belief in our destiny with all my heart, despite how shaky my own feelings were. "Ronan's been up for a while. He's an even earlier riser than I am."

I said nothing, unsure if I had it in me to face him so early in the day. Hangovers always brought with them crushing anxiety, and I would have preferred to spend the day in bed, ideally snuggling Dom in the process.

"Julia, I know Ronan can be insensitive sometimes, but he's one of the good ones. I promise. You don't have to like the man, although it *would* make things simpler. But we do have to work with him as he's probably our best ally in all of this."

I realized then that I hadn't actually asked what his role was among the Druids working for "the cause." Dom thankfully followed my thoughts with ease.

"He's the head of intelligence around the Druidic forces mustering against Cassius's Wraiths. Sort of like a section leader, although I don't get the sense that Druids follow any kind of hierarchal structure; it seems to be more of a 'time served' kind of thing that determines your role."

"Where does that leave you?" I asked, genuinely curious but also somewhat afraid of the answer. A man such as he was destined for leadership, his ancestry alone being the most significant indicator.

He furrowed his brow momentarily and was about to speak when his phone went off with a loud vibrating buzz; I really needed to show him how to shut that off.

He sat up and checked the screen, then let out an exasperated groan.

"Text from Ronan; he's got to go. Emergency at the hospital or something. Christ."

Without another word, Dom swung his powerful legs off the bed and strode from the bedroom wearing only his boxers. I debated between staying hidden in the bedroom or following in his wake as backup, but I chose the latter; I was tired of choosing the safer route.

By the time I made it to the front step, passing by an immaculately clean kitchen—Ronan's doing no doubt—he was already backing out of the driveway.

"All is well," Dom said, still facing the retreating SUV. "It's a legitimate medical emergency at the hospital. Ronan isn't one to lie. Although, I did get the sense he was relieved for an excuse to leave. Oh, and he took his compass back."

Eyeing his practically naked frame as I leaned on the doorframe, I breathed in the cool and bright morning air on the mountain with gratitude and sighed. Despite everything, here we were, and I couldn't think of anywhere else I would rather be.

CHAPTER 18

Ronan left before we could discuss their espionage in Vancouver further or what "next steps" might be for Dom and I over the coming weeks with regards to the greater picture. Pressing Dom on the matter, it turned out I had quite falsely assumed that Ronan would be the one influencing these choices for us in *any* capacity.

In fact, these types of logistical decisions actually lay wholly with Dom.

"So . . . you're the leader then?"

Dom grimaced, clearly reluctant to have any sort of title.

"I suppose in the truest sense of the word, I am. But like I said before, with the Druids, things don't really settle into the usual hierarchy anyways. I think I'm just . . . the oldest? I mean, I've been fighting Cassius the longest, obviously. So, the job lands with me."

I nodded, curious why he had decided to keep this specific detail locked away. Perhaps he simply didn't want to add undue pressure onto me as his partner, what with all the other adjustments I had been asked to make over the past week alone. Regardless, I didn't belabour the issue.

The days between Ronan's visit and the festive season passed with surprising ease, all things considered. We found ourselves settled into a shy rhythm, almost like we were now *consciously* becoming reacquainted, rather than diving in on first impulse. Our daily ritual now included long hikes, some more challenging than others but all culminating in perfectly pink, chilled noses and sloppy, soggy boots.

It was immensely restorative to be out in the fresh air, moving our bodies in tandem as we worked through the complexities of our new life together. We hadn't revisited more carnal explorations in the bedroom since the first night of our arrival, so the physical exertion discovered in our outdoor forays had soothed us both on multiple levels. While we still shared a bed, at this point it just hadn't felt right to reconvene beyond intimate snuggles and pillow talk.

One sunny afternoon, we decided to climb a trail up Mount Erskine. The weather had been unseasonably warm all month, and before long, I had tied my jacket around my waist and had streams of sweat dripping down my back. The hike had been majestic, passing by countless orange-barked Arbutus trees with their peeling flesh and dark green leaves heartily retained throughout the winter months. Conversely, the gnarled and mossy Garry oak groves we came across looked undoubtedly spooky, and I couldn't help but feel transported to another realm or time altogether.

Dom delighted particularly in the hidden fairy doors dotted throughout the ascent.

"The tales of the fairies from our youth weren't *nearly* so whimsical though."

I chuckled. "Our youth?"

"You know what I mean," he said. "The stories told that it was best you behave lest *'the Other Folk'* cause you trouble. The *Gentle People*. Morally grey they were, which was more than likely a means of social control, besides the church, of course."

"I can't see the church liking the fairies very much."

"Well, that's also true. Especially in the early fifteenth century; the Catholic church decided that Witches and fairies were the root cause of the people's woes. It wasn't a very nice time to be alive then . . . horrific actually."

It was a grim notion.

"But when burning people at the stake didn't *actually* solve anything, the Irish people went back to minding the fairies as they always had. And they still mind them today. You should hear all the difficulties around roadway expansion throughout the country; it sounds totally mad, but it really isn't a good idea to take down a fairy mound for the sake of development."

"Do you believe in them?" I asked playfully.

He deadpanned. "Well, I'm certainly not going to be lingering around these doors if that's what you're asking me."

I really couldn't tell if he was affirming my question or not.

When we finally reached the low mountain summit, I plunked to the ground, gasping for breath. I liked to consider myself as being in relatively good shape, but something about vertical climbs always kicked my ass. Meanwhile, Dom probably could have sprinted the entire way and still considered it only a refreshing walk. We sat side by side, looking out across the Sansum Narrows towards Vancouver Island. I had the distinct sense that we had gone through these exact motions at many points in our shared timeline and relished in the familiarity.

"Hey, so . . ." I said finally, breaking the silence once my breath and heartrate had slowed to normal intervals, "you still haven't told me how *you* became reborn in the first place? How did you manage it?"

He stretched his arms above his head, and I noticed that he too was drenched in sweat, but his breathing was considerably lighter than my own.

"Well, that's a bit of an exciting tale, if I do say so myself."

"I'm intrigued," I said, deeply curious about what it had been like for us, back in the late tenth and early eleventh centuries.

"Well . . . after you *literally* disappeared from my arms while your granny's hut burned, I actually considered dying myself . . . to follow you, wherever you had gone. I could imagine myself walking into the fire in some kind of brazen attempt to grab hold of some of the magic you left behind, and then chase you into the Otherworld," he said, smiling unexpectedly.

I looked at him in disbelief. "Really?"

"I was rather fantastical then. We all were. Life was . . . simpler. Grand acts of passion and the heroics. They made sense. Also, people *actually* believed in magic back then too, despite what the Catholic church says in their recorded histories of the time."

His eyes were distant then, momentarily lost in memory of a time long gone.

"But clearer thoughts prevailed, and I presumed that you had fallen victim to a misguided curse. Your old grannie was a bit of a martyr when it came to magic, truth be told. So, then I sought out the next best thing: Druids! See, we had only just met several months previous, but I'd known, as soon as I first laid my eyes on you, that our destinies were fated alongside one another." He looked at me adoringly. "You had told me as much as well. And who better to contend with fate than the Druids? They were, and still are, exceptional Diviners. But the Druids of our time, well . . . they were different."

"I can't get a dowsing rod to work for the life of me."

His face darkened. "No, not that type of divination. What these Druids did was *much* more sinister stuff. All the talk about ritual sacrifices is true, for the most part. The Druids we know today have long since deviated from the practices of back then. It's rumoured that there are still Sorcerers who take part in the ritual, and that's our current theory around Cassius. We think it's how he manages to stay one step ahead of us so much of the time, magically speaking. That . . . and all the missing girls." He paused.

I stared at him, suddenly struggling to take it all in.

"Sorry, I'm getting ahead of myself. Stay with me," he said, though it wasn't altogether reassuring.

"We were planning to run away together as soon as we could manage it. I had obligations to my father's cause, but it was never my calling . . . and I would never be High King anyways. I had far too many brothers ahead of me in the succession, several of whom wanted it *quite* badly. I was a decent warrior though. We all knew how to fight back then, our family especially." He paused, taking my hand into his own. "But I knew my—*our* destiny, lay elsewhere."

I was shivering now, the sweat having cooled proportionately with my body. I urged him onward, however, despite my falling temperature.

"The Annals of Innisfallen breeze over any of *my* contributions fairly quickly," he began, counting off a very short list on his fingers. "First, they describe a raid at Cenél Conaill I participated in with my half-brother Murchad . . . and then later it says I died of natural causes in 1012 AD. Which I guess is close enough to the truth. The monks certainly wouldn't have acknowledged that I'd taken off with a hoard of Druids and never come home. Natural causes would have served as a much simpler explanation for everyone, to be sure."

A distant, hazy part of me felt like I knew all of this, but the larger part of me was absolutely mind-blown with the words coming out of his mouth, just casually remarking on some of the major points of history at the time.

"Anyways, I *did* go to the Druids. I was frantic and terrified that I had lost you forever. And at first, they said there was nothing they could do to help me. That it required a sacrifice and that it wasn't the type of magic they took part in anymore. Frankly, I think they were shocked I would even ask, but I *knew* Druids, and these ones definitely had the capability." He frowned at the distant memory of their reluctance and cracked his knuckles menacingly. "Plus, I did have a sacrifice for them. Regardless of why, your mother *had* died at the hand of another, either yours or your grannie's during an act of magic. That much was plain when I walked into the hut and saw you standing there."

He paused as if waiting for me to react, or even wince, but I had seen this vision in full detail from my own perspective already. The circumstance of my curse wasn't news to me, as grizzly as it was.

"And so, since we *did* have the sacrifice, one which was inexplicably tied to you, they agreed," he continued. "We returned to the cottage, which was naught but a pile of cinders at this point but as of yet not discovered either. The Druids were pleased it hadn't been disturbed, and started hopping around and sorting through the ashes, searching for something to tie the sacrifice to. It turned out to be your mother's rib bone with the knife *still embedded.*"

He paused for effect, and I shoved him impatiently.

He went on. "Pleased with their finding, they instructed me that we would have to travel to a remote Druidic site before the winter solstice. It was from there that I would be sent to the Blessed Isles, a place of transformation, and hopefully my soul would be re-routed, or reborn towards you in time, or something like that. One of them had called it a transmigration of the soul, but I never fully understood it, truth be told."

It was just like something out of a fairy tale, or some kind of myth tied to Arthurian legend. I remembered reading about King Arthur and the Lady of the Lake as a child, being drawn to the magic of a place called Avalon. He was right; his tale was certainly more exciting than my own ill-fated sequence of curse-related events.

"Anyways, it worked, and I was reborn a handful of years later on the morning following the winter solstice—disoriented, but whole. The Druids had waited for me, taking turns in watch. For you see, they too had learned of and kept the Prophecy. And from the first rebirth, I set out to find you."

He folded his hands neatly across his lap.

"Unbelievable," I said.

"That's one word for it. But it explains why our . . . patterns? . . . are so different. Mine is tied to yours, I think somewhat indefinitely. And in turn, *you* are tied to the Prophecy through your grandmother's curse. And so it goes, round and round."

He looked away then, stealing away some unseen emotion.

"Round and round," I said, staring back towards my own fragmented memories.

Suddenly, arching his back and kicking his feet out in front of him, he popped up rather athletically, landing solidly on the balls of his feet.

"I'm famished. Are you ready to head back?" he asked.

"I am."

The week before Christmas arrived with the magic of heavy, wet snow. It was a rare occurrence on the West Coast at the best of times, so it felt utterly enchanting to peer out the window and see the garden adorned in festive white as the thick flakes fell to the earth. Mother Nature had also decorated many of the trees around us with light green lichen, which would dangle and blow in the changing winds like tinsel. Clouds came and went like heavy cotton batting over the mountain tops. They brought yet more precipitation that only seemed to enhance the effect of being socked in.

Apart from our now snowy hikes, we spent most of our days doing what Gertie would have called "reclaiming comfort," as lovers do after surviving some kind of trial or great discomfort. Yet, for the most part, there had been very little combat between us, verbal or otherwise.

I would have been lying to myself if I said there wasn't an un-germinated seed of doubt sitting somewhere in my belly. No doubt it was a hypervigilance tactic I'd learned that signalled things *could* change at any given moment.

However, I simply wanted to bask in the sunshine of the man beside me . . . and think about what our meal plan might be for the holidays; he *did* love his food.

In fact, Dom and I had arrived in a place of perfect harmony around food and drink. He was happiest when facing a large portion of meat and vegetables he could scarf down at regular intervals. Meanwhile, I was more content to snack throughout the day as the mood struck, and then consume an arguably more reasonable portion at mealtimes. This meant we needed groceries both for tasty meals ready to cook as well as an assortment of nibbles like charcuterie and fresh fruit on hand at all times for lighter snacking. Thankfully, Dom also was a skilled cook.

"You probably think I'm an absolute glutton," he said one evening as he polished off a steak the size of a war hammer. My own steak had been a hearty six-ounce, and I was bursting after consuming the entire juicy strip loin to myself.

"Of course not . . . well, not entirely," I said with a wink as I deftly dodged a bread roll flying past my head in reply.

"I think there is nothing I love more than sitting down to enjoy a meal with you," he said, sipping fully from his glass of red wine, cheeks flushed pink from the warm fire and rich foods.

"Is that all?" I said, eyebrow raised into a cheeky question mark.

"Well, there are other things . . ." he said, his hand sliding along my thigh, trailing inward and giving in to his own temptation.

"Hmm!" I said, and scooted back into my chair, feigning innocence and propriety.

The days had gone on much like this, playful flirting, but never really engaging past giggles and extended make-out sessions on the couch. Gertie would have described this phase of our romance as "hot and heavy," a phrase that always made me laugh for whatever reason.

Indeed, our kisses had been long and delicious. I reveled in the moments we spent intertwined by the fireside, getting to know each other more, but I had thought that by now we would have translated that early tension and passion into something more carnal. Because frankly, I was horny. And frustrated.

TIDES OF THE SOVEREIGN

That being said, since I had experienced the vison of his death on the icy cliff that first night at the cottage, followed by his impenetrable stone wall, I'd felt a strong instinct to wait. It felt necessary to firm up our foundation before putting myself at risk of another "death-blow divination." Deep down, I also knew that my inner magic was still in the process of settling after all the abrupt changes I had encountered this month. My Witch's fire seemed to now be steadily ablaze; however, it still threatened to burst into inferno with one wrong move. Time was what we needed, and it thankfully seemed to be in abundance, for now.

Late in the afternoon on the winter solstice, which also happened to be Dom's birthday, we decided to take a long walk closer to home. It started out just as pleasant as any other, with Dom regaling me with tales of adventures past with the Druids. I had gifted him a new sweater, a much more Canadian version of the wool sweater commonly worn by Maritimers on both the East and West Coast alike.

"Julia! You remembered."

I grinned broadly, having picked up the rough woolen shirt on one of my grocery trips earlier in the month. His joyful response was priceless.

"Is this your *real* birthday though?" I asked as he was unwrapping his gift.

He chuckled. "It isn't. I think I was born in late June sometime. But honestly, it was such a long time ago that I couldn't tell you the exact date. Plus, the calendars weren't the same anyway. The winter solstice has always just felt like my adopted birthday."

Dom pulled me into his arms then, holding me tenderly in sweet gratitude for the gesture. "You didn't have to."

"But I wanted to," I said, and planted a big old birthday kiss smack on his mouth.

Thankfully, the sweater was a perfect fit, with Dom pulling it on enthusiastically as we walked out the door and towards the road. We had mostly driven to our hiking destinations, but between the slick roads and the joint we had shared earlier, hopping in my old truck didn't feel like the safest decision. Our walk was slow and leisurely, and when we eventually turned towards home, with clear heads and open hearts, the sun was quickly beginning to fade. I shivered as the long shadows fingered their way through the bare trees darkly, beckoning us to join them in their winter slumber.

"Julia, have you ever thought about . . . being a mother?" he asked, shyly looking down at his slushy, mud-caked boots as we turned up another road towards home.

Oof.

I could hear both the mixed hesitation and curiosity laced through his question. My pulse beat heavily into my throat as I swallowed back what felt like my stomach trying to climb its way out. This had all of a sudden become *very* personal.

"Well," I said with a gulp. "Yes, someday, I suppose. It's never really come up with anyone before though."

My brain was working at breakneck speed to find a simple way to summarize my stance.

I could feel his broad body beside me, our fingers still intertwined as we worked our way along the slippery road, cautiously supporting one another through the icy puddles and ruts. He was neither tense nor relaxed; there was just the honed anticipation of a warrior.

"I haven't really shared much about my childhood with you, this time around. But my mother wasn't exactly a sound parent, I guess. And I never met my father." My own hesitation was evident.

He waited in silence.

All the years of heartbreak I had experienced while watching my mother try and fail to cope with the demands of daily life washed over me. I knew it wasn't entirely her fault, but I also knew that, in order to raise a child, I would have to completely re-parent myself first. And honestly, I wasn't sure I had it in me; perhaps the cycle was best left tied into a neat knot.

And then I thought, *Maybe that isn't what he's asking about at all.*

"Are you worried about contraception? Because you don't need to be. I have an IUD."

He nodded. "Mm. Yes, that is something that's different this time around. Last time too, actually. Although in Ireland it still wasn't so easy to explain away the need for *family planning.*"

I laughed in spite of myself, but Dom continued to look uncomfortable.

"Yeah . . . but you do agree it's a woman's right to make her own choices about her uterus, right?" I asked, somewhat defensively.

"Absolutely," he said, giving my hand a squeeze.

I took a deep breath and let it out slowly. "I think someday, once I feel settled again in my own mind and body, I might consider it. So much has happened recently." I hadn't really given an answer that held any weight, but that was the best I could come up with for the time being. And it was the truth, for what it was worth.

After what felt like an unbearably long moment, and one in which I would have slipped and fallen into the prickly snow-covered ditch several times if not for Dom's reassuring grip, he answered simply: "I think that makes complete sense."

"What am I even talking about?" I said, my heart dropping. "This is all assuming we even live past the summer solstice."

"Well, there's that," he said, now carefully guarding his emotions. "I don't know if you remember, but we've conceived before, a few times actually. But . . . we never lived long enough to make it past the early days of your pregnancies."

"There would have never been enough time."

Slowly at first, a door opened within my memory, its hinges rusty and seized with age. Before I could brace myself, a deep-seated grief of my own poured through it. While new to *this body*, it was all too familiar and indescribably painful.

"Oh, Dom . . ."

He stopped me flat in the middle of the road and pulled me into a roughly powerful and protective embrace. I sobbed openly into his scratchy sweater, feeling a rumble deep in his chest that, without a doubt, mirrored my own sorrow.

Suddenly, headlights were upon us, and we had to duck to the side of the road to avoid a bright-orange snow plow that had finally made it towards the upper roads. We walked along the side of the road in silence then, hand-in-hand in our shared grief.

After a time, I had an idea. "Do you think that could affect the Prophecy at all? That right now I *can't* get pregnant? Or at least, that there is a very slim chance."

He stopped in his tracks. "I hadn't thought about that."

"But I guess . . . does destiny even care about birth control?"

Dom explained then that we had often speculated whether or not the Prophecy actually spoke of me or of our unborn child. "But since you were always the one who was hunted down in the end, it didn't really matter." We continued on in more measured silence, trudging slowly upwards towards home. I could tell he was reaching his emotional capacity on the topic, but I had one more question.

"What about you? Do you . . . want kids?" I asked, throwing all caution to the wind as the quickly engulfing darkness obscured our faces. It somehow felt easier to hear his answer if I didn't have to look into his eyes.

We had reached the end of the gravel drive at the cottage, and finding myself grateful for the additional traction the small sharp stones provided, I dropped his hand.

"I think I would like that, yes. But I don't think any time soon." He sounded sure of himself, despite the fact that he had ripped his toque off and was running his fingers through his thick sandy locks. "The threat seems so much bigger this time around, and the stakes are higher than ever. We need to be smart. And calculated."

I wasn't sure how he thought babies were made. As far as I knew, something like fifty percent of the time they were definitely *not* created under smart and calculated circumstances.

We spent the next several days enjoying each other's peaceful, albeit modest, company. I had recently torn into another one of Gertie's smutty romance novels from the lowest bookshelf, the one she didn't think I knew about, and giggled heartily at the idea that she had filled so much of her latter days with such indecency.

Dom thoroughly enjoyed my squeals from across the room as I delighted in absurd premises and the preposterous adventures that ensued. In fact, he had positively giggled with mirth at one point when I threw the book across the room dramatically at a point of contention between the overly melodramatic characters.

"I'm trying to work here, you heathen! Keep your filthy little books to yourself," he said, slamming his laptop shut in hilarious indignity as he chucked a worn velvet-brocade throw pillow at me from across the living room. I smiled devilishly in response and dove back into my steamy paperback.

While we had found a new, or I guess renewed, sense of comfort together, I could still sense the private sadness that he carried with him in the quiet moments when he didn't think I was watching. He almost always woke several hours earlier than me, usually under the guise of considering the time change for his work with the Druids overseas, or to catch Ronan on the phone over in Vancouver between shifts. But I knew that it was also because he craved time alone to wander his internal halls of stone in solitude.

Indeed, I had found myself awake in his arms one night, having cried out despairingly from the now-recurring vision involving his death on the cliff. He comforted me, then uttered soft words of safety to ground me back into place. It was deep in the darkness of the night, while holding back his own unexpected tears of grief and self-imposed guilt, that he had promised he would never again retreat to those dark places if it meant leaving me vulnerable and alone as a result.

"It's just, it's so hard to witness you in pain with the visions while reliving my own . . . story . . ."

"Dom, who am I to tell you how to process your grief? And all the memories? I can't even imagine . . ." I was still struggling to comprehend the gravity of what he was contending with.

"But Julia, I've had *how many* lifetimes to process our lot? I always get a handle on it eventually; it's just that, this time it's a bit more of a battle than I anticipated."

I had a few guesses as to why it was harder this time around, largely because he had more than likely developed some kind of complex post-traumatic-stress response to the repeated horrors experienced throughout his lifetimes. On top of that, when I considered all of the social change that had occurred in the last several decades alone, it was no wonder he felt rather disconnected from me and disoriented by this life. What must it be like, being reborn in an entirely new generation, only to find the love of your life fully versed in its customs? Meanwhile, you're stumbling along, attempting to get your bearings. In truth, he was a marvel for having adapted so keenly.

I also knew that it hadn't always been like this with each rebirth. In fact, it was completely plausible to imagine that there may have been times where he didn't find me at all or was too late—that I had already been captured and we both died in the struggle before even finding one another. I could sense *these* memories when I searched deep within my own fragile recollection. But it was like trying to catch lightning in a bottle; the premonitions always escaped me, and Dom seemed hesitant to re-tell any of his failures for the time being.

CHAPTER 19

Late in the afternoon on Christmas eve, I found myself tucked happily into my usual couch nook. Gazing out of the quirky, custom, wood-paned front window, I sipped peacefully on a giant cup of steaming black tea, spiked heartily with whisky by Dom. All of a sudden, a large slab of snow and ice slid off the roof, crashing onto the ground with a large *thump!*

It had been unusually warm over the last twenty-four hours, much of the sodden snow having already melted away, its freshwater flow washing gracefully towards the salty shoreline and out to sea. The lawn bore patches of green once more and was wet and spongy under foot. However, the forecast was calling for more snow at any moment, so we knew it wouldn't last. I thought dreamily of what Christmas morning would feel like, celebrated with Dom with a fresh sheet of snow on the ground.

We had been enjoying a peaceful afternoon, listening to tacky Christmas music while Dom marked his final papers and essays for the term. I had to give him credit for upholding his responsibilities, because from where I sat, it all seemed like such a royal waste of time.

The night before, we had engaged in a hearty discussion on his marking schemes when he assigned me a final grade of eighty-three percent.

"Eighty . . . three?" I had asked, somewhat shocked at his restraint. He'd run his long fingers through his hair, followed by a hearty scratch of his beard, seeming perfectly calm and resolute in his decision.

"I'm not the kind of professor who plays favourites, Julia. However, you were still top of the class. And if I *might* add, you earned it."

I rolled my eyes. "I'm sure I earned it in more ways than one, *Professor*." What followed was the closest we had come so far to giving in to the fullness of our desires, but it was cut off abruptly by a glass of water spilled onto some of his more important paperwork.

My current musings were interrupted by the sudden crash of the snow leaving the roof. As if on cue, Dom snapped his laptop closed and hopped up enthusiastically, heavy feet crashing to the floor with a resounding thud. The boisterous combination of the snow falling and his abrupt action made me jump. My cup lurched forward, spilling tea all over the cream cable-knit sweater I had stolen from Dom's luggage; obnoxious spillage was fast becoming a trend around here.

He had hesitated to unpack his clothes into any of the empty drawers I had offered, which at first stung me slightly. My offer had literally only been to make his time here more comfortable and certainly *not* some clingy maneuver that I might have made in the past. After a time, I decided his resistance was more likely due to his constant need to be able to leave at a moment's notice; his awareness of constant threat was very real, and I was trying my best to respect this aspect of his countless lifetimes upon this earth.

"I'm done!" he said triumphantly, his glee over completing his marking and submissions spreading readily across his thickly bearded face.

Then, as if by an act of magic, the playlist shifted from a perky modern Christmas tune to one of the more classic numbers oozing with sentimentality. For a fleeting moment, I could see Dom's mind travel to a distant place of memory, but he soon returned to the present in one long stride towards me. Offering me his welcoming hand as I clamoured to my feet, he scooped me close to dance sock-footed through the sitting room.

"I've always been such a sap when it comes to the holidays," he said, lowering me into a romantic dip, then swaying me back up into his arms with a kiss on my nose.

"I think I like it," I said, enjoying his confident dance steps and the sudden warmth of his hand on my lower back, which he had casually slid under my shirt during his most recent maneuver.

"There's just something about it, Christian, Pagan, or otherwise. It's just . . ."

"Magical," I said, finishing his sentence as he kissed my hand following a dramatic spin towards the fireplace.

Upon my return to his arms, with my back to his chest and looking up into his kind eyes, I felt with surety that I was safe to let down my guard and share all of myself with him, all over again.

"Dom?" I asked, swaying in time with him to a slow and romantic number.

"Yes, my love?"

"Is it painful for you? How little I remember of our past?"

He took a pause before mustering his reply.

"Yes. Sometimes . . . I wish you could remember days like this in the past, like I do. Sometimes, it feels like they were only dreams. But other times, I really do just live in the moment. Honestly, there's a whole ocean of memories behind us. I don't always recall every detail myself unless I'm reminded."

"I don't mind, you know. If you want to tell me about . . . things."

He smiled and kissed me softly on the top of my head, our slow dance coming to a gentle close.

"I will. In time. When we're back in Ireland, I'm sure more will come up. I have many . . . mementos, you might say, scattered throughout the house. Reminders that will hopefully jog your memory."

"Hopefully," I said, suddenly wistful.

We had decided to leave for Ireland just before the New Year, largely because it was by far the preferable location to work together with the Druids on the cause. Additionally, since it was technically the ancestral home of both of us, Dom had hoped that it would reconnect me to some of my old magic, and perhaps even lost memories. In his defence, I too had wondered if certain items from our shared life together might carry embedded memories, as I certainly tended to leave behind thoughts or ideas on items wherever I went. It was an occupational hazard of having the Sight, truth be told.

This brought my mind back to the quilt. *Aha!*

"Dom, do you think there are any mementos in the quilt? Like, do you recognize any of the fabrics or patterns?"

He tilted his head thoughtfully, then squeezed his eyes shut.

"There's something to that, I think. Sort of like the tattoo."

The song ended and both the moment and the memories twinkled away. It was followed by a particularly gaudy holiday tune, and we chuckled, shying away from more dance steps and heading towards the kitchen.

We had prepped salmon Wellington earlier in the afternoon. The buttery puffed pastry was wrapped tight in parchment in the fridge, stuffed with Pacific salmon, artichoke hearts, spinach, onion, and parmesan. I had requested beef, but he was insistent that it needed to be seafood tonight, so that was where we had landed.

A simple tossed salad and baked lemon-and-dill potatoes would serve as the sides to our meal, followed by homemade crème brûlée for dessert, which Dom proudly claimed was his speciality, knowing that it was one of my favourites.

While I couldn't disagree, I was curious how he would be making the caramelized sugar top without any kind of kitchen torch. Grandma Gertie's kitchen was surprisingly well stocked, all things considered, but it was painfully lacking in this aspect. He assured me he would make do with the oven set to broil.

"I've made it for you several times before, or some version of it, and you didn't complain. I promise!" he said, giving me a little shoulder nudge as we prepped our dinner together. I was quickly discovering how much I loved when he shared happy memories.

"I believe you! But I'm giving you fair warning that the oven is old and unreliable, so if it doesn't work out . . . you're in charge of chopping and stacking the wood for the rest of the week!" I responded playfully as I pulled out the mismatched dinner plates from the simple raw-pine upper cupboards.

A hint of mischief crossed his face. "Julia, please. I've said from the start that I'm more than happy to do that. You'll have to think of a better wager than that."

"Oh ho! It's a wager now!"

"Indeed, it is. And I think the odds are drastically stacked in my favour. Think of something else," he said, hand barely dragging across my denimed backside as he moved to courier the cracked vintage bowl of side salad towards the table.

True to form, Dom had poured me an overfull glass of the local white wine I'd picked out from our neighbours on Vancouver Island. It happened to be my absolute favourite, and its slight effervescence and fruity bouquet went down with unsurprising ease. It was a lovely match for our fish tonight, so I had insisted we bring home several bottles for the evening's meal.

"Hmm . . ." I pondered as I switched on the oven light to eye the progress of the browning puffed pastry. It wasn't yet golden, still holding onto the sheen of not-quite-doneness. Dom eyed me speculatively as he leaned on the fridge. His own glass of wine was already half gone, his cheeks flushed from both the heat of the oven and the increasing heat of the moment.

He truly was the most magnificent creature I had ever laid my eyes upon. Broad, powerful, and formidable, he was every bit the warrior prince. But instead of being intimidated by his stature and history, I was drawn whole-heartedly to him like a moth to the flame. On the balance, he also held such a welcoming softness and natural joviality that he was equally as magnetic in his comfortability too.

"My wager . . ." I said, taking a long, seductive sip of my wine, vastly enjoying the provocative weight of the moment as I considered it. I could smell the puffed pastry reaching its perfect "doneness" in the old oven and the scent of the last pair of Gertie's natural beeswax taper candles burning on the waiting table, both of which filled the room with pleasant familiarly. Overwhelmed with a sense of home and fuelled by the beginnings of liquid courage, I felt profoundly resolute that, as this was *my* turf, I would wager as I pleased.

He raised his light-brown eyebrows in wait, but I noticed that his breathing had become fractionally heavier. Was he waiting in anticipation for the wager to transform itself into some form of an invitation? It reminded me of playing strip poker as a teenager on a Friday night in a friend's basement. We didn't really know *how* to play poker, but that wasn't really the point.

"I wager, that if your dessert is a flop, I get to ask you one truth," I said, aware that this came with great risk of being met yet again with a stone wall, but my intuition practically screamed that this was my moment. "And if it isn't, you can ask me anything your heart desires, and I promise I'll tell *you* the truth."

"Well, that's not nearly as naughty as I was expecting," he blurted out with a laugh. "I was thinking like a week of back massages or something. Alright. One truth. If I fail, which I won't," he said with a wink, "it's yours."

223

"Ah shit! Your idea was way more fun!" I said, choosing distraction now and pulling the pastries out of the oven with satisfaction. They had turned out perfectly, and I was beginning to think the old oven would prove the wager in his favour after all.

We enjoyed our meal immensely, as well as the wine, and our conversation for the next hour. Dom regaled me with his adventures of acclimating himself to this most recent time period, poking fun at his clumsy adjustments in particular.

"If you can believe it, I actually tried to dismantle a security system in the middle of reconnaissance by ripping it off the wall."

"You did not!"

He had tears running down his face in mirth. "Well, believe what you want. But I assure you, I *did*. And it went about as well as you can imagine too. The police were there so fast, chasing after me and everything! Thank God Ronan was nearby, and I was able to hop into his car."

Evidently, he had learned to use humour to gloss over some of the more embarrassing stumbling blocks of his fate, which I found to be a most admirable coping mechanism.

"Well, my love, I think . . ." he rose from the table at last and rested his hand on my shoulder, "it's time for me to *win* our wager." A cheeky grin spread across his face as his Irish lilt grew thicker with each glass of wine.

"Do you want my help, or does that sully the odds?" I asked, bringing the remaining plates and dishes to the sink.

He practically shoved a refilled glass of wine into my hand. "Absolutely not!"

"Okay, okay!" I said, raising my arms in surrender and making my way to the couch. The fire was going out, so I focused my attention on that while he busied himself with dessert.

What *was* my question?

Admittedly, I hadn't entirely thought out *that* aspect of our wager. The truth was that I was looking forward to cracking into the bubbling golden top and creamy delicacy of the dessert, followed by his chance to voice his heart's question. Sure, there was a risk he would botch it and ask me something wasteful like who my guiltiest celebrity crush was, or my most embarrassing moment, or worse, something about past lovers. However, the romance and festive mood of the evening had been consistently reticent of magic, and I felt a deep trust for the direction things were going.

Unsurprisingly, by this point in the evening, my intuition had been utterly correct. The crème brûlée was perfect, flavours of vanilla and coffee bean dancing a bold tango across my tongue with each delicious morsel. Dom was revelling in the merriment made both by his delicious offering to me and his victory, even if he was trying his utmost to be a respectful winner. Ever the sportsman, it would seem.

"Well?" I said, preparing myself for whatever would come next. "I'm ready."

"Hmm . . . I need more time to devise my question, so you will have to wait," he informed me with delight. Perhaps not as respectful a sportsman as I had previously given him credit for.

"You're the winner; you get to decide," I said placidly before crouching down to open the ancient box of decorations and tangled white twinkle lights I had hauled down from the attic crawl space earlier in the day.

He gave me an all-too-charming grin in response.

We moved forward with trimming and decorating our lopsided tree. Dom had cut it down and brought it inside yesterday, allowing its limbs time to relax. It was short, crooked, and decidedly *Charlie Brown*. I loved it.

I was nervous what memories or visions might be borne from handling the cracked old ornaments, but surprisingly, they were only warm visions of opening presents together as a small family. The images passed quickly and left me feeling sentimental, if a bit sad. My grandmother had always safe-guarded any special occasions or holidays at her cottage, no doubt weaving her own brand of magic into the events. I did remember my mother being angry on several occasions that Gertie wouldn't welcome any of her many boyfriends into our holiday festivities. Looking back now, I was eternally grateful; no triggers here in this box of assorted holiday baubles.

Once the tree was decorated to our liking, dotted haphazardly with vintage green, red, and gold orbs throughout, plus a handful of home-made ornaments crafted by yours truly in elementary school, we settled onto the couch together to observe our good work.

Tiny white lights twinkled merrily throughout, and even though there were fewer than I would have hoped for initially—three out of five strands having burnt out some time ago—it absolutely oozed Christmas spirit.

Realistically, I could have probably lit the strands using magic, but I felt a strong intuitive sense to resist using any magic tonight to solve our problems.

I leaned back happily into the warmth his chest, his long arm wrapped around me as he stroked my thigh absently, his entire body relaxed and welcoming.

"Can I tell you a secret?" he asked, gently stroking my hair back before kissing me on the soft recess below my ear.

Heartrate rapidly rising now, I was shockingly unsure whether I would be able to divide my attention between his words and his body for much longer.

"Of course."

"I had hoped, well, wished really, that we would be in each other's arms in time for the holidays. Just like this. And with the way the curse has been going each cycle, well . . . I just really wanted to be here with you, in this moment. It feels like a miracle."

I turned to face him properly.

The effect of the low light from the tree shining on the sandy waves of his hair, along with his thick, coarse beard, made him resemble nothing short of an ancient king, conversely perched proudly atop his couch-cushion throne. I often ignored the fact that he was indeed centuries old, even if he seemed so real in our present time. And in that moment, gazing at each other in shared adoration, the cord that bonded us together throughout the centuries tightened around my heart completely; I knew then with utmost surety that, in all of my past lives, I had been utterly correct in choosing *him* every time, without fail.

Eventually the spell broke, and I smiled, heart full of new (or renewed) love, and leaned forward to kiss him purposefully. I could taste the wine and crème brûlée on his lips, his rough beard grazing my chin in contrast. I found the increased sensory influence additionally arousing. I had always had a thing for beards.

Quickly, the tide between us began to rise at the meeting and parting of our mouths, and much as waves rise with increasing enthusiasm during a storm, we were both soon silently speaking the unbridled intentions between us, as surely as the sea finds the shore. Lost in time together once more, bodies intertwined precariously on the small couch, Dom pulled me into his chest and kissed the top of my head, followed by a bearhug.

"It's *time* for my question," he said.

I breathed in his deliciously masculine scent, and placing more meaning behind the phrase than simply being ready to answer his query, I said, "Okay. I'm ready."

We sat in silence for a while, Dom suddenly pensive and clearly re-framing and re-wording whatever his query might have been.

I noticed that the familiar melody of coastal rain dancing across the metal roof was rapidly shifting to favour the loud howls of a tempestuous wind as relentlessly heavy sleet slashed harshly into the single-pane windows. The false shutters quavered with each violent gust, but our stronghold remained cozily buttoned up against the oncoming storm.

When the lights flickered momentarily, we shared a playful smile, but the tension between us was rising in perfect unison with the weather beyond the cottage, making it difficult to make light of our situation for much longer.

"I suppose you have other candles," he said practically, nodding towards the tapers on the table, which had by now, of course, burned down to their bases.

"I do . . . but that's not your question."

The power went out fully this time for several moments, and then flashed back on. At this, our music had also come to an abrupt stop, and I took this as my cue to steer our conversation, and physical location, elsewhere.

"*Oh, the weather outside is frightful . . .*" I sang festively, and stood up before him, stretching with leisure onto my tippy toes. He smiled only slightly, and I noticed that his eyes had clouded over in some sort of dreamlike state.

I was beginning to think there would *never* be a question at this rate.

Biting my lip, I held out my cool hand to grasp his much warmer one, and guided him up and away from couch, as well as from the discomfort of his internal machinations. He took my prompt without protest and rose to meet me, but his expression was still curious.

Turning silently towards the bedroom, I held his knuckles at the base of my spine and swayed my hips gently to lure him onward, not that he needed any encouragement. I could hear his breath changing, hitching, with each measured step in my wake, his baritone voice occasionally letting out soft sounds of deep longing. Perhaps it was the magic of the season, or simply the wine, but our synchronized movements towards the bedroom felt almost ethereal, as if we were walking the fine line between all of our lifetimes at once.

Crossing the threshold of the dark bedroom, the air met us in cool contrast to the warmth of the fireplace—electric baseboard heating had its limitations—and I found the effect oddly sobering as my senses sharpened. Immediately, I could smell the lingering scents from the evening's dinner, slight whiffs of salmon and cooked onions having settled comfortably into the cool recesses of the home. My mind wandered to where the emergency candles could be found, and whether or not the roof leak would hold against a storm of this magnitude.

Focus, Julia, I thought loudly, suddenly nervous.

Dom had regained control of his station just in time and was already angling his body between me and the bed. He could read me like one of his favourite books and steadied me against his powerful frame to keep me connected to the moment.

"Julia . . ." he said, brushing my hair slowly back from my face, the warmth of his fingertips a delicious contrast to the cool air of the bedroom.

He continued to run his fingers through my hair in a rhythmic motion, kissing me gently along my jawline, his lips flickering across my own in sweet, gentle passes.

"Mmm?" I said, pushing into his palms like a greedy cat; I loved when he touched and played with my hair, and even more so when he kissed me *just so.*

"Can I ask you . . ." he paused, and I looked up into his dimly lit face, which had taken on a sort of angelic quality. I waited, shivers running down my spine at his touch. "Can I ask you . . . to be mine? Only mine?"

I laughed in spite of myself. Was he honestly worried about *fidelity?*

"I already am . . . aren't I?"

His face remained serious, and he took a deep breath. "I mean . . . will you take *me.* To be yours, and yours alone?"

"Are you asking me to marry you?"

I had half expected this. He had done his best to adapt to the modern world, but certain beliefs and habits were sure to arise in undertaking certain intimate acts.

"Oh, no, no! That's not what I mean. We don't need to be married, not yet anyways. I mean, it's not that I *don't* want to be, I do . . . and we already were . . . are . . . anyways . . ."

He took another moment to steady himself.

I waited.

In the past, this would have been my cue to run, but this man already had my heart and soul in his full possession. In fact, I was shocked to feel my heart beginning to beat in excitement at the prospect of a civil union for the first time in this entire life. But we were clearly getting ahead of ourselves once more.

"I mean that, I just want to ask you if *you* truly want this. Us. All of it. I can't help but feel sometimes that our union is condemning you to your own death. You don't have to do this you know. You could walk away from it all. Maybe that's why you don't remember much of our past anymore. Maybe it means we aren't supposed to meet anymore . . . maybe . . ."

I could sense a concerted effort growing behind his stiffening jaw as he tried to stop himself from either shaking, or crying, or screaming. Perhaps all three. He suddenly seemed terrified at my response, frozen in time—in *all* of our time, together. I blushed in spite of it all. Most honourably, he was doing his best to consider my role in all of this, at his own pain and personal determent, which only made me love him more deeply than ever before.

"Domhnall, stop."

It was my turn for a breath, but I felt surprisingly steady, all things considered. I placed my hand on his cheek. Another deep sense of déjà vu had arrived, but my inner fire crackled in some wholly new formulation, telling me that this time it was different; this wasn't the first time we had uttered a private vow of commitment to one another, but somehow, this time . . . it was still completely new.

And he was giving me an out.

As unfathomably painful as it was for him, he was offering us both truthful honesty around all that this relationship could, and would, entail. The risks, the rewards, the potential for loss, and the tentative promises of a real future. And that my opinion, my autonomy, mattered. He was asking for my affirmative consent.

I continued, placing all the truth and reassurance I possessed onto each word.

"I *am* yours, and yours alone. I can't imagine wanting anything more in this world than this life with you. I don't know what this next turn around the wheel of time means for us, and I think you're right, something *is* wholly different. But I do know that there is no part of me that wishes to do this without you. I've never been so sure of anything before, in *any* of my lifetimes."

He stood now, looking deeply into my eyes, still suspended in the moment as his jaw clenched tighter yet. Suddenly, I felt very vulnerable. This was a *much* bigger question than I had anticipated.

I continued. "For the first time in . . . well, in this life, I know where I am supposed to be. And who I am supposed to be with, if not when or where." I cleared my throat, which had become raspy and dry. "But . . . do *you?* Want this?"

And then it was as if the spell of the moment had been shattered into a thousand tiny crystalline pieces, his body replying with a massive shiver of relief.

"As if that's even a question."

It was then that his walls came crashing down before me, and at long last, I opened myself to him fully in turn.

Unable to contain his hunger for me any longer, he pulled my hips forcibly towards his and uttered a deep mingled sound of relief and anticipated pleasure as he pushed his lips firmly onto mine. He was as solid as a brick house, but that didn't mean he wasn't tender. Never had I ever felt so safe, and so protected, and so loved beyond measure.

The storm outside was banging in its climax, winds ripping past the cottage at unearthly speeds, causing the whole structure to shake and bang in its wake. A door slammed upstairs, some gusty draft making its way through the upper bedrooms in earnest.

We were suddenly frantic then too, wrapped up in the energy of the storm and our own overflowing desires at long last. We stood facing one another in the middle of the room, ripping off clothing at an inhuman speed.

Then, with a bright surge followed by a flicker and what felt like a deep sigh by the cottage itself, the power finally went out.

Still riding on the coattails of passionate haste, I flung my arm mindlessly in the direction of the varied candles placed in their usual vantage points around the room, igniting them with mindless ease. My earlier worries seemed so miniscule then; of course, we had an excess of candles. This *was* a Witch's home after all.

Another spell cast over us then, as if arriving on the wings of the storm itself.

Standing there, goosebumps raised on my air-chilled body, it was in that moment that I finally, truly, saw him. Raw and open and so beautifully vulnerable. Destiny would have her say at long last, and we would do our best to fucking listen.

He was impossibly perfect, still every bit the Celtic prince I'd fallen in love with more than a millennium ago. He stood before me, drawn up to his full warrior height, chin raised in full acknowledgement of the battle that stood before of us, fully prepared for the weight of what this moment *truly* meant between us. He was undeniable, and I knew intuitively why both the forces of destiny and the Goddess herself had taken him into her fold; he was practically Godlike in his own right and demanded notice from anyone who stood within his gaze.

In the same breath, I witnessed his modern-day rendition, the one who had *truly* drawn me in, this present version of myself. I thought of the kind creases beside his eyes when he smiled, and the ease with which he fell into fits of mirthful laughter when we were together. This very man, who strove to embrace and embody change, despite his own seemingly fixed story in time.

Welcoming and full of light, he was a safe harbour to come home to as I explored the rough seas of my own lived experience. Better yet, he was a shipmate, a co-captain, more than willing to ride the waves alongside me as they came. I had always imagined I was capable of doing this life on my own, and I was, but it was all the more wonderful to share it with one such as he. I was indeed a ship meant to sail, but what better way to go through life than alongside the perfect complement to your soul?

He was a culmination of all his parts and stories; the good, the bad, and the ugly. But standing here, he was about as far from ugly as one could possibly perceive. All muscle and tendon and limbs, long lines and capable movements. Perfection. I could tell by the look on his face that he was processing a similar internal dialogue, and I blushed, deeply in wonder at what he could possibly be thinking about me in that very moment.

Gently now, he led me onto the bed. And, at long last, we met together, sum parts to the whole of our shared destiny. His entry into me felt like a homecoming. I let out a deep moan of my own pleasure and a centuries-old relief.

He was dreamily slow at first, and I drank in every vigorous thrust, my own body responding with transcendent feminine rhythm. Soon, everything around me blurred, but this was no vision. All I could see now was him, in this very moment, and the magic created between us was the light, beacon, and advent of something far greater than anything we had ever imagined before.

Dom's pace quickened, and in moments, the chill in the room was negligible compared to the steadily growing heat between us. His movements were precise now, powerfully charged as he drove the depths of his loneliness, loss, and eternal love hard into my soul.

When we finally reached our climax, the fire within me was lit to an inferno.

I cried out in unison with his deep howl, and when he finally shuddered into me, pressing down his weight at last, I couldn't recall a moment where I'd felt closer to divinity.

After a time, I kissed his shoulder gently, the residual sweat of exertion salty on my lips.

"I love you."

He buried his face into my own hair once more, before pushing back and rolling onto his side, tucked close to me still.

"I love you, too," he said, and closed his eyes as pure peace settled across his brow.

CHAPTER 20

As is the custom, the lapse of time between Christmas Day and New Year's Eve felt like a strange food-fueled time suck. I assured Dom it was entirely usual to be busy all day but feel like you've done absolutely nothing and to fill your face with Christmas chocolates and leftovers to compensate for the profound effects of the unusual holiday limbo.

"Don't get me wrong, I'm *absolutely* pleased about the excess of food . . . and the sex," he said with a cheeky grin, "but I'm also starting to feel a bit squirrelly."

"Here, have some nuts then!" I said, and tossed a half empty bag of candied cashews towards him, which he obediently held up to his chest, positively squirrel-like.

I was working on cleaning out the fridge and pantry, and Dom was doing his part by polishing off anything I threw his way.

He wasn't wrong though. I was also anxious to get packing and be on our way to Ireland, and since we had tied up most of the loose ends for our departure well before Christmas, we were mostly just lying in wait until it was time for take-off.

Dom started to take long runs each day to manage his pent-up energy, but I didn't share the same need for movement, not *that* kind at any rate. He seemed to have endless stamina, but perhaps that was the warrior in him, always with a mind towards training to some degree.

When the time came to finally decamp the cottage, I felt surprisingly bereft to be leaving it behind. It had always been my home away from home, but now it was so much more than that. Bill would take good care of it while we were gone, of course, and I could decide next steps when the time felt right. Time, after all, had taken on a whole new meaning these days.

Between the money I held in savings, as well as the equity in the house, I felt relatively stable on a practical front. The mortgage was long since paid, so I simply had to consider property taxes and its upkeep, which would be easily covered by the small sum of life insurance Gertie had left to me in my name. I laughed at the memory of the birthday cards she would receive each year from her insurance provider with a five-dollar scratch ticket inside; something about it had always felt so humorously macabre.

Dom had also assured me during our trip planning that he, or rather *we*, had plenty of money set aside, in addition to a modest and comfortable home located somewhere in the West Irish countryside.

"Don't worry, Julia, we're all set," he said with a wink. "Not to mention, the money's accumulated considerable interest over the past century."

"Isn't that cheating somehow?" I asked.

"Of course not," he puffed out his chest in jest. "Plus, we *are* working for the greater good. It's honest income by all accounts."

I wasn't entirely sure how I felt about combining our assets, as I had been accustomed to managing my own finances since I'd started my very first job at fourteen. My mother had been grateful when I'd begun to accumulate my own pocket change. I had taken it with great pride of person when I was able to eventually purchase my very own car at sixteen: a "Rio Red" Subaru Justy, with only *minor* rust damage (I was quite proud to add). Plus, it was cheap on gas, so it had that going for it too.

Dom had insisted he pay for the flights, as well as any transportation between the cottage and the airport.

"I'm the one dragging you off to Ireland after all!" he said, "And I've got a surprise arranged for us on the other side, but I'm not giving you any clues. So, don't even ask!"

"I'm intrigued!" I said as I threw in what I hoped was the final load of laundry before we left; we had gone through several sets of sheets since the events on Christmas Eve.

Since Dom had barely unpacked in the first place, he was prepared for our departure long before I was. I was actually struggling slightly in that regard. Doing my best to bring only the essentials, I also knew we would be somewhat isolated for a time and didn't want to forget anything that I *might* need on short notice. Regardless, I needed to pack light.

"Unfortunately, we'll have to stay in hiding for a time, at least until we get a sense of what Cassius is up to. If the convergence of the dark forces around Vancouver are any indication, he's no doubt got a sense of where you might be now."

I shivered nervously at the notion. "So, he will probably be tracking us?"

"Not necessarily tracking. I have a hunch your protection magic will be helpful on that front anyway. But he's addicted to control. He will want to know if you've moved, and the rough location of your new whereabouts."

The weather near Galway sounded remarkably similar to the West Coast of Canada, so thankfully my wardrobe wouldn't need any updating; sturdy boots, a solid raincoat, and warm sweaters were already my usual armament against the forces of nature.

After some debate, we decided it was likely safest to bring along the quilt as a carry-on, even if it might raise some eyebrows in its unusual makeup. While we doubted anyone would actually *steal* it from our checked baggage, largely due to its own protective qualities, we also couldn't risk it being lost in transit.

I was surprised to discover, upon booking our flights, that Dom actually held dual Irish and Canadian citizenship.

"I did tell you we've been married before," he said sheepishly.

"Oh, and let me guess, you had one of your pals doctor up the passports to catch you up to the times?" I grinned at him.

"Well, that part was easy. We have connections in most of the commonwealth intelligence agencies. But aren't you curious about *how* I got my Canadian citizenship in the first place?"

What started out as a delightful tale about a rather brazen trip to the courthouse together in the late 1960s quickly devolved into a much more *physical* re-telling by Dom about what had occurred proceeding the more formal aspects of the matter.

Yes, he had definitely earned his Canadian citizenship.

Finally seated together on a red-eye routed from Vancouver through Iceland, we would eventually be touching-down in Dublin sometime around mid-morning. Dom, it would seem, was a bit of a nervous flyer, but as he was so adept at napping almost anywhere and in any position, he turned to sleep as a coping mechanism. Lucky bastard.

True to form, I barely slept. Dozing off and on, I committed myself to listening to an entire audiobook on condensed Irish history. Unfortunately, the delivery medium failed to jog any of my past memories and mostly left me with a feeling of embarrassment around how little I actually knew about my ancestral home.

Groggily arriving at customs, Dom and I quietly stumbled through the usual rigmarole of declarations, slower, perhaps, than he was used to since my passport didn't mark me as a member of the EU.

"We're going to have to do something about that," he said, pulling me close into a one-arm hug as we moved slowly forward in the queue. I wasn't sure if he meant having one of his people arrange an Irish passport for me, or if that meant *actually* getting married. I was pretty sure that required having permanently resided together for more than three or four weeks, but since they had already somehow magicked up a three-month travel visa for me, I had my suspicions there was a likely solution somewhere.

At long last, we stepped out into the early morning air, gratefully leaving behind the hustle and bustle of the busy international airport. Taking a deep breath, I marvelled at how powerful the initial scent of a new place could be, realizing at once that it was certainly enough to imprint a sensory memory. Or perhaps, to trigger one.

I paused, curious about any potential feelings or visions while closing my eyes momentarily.

"Surprise!" Dom said, gesturing proudly towards the road. I jumped slightly, jolted from my brief reality break.

A soft-top, signal-red MGB Roadster sat beside the curb, no doubt a delivery from one of his varied connections. Dom assured me that this particular vehicle was the favourite in his possession, and more than essential for our next adventure. I watched as he tipped the valet handsomely, all the while eyeing the car scrupulously for damage.

"How many cars *do* you own then?" I asked, impressed by the sheer cheek of the little red number. I didn't know a lot about old sports cars, but Dom was already proving that he would be providing me with a crash course whether I liked it or not.

"Oh, a few," he said vaguely with a wave of his hand.

The grin spreading across his face betrayed his casual air, and I was more than curious to know what other vehicles I would have the pleasure of becoming acquainted with over the coming weeks.

After popping our few items of luggage into the surprisingly roomy trunk that contained naught but a spare tire, Dom helped me with the sticky metal door handle on the passenger side. After an awkward twist of his elbow to open and close the door, I sank into the low-slung leather seat.

"Takes some getting used to, being so low to the ground, but you're going to love it," he assured me, scarcely hiding his pride.

I smiled up at him with assurance as I fussed with the tricky seatbelt. "I'm sure I will."

The initiation to his favourite car felt a little bit like a test, and since I wasn't sensing any remnant visions or sensations indicating I had sat in this particular car, it would have to be trial by fire. On that account, I pledged to think of any unexpected memories that might pop up during the journey as little notes or keepsakes that I had left for my future self. I would do my best to welcome any visions as a sort of "Coles Notes" version of our life that might help me out in the future.

Dom walked with a definite spring in his step as he rounded the artistically designed back end of the car with unabashed enthusiasm. I couldn't imagine how a man of his stature would sit comfortably in a vehicle so small. I was soon freed from my wonder as he slid gracefully into the driver's seat, his long legs accommodated with ease by the sheer length of the driveshaft.

"Bigger on the inside," he said with a wink as he popped the key into the ignition, which was almost solitary on the silver keychain but for a leather tag with a plastic MG insignia.

"Where are we headed then, Doctor?" I said in my best Yorkshire accent.

He chuckled, eyebrow raised. "Where? Or *when?*"

The *Doctor Who* reference wasn't lost on either of us, and I smiled broadly, appreciating the familiar ease we had settled into since our time at Gertie's cottage.

On the open road at last, we were soon tripping gracefully through the Irish countryside in our right-hand-drive classic sports car; its slipstream trailing behind as we rocketed towards Dom's country home on the western coast of Ireland. It felt like a dream. Reminding me surprisingly of the Prairies, a broad expanse of open sky welcomed us as we traversed the busy highway westward, the land beckoning us into her arms with hospitable ease.

Having flown all night, my face bore the oily remnants of not enough air shared with too many people in what was essentially a tin can propelled through space. Dom wasn't entirely wrong in being a bit leery about flying.

I unrolled my window with some effort, the rolling crank yet another aspect of this voyage that required a bit of finesse to get right. Poking my head out into the morning air, my hair whipped around my face aggressively as our brisk highway pace made it practically impossible to tolerate the moment for long.

"It's a bit cool to put the top down just yet," Dom commented as he gave the gas a good punch, engine purring with pleasure to his urgings onward. He was now wearing a pair of vintage club-master-style sunglasses, horn-rimmed in tortoiseshell with a subtle gold rim around the lens. How did he always manage to look so effortlessly cool?

"That's okay. I just wanted to smell the air," I replied. I realised in hindsight that it was a bit of a strange thing to say, but he didn't seem to notice.

In fact, it would seem Dom was experiencing a similar magic as the familiarities of home welcomed him like a warm blanket. He smiled intermittently, noticing some familiar landmark or acknowledging a memory floating through his thoughts with peaceful pleasure. I thought briefly of the quilt rolled up in my carry-on luggage in the trunk but pushed the memory aside for more present matters.

"You're happy to be home," I said, shifting my body in the slippery seat to face him a little bit more directly.

He nodded in agreement and turned the wheel with enthusiasm as we rounded yet another bend, down-shifting gracefully through the gears as if he could anticipate each upcoming turn with his eyes closed.

I found myself torn between the excitement of viewing the new-to-these-eyes countryside and an ever-mounting desire to take in the raw sight of him instead. The soft waves of his sandy hair were swept back as gracefully as ever in his distinct devil-may-care style as the chilly morning wind rustled through a gap in the window. His slightly overlong nose and thick but short cropped facial hair were the perfect frame for his full lips. Those very lips that had already done plenty of travelling over, under, and across my own landscape during the past week.

Goddess help me. I was positively besotted with this man, and there was no turning back.

Dom must have noticed my increasingly amorous glances and did a quick double take in my direction before signalling to pull off the main road.

"Can I help you?" he asked, a devilish grin spreading across his angelic face.

I gulped. The wanting, which I had expected to fizzle slightly once we finally had full physical knowledge of one another in this life, had not waned. In fact, it was mounting each day with an increasing fervor, my inner fire stoked at even the slightest glance my way.

"Not sure. I think I might be a goner," I said, blood rushing to my lips and cheeks as I greedily drank in more of his presence with my eyes.

The clear connection between this love and the increase in my own magic was far too symbiotic an occurrence to dismiss. I needed him like I needed the air I breathed, and my magic relied on my willingness to be open to the powers of love, vulnerability, and fate.

"Oh? That can't be good," he said. He quickly snapped the car off the motorway and onto a side road, hastily placing the car in park and unbuckling his own seatbelt with matched urgency. I had no idea where we were, and I didn't care.

The size of the car was increasingly becoming an issue, however, as we struggled to meet somewhere in the middle, hands and lips locked in frantic exploration all over again. The smell of leather and rich engine oil mingled exotically with our own unique lustful scents; the effect was nothing short of intoxicating.

The gear shift dug into Dom's thigh as he struggled to remove his sweater, broad back pressing into the convertible's soft top. He swore colourfully under his breath.

"Should have taken the top down after all!"

He silenced me with a forceful kiss, hands first grasping me by the hips, and then travelling more enthusiastically still up the back of my sweater, unclasping my bra with adept precision. What followed included dragging his fingers around my ribs in an act of pure need before cupping my breasts, stroking my raised nipples with his thumbs.

"God, I feel like I'm in rut," he said, his eyes were indeed taking on the signature dark hue of a dominant stag, pheromones surging and nostrils flaring as he looked down to me.

I responded in kind, heart racing and hormones rushing to the surface as I welcomed the oncoming storm. He could have me here, there, or everywhere as far as I was concerned. My sensibilities had taken leave willingly, as I couldn't remember any point in my life where I'd felt more alive than when I was entangled with this ancient Celt.

It was in that moment that there was a slight tap on the window, and we both jumped, hitting our respective heads, mine on the doorframe and his on the rear-view mirror.

"Sorry, but you can't park here!" the voice of the woman came from somewhere behind us as she crunched away on the gravel, all too easily heard through the soft top. I looked out the window to see that she was already retreating to the roadside café she had wandered out from, a no-parking sign sitting clearly beside our very much parked vehicle. She was obviously expecting her early morning breakfast crowd and that did *not* include us.

Dom burst out into booming laugher and slumped back into his own seat, hitting the horn on the steering wheel with his ample behind on the way down.

"Jesus!" he said, shaking his head.

"Didn't you look where you were parking?" I said, blushing deep crimson and meeting his mirth with my own embarrassed chortle.

I snorted in spite of myself, which made him laugh harder still. It was very much like trying to have sex in a tent when others were camping nearby, that awkward moment that comes when you are reminded that the thin walls only serve as a visual barrier, doing nothing to stifle the sound.

"Oh yes, but you seemed to have more pressing matters to discuss, and I know you hate when I tell you no," he said, scolding me for my evident indiscretions.

"Really," I replied, eyebrows raised as I gestured with my chin toward the bulge in his light-blue jeans. "My most sincere apologies, good sir."

He greeted my gaze with the most heart-melting smile, grey-blue eyes crinkling with unbelievable sweetness. I had mused, as of late, that he must have gotten away with almost everything as a child with a smile like that, and this was no exception.

Dom gestured towards the road as he righted himself in the driver's seat. "We really should keep going though. Morgan will be waiting for us with the dogs. And besides, I would far prefer to shift you without a steering wheel digging into my arse."

The residual broad smile across his face was evidence of his continued amusement at my embarrassment for being caught out like a pair of teenagers necking on the proverbial lover's lane.

"I am never so happy as I am when I'm with you, Julia. Truly. There's never a dull moment," he said, shaking his head, white teeth gleaming through the joy of his smile.

I reached across the car and gently patted his thigh much like patting a dog atop its head after performing a particularly good trick. "I'm glad I can be a source of entertainment for you."

"It's really the only reason why I've kept you around all these years," he responded, ducking to the right to avoid the impact of my oncoming playful smack to his shoulder.

"Always a ham!"

"I am hungry, now that you mention it. Hopefully Morgan has already stocked the pantry."

I rolled my eyes internally at his constant hunger, but I still had more pressing questions about the elusive Morgan, as well as Dom's country farm-house. Indeed, it was sounding more and more like something considerably larger than the secluded, rustic stone house on the hill I had pictured.

"You haven't told me much about Morgan. Who is she?" I asked, wondering (not for the first time) about the generations of people who had been enlisted to maintain his varied estates over the centuries, often during his absence from this earthly plane.

"Morgan is a he and lives in my gatehouse. Morgan is his family surname though, so sometimes Morgan *is* a woman. Depends on the year, or decade, really."

Gatehouse?

My suspicions about the size and value of Dom's current estate were becoming clearer with each passing kilometre. The countryside opened up before us while the roads had significantly narrowed. Soon, there were fewer individual roadside structures and farmsteads and more of what looked like large land holdings; we were travelling to where the back roads stopped, it would seem. Towards home.

After passing through a toll stop, we travelled for another twenty minutes in easy silence, Dom slipping in comments here and there about significant landmarks or cute farm animals gathered happily, munching grass between low stone fences. With our wheels continuously in motion, they mirrored my thoughts as we hurtled towards the next chapter in our story.

Without question, I knew that I would more than likely encounter bewitched items and memory-bound mementos dotted throughout the estate home once we entered, but for some reason, the closer we got, the more anxious I felt about it. My positive resolve from earlier was fast fading, and I was suddenly worried about the potential magical onslaught ahead.

That, or perhaps I was just hungry like Dom.

I rubbed my chilled fingers and clammy palms on my jeans, noticing a slight change in Dom's posture as well as we pulled off the main road and onto a narrow tree-lined country lane.

"Are we getting close?" I asked, straightening in my seat, black leather creaking beneath my quite-numb butt and thighs. I would certainly welcome a chance to get out and stretch my legs soon.

Dom pushed his sunglasses atop his head and leaned forward, squinting heartily as if to see the world more clearly as we approached what was quickly revealing itself to be a vast estate.

"Very."

Turning left, we passed through a fairly unassuming set of wrought-iron gates, wide open in what I assumed was anticipation of our arrival. I held my breath momentarily, but still, no memories were jogged.

Soon, we were scooting past a modest white Victorian-era gatehouse surrounded by climbing roses that were supported by faded lattice and a low black metal fence.

"That's where Morgan stays when I'm home. I've offered him one of the greater cottages on the estate, but he always says he prefers to be closest to the frontline," Dom told me in passing. "Ronan figures it's probably because he prefers the proximity to the pub in the village."

I looked at him, jaw dropping in disbelief. "One of the *greater* cottages?"

"Well, he stays in the servant's quarters of the manor house when I'm not here. It's not like he's *that* cramped for space all the time."

"Servants quarters?" I echoed, no longer hiding any incredulity. "Okay, so you may have left out a few details when you said we would be staying at your . . . what did you call it? Modest farm estate?"

"Oh, Julia. You're reading too far into this. It just wasn't important to elaborate further. It's just a house. We still eat, sleep, and shit in there, you know?" he said, his levity faltering at the look on my face.

The car slowed as he diverted his attention from the road towards me.

"Oh, love. Come now. It's your home too, remember? Give it a chance."

"I have no doubt I'll like it. I just feel underdressed and ill prepared for the world of a prince."

I looked down at my battered boots and faded black jeans and muttered under my breath. "Servants . . ."

"I'm hardly a prince in modern times," he said, cranking the steering wheel around another bend. "And I don't have servants. Morgan and his family are employed by the estate to manage my affairs while I'm away. That's all. I cook my own eggs for breakfast, for God's sake."

As if that settled things. A million questions were exploding inside my head, but I was learning quickly that Dom answered any pressing inquiries better with a satiated stomach and a recumbent form. As neither were currently the case, I trusted my own instincts that this would be a discussion best suited for later.

A pristine lake had presented itself in front of us, and just beyond, I could see a grassy slope that led up to the looming form of an eighteenth-century Georgian manor house. Several deer were grazing peacefully in front of the vine-covered façade, the central rounded turret sticking out slightly from its large rectangular footprint.

An exhale through my teeth was all I could muster verbally in the moment.

Dom, for his part, was practically vibrating in anticipation, tapping his fingers in delight on the wood-grain steering wheel.

"I can't wait to see my dogs!"

His heart-melting smile was as contagious as ever, and to my surprise, I felt excitement building within my own being, not just for the dogs but also to greet the place Dom so affectionately called home.

As we rounded the lake and approached the drive, the deep-burgundy front door swung open unceremoniously, followed by three blurred and charging dogs of varying sizes, now exploding towards the sportscar.

"Oh God, they're going to scratch the paint!" Dom yelped as he slammed the car into park in the middle of the driveway and hopped out of the driver's seat at breakneck speed.

He greeted his furry companions in a rolling ball of wagging tails and lapping tongues as they sprawled across the grass. The image was perhaps the most crushingly heartwarming thing I had ever seen.

I was no stranger to dogs, but it had been years since I had owned one of my own. As a child, we'd had an English cocker spaniel named Ginger who was both clever and naughty in equal measure. In high school, I'd adopted an aging chocolate lab cross named Bruce from the humane society who had a short but fulfilling life with me as his companion.

These dogs, however, were new to me and overfull of wild canine energy. Animals bore a special kind of magic, and even at this proximity, I felt a wave of raw power in their presence. I was no stranger to this aspect of the Witch's familiar, and took heart that Dom was an animal lover. I had a hard time trusting people who didn't like dogs.

"Oh, you are good doggies, you are! I missed you! I did!" Dom was saying on repeat as he scratched behind each dog's ear in turn, as each of them lapped kisses onto every exposed inch of skin they could find.

With some difficulty, I opened the creaking antique door to the convertible, leaving it open behind me for fear of damaging it upon its closure. Crunching across the packed gravel driveway, I loped towards Dom and his playmates, enjoying the view immensely.

A medium-sized blond terrier with a messy beard heard my approach and bounded gleefully towards me, bouncing up on his hind legs and slamming his front paws onto my thighs.

"Hello you!" I said, steadying the licking dog back towards the ground, following the move with a scratch behind his ears just as Dom had done.

The dog coiled himself behind my legs with a wiggle and was soon back in front of me, jumping up again for another greeting. Clearly, he was the kind of dog who took great pleasure in having company and had little self-restraint. Frankly, he was the perfect match for Dom.

"That scallywag is Sully, and that's what they call the 'wheaten greetin'!'" he said as he clamoured back onto his own two feet and walked towards me.

Meanwhile, I was unsuccessfully wiping muddy paw prints from my jeans.

"Sorry about that," Dom said as the other two dogs followed suit to their fuzzy pack member, though neither jumped up.

Oisín was Dom's Irish wolfhound, whose long and elegant form glided towards me with an ancient grace I recognized from some foggy memories of days past. This was certainly the dog of a Celtic prince, and I was in awe of his sheer size as he leaned up against me for his own turn at scratches behind the ears. His greyish coat was surprisingly rough to the touch, but his eyes were soft and wise.

"Mags is a bit skittish with new people, but she'll warm up to you. Especially if you give her oranges," he said in reference to the third dog, a beautiful reddish-chestnut-coloured Irish setter.

"Oranges?" I asked, taking care not to startle her as she paced nervously nearby, just out of reach.

"She's a bit of a weird one. She also has a penchant for stealing bread off the counter when you're not looking."

"It's okay, sweetie. I like carbs too. We can have a snack later," I said, passively extending my hand to let her steal a few cautious sniffs as she went by.

Dom stepped directly in front of me now, arms wrapped protectively around my waist as he pulled me in close for a kiss.

"Really though, Julia. Welcome home."

CHAPTER 21

om had apparently acquired the home in significant disrepair during the early 1960s from the Irish Tourist Board. He had subsequently poured himself into its reparation as a means of distracting himself from the agony of waiting to find me once more. Allegedly, it had been a bit of a foolish investment at the time, but from where I stood today, it looked spectacular.

In a flight of passion, he had boldly renamed it *"Caisleán na Spéirmhná,"* with its original name being far too English for his preference.

"The last bit translates to 'sky woman,'" he said, suddenly blushing deep crimson. "I actually named it for you. For your beauty . . . As fair as the sky."

This was indeed the most romantic thing anyone had ever done for me, at least in my current memory. But on the other hand, it felt *well* above my station as I looked down embarrassed at my rough travel clothes and the fresh collection of muddy dog pawprints on my pant legs.

As for its status as a castle, this seemed to be a nod towards the more traditional nomenclature used in the region, the Irish far preferring to use this term over more English words like hall or court. However, I knew already that my comfortability around referring to my own home as a castle was practically non-existent.

"I don't know what to say," I said, taking my own turn to blush. "It's incredible."

I decided then to refer to it, at least in my head, as the manor house, since that sounded slightly less frivolous to me.

The interior of the home was set to be even more impressive than the outside. From what I could gather from my vantage at the front entrance, it seemed to be outfitted in an eclectic mix of pristine period furniture and artwork, intermingled with some cleverly chosen mid-century modern pieces, all of which had been dutifully maintained by the Morgan family for decades.

I noticed with some trepidation that the interior was *also* outfitted with a crushing sense of déjà vu; I had definitely been here before, whether or not I remembered any specific events.

The mysterious Morgan stood waiting patiently for us just inside the doorway, stepping aside and already prepared to avoid the flurry of dogs surrounding Dom and myself as we lumbered in. He was a shorter fellow, adorned from head to toe in a mix of brown tweed and wool and wearing a pair of smart rubber boots. Dom strode forward confidently to greet him with the professional kindness attributed to one well accustomed to being the master of the house.

"Morgan! Good to see you, man. The cold weather hasn't been too hard on your joints this winter, I hope?" Dom asked, grasping his housekeeper's outstretched hand with thoughtful consideration to what seemed to be the beginnings of arthritis, judging by the knobbed knuckles clutched around the moss green cap in his left hand.

"Keeping well enough. Nothing to report. Well, the dogs have been a bloody handful," he replied grumpily in his thick country accent, but something about his tone told me he was actually *quite* fond of the dogs.

Dom was attempting to convince Oisín to follow the other dogs to the kitchen for a drink of water, with the wagging tails of Sully and Mags already rounding the corner ahead, but the regal dog was determined to remain by Dom's side for the immediate future. Clearly, this particular creature carried a piece of Dom's heart.

"Pantry's stocked, and your rooms upstairs should be plenty warm by the time you're ready for bed. I haven't opened up all of the guest rooms just yet, or the dining and sitting rooms, what with the fact we won't be expecting visitors for another week or so."

Visitors. *Right.*

I had momentarily forgotten how quickly we would be welcoming the oncoming hoard of Druids and other allies to our shadowed cause. When Dom first told me of the plan, I had felt quite frustrated, strangely sensitive about not being considered in the details before he'd extended the invitation to the others.

In my heart, I wished fervently to spend the next several weeks getting to know Dom on his terms, and in his own space. While my magic was still steadily re-awakening within me, it felt inexplicably tied to my relationship to this ancient prince, and my instinct was that we still needed time to find each other before diving in headlong to a foretold path of destiny. On top of that, I was also silently hoping that, during the time spent in the comforts of his home, I could maybe learn a little bit more about our lives together *before*.

"That's excellent, Morgan. Can I give you a lift back down to the gate-house?" Dom asked routinely.

"Oh, no. I like the walk. If that will be all then?"

Dom answered with a courteous smile and nod, and soon Morgan was gone, crunching methodically down the drive, cap placed back onto his mottled grey head. He reminded me a lot of my neighbour Bill back on Salt Spring. Kind, but clearly the kind of gentleman who preferred frank discussion that dove straight to the heart of the matter.

Dom trotted out behind Morgan to retrieve the car, door still agape from my awkward exit, and pulled it up to front door with haste. He had insisted that he grab our luggage himself, and while normally I would protest, I was quickly realizing how unbelievably exhausted I was.

Somewhat unsure what to do next, I waited quietly in the broad doorway, absently scratching the great wolf of a dog behind his ears. He leaned in affectionately, and I suddenly felt immense gratitude for his presence.

I knew that long ago, before the European Witch hunts of the sixteenth and seventeenth century, animals were believed to have much more agency than they did even today. No wonder the persecuted Witches were disallowed their relationships with animals during this dark era. There was a great power hidden within all creatures, not least of all those who endeavoured to spend their time cohabitating with humans on a daily basis.

On cue, Gertie's words entered into my thoughts with their familiar warmth as I attempted to ground myself in the situation. *"Never underestimate your familiars, Julia. Even the chickens scratching in the garden can lend us magic when we have need of it!"*

Dom strode confidently up the front step, and true to form, he had transported all of our bags in a single trip.

"He'll warm up to you, just wait," he said, gesturing his chin in the general direction of the gatehouse as he set all our bags on the floor with a clatter. "His family has always been incredibly loyal to the O'Briens, and we have what you could call a 'don't ask, don't tell' policy, built on decades of trust. And besides, you're one of us."

Oisín swished his long tail back and forth at the sight of Dom finally returning to the old house and closing the latch as if now that he was inside it was his cue that things would soon be back to normal. I couldn't imagine what it had been like for the great beast to be separated from Dom for so long, and I could almost taste the relief in the air as he tamped his paws on the ground a few times as if to say, *"Hurry up! I'm thirsty,"* clearly parched but only willing to indulge once his master was settled.

Dom gestured his hand in the direction of the hall leading to the kitchen, and his loyal hound happily trotted off in the direction of the other dogs.

To my surprise, the kitchen was smaller and more welcoming than expected, although I'm not sure what I *had* expected. I was certainly no master of eighteenth-century architecture. A long and well-worn wooden table stood in the middle of the room with a cracked stoneware bowl filled with apples set in its centre. Several newspapers were strewn about, and I could detect notes of relatively fresh pipe-smoke, presumably remnants of Morgan's occupancy only moments before our arrival.

I noticed with pleasure that there was also a steaming pot of tea wrapped in a quilted cozy set on a sideboard near the door with two clean porcelain teacups set out invitingly beside it. I was beginning to like this Morgan character more and more.

The dogs had settled themselves in front of a deep yet practical hearth fireplace along the outer wall; evidently this was *their* domain. Across from the mantle, a large stainless-steel gas range stood in front of a shiny, black-tiled wall. I assumed this was an upgrade from the kitchen's original layout, but it still bore that well-used quality that said it wasn't new to this decade, or even to the last.

"I hope he was able to get everything on my list," Dom spoke into the large pantry, eyes crinkled in overblown scrutiny. "Looks full at any rate."

The pantry was more like a long room off the main kitchen, which housed shelves for non-perishables as well as an older walk-in fridge with a large stainless-steel door, obviously another upgrade over the past century. I noticed another shorter wooden door with a padlock that I assumed must just be more storage, or something that had once led to a cellar. I wasn't surprised in the least that the kitchen had been retrofitted over the years to meet the emergent culinary needs of a hungry Celt.

Reaching my arms above my head into a long stretch, I was surprised at how low the ceiling was in the room. I shuddered as my arms dropped down to my sides, and I stifled a yawn. I was both hungry and exhausted in equal measure and could feel a familiar chill creeping into my bones.

"Hmm. I think I'll need a snack and a nap. In that order," I said, taking stock of my steadily lowering blood sugar and eying the pantry. "Sorry."

Dom reappeared with a loaf of French bread tucked under one arm and a carton of eggs and a stick of gold-wrapped butter from the cooler in the other.

"That can be arranged," he said, backing out of the pantry, flashing me a broad smile as he waggled the butter in my direction. "Irish butter is the best."

It was a statement of fact, no doubt, and I accepted his authority on the matter without discussion. I watched sleepily as he grabbed a small cast-iron skillet from a hanging pot rack along the way to the range. Soon enough, the smell of gas, hot butter, and fried eggs filled the room.

Busying myself in the mindless work of toasting our bread, I noticed that the blond terrier, Sully, had quietly risen from his resting spot by the fire and was nosing me from under the long table.

"Oh, you like butter, do you?" I asked him, knowing full well that was *exactly* what he was after.

For some reason I loved dogs with bad manners, and so with Dom's back still turned to the stove, I slipped the mooching dog a little tab of the golden butter, which he took gratefully.

"Sully's got no shame," Dom said, shoulders moving slightly with gentle mirth as he flipped the eggs in the pan; apparently, this was expected behaviour.

Soon enough, we were seated together at the end of long wooden table, tucking into a simple yet extremely satisfying breakfast. Dom had returned to the pantry to snag a few out-of-season tomatoes and blistered them in the pan after the eggs were cooked.

"Morgan won't have been pleased with the price of these."

I shoved another forkful of eggs into my mouth and turned my attention to the rhythms of the house. The dynamic would take some getting used to, as I was far from familiar with the kind of life where someone else did your grocery shopping, even if you pre-approved the list.

"What else does Morgan do around here?"

"Oh, the usual things. He attends to the grounds and the animals, makes sure the house is running efficiently with both food and heat when necessary." He thought for a moment and then chuckled. "I suppose his main role is to keep things alive around here."

Ah yes, the basic physiological needs of all beings: food, water, shelter, rest. How many times had Maslow's "Hierarchy of Needs" been hammered into my brain during my time as an undergraduate? However, it would seem there was some truth to it all.

"He also takes care of any . . . personal biddings I might need sorted out on short notice," he said, failing to conceal the air of mystery that still surrounded so much of his life.

"Hmm. So, a bit of a 'jack of all trades,'" I replied, sipping what was now a tepid cup of breakfast tea. It still tasted wonderful, however, and I took a moment to appreciate the simplicity of a cup of tea and a hot breakfast.

"He is, but he's actually rather good at it all. Apart from managing things while I'm . . . *away*, he also takes care of any non-magical security. Oh, and my cars."

He grinned mischievously, piquing my own curiosity as to what other vehicles he had in his possession

"So, is Morgan a Druid?"

"No. He's like me. Obviously not a Bearer, and he has never seemed inclined to assess whether he could Wield. It's come up in the past, one of his distant relatives had a hint of the gift and was curious, but it seems to have faded over time. Like a lot of things have."

The sadness I expected from his words had indeed shown up in his expression, and I reached across the table and squeezed his hand gently.

"There is a lot of history in this place. I'll give you a tour once we have a rest," he said.

I nodded in agreement.

We washed the dishes in peaceful silence, Dom quietly humming in his low baritone as the dogs revelled in the leftover corners of toast that Dom tossed to them by the fireside.

"I probably shouldn't have fed them that," he said, but it was clear he was trying to make up for lost time. "They really are spoiled." There was no trace of shame in his voice.

"Gertie always said you could judge someone by how they treated their pets." I leaned into him playfully. "I like it."

He chuckled and muttered something like, "Just wait until I start spoiling you . . ." as we finished the last of the washing.

"Where to next?" I asked lightly as I dried my hands on a red-checkered tea towel I'd found folded beside the deep farm sink. I was looking forward to possibly exploring more of the house on the way to bed, my previous exhaustion quelled momentarily by our breakfast and the strong tea.

Dom paused unexpectedly, his hands briefly white-knuckled on the edge of the white enamel sink as he closed his eyes and cleared his throat simultaneously.

"To my—*our* rooms, I suppose," he said at last, breath now deep and measured.

He wore a strange look on his face, a pained expression that I wasn't entirely sure I had encountered in this lifetime. At least not in the daylight. I could soon feel the beginnings of an anxious stomachache forming deep within my belly, overwhelmed exhaustion waiting readily in the wings.

"Well, we don't have to. I'm more than happy to catch a nap on a couch somewhere. Truly," I said, shrugging my shoulders to signal ease of passage. Frankly, at this point, I was content to sleep curled up beside the fire with the dogs, my muscles aching from far too much time spent sitting over the past forty-eight hours.

"Don't be foolish, Julia. Let's go." He paused a moment, wincing at his own reaction. "I just mean . . . Sorry. Everything will be fine. Don't worry."

And with that he was off, running his left hand through his hair as he gestured with his right towards the dogs. I wasn't sure if his latter command was meant for me, them, or both of us, but I followed along dutifully a few steps behind in their wake.

Dom's unexpected mood-swings had seemed to be lessening the more time we spent together; however, it's hard not to fall into old habits when you arrive home after a long journey. I knew this all too well, a lesson recently revisited after spending time at Gertie's cottage before Ronan's visit. My intuition was to ride the waves with him, choosing to offer him grace over conflict as he navigated his own complex emotions, whatever they were. In truth, I didn't think he was hesitating about sharing his living spaces with me; he was far too nomadic to be private or possessive about such trivial things. But there was definitely something else behind his shift in behaviour.

"Just this way," Dom said, his back towards me as he bounded up the curving staircase towards the second floor.

Soon, he had reached the upper landing before what I assumed was his wing of bedrooms, and I could sense a softness rounding through his shoulders that either meant he was feeling a great relief to be home or something else still yet undiscovered.

I stopped climbing, waiting several steps below.

"The last time we were here, it was the last time we were alone together."

His voice shook slightly.

"It's the memories of you. Here. Well, anywhere really. But it feels more . . . difficult, the closer I am to home."

He was stumbling over his words slightly, almost as though he were struggling to convince his mouth to cooperate with his thoughts. He dug deeper.

"I've spent the better part of the last decade searching for you, having nightmares practically every night about losing you all over again. And now that you're here, in Ireland," he said, turning slowly towards me, "it just feels so different this time around, like it might be our last chance. I don't know if I'll be able to bear losing you again, let alone manage to find you once more, before time runs out . . . again . . ."

He was beginning to ramble, and I was beginning to sense he knew something that I didn't around the longevity of the curse, or at least our combined involvement in it. However, something felt final to me this time around too, even if I could only recall a fraction of our memories.

"I know," I said quietly.

"It's not that I'm afraid . . . No, not like that," he said, staring down at the suddenly fearful look on my face. "It just all feels so . . ."

"Delicate."

I looked then into his beautiful grey-blue eyes, his worries obviously weighing excruciatingly on his thoughts, even with the hearty breakfast behind us. Reaching out, I placed his powerful hand into my considerably less meaty though similarly long fingers. I still marveled at the perfect fit between the two of us.

"Hmm. I need a shower to wash off all this dog slobber," he said, a sudden twinkle in his eye. "You coming?"

I smiled wickedly in reply, having discovered recently that words were not always necessary with this primal human during times of abrupt passion.

He pulled me to the top of the landing and quickly down the hall to a room on the left, dogs lumbering behind him enthusiastically. The doors that lined the hall were of dark polished hardwood and closed tight. It was going to take some serious mental mapping to get the hang of what was what (and where) around here.

With a note of command not to be trifled with, he instructed the dogs to lay down outside the bathroom door. Considering the previous enthusiasm of the motley crew of canines, I was shocked to see them obey and lay quietly in the hall.

"As long as they know where I am, they usually settle down," he said, reading my mind.

A small-ish bathroom that was fitted floor to ceiling in lavish grey marble opened up before me. At first glance, I noticed it was stocked practically with fluffy white towels of various sizes folded neatly on the edge of the bath, and that there were two thick terry-cloth housecoats hanging by a second door, which was painted white. It instantly reminded me of a bed and breakfast or boutique hotel bath, but I supposed this was customary when you had a housekeeper and cleaning staff who made regular rounds. I lifted up a raw-edged bar of soap from beside the sink, admiring its simple paper wrap, cream-coloured with a sprinkling of dried flowers across the top edge.

"Mmm . . ." I said, drinking in the clear scents of lavender and bergamot with mindful pleasure.

Looking up, Dom's eyes had taken on their familiar shade of elemental desire as I floated through the bathroom, gently dragging my fingers across the cool marble. I rather enjoyed teasing him as he worked himself into lustful, sometimes fitful impatience.

"Shall I shower first or you?" I asked not so innocently, batting my lashes and licking my lips once to sweeten my inquiry.

"Don't tease, Julia," he said, teeth clenched as he ripped his sweater over his head. "I'm not in the mood."

Clearly, however, he *was* in the mood, as best indicated by the ferocity with which he unbuckled his jeans and threw them to the glossy floor in a heap.

The image that followed was tantalising.

As always, he wore simple black boxer briefs that hugged his thighs alluringly. Today though, his raw stature stood out in great contrast against the smooth marble that surrounded us, heightening the effect of his masculine figure ten-fold. I couldn't comprehend how he could be even sexier than before; it had to be *some* sort of magic.

Finished with playing tease, I efficiently pulled my sweater over my head while inadvertently pulling my static attached t-shirt off along with it. The hasty removal had also pulled out my ponytail elastic, causing my travelworn hair to tumble messily over my now bare shoulders—bare save for the straps of my transparent lace bra.

"Jesus," he said, eying the delicate coral-pink lace number I'd worn hidden underneath my rougher travel clothes. Looking down, I could see that my nipples were making their meaning quite plain in the cool marble capsule of the bathroom, despite my playful resignation.

I smiled shyly.

"I didn't want to pack it in my luggage in case some creepy customs agent rummaged through my bag."

It was a bit of a lie, knowing full well this was fairly bland content to discover in someone's luggage.

"Indeed," he said, biting his full lower lip, eyes hungry with his full focus on my figure. "I didn't notice it when we were in the car."

"In your defence, you were a bit . . . frantic."

He gently dragged both thumbs simultaneously over the thin lace front of my bra and the outline of my nipples. Then, running his fingers down my sides towards the top of my pants, he jammed his thumbs in my beltloops, pulling me close.

"In my *defence*," he said, drawing out his words as he looked down, eyes wracked with desire, "I'm rather frantic right now."

I raised my chin and chest towards him simultaneously in response to his own rising need and breathed in deeply before he kissed me with little reservation.

He had my full attention now.

I hastily unbuttoned my jeans and jammed my pants and underwear down to the elegant floor with little ceremony; my bottoms weren't nearly as sexy as my top in this particular ensemble, so I preferred to keep his attention "upstairs" as I wriggled out of my worn wool socks one by one, stepping on the ends of the fabric to help pull myself free.

Not entirely graceful, but he either didn't notice or didn't care in the least.

He paused momentarily in his frenzy to turn on the shower for us, long arm reaching gracefully as he bent down slightly to set the nozzle to full blast.

I sighed with exaggerated relief. "I *desperately* need a shower."

It had been an exhausting journey, and I anticipated a delicious post-sex nap in our future as well, if all things moved in our favour.

"And I need you," he said, running his fingers through my hair once before unclasping the back of my ornate bra with his other hand. Admittedly, the garment wasn't entirely my personal style, but his reaction had been worth every bit of discomfort on the flight across the pond, its underwire jabbing rudely into my ribs while I tried to nap.

We stepped clumsily into the steaming shower together, tossing back the simple white shower curtain with a very real threat of ripping it down in the process.

Within moments, a vision moved through my thoughts to deliver me to a distant land. The memory was unobtrusive, however, simply a glimpse, visiting briefly in the moment. We were standing embraced similarly under a waterfall in some faraway green place, clothing long discarded under some tree somewhere and hands barely able to keep still with the longing. The water was very cold there, and in my memory, I could feel the goosebumps on our bodies rising in contradiction to the heat burning within.

I was quickly brought back to my senses as the hot water and Dom's forceful lips washed over me, taking my breath away and demanding, with little patience, that I remain in the here and now. Then, as if to drive the point home, his hands trailed down and found my warmth, gently exploring the outermost regions of my femininity before grabbing me forcefully from behind and pulling me closer. His cock pressed hard into me, and I stroked him with the clearest invitation I could muster.

"I need you in my bed. *Now,*" he said in a low growl as he abruptly pulled away, "I'm done waiting."

On the contrary, and much to my pleasure, he *could* wait a little bit longer.

Passing through the white door this time, the transition from the heat of the shower to the cool cotton sheets of his massive four-poster, king-size bed was utterly tranquilizing as I looked up at his powerful figure above me with complete vulnerability and surrender.

Naked and malleable from the hot shower, I pulled him close, drawing my hips wide and urging him onward with my heels behind his full ass. He looked down, nostrils flaring once again in urgency and taking in the vision of my open feminine form with pleasure.

"You are the most dangerous creature I've ever encountered," he said. "I could all but drown in your ocean and be the happiest man alive."

His brogue was thick and anciently poetic, and I couldn't bear the suspense any longer.

"Then get on with it, sailor!" I commanded, bordering on giddiness with my own impatience as he dove in.

After being especially mindful of *my* pleasure, he pulled his shoulders out from under my thighs and lurched forward, plunging himself deep, my own tide rising still as he crashed against me.

I squeezed him as close and as deeply as I could muster, my own need to devour him becoming immediately plain. Again and again we met, until all our worries of the day subsequently washed away.

After all was said and done, we cuddled serenely as the late-day sun streamed brightly through the windows, giving the room a distinctly supernatural air.

"Every day with you is the best day of my life," he said dreamily as he planted several more kisses on my shoulder.

"Lives," I said through a stifled yawn.

Indeed, he was truly the tether that kept me safely ashore though my tumultuous gales of the Sight. And as I drifted off into a dreamless sleep, I thanked the Goddess for our plight, as terrifying as it might be. For in the balance, I also had the pleasure of truly knowing *him*. And for that, I would give anything, over and over again.

When I awoke serval hours later, Dom was still sleeping comfortably beside me, a slight rumble coming from deep within his nasal passages; he was well and truly relaxed, at long last.

I discovered, after a kick in the ribs from above the covers, that the dogs—who had quite plainly been commanded to remain in the hallway—had pushed the door open and crept into the bedroom once we were finally asleep. Evidently, they were used to spending their nights in here, and I giggled at the sight of the three beasts scattered throughout the room in what I assumed were their usual sleeping positions.

I then drifted back into my own peaceful slumber, heart filled with gratitude for the beauty of this simple moment in time.

CHAPTER 22

T he next week was spent recalibrating to one another in our newly shared environment. We eventually moved away from our time being solely divided between the bedroom or kitchen and instead spilled out casually into the other rooms of the vast home. Dom had opened up the sitting room, despite Morgan's protestations about the cost of heating, and it quickly became our favourite place to enjoy a morning cup of coffee together. I also enjoyed learning more about the house itself.

"It's a bit farther north than my ancestral home, of course," he said, gesturing idly to somewhere off in the distance. "But when it came up for sale, I had to jump on it!"

"Was the . . . *castle* . . . expensive?" I asked, not that I had any point of reference on the matter.

He laughed. "Honestly, it was a total steal, all things considered. And I had money to burn. It was quite run down, and the area had only just recently been electrified with power poles. But that wasn't all that strange in Ireland at the time. Things moved slower in those days out here. I had quite a bit of fun renovating it, though!"

I was surprised how much I liked the idea of Dom participating in home-improvement projects, picturing him diligently sanding and painting door-frames, stripping wood and hammering down floorboards, or agonising over paint colours while picking out new furniture.

"I can tell," I said, gesturing towards the eclectic mix of retro and antique furniture dotted through the room; it was certainly an unusual combination, but somehow it all worked together magnificently.

"Well, you had a bit of a hand in the décor too. Don't forget, you were here for a time," he said, smiling into his coffee cup while drinking back some distant memory.

"Dom . . . do you have anything that was mine? From then, I mean?"

He flushed. "Oh, to be sure. Did you . . . want me to show you?"

Suddenly *very* eager, I agreed enthusiastically as I hopped up off the low green couch.

He led me from the sitting room and up the curved stairway, eventually landing in front of the bedroom next to ours, this one being situated smack in the centre of the house above the entrance way. He paused, facing the closed door while running his fingers through his hair.

"This was our bedroom last time. I was nervous about bringing you in here when we first came back. Just in case . . ."

I placed my hand on his arm. "It's okay, Dom. I understand."

Pushing the door open ahead of me, he let me step through first, waiting silently in the hall for my reaction.

The room was very similar to ours now, although slightly larger with a rounded front wall and three large sash windows, all of which offered a beautifully clear view of the lake. I could see why it had been our first choice, but on the other hand, I also completely understood Dom's reluctance to move us back into the space. His memories no doubt haunted him of my absence upon his own return.

"I don't sleep in here anymore," he said, appearing behind me without warning and placing his arms around me in a soft embrace. "But I did . . . for a time."

We stood locked together for a moment, breathing deep in unison. I completely understood the desperate need to feel close to a lost loved one and hoped that he didn't feel embarrassed or ashamed for his innocent act of longing.

"Come," he said, breaking the silence. "I've got a few boxes of things stashed under the bed you might enjoy."

He crouched onto the carpeted floor and flipped up the cream-coloured bed skirts to expose two faded-brown cardboard boxes. I plunked down beside him, nervous and excited all at once.

"It's not much," he said with a chuckle, "but you *really* did enjoy this era."

The first box contained an assortment of clothing, which at first glance included a leather purse with a narrow strap and an abundance of tassels, several pairs of flared women's blue jeans, a few plain cotton t-shirts, as well as pair of white plastic boots that were *clearly* my size.

"I saved some of your favourite clothes . . . and also some of mine," he said, grinning sheepishly.

"Oh really?"

I dug frantically towards the bottom, past several unassuming men's sweaters and a few more pairs of denim pants, at last pulling out what was obviously a Dom-sized floral pullover tunic.

"You didn't!" I said, rolling back onto the floor and giggling with uncontrollable delight.

He lay back with me at once, joining in heartily with my fit of laughter. "Well, no. I didn't wear it much, not really. Only when we took a trip to California."

California. I had almost forgotten about my plans to travel there next month and made a mental note to contact Alice as soon as I could about my cancellation. It felt so strange to consider my life before all of this, all the while still so bloody unaccustomed to the "now."

Something else *was* striking about the shirt, however, and turning it over in my fingers gently, I noticed that the fabric felt *quite* familiar. As if by default, I tapped into the Sight, closing my eyes to focus my energy, and was rewarded with a few brief golden glimpses of memory. Dom was wandering ahead of me across a jewel-green park, sun shining down, and wearing yet another pair of effortlessly cool sunglasses, well suited to the time, of course. He wore the floral shirt, and I was surprised to see that he had bare feet. He turned back and beamed at me, and I realized then that I was actually taking a picture of him.

Pulling myself from the memory, I sat up abruptly, barely breathing. "Dom! Wait! Are there photographs?"

"There are."

He rolled onto his side, pulled out the second smaller box from under the bed, and shoved it towards me. Hands shaking slightly in anticipation, I gently opened the lid.

Inside, stacked neatly, were several cracked photo albums as well as a handful of loose photos scattered throughout the bottom of the container.

"Oh . . ." I said, lost for words.

There *were* pictures. And so many of them.

"You were quite into photography then, so most of them are of me unfortunately," he said, laughter escaping in a low, yet wistful rumble.

Most of the images were in black and white, especially the artsier ones, which I had apparently taken, but there were also a select handful on colour film. We spent the next several hours pouring over the old photos, spreading them out across the bedroom floor as Dom reminded me of the corresponding stories and adventures, as well as regaling me with the who's who of each image.

"That's Peggy and Malcolm there—two of our guests that are coming," he said, pointing to a couple in the distance of a wide-angle photo, the pair of them leaning back on a slick-looking sports car in the driveway. "Oh God, they look so young there. Freshly married, I think. I'll have to show them when they arrive."

The memories that returned to my consciousness didn't feel entirely secure, per se. But I found that, between the photos and Dom's detailed explanations, I felt closer to that version of myself and that time than I had felt about any of my lost memories to date.

At one point, he had abruptly shuttled downstairs, allegedly to grab something from his duffel bag, which he now kept tucked away safely in his study.

"I usually keep these with me when we travel," he said upon his return, slightly sheepish and short of breath.

He then handed me three well-worn photographs of *me*.

"Like I said, you were usually behind the lens. But every once in a while, you would let me capture *you*," he said, scarcely hiding his affection.

In the first, a colour photo, I was lounging back on a low metal chair on what appeared to be the front lawn of the manor house, wearing a high-waisted white bikini and holding out a cocktail, in what I assumed was Dom's direction, with an inviting grin.

"It was a *really* warm spring that year," he said, smiling fondly.

The second and third photographs were much more candid, and both in black and white. In the smaller of the two, I was seated in front of a window, looking out pensively towards some unknown notion in the distance. I had to admit, I looked beautiful there, my dark hair long and straight, and a high turtleneck highlighting the angle of my chin before the light of the window.

Dom stroked my present-day hair back behind my ear, having tucked himself comfortably onto the floor behind me.

"The other one is my favourite though," he said, pulling the third picture forward.

We were seated side by side along a stone wall, with Dom's arm wrapped protectively around me as I tossed my head back in laugher, his face turned in profile with a broad grin of his own.

Suddenly, I could remember *vividly* how adoringly he had looked at me on that day, and so many of the days we spent together during that time, and my heart positively leapt.

"You were making some stupid joke about having to wait for supper because I wanted this picture."

"I was," he said, eyes filling with tears.

I kissed him then, long and slow, before pulling back and scrunching my nose at him. "You still think you're funny, *and* you're always hungry. I guess some things never change!"

We doubled over in a fit of laughter together then, happy tears flowing as we found ourselves in a tender embrace on the carpet. We had clearly enjoyed so many wonderful friends and beautiful times together, despite the ominous fate that always laid ahead. It truly felt divine to reminisce with him there in the rounded room and breathe some life back into a space he had so protectively locked himself away from.

Not all the feelings of memory and magic in the manor house had been so easy to digest. However, I *was* surprised at just how quickly I adjusted to the vastness of the manor; so that was something. As if to reinforce the point,

Dom assured me all along that it was quite modest compared to others in the area.

"Modest? Hmm," I said as we were putting on our shoes for a brisk walk around the grounds.

The sun was shining. It was unseasonably warm for January, and we both agreed that our daily fresh-air routine from Salt Spring was worth continuing. Dom whistled to the dogs as we passed through the creaking front door.

"You'll see."

While I was becoming accustomed to the size of the home, I was quintessentially *not* accustomed to the magic woven throughout. The more comfortable I became in the various high-ceilinged rooms, the more it seemed objects were reaching out to me to tell their stories, whether they were yarns from our own past or an unfamiliar skein left haphazardly strewn about for me to tangle myself into.

Gertie's cottage had always boasted a most familiar magic, one that was welcoming and always attuned to my own fluctuating energy. It had almost felt as if the cottage would breathe a deep sigh of relief any time I came to call. This place, however, was decidedly unsure of me, tentative if not slightly defensive. All of this wasn't helped by Dom's tendency to collect things from our past and scatter them about as relics. As a result, I struggled with even the simplest acts of practical magic about the place.

His study, which was essentially a sunken room with stone walls located just off the main sitting room, was full to the brim with antiquated objects and dusty old books, alongside his rugby paraphernalia and a sleek silver computer atop a well-aged oak desk. It was also a positive treasure trove of jarring memories and untamed magical energy. I felt a keen desire to avoid it at all costs, being wholly unprepared emotionally for what might greet me.

Today, as it happened, I was not feeling particularly strong, which meant I was eager to accept Dom's suggestion to be outside.

Having just completed a wide pass around the west side of the lake, fields were now opening up in front of us, with only small copses of trees now dotted about throughout the wide, agrarian landscape. Fooled by the mild weather, my running shoes were already positively soaked, and I kicked myself heartily for not wearing rubber boots.

Dom, for his part, had spent the entire walk practically buzzing in anticipation around our upcoming houseguests and speaking almost a mile a minute while doing so.

Meanwhile, I was actually craving silence. I had just shared with him how overwhelmed and exhausted I had become by all of the new visions this past week, which had ultimately been affecting me both day *and* night. As such, I was not feeling prepared for company whatsoever.

"You know, I had wondered if you might not recognize more of the magic around the place by now. Does *any* of it feel familiar?"

"Oh. Well, I recognize some . . . but a lot of the magic is so old, it's as if it's speaking a different language," I said, feeling slightly dismissed.

"Well, it probably *is* a different language. This form of modern English certainly isn't our first, or second, or third tongues, to be sure," he said, carrying on enthusiastically. He really was eager to talk and think out loud today, and I did my best to keep up in spite of how taxed I felt.

"That explains why you were drawn towards Linguistics . . . what with having to jump in and learn new languages with each cycle," I said, my replies degraded to merely participatory.

He threw a big stick into the distance for the dogs, and as always, I was impressed with his athletic prowess. Sully proudly captured the prize, which was about twice the length of his body, and dragged it along gleefully with the rest of the pack.

"Too true. Thankfully, I have the mind for it!" Dom said.

The linguist in me *was* still particularly perplexed at that aspect of our evolving timeline, but it felt like a rather big topic to unpack, and I certainly didn't have the energy for it today. I had slept terribly all week, which wasn't a total surprise, as I always needed time to adjust to new places.

"You do; it's incredible really," I said as I smiled tightly at him. "But that's not what I mean. It's like I've forgotten how to decipher it. That's what the quilt feels like too, but this place makes the unknown energy in the quilt feel like a handkerchief by comparison."

I thought of the quilt, which had been tucked away safely in a canvas bag in the bottom of Dom's vast wardrobe almost immediately upon our arrival. Oddly enough, I only ever seemed to consider the quilt's existence on the occasions where I was attempting to decipher how *my own* magics worked in the greater world, past and present.

I closed my eyes momentarily before reaching out from my inner core, sensing. "There's other magic too, throughout the grounds. And it's definitely *not* mine."

"I wonder if because it's such an ancient place. There are just more traces of magic scattered about . . . certainly more than 'back home.'" Dom said, rubbing his hands together.

This was quickly exhibiting shades of our seminar, with Dom purposely delivering topics to engage me in debate. I sighed. "Well . . . *Canada* is full to the brim with magic; it's woven into the bones of the land. But it is a language I don't speak, if that makes sense? Here . . . it's more like I've forgotten it altogether, which is frustrating."

He nodded eagerly, though clearly not hearing my words or exhausted tone as he pivoted once more. "What about the physical element of existing dwellings and their ability to hold the imprints of the magic left behind? I mean, the ancient Pagan monuments alone! That's got to be different, and there's tons of them."

"I think the same exists over there too, ancient communities and artifacts, but you're probably right in that it's not nearly as concentrated as it is here, I'll give you that. Canada is massive. And also, *so much* was destroyed when it was colonized."

"Right, that makes sense," he said.

We had reached the roadside edge of the property, and after climbing a low stone fence, were soon walking along the narrow road that met up with another estate nearby. A massive home sat back several hundred metres from our vantage point, and the size of the manor house did indeed pale in comparison. Dom raised his eyebrows as if to say, *"Told you so."*

We walked along the narrow road for a time, back towards the entrance of the estate as Dom continued to batter me with more tales of his past and his opinions on the current state of the world.

"My father was so enamoured with Charlemagne. The way the Roman armies functioned, conquered, and dominated things. And then of course there's the whole 'island of saints and scholars' element, and the preservation of language in the Catholic church during the dark ages! It really was the foundation for so much of our world today. And so much of it was just, well . . . they got it wrong," he said, laughing heartily.

Dusk settled in as we approached the manor house once more, soggy and starving. The afternoon had been warm, but the setting sun brought with it a bone-deep chill, and I was shivering by the time we rounded the back of the house. A soft light was aglow through the lower windows, and we entered through the kitchen, much to the dog's collective pleasure.

"Supper time!" Dom called out as he headed to the fridge to fetch each of their dinners.

I yanked my sopping runners off and threw them by the door.

"I've never really known how to tap into others' . . . What did you call them earlier? Mementos? That's new to me. I've never really needed to in the past. Honestly, my magic always just felt like an aspect that was just *how it was* for me, never really a true purpose. I mean, I barely use my magic as it is."

Dom made each of the dogs sit obediently before he placed their bowls in front of them. I was initially surprised to notice they each had custom meals, all of which contained a mix of raw meat, bone, and organs. However, once I got over the shock factor, it made perfect sense.

"Well, we will just have to find someone who can help you! There's got to be someone who can. I'll set the Druids on it."

I hesitated. "Dom, it needs to be a Witch."

Reservations had already been brewing within me about the eagerness and availability of Druids in the cause. Where were all the Bearers? Or the women, for that matter?

"Of course, you're right."

He nodded dutifully, but I wasn't entirely sure he felt the weight of my request.

"Morgan is going to bring in a massive load of groceries tomorrow afternoon for our guests. As for the cooking, I wonder if we shouldn't bring up Maureen from the village. She's always keen, and we've already got the cleaners in anyways. Are we going to want to worry about cooking?" Dom trailed off, wading into planning mode once more, focussed on what obviously felt like the most important aspect: the provisions.

"Surely we can cook for ourselves?" I said, frustration mounting.

"What? No!"

He rambled on for another several minutes about food and comfortable accommodations, but at this point, I had stopped listening altogether. All afternoon he had essentially ignored my discomfort around the series of micro adjustments to my new life in Ireland, either by driving the conversation in a different direction or by feigning overbearing positivity. Actually, he had suddenly seemed completely hellbent on controlling the situation, and it wasn't tasting very appetizing in my mouth.

"I know you're nervous, Julia," Dom said, interrupting my altogether unnoticed contemplations.

He plunked down at the table across from me, grating his chair irritatingly across the stone floor, with a whole cooked chicken, half a block of cheese, and a dried-out dinner bun crammed on a white porcelain plate before him. He squeezed an inhumane amount of mayonnaise from a plastic bottle onto the side of the dish before speaking again.

"You couldn't have predicted what Ben would do back in Vancouver. It's as much my fault as anyone's. And besides, your magic was *down*, for all intents and purposes. This will be different. I'm sure of it."

I bristled.

He was right, I had failed to detect the sinister motives of my ill-intentioned roommate, and it *had* almost inadvertently cost us our lives. But what he didn't know, or was neglecting to notice, was that even now my magic continued to be shoddy, at best, and downright dangerous at its worst. I felt completely vulnerable and exposed in this new life, and all I wanted was his support.

I watched as he used a butter knife to dig aggressively into the roasted chicken carcass before him, the sounds of the cracking cartilage and bones bordering on nauseating for my utterly taxed body and mind. As this wasn't the first time I had witnessed him devour an entire bird in one sitting, I could only assume he intended to consume the whole thing while discussing more plans for our upcoming assemblage.

There was no way in hell I was willing to sit through this.

"What happened with Ben was a mistake that I will *never* make again," I said, pushing my chair back without thinking as it clattered to the floor. Taking wing in a flight of anger, I marched over to the polished farm sink and dumped my cold cup of tea with what my grandmother would have called an "exceptional flourish."

"Julia, you know I didn't mean it like that," he said, mouth still full of chicken, confusion across his brow as he braced his long fingers onto the worn table for battle.

I looked him square in the eyes as I resolutely set my jaw, and for the first time, I felt pity. "I know you didn't."

Since returning to Ireland, I was beginning to see how painfully bound he was to his predetermined mission, so completely hyper-focused on how it had always been that he couldn't imagine that things might look differently this time around. Or that my opinion on things might bear some weight.

It all felt so limiting, and I was already so tired.

"Feel free to bring in Mrs. Tibbles the cook or whoever you think will best serve the cause, *Domhnall*. I'm going to go lay down for a bit. As you *may* recall, I slept very poorly last night. I don't want to be a total zombie when our *guests* arrive."

I was struggling to overcome the venom that had bubbled to my lips.

"Julia! Oh, come on!" he called out after me.

"Thanks for dinner!" I called back, but I was already headed down the hallway.

Sprinting up the stairs, I thought of how it was only going to get worse when Ronan arrived. The two of them would continue to plan our destiny based on Dom's first-hand accounts, bickering like siblings over the best laid plans while the rest of us looked on, impressed with *how clever* these two masculine figures were. I had absolutely no interest in participating at that level, not if the odds were indefinitely stacked against me anyways.

My inner fire had kicked into full inferno now for the second time in just over a month, and once more, I needed time to move through the feeling before we spoke again.

Before I knew it, I had locked myself into the marble capsule bathroom and was turning on the shower. I was flooded now by the contradictory joy from the first day we'd arrived at Dom's house, the scent of bergamot and lavender soap in the room greeting me familiarly. *What* had I gotten myself into?

Having watched my mother be destroyed by her proclivity to let others design her personal constellation, I had spent most of my life running from men who, intentionally or not, attempted to control my destiny. No, I flat out refused to let this be the case for my own life, even if up to this point my own story had been on repeat for decades like some fucked-up prophetic rendition of *Groundhog Day*.

Before stepping into the shower, I pulled out my phone from my crumpled jeans on the floor. No messages, but that wasn't a surprise. While Dom had adapted to most modern things with surprising grace, he was not the kind of person to meddle with an apologetic text after a fight. As for texting any of my friends, even just for a feeling of connection, the fact remained that I had been successful over the past year in reminding them that I needed space. Not that I had any of their contact information on my replacement phone anyway.

And now . . . I was just so damn lonely.

I slept for an unknown amount of time following my tear-filled shower, awaking to the placid dark of Dom's vast bedroom. Pushing the sleep from my eyes, I groggily attempted to gain my bearings. Through the window, I could see dappled shades of the moon, the ripples of soft grey and blue velvet dancing against the night sky, but she was as yet veiled to me by fast-moving clouds high up in the atmosphere.

I guessed it was nearing the Witching hour.

Dom was well into his own deep slumber atop the covers beside me, arms crossed and so stone still that I almost wouldn't have noticed his presence if not for his low, measured breath. He smelled vaguely of pipe smoke, which I thought was unusual; perhaps he had met with Morgan to finalize arrangements for the days ahead while I slept.

Goosebumps soon spread over my drowsy form, and I shivered in delayed realization that I was still completely naked under the white feather cocoon of Dom's king-sized duvet. The fire had long burnt out, and I momentarily wished he was under the covers beside me, his body a thoroughly dependable furnace against the winter chill.

But I didn't dare wake him. Not now, and not after what happened. I felt unexpected shame well up inside for my behaviour earlier, not that I didn't *also* still feel a mounting frustration towards the command structure evolving before me. Regardless, I wished that I had handled the whole situation with a bit more tact.

Sitting up carefully so as not to wake the prone form beside me, I gazed blearily out the ceiling-height window as I grappled with my own embarrassment. As if on cue, the clouds parted and the moon gently spoke her cool clear language through the glass.

"Grace, Julia. Give yourself grace."

These truly were unprecedented times, so why had I expected myself to handle it all like a seasoned Witch? Perhaps because I had already done so, allegedly, countless times before. I felt like I was failing Dom, the cause, and if I was completely honest, failing myself too.

Knees to chin and eyes locked on the moon, troubled thoughts passed in and out of my consciousness like the heavenly clouds flickering across the face of twilight. Time passed, still unmeasured. Eventually, I lost the moon behind the clouds once more and turned my gaze towards my lover.

Muscles stiff from my night watch and resisting the urge to wake Dom, I stretched my legs out slowly before snuggling back down under the covers as close as possible without disturbing him, his body akin to a paperweight atop our shared bed. Anxious about how my haphazard sleep would disrupt the day ahead, I finally mustered the courage to roll over and peer at the alarm clock on Dom's beside table. It had been well over seven hours since I'd first drifted off; however, there were still many hours ahead before the day would begin.

"You can always just rest your eyes, Julia, even if you can't sleep."

This time the words that interrupted my reveries were Gertie's, and her memory from my childhood brought its usual comfort before I gave in to the peaceful solitude of the night.

CHAPTER 23

When I awoke for the second time, I was alone. The room smelled warm and familiar, like wood smoke and something else more savoury. It would seem Dom had silently re-lit the fire while I slept, although he must have left the room some time ago, as it had fully burned down to the coals once more. While the majority of the house had been updated to steam heating centuries ago, Dom had apparently insisted that the upper bedrooms maintain the capacity for wood heat as well.

I *also* knew for certain it would have been Dom who lit the fire. The house cleaners had been specifically instructed *not* to come into these rooms if occupied, a lesson learned rather unfortunately three days prior when they had walked in on the pair of us in a rather compromising position for the middle of the afternoon.

"Jesus, Mary, and Joseph!" Dom had shouted, before hastily gathering the bedclothes around us. Clearly mortified, the cleaners had slammed the door immediately before rushing downstairs and turning on their vacuums loudly in unison. I realized then that I couldn't actually remember what their names had been, but I was fairly certain they didn't share them with the Holy Family. Sarah and Jane? Or maybe Jenny? They had looked so similar and had completely avoided eye contact with me when I'd first met them that morning, but I made a mental note to properly learn both of their names once the embarrassment subsided.

Dom, who was apparently *far* more accustomed to random strangers in his home than I was, had merely laughed about it afterwards. He swiftly rectified the situation by issuing specific instructions around which rooms were a priority, as well as the appropriate time of day for each task. For my own part, I had practically died of embarrassment, diving under the covers and effectively hiding there until they were gone.

While I still felt like it was ridiculous to have an active house staff, even if they were only here twice a week, I also wasn't entirely enthused about the idea of cleaning all of these rooms alone. Dom had made it quite plain he wasn't interested in the task, even if he was fairly neat and tidy by nature. I also had the sense that the kinds of people who visited here with frequency were already well accustomed to the luxuries of the house as they stood.

And it *was* a luxurious home. I felt somewhat cheated by how little time we'd gotten to spent alone in the manor house before welcoming in cleaners and cooks, and now today what were sure to be some *well-received* company. I rolled my eyes, picturing Dom downstairs greeting the first of our company, charming as ever and making everyone feel *completely* at home through proffered food and drink.

Then I realized how desperately hungry I was.

Having skipped supper entirely, I now felt the aggressive pangs of an empty stomach on top of my anxious and lamentably grumpy sense of anticipation. Groaning audibly, I rolled onto my side while pushing the plush down duvet away, my post-shower hair askew in every possible direction as I took in my bearings.

Eying the bedside table to check the time, I discovered a plate of cured meat and cheeses, along with a small handful of crackers, a bunch of grapes, and a low glass of water on a napkin; Dom's handiwork, no doubt. I reached frantically for the food, stuffing my judgement aside from only moments earlier. I then noticed a small box tucked slightly to the right of the alarm clock, no bigger than the palm of my hand. It was surprisingly heavy, wrapped in light brown paper with a rolled-up note that was carefully tucked into the bow-tied twine.

Curious now, I picked at the twine with some difficulty. It was *definitely* from Dom, the tightness of the knot being a dead giveaway. I shoved several grapes hastily into my mouth while spending a few more clumsy moments working the knot. At last, I unrolled a short message written in Dom's tidy cursive:

> *Julia,*
> *I was saving this for a special moment, but now is as good of a time as ever.*
> *It's a modern replica of something that I gave to you a very, very long time ago. I had it re-made several years back. I hope you still like it.*
> *I really am sorry for yesterday. You are my eternal companion, and this is your home as much as it is mine. I am so proud to greet our guests with you by my side.*
> *I'll see you when you're ready to come downstairs, but please take any time you need.*
> *Yours endlessly,*
> *Dom.*

I had to admit, it was a start. I could still feel the coals of my anger simmering with a vibrant crackle deep within; however, I was far more intrigued about what was in the package.

He hadn't used tape so I easily folded back the brown paper. Within the box, I found a single weighty object wrapped in a scrap of soft white linen. I closed my eyes and felt the fabric with my fingertips for a moment, noticing the similarity of this piece of fabric to the shirt he had worn the first night I had seen his tattoo, when we had set the clock well and truly into motion.

At first, the memory of that night moved through me slowly, the vitality of Dom's gold and blue essence weaving effortlessly between the deeper shades of dark green and silver that lined my own aura. So often my visions would arrive in blurred tendrils of vibrant colour but then morph into a muddy mix more closely resembling dirty paint water than the brilliant illuminations of an ancient storybook. Never before had I seen images with such consistent clarity, at least not before reuniting with him.

Closing my eyes and allowing the recollection to wash over me further, I could soon smell the rain from that fated night and could hear—almost *see*— the pain in the room as he'd urged to me to release the tattoo's magic from his body. I wondered then what it must have been like for him to literally carry the physical weight of our story on his bare shoulders.

My attention was drawn back to the present moment by the weight of the package, and I released the vision with a flick of my hand. This was a new, albeit clumsy, skill that I had gained since exploring the manor house. Right now, I was *far* too curious about what was directly in front of me than in dwelling on the sensory memories of the past, no matter how distinct they were.

Carefully unwrapping the folded fabric, I discovered a small disc-shaped gold pendant affixed to a comparatively thick gold chain. The adornment itself was about the size of a loonie and centred with a polished garnet cabochon. In between curls of delicate golden filigree, the red stone was surrounded equally on each side by four petite white pearls. Unfurling the heavy chain, I noticed that it was quite long, which would suit my neck and body very well, if I ever mustered the courage to wear the regal piece.

My ears burned hot as a powerful vision overcame me. This time, its unexpected force pounded through my thoughts and body like a freight train; this vision was definitely *not* within my control.

I landed in the vision with an astonishing weight behind me.

Looking down, I could immediately confirm that it was indeed *my* body that I occupied, mostly because I was completely naked. Well, not technically; I was wearing the pendant, or some ancient version of it, but nothing else. Something about my body was different though, almost as if it were blurred around the edges, illuminated. I was laying back on what must have been considered a bed, composed of lumpy wool and various furs and woven fabrics strewn heavily about the earthen floor.

And I felt *powerful*.

Dom was standing, hunched slightly, within the folds of the low-slung linen tent, looking down with a familiar lust, grey-blue eyes burning with intense ferocity. His hair was long and unbound, but he looked younger, almost raw in his masculinity. A man in his mid-twenties, virile and reckless. Apart from his short sword, he had discarded all other weapons outside. He was fresh from battle, splattered in mud, blood, and sweat, and something else that smelled as foul as it looked.

I knew then with certainty that the vision was from a very, *very* long time ago.

"You've returned," I said, arching myself in his direction as I moved to my knees.

The night air was cool, causing my flesh and nipples to pucker in apt response. There was something unfamiliar about the way my muscles flexed towards him with each taut movement. My frame was demonstrably lean, and hungry. But there was also an unwavering strength there, and I could feel my Bearing magic almost crackling within, eager and electrified.

"And you . . . are a vision," he said, breath heavy and heart still pounding with residual adrenaline as his eyes grew wide at the sight before him. He spoke in an old form of Irish, but I understood every word.

I beckoned for him to join me in bed, a queen in my own right, holding fast in my seat of power. Both his allegiance and my sovereignty would be observed this night as it had been so many nights before.

He was a man worthy of my strength.

The vision trickled away with much less force than when it had first arrived, and I stepped back into my present consciousness. I looked down at the necklace, its gravity weighing heavily in my palm, almost like a talisman. Was it grounding me in the present, or perhaps, even to Dom himself?

And I knew what the vision had meant. The necklace had been given as a symbol of his devotion prior to a dangerous raid, one from which I had demanded his promise of return. The bartering nature and playful wagers between us seemed to originate in the beginning of our story. I knew with surety that *this* wager dictated that, should he return in one piece, I would be ready and waiting for him, naked, in his tent.

We *belonged* to each other, balanced and harmonious in our power.

In fact, it was incredible to witness myself so raw and knowing in my own strength. Perhaps it had been a sign of youth, but I couldn't remember ever in my current lifetime feeling remotely that much freedom, strength, and untamed magic surging through my veins at any one time.

"All of my brothers married these bland and overwhelmingly chaste Christian women," he had told me only very recently, when I was being *exceptionally* enthusiastic in the pleasure he was offering, *"prone to propriety and*

feigning great displeasure in the bedroom. Pagan women, however . . ." Pagan woman, indeed.

My desire for him both then and now was undeniable, but sitting alone on the edge of the bed in my present moment, I felt woefully unsure if I would ever be able to live up to *this* particular memory. I eyed myself disparagingly in the long mirror leaning casually on the wall opposite the fireplace. I still bore the dark circles of underlying stress below my eyes, but at least my complexion was much brighter overall than it had been the night before.

Tentatively at first, I lifted the replica necklace over my head, its weight heavy on my shoulders, a metaphor that was not lost on me. While the chain was cool, the talisman was surprisingly warm against my bare chest. Despite my mounting insecurity, I was quite certain the current image would have floored Dom now just as it had then.

With the chill of the bedroom fast becoming a discomfort, I attempted passively to ignite the coals with some Wielded magic but to no avail. Still as inconsistent as ever it would seem. Instead, I turned my thoughts towards the towering oak wardrobe in the corner of the room and some more appropriate wrappings. What did I own that would even begin to honour this timeless piece? It felt unfathomable to tuck the necklace underneath one of Dom's sweaters, or one of my own casual t-shirts.

I felt a stinging regret as I opened the wide doors and revealed my suitcase, hastily shoved within and still almost completely packed, but for some dirty laundry shoved beside it in the corner of the cabinet. Recounting with shame my own annoyance towards Dom when he failed to unpack his things at Gertie's place, I made a mental note to properly settle into our new life here as soon as I had the chance.

Doubtful that my search would bear any fruit, I began to rummage around hopelessly. I eventually pulled out a short-sleeve black bamboo romper that I had packed in what I now considered a rather weak attempt at formality, especially when I considered the state of the manor house. The outfit *did* fit me well though, with its relaxed low V-neck and flattering wrap tie situated at the waist. The legs tapered elegantly at the ankle and somehow miraculously fit my long stems without the uncomfortable bunched effect in the groin that I had come to expect when donning single body garments.

Plus, I was pleased to report that it would frame the necklace rather well too, all things considered.

My hair had now completely taken on a life of its own, as it always did when I feel asleep before having a chance to dry it fully. Messy auburn waves tumbled down my shoulders, the look planted firmly somewhere between a disgruntled lion and an over-wrung mop.

I was surprised at how much I suddenly cared about all of this. Was it a built-in response to the cultural expectation of being the "woman of the house," or was it simply consideration for the significance of first impressions? Or perhaps it was merely a when-you-look-good-you-feel-good confidence I sought. But it didn't matter now, I had been due downstairs over an hour ago.

Simultaneously gobbling down the remainder of my breakfast, I hastily ran a comb through my matted knots, resigning myself to the fact a pony-tail was my choicest option in the moment, roughly pulling back my mane before venturing onward. The first of our company would undoubtedly be Ronan, a fact that was confirmed almost immediately as I descended the steps and moved towards the sitting room at the end of the manor house, where I could hear both he and Dom talking somewhat spiritedly and . . . was that grunting?

Standing in the wide doorway, I discovered with dawning confusion that the bulk of the mismatched furniture had been stacked or pushed impulsively to the side. Meanwhile, the two men were locked in some kind of awkward embrace in the middle of the massive ornate Persian rug, sweating and indeed grunting.

Dom was clearly at an advantage due to his raw magnitude, but Ronan was holding his own, more likely due to sheer pigheadedness than strength. That was one of the more infuriating, yet interesting, things about Ronan. Stubbornness was more than a personality trait with him; it was almost as if it were a way of life. Dom had said to me once that, if obstinance was a virtue, Ronan would be akin to a saint.

I continued to watch patiently for a few moments, gathering that this was some form of impromptu battle ballet, what with all the balance shifting between their feet and heavy nasal breathing. Their movements were laced not so delicately with profanities, all of which passed forcibly between their teeth, along with low growls.

In fact, the sparring resembled some sort of rugby-meets-wrestling-meets-hand-to-hand combat. Dom's head was tucked firmly under Ronan's armpit, with his one arm wrapped around the bulk of his body and the other fist on the floor, legs braced wide and his butt in the air. Honestly, it *was* positively scrum-like, if not for the fact Ronan was twisting his body and pulling on Dom's t-shirt simultaneously, a major penalty if I had ever seen one, and I knew next to nothing about any of the tactics at hand.

They reminded me of a pair of gorillas fighting, and I let out a snort of laughter, giving myself away at last. Dom's head popped up, keenly alerted to my arrival, and Ronan took this brief moment of distraction to heave his advantage over Dom, flipping himself 180 degrees and slamming Dom flat out on his back with an impressive *thud!*

Ronan landed lightly on his backside beside him, the clear victor in whatever you called their game. "Thanks, Julia! I was beginning to think he might out-last me."

"Ape!" Dom hurled in Ronan's general direction as he clamoured to his feet, but his eyes were entirely locked on me.

He beamed at me, hands outstretched. His face glistened with the sweat of exertion, and I drank in the fact that his hair was tousled in the way that had so consistently turned my legs to jelly.

"Julia," he said, taking my hands into his own while kissing me softly across my comparatively dry brow. "Did you sleep well?"

"I did," I said, releasing my right hand from his and instead resting it on the heavy necklace around my neck. He smelled of physical effort, his usual intoxicating masculine essence clouding my senses momentarily as I greedily breathed him in.

Unexpectedly, my eyes began to well with tears. What the hell was happening to me?

He looked momentarily concerned, and I extended my chin in a signal of strength, despite the gathering emotion on my face. In that moment, an invisible waterfall of unspoken words came pouring down between us.

I grinned, embarrassed now.

"I feel like the emotions are coming back before the memories or something. It's so strange," I said as I wiped the incongruous tears from my eyes.

But it wasn't only that. The magical connection between us today was as clear as the brilliance of a blue sky following the passing of a spring storm, the sun pouring so gleefully through the recently cleansed air that I could almost smell the petrichor as we settled ourselves in front of the ornate fireplace.

I perched on the blue slouchy chair in front of the fireplace, which had quickly become one of my favourite stoops, and Dom knelt at my knees. I noticed that Ronan had silently exited the room during our relocation; perhaps they had discussed our argument in some form or another. Or maybe Ronan simply valued his life.

"Oh, my sweet love," he said, resting his head on my lap.

It was such a submissive gesture that I found myself slightly taken aback and would have bet the farm that I would be the *only* recipient of such in his life.

"I really am so, so sorry. I get so caught up in the planning and control that . . . well, sometimes I forget to just live," he cleared his throat. "Drawing up battle lines seems to be the best way to cope. Organize and plan, find logical solutions—"

"And gather provisions?" I offered, eyebrows raised.

He stuck his nose between my knees and placed his hands on either side of my thighs. He laughed in muffled embarrassment. "And gather provisions, yes."

"It's alright," I said, stroking his golden-brown waves back from his forehead as he looked up at me once more. "It's not always going to be easy. It's about the only thing I'm sure of really. That and how much I love you."

I continued to run my fingers through his hair, and he sighed in audible relief.

"I love you too," he said, and taking a deep breath, he pushed himself back onto his knees before me. A cheeky grin then spread across his perfect face.

I grinned back but narrowed my eyes in equal measure. "What?"

"The necklace." He ran his long fingers inward along my thigh, sultry memories obviously fuelling his current motives with an increased urgency. "Do you remember?"

"Oh, you mean this old thing?"

In one swift move, he pulled me down onto the floor with him, laughing heartily. "Yes, *that* old thing!"

DING-DONG! DING-DONG!

"Ah! Fuck!" Dom said as he extricated the hand that he had somehow so deftly slid through the crossed fabric at the front of my romper during our recent descent to the ground. The body control on this man, *honestly*.

"Looks like it's time for company, Julia! Look alive!" he said as he hopped up, pulling me up shortly thereafter.

"Speak for yourself," I said, staring directly at his erect cock making its own arrival known through his thin jogging pants.

He kicked his legs out sideways several times, flexing his quads in turn. He then performed several jumping jacks and smiled devilishly over his shoulder before striding from the room. I followed warily in his footsteps, suddenly wishing for one of the dogs at my side.

No sooner had the thought crossed my mind than three barking dogs rocketed enthusiastically around the corner from the kitchen and into the entrance hall. Mags and Sully were their usual overly exuberant selves as Ronan struggled to open the door between their wagging tails and lolling tongues.

"Christ, man! Get ahold of these damn dogs!"

"Would that I could, my friend," Dom replied. He crossed the entrance hall towards the door in three long strides. "Only the big fella listens when there's visitors."

The great dog, who had cleverly avoided the chaos at the door, now leaned obediently into me, and I scratched him gratefully between his ears as we braced ourselves for what would come next.

CHAPTER 24

I t felt like we were about to play a strangely upbeat real-life rendition of *Clue*, each guest arriving with their own unique story and flair to add to the complexity of our mutual cause. I silently hoped no one would show up wielding lead pipes or candle sticks; however, at this point, how was I to know? And knowing what we did so far about Cassius's current whereabouts, which was allegedly somewhere in the Los Angeles area, it really *was* a who-dunnit as to when our foe would next make himself known.

Several days prior, Dom had explained to me that even during the phases when he and I were inactive in the cause, forces for good continued to forge bravely onward in our absence by making attempts to thwart the Wraiths and heartily aligning themselves against "the Child of Rome."

"Well, in truth, we haven't the same level of support we once did," he'd said, sighing with decided resignation to this fact. "It's not that they don't believe in *us*; I mean I'm fucking real, aren't I? It's not every day a grown man is born into a tomb."

He flexed his biceps in jest, but his shoulders fell at the look on my face as I asked, "What do you mean by 'don't believe?'"

"Well, it's just that times have changed, Julia. I know you grew up in the *now*, but the world just isn't the same as it used to be. It's hard to convince modern minds that the best way to destroy a Sorcerer is by going back to the basics. People just aren't really willing to die on the battlefield anymore."

"Okay . . . and what exactly are the basics?" I asked with a grimace.

"You know, swords, shields, and clever divisionary tactics. Offensive magic, spells. Brute force."

I watched as his gaze travelled deeply inward, grappling painfully with a memory from of another time. He hated the failures more than anyone, and I felt deep compassion for the guilt he placed upon himself for the repeated losses. However, if I was being honest, I wasn't entirely sure I disagreed with my modern counterparts.

From the disjointed fragments I had managed to accumulate about Cassius, both in this life and from the jagged memories of the past, I knew that his network was inconceivably vast and immensely powerful. He was the kind of man who stopped at nothing to take what he wanted by any means necessary. And, unlike Dom and I, he showed little fear of the future, which was no doubt a result of our continued failures to thwart him fully. One had to wonder if he believed in the Prophecy at all anymore.

Most of Cassius's networks contained non-magical beings, completely unaware of the masked darkness that drove them onward, but that didn't matter. He was hellbent on power, whatever that looked like. After all, the capitalist corporate structure was the perfect place to hide psychopaths and Sorcerers alike.

"So . . . who's coming to stay?"

He grinned then, excitement easily overriding his feelings of disappointment. "Oh! Well, it's not a great number, and there are a few who can't make it, but they will be kept informed. Several from the last time are dead now, but it's no matter. There will be six coming, if you include the Witch."

I blatantly ignored his flippancy around the dead. "Witch? You've found someone?"

"Ronan did actually. Daughter of a friend of a friend? Something like that. She will be coming down from Northern Ireland. Been some logistical issues, but he says she's keen to help in any way she can."

While I was relieved to hear I would soon be sharing the space with another Bearer—it had been far too long—I was also apprehensive to add *more magic* to what felt like an already overbearing atmosphere.

Our first guest, apart from Ronan, arrived smoothly astride the back of a sleek black motorcycle, the type that my friends in high school would have crudely referred to as a "crotch rocket." Dom peered out of the door curiously, but I knew that his personal style was more suited towards vintage bikes. The fact that he had several tucked away in his horse-stable-turned-garage was proof of that.

Lennie Crandall wore a practical matte-black travelling backpack over his fitted leather jacket, and simple black jeans that looked deceptively expensive. He was rather thin in the hips and stood several inches shorter than me, even with his heeled motorcycle boots. Based on his appearance, I surmised that *incognito* was more than a just lifestyle choice for him. What little I had learned about him from Dom and Ronan aptly managed to bolster my first impression.

Roughly my age and English, he had spent his early twenties as some sort of computer whiz who managed to get himself kicked out of Cambridge for ferreting into the school's finances, allegedly outing several instances of corruption and kickbacks between several prominent members of staff. His actions hadn't reflected kindly on the institution, and they'd preferred to make an example of him.

Brains like that didn't go unnoticed by the facets of global intelligence, however, and he had supposedly been swiftly taken on by the British government after his expulsion. Whether that was for his prodigious skills or simply to keep him from joining a more underground sect was unclear—perhaps a bit of both. Both his government and Druidic connections were apparently *quite* prestigious, although he himself wasn't technically a practicing Druid.

This explained how he had crossed paths with Ronan, but it didn't exactly explain why he had been committed to this particular cause, especially when Dom seemed to find him rather irksome. He was of immense value to us though, not least of all because of his ability to think like Cassius's own intelligence league. The other curious element was that he was still *very much* a Wielder, even if he didn't adhere to his alleged Druidic lineage; I could feel it the instant he walked into the room.

"Lennie! Good to see you!" Ronan chimed. "How was the trip?"

"Same as usual. Nothing to report," he said simply.

Evidently at ease in the great house, he immediately bolted towards his usual upstairs bedroom without a second glance, boots still on and shiny black helmet in hand. Dom had already informed me that several members of our band had regular rooms and were altogether quite familiar with the ways and customs of the place. This, however, felt rather presumptuous considering the reason behind our gathering.

Coughing assertively, Dom introduced me to our new visitor's back: "Julia, this is Lennie."

"Oh, sorry Domhnall. Forgot myself." He turned slowly towards me and held out his hand in a proper greeting.

He wore his mousy brown hair cropped short and had beautifully bright skin on his clean-shaven face. His fingers were slender and strangely cool to the touch, and I got the sense from the twinkle in his light-green eyes that he knew *a lot* more about me than I did about him.

"Pleasure to meet you," I said, surprised at my own formality.

"Sometimes Lennie forgets he hasn't actually met someone in person when he already knows far too much about them," Dom said through gritted teeth.

Evidently, a line had been crossed at some point, and Dom gave me an *"I'll tell you later"* look as Lennie turned once more to climb the staircase towards his usual lodgings, skipping every other step in his expedited ascent.

Within moments, the tension cleared.

"Lennie is a bit of an elusive cat," Ronan mused. "He will be back down soon though, and probably in a better mood. He's always anxious to catch up on what he missed while out travelling. But he's *one of a kind.* Invaluable, really."

"That seems to be a common term of endearment around here," I remarked, not clear whether this was a good thing or not.

Dom let out a barking laugh and kissed me gently on my cheek. "I'll put on some music!"

We wandered back in the sitting room where Ronan was already pouring drinks, apparently quite used to the rhythm of days like these, despite the fact that it couldn't be past midday.

"I suppose it's happy hour somewhere," I said as I awkwardly plunked down on the love seat adjacent to the fireplace. I gratefully received a heavy-handed glass of whisky, my choice over the white wine first proffered.

"Suit yourself, darlin'," Ronan had said, pouring himself and Dom similar glasses, although theirs didn't contain ice. *"Sláinte mhaith!"*

I decided not to let the tone of his comment or the presumed addition of ice irritate me. Instead, I took a deep draft of the amber liquid, focusing in vain on the apparent subtle grassy notes of what was a young bottle. Regardless of what I didn't know about sipping whisky, its warmth trickled down my throat with welcome. I eased back onto the couch, pulling my feet up underneath me for warmth.

To my amusement, Dom had worked himself into a fit as he fussed with the record player, his tone and body language steadily increasing in levels of aggravation. A delightful stream of what I could only assume were Irish profanities were being hurled at it with verbal force to no avail. The device in question, situated unassumingly atop a very ornate-looking dresser in the corner of the room, continued to sit proudly in mocking silence.

"The thing's fucking banjaxed!" Dom said as he plugged and unplugged a worn and somewhat shredded black cord. Much to his consternation, the connection between the record player and the aged amplifier seemed to be permanently faulty. I snorted audibly at Dom's plight; the man really was hopeless with electronics.

Just as he was about to give up, Lennie strode into the room.

"At it again, are we?" he asked, clearly sharing the opinion that Dom was a complete Luddite.

Dom bristled slightly, but then changed tactics. "How about your fancy wireless speaker then, the one named after old King Harald of Denmark. He died just before I was born the first time, I believe."

The look on Dom's face was nothing short of smug as Lennie rolled his eyes and Ronan chuckled; this was evidently not a new game for any of them.

"I think you just proved my point, Domhnall," Lennie said, and Dom snorted as he sat down beside me. Before I could decipher who had, in fact, won the joust, Lennie shifted his attention towards me.

"So, Julia, how was your flight? Any troubles at the border?"

"Lennie . . ." Dom said, and I looked between the two of them, perplexed.

"It was alright. Why?" I wondered why he would question my clearance at the airport, which had of course been no issue.

Dom glowered, and then it all started to click into place.

I knew the man was some sort of British Intelligence, though it was never actually mentioned outright. Regardless, he had undoubtedly looked up much more than my address after they'd discovered my whereabouts last summer.

"Oh! If you're referencing the arrests? The first two I was released after questioning. And the third? Charges were dropped." I looked at him serenely over my glass. "Would have been pretty hard to follow my plan to visit the States this year with that on my record, no? Or what about potential law-school applications? Not a good look in the long run, I don't think. You must know all about that too then, since you're *so* curious. I'm no eco-terrorist or anything if *that's* what you're worried about."

I offered him a self-satisfied smile and took another well-earned sip of my whisky.

Admittedly, I had gone through a bit of a phase in my early twenties where I seemed to attract the attention of the law. Once when I was twenty, I'd worked in Northern B.C. for the summer tree-planting. Some of my co-workers had gotten into a bit of a small-town brawl with some loggers at the local bar; it was a very wrong-place, wrong-time situation for me. And then I was arrested twice when I was twenty-four for crossing the boundaries of a pipe-line protest just outside of Vancouver, the first foray being fueled by curiosity and youthful exuberance, the second by pure cheek. I never did like cops.

I noted that I would have to tell the stories to Dom; I knew he would enjoy them. As if to affirm my intuition, he offered me a mingled expression of pride and surprise while I blushed slightly, yet I wasn't finished making my boundaries perfectly clear.

"You probably already told Dom all of that, I assume? And, I'm guessing you didn't have a hard time digging up other unnecessary intelligence on me? I'm an *open book*, so . . . what else do you want to discuss?"

That wasn't entirely true, being someone who actually liked their privacy quite a bit, thank you very much, but I was positively aghast that someone would feel it's their right to dig so deeply into my personal domain, regardless of their intent.

"That depends," Lennie said, although he didn't seem threatened by my tone in the least. I could immediately see how he had the proclivity to get under Dom's skin.

I continued. "Credit card history? Old boyfriends? Dom met one this summer I believe. Jake *has* been a naughty boy, hasn't he?"

I teased his accent, and Dom let out a deep sigh, but I was just getting started if Lennie wanted to unpack this shit to embarrass me in front of the others; I had no patience for the kind of men who liked to embarrass women to boost their own ego.

"Like I said, Julia, Lennie likes to nose into places he shouldn't. It's of no consequence now."

While I appreciated Dom's restraint, he also knew all too well I could handle myself in a verbal spar, and he seemed to be enjoying himself more than a little, despite the "dirty laundry" being so rudely aired.

"Can't be too careful," Lennie said, clearly trying to decide whether he should press the matter further.

Ronan stood up from the corner and clapped his hands together. "Good. Shall we move on then?" He had been uncharacteristically silent throughout the conversation, although he'd kept attentive watch on the discord. I saw him exchange looks with Dom more than once as he boasted a very *"I told you so"* grin. Perhaps Ronan had decided that I *did* have the moxie to handle what our situation required after all.

As if by divine intervention, the sound of wildly barking dogs signalled the influx of three more visitors, the penultimate wave of new arrivals. I was grateful for the break in conversation and stood carefully, stretching out my coiled limbs. The whisky and fire within me had served as a slight boost in bravery, but I had also been habitually tensing much of my body in anticipation of a threat.

The real threat had nothing to do with Lennie but rather my growing concern as to what might happen when I met Peggy and Malcom. *Again.* When Dom and I had looked through the photos from our last meeting, I'd felt a vague familiarity around the pair but nothing that could be considered concrete by any means. I was worried now that I might experience some kind of overwhelming vision, one that would leave me embarrassingly incapacitated, effectively outing my frailties as a Bearer for all to see.

Dom hopped up eagerly to welcome our guests, but not before planting a deceptively sweet kiss on my cheek. He whispered something definitely *not* meant for polite conversation into my ear, and I grinned devilishly in reply. Without pause, I followed the momentum of energy towards the front entrance, ready or not.

Driving a green, *very* British-looking two-door vehicle, a sensible-looking couple rounded the drive at an unprecedented speed before slamming on the breaks coolly, perfectly aligned at the front door.

"They brought the Traveller! Oh, look at the wood," Dom shouted, laughing heartily while clapping his hands in delight. He stepped down onto the drive, arms soon spread wide in greeting.

Indeed, it did have *actual* wood framing the rear half of its body, along with interesting twin rear doors and an overall appearance of a well-rounded and relaxed touring vehicle.

"Well, it can't be good to drive it like *that*," I said to Ronan who shook his head, chuckling along with me at the spectacle. We stood slightly astride one another at the doorway, but still within the confines of the house. Lennie hadn't left his seat in the other room.

It would seem that Malcom shared Dom's love for what were now considered classic cars, though I supposed when they had first met, their shared adoration had been rather contemporary. I peered over Ronan's shoulder and noticed that sprawled across the back seat was something, or someone, rather resembling a large black bear.

"I'll tell you what, Domhnall, they completely botched the almond green! Had to get the *entire* thing re-done!"

I heard what I assumed to be Malcolm's voice hollering out towards Dom, clearly so indignant about the situation that it was his critical first utterance. Dom shouted something enthusiastically in reply, but I was standing slightly too far away to decipher their mutual annoyance towards amateur workmanship.

Malcolm's catapulted words and bold Cornish accent hadn't jogged any particular memory, but surely voices changed with age. Perhaps his face would bring something back if I could look a little bit closer. I felt like a small child peering out from behind the curtain towards the crowd before a recital. Instantly, I felt embarrassed for my reservations in greeting our guests. Dom had made it quite plain this was my home as much as his.

Peggy's sing-song voice rang out in greeting as she opened her car door. "Hello, Domhnall! We made it! And in one piece, if you can believe it!"

She gestured her thumb humorously towards Malcolm, who was already unloading their bags from the back, twin doors swung out wide, shaking his head in reply.

"Peggy!" Dom said, and strode to embrace her with warm, open affection.

She was tall for her generation, with cropped grey hair that elegantly highlighted her dangling sea-glass earrings and a rather funky pair of purple eyeglasses. She wore a travelling scarf around her neck and a long black rain-coat, a look that was both practical and effortlessly chic. Her style was akin to women I knew on the West Coast, but as for she herself, I didn't feel any keen sense of remembrance. At least, not yet.

Malcolm, in spite of his initial entrance, seemed smaller and less boister-ous than his wife. However, the gusto with which he drove his car still led me to believe that there was more than meets the eye when it came to this particular human. He was dressed head to toe in various textures of wool and tweed and boasted the distinct vibe of a schoolmaster or professor, if not for his casual brown corduroy cap and light-brown boat shoes.

"Lifelong Druids," Ronan said. "I've known them for ages. They aren't the fighting type, not anymore at least, but they have a wealth of knowledge we'd be remiss to ignore in our *current* circumstance."

"Mal was jumping about that paint, I'll tell you!" I heard Peggy say gleefully as she tilted the passenger seat forward to release their apparent live capture.

Out of the low back seat emerged Thomas Storey, who was clearly the third wheel of the group. Ronan informed me that he was training under Peggy and had become almost a surrogate son to both she and Malcom, his own family disowning him for following an alternative path to the rigidity of Christianity.

He was a lumbering figure of a man, with long dark hair and a thick beard well matched to his booming voice. His smile was broad, and he greeted Dom with a massive embrace. It was difficult for *anyone* to make Dom look small, but somehow, Thomas pulled it off with ease.

The new arrivals made their way happily towards the door, and I stepped back into the shadows nervously. Peggy handed Dom a brown-paper gift bag tied with a neat red raffia bow before passing through the threshold.

"Something for you to enjoy."

A massive grin spread across Dom's face when he peered inside. "Oh, Pegs, you're too good to me."

She patted him on the arm politely, plainly inferring it was no trouble.

Thomas managed to knock over a coat stand as he moved into the entrance hall in order to give the dogs more attention; they clearly adored him. Ronan stood beside me throughout the chaos as we backed slowly towards the drawing room, evidently preferring to avoid the boisterous greeting. I also felt like he had perhaps been tasked to stay my side by Dom, not that I was complaining. For my own part, I *was* avoiding introductions, anxiously trying to suss out if I was about to be transported violently to another time.

Ronan had finished his whisky and held out his hand to take my identical glass for a refill. I spoke to him quietly under my breath. "Thomas looks like the kind of guy who enjoys LARPing or something."

"Funny you should mention that. *He is.*"

I paused to look at him square on, both surprised and embarrassed at my own accuracy.

"Live action role-playing is a more practical hobby than you might think, Julia."

I could remember watching the mock sword fighters practicing in the park across the street from my childhood home in Victoria, always impressed with the details of the costume and the accuracy of the combat. And the repetition. Over and over, until everyone was grinning broadly, exhausted and thoroughly drenched in sweat. Apparently, there were even some very complex live-action campaigns and thematic games that could be played over weekend retreats and the like. If not for the bitter taste of truth in my mouth around the realities of historical magic battles, I might consider the notion fun.

"I guess it's not just for pretend."

Ronan chuckled wryly and looked over to where Lennie was still focused intently on his phone in the corner. He had rapidly sorted our music problem with a small yet very impressive speaker that was currently playing the Rolling Stones.

"Whisky again or wine?" Ronan asked, this time in non-judgement.

"Wine," I conceded. "White . . . please."

Ahead of our new guests, Dom suddenly appeared at my side. "Are you alright?"

His concern was genuine, and evidently my hesitation had been duly noted. Placing my hand on the talisman, I recalled the vision from earlier and the power I once held.

"Yeah, I'm alright. Why don't you *re-introduce* me—"

"Peggy! Malcom. You'll remember Julia."

The two stood shoulder to shoulder in the doorway to the sitting room, outer apparel removed but now wearing what seemed to be their "indoor shoes." I wiggled my toes within my socks, still feeling underdressed. Dom squeezed me tight, and I smiled with as much grace as I could muster.

"It's so wonderful to see you, Julia. It's been *such* a long time," Peggy said, confident in her understanding of our circumstance and not wishing to belabour my apparent discomfort.

"It's nice to meet you," I replied simply.

They paused in the doorway for a moment before Dom encouraged them to sit. I nodded in polite silence. I noticed with interest that, while neither had reached out to physically touch me, I could still feel the distinct flickers of gentle Wielding magic probing at me in greeting. I felt at ease in their presence, however, even if there were no sure memories or visions surrounding the pair of them. Plus, I hadn't fainted, so that was a bonus.

In fact, I found myself instantly drawn to their infectiously musical and spritely presence. They seemed to be such pleasant and happy people, and I could feel the strength of their individual magics dancing around them—a *very* welcome addition to our current mix of personalities, no doubt.

Enjoying the reprieve from doorbells and bounding dogs, we settled comfortably into the re-assembled lounge. It was soon plain that the others had visited Dom's place several times before, mostly because they all immediately settled into spaces that suited each of their personalities perfectly.

Dom was soon lounging beside me, his arm resting in casual protectiveness along the back of the plush green loveseat; this was clearly *our* spot. Ronan sat in the blue armchair I had occupied earlier, nearest to the fire, and seemed a completely natural fixture to the place. Lennie sat still distracted in the chair opposite Ronan's, boots kicked up onto a squashy brown leather ottoman, which I thought was rather rude. No one else seemed to care or notice.

Peggy and Malcolm, for their part, had comfortably situated themselves on the more modern sofa opposite ours.

"We had *quite* the adventure on the drive here," Peggy remarked as Thomas handed her a glass of water, followed by a short whisky for Malcolm. The dogs were still at his heels, and he soon settled himself onto the carpeted floor to give them the attention they were apparently extremely overdue.

"Mal of course was worried we would be late, but with how he drives," she wagged her thumb affectionately in his direction once more, "that was never a real risk."

Malcom chuckled, smiling conspiratorially towards the group. "I've only been driving us around the countryside for about forty years, and yet . . ."

"I thought I was going to throw up around some of those curves!" Thomas added joyfully, but evidently the event had tendered no real after-effects.

Peggy and Malcolm Davies resided on the coast of Cornwall during the bulk of the summer months, and otherwise wintered somewhere in the west midlands. I was still altogether quite confused around which region was where in England, having never been there myself, but it was my under-standing that they had quite a large extended family, most of whom were Druids they liked to visit throughout the seasons. It was already obvious they enjoyed socializing and lively conversation, along with a solid bit of magic heartily added into the mix.

Their energy was positively magnetic, oozing with the natural magic of a couple very much in love who had experienced much in their well-lived life. I could still sense their Wielding prowess from where I sat, but it was such a pure and light formulation that it only served to add to the atmosphere, rather than confuse it.

They regaled us with wonderful tales of Druidic gatherings and past sailing adventures as we all sat together, myself in particular getting to know everyone. Dom positively delighted in his own retellings of recent adventures, with Ronan providing a well-measured barometer on the truth of the tales. Even Lennie had been surprisingly loquacious in conversation once the party of three had arrived, his parents being old friends of Peggy and Malcolm.

Time was soaring by, but as expected, the conversation returned to me.

"Julia! Dom hasn't told us much about you, other than the obvious. How are you finding Ireland? Must be a change from where you're from?"

"It's probably not that different, Peggy. I visited Victoria a long time ago, when I was a much younger man," Malcom added with a wink.

"He's right. It's actually quite a similar climate. What I'm not used to is all of the magic awaiting me around every corner in the house itself."

I was surprised at how quickly I had landed at the heart of the matter.

"Too right!" Peggy exclaimed. "Dom keeps quite the shrine of charged artifacts around here. I would be overwhelmed too if I could pick up on even half of it."

She waved her hand in a broad gesture around the room. "Wielders don't have the ability to read magical items the way some Bearers do, although we can feel some of the tones or shades of the energy, if that makes sense."

"You're not wrong. It's a bit overwhelming, but I'm getting the hang of it, slowly."

Dom beamed at me with pride, clearly at ease both with his collection of things and my acclimation to the space. Soon enough the conversation migrated away from me once more, and in this case, back towards the collection of cars stashed in Dom's garage.

Being able to speak freely around the truth of our history was an obvious benefit to the shared space with Druids. After all, they (and their kin before them) had allowed Dom safe passage each time he had arrived earth-side, all with the utmost secrecy. But beyond that, this group was very clearly Dom's chosen family, having been with him since his rebirth.

And for that, I was eternally grateful.

CHAPTER 25

The generally cheerful atmosphere of the room had gradually devolved into something much more sinister over the following hour. Three o'clock had come and gone with still no sign of our final house guest, and soon our magically inclined hive mind tuned towards the notable passage of time.

Sandwiches had been brought out from the larder at Dom's behest. They had been prepared in advance by the hired cook, Maureen, to accommodate that day's revolving door. Still somewhat bitter about Maureen's role in all of this, I found myself equally grateful for the nourishment, realizing with some shock that I had still barely eaten all day.

Gobbling back several sandwich halves, I watched Peggy gently hold the talisman that hung around her neck. It was flat and looked like a polished moonstone with a Druidic symbol carved into it. She was silently reciting an incantation or prayer; I couldn't quite tell which. I placed my hand on the necklace Dom had given me, but felt little assurance, comparatively speaking. In truth, I wasn't very familiar with Druidic magic, but it did fascinate me to see it peacefully in practice. Beside her, Malcolm had leaned back and closed his eyes, but he was far from asleep, as his lips were moving slightly in his own recitations.

"I'll be back in a moment," Ronan said, briefly exiting the room, but soon returned with a black leather bag, which he deposited on the floor just under the front windows where he stationed himself as lookout. I was fast learning that everything was strategic when you were stationed under Domhnall O'Brien.

For his part, Dom had just popped onto the phone to alert Morgan of the delay in our final party member and mumbled something about surveillance cameras. Lennie had pulled out his sleek black laptop. When in doubt, apparently, check the computer.

"Lennie will eye the surveillance, but it can be a bit faulty with all the magic around here," Dom said to me. I realized I knew next to nothing about how the manor security actually worked, but I now assumed it was *much* more substantial than I had previously considered.

Of course it was.

Meanwhile, Thomas continued to pet the dogs, cocking his ear in response to any noise alongside them, almost as if he was attuned to the pack itself.

"Can I get you anything?" Dom asked me tenderly so that only I could hear, his protective nature kicking in. He clearly managed stress well, although I noticed he had moved closer, arms wrapped around me like the vast wings of a great falcon.

I leaned back, signalling my increased need for closeness as well. "No. I'm okay. Although . . . hold on . . ."

"What? What is it?"

The room went silent, and all eyes fell on me. Lennie cut the music, and the dogs and Thomas were suddenly alert. A strong vision fast approached, and I had no choice but to bear it. I closed my eyes and dug my nails into the soft velvet of the couch. Soon the icy touch of frigid water surrounded me, pushing in without a care for the oxygen currently in my lungs, effectively dragging me under.

I can't breathe!

In my mind's eye, I could see that Dom had jumped up in front of me and was shaking me by the shoulders like a ragdoll. But I couldn't feel anything in my present body.

Suddenly, I was able to gasp for air, the room swimming violently in front of me once more.

"Julia! Julia!" he yelled as the others surrounded me.

"I think . . ." I said, gulping back heaping gasps of air. "I think she's here. On the property. But she's . . . in the lake?"

How the next several minutes had played out I would likely always struggle to recall; my mind was clouded inexorably from lack of oxygen and the severe disorientation from such a *forceful* vision. Dom, naturally, had burst into immediate action, directing Lennie and Thomas out the door. Peggy and Malcolm had bolted from the room, but it sounded like they had headed for the kitchens, hollering back something about a store cupboard.

"Go, man!" Ronan yelled at Dom as he lingered for a moment. "I've got Julia."

I was dizzy, perplexed, and shaking from the perceived cold, but there was no way in hell I was going to stay prone like that on the floor when one of my few Bearing sisters struggled for dear life in the middle of a lake. She had clearly cast me that vision—a *Send*. It was a skill so completely foreign to me, but I knew with surety that I now needed her more than ever.

My hands felt clumsy with frigid stiffness as I pushed myself up from the ground. After several sobering deep breaths on my knees, I was finally on my feet and began to make for the door.

"Don't—"

Ronan had started to protest but then shook his head. He knew as well as I did that we were both needed outside. And he, unlike Dom, only felt *so* protective of me in these instances.

"She's alive, but something strange has happened . . . I can't quite . . . place it," I said to Ronan, who had thrown his mysterious black bag under his arm only moments before pulling out a small black pistol with a silencer. I raised my eyebrows in genuine surprise as we bolted through the door, Oisín steadfast by my side.

"Not all foes are magical, Julia. This entire property is guarded against dark magic by a whole host of charms and deterrents. Surely you felt *that* when you arrived."

His tone was condescending, clearly frustrated at my inability to see clearly or handle my visions with any skill.

I hadn't asked for much information beyond what Dom had told me about a variety of protections in place. In truth, however, I felt rather foolish for not knowing more about the surrounding battlements, but I wasn't going to give Ronan any satisfaction at the apparently ever-growing gaps in my knowledge.

"I felt a lot of things when I first arrived," I said simply.

While I was still gasping for air somewhat, fresh adrenaline had finally worked itself through my system. I was soon able to jog beside Ronan without too much struggle, although I was developing quite a painful stitch in my side.

Running in silence into the gathering dusk, we soon crossed the grounds to approach the edge of the lake. The scene that unfolded before us was utterly bizarre. Morgan was there, holding a large hunting rifle with what looked like a body heaped at his feet. Thomas and Lennie were nowhere to be found, but I could only assume they had split from the group to search the grounds further.

Domhnall stood holding the motionless body of a waiflike woman, both of them completely soggy with lake water, but the look on his face was calm enough; she was alive.

"Ronan! We need a doctor," he called out. Ronan had yet to holster his gun.

Soon the three of us were kneeling around the unconscious figure. She couldn't be more than fifteen or sixteen years old, her skin a pale and almost translucent blue. Atop her head she bore dark, thick curls.

"What . . . is she?" Dom asked, first looking to Ronan and then towards me.

She was a Bearer, that much I was certain of. But there was something otherworldly to her, almost as if she carried the spirit of the faeries of old.

"Aisling . . ." Ronan said, speaking calmly into one of her ears and then the other. "Can you hear me?"

Soon, Peggy and Malcolm arrived on the scene carrying a basket full of blankets, an odd assortment of what looked like herbal medicaments, and some less friendly looking implements in black leather pouches.

"Wha—"

"Just in case," Malcolm said, covering the pouches with a linen tea towel as Peggy began to wrap the girl in a rough woolen blanket. She was breathing, but it was shallow.

Ronan had checked her vitals, and it looked like Peggy was doing more of a magical evaluation of the girl, the two working seamlessly together in their ministrations. If not for the deep-rooted fear in my belly, it would have been a spectacular sight to witness.

"I think she's alright," I offered, with absolutely no idea where my surety had arrived from. All four conscious faces stared at me.

"I mean, she managed to get the Send to me, and then Dom pulled her out before she drowned. I think she's just . . . shut down for a bit."

Morgan's voice suddenly piped in over us like a loudspeaker.

"And what about this fella?"

Dom popped up, returning to reality just as Thomas and Lennie jogged back towards the group.

"He's not a Wraith, is he?" Thomas asked, clearly not having encountered one in person. They were impossible to forget.

"There's no way a Wraith could have made it through the outer protections," Ronan said as Dom kicked the still form over onto his back.

"You didn't shoot him, did you?" I asked, shocked at the sight of the bloodied face looking blankly at the sky, which was now almost completely dark.

"Nope, got him with the butt of my gun after Domhnall wrestled him to the ground."

I noticed then that Morgan, too, was entirely soaked.

"We need to get her inside," Peggy said as she gestured to Thomas to lift the still unconscious Aisling into his arms. She looked like a doll compared to his mass, and along with Peggy and Malcolm, he trudged towards the house without a single glance back.

"Ronan, I'm going to need you to attend to his wounds. Lennie, you had better come too. Let's take this bastard to Morgan's for interrogation once he wakes up."

The look on Dom's face was menacing, and I wasn't altogether sure if Dom was referring to his current wounds or others he had yet to receive. Morgan had already slung the rifle over his shoulder and was headed down the drive towards the gatehouse, boots squelching loudly with each measured step.

I stood, utterly frozen between the two groups, momentarily unsure where I fit into the whole mess of things.

"Julia—" Dom started, but I cut him off before any waffling could begin.

"I need to make sure she's okay." As much as I wanted to stick close to Dom after such a frightening escapade, my intuition told me that where

I was truly needed was at the side of the only Bearer I had spoken to in months. She had called out to *me*, and therefore I needed to be there when she woke up.

He nodded in what was clearly apprehensive agreement but soon turned to join the others, jogging to catch up to Ronan, who had easily slung the inert body over his shoulders in a fireman's carry.

"Oisín!" Dom shouted back. With a subtle motion of his head, he commanded his trusty hound to join me as I returned to the manor house. The dog needed no further direction as he trotted towards me.

After all was said and done, we would discover that the man who had stalked and consequently attacked Aisling had been hired to track her if she were to leave her previous location, ensuring that her whereabouts were always known. And if it came down to it, to restrain her by any means necessary.

Much like the situation with Ben, someone had predicted there would be magical forces protecting her, and so had cleverly enlisted a non-magical person to do their bidding. But either through deception or Sorcery, they ensured the hitman couldn't disclose who had sent him. It reeked of Cassius and his Wraiths, Aisling being clearly marked for their dark intentions. A small part of me wondered if this individual had been tricked and coerced just as Ben had been, or downright bewildered, but even my compassion had its limitations.

She awoke about an hour after Dom found her unconscious, floating atop the water on her back. Thomas, Peggy, Malcolm, and I had gathered around her on the drawing-room floor when she suddenly sat up, completely disoriented and grasping for her surroundings.

"It's okay, dear; you're safe now," Peggy said, and gently encouraged her to lie back down.

She looked somewhat older now that the colour had returned to her checks, perhaps in her early twenties, but she still bore a youthful, ageless quality about her. Almost otherworldly.

"Not very 'Lady of the Lake' of me to almost drown," she said, and the Druids laughed in turn. I wasn't particularly well versed in the mythos of the Blessed Isles; however, I caught what she was throwing well enough. "Anyway, I'm Aisling."

We took the next few minutes to introduce ourselves before she told us what had happened.

She had apparently felt the presence of her stalker several times on her journey towards the manor but had failed to shake her tail completely. When she'd finally arrived, it had actually been on foot in the hopes of eluding him by hiding in the bushes several miles down the road from where she had exited her taxi. She was shocked to discover, while navigating through the magical enchantments around the grounds, that he had been able to follow her through, as if a trace had been placed on her person somehow.

Panicking, she had thrown herself into the lake, hoping it would deter him long enough that she could get a message out, or that it would remove whatever dark spell had been cast upon her. What she hadn't bargained on was him following her into the water, or almost drowning herself shortly thereafter.

"I got your message, the Send. It was incredible," I said, openly in awe of her talent.

"I have to apologize for that; it probably came on a little bit . . . strong."

I shrugged my shoulders. "I survived."

She laughed lightly, which reminded me of the twinkling of a wind chime.

"Well, *I* almost didn't. I passed out from the effort and almost drowned myself. I think my stalker thought he'd killed me and panicked."

Just then, Dom, Ronan, and Lennie waltzed into the room looking rather pleased with themselves. I noticed blood spattered on Dom's still-damp joggers, and Lennie's knuckles looked like they were beginning to swell. Ronan, as usual, was spotless.

I eyed Dom speculatively, and he shrugged but showed no guilt.

"He won't remember where he followed you to, Aisling," Ronan said as he crouched down beside the young woman. "And he certainly won't be bothering you any longer. We saw to that."

"You didn't kill him, did you?" I asked, suddenly fearing the worst.

Aisling too looked nervously between me and the three strangers who had just entered the room. This was the first time she had met any of them actually, although she seemed to have had an intuitive sense of me from the get go.

"Of course not, Julia," Dom said. "What kind of monsters do you take us for?"

At this point, I honestly wasn't sure. There was *a lot* of blood on his pant leg.

"He had a nosebleed is all."

"And Lennie's hand?"

The three of them looked at each other, feigning innocence as Lennie shoved his hand into his pocket.

"No idea what you're taking about."

It would seem there was some sort of unspoken code about how these things went, since Peggy and Malcolm seemed completely unburdened by the telling, or rather, un-telling of their tale. Everyone settled back into their usual positions with a collective exhale, Aisling joining Malcolm and Peggy on the longest couch.

"I'm so sorry for the inconvenience, everyone. Truly. I thought I had shaken the bastard, but he was a resourceful fucker," Aising said, her language notably brash against her spritely demeanour.

"They tend to be that way," Dom said in agreement. "We're just glad you made it. I know you and your mother were unsure about all of this." Clearly, I had been left out of some of the more critical details of this plan, but I was so eager to learn more, I set my annoyance aside once more.

"She still is. Was right pissed when I decided to go. But it's important I do what I can to help. I can feel the threat growing too."

The atmosphere of the room quickly shifted from the adrenaline-fuelled frenzy of earlier in the evening to a much more serious discussion of what was at stake.

"Has Ronan filled you in on the Prophecy?" Dom asked her, and I held my hand up in what would prove to be a vain attempt to slow things down.

"Hold on; she just got here. Give her a minute," I said, defensively.

"It's alright, Julia. I only have so long with all of you. We can't afford to waste a minute."

There was something ominous in her tone that sent a cool ripple down my spine.

"I didn't really, only what she apparently already knew," Ronan said.

"My granny was a great Diviner, but she's long since passed. She knew of the Prophecy though, or some variation, I assume, and passed it down to my mum, which eventually came to me after a bit of prying." She looked around the room with a half-smile. "She doesn't think it's a good idea to get mixed in with all of this. I probably won't tell her about the lake . . . Anyways, it foretold of someone who would arrive, apparently out of the mists, and gather us together to defeat our greatest foe."

"Right," said Dom. "And did it explain *how* they would come . . . or *when?*"

He had settled in close beside me on the couch, and I wondered absently if he felt the same deep ache I felt when we weren't in close proximity. He squeezed my thigh gently and demonstrated our unified front, and while I appreciated the sentiment, he also smelled a bit like a wet dog.

Aisling shook her head, but Lennie interrupted her before she could utter a reply.

"You know, I'm not entirely sure I understand how it all works either. You've been a bit vague on how this all works, and why it's so important to adhere to the way it's always been done."

Lennie was seriously starting to grate my cheese, but Dom spoke up first, ignoring Lennie's tone entirely.

"Julia and I were both born in the late tenth century. Well, our first births, that is."

Aisling looked impressed but not altogether surprised, and the others remained silent, already aware of this magical aspect.

"We regenerate differently, which is a tale for another time. But the long and short of it is that Julia and I, and potentially our future child if you choose to interpret the Prophecy that way, hold the key to defeating Cassius once and for all. It's because of our individual curses that we continue to have the chance to do so, learning more each time, inching closer to what will hopefully be the final victory."

"But you—well, *she*—has been forgetting," Ronan said flatly.

Dom shot him a dirty look, but I stilled him.

"No, Ronan is right. Something is happening each time, where I remember less, and we aren't sure if it means the strength of the curse is fading . . . or something else."

It was the *something else* that I was most afraid of . . . that the winds of change were upon us, and our destiny was steadily veering off course for good. More than anything, I was now terrified that, if we failed this time around, we would lose each other forever.

"But that still doesn't answer why we put so much stake in an archaic Prophecy," Lennie said.

"Well, thus far, it's the best guide we have. Unless you have any better suggestions?" Dom said, leaning back into the couch, his muscular arms crossed aggressively across his chest.

Ronan shook his head in frustration and stood up, evidently *this* wasn't a new argument either. "What we do know, Aisling, is that there is always a moment in time where it all comes together, whether it be when the good guys are forced to meet Cassius in some sort of 'magic-users-only' battle . . . or Dom and Julia are killed before we even get the chance, and it all starts over again."

Ronan was pacing the room now, visibly uneasy around either of these options. I was beginning to wonder if Ronan's distrust around the Prophecy wasn't entirely pragmatic but rather born out of deep concern for losing his dearest friend.

"Lennie's quite certain we could find a work-around for a physical battle, beating him on a different playing field, digitally and without modern weaponry. But Dom assures us that the battle, if he and Julia make it that far, is *always* fought in the old magical way, as that's how it's written in destiny."

"Even if we try to fight him some other way, it always comes to a head on the battlefield," Dom said, as if to strengthen his point. "That or we're killed anyway."

Aisling looked around the room, then let out a soft whistle.

"Well, I'm not sure how I can help, but I would like to, if I can."

"I need—" Dom said, but then stopped himself. "*We*, that is Julia and I, need you to try to help her regain some of her memories or access to her powers. The older ones. Your granny was a Diviner, right? Perhaps you know something we don't, or some way to unlock secrets of the past that could help us find a way around or through the battle. The odds seem greater than ever this time."

Dom looked at me with reassurance, but the old gnawing of uncertainty at the pit of my stomach had returned once more. What I needed was to get Aisling alone so we could talk frankly about all of this—and about the quilt.

The quilt.

Once more it had slipped my mind, but I was going to be damn sure I remembered it when I finally had a chance to pick Aisling's brain. We had reached a natural pause in our discussion, Malcolm having dozed off on the couch and Peggy herself yawning through her hand as she listened to Lennie and Ronan spin off on a debate around the potential for the integration of technology and magic.

"It's already being done all around us!" Lennie yowled, and Ronan rolled his eyes in annoyance.

I leaned into Dom, who stroked back a stray strand of hair from my face.

"I'm ready for bed, love, if you are?" he asked.

I was utterly exhausted, but unfortunately expected that any sleep ahead would be plagued with nightmares of drowning in our own destiny or something of the sort.

"Please," I said, yawning through my chilled fingers.

"Aisling, I can show you your room," Peggy said kindly, alleviating us of our hosting duties and allowing us a direct descent to bed. I was seriously beginning to like Peggy.

Finally tucked under the covers together, Dom having first insisted he take a shower to wash both the lake and the stranger's blood off himself before joining me, I felt an overwhelming sense of relief. The day was done, and at long last, I was horizontal.

I had placed the priceless necklace back into the linen square and into the box on the bedside table, making a mental note to find a better way to store and protect it in the future, when I wasn't wearing it.

"Never a dull moment," I said, snuggling in close to my freshly bathed Celt.

His laugh rumbled low and sure, reverberating through me like a soothing hum.

"I was proud of you today."

"Oh? What for?" I asked.

He nuzzled into my collarbone. "Hmm . . . lots of things. But mostly for just being you."

If he was referencing my attitude towards Lennie, he had a point; that was definitely an authentic inflection. Otherwise, I still felt like I was completely winging it and somewhat guarded in most of my interactions. After all, I was used to protecting myself.

I stroked his hair gently, I could hear his breathing slowing considerably, and before long, he was fast asleep. With his warm and weighty body draped halfway across me, and his muscular left thigh bent comfortably on top of my own, the deep pressure of his frame dragged me into my own slumber shortly thereafter.

I did dream that night, but they were of a surprisingly more erotic nature, including a very beautiful gold necklace and a certain brawny Celt who had just returned victorious.

CHAPTER 26

The following morning, it was made immediately clear that not only did the others have their usual rooms they would occupy but also their own individual routines within the space as well.

Ronan, naturally, was up at the crack of dawn and had already been for a run and completed his breakfast by the time we found him in the kitchen. Dom usually would have joined him; however, I had made it *quite* plain that our athletic pursuits this morning involved a certain necklace and a particularly sultry re-imagining from last night's dreams, which of course he had no difficulty obliging to.

Peggy and Malcom were also early risers it would seem, already seated comfortably around the long kitchen table with Ronan, their plates empty and cups thoroughly drained.

"Good morning, Domhnall!" Peggy chimed lyrically, while Malcolm looked up from his paper with a nod.

"Lennie is still upstairs, as usual, but I'm certain he's awake," Ronan said.

"I'll take him something to eat shortly here," an unknown voice piped in from over beside the stove; this must be Maureen.

Apparently, it was entirely usual for Lennie to hole up and work while he was here, the privilege of remote access I supposed, and Maureen was more than happy to accommodate this as well. This really was a well-oiled machine.

"Has anyone seen Aisling?" I asked, distracted by Maureen's ministrations beside the stove, already plating up what looked to be Dom's favourite breakfast, but no sooner had the words left my mouth than she appeared in the doorway behind me.

The backpack containing her belongings had been retrieved by Thomas and Lennie on their second patrol last night before bed, and she was dressed simply in dark skinny jeans and a soft light-blue knit sweater, her dark curls pulled tightly into a knot atop her head and a large, shiny silver hoop earring dangling brightly off each lobe. The overall effect added to her height only slightly; she really was quite a petite woman.

"Good morning, everyone," she said shyly.

Naturally, between the combination of Peggy's vivacious attitude and Maureen's efficient, if not almost militant, ability in the kitchen, everyone sat welcome in the space. Well, almost everyone. Between the piping hot food, as well as Peggy and Malcolm's proclivity to break out randomly into what were apparently Gilbert and Sullivan numbers, I *should have* felt completely relaxed and at home. Instead, I found myself clutching onto a deeply embedded pang of regret for not finding this type of skill naturally within myself. Hospitality had never been my strong suit, and I wondered if this bothered Dom at all, as he too seemed to ooze a natural proclivity for providing others with ease of comfort in most situations.

Before I could dwell any longer, a large shadow appeared behind Aisling in the doorway. Thomas joined us at the breakfast table then, and the dogs were beside themselves with delight that he had joined in the fray.

"He feeds them more table scraps than you do!" Dom said to me with a grin as he took a massive bite of amply buttered toast, white teeth gleaming.

The atmosphere *was* pleasant, and the conversation flowed as freely as warmed honey, sweet and bright and easy to swallow. Even Maureen seemed agreeable enough, and quite familiar with most of the group. I wondered absently if her family too had served the O'Brien's over the past centuries, well accustomed to the haphazard comings and goings of the most varied dinner guests one could imagine.

Thomas was in the middle of telling a rousing story involving his wearing of an extremely heavy suit of armour and a very poorly timed encounter with a goose.

"Julia, I was wondering if we might take a walk after breakfast? Away from everyone," Aisling said quietly, so the others wouldn't hear. Evidently, she too felt the need to break away from the fracas and speak more plainly, Bearer to Bearer, Witch to Witch.

"Absolutely. I can meet you at the front doors once we've finished up." I gestured at the gratuitous breakfast spread out before us. "Did you bring rubber boots?"

She looked down at the silver ballet flats on her feet and shrugged.

"My trainers should be dry enough from last night. I left them by the fire."

"Perfect."

I was suddenly feeling rather suffocated by so many people crammed into such a small space. Even though the long table fit everyone with ease, the low ceiling of the kitchen was not helping with my claustrophobic leanings; I was anxious to speak with Aisling now that we had a scheme in place. I twisted awkwardly towards Dom to tell him I was headed out for a walk, and he responded only half attentively, mumbling, "Absolutely, love," and kissing me on the cheek before returning to the energized conversation at the table.

I gave Aisling a quick nod, slid silently from the kitchen, and walked distractedly towards our bedroom to grab another sweater. Lost in my own thoughts, I was completely startled when I almost ran headlong into Maureen on her way back from what I assumed was delivering Lennie's breakfast.

"Oh! I'm *so* sorry!" I said, and helped right her tea tray, my face full of honest apology.

"Mm," she said with a curt nod, and hustled past me back towards the kitchens without another word. Strange, that energy was *very* contradictory to what had been expressed downstairs. Had Lennie said something offensive? More than likely.

Soon enough, I was back downstairs and waiting for my new walking buddy beside the front door. I wished Oisín would be joining us, but he was likely with Sully and Mags, mooching heartily from Thomas at the breakfast table. After several minutes, Aisling arrived with a semi-soggy pair of runners on her feet and a pack of cigarettes in her hand.

"You don't mind, do you?" she asked as we headed off the front steps and into the wild.

"Of course not."

Although the morning was clear, a frost was still thoroughly blanketing the lawns. We walked in peaceful silence for a time; something about her invited calm and pensive thought. When we made it about halfway around the lake, she finally spoke.

"I know a bit more than I shared last night, about the Prophecy," she said in almost a whisper. She had finished her first cigarette and was in the process of lighting another. I hadn't noticed her smoking habit last evening, but perhaps she was just nervous.

"I wondered," I said.

Why else would she have come? It seemed a random request to join a group of strange Druids and their kin in the countryside on short notice. Not to mention that her arrival had given me the strange sense that more strings were being pulled beyond our earthy reckonings than we knew.

"My granny, she knew you would be coming. Well, returning. You knew her then, although she was fairly certain you wouldn't remember her. But it's not important, because I'm here now to pass on the message."

She had my full attention now.

"I can't stay long. Mostly because I'm fairly certain I'm marked by *him.*"

"What do you mean?"

Something as heavy as a stone dropped into the pit of my stomach as she took a long and slow draw on her cigarette.

"I'm going into hiding after this. I really should have gone some time ago, but I was also waiting for you. You sure took your time finding Domhnall again, didn't you?"

I tilted my head slightly, curious what her somewhat altered interpretation of the matter had been and what else she might be holding back.

"Do Dom or the others know that you've already heard of the Prophecy?"

"Of course not!" She laughed, the sound of twinkling bells surrounding me once more. "This is Bearer's business. And I'm here to teach you, and as quickly as I can, mind you, so pay attention . . . Please."

She had obviously added the latter part of the request as an after-thought.

It was almost dizzying the pace at which she was doling out what she apparently viewed as facts on the matter; there was absolutely no mistaking that she was feeling pressure to get moving.

"I need to teach you how to perform *a Send*. I am one of the few left in this part of the world who can still perform the skill with any effectiveness, although last night was a very poor demonstration. Sorry about that. But I'm afraid you're stuck with me."

She laughed again, stopping in her tracks to stomp out her second butt. She looked to be considering a third one, but momentarily thought better of herself.

"Do you have any idea how it works?"

"I've only ever heard of them though stories, and last night was probably the first time I've ever been on the receiving end of one, at least knowingly. My grandma Gertie told me about them once a long, long time ago. It's a rare and ancient gift you have."

"And it's one you're going to need if you're hoping to stand half a chance this time around. My granny said to tell you that time was most certainly running out. You'll need all the help you can get."

She spoke with such surety; clearly her granny's word was law.

"And if I can be completely honest with you, Julia, the others are placing far too much emphasis on the possibility of a final battle before the solstice. You're going to need much more in your arsenal than what you, and *they*, already know, if you hope to defeat him. Well, that's what my granny told me, anyway."

I let this roll around in my head for a few moments, and then thought of the quilt.

"I found an enchanted quilt, and I think there is some important magic embedded in it. Some sort of message, or puzzle. Or . . . well, I don't know really. But I can't seem to crack it. It's all chaos and confusion when I do try, and I mostly just seem prone to forgetting about it all together most of the time."

"Sounds like it's important."

She looked up and considered me for a moment before finally deciding to pull out a third cigarette. "I can't help you with that though. I'm so sorry. I was given specific instruction by my granny to teach you to Send, and then it would be high time for me disappear for a while. I'm amazed I even made it here alive."

"I understand," I said, even as my heart sank further.

For her part, she didn't look too concerned.

However, I had been desperately hoping she would have some sort of wisdom around the kind of magic that had been placed on the textile. I had such a strong intuition that it was important, but I seemed to be about the only one involved with the cause so far who thought it was important, besides Dom, and even he seemed to have his doubts.

"Julia, I know you want to figure out what the quilt means, but we are here now, with the Druids. I really think it's important to focus on the task at hand while we have our resources all gathered under one roof," he had said when we first arrived.

I carried the discomfort of the quilt's burden with me as Aisling and I walked farther away from the manor and towards a small copse of trees.

"I don't think you should tell the others I'm teaching you how to do this. It will put a greater target on your back. But I think it's worth the risk."

I looked at her with serious inquiry. *More danger?*

"I mean, tell your Domhnall, of course. He'll need to know, as he's going to need to help you practice. There's a considerable magical bond between the two of you, in case you hadn't noticed."

I heard the distant chiming of bells, Aisling's own magic very much present around us in the current moment; she was starting to focus her energy. It felt like ages since I'd last basked in another Bearer's presence, and I realized how desperately I'd missed the company.

"Is it at all like the Sight? I'm afraid I'm awful at controlling any of that," I said.

She nodded sombrely. "It is. My granny could do both. She said that most with the Sight could learn to Send and would be adept at receiving them as well, but not all who could Send were born with the Sight. Like me. That doesn't seem to be deterring Cassius from hunting us down, though."

Magic was certainly a complex weaving of riddles and word games, which made sense, as you were trying to put earthly words to something completely otherworldly.

"How do you know so much about . . . *him?*"

"Those of us who are born descendants of the Witches of old . . . well, in one way or another, we were all told in secret about the dark force that hunts us. It's the reason we're all hiding, Julia. Surely you know that much."

Not entirely. So much of the mythos and illuminative lore of previous generations had been stomped. Countless women and Witches, all wrangled and controlled, oppressed and suffocated in the name of modern patriarchal society. Perhaps living in the New World had also given me a false sense of security, even if I hadn't known it.

"Okay, I'm ready. Teach me."

She nodded, agreeing that we were wasting far too much time on the hypothetical.

"So. It's almost as if you can sense a cord between yourself and someone, and it's a lot easier if you have an actual personal tie between the two of you. For me, finding you has been written in my destiny since I was born. But as I had never met you in person, I put rather too much force into the Send and almost drowned myself in the process." She laughed again, but there was no smile on her face, nor were there bells in the air.

"Your best bet really is to start with Domhnall, as you know him best."

I realized with a rush of regret that he was about the only person of any consequence in my life at the moment. However, he was also the only person I had ever felt a full physical bond to, besides my grandma Gertie . . . and my mother, sometime long ago.

"Is he in your mind?" she asked, and I nodded.

"Good. Now, you have to imagine the core of your magic."

"It's—"

"No, don't tell me. Just picture it, as that is where your source originates. I'm assuming you already knew that, but it really does help to picture it. It's obviously different for every Bearer . . . but however you see it, that's where it is."

I imagined hers must have included a great silver pipe organ with endless chimes and bells of all sizes, all of which culminated in an elaborate cacophony of wind and bright light.

I then thought of my own inner fire, which resembled more of a great hearth, an eternal fire that contained not only my own magical essence but also the fires of the countless generations of Bearers before me. This great combined fire was carried on, generation after generation, cycle after cycle, for better or for worse. It lived deep, deep within, perhaps in the most remote part of my entire being.

"Now, you're going to need to Send from *that* place, and that place only. You can't Wield this kind of magic, as there is no way to source it or restore its cost back into the earth. And that's precisely why *he* wants it. It's useful, and powerful, and its *wild.*"

Wild magics. I had heard of these; the ancient Bearers had used them freely throughout history, but they had been the first magics to be stifled by the Witch hunts. It was similar to Wielding, as it was cast outward from the magic user, but it was exponentially more powerful. Sorcerers were known to use this type of magic freely, and if he was looking for it, I could only imagine what he would do with it once it was captured.

"You're not thinking of Dom. You need to focus. I won't be here after today; time is running out," she said, face still eerily unafraid.

I held the first image of Dom that came to mind, a particularly delicious image that I had seen only this morning when we first awoke, long and languid in his raw masculine form; now *that* was an image I didn't struggle to conjure up.

"Good. Now reach into your magical core and Send! Almost like throwing a single word or idea towards him."

I looked at her, bewildered.

"But what's the point of it all?"

She thought for a moment. "Well, I suppose, in its simplest form, it's a way to call for help. More complicated . . . it's a way to communicate, pass on knowledge to others at a distance."

I nodded slowly.

"I know it sounds simple, but you have to start simple. Plus, it's harder than it looks."

She was becoming impatient, digging around in her empty cigarette pack, and I soon had the distinct sense this meant I was now well and truly on the clock.

A word. An idea. What would I choose?

She gave me a withering look, as I was obviously wearing my over-contemplation across my face.

"Got it?" she asked.

"Yup."

"Now . . . Send it!"

I sent the first words that came to mind: roast chicken.

And then I waited.

As it would turn out, my first Send had been an abysmal failure. Aisling had purposely not alerted the others to what we were doing out near the trees for several reasons: first and foremost, for my own safety. Second, it was so that Dom wouldn't catch on to what was happening, and so we could have a completely clean slate the first time we tried, in case by some miraculous gift, it had worked.

It hadn't.

Though on his way to take his dogs out for a run after breakfast, he did say he'd felt a strange sensation while he passed through the kitchens as Maureen was cleaning up. It had apparently felt almost like a brief disorientation, but it had passed as quickly as it had arrived.

After the three of us returned to the manor house from our varied excursions, Dom, Aisling, and I were sitting privately in the sitting room, discussing my recent learnings, when she suddenly popped up and made her excuses about it being time for her to go.

"Already? But you've only just arrived."

"And Julia has learned all that she can from me. Now, all she needs to do is practice."

I slumped back onto the green-velvet couch and let out a long groan.

"Are you sure?" Dom asked, looking between the two of us, evidently uneasy about this new turn of events.

Aisling dug around absently in her backpack, presumably searching fruitlessly for another pack of smokes. Several short curls had fallen down from her bun on our way back towards the house, and she looked much younger again than she had when she was teaching me outside.

"And remember, Julia, you really shouldn't tell anyone about this, or the extent of your divining abilities, really. Even if they are dodgy. It's just so fuckin' dangerous for us all out there. Keep it a secret for now, won't you?"

I still had the distinct sense that she was keeping something else from me, but I was also sure she had been truthful in all of the words that had left her mouth.

"I'll have Morgan drive you out, along with Ronan. Shouldn't have any problems then," Dom said, standing up to escort her out.

"Thank you, I appreciate it. You likely won't be hearing from me again, but . . . oh!" She jumped with unexpected remembrance. "There's someone, like you, with the Sight, who could perhaps help with your quilt situation. I don't know why I didn't think of it before. She was a friend of my granny's, her name is . . . um . . . Agnes! Agnes Sweeney. Yeah, that's it. And if she's still alive, she's a mighty powerful Witch too. Was always a bit funny in the head, Granny said, but I would say she's worth looking up. I think she's over in England somewhere."

This new information boosted my mood considerably, and I thanked her again for coming to see me, despite the circumstances, and watched her and Dom leave the room together.

I would be sad to see the only other Bearer in the house leave after having only just arrived, but it gave me hope that if she was out there with this tidbit of help, maybe someone else out there would be willing to help me unlock my lost memories and magical abilities. Agnes Sweeney, for one.

Prior to meeting Dom, I really had no idea how truly dangerous it was to be a magic Bearer in these times. I felt a crushing sense of naivety about so much of the greater magical world. Now, after speaking with Aisling, it was abundantly clear to me that, while I had thought that the great covens of the world had long since diminished under the pressures of the new world order, it was indeed Cassius who had been well and truly at the helm of their destruction. The main culprit for their disintegration being the need for secrecy and safety from *him*.

I moved to a low bench beside the window and watched anxiously as Aisling loaded up and drove away from the manor house. Within moments, Dom had returned, having also apparently tasked Lennie with locating a "Ms. Agnes Sweeney." Surely, he would be up for the task, as it fed preferentially into the "alternative to the Prophecy" vein of strategy.

"Julia, I know you are anxious to understand the quilt," Dom said.

"I am, and I just don't understand why we can't place a greater focus on that. I've seen the maps in your study, the lists of names of people waiting to come and support the cause; you're preparing for a *battle*. But what if the battle could be avoided altogether? Something tells me the *quilt* could hold the solution."

He ran his long fingers through his tousled hair; he hadn't yet had a chance to wash up since his run and the effect left his hair standing almost on end. At this rate of growth, he would soon be able to wear it tied back. He lowered himself onto the bench beside me.

"I understand your concern. But the fact is that it almost always ends up in a battle. That . . . or we die before. We would be remiss not to at least have our resources at the ready and a solid plan in place. Ronan agrees and—"

"And Lennie doesn't. So, where do I fit into all of this? What about Peggy and Malcolm? Thomas? You saw what happened to Aisling. She was literally hunted down trying to help me, and thank the Goddess the fucker didn't have any magical abilities. What then?"

I was becoming increasingly tired of living on the edge of conflict with my newfound yet ancient lover. I spread my knees wide, placing my head into my hands, once again overwhelmed and exhausted.

Dom slid closer, taking my chilled hands into his much warmer ones. He smelled of cooled sweat and exertion, and a bit like the dogs again. I closed my eyes and was easily transported to an endless array of memories with the same atmosphere and feelings of desperation. I couldn't quite place my finger on any single one, but I knew we had been here far too many times before.

"Peggy and Malcolm remember what happened to us—to you—the last time we were here. Understandably, they don't want a repeat."

I stared at him in silence. He made a point of *never* speaking of the circumstances of our deaths, but I knew that our most recent one had been swift and brutal, with me passing before Dom could save me. I also knew there hadn't been battle in 1968, even though I had locked away any memories of my own death entirely.

"I wish we could . . ." He left the thought unfinished.

I looked up at him, grief swimming once more in the pools of his eyes. I already knew what he wished without him completing the sentence, because

I also felt it so strongly that it hurt. With all of my heart, I wished that we could run away from it all, together, and escape this ill-fated destiny for good.

"I know, Dom. I do too."

He drew me close as I held tight to the tiny spark of hope embedded deep within me that there *had to* be another way out. If he could protect us for a just little bit longer, perhaps I could find, within myself, the answers I so desperately sought.

CHAPTER 27

A s the days wore on at *Caisleán na Spéirmhná,* I found myself worn continuously thin by the unspoken expectations put upon me, both as the only Bearer in the space as well as the one around whom the Prophecy would most closely revolve.

January had nearly drawn to a close, and the others were preparing a small party for February first to celebrate Imbolc, a traditional Gaelic festival, but I found it hard to get in the mood. Dom and Ronan also seemed uninterested in any kind of ritual frivolity, as they continued to spend countless hours drawing up battle plans, scouting battlegrounds, seeking allies across the world, and configuring every possible hypothetical result if the threat were to come to us . . . versus if we took the offensive.

I continued to avoid Dom's study like the plague, far preferring to spend most of my time outside, or in the kitchens if Maureen wasn't around. Thomas joined "the lads" in the war room regularly, his own experiences with live action role-playing proving to be an asset in its own right. Lennie too was part of the complex schemes and arguments, although he continued to prefer to conduct his work from his upstairs lair.

At least on paper, Dom had continued to be supportive of me, promising that when the time was right, we would seek out and find the answers we needed. Lennie had easily tracked down Agnes Sweeney, so Dom suggested we visit her in the spring, once they had their plans firmly settled.

"Think of it as a contingency plan," he had said in reference to their work, though it hardly felt like that with the intensity with which they undertook it. I wondered—for what felt like the hundredth time—what the point had been of even dragging me into all of this, other than the fact that I was some sort of keystone in setting the final wave of the Prophecy into motion. While the smile across his lips was reassuring, it failed to reach his eyes, giving way to the anxiety locked there. We were running out of time to gather the intelligence we needed, and the quilt just wasn't important enough to get in the way of things.

Aisling, of course, had left me with the task of learning to Send, which was not only going very poorly but had caused even more conflict between Dom and myself as a result.

"I need us to find some time to work on this . . . to *connect*. I can't do that properly when you're in *there.*"

I had been talking, of course, about his study, so cluttered with artifacts and what he had called mementos that I couldn't seem to get even a fragment of a Send through all of the bloody magical *noise*.

"I'm sorry; we will. I promise. It's just that we're onto something right now. Soon, alright?" he'd said one morning as we lay in bed after I'd had a particularly tumultuous sleep, and he had been thoroughly *not* bedded. He was also hungry and distracted.

Admittedly, it wasn't the best time to bring it up for either of us, but I'd been struggling to find any time with him alone.

"Fine!" I had shouted, rather childishly, before burying myself under the covers until he had dressed and left the room. Fuming, I'd thought of the story where I'd begged him to not let me forget him. *What now, Domhnall? I'm sitting right here!* He didn't seem to think I was all that important, after all.

What I really needed was someone to talk to who wasn't Dom, or any of the other war mongers in his study. While Thomas and I had grown closer throughout many of the group gatherings, he was an integral piece to the planning puzzle, so I didn't see him much outside of mealtimes.

I was disappointed to learn that Peggy and Malcolm were planning to leave mid-February to go home for a while and rest. Having supported Ronan as best they could with any Druidic ministrations and queries, they wished to reconnect with their family and would return in a few months to help us further. Sooner if needed, of course, but hopefully not. However, they would be leaving Thomas as a continued support.

I met them both in the kitchen one morning after taking a slow shower and dressing warmly for yet another day spent wandering aimlessly outside, attempting to Send and otherwise contending with my demons. I noticed that Peggy too was dressed for the outdoors, and she looked at me expectantly. Malcolm was hidden behind a newspaper, apparently engrossed in the current events of the day.

"I thought we might take a walk. You've been looking like you could use a friend the last while."

She had clearly picked up on my deteriorating mood, which I had all but given up on hiding from the general mass of the house over the last few days.

"Sure, I was heading out anyways. The dogs have gotten used to it now, so I don't think they would tolerate if I *didn't* go," I said, feigning lightness.

Peggy smiled patiently as I slid on my rubber boots and sorted the dogs around me before heading out into the sunshine.

"You really don't remember us from last time, do you?" she asked.

"No, not really . . . I'm sorry, Peggy."

She laughed heartily. "There's nothing to apologize for! We're old codgers now anyway, especially Malcolm. It was a long time ago. I barely remember much of it myself!"

I assumed she wasn't completely telling the truth but appreciated the white lie for my sake anyways.

"What I will say, though, is that your love for Domhnall is much the same, at least to my old eyes. He still looks at you like he did then, which is quite miraculous to behold! But of course, you weren't without your struggles then either. These . . . frustrations, shared between you, were much the same as well."

I groaned. "I'm not sure that makes me feel any better."

"Oh, Julia, come now. Think about it. You only ever have so much time together, and each time it's completely wrought with fear and anticipation of your *imminent death,*" she said dramatically. "Surely, you can imagine how that would cause some strife. Hell, the two of you barely ever have enough time to go through the normal growing pains of a couple, let alone process the grief of countless lives passed. Besides, do you think Malcolm and I don't have our moments?"

I chuckled; there was absolutely no doubt they had done plenty of growth together throughout the years.

"Believe me," she said raising her eyebrows playfully, "there are *moments!*"

We walked in amicable silence for a time, Peggy occasionally pointing out a particular tree or stone of significance about the place but mostly seeming to be waiting for my mood to settle. She was very attuned to how tightly wound I had become, and I sensed we had been on walks like this before, even if this was *our* first. The morning sun was shining heartily onto the moisture rising off the grasses, the effect creating a brilliant gleam all around, and I immediately regretted not bringing my sunglasses.

"Ireland is chock-full of free-flowing, ancient power," she said, the voice of a teacher speaking now. "The whole country is practically a thin place. Honestly, the closeness to the Otherworld here is so intense in some areas that it's almost palpable."

I was pleased that I could stumble along so far in her telling. I recognized that soon she was going to cross into the spiritual, sacred, and secret teachings of the Druids, and I felt humbled to be privy to her wisdom.

"So, you can imagine that the Celts, having lived and prospered in such a magically imbibed location, had no difficulty believing in the continuation of life beyond physical death. This belief exists in *your* bones as well, even if you can't remember your past. You are as much a part of the Celtic landscape as myself or Malcolm, Domhnall or Ronan, or anyone else here. And I'm sure this is also largely why you are so disoriented right now."

Evidently an experienced ambler when it came to countryside exploration, she continued ahead of me through a more difficult and soggy section of land. Her knee-high, black rubber boots squelched fashionably across the glade as if it were nothing, while I stumbled along clumsily in her wake, doing my utmost to keep up with her on all fronts.

"I've never felt like I truly belonged, anywhere," I said. "Maybe at my grandmother's cottage, to a point, but otherwise, I've felt so . . . displaced." I caught up to her on steadier ground at last.

"And now you know why. You were living, but you weren't yet walking your intended path. Here at the manor house, your soul recognizes some of your previous paths, even if your mind does not. But it's not surprising there is a disconnect. And if I were to guess . . . you're struggling to trust your own intuition about it all."

I shrugged, non-committal.

She paused for a moment, rewording her thoughts. "Julia. You have been wholly disconnected from your inner world, unfairly in most respects. Especially when you consider your complex, and might I add rather spectacular, interactions with the Otherworld, your curse, *and* the Prophecy. I think how you have been feeling lately is more than understandable. Frankly, I'm surprised you're not completely flat-out right now!" she said, chuckling compassionately.

With her words working an unknowingly long-awaited permissive spell, heavy tears soon began to run down my cheeks, grief welling over from so many years of self-denial. She walked beside me in silence for another few moments as I collected myself, but I had the distinct sense that my work had only just begun.

The emotions that arose were crushing as I grappled with how deeply I craved a more meaningful connection to the world, with other women, but most of all, I longed for a connection to *myself.* It made me think of my time at Gertie's cottage, after she died but before I returned to school. Indeed, I had felt distant from what she had referred to as my "inner world" for so long that it was no wonder my magical abilities were either sputtering weakly, or conversely exploding everywhere, unchecked. I had absolutely no sense of "clear source" or "knowing intention."

"If I'm completely honest, Julia . . . I am unsure why the guides have decided you should gradually lose your memories with each re-generation, while Domhnall should keep his." She paused for a moment. "But they *will* have their reasons. Do you know much about that place? The Otherworld?" she asked.

"I'm sorry. I don't."

"It's of no consequence. You'll need *years* to explore a true understanding of the connection between worlds. But what you *do* need to know right now is how imperative it is that you lean into trusting your own intuitive voice. This is the foundation of the knowledge of the Divine Feminine, and ultimately, our collective understanding of what it is to be a human being in this life and into the next.

"Our current world hinges so heavily on the value of knowledge over inner wisdom. Intellect over intuition. But it is actually the marrying of these parts that will bring us the clarity we so badly need, and of course, the enlightenment that we all crave so desperately on our individual paths, as well as within the world at large."

She was clearly a wealth of knowledge, and I found myself suddenly overwhelmed with the information I was receiving. "Feels like a big task."

Slogging through yet another soggy patch, I was now completely covered in mud.

"You're stagged now, Julia!" Peggy called out, but I was unfamiliar with the term.

At last, we had arrived at a small copse of trees, which I now realized had clearly been her intended destination from the get-go. There, completely unnoticeable at first glance, were the crumbling ruins of a long-since collapsed stone well. The ground was densely wet, with clear surges of groundwater pulsing up from different recesses across the ground.

"The wells," she said, gesturing towards the sodden earth. "*These* are known places of connection between the worlds, and if you would allow me to, I would like to direct you towards them now, as an aid on your current journey."

I tilted my head, taking in the sight before me with some confusion. It looked significantly wet but not altogether remarkable otherwise. She placed her hand on her heart and nodded slowly; she clearly didn't mean to direct me visually.

"Where I'm from, over in Cornwall, we have many, *many* wells. The Christians, of course, have attached saints to most of them, but the voices of the wells . . . well, that's a story far older than any of all that." She continued to look serenely towards the wellspring. "The wells are a place where we can *truly* listen to the land, our mother, as she speaks to us now. There is much to be learned from the magic there, and so I visit them often throughout the cycle of the year, especially in times of need. And, would you believe it, I *still* leave with something new to consider each time!"

"It's like . . . somewhere to ground into place."

"Precisely," she said, beaming.

Closing my eyes, I glanced inward for a brief moment before casting my thoughts outward and into the well. They carried on their wings my own unique form of Bearing magic, calling out my name, and existence, to the worlds. Almost immediately, I felt an overwhelming pull towards some kind of dense centre, as if there was now a game of tug-of-war between myself and the energy emanating from within. However, I remained surprisingly steady. I could almost sense the finite balance between light and dark, sun and moon, masculine and feminine, all pulsing freely from deep within the well.

I thought of Dom then, and what felt like a crippling overreliance on the knowledge of our shared past, which he carried so dutifully. Coupled with my own complete lack of knowledge on most subjects, along with the significant disconnect between my current path and my intuition, it was no wonder we were fumbling along so painfully towards our perceived finish line. The trouble, it seemed, was that we still had no idea how to properly marry the two together before time ran out.

After grappling with my problems for what seemed like an infinite period of time, I opened my eyes at last and was blinded by the scorching light of the sun directly above me. I couldn't be entirely certain how long I had stood for, but my grumbling stomach suggested to me that it was likely high time for lunch. Maggie and Sully must have returned with Peggy, but the stoic Oisín was standing just up the slope, on much drier land, diligently awaiting our next maneuver.

While I was sad to see Peggy leave the manor house, she had left me with a priceless gift. I found myself travelling to the wellspring with regularity now, if not simply as a daily reminder of who I was and where I had come from all those years ago. I thought back to the oak tree at UBC, which of course now felt like a lifetime ago, but its sentiment had been similar. It now felt like a much simpler scale, but I was heartened by my intuition all the same.

Tensions between Dom and I had settled considerably now that the initial push of planning began to wear down, at least for the others. His stamina for strategy still seemed boundless, but I could tell that Thomas and Lennie were particularly weary of talking in circles, and Ronan was anxious to return to work for a time. While he had managed to continue much of his research remotely, especially with the welcome help from Peggy over the past month, he would soon need to return to some sort of hospital to continue the non-magical groundwork.

"I won't be going back to Vancouver this spring, and unfortunately, they aren't very pleased about it. But I did manage to get them to extend the research contract to return again in the fall," he said sombrely during dinner one night.

We all knew he meant "if I'm still alive in the fall." I gulped back a particularly large spoonful of soup, choking somewhat before Dom firmly patted me on the back several times to dislodge the chunk of potato.

With a slight increase in free time available to us now, I was delighted to discover that Dom actually had quite an extensive classic-movie collection, a relative term of course, with his favourites ranging anywhere between the Monty Python movies and *Jurassic Park*. Thomas was equally as eager, and the two of them had designed a handful of weekend watch parties for the group. Even Lennie joined in from time to time. While I was neither here nor there on the movies themselves, it was nice to gather peacefully for a time. However, Ronan and I both drew the line after what I was pretty sure had to be the fourth or fifth *Alien* movie. I had entirely lost track and interest and soon found myself alone once more on a walk across the grounds, with Ronan heading to his room to work.

The early March air smelled heavily of recent rain and subtle hints of new growth in the forest. The trees were still holding onto their early buds, waiting patiently for the sweet release of spring. I had always sympathised with the trees during this time of year, as if they were waiting in painful anticipation for a chance at the true expression of their own magic.

I supposed it was no surprise that a part of me felt a bit of comradery to the trees these days, or perhaps I was just searching for the presence of like-minded company. Winter could be long and hard, a time of concentration and rest, and I was anxious to break out of my inner contemplation and start to grow outward instead.

While the other two dogs were often hit or miss, Oisín was always keen to keep me company during my daily walks. Exiting through my usual escape hole in the kitchen, he popped up dutifully from his prone position at the fireside. He truly was the heart outside of Dom's body, and I found his presence immensely comforting, especially on the still somewhat unfamiliar sprawling grounds ahead of me. So far, I had only managed to get lost once, but with the help of the great beast, we had managed to sort ourselves, and since then, I had almost insisted he accompany me.

Walking through the grass now with Oisín, I was mindlessly singing a song about a pirate king, which I didn't really know the words to but had picked up from Malcolm simply by means of proximity. Peacefully releasing my worries, I had admittedly let my guard down for a while, watching intently as a pair of swallows ducked and dove through the air, feeling decidedly content at another sure sign of spring.

Head in the clouds, I jumped when the wolfhound suddenly had his hackles raised, snarling and snapping at something beyond us in the trees. At the same moment, a thick fog began to creep in at an alarming rate around us; we were being surrounded by some kind of magical entity or newly cast spell.

"Who's out there?" I called out into the mist, but my voice failed to travel beyond my lips. Ahead of me, Oisín was still snarling towards a crop of trees where I knew seven or eight broad oaks stood beyond a small ditch, but I could barely see beyond the dog to discern who was hiding down below.

As if in response to my voice, the wind began to pick up and swirl around me. This wasn't only Wielding magic, not technically. I could feel the distinct sense of some kind of spell or incantation being used, much like the Wraiths had done in Vancouver, but there was also definitely Bearing magic laced in somewhere.

It would seem there was a Witch in the ditch.

I closed my eyes, feeling a distinct strain as the natural energy around me was pulled at and commanded into the swirling mists. I felt the fire within me crackle with anger. How *dare* they attempt to use magic against me at *my* home.

In the past, my fear would have stifled my abilities and led me spiralling downwards into irrational panic, but instead I felt a quiet confidence growing within me as I searched outwardly towards where the force was originating. I admittedly still had no offensive skills, but I was becoming fairly adept at locating threats, which was really half of the job in this sort of combat anyways, finding the source of the power.

Aha!

It was weak, not a true threat considering all the power housed by our congregation, but it was undoubtedly and infuriatingly familiar. If I could just clear the air ahead to allow the great hound to charge forward towards our foe, we would be more than equipped to manage this new threat.

"How long have you been watching me leave through the kitchens, Maureen?" I asked, voice suddenly loud with anger now that the mist and wind weren't strangling me.

"Long enough to separate you from the group today, you . . . you useless woman!" she spat, her clear distaste for me on full display.

She was still wearing her white apron, hair pulled back into an aggressive bun at the nape of her neck. The effect made her look like an angry toad perched clumsily upon a crumbling toadstool, croaking down below me in the ditch by the glade.

"What have I ever done to you?" I asked, voice stifled by the continued snarls of Dom's hound. I was genuinely confused now. I couldn't sense any evil in this woman. On the contrary, there was simply a fragile weakness and many years of long-harboured grief.

"It's not so much what you've done, but what you've taken away from me . . . from us!"

Her eyes were frenzied now, darting left and right as the emotion grew within her.

"I'm sorry? Taken *what?*"

"My daughter Jenny has been sweet on Domhnall for the better part of a decade; don't you see? She's been working in his house and on the grounds for ages, and just as he was taking a shine to her, he left. Now with you coming here and taking all of his attention, he hasn't batted an eye in her direction. She's heartbroken!"

Ah, yes. I had wondered about Jenny, who I often found staring at me reproachfully as she cleaned windows or vacuumed the various rugs throughout the manor. I *knew* it was a mistake to keep a regular cook and housekeepers and would be having a discussion with Dom later about the necessity of staffing our initiative beyond the essentials.

I took a deep breath of the heavy air, moisture still lingering around us from her likely stolen elemental spell. I spoke slowly then, so as not to aggravate her further, but also to make my meaning quite plain.

"I am not entirely sure anyone has the right to take claim over anyone else's heart, Maureen. But I am genuinely sorry to hear that Jenny is feeling hurt by my arrival."

She didn't know about the Prophecy, nor that Dom and I had been lovers for the better part of a millennium, eternally bound by our so-far ill-fated destiny. And, in that moment, I truly felt pity for the woman sitting there in outraged desperation.

She wasn't having any of it, however.

"How *dare* you speak down to me!" she said, charging towards me in what seemed like slow motion.

I raised my hands in an offering of peace, dreading the thought of using my own magic against her in response. Not that I knew how, of course, but I would do what was needed to spare her any further humiliation. Oisín lurched forward first, placing his massive paws on her shoulders, sending her rolling backwards further down into the ditch. I dropped my arms, and stood limply, watching the scene below.

Thundering footsteps approached us from behind, and in a swift change of direction, the great wolfhound turned and leapt past me towards his master's side.

Dom arrived, face flushed with anger, polished dagger raised in his left hand.

"What the hell is going on here!" he boomed, clearly disoriented by the scene that had unfolded before him.

He sounded fearful and angry. In his defence, it *was* a rather unexpected scene to encounter. Maureen was now curled in a disoriented heap, Oisín having clearly defended his ground against the spiteful cook. Dom must have seen the last moments of our conflict from afar as the quieting mists had slowly cleared away, though I wouldn't have been able to hear him until he was directly behind us.

Ronan, Thomas, and Lennie soon charged up behind, Dom's sheer power and speed having left them all in his wake as he'd surged towards me. The three men shared looks of equal confusion as they approached us.

"Oh *fuck,*" Dom said, a look of realization dawning across his face as he closed his eyes and raised his eyebrows in an expression that seemed to ask the lord to give him strength.

"I had wondered if this would be a problem. Can someone fetch Morgan for me?"

He ran the long fingers of his dagger-free hand through his hair, placing his other arm around me while bracing the weapon against my side. He was clearly relieved that this foe was merely a spiteful staff member, but I wasn't quite so confident on the matter.

My grandma's sage advice rang through my mind as I recalled the summer with Jake, and the handful of other lovers I had left behind, hearts utterly shattered in my own wake as I followed my own destiny: *"Unrequited love can be incredibly dangerous, Julia; be careful with the hearts of others."* I had always wondered what damage I had inflicted on their paths as a result, but I learned quickly that you also can't control other people's behaviours . . . or lives.

However, you *can* control who you employ.

We made our way back to the house after Morgan had arrived, Dom giving him specific instructions that both Maureen and Jenny would need to seek other places of work.

"Did you know she was a Witch?" I asked.

I hadn't sensed much active magic within the woman, only the creative energy of a sturdy cook and doting mother.

"No, I didn't. Although her bolognaise had a real element of magic to it, didn't it?" Dom said with a chuckle. I wasn't sure I was in the mood for jokes just yet, but I smiled at how the conversation had come around once again to food.

My stomach growled; I was suddenly very hungry.

"I wouldn't trust anything she cooked for us today, Dom; she probably put a laxative in it or something," Ronan said, laughing as we entered the kitchen, all of us suspiciously eyeing the stew boiling on the stove. "Although, I *do* think she stole that pouch from the store cupboard. We will have to do inventory."

"I'm on it," Thomas said. He had an intimate knowledge of the Druidic casting pouches apparently stored behind the mystery door in there, having formulated most of them with Malcolm as part of his training.

"Looks like we're ordering pizza!" I readily offered, and the others nodded in rapt agreement. I was relieved that we wouldn't have to debate over what we would eat for supper just yet, although with this particular group, I sensed this would soon become another bone of contention.

The others removed their boots and hung their coats on the rack by the door. Meanwhile, Dom wrapped himself around me as the others filed through the warm kitchen towards their respective corners to change before dinner and what they anticipated to be yet another night of strategy or perhaps another movie instead.

Dom ran his long fingers around my waist and under the front of my sweater, pressing his thumbs into the space between my ribs just above my belly, and pulled me close. Breathing deep, he kissed me the soft spot behind my ear, sending chills down my spine, despite the warmth of the room.

"You scared me today," he said, but there was no trace of fear in his voice now.

"I had it under control." To my surprise, I wasn't actually bristling at his protectiveness.

His hands travelled downward now towards the backs of my thighs, fingers searching with increased enthusiasm as he pressed his hips against me.

"I know you did. I can see that now."

Danger was clearly a turn-on for this beast of a Celt.

I leaned my head back into the crook of his neck. "How did you know where to find me?"

"I always orient towards you, Julia. I don't know how to explain it, but it's like there's a magnet between us."

I didn't think I had finally managed to pull off a Send, since it hadn't even dawned on me to try. But he was right, there *was* something about the connection between us that was more than unusual.

"It takes immense mental energy to keep me from your side. Take now for instance."

I watched as Thomas exited the pantry and left the kitchen, hopefully having accounted for all the pouches, save for the one Maureen had nicked.

Seconds later, Dom turned me abruptly towards him, mouth instantly searching as he ran his hand instinctively into the space between my ponytail and scalp. He was growing desperate now. I could smell his masculine essence surrounding me, salt and sea churning and frothing around us more with each passing moment, searching for harbour with one another.

"There's time before dinner," I said, pulling myself back momentarily and eyeing him playfully.

He grinned widely in reply, eyes twinkling. I finished my proffered thought with mock thoughtfulness, head tilted. "Time for a game of *Scrabble*, that is."

I could only describe the sound that came out of him next as a mix between a frustrated growl and a barking laugh as he gave chase towards our upstairs bedroom.

CHAPTER 28

M arcus Cassius Longinus could scarcely remember what it had been like all those years ago. The fall of Rome had come swiftly in comparison to the crawling passage of time since, especially when he considered all the things he had learned and done since then. Indeed, the further he ventured into the future, the less his origins seemed to matter to him. Still though, he would face unfortunate moments where the memories were almost impossible to stifle; a jarring, ever-present reminder of his one true weakness.

"You remind me of someone I used to know," he said, grinning maliciously.

The girl looked up at him, eyes pleading hysterically for release. When she couldn't keep that up, she looked desperately around the dim hotel room for an escape. The tears had long dried on her face, leaving black streams of makeup across her young, supple cheeks. She still had fight in her, and he liked that.

He would soon release her, but not in the way she had been praying for.

At his behest, she had been bound and gagged and placed at the end of the bed across one of the standard velvet foot-covers so common in modern hotels. It painted a pretty picture; she at the foot of his bed and him looming above her like a harbinger of death, moments before extracting the last vestiges of her essence for his own consumption.

Lately, he had grown weary of the dim hotel-room scenes that had played out before him over and over throughout the past several months, but with modern surveillance and his need for an ever-changing location, this was by far the easiest method for extraction.

She screamed again, but he silenced her with a flick of his wrist.

Boredom with the repeated environment was easily overshadowed by the growing thirst, hunger, and pain within his own body. Sensing his own mortality was never a feeling he wished to sit in for long. He would need to extract her *being* before the agony became too engrossing, and he would have to struggle to focus on the task at hand.

His hunger had grown over the past several hundred years, with the pangs never truly abating now. As a result, the spacing between extractions had become significantly shorter and his withdrawal symptoms considerably worse. As a rule, he used to assign a divination to each sacrifice, not wanting to waste a perfectly good body in the process. However, his need had grown so exponentially over the past decade alone that he had taken to consuming bodies without seeking any portents at all.

He knew the feeling of hunger, and he abhorred it.

Unknowingly born with the abilities of a great Sorcerer, his childhood as the bastard of a *meretrix* on the streets of Rome had been much as one would expect. The turn of the second century of the common era was being ground under the weight of the Roman empire just as he had been. His memories of that time were disgustingly flavoured with the fruits of pain; his mouth constantly dry with thirst and hunger and his stomach full of desperation and loneliness.

His mother had shown no interest in him. She'd met only his most basic survival needs before weaning him to other nursing mothers in the brothel and eventually abandoning him altogether. He had no recollection of her face but could easily remember the heavy curves of her naked body facing away from him as she led yet another Roman son or soldier into her soot-filled chambers.

The other women in the brothel might have been more maternal to him than his own mother if not for their own loathsome circumstances. He'd truly never felt any compassion for his mother, nor any other woman, and when he had learned of her violent death some years later, he'd felt only vindication; she had probably deserved it.

Whomever his father had been was of no consequence either. He'd likely had half-siblings out in the world at some point if they had survived past infancy. He didn't care to know. He had learned from birth that survival was to be obtained by any means necessary.

He couldn't remember his original name, so he had chosen his own instead. After all, he was a child of Rome.

He'd begged on the corners for scraps of food; too old a boy to stay in the brothel but too young to be a man. The constant pain of deep hunger had soon become his ever-present companion. It was without surprise that he would spend the succeeding millennia with an insatiable hunger for power, unable to fully quench his almost crippling thirst for magic. In fact, this overwhelming feeling had been what led to him discovering his ability to take, and then Wield, magic of his own.

Sorcery, it would seem, was his destiny.

Returning his attention to the present, he reached down to the bound girl, irritated by her incessant shaking and vain attempts to draw her knees protectively around her belly. He noticed she was pregnant, or rather, he sensed it. There's no way the Wraiths would have been able to tell at this point in time what a supple gift they had brought him. It was early, although it was very likely she knew, based on her instinctive posture.

This changed things considerably.

"You're with child, I see," he said, stroking her blackened cheeks with the end of his dual pronged blade as he dragged his other hand seductively across her hip.

He then pushed her onto her back with little consideration for what grew inside. Bearers had an uncanny ability to protect what grew within, but it was of no consequence. Jealousy spread through him at the thought of her ability to keep her magic concealed from him, which quickly transformed into the rage he had become so accustomed to as of late.

Her eyes shot up at him, fear further magnified by his ability to name her truth.

"Don't worry; no one will *ever* know," he said, a lethal smile spreading across his parted lips.

She looked as if she would faint from his sudden scrutiny, consciousness leaving her body in an attempt to momentarily free herself from indescribable fear. He had never had patience for dissociation, and slapped her with the back of his hand, bringing her back to him with abrupt violence.

"Good. Now . . ." he said, clapping his hands together while still holding the blade. "I need you to wait a while. I am going to bring someone in who can help me with the task at hand. And I'll need you to stay awake for it."

His hunger was screaming into his throat now, almost as if a fever were burning into his ears and threatening to overcome him at any moment. Perhaps it would be best if he tapped into her power now while he waited for Desmond to join them. He wasn't convinced he would be able to stop midway through the process, however, and then she would be lost for divination altogether. If not for the fact that she was pregnant, he wouldn't care, but he wondered with a mounting curiosity if she could be the one to answer his biggest questions.

He lifted his phone to his ear and waited for the answer on the other end. A muffled voice came in reply, but Cassius had no time for pleasantries.

"Desmond, I need you. *Now!*"

There was a click on the other end of the line, and he stood in wait. Desmond was situated in the next room over, his presence a constant insurance policy. It was unfortunate to have to travel with such a pathetic companion, but needs being what they were, it was essential.

Within moments, there was a soft knock at the door. He unlocked the latch with an upward curl of his finger. It was foolish to squander the last of his magical reserves, but he couldn't afford for Desmond to clue into the precariousness of their current situation.

"The girl," he gestured towards the bed. "She needs to answer a question for me. Make it quick."

Dressed in ill-fitted khaki slacks and an endlessly crinkled dress shirt, the Indovino hurried over to the girl curled on the foot of the bed. If not for wishing to preserve his energy, Cassius would have mocked the absolutely disgusting state of Desmond's current dress.

To Desmond, the room smelled of sweat and something more sinister, almost akin to the putrid scent of rotting flesh or long-spoiled meat thrown into the trash and set in the sun. The air was almost acidic, prompting stomach-churning nausea; he almost expected to see maggots crawling about the room. In fact, Desmond had been silently noticing the smell's increased presence over the past months and wondered what new diabolism Cassius was attempting during his private rituals.

The girl began to panic and thrash at the sight of him, frantically hoping this new arrival would free her from her bonds in rescue. It was a common reaction to his mild appearance, and it pained him greatly to see their last throws of desperation cast in his direction. As usual, he avoided eye contact entirely as he drew his silver sickle from its sheath at his waist and set to work.

When all was said and done, blood spattered from floor to ceiling, Desmond sat in a heap at the floor, and it was in this rare occasion that he felt drawn to look Cassius in the eye.

"She . . . she was pregnant," he said, surprised at the shock in his own words.

"Yes. Very convenient." Cassius nodded, pain screaming through his own body as he barely maintained his composure in the moment. "I need you to tell me what you saw."

Desmond's face was glistening with cold sweat, and he could barely feel his own fingers. He cleared his throat and pushed his glasses back, the combined reaction almost slamming his glasses into his eye sockets. He winced.

"There is a growing power . . . in the birth of a child," he said, clouded images swirling before him. "I'm unsure who the child is . . . I . . . cannot see their face, but at maturity . . . they stand at the precipice of a great cliff, holding . . ." He paused.

"Holding?"

The rage and pain would soon spill over, and he didn't wish to kill Desmond in the process, despite how infuriating the abject man could be.

"Holding your spear," Desmond answered, eyes dropping to the floor.

"Out." It was all Cassius could muster, and Desmond scrambled to his feet in a flurry of creased cotton and blood-stained dress pants, slamming the door behind him.

Cassius was swift then; there would be no time for extended ritual. He aggressively inserted the two-pronged instrument into the girl's solar plexus, and as the final burst of air left her lungs, he fell to his knees, closing his eyes as at last the euphoria overtook him.

His thoughts swirled around him, new and ancient notions mingling together in some kind of baseless, contorted dance. The girl's magic at last reached his hollow core, filling him once more with the nectar of stolen life force. He had been so close to losing control and possibly even his life just then. But it had all been worth it for what he had discovered, with the dire risk to his survival offering a sickly-sweet reward.

He could hardly remember the first telling of the Prophecy now.

After he had taken the Oracle's life, he'd grown steadily in power with the knowledge of how to extend his own through dark Sorcery. Hundreds of years passed with no threat to his existence. It had been so long ago that eventually he took it as a false portent. But then, one dark day at the end of the tenth century, it had come again, this time in the form of a vivid, terrible dream vision. *She* had arrived and was now situated across the sea on a vast and mostly untouched isle, Hibernia. The Romans had, of course, never occupied the region; that didn't mean they didn't know exactly where it was.

And so, he had sought her out, only to discover that she and her protector had somehow evaded him. Since then, and over the past one thousand years, each and every Oracle, Indovino, and Soothsayer had continuously foretold that *she*, the Witch, would serve as either saviour or destructor of his mortal essence.

Staring at the lifeless form of the girl before him, she who had borne the magic of a newly minted child, he now shared a much different perspective. Perhaps it wasn't *her* after all, but rather her child who would attempt to usurp his power. The same child whose inner magic could also hold the cure to his mortality, if he were to extract it. Cassius would, of course, gather more intelligence to be sure, yet he felt a growing confidence that this was the *truest* fortune-telling of all.

Maybe it was simply the compounding strength of the magic gathering within him now that was bolstering his surety. But the fact remained. The cliff, the dagger, the image. How many times before had they stood at that place? And how many times had they used *her* as a lure to draw him out of hiding? It had always made the most sense to simply kill her, eliminating any threat to his life in one swift motion, with the occasional opportunity to try to extract her power.

Early on, Cassius had taken immense pleasure in the thrill of the hunt. He positively delighted in the routine destruction of the "*World Ruler*" with each attempt to protect his ill-fated lover. It had been especially vindicating if he could get to them before they had time to assemble any of their meagre forces against him and attempt to truly invoke any aspect of the Prophecy. He had relished in the control he'd held over their destiny, and despite the fact that he never seemed to be able to harness any of *her* power, their deaths had affirmed his dominance. They'd also gifted him with the great privilege of time.

Now, time was beginning to bend almost violently around him and *not* to his will. With each subsequent defeat of the Witch and her Celtic protector over the years, the spaces between their union had drastically grown. The increasing distance only further fed into what was now becoming a degenerative cycle; each calculated death added to the feedback loop. The Prophecy spoke of the summer solstice being the divine timing for their demise, but he was beginning to wonder if this still held true.

It had been centuries since he had dedicated any of his own energy towards hunting them. The only exception being their previous appearance in the mid-twentieth century. That had been an unfortunately hasty decision on his part. He had acted on impulse and rage, rather than calculated thought, and it had almost cost him his life.

He would *not* make that mistake again.

Unbeknownst to them, his existence increasingly stood on the edge of a knife. In fact, he wasn't sure that he could survive the long wait through yet another regeneration cycle without the power needed to secure his immortality. Precariously held in the balance, it was time to change his approach.

With thoughts steadily clearing after the rushed extraction, Cassius slowly returned to his methodic ritual of cleaning the blades. Quicker than usual, he polished the thick, cool blood off each prong, its coppery tang barely overwhelming the putrid scent of his own rotting flesh. His fragile heart was beating frantically now, the magic of not one but two heartbeats surging through his decaying arteries and valves further suspending his existence for just a little while longer.

Changing his perception of the Prophecy had always seemed dangerous, and it felt a great risk to alter tactics after all this time. Still, he *was* weakening at an exponential rate, and had come dangerously close to death today. Perhaps this was the cost for the enlightening information at last divined.

But he needed something stronger.

He picked up his phone and punched the single number again. "Desmond. Get the jet ready to fly to Heathrow . . . Yes, tonight." He paused, listening to the voice on the line and licking his lips as the magic continued to surge deliciously through his entire being. "I guess you'll have to deal with it quickly then," he said implicitly in reference to the gruesome scene in front of him. It wasn't a request.

He hung up. To his knowledge, there were still several remaining Witches in the UK who held onto the *old power*. He had been saving their existences for just such an occasion. Their wild magics could satiate him for weeks, rather than the mere handful of days he was accustomed to from his recent victims. Although today's consumption had been especially substantial, he had to admit. They may also be able to confirm his renewed hypothesis, and *that* gave him a hunger he'd not felt for quite some time.

CHAPTER 29

I t felt like ages since Aisling had so swiftly come and gone from our presence, but her message to me had been plain enough: There is more to the Prophecy than meets the eye, and I had best start practicing my unique gifts as a Bearer if we wanted to stand a chance in hell against Cassius. Simple on paper, much more difficult in practice.

Peggy, of course, had left me with her own version of what I now considered to be the same memo—a firm reminder to connect inward before working my magic outward. Being solely a Wielder, her interpretation of this was different than mine, but the sentiment remained the same. Bearing magic took some serious tending to. I had also learned quickly that this wasn't a skill to be learned overnight.

By the time the end of March arrived, I was hardly any further along than I had been weeks ago. The sole exception being that I managed to quell my inner sensitivity against the onslaught of magical trigger points throughout the manor house. Ultimately, I wasn't sure if it was because I had simply grown accustomed to the rhythms of the place, and it to me, but I did think I had at least made some headway in my tolerance of it all. And that counted for something.

I found myself thinking of Grandma Gertie less and less with all the distractions of the cause and couldn't decide if this was a betrayal of her memory or perhaps a sign of healing. While I had spent much of my time thinking of grief and loss at the manor house, I was surprised when I discovered that a year had passed since she had died. I almost would have missed the date altogether if not for a completely unrelated and jarring reminder from Ronan.

He had just returned from two weeks at the teaching hospital in Cork and was in an uncharacteristically bright mood.

"Hello!" he proclaimed, sitting down loudly at the kitchen table beside us. "And how are we all today?"

Dom grinned from ear to ear. "Oh, fine, and you?"

"I am well, thank you *very* much. And do you want to know why?"

"Tell us, Ronan," I said, voice playfully flat.

He clapped his hands together in delight. "Well, you should know that I've made *huge* progress over the past few weeks in my research around the regenerative healing of Wraiths! I figure it will be critical when we *do* finally move into battle, though I'm not sure how just yet. You see, the only reason they are still alive is that their cells are *suspended* by the magic, not nourished by it. It's a bit more complicated than that, but . . ."

He went on for over twenty minutes explaining complex degenerative cell patterning and what actually happens to Wraiths when they are injured versus when they are actually dead. He was exceptionally enthused during the more graphic descriptions, which left me feeling slightly woozy.

"So, did you get hold of some Wraith bodies? Or . . . ?" Thomas asked, also grimacing.

"I did, but that's not important," Ronan said, making brief eye contact with Dom. "What *is* important is that the way the Wraiths seem to acquire their long life is not a matter of increased cell production or exceptional durability but rather that the cell death is actually almost paused. I had been following a model similar to some cancer research around cell damage at the place of production, but this is a much different angle. And if I'm honest, it makes them much less infallible. The longer they live, the *deader* they actually become!"

Dom tilted his head with his mouth slightly agape, followed by a quick snap shut, clearly at a loss for words. Lennie seemed to be following along so far, but even he looked perplexed at this point. I thought of Gertie then, and her own battle with cancer. And then I realized the date.

"Oh . . . shit," I said under my breath, but only Dom heard.

"What is it, Julia?"

"It's nothing. It's just been a year since Gertie died, and I almost forgot."

He took my hand into his. "You've had a lot on your plate."

I smiled his way but my heart felt heavy.

The initial high of Ronan's discovery had lasted for several days, but soon we had moved back into our more usual, and much darker, modus operandum.

We were no closer to finding a solution to the threat than we had been at the beginning of the year. Meanwhile, the used and discarded magical bodies that continued to pile up weren't helping anyone's anxiety. Now, it seemed, Cassius had jumped the pond and was somewhere back in London. Lennie's agitation, in particular, around the proximity of the threat had grown exponentially. Frequent arguments had broken out between he and Dom at the dinner table regarding the plausibility of an all-magical battle in a technologically advanced world.

"I understand what you're trying to say, *Lennie*, but you weren't *there!*" Dom slammed his fork down in anger, though the effect was lost on the obstinate Lennie.

He snorted. "You're correct, *Dom*, I wasn't. And guess what, in *this* time-line, you bloody well know he's got just as much access to the intelligence and technology as we do. It's only a matter of time before he strikes! This is new territory, and we need to be one step ahead. That sure as hell isn't going to be on some remote magical battlefield at the ends of the bloody earth."

Dom stood up aggressively, tossing his chair loudly backwards as a result.

Ronan spoke in an attempt to keep the peace. "You said it yourself, Lennie, that it's more than likely he's advanced well-past anything we'd have access to, especially on such short notice. Money talks in his world, and the reality is, we are probably woefully ill-prepared for any non-magical weapons he might possess."

"That's my point! Why the need for any weapons at all? We can outsmart him in other ways. You're both so hell-bent on an outright battle! That just isn't how wars are fought these days!"

Dom and Ronan looked at each other in what had become a well-worn expression of exasperation. Realistically, with his modern-day military experience, Ronan knew better than anyone what real weapons might be a threat. If he said things needed to be fought on the magical playing field, he was more than likely correct. Simply put, in any other arena we would be outgunned.

Lennie's ego was getting in his way when it came to his ability to conceptualize winning a virtual battle. There was still the fact that Cassius had to be destroyed, *in the flesh*. And that would take a hell of a lot of force, magical or otherwise. In truth, a good old-fashioned magical standoff was probably the only place we could stand a fighting chance against the impregnable Child of Rome, or at least where we could begin to hope, or dream, of gaining the upper hand against his dark forces.

"But how are we going to draw him towards a positively weighted playing field?" Thomas asked. "Or even an equal one? He's obviously smarter now than he's ever been, and with his endless web of spies and his *Conventos* of Wraiths gathering on what feels like every corner . . . I mean, how could we possibly hope to lure him into a place where he would be at a disadvantage?"

I was beginning to understand why they had kept him around, aside from the many obviously positive attributes of his character. Thomas had an impeccable mind for strategy. Both he and Dom had connected very early on around the tactics of the Roman legions, of which Dom's father, and consequently Dom himself, had also been a student.

Then, as they always seemed to do in these situations, all four sets of eyes had landed on me, and once more I felt the suffocating strain of the varied expectations around my role in the Prophecy.

Ronan looked strained with concern, which was usual when my capabilities and purpose came into question. Lennie's face bore his customary shade of intentional indifference. Thomas's expression was warm with compassion, which I appreciated more than he could ever know, especially since the grimace across Dom's face was one that shattered my heart into a thousand pieces.

In one form or another, the collective mind was that the best purpose for me these days was as bait. I had heard the rumblings that emanated from the study when Dom was fighting for my autonomy in the matter, but ultimately, he too could see no other alternative. A well-designed lure into the magical arena, where we would hopefully arise victorious, was the only way to entice Cassius.

Timing was everything, however, and at the moment, we had no idea when the tipping point would arrive. It was why Dom had poured himself into what he deemed to be the most critical level of preparedness. We had until the solstice on June 21 this year, or at least, having never survived past that rough date before, we could only *assume* that this was our potential time-stamp this time around as well.

Every time I *really* thought about the matter, bile rose to the back of my mouth. But I also grew incredibly weary of the assorted hands groping at my impossibly short destiny. At last, it was time for me to make a move.

"I need to visit Agnes Sweeney. In England."

The silence that followed only amplified the already exacerbated looks spread across their faces.

"It's time. I have this constant feeling that the answers we seek, to *defeat him*, are hidden, embedded in the quilt somehow. Why else would I have it? But I have no clue how to read it. I need help from another Bearer . . . from someone who has the Sight."

The others looked to Dom in the hopes that he could talk some sense into me, but he knew better.

"Alright, Julia, we'll go. You're right; we've put it off long enough."

There was no further need for discussion. When it boiled down to it, as far as the others were concerned, Dom's word was law. While I appreciated his admirable qualities as a natural-born leader, I felt instantly irritated. They looked to him for discernment around the aspects of my request rather than listening to my needs and intuition and instead placing their trust there.

I had shown all of them the quilt early on, the only person not having seen it was Aisling. The general consensus was that it was indeed a powerful magical artifact, but the magics woven into it were confused, even though it was enchanted with intention. The response had been thoroughly underwhelming, and since then, it had been sitting silently in our bedroom, waiting ever so patiently to be recalled at long last.

After the argument at dinner, Dom and I made our way back up towards our bedroom together. We both wished fervently for a long break from house guests, but each for our own reasons.

"I swear to you, one of these days, I'm really going to wind his neck!"

I rolled my eyes. "Come on, really? I mean, I know Lennie's an asshole . . ."

He sat down on the edge of the bed, visibly frustrated beyond his limit. "Well, maybe not now. But in another time, I would absolutely have at least belted him by now, for certain."

He clenched his fists while I climbed up behind him, kneeling close as I draped my arms loosely around his shoulders. I knew he was right. In another time, it was more than likely that Dom wouldn't have dreamed of working with someone as insolent as Lennie, but times being what they were, he had little choice.

"Julia," he said, "I'm sorry about the bait plan. I really am. I've tried—"

"I know," I said, suddenly wracked with anxiety of my own.

He turned towards me, attuned. "What is it?"

I flopped back onto the bed with a great sigh. "Ugh. It's nothing."

"Oh, really!" He snorted and dove onto the bed beside me, its timber frame groaning in unison with him. "Oof! I'm getting too old for that."

"But that's the thing, Dom. Are we even going to get older?"

It wasn't exactly a great time for an existential crisis, I had to admit, but with our situation being what it was, the question held true.

"Hmm," he said, his baritone purr instantly grounding. "I don't know. But does it help you to know that, after all of this time, I still *want* to grow old with you?"

I laughed in spite of his romantic sentiment. "What's that supposed to mean? '*Still?*'"

"Oh, for Christ's sake, Julia. I'm really trying here!" he said, then proceeded to grab a pillow and squish it into me playfully.

We laughed for a time, but before long things became serious once more.

I sighed. "It's just . . . I keep thinking about something Peggy said to me. How we've never actually had the chance to *grow* together. Really 'go through it,' you know? We're so dominated by the doom and gloom that we never actually get to *live* our life."

It wasn't exactly what she had meant in the sentiment, yet it had me thinking.

He was silent then, even though I knew all too well that this was something he had turned over in his mind an infinite number of times as well.

"I guess that's exactly why we need to go and see Agnes Sweeney," he said simply.

I snuggled in close to the bulk of his frame then, effectively holding on for dear life.

By the beginning of April, spring was well into its full-blown splendour, each tree dotted with broad green jewels of new growth, while the fields and ditches of the countryside were fast becoming a rich tapestry of cheery wildflowers and freshly born grass. The earth smelled positively vibrant each morning, and I could feel the magic surging beneath my feet with each step across the springy ground outside of the manor house. In fact, I was becoming quite attached to the landscape here and was surprisingly hesitant to leave.

Only Dom, Ronan, and I would be travelling to visit Agnes in the dementia hospital in York. Meanwhile, Thomas and Lennie were headed to Leeds to watch some "footie" before meeting up with us to discuss our findings.

I had mixed feelings about the arrangement but tried to take heart in the fact that the three of us should be more than a match to visit an elderly scholar in a nursing home. And *really*, we only intended to ask a few pointed questions. I did wish we had planned to have backup nearby; however, Dom and Ronan both assured me that a stealthy trip was the safest option.

"It sounds like some sort of bad joke: A Witch, a Druid, and an ancient prince walk into a bar," I said to Dom as we loaded our bags into Ronan's practical black sedan.

I still felt misplaced guilt over the fact that Ronan had essentially put his entire medical career on hold to attend to our current needs. Then again, it seemed this was just the way of things, particularly when you were a part of an underground Druidic order attempting to overthrow the greatest dark Sorcerer and tangible magical threat of the past several centuries.

Small potatoes, really.

I had tucked the quilt safely into an unassuming canvas bag, yet I still felt inexplicably nervous bringing it into the open. Privately, I had been theorizing that there really *was* more to it than meets the eye, particularly when it came to my own magical core. However, to any passive observer, it would just be an eclectic quilt that I was bringing to my ailing grandmother in the care home. My thoughts travelled to Gertie then, but I shook the grief from my mind. It was imperative that my magic was fully accessible for this journey, whatever form it took.

Dom dutifully laughed at my joke. "I would *much* rather be walking into a pub than into some sour-smelling care home."

Ronan shook his head in obvious impatience; he had been ready to go for hours.

Taking a ferry between Ireland and England was a decidedly extraneous route, but it was preferable to flying and the traceability that came with airports. It was quite a journey between Belfast and Liverpool, one which we would be taking overnight. Lennie had assured us this was the best route with the least possibility of being tracked, whether from cameras or documentation, other than the usual declarations, which *he* had full access to once we crossed into the UK anyway.

For their part, Lennie and Thomas would be flying, and while I felt a pang of jealousy at their experience, I knew our mode of transport would be Dom's preference too.

"Took you both long enough. Let's go!"

Ronan's voice was icy, but he didn't seem too terribly annoyed.

Dom rolled his eyes and gave me a quick kiss on the cheek as he strode past me on his way to the passenger door. His body positively vibrated in anticipation of the days ahead. It had been a long while since we had gone anywhere beyond the manor house.

In fact, we had been delayed leaving the house precisely because of that very energy, which I was told by a certain Celt needed burning off to be sure he would have his wits about him on such an important day. *Right.*

Dom offered me the front seat, but I shook my head. Ronan and I had arrived at a sort of truce between us over the past several weeks since I'd requested we make the journey to England, but I wasn't interested in small talk with him this morning. I tried to distract myself in the back by listening passively to their discussions, which had turned into a rousing debate around a raid Dom had led against Ronan's ancestors at Cenél Conaill all those years ago. The row soon devolved into a more heated discussion about who had been the most influential High King of Ireland, Ronan's distant relation, Niall of the Nine Hostages, or Dom's own father, Brian Boru.

They had lost me at that point, and I went back to processing my own worries.

We had recently received some disappointing news that had almost led us to cancel the trip: Agnes's health had decreased substantially as of late. This, of course, came as a great frustration on my part. Had we travelled to England when I'd first suggested it ages ago, perhaps we would be dealing with a different level of capacity. However, Ronan assured me that we should still be able to communicate with her well enough. Having managed to successfully secure our passage into the dementia ward in York, the visit was expected to go smoothly. With any luck and a bit of magic on our side, we would have our answers on how to release the spell on the quilt and ideally find some clues about how to defeat Cassius.

It still made me incredibly uncomfortable to be around the quilt. I could feel power surging through it and into me as it sat on my lap during the ferry ride, my own heartbeat in undeniable unison with the piece. It almost felt alive, but I was unsure where its power source was located. Surely it was because many parts of my own story had been woven into it, much like the enchanted tattoo I had placed on Dom's back, but it still made me wary that I couldn't recall the spell I'd placed on it, or why. It also made me nervous that Dom couldn't remember its origins either, as if a spell had been placed on him too in order to protect its truth even from him.

The drive between Liverpool and York would be relatively short now that we were in England. I felt disappointed that we wouldn't be stopping to visit any of the landmarks I had always dreamed of visiting in the past. I also knew those dreams would never become reality if we didn't find a way to stop *him*.

At Dom's insistence, we budgeted ample time to grab a quick bite to eat before we visited the ward; Ronan would have preferred to drive straight through, of course. I sat quietly in the corner of the booth while we ate, tucked close beside Dom's broad frame. I felt oddly shaky as I worked my way through a dry club sandwich, barely tasting each morsel but being sure to at least attempt to nourish myself.

"Julia, are you alright?" Dom asked me when Ronan rose abruptly to go to the bathroom. "You're so quiet. Did Ronan say something?"

"No, no. He's been fine. And I think so." I leaned into him then, breathing out a deep sigh and focusing on my breath for a moment. Anxiety had been welling inside me for hours, not to mention the fact that I had barely slept on the ferry ride over. I had now taken to regularly flexing my hands and fingers in order to keep the feeling in them.

"It's just that, the closer we get to the ward, the more uneasy I feel. It's like . . . well, I can't quite put my finger on it, but something doesn't feel right. And don't say it's just nerves," I said, cutting him off before he could attempt to pacify my worries.

"Do you think it's a warning sign?" he asked.

To his credit, Dom had been making considerable effort to take my intuition seriously during the trip. Perhaps because, after learning of the deterioration of Agnes's health, he had been feeling guilty for not acting sooner. Nonetheless, I appreciated the gesture.

Ronan returned to the table and cocked his head to the right at the sight of our concerned faces.

"What's happened?"

"Julia is having some negative premonitions about this visit is all," Dom said, and squeezed my hand protectively.

"Hmm. How negative?" Ronan asked, before glancing at his watch.

"It's fine. Really. Let's go," I said and slid out of the booth without a glance towards Dom.

I was worried that if I stopped to process too much, I would panic and back out entirely, or that Dom and Ronan would. Regardless of how I was feeling, we needed this information more than anything else right now if we hoped to find a tangible way to avoid what seemed to be an unavoidable fight ahead.

CHAPTER 30

The car ride to the dementia ward was uneventful. I found myself lost in thought around what would come next and tried desperately to open myself up to what exactly the warning I was sensing meant. Meanwhile, I could practically hear Dom's internal gears grind into action; he was readying himself for the possibility of battle, and his intermittent glances towards me in the back seat didn't do anything to help my nerves. Ronan simply looked passive and focused.

The air was heavy with humidity and it was difficult to differentiate between the smell of the actual storm brewing and that of foreboding magical premonition. Gertie had often encouraged me to regularly look to the skies and the earth for my divination practices. However, I had never mastered what she would have called a "Druidic sense of the weather." Whatever that meant.

The temperature had cooled significantly since the onset of our journey, and the distinct drop in barometric pressure was causing difficulties with my hearing. I always found this sensation so unusual, the air outside seeming oddly quiet while the pressure within your ears popped and bubbled. I plugged my nose and blew out against it several times, releasing only some of the pressure. Dom gave me a quizzical look.

The entrance guard to the staff parking lot greeted us with an easy grace, the pleasantries of his Yorkshire accent bright and cheerful in stark contrast to the foreboding sky. Ronan flashed him an unfamiliar medical badge and stared nonchalantly towards the parking lot.

The older man put his hand out for the ID, sliding his silver-rimmed eyeglasses up his large and shiny nose. I wondered silently how many of these convenient access cards Ronan carried and how many doors they would open around the world.

Ronan handed it over reluctantly, and said, "Visiting specialist. Neurology."

The guard lifted his glasses to take yet a closer look, squinting aggressively and looking back and forth between the ID and the driver several times. I noticed Ronan slowly reach his left hand down towards the black medical bag at his feet. I hadn't noticed that before.

"Who are you here to see?"

Ronan cleared his throat. "That's confidential."

The man bristled, and Ronan changed tactics swiftly.

"It's a special case. A woman on the fourth floor . . . you know . . ." And he cocked his head at the man, intimating that they both *knew* what he was taking about. He didn't.

My own magical sense was going haywire, and I couldn't make heads nor tails of what was happening around us. It had to be the weather; it was just so strange outside. Everything felt off, but I also desperately needed answers.

"And them?" the guard asked, sunny disposition suddenly darkening in concert with the clouded sky.

"Students," Ronan said simply.

We hardly resembled anything like what I naively assumed medical students would look like. Dom sat formidably in the front seat, glowering across to the window, unable to hide his contempt for the delay. His shaggy hair and substantial beard gave him more the look of a wild man than a student. I was severely underdressed for a professional outing and smoothed my fleece sweater down over my front self-consciously.

After another painfully long moment, it would seem the guard believed our story.

"Ah . . . right! Of course. Midge mentioned you would be coming today. Sorry, can't be too careful around here. These patients are under strict safety lockdown, and we've had a few attempted security breaches as of late." He paused as if pondering whether he had just divulged too much information to a carload of strangers. "You can park straight through there." He gestured randomly at the large L-shaped parking lot before handing Ronan back both his medical ID and a light-blue parking pass to be placed on the dash.

Ronan's hand released the medical bag, but Dom's jaw was still tensed threateningly.

Driving all the way around to the back of the building and the very edge of the staff lot, Ronan parked adjacent to the back-exit doors. This meant we would have to walk all the way around the building to reach the front entrance, so I looked at Dom, puzzled.

"Escape route," he said before I could open my mouth and gestured at the back doors.

I knew they had spent time analyzing a map of the hospital for several days before we'd left but had dismissed it as just part of their usual pre-mission ritual. If I was honest, I had scoffed at their over-preparedness, but as this was my first real mission with the two of them, I'd refrained from asking too many pointed questions or teasing them for their over-zealous planning.

Plus, I'd had my own worries to deal with.

The air felt heavily blanketed as we travelled along the sidewalk adjacent to the brick walls. Ronan travelled in front of me, carrying with him his mysterious black bag, which while mimicking a doctor's briefcase, definitely did *not* contain a doctor's usual implements. Evidently, this visit was riskier than had been initially intimated, and the mounting tension made it feel much like a clandestine mission.

I felt the hair on the back of my neck raise ominously, a feeling that easily overrode my brewing irritation at being left out of the loop in terms of what seemed to be fairly significant details. Dom followed silently behind me, his stature distinctly shifted from his usual air of easy confidence. Instead, I could practically feel his sharp edges slicing through my wake; he was a weapon alight, ready to spring and snap into action at any moment.

I carried the simple canvas bag containing the quilt close to my chest and had left the rest of my personal items locked safely in Ronan's trunk. It was surprisingly light, which no doubt had to do with the magic it contained rather than the fabrics themselves. It almost seemed as if its weight changed depending upon my need of it. I had no doubt that if I were to snuggle up underneath the unusual blanket, it would feel heavy as lead. However, I had no intention of cozying up with something *that* magically powerful without understanding its uses first.

We reached the front entranceway, and Ronan stepped forward confidently towards the front desk. Dom gently grabbed my elbow to momentarily hold me back.

"I don't have a good feeling about this," he said.

"Neither do I. Something smells . . . wrong. And I don't mean the astringent hospital smell either. I smell dark magic."

"Ronan clearly senses it as well," Dom said, almost imperceptibly jutting his chin towards the black bag Ronan held. I could hear his deliberately paced breathing as he stood uncharacteristically close to my side.

My Bearing magic remained confused in the space, like when I couldn't get a clear signal on my cellphone. Patchy and unreliable. But it crackled loudly within nonetheless.

We watched at a distance as Ronan fluidly undid the top clasp of the bag as he spoke to the receptionist, clearly anticipating resistance, and then just as quickly closed it once more. He had apparently gained us access through the security doors to the right.

He beckoned us forward and smoothly handed us ID tags to pin to our fronts.

I am not sure what I had been expecting. Perhaps some sort of sunny dementia ward with false front steps and happily cared-for patients. Apparently, this place *did* house that style of ward; the handful of pamphlets stuffed into a clear plastic stand bore the faces of models who were pleasantly at peace in their surroundings. To our left, signs pointed towards a music and games room and even a movie theatre. I wondered absently if they allowed the patients popcorn and liquorice before snapping back to attention.

The ward we were entering had a distinctly different energy. We were practically frisked by a new guard who asked us to remove anything from our possession that might be used as a weapon. Ronan glared at the man as he stepped forward, all the while casually barring Dom from reacting with open hostility when the guard yanked my canvas bag from my hands without warning.

"Hey—" I said, but Ronan interrupted, even as Dom let out some kind of strange primal snort.

"*This* contains necessary medical implements, which are of no business of yours," he said, his eyes practically daring the guard to try to remove it from his possession. "*That* is a quilt for the ward. Nothing more." Ronan didn't break his stare with the guard, who continued to eye his medical tag with further skepticism. The guard paused for a moment and then handed my bag back to me rather unceremoniously, the effect causing me to almost drop it on the floor.

Ronan was in full command of the situation, yet I was still relieved when the guard finally opened the security door with a satisfying *click*. I had no doubt Dom would have stepped in next if they'd tried to remove the quilt once more, and I could only imagine how smoothly *that* would have gone.

For his part, Dom carried nothing on his person, but the man himself was dangerous enough without any weapons. And then to my surprise, he winked at me before grabbing an empty clipboard off a side table as we passed through the door, clearly not wanting to be without an item of encumbrance of his own. I would have burst out laughing were the circumstances not so serious.

The halls were lined halfway up with white subway tiles and uncomfortably lit with cool-toned fluorescent lights. The combined effect made it feel like we were walking into an empty refrigerator. We took a short staircase towards a different wing, which branched off from the main corridor we had travelled down, and Ronan swiped his guest tag through the next security door.

It was then that I knew we had arrived at our intended destination; the air was positively thick with the foul stench of Wraith magic. The charge nurses on the floor didn't seem to notice anything out of the ordinary and went on about their business. They did look pre-emptively annoyed, however, at any possible disturbances we may cause.

We had ventured into some sort of common area where various patients were scattered about, participating in activities that ranged from backgammon to painting. A small flatscreen TV played what looked to be a popular English soap opera.

Ronan nodded pointedly at one woman in particular, ignoring the rest.

The nurse in question must have been Midge, who we'd been advised to speak to. After tucking a flannel blanket with satin trim around a woman sitting in front of a barred window, she walked slowly over to greet us. The rain had started and was pelting sideways. It covered the windows in streaks and droplets, the effect making it very difficult to see outside, though I could tell that we were indeed at the back of the hospital now. I could now see why Ronan and Dom had elected to park on this end of the building. I had no idea how we would break out of a high-security floor like this, but I had no doubt they had considered that fine detail as well.

"You'll have to be quick, Dr. Gallagher. She's easily agitated, and we won't be best pleased if we have to administer an extra restraint today." She shook her head sternly. "We're short staffed."

Ronan nodded with what was obviously feigned compliance.

"I don't know what it is you're after," she said after a moment, looking ominously towards the next locked corridor, "but I doubt you'll get a whole lot out of her. She's been deteriorating pretty much daily. If I'm honest . . . I'm not sure how long she has left in this world."

Ronan nodded, gesturing her towards the final locked door.

Our trio plus Midge now stood just inside a short hallway containing four wide doors, two on each side of the berth and two side-by-side at the end. Apparently, Agnes was in the room on the front left.

Midge knocked gently on her door, though there was no reply from inside. She didn't seem to expect one. The stench was almost unbearable. Only Ronan and I seemed to notice it, although he was doing a much better job than I was at maintaining his composure. I put my arm up over my nose and mouth, pretending to be about to sneeze so as not to raise any alarm from our escort.

"I'll be back to let you out in thirty minutes. If you need out sooner, press this buzzer, and I'll come for you." She left then, the hallway door closing loudly and locking automatically behind her.

"Great, so now we're locked in with this wretched stench and an unknown magical entity!" Ronan said as he reached for Agnes's door, almost collapsing in his fight to maintain composure.

Dom looked perplexed, and I let out a stifled laugh that came out more like a choked gag.

"At least Dom won't faint from the smell!" I coughed. "He's the strongest anyway, so he can drag out our limp bodies if we pass out." Dom shot me a forceful look, and Ronan shook his head at my absurdity as he turned the handle; not the best time for jokes perhaps.

To my relief, the small room didn't greet us with nearly the same level of stench as the hallway, and both Ronan and I clamoured inside somewhat desperately as Dom closed the door behind us with a much quieter *click.*

The room was dimly lit and sparse. It contained a rocking chair, a plain flat bed with padded rails on all sides, and a single boxed-heating register below a south-facing window. I was glad to know she could still feel the sun on her face from time to time.

Dom remained standing in front of the door, looking menacing, arms crossed around his stolen clipboard.

Quick to work, Ronan crouched down beside Agnes Sweeney, who was sitting quietly in the chair. She was very elderly, her face deeply etched with the long lines of age. I noticed too that her eyes were an almost milky blue colour; evidently, she was also blind.

"Hello, Agnes," Ronan said, and gently touched her hand.

She had wide, almost buttery-skinned fingers crossed simply on her lap above a plain grey-wool blanket. Her face remained impassive, and I was unsure if she even knew we were in the room.

"My name is Dr. Gallagher. I was hoping to ask you a few questions today. I've brought my friend, Julia. She is a Witch . . . and a Diviner . . . like you."

The woman slowly turned her face towards me, and I could feel her powerful, scattered energy gathering within the confines of the room. The sensation was unnerving at first as it passed over my skin, arriving at its intended target with a prickly itch; she very clearly didn't need eyes to identify another magic Bearer in the room.

I pulled the ends of my fleece sleeves down tightly into my fists and wrapped my arms around my waist protectively. Ronan quietly opened his bag, which had been placed conveniently between his low-crouched legs.

"Round and round the garden. Like a teddy bear. One step. Two step. Tickle under there!" she said suddenly, voice breaking and raspy from ill-use.

Ronan pursed his lips and took a deep breath through his nose. He squeezed her hand gently again. "My friend Julia . . . she was wondering if you could look at something for her."

I felt more magic pushing in my direction, but this time it was smooth against me, albeit arriving with much more force. The sensation reminded me of a cool river stone or a marble. It gently pressed against me, rolling past as if it were testing the edges of a poorly sealed container.

"Ronan, let me try," I said and stepped closer to the frail woman.

Her clouded eyes hadn't left me since Ronan had announced my presence in the room.

I arranged myself at the end of her bed where there was a short gap between the footer and the side rail. Ronan turned her rocking chair to face me directly, then stood behind her, still fingering around in his black bag.

It was incredibly distracting, and I gave him a forceful look.

"Agnes. I've brought something to show you. I was hoping you could help me figure out how to unlock the spell that's keeping the magic hidden . . . from me."

The swirling, rolling forces around me quelled slightly. She was definitely listening now, although I could sense it was taking great effort on her part to keep from bursting back into the scratching, itching, sporadic efforts from before.

"I know some of my own magic is trapped inside, or at least . . . well, I think it's maybe some of my own memories. I can feel it like my own heart-beat sometimes. Like a missing piece of me."

I heard a collective intake of breath from both Dom and Ronan.

Evidently, I had failed to fully elaborate on my theories of how the magic within the quilt actually worked, or how deeply I sensed it was connected to my past. I avoided their gaze but could feel both Dom and Ronan's eyes on me heavily, watching every move with even more rapt attention, if that were possible.

"Am I the one who needs to unlock it somehow? Or did someone else curse it? Help me . . . please."

I was desperate now. How long would she be able to pay attention before the churning forces overtook her mind once more.

"Teddy bear under there. Round the garden."

I attempted to yank the quilt from the depths of the bag, but it suddenly felt immensely heavy. More unruly magic pulsed around me as I placed the quilt across her hands and lap and waited.

"Two step. Over there. One step."

Slowly lifting her hands on top of it, I could immediately feel the sheer effort it was taking her to explore the bewitched artifact before her. She was barely touching it now and ever so slowly feeling for the magic. Even from their vantage points in the room, the others probably couldn't detect the imperceivably small movements, but I knew intuitively what she was doing.

She was attempting to map the containment spell.

Dom was silent as a stone by the door. But in that moment, I could somehow sense him reaching towards me with his mind, desperate to offer me protection, even from across the room. It was so strange how I could *feel* him in the room with me. Incredible really. I saw a brief smile flicker across her face. Could she also feel his reach?

"Garden bear. Under there."

And then she was lost to us again.

Within moments, her magic was writhing, a tumult pushing against me and the four walls around us. Confused. Lost. Searching desperately for an escape from this prison and the prison of her mind.

No longer cool and rolling across me, her magic had transformed into something harsh and jagged, and my skin felt raw from the assault. I gathered up the quilt from her lap and hastily shoved it back into the canvas bag, its weight now suddenly, and conveniently, featherlight.

Behind her, Ronan pulled out a small white pouch and balled it into his hand, his middle finger and thumb looped carefully into the silvery drawstring.

"I think we will leave you for now, Agnes. We're sorry to have disturbed you," I said, standing up gingerly before her. It turned out my bed-end perch wasn't particularly comfortable, and I suddenly felt a dull ache in my hips.

With a startling jolt, she looked up at me, grabbing my wrist with surprising force.

Dom started forward, eyes wild and nostrils flaring as he snapped the clipboard in two. I threw my other arm up to stop him. Ronan had his own arm extended just behind her head, holding the hidden white pouch, no doubt some sort of Druidic spell at the ready.

"Round and round the garden. Like a teddy bear. One step. Two step. Tickle under there."

She repeated the verse several times more, but the words were becoming increasingly jumbled and her cadence wild. However, in my own mind, her whispered voice passed through my thoughts.

You wove the protection spell onto the quilt to protect your secrets from years ago . . . Anyone who discovers it will quickly forget . . . That's the trick . . . Only you can release the magic within, when the time is right . . .

Her grip was becoming increasingly painful, and my discomfort was now notable to the others. Their nervous glances indicated a ticking timebomb; it was only a matter of seconds before one of them would step in. Yet, I knew the strength of Agnes's grasp was directly correlated to the grip on her own consciousness.

"What do you mean?" I asked aloud.

Dom took several steps towards me, but I held my hand still firm. Ronan was softly chanting under his breath, preparing himself.

I could barely hold on now. The pain of her grip and the splintering edges of her magic slashed across me, unseen to Dom, and I assumed only mildly sensed by Ronan.

"Who did this to you?" I asked, bile rising in the back of my throat; I already knew the answer.

"Round and round and round and round!"

Cassius . . . He knows you are looking for other Bearers . . . He's been killing us one by one . . . to get to you . . . He wants the baby now . . .

Her outward ranting grew into a frenzy, and she soon began to wail. A shrill, pained scream ripe with grief filled the room. I looked down towards my completely numb fingers, which were now turning an odd shade of greyish purple.

"What baby?" I gasped, my own resolve on the edge of a knife.

"That's *enough*, Ronan," Dom boomed to his second in command, and Ronan dropped the contents of the white pouch over the aged woman's head, sprinkling what looked like glittering white sand across her shoulders and lap. Her eyes closed, and a soft smile spread across her now-tranquil face as the magical dust slowly disappeared from her brow.

I looked down at her slackening fingers, knuckles already changing back from white to pink. She was wearing a knit sweater with tiny yellow and blue forget-me-knots stitched along the cuff of the sleeve in a very familiar pattern.

My heart sank as dark, heavy dread spread through me like magma. This Bearer, who had been irreversibly damaged by dark spells that seemed to violently force her own magic inward, was yet another horribly woven piece of our ill-fated destiny.

We did this to her. And the cost of our truth suddenly became too much to bear.

Before I could protest, Dom led me out towards the door with his arm firmly around my back.

Ronan tucked Agnes in gently, and I noticed out of the corner of my eye, while he turned the rocker towards the window, that a single beam of sunlight had broken through the clouds and fallen across her face. The remnants of her surging, frothing will, as well as the contents of Ronan's pouch, had all but disappeared, and the room now seemed untouched by magic once more.

We were soon met again by the horrendous stench in the hall. But just before the door clicked shut behind us, almost imperceptible even within my own mind, I heard her speak one last time.

It was always you, my dear.

Ronan tilted his head, and then shook it dismissively before buzzing us out. We had barely lasted fifteen minutes, but it hadn't felt that long.

Dom and I exited the locked ward without uttering so much as a word to any of the attending staff. Ronan handed me his clearance pass to make for a quick exit. He would be staying behind to cover off any professional courtesy that was due and would meet us at the car when appropriate.

I moved silently down the first flight of stairs and back down the white hallway. The exit voyage felt considerably more expeditious than our arrival. In fact, I was moving at such a pace that I could feel the cool, soothing air of the hallway moving against my magically chapped cheeks and lips. Dom followed behind, a protective shadow once again, though far closer than normal. I could almost feel his hot measured breath on the back of my neck, and something about it made me uneasy.

For my own part, my heart was pounding an irregular and rapid rhythm against my ribs, while beads of sweat were quickly collecting on my hairline and dripping down my neck. Conversely, my hands had completely turned to ice; I ran them over my face, the effect serving to further numb the invisible pain there. It felt a lot like a panic attack, but I knew there was a lot more to it. Magical disturbances like *that* don't go unnoticed or unmeasured by other magic users.

Shockingly, I wished I could speak with Ronan about what was happening in that moment, not Dom.

"You're going to have to explain to me what the hell just happened in there," Dom said through gritted teeth once we were finally out of the security-clearance areas and could see the front exit ahead.

"I don't—"

"No. Not here. Outside," he growled.

I could barely remember my feet carrying my body between Agnes' upper-corridor room and the front door of the hospital, but I would certainly remember the journey between the exit doors and Ronan's car. Roughly grabbing my arm once we were out on the street, Dom then steered me towards the car more firmly than was to my liking.

"Ease off, Dom!" I said as I furrowed my brows and pulled my still-tender wrist back towards my chest, rubbing it gently. "We're outside now; it's alright."

He proceeded to take my arm again and tuck it into his own, clearly intending to dive directly into the crux of the matter. "It's not safe here, and you know it! You knew it *before* we even went inside!"

"Well yeah . . . and I said as much."

We passed a cluster of nurses smoking outside a fire exit, eyeing us speculatively, but Dom forged onward without a second glance.

I struggled to make out the complicated look on his face as we arrived at Ronan's car. Something familiar, but perhaps from another timeline, had settled there. I scrunched up my eyes for a moment to try to grasp a vision or memory that would give me the answer, but it was as fruitless as trying to catch sunshine in a butterfly net. I opened my eyes as he unceremoniously handed me a bottle of lukewarm water from the trunk and stood with his arms crossed and eyebrows raised accusingly.

"What's your issue here?" I said, frustrated and no longer able to temper my own anxiety while trying to process the dysregulated emotion he was hurling towards me. "You're freaking out because you don't understand what happened to me, but clearly it wasn't the same as what happened to you. Is that it? Well surprise, surprise! I'm a Witch!"

"You didn't say how *unsafe* it was for you! To be there! We should have left immediately."

"How could I have known that?"

He didn't answer but ran his fingers through his hair, which was damp with sweat.

"Well, for starters, *Julia,*" his voice was low and formidable, "it would seem you've kept a fair few details to yourself regarding the quilt and its magic—"

"I told you what I *knew!* And it's not like you've been around much to even *talk* to me about any of this anyway!" I interrupted, angry tears now forming in my eyes. How dare he accuse *me* of purposely keeping important details from him. "And what about you and Ronan? Clearly you kept a whole list of safety and logistical details *from me! You* knew it would be dangerous too! I mean what the fuck?"

Evidently there was a reason why I'd hidden the magic in the quilt, and it had nothing to do with him. For all I knew, he was *included* in the spell as another protective measure to keep its secrets guarded until the time was right. *Nothing* I had done, or kept from him, *was* personal. I just didn't fully understand my feelings or intuition around it. Not yet at least.

However, keeping escape plans and risk assessments for our journey here a secret *did* feel personal. Suddenly, I didn't feel like sharing the details of Agnes's message to me, at least not immediately. It didn't matter because Dom's emotional sensibility while in warrior poise was as impossible to reach as a stone keep.

He rolled his shoulders back several times, then growled, deep in his baritone, which I took as a warning sign that he was about to blow. "How the hell am I supposed to keep you safe if you don't tell me *what the fuck* is going on?"

As calmly as I could, and ignoring my shaking hands, I stretched to my full height and looked directly into his grey-blue eyes. I knew this would either have the effect of calming him, or precisely the inverse. Sometimes he reminded me of a great wild stallion, and unfortunately, I knew next to nothing about horses.

"How *dare* you?" I said, acid forming on my lips.

A woman walking by looked completely appalled at the impropriety of our public display, but I didn't flinch. Dom stared back at me, lips tight and nostrils flared. I could see the familiar pools of grief behind his eyes, but the anger on his face was so palpable that any sane person would have taken several steps back. Instead, I leaned in and raised my chin in clear challenge to make my meaning crystal *fucking* clear.

"I guess you'll just have to learn to trust me," I challenged him once more.

He dropped his hands loudly onto the sides of his thighs and shook his head ruefully. An open-mouthed smile borne from disbelief spread across his face.

"You think I don't?" he scoffed, appalled at my insinuation.

Shoulders raised, I tilted my head and tightened my lips in a *"you tell me"* manner that was more than likely going to goad him. The thing was, I wasn't going to back down. Not on this one, and especially not after what I'd learned about Agnes's tragic decline. Too many people had been hurt already. I was done with sitting back and being the *good girl*.

He looked away then, jaw tensed into knots and long fingers drumming on his thighs in a sporadic pattern. I sank down onto the parking-lot's curb and put my head in my hands. Clearly there was more to this argument than was on the surface, but this was neither the time nor place.

And I was just so dizzy all of a sudden.

After what felt like a lifetime, Ronan appeared at my side, positively humming with uncharacteristically ignited energy.

"Julia . . . Did you feel it? Her magic! I've never felt anything like it!"

I gave Dom a quick glance. He was refusing to meet either of our eyes as he leaned casually on Ronan's car several feet away, arms crossed angrily on his broad chest.

"They got to her first," I said flatly and ran my fingers through my hair once more. I could smell the stress sweat on myself now, and my palms were uncomfortably clammy.

His face fell into a scowl. "I know. I could smell it everywhere, the stench of dark magic. Like they had boxed her in there. Fucking Wraiths."

I shuddered.

They had gotten to her alright, and I was already dreading the dreams that would follow tonight after having pressed so closely to such volatile and insidious magics.

"It would have taken more than an underling to do this kind of work, Ronan. This was pure sorcery. I think *he* did this to her. *Himself.* The Wraiths only created the container to keep her volatile magics *in.*"

Both men stared at me in disbelief, and I continued. "She was immensely powerful . . . like nothing I've ever encountered. You could feel it like rolling electricity through the air. Shit, Dom could probably even feel it, even if he didn't know what to do with the information."

It was a low blow, and I knew it, but I was too dizzy from trying to process all that had happened to make amends now. I put my head back down between my knees. My own energy was utterly spent, and I felt so angry with Dom for making this personal when I clearly had enough to process in the moment. It was all too much.

Ronan paused, his voice suddenly tentative. "Julia . . . are you alright?"

I looked up again slowly, taking several deep breaths to steady myself.

He continued, gesturing towards the brooding Celt standing several feet away. "It affected you more than it did me, or Dom . . . you're right."

Ronan had finally picked up on the tension between us, which had only moments before been on full display in the parking lot for all to see. Now, however, Dom was doing his best impression of a tree, though I knew he was listening to every word with raging, rapt attention.

"She spoke to me, Ronan . . . in my head," I said in a whisper, eyes filling with tears once more. "It's never happened before, not like that. I mean, I've heard whispers here and there, but that . . . was exceptional magic. It wasn't like a Send, all fleeting and wild. It was controlled. And she just . . . walked right in."

I knew that many Bearers had their own special talents, much like I could Divine, and Aisling could Send. But this was something wholly different. I felt guilty I hadn't shared this detail with Dom when we'd first arrived outside, and under the right circumstances, I would have.

But things had spiralled out of hand so quickly.

"I think it's time to go. There are too many watchful eyes and mistrustful ears," Dom said, doing a poor job at keeping his commanding tone in check.

Ronan offered me his hand to get up, but I thought that might be a saltier move than Dom needed from me at this point in time.

And I was okay to stand on my own, really. I always had been.

CHAPTER 31

Thankfully, the distance between the ward and our accommodations for the evening in the heart of Leeds wasn't too terribly far. Its location had been selected largely because of its proximity to Elland Road, where Thomas and Lennie were currently watching the soccer match. Apparently, the terracotta-fronted, Victorian-era, boutique hotel was not only well situated for our reunion with the rest of our party but also met Ronan's unusually high standards.

"I mean, I really don't think it's that unreasonable to want comfortable lodgings, especially after a day like today!" Ronan said, trying to keep the conversation light.

The drive had been mostly silent, with Ronan interjecting from time to time about traffic or the weather and now about the hotel. Neither Dom nor I had responded throughout with much more than a nod apiece. If not for our combined dark mood, I was quite sure Dom would be rubbing Ronan about this all being rather fancy for a military man, but as it stood, the brooding Celt seated in front of me was as silent as a boulder.

Surprisingly, I looked forward to re-connecting again with Thomas and Lennie on their return, if simply as an excuse to avoid Dom's gaze a little while longer. In the meantime, it would be easy enough to pawn him off on Ronan, at least until the others joined us. There was obviously more than meets the eye to his reaction, but right now, I just didn't have the emotional bandwidth to help him unpack it all. I desperately needed time to process what had happened with Agnes Sweeney and to do so at my own pace.

It *was* me who had protectively sealed in the quilt's magic, almost as if I had left myself a trail of breadcrumbs that only I could find. While I had suspected as much before, this new confirmation had slightly bolstered my confidence in my ability to unearth its truth. Or at the very least, it strengthened my argument against leaning so heavily on the Prophecy and the looming final battle.

The problem was that I still had no idea how to crack the code.

Ronan parked his car directly in front the hotel in one of the few available parking spots, and I shook my head at his luck once again. He promptly unloaded our luggage from the trunk and set them on the curb. Dom quickly scooped up our bags, as well as somehow managing to wedge the canvas quilt bag under his arm. I held onto my purse possessively and eyed him in the moment. I couldn't decide if he was feeling guilty and overcompensating, or if this was just more of his aged chivalric habits at play.

Regardless, he looked ridiculous.

"*Well, fellas* . . . *I'm* going to go for a walk," I said, attempting to feign casual indifference to the obvious discomfort we had all endured during the past forty-five minutes. Unfortunately, the desired effect wasn't achieved, and I only managed to sound more awkward than usual. Dom stared dumbly at me on the busy downtown street, like an over-encumbered and exhausted pack-mule.

"Julia, you've *got to be kidding me right now*," he said, putting heavy emphasis on the latter half of the statement, almost stamping the words out.

I ignored his tone as I dug around in my bag, searching for my phone.

"I'll meet you inside, Dom," Ronan said, already turning towards the hotel. The man clearly had enough sense to get away from this potential combat zone posthaste.

I let out a resigned sigh. "No, Domhnall. I'm not kidding. Please don't follow me."

Dom dropped the luggage to the ground and slammed his fists on the top of Ronan's car. "Oh, for fuck sakes, Julia! This is *dangerous!*"

"And I said I just needed a *fucking minute!*"

I slung my bag over my shoulder, and without another glance back, promptly strode down the busy street towards the area Ronan had referred to as the "Headrow" on our drive in. Before I could ask how he was so familiar with the area, he had brightly informed us about his more recent stint at "Jimmy's," which was apparently just up the road.

"More Wraith research, of course, and where better than at Europe's largest teaching hospital. You would be surprised at how many other magic users have turned up there over the years!" he'd said enthusiastically. Dom had replied by flexing his crossed arms even further, while I had at least offered up a polite, "Hmm."

Walking freely now, I was desperate to find a park or a green space where I could just *breathe*; so far, all I had been met with were high red-brick and stone buildings intermixed with a handful of more modern structures. Shops, restaurants, and plenty of tourists, but no greenery.

I wandered aimlessly for several minutes through this newly unfamiliar territory and increased my pace while redoubling efforts to clear my anger and my head. I wasn't exactly certain where I was going, but it surely wouldn't serve me to blow up in the middle of a strange place either. I knew I had my phone with me in case I got lost.

After a time, I realized there was still no sign of my magical reservoirs refilling, and I couldn't find any greenery to ground myself with. So, I resigned to head back in the direction I had come. Fortuitously then, a city bus rumbled up in front of me and lowered to the curb. I boarded without a further thought, using some leftover small change in my pocket, from the ferry ride over, as fare.

Perhaps there would be a park on the route I could visit. Or better yet, a pub!

I intended to return without too much delay and would probably only ride the bus one or two neighbourhoods over before disembarking towards the closest drinking establishment. A pint would serve much faster to calm my nerves than nature and meditation, and desperate times called for desperate measures.

I stumbled towards the back of the bus, which had already taken off, and noticed with increased discomfort how much sweat was dripping down the back of my neck. The morning's chill air had transformed into a supremely muggy late afternoon, and I had unfortunately made the mistake of dressing in heavy jeans and a pullover fleece sweater. Gertie had always called weather like this "close," and it was certainly that.

The bus was crammed full with all sorts of riders, all of whom kept their heads down, focused intently on their own business. I had the distinct impression I should likely mind my own as well, rather than staring around like a tourist.

I ran my fingers through my increasingly frizzy auburn locks, cursing the fact that I had decided to wear my hair down today. I felt anger bubbling inside me at the thought of Dom's idle opinions on my dress influencing even *this* direction of my day.

Moodily digging through my bag in search of a hair elastic, I swore quietly. I had left my wallet in the back of Ronan's car, or maybe even dropped it on the ground in all the commotion. Hopefully Dom had seen it, but in the meantime, my remaining pocket change would have to do. Or better yet, perhaps some kind person would take pity on me and buy me a drink. It was worth a shot anyways.

Memories of my early twenties flashed before my eyes as we thundered down the road. I yearned then for the invigorating magic of living freely on my own two feet and blindly following my own path of destiny. *That* path hadn't included Prophecy, imminent death, or the birth of an aforementioned child who would defeat the all-evil one. Nor did it include some ratty quilt that was apparently an unsolvable puzzle I had created for myself like some inscrutable, twisted genius.

The bus rumbled through a greener strip for a time, but I had my sights set firmly now on a cold pint and so resisted the urge to disembark. Entering a new area with significantly less red brick than the previous few, I spotted an old stone pub located on the corner of a busy intersection, kitty-corner to an ancient-looking church. It was perfect, and I would simply hop back on in the other direction in a little while, once I was feeling more settled.

"Easy-peasy, lemon squeezy!" I said aloud, and hopped gleefully off the bus, patently ignoring the strange looks I was receiving.

I smiled shyly at the bartender as I entered the low-lit establishment. He wore a button-down white shirt and a green-grocer apron around his waist. Well-worn, faded-black slacks with tattered bottoms completed the ensemble, along with the slight sneer on his face. A sign above him read, "No Swearing and No Electronics."

Resisting the urge to check my phone, I sidled up to the bar while absently digging around in my pockets and across the bottom of my bag for some spare change. I cringed momentarily as mystery lint and last summer's sand caught under my nails in the process, then sighed. There was enough for at least one pint and then the return fare on the bus.

"What will it be?" the bartender asked, polishing an oblong pint glass with a dirty-looking rag, looking irritated at the interruption. He was watching a small rectangular TV with a rounded screen and antenna preferentially tucked between a collection of whisky bottles and an empty dish tub.

"A pint of . . . whatever's most popular." I said, eyeing the various sizes of taps of unknown lagers in front of me.

He gave me a sideways look for just a moment, and then filled the glass he had been polishing for what I could only assume was the better part of the last half hour as he tensely observed his favourite team miss yet another goal.

The pub was mostly empty, save for an older couple situated in peaceful silence in a wooden booth in front of the greasy-paned front window. Another group of gentlemen sat around a wooden table in front of a non-functional fireplace, their attention drawn towards a small flatscreen TV precariously perched above the mantle. Apparently, the no-electronics rule didn't apply when soccer was on—or "football" as they called it here. My attention was momentarily drawn to the stadium where I assumed Lennie and Thomas must be.

After taking a mindful sip of my treasured pint, I noticed a final patron watching me from across the room. I hadn't noticed him when I first arrived, but he was now gesturing towards the seat across from him.

I was feeling rebellious, and he looked friendly enough.

"Come! Sit," the man announced, his accent somewhat unfamiliar but welcoming nonetheless.

"What the hell," I said under my breath, and then eyed the barkeep for possible repercussions for my apparent indiscretions. The match seemed to have just ended, and in what I assumed was a loss based on the foul look on his face as he slammed around more dirty glasses.

"There's no reason for either of us to drink alone on this beautiful day!" the man called over to me.

My attention returned to my new acquaintance. His voice lingered on the word "beautiful" as he eyed me from top to bottom, eyes bright as a broad smile spread across his handsome face.

His charm was well seasoned, no doubt, and I ventured a guess that he rarely encountered anyone who had the nerve to turn him down for at least a short conversation, or in my case, a pint. I knew damn well to be wary of men like this, but as I was well within view of both the bartender and the older couple by the window, it seemed safe enough. Plus, I couldn't sense any magical danger, *per se*. Although that wasn't saying much considering the current state of my inner fire.

"What brings you here? You don't sound like a local," he asked, eyebrows raised in enthusiastic welcome, and with almost a hint of mockery towards our present company, as I approached.

"Nor do you," I said, my eyes looking him over from above my drink as I took a long sip.

He smiled serenely.

"I'm from Canada. The West Coast actually," I offered before returning my attention to my pint, which was unfortunately already half gone.

"Vancouver perhaps? Oh, I love Vancouver," he said, and as he clapped his hands together, I noticed he wore a gold signet ring on his right pinky finger. "In fact, I have done a lot of business there in the past."

"Kind of. I go to . . . well, I *went* to university there."

I took another long drink, the bottom of the glass now within sight.

This man was magically charismatic, but I was unsure if he was a magic user or simply someone with the unexplored potential to Wield it. Certain individuals had always proven difficult for me to navigate, especially without a physical touch or some kind of back story.

I noticed that he kept his hands folded neatly on the table before him when he wasn't clapping them together or reaching for his glass of red wine. The glass itself was aged and short. I looked around the room and gleaned that wine was a bit of an odd choice for a pub such as this. But who was I to judge?

"So, tell me about yourself! What brings you here, all the way across the pond?"

It hadn't gone unnoticed that he had now asked about my personal business for a second time, while revealing very little about himself.

"Travel mostly. I just finished school and was chasing some adventure before tackling the real world." I smiled at him over my almost-empty pint glass, wondering shamelessly now if he was the charitable type.

"Wonderful!" He looked towards my left ring finger for a moment before dragging his eyes back up towards my own.

His were a steely grey, which stood in great contrast to his lightly olive skin. His hair was impeccably cut, with the perfect dash of salt and pepper throughout, almost as if that too had been precisely calculated. I noticed then that his clothes, while simple, practically screamed money. The casual way he had rolled up the sleeves from his dress shirt made him look approachable, but the pattern and thread of the cuffs were extremely neat and fine. The heavy gold watch secured on his left wrist served to underscore my assumptions.

There was something oddly familiar about him too, but I was struggling to place exactly what it was. He had the charisma of a celebrity . . . or maybe a news personality? But I shrugged it off as this was one of the many occupational hazards of being both a Witch and a Diviner. Gertie had once called it "false familiarity."

"No one special out there waiting for you? A *beautiful* woman such as yourself must be betrothed to a real prince of a man," he said, smiling smoothly from across the grimy table. This felt like an oddly specific phrase, but I chalked its accuracy up to his possible romantic leanings rather than any awareness of my own truth.

Still, my magical intuition remained silent within.

"Yes . . . there's someone," I said, not wanting to give too much away about my current circumstances. This was quickly starting to feel a bit like an interrogation. "But we've only just met recently. It's new."

I had been grappling with this fact for weeks, the juxtaposition between our shared history and our present-day reality. I had known Dom in the here and now for less than a year but was supposed to act as if I remembered spending the eleventh, fifteenth, or seventeenth century with him with surety.

He smiled conspiratorially.

"You'll want another pint then!" he suggested, clapping his hands together enthusiastically once more.

I shrugged and opened my bag towards him, demonstrating a distinct lack of *tuppence*.

"I forgot my wallet at the hotel. That's it for me."

"Nonsense!" he boomed, barely allowing me to finish my sentence as his gregariousness oozed into the space between us.

I raised my hands in both resignation and thanks. "Well, if you're sure, then sure."

"Wonderful!"

And as if by magic, the bartender brought him over another stumpy glass of his bright-red wine, followed by a second warm pint for me; England was weird.

"Now tell me, it was Julia, wasn't it?"

I wasn't sure I had mentioned my name to him yet, but I also wasn't entirely sure that I hadn't. The entire journey from the hotel to the pub had been a blur, and the beer was having its way with my empty tummy. It had to be approaching supper time.

I smiled. "Yes, it's Julia."

"After Caesar! Or perhaps Julia the Elder? Although I'm not so sure you would want to be named after her," he said, laughing at his own brevity.

He carried on for a while about some ancient collection of Latin love poems by someone called Ovid, which were allegedly written about the Elder Julia, although the notion was up for debate. I nodded politely as he occasionally prompted me for response; it was a blatant attempt to draw me into the conversation at a deeper level. I was hardly keeping up, my attention busy floating somewhere between my first and second pints on a notably empty stomach.

With my insides gurgling and attention now thoroughly waning, I looked at the time on the wall, realizing that it would be dark before long. "What did you say your name was? Sorry, I'm terrible with names."

His eyes darted towards the door briefly. "Marcus Long. But you can call me Marc."

We chatted freely for another few minutes until I finished my second pint, after which I attempted to gracefully dispel his offer for a third.

"I insist! One more, and then I'll let you on your merry way!"

"No, no, I couldn't possibly." I was growing uncomfortable with his persistence now. "I've got to be getting back."

If I hadn't been looking directly at him, I might have missed the dark shadow that darted across his face at my rejection. And although it was only for an instant, it was more than enough to send me packing. I reached within; still no magical alarm.

Strange. But clearly this man was dangerous on *some* level, and basic human instinct screamed that I should run.

"Come now, Julia! Another!" he said, features softening once more as he gestured to the bartender. However, the residual warmth failed to reach his cool grey eyes.

How had I missed this feature before? He was suddenly utterly terrifying; my mind recounted our conversation and the way his voice had exuded what I now perceived to be vanity.

My magic sputtered feebly within me as my human memory scraped helplessly across its recesses to place his familiar face.

I stood up abruptly, swaying slightly on the spot before shoving my chair back with a clatter. I turned and looked towards the bartender to signal that I was no longer interested in participating in this conversation. In that moment, I came to greatly appreciate the seasoned awareness of the scowling man behind the counter, watching him deftly redirect his scowl instead onto the man before me.

Marc raised his hands in surrender, as if there had been some great misunderstanding and that he would of course let me leave freely; no harm, no foul.

I had no recollection of it taking more than two or three steps to reach the creaking pub door. Before I knew it, I was standing on the street, and to my surprise, dusk was quickly gathering around me. I reached into my bag for my cellphone to call Dom. He was probably starting to worry, and I was suddenly missing him desperately. No cellphone. *Shit.*

I turned around to grab the pub door before it shut behind me, gaze travelling back inside towards the bar top and table. But then I distinctly remembered having *not* removed it in the first place. Strange. I noticed with great discomfort that the mysterious Marc Long was no longer seated in his corner booth.

The now cool, damp hair on the back of my neck prickled ominously.

I would get on the first bus back towards Dom, and then I would bring him back to the pub with me to search for my cellphone; there was no way in hell I was going back in there right now. My adrenal system had suddenly shifted into overdrive, urging me onward into flight from the current situation in increasing waves. Parallel, almost laughably, my Witch's fire was still completely burnt out.

I turned right onto the high street towards the first group of people I could find, but I didn't even make it close enough to see their faces. Before I could register what was happening, I was being shoved headlong into the back seat of an unmarked van.

In the distance, somewhere outside the vehicle, I could feel what I now knew was Cassius's malignant aura reaching in my direction.

CHAPTER 32

"**L**et me go!" I screamed as loudly as I could, kicking blindly in the direction of my abductors. I tried to remember self-defence movements from the class Virginia had demanded I attend when I'd first moved to Vancouver. But there was no use; their combined efforts easily outmuscled my own and made it clear that fighting was futile.

Soon, I could feel the rumble of the engine as we sped away down the road.

How could I have been so stupid as to leave Dom and the others? My magic was always fucking unreliable under duress! Who did I think I was? Claiming my independence in such an unfamiliar place when I was *clearly* being hunted?

I replayed the abduction in my mind. Someone already in the back of the van had quickly bound, blindfolded, and gagged me in quick succession as the two goons who'd grabbed me hopped in behind. For good measure, one of them gave me a solid shove into the back of the passenger seat, where I subsequently bounced my face off the side panel of the van. Then, as the driver took a hard left, I hit the floor with a final *thump!*

The floor smelled sourly of urine and beer, but the smell that was emanating from the cloth bag lying beside me was otherworldly. *Wraiths.*

"Stay queenright, Julia. You were gifted with more than magic in this world!"

The thought of Gertie's words brought me back into clear consciousness as I attempted to gather what information I could about my surroundings.

Reaching out from within, I could definitely feel a web of dark Wielding magic surrounding the body of the van; there was clearly no escaping the vehicle before we reached our intended destination. Based on their boisterous conversation, I was fairly certain that, in front of me, there was only the driver plus the two goons who had shoved me into the van, both of whom were now seated in the middle row. That left one Wraith remaining, seated behind me.

Cassius certainly wasn't the type to ride shotgun with his henchmen, and I easily pictured him following behind in a stately black car.

I was significantly outnumbered, and despite the clear indication that these were dark-magic users, I couldn't sense any tangible magic among them. I tried to remember what Dom and Ronan had explained to me about the Wraiths, but my head was swimming.

Wraiths *were* magic users, but not technically Wielders in the purest sense. They relied heavily on pre-concocted alchemical potions and powders and enchanted weapons to do their work, but bore no consistent spontaneous ability. They shared many similarities with Druids in how they collected power, although their more sinister methods were focused on consumption over propagation.

I had landed myself in a real pickle.

The dank-floored van screeched onward towards some unknown destination. I tried in vain to keep track of every time we turned, or how much time had passed—to estimate the distance travelled—but it was pointless. How was I to know they hadn't driven around the block, or circled back several times to confuse me? They didn't *sound* all that smart, but then again, I was the one bound and gagged on the floor of the van, not them.

At last, the van stopped, and the door slid open before anyone had moved from their seats; more Wraiths outside, no doubt.

I was dragged unceremoniously to my feet as filthy fingers entwined violently in my hair and hands grabbed me under my arms.

"Walk!" a rough and unfamiliar voice said, and I did so, not really having any other choice in the matter. Try as I might, I was unable to muster any magic, and my visible attempt was promptly met with an aggressive smack.

"Try that again and you'll pay in more than a blow to the head!"

I had still never used magic offensively, and once again felt woefully unprepared for any kind of forceful attack I might face.

I was a fool caught in a clever trap. Only, the trap didn't feel clever as much as I felt the fool. Terrified, I shuffled onward in silence, gagging at the smell of the sour body odour emanating from the man closest to me. I choked back the beer-laden vomit that rose to my parched mouth.

Someone roughly removed my blindfold, but I could see little as we descended into an almost pitch-black space. The air smelled heavily of dust and mould, and there was a distinct echo in the room as the others shuffled and moved into position around me.

I was then shoved onto a splintered wooden chair, still helplessly bound and gagged against my will. They kept the lights off, and I listened intently as the voices around me chatted on about duties and expectations, trying my best to gather some sort of indicator as to where we were and what would come next.

Suddenly, I felt a distinct shift in the Wraiths' mutterings. Then a door crashed open and the lights flew on as the echoing bodies around me scattered like exposed rats through a barn door, scratching and clawing, frantically attempting to get away from the apex predator.

"Out!" a now-familiar voice commanded.

He was here.

I squinted feebly, adjusting to the sudden brightness as I struggled against my bindings. We were indeed in some sort of auditorium, but it was no use trying to escape. My magic was effectively smothered; the knots around my wrists were tied with experience as if to emphasize the point.

"Julia . . . now! Where were we?" he laughed again at his own wit and clapped his hands together for what I was pretty sure was the tenth time in less than an hour.

Still heavily gagged, I couldn't answer.

Then, with a sudden force of cold air, all my bindings sprang free.

"*So* sorry about that! They can be such brutes," he said, striding slowly towards me.

He wasn't particularly tall or broad, but his presence bore a menacing quality in its own right. His clean-shaven face was indeed handsome, with its long Roman nose and expressive eyebrows; it was hardly the face of a

Sorcerer. I had somehow always pictured them as being hunched over, with long tattered beards and gnarled fingers fussing over great grimoires and charred cauldrons. Perhaps even a raven on their shoulder and a missing eye for good measure.

No, this man, if you could even call him that, reminded me more of a beguiling CEO, or a spin doctor from some American political program. Sure, his charm was present on the surface, but underneath, he oozed malice in which absolutely no warmth could be found.

"You Witches are so damn predictable! It took almost no effort to have you and your foolish Celt spring the trap!"

I stared at him, daring him to elaborate, which of course, he was dying to do.

"I *almost* killed Agnes Sweeney . . . and would have if I didn't think she would serve perfectly as bait for you." As he stepped ever closer, I noticed he looked considerably different than he had in the pub, or even as he had from farther away across the auditorium.

Then an all-too-familiar, mirthless, evil grin crept across his face. I recognized it at last as the face that had haunted my dreams and plagued my visions over not only the past several months, but lifetimes, infinitely destined to darken my door.

I realized shamefully that he must have used some kind of glamour on me when I'd first met him at the pub. How else could I have failed to detect his identity and the malevolent intent so clearly present now? Any magical awareness I normally had was gone due to my own anger and lack of control, and as a result, I'd fallen flat on my face and right into his spellcasting.

"Now!" he said. "I want to test something, Julia."

I hated how he said my name, like he *owned* it.

"I'm going to measure your magic!"

I would have described him as practically gleeful if not for the sinister look he bore, and I glared back at him, still wordless.

"Oh, don't worry! You won't have to do anything; it's on me!" he winked, as if an obvious extension of his earlier favour. "I'm told its *incredibly* painful, though."

I attempted to burst from my chair and run but couldn't move a muscle. He evidently didn't need the bindings to keep me still after all, his own method of paralysis available to him at a whim.

I was his to play with as he pleased.

"Sorcerer!" I spat at him instinctively.

I still had the use of my mouth it would seem. Good.

"Oh, come now! You shouldn't use someone else's name in vain! *Tsk. Tsk.* How prejudiced of you! You should know better. What would your mother think? Wash your mouth with soap!"

Eyes manic, he laughed darkly as he quickly spewed the words at me.

Out of a sheath at his hip, which I hadn't noticed before, he pulled out an ominous short-sword-type weapon. Only it wasn't *quite* that.

"It's a bit of a fun play on the old 'Spear of Destiny,' don't you think? You know, the Lance of Longinus! It is my namesake after all . . . I named myself, actually. Did you know that?" he asked sweetly, as if sharing a delicious secret with an old friend. "Anyways, now I've made my own version of the spear. You won't have seen it yet. It's not the original, *obviously*, but don't worry, I won't need to break your legs either. Not unless you make this difficult on me, like Agnes did." His face darkened.

So, Agnes had put up a good fight. I felt both pride and sadness for the elderly Witch at the closed ward, the events of earlier feeling a million miles away. As for the spear, I had no idea what he was talking about but continued to hold my face in impassive disgust.

The horrific implement had two polished, bladed prongs that ran perfectly parallel to one another, like two gleaming silver dinner knives. One was short, maybe six inches, and the other something closer to twelve. Their adjacency spread from a dark-black, unpolished hilt, which looked like some discarded thing on the floor of a blacksmith's shop in contrast to the blades. He evidently took great care in keeping them gleaming and ready for use at all times. My stomach took a harsh turn thinking of how many bodies had been pierced before mine, followed by his tender cleaning of the device.

"Its use is two pronged . . ." He paused then to laugh at his own joke, but it came out more like a stifled, wheezing sound. "But its *most important* use is as a magical divining rod. The other? Well, that's *my* secret."

He batted his lashes.

His pride was nauseating, but I continued to hold my silence. A man like this would hurl your words back at you as weapons in an instant. But in essence, I was doomed . . . and I knew it. I had no access to magic, not that I had any offensive skills anyways, and no escape plan. My mind wandered to Domhnall then, and I felt deep regret at how I had left him, even if my reasons were honest. I hoped against hope that he would find me, but the chances were marginal at best, and for that, only I was to blame.

Cassius walked slow circles around me, once . . . twice . . . three times . . .

"Round and round the garden."

Agnes's inner voice filled my mind then, and my heart began to pound in terror, panic violently setting in. This was exactly how he had begun the torturous process with her as well, and he had driven her to madness as a result.

I choked back more bile. "What do you want from me?"

He said nothing, his rhythm notably shifting as he became transfixed by his own ritual.

Once again, my mind was with Domhnall, and I was reminded of the harsh words from our argument earlier. That, too, felt like a lifetime ago.

Around me, the air began to swirl and constrict my body as I was slowly lifted from the chair and suspended in the air, my feet hovering several inches above the asbestos-tile floor. He tossed the battered chair to the side with a flick of his wrist and stepped closer yet, inspecting me before him like an animal carcass after the hunt. At this proximity and without his glamour, he smelled absolutely rancid, like rotting flesh or spoiled milk. I wouldn't have been surprised to find maggots crawling across his skin if I were to inspect the folds of his body.

The beer in my stomach sloshed; I writhed convulsively and vomited spectacularly onto the floor below me. He stepped out of the way deftly; clearly, he was used to it.

I blinked several times afterwards, still retching, but he was now out of sight. I could still feel him standing close, though, the dark magic of his spear humming loudly as he brought it nearer yet.

He pulled my hair back with unexpected gentleness, running his fingers along the top of my ear as he did so, and whispered, with his wretched tongue, into the very depths of my soul. "You're mine now, dear Julia."

My heart told me to beg for mercy, to give him whatever he needed in a vain attempt at surviving this ordeal. But my mind knew that this type of behaviour would only enrich the process for him, so I held my tongue defiantly.

All at once it hit me, like a force of a thousand blows from a red-hot smelting hammer. Shattering pain like exploding glass rippled throughout my entire being, shredding into the recesses of my mind and searching with extensive force for any traces of my magic. Still suspended, I had been violently skewered from behind, the spear's twin blades piercing exactingly through the gaps of my lower right ribcage.

A moment, or a lifetime, passed before my eyes.

Splintered apparitions danced through my head and into my vision. I saw images of my past lives doggedly swim before me, their meanings confused and tragic, as they had always felt to me in this lifetime. There were no future dreams to witness, long gone before I could even begin to grasp at them. And the present was black as night. Time held no meaning in this place, my existence was both infinite and pendulous between life and death.

And then, a stronger sense of peaceful knowing arrived, nudging me gently out of the darkness like fingers of mist across the spiritual plane. Was this what death felt like?

"You need to hold onto the deep secret of your magic for just a little while longer, Julia. Hold on."

"What secret?" I asked silently into the mists, but there was no reply.

I realized then that, somehow against all odds, I was still alive. Despite all the pain my physical body was enduring, my consciousness seemed untouched. And even more surprisingly, I still had my faculties. Instinctively, I fought hard then to remember the beauty in this world, rooting myself deeply in the power of the earth.

The place where *all* our magic was so purely born.

I thought of the bees and the taste of a supple honeycomb freshly drawn as the sweet liquid ran down my cheeks with each bite. I remembered the sound of polished stones as the waves crashed in at the beach near my childhood home in Victoria. The smell of bleached driftwood and salted seaweed surrounded me, and I could almost feel my wet socks from the surf as a glitter of sunshine scattered itself freely across a warm ocean. I thought of the way the sun held onto the air during the golden hour at Gertie's cottage in high summer, so akin to the golden essence that surrounded Dom each and every day.

Slowly walking me home, my mind had meandered to him once more. My Domhnall.

I reminded myself of how his smile reached all the way to the corners of his eyes when he laughed, and how he delighted in the simple things in life like playing with his dogs or sitting down to a freshly roasted chicken. I warmed at the memory of his flirtatious wagers and the playful, passionate delight with which he made love. I thought of his powerful frame, so capable of destruction, but how he chose only tenderness towards the ones he cared for.

I ached for his ever-grounding presence in a tumultuous world. A beacon of hope, a protector, my anchor.

And so, I *Sent* my love to him, wherever he was, hoping he would feel something of me in these last moments. I leaned into his memory as hard as I could, its gentle protection enough to hold me until the darkness finally overtook me.

Except it didn't.

Cassius abruptly removed the spear from my ribs, and I cascaded to the ground with a solid thump. My face smashed headlong into the linoleum floor below in the wake of my limp body. As I lay there slumped in a heap, the pain was still radiating through my insides, directly into the core of where my witch's fire burned, or where it should have been. But it remained snuffed, for better or for worse. And that's when I heard *him* speak again.

"As I . . . expected . . . you're . . . weak. Nothing. No threat . . . to me. After . . . all this time."

He sounded drunk, his words slurring almost into incoherence. Evidently, the ritual had taken a considerable amount of his own power to perform, and he was struggling to stay upright.

After coughing up bright-red blood from what was likely a broken nose onto the already drying vomit on the floor, I looked up at him, confused as to why I was still alive.

I could only assume he wasn't finished with me yet.

"I'll . . . leave you now," he said, striding slowly towards the exit, "but . . . I'll see you again . . . Julia. Very soon."

With that, he was gone, but no Wraiths returned.

My head began to spin as my consciousness threatened to pack up and leave without me once more. Then, out of the void, another vision came to me.

It was Cassius, on his way to perform the same ritual on another woman tied with bloody ropes in what looked like a dingy hotel room. I knew then that she wouldn't be allowed survival as I had been. He was going to use the spear for its other intended purpose. He would consume her magic whole and discard her, a mere commodity to be spent for his cause.

Darkness came then, at long last.

CHAPTER 33

Domhnall O'Brien had never been the sort to shy away from conflict, and being who he was, it's not like he had ever been given any choice. Indeed, when your father rose to greater heights than ever imagined by any of his supporters, or more importantly, his enemies, and you stood in that man's shadow . . . *that* came at a price.

When times were peaceful, he often mused what life would have been like had he not been born into such a prestigious, if not contentious, family. A life where he and Julia could have followed their plan to run away together, homesteading somewhere quiet with running water, trees, and perhaps a small flock of sheep or a few head of cattle. But it was a mere fantasy, as he knew all too well by now.

His father had idolized the life of Charlemagne and the strategy of the Roman Legions. The High King's aspirations had been matched only by his cunning skill and his diplomacy, balancing appeasement of the Christian church and the deep-seated history of warring Irishmen. The legends that grew in Domhnall's bones were born of a time and spirit far greater than anyone knew. He had been destined to the life of a warrior prince, managing the complex layers and permutations of any conflict, regardless of which realm or century he occupied. He'd always known this to be his destiny, and as such, the helplessness dealt to him of late was not a feeling he was *particularly* comfortable with.

Fire burned in his belly as he watched Julia storm off down the busy street, long legs creating considerable distance between them with ease. It's not like he had done a great job of quelling the obvious tempest brewing within her throughout the past months, or even days, but she just had such an uncanny knack of goading him into acting like a child when he was heated.

He stood stupidly on the street with their luggage scattered at his feet, feeling ashamed for his mulish reaction at the dementia ward and here on the street only moments before. The mounting discomfort of shame was piled on top of his already burning, helpless anger.

She had pressed him several times in the past weeks and months about her discomfort in delaying their visit to Agnes, but he'd dismissed her fears instead and emphasized the greater mission's importance. Agreeing to her request at last, he and Ronan naturally *had to* consider logistics and a vast array of contingency plans. Plus, they had to work around the football match for Lennie and Thomas; it was only considerate. And when they finally *did* go, he'd had the *gall* to criticize her for not knowing better than to enter into such a dangerous scenario?

"For fuck sakes," he breathed.

It was no wonder she was furious with him. He knew now, with the clarity of hindsight, that he had failed to support her in finding the calm in the chaos over the past weeks. He'd locked himself away from her with Ronan and the lads, obsessing habitually over their dark, looming future. Their interactions were reduced to pacifying her in the in-between moments with distractions of food, comforting words, and sex.

Well, the sex *had* been good; absolutely no regrets there.

But Julia didn't need to be pacified. He'd actually struggled each day when she left for her long walks across the grounds; he was familiar with the crushing isolation created by realities of their *shared* fate. He could have communicated with her then about how well he knew the vast loneliness she contended with.

He ran his fingers through his hair and let out his frustration with a low groan.

Having the privilege of loving her through countless lifetimes was a luxury he wasn't willing to take for granted. He never had, and he sure as hell wasn't about to start now.

Dom looked down the high street as he gathered up their luggage, hoping in vain that she had changed her mind and was on her way back to him. He would need to apologize.

Frankly, he had been aghast at the state of Agnes Sweeney. Even to his untrained eyes, she had clearly been irrevocably damaged by some form of dark magic. Afterwards, when he'd found out that it was indeed Cassius himself who had performed the sinister act, it had been the final straw, and something within him had broken. The notion of having Julia's magic turned against her in this way was unfathomable. And when Julia spoke of Agnes's words inside her head, he'd felt the cold hand of time dragging its fingers down his spine. It was an ill omen if there ever was one.

Ronan silently appeared at his side. "Should you—"

Dom cut him off with a sharp glare. Where had he come from? *The sneaky fuck.*

Without further comment, Ronan grabbed Julia's bag from Dom, and the two Celts headed towards their hotel rooms on the third floor.

"I've checked us in. Lennie and Thomas stopped here before the game, but they should be on their way back shortly to beat the crowds." He gestured to his cellphone. "Leeds is losing miserably to Chelsea, and Lennie is ecstatic. He said Thomas is already fully locked, and they are up for trouble tonight."

"Grand!" Dom said, perhaps a bit over enthusiastically, attempting to act normal as they headed towards their rooms. He still couldn't shake the feeling of foreboding that clouded his thoughts, or maybe it was just guilt. He carried a lot of that these days, and with good reason.

Even if Julia couldn't remember all of their cycles, her soul's memory was as discerning as ever. It was almost as if, with each rebirth, she was further weakened by the unconscious grief she carried from each failed attempt to defeat Cassius. He felt immensely culpable for this continued burden on her soul. It was the same grief that drove him harshly into the dark places of his own reality.

Ronan mumbled something about needing a shower as he headed towards his room, and Dom locked himself into his and Julia's without another word. The empty queen bed stared back at him. He set their bags down unceremoniously at its foot, atop the blood-red boot protector, and promptly began to pace.

It had been pleasant enough in their seminar to get a rise out of her. Her intelligent rebuttals and charming wit a true delight, he had always taken pleasure in teasing her *just enough* to bring out her feisty side. And all the better if she felt the need to remind him of her power in the bedroom. Those were the good times, and their natural state of affairs, truth be told. It was almost impossible to describe the effects it had on his physical body, let alone the spell she cast on his mind.

But this was different, and he took no pleasure in the result of their conflict.

More time passed. He checked the window for a tenth time in as many minutes and detected a new commotion in the hallway but heard only deep voices. Lennie and Thomas, no doubt. And still no Julia.

This was madness!

He should be out there searching for her. It wasn't safe for someone with her abilities to be wandering aimlessly in a strange city when she was so *clearly* marked for the hunt. Adrenaline rising and heart suddenly pounding, Dom launched into the hallway.

The recently returned men paused abruptly at the look on Dom's face and quickly turned towards Ronan—who had just popped his head out of his doorway while rubbing his hair with a small white towel—for guidance. Dom breathed out forcibly through his nose, a poor attempt to maintain composure. Frustration was fast mounting within him for their lack of gumption towards the current status of their group.

"Bit of a complication. Julia's gone for a walk," Ronan said, breaking the silence as the others stared back at Dom.

"Is she alright? Should we go after her?" Thomas asked, speech slightly slurred but with genuine concern spreading across his brow. Dom knew he was fond of Julia, and that he too would worry for her if he understood the danger she was potentially in.

Ronan gestured them all into his room.

"I'm not sure I understand what the big deal is," Lennie said as he closed the door behind them.

Dom cleared his throat and unclenched his fists, wiping his sweaty palms on his blue jeans and attempting once again to sustain some level of control. "It's probably nothing, but she left in a weakened state. And . . . well, I just have a bad feeling about her being out there alone right now. Something doesn't feel right."

Ronan updated Lennie and Thomas around the events surrounding their visit to Agnes Sweeney. Thankfully, for Dom's sake, he didn't mention the argument that had followed. The last thing he needed was judgement from Lennie, or an explanation to Thomas as to why he had let Julia down so badly.

The others stared at him in subdued silence, waiting for his word.

Quickly, he wracked his brain as to what she might be playing at. Instinctively, he expected that she would have taken a walk around the block, trying to find green space somewhere to sit and think. He shook his head; no that wasn't quite it. He thought of her then, chatting up some unassuming barkeep; no man stood a chance in hell against *that* charm. Dom had worked hard to keep his jealousy in check over the years, but she had always been a great beauty and easily attracted the attentions of others. There was no denying the raw magic and energy that surrounded her.

It had always been this way.

"I noticed several pubs along the main road; that's probably where she went. I'll maybe go join her," Dom said, and the others nodded some-what cautiously.

"Alright. Let us know if there's anything we can do to help," Ronan said, eyeing Dom speculatively. Could he sense the growing disturbance too?

He turned to exit without another word, pausing only momentarily at the doorway to check his phone for messages from Julia. Nothing. Of course, he hadn't sent her any messages either, being far too busy pacing to use any sort of common sense.

Walking along the empty hallway, he swore loudly.

If he could just find her somewhere, tucked away from all the others, he could apologize, and then finally tell her how terrified he had been since what had happened *the last time* they'd been together. Or not. He might just like to sit and enjoy her company for the vibrant and beautiful human being that she was. Good God, suddenly he yearned for her. He desperately wished to run his fingers through her gorgeous mane, and then slowly trace them down her back, making her arch wide with pleasure. It had always felt like a homecoming when they were able to find each other in that way.

Each reiteration of their story had borne new difficulties, distances, and dilemmas. Yet, he somehow fell in love with her deeper richness each and every time, despite the fact that she was steadily moving away from their shared narrative. In this life, he had found that he loved her more than ever; the new challenges she had thrown his way were enthralling, seeming to say, *"Grow with me or don't bother coming along for the ride."* She was *so* powerful.

His heart sank at his own foolishness. But at that moment, something much more primal clicked within him: a gnawing sense of dread situated somewhere just behind his navel.

"Fuck!" he boomed, turning around abruptly. "Ronan!"

Ronan and the others streamed from the room, disorganised but all present and accounted for. Ronan was still only half dressed and looking rather annoyed at Dom's mood swings

Dom was beside himself now. "She's gone. She's left." While he had expected her to do things differently this time around, he hadn't expected her to up and leave the area entirely. His face began to fall.

"Yes, we saw that . . ."

"Weren't you . . ."

Shared looks of confusion spread across Thomas and Lennie's faces, but not Ronan's.

"You mean you can't feel her anymore."

"Yes, that's what I *fucking* mean, Ronan!" Dom snapped.

The rage had returned. But that was not a problem; he always thought more clearly when he was angry, in an *actual* crisis at least.

Few of their allies comprehended this aspect of his relationship with Julia, except perhaps Ronan. They were close enough friends that, much to his irritation, Ronan had been able to sense Dom's physical discomfort any time Julia wasn't within a three-kilometer radius of him. They were bonded by something greater than romantic love, which Dom had always assumed was some aspect of his own curse. But when he had intimated to Julia about this feeling of tension at her absence, she said it had reminded her of the maximum range bees would travel from the hive. They only went *so far* away from the queen pheromone to forage, ever conscious of the greater needs of the colony. It wasn't out of a need for control but rather simple survival.

Countless times, he had warned her about travelling too far from the group. Now that the Prophecy had well and truly been invoked, there was no question that Cassius and his wraiths would be looking for her at every turn. And with modern technology, especially now that they were in the UK, CCTV channels would be used against her with utmost certainty; Lennie had basically promised them as much. This was the whole reason they'd planned to leave England as quickly as possible and return to the safety of the manor house.

"Well, if you're *that* worried, why don't you just track her phone? Your phones *are* linked after all," Lennie said, a little too obviously for Dom's deteriorating patience.

"Well! *Do it* then!" Dom said, shoving his phone at the slender man, teeth gritted. The following moments were agonising.

"Okay, there! She's headed northwest, and judging by the route, she's on a city bus. Give me a moment," Lennie said, hammering away on the phone and sweating slightly under Dom's scrutinizing gaze. The young, self-identified techno-Pagan—apparently a reference from some television show Julia had also liked from the early 2000s—had swiftly pulled up the routes for all the busses in the area. "Yes, okay. Great."

Dom rolled his eyes skyward. "Get *on* with it, man!"

Ronan rolled his eyes and moved to put his shoes on. The bastard was always so flippant when Dom was in a mood, which actually reminded him of Julia.

His heart sank further yet. Where the hell was she?

"It looks like she's just going for a bus ride, so far," Lennie said. "But we might as well wait until she gets off before moving to follow because the route is a loop, and she may just ride the bus all the way back towards us. We don't want to be back ended . . . double-backed?" He raised his eyes towards Dom from the screen, visibly annoyed now with Dom's forceful attention.

Dom often had that effect on his friends when he was angry. "I'm going outside," he growled, and stomped down the hallway, the others following silently in his wake.

Walking together towards the bustling Headrow, several busses passed the disgruntled group in either direction, but Lennie assured Dom that she was still on a different one. "It should be back within the hour if we wait, or she doesn't get off first."

"Do you think she would?" Ronan asked Dom.

"She might," he said, wringing his long fingers together before jamming them into his pockets to keep them still. It didn't help, and so he crossed his arms instead, pinning his hands flat under his biceps.

Carefully, Ronan said, "The unfortunate thing is that England is so incredibly dangerous for her, Domhnall. Didn't you warn her about the risks of being followed?"

A low growl escaped from Dom's throat. "Of course I did. Do you think *she* gives a shit about that?" He was angry at her now too for putting them all in this situation, but still more so with himself for failing to keep her safe once again.

They stood in silence now, the others clearly hesitant to agitate him further.

Lennie broke the silence at last. "There, the bus has turned back. Looks like she's still on it. Hopefully this has all been a false alarm."

Dom failed to bring words to his mouth and stuck with nodding in response. Ronan and Thomas went inside to their rooms briefly while Lennie stayed behind, leaning casually on a light post. The following moments passed with agonizing stillness. This was wholeheartedly *not* a state Dom was comfortable existing in.

"Where is she now?" he asked finally, about ready to burst into flames in either impatience or fear. The others had only just returned and startled at his forceful question.

"Minutes," Lennie said as he looked down at the phone once more.

At last, the bus had arrived at their sidewalk vigil. Dom strode forward before the bus had even lowered to the curb and gestured commandingly for the driver to open the doors.

"Julia?" he yelled, as he cleared the several steps onto the bus with ease.

"Oy! You've got to pay to ride!" the bus driver shouted indignantly.

"I'm not here to ride your bus, *sir*. I'm looking for a woman. Tall. Dark reddish-brown hair, black jeans, and a brown bag. A fuzzy pullover sweater. Have you seen her?"

Dom searched fruitlessly for Julia aboard the stifling transit bus. It stank like body odour and something reminiscent of a street hot dog doused in warm mustard. Perhaps he'd missed her as he jumped on? The haste at which he'd boarded had been unexpected even to himself.

Ronan, instincts holding true, gave him a shrug from the side door. She hadn't excited the bus while Dom boarded, and by his observations, she wasn't on the bus either.

Dom scrambled to make sense of the situation. Then it hit him. "Her cellphone, it's on the bus," he said flatly to the bus driver as he strode down the aisle without paying. The driver hollered back with aggravation that he had a schedule to keep. Dom ducked down to the floor, much to the dismay of a dotty woman in the midst of knitting what looked like a gaudy orange tea cozy. There it was, stuck to some unknown substance on the floor. He noticed the battery was at seven percent and very much abandoned.

"Shit! Ronan!"

While it was very much like Julia to storm out of a confrontation without considering how unsafe it was, it was altogether unlike her to leave her phone in a strange place; she *had* grown up in this world after all.

Leaping from the bus, he shoved the device forcibly at Lennie to check for clues.

"There's nothing since her last text to you earlier in the day, which it looks like you've already read," he said, handing the phone back to Dom after a quick check.

Julia had sent him a playful text from the back seat on the way to the closed ward, making fun of the rooster tail at the back of Ronan's hair. It felt like a lifetime ago.

"Domhnall, we need to split up," Ronan said.

He knew that already.

"Thomas! Head up the main street and start checking in any pub you find."

Thomas nodded without question and took off.

Lennie turned towards the hotel. "I'll start trying to hack into the security cameras for the area, perhaps I can find her on there."

"Perfect. Ronan . . ."

Ronan was already on his way to his car, no doubt to dig into his black bag of tricks. Dom hoped he might be able to sense some magical disturbances in the area, or set a tracking spell, or whatever he did with all his pouches and potions. Regardless, Ronan didn't need his instruction right now; he knew full well the severity of the situation.

"I'll have my phone on me," Dom said as he took off in a run up the main street in the direction the bus had come from.

He was hoping he could trust his instincts to find her, but the modern world was so full of people and endless distractions. If he could track her somehow, or feel a trace of something or somewhere her magic might have passed, perhaps he could find a direction at least.

More than anything, he also just desperately needed to *move*. Foolishly, he had left his weapons behind at the hotel, so fisticuffs it was. He smiled in spite of himself at a recent memory in which Julia had been trying to convince him to actually name his fists.

"What about pleasure and pain," she had said mockingly with a smirk, ducking away from him playfully as she danced around like a boxer. "Or is that too obvious?"

He ached to be near her once more, to hold her and aggressively cast away the dark thought clouding his mind, reminding him that there might not be a last embrace this time around.

Now was the time to *think*.

The *best* worst-case scenario was that she was lost. Hopefully, the worst was that she had gotten tangled up with Wraiths, and he would be able to deliver them some serious punishment before bringing her home safely. He desperately wished she had figured out how to perform a Send, or that he had done a better job in *helping* her learn to do so. But it was too late to worry about that now.

He jogged down the street for several more minutes, ignoring the confused looks of the various pedestrians as he eventually crossed onto less densely occupied streets towards what looked to be a university campus. Clearing his mind in the process, he tried to detect even some infinitesimal trace of her magic.

Something deep inside screamed then that it was time to *run*.

He took off at a flat sprint. After about fifteen minutes, his body had settled into a canter while his fear urged him forward. He at last rounded the corner into a visibly seedy neighbourhood. There he discovered several blocks of perfectly aligned red-brick houses; they were thoroughly graffitied and neatly culminated in a wide dead-end street. At the end, he saw a large, abandoned building.

Two significant things happened then in quick succession.

First, he felt a soft breeze ripple across his brow, carrying with it a scent that reminded him of Julia's shampoo at the cottage, followed by what felt like the soft caress of lips across his sweaty cheek. Then the air suddenly felt forcibly restrictive, slowing his pace significantly due to the lack of oxygen making its way into his lungs.

He pulled his cellphone out of his jeans with some difficulty, and then leaned down to catch his breath while he dialed Ronan.

"I think I found a waypoint," he panted.

"I see you," Ronan replied from down the street behind him, where he'd only just thrown his car into park.

"How did you find this place?" he asked when he finally caught up to Dom, black bag in hand once more.

Dom shook his head. "No clue. Just felt right."

Ronan looked somewhat dubious. "Bit of a risk just running off like that. What if you'd gone in entirely the wrong direction?"

"Well, I still might have . . . but I never am wrong, am I? Not when it comes to finding Julia."

The two men paused, looking down the road. It was a conscious moment to gather their might for what could be a fight for their lives. They were both soldiers in their own right, fully capable of handling this dire reality, and Dom was reminded heartily of yet another reason why they had grown so close over the past decade.

"Wait. What brought you here?" Dom asked, suddenly puzzled as to how Ronan had ended up in the same locale.

He shrugged and pulled out his compass. "Wraith magic is sloppy. It's hard to miss when you know what you're looking for."

So, it *was* the Wraith magic he'd sensed clogging up the air, even if he couldn't sense it as clearly as Ronan. He did, however, have countless decades of experience tracking the bastards and suddenly felt very, very alive.

"Well, I think two for two confirms it. This has got to be the place."

Ronan sent a location pin to the others and shoved his phone into his back pocket.

Far down at the end of the road, a large and rather contrary beige building stood punctuating the end of the well-organized street. It looked like an abandoned community centre of some sort, adorned with safety tape and bright-orange barricades at each entrance.

Without a word, the two Celts forced their way down the street though the thickening air, finally arriving at a sign in front of the old building.

POSITIVELY NO ADMITTANCE
HSE Asbestos Restoration Project
Call office for access.

"Oh wonderful," said Ronan flatly.

Dom was already on his way towards the front entrance. This was *exactly* the kind of place you would take someone if you didn't want to be interrupted. It was also the kind of place where you could be exposed to harmful particulate, but what did any of that matter if Julia was dead?

The front doors were locked and taped, but peering in, the building looked untouched and demolition work had yet to begin. It *was* a Sunday after all.

"Praise be for small miracles," Ronan said under his breath. Dom took off to circle the left side of the building, hopeful that he would find a loose or broken window, but he would force his way in if necessary.

Ronan followed, clearly feeling (and smelling) the distinct filth of Wraiths all around them.

Dom stopped momentarily ahead of his friend, suddenly feeling as if he had been stabbed in the heart. "I can feel her, Ronan. She's here somewhere. But something feels . . . wrong."

He was in a cold fury now, warrior mentality fully engaged. He would obliterate anyone who got in his way with the same ferocity as the Viking berserkers he had fought centuries ago. As he rounded each corner though, there were no actual Wraiths to be found, or fought, only the constricted air that burned the inside of his nostrils.

Dodging two large metal waste-disposal bins, Dom finally reached the back of the community centre, discovering what looked like a poorly maintained gymnasium. Its metal double doors were flung wide open, taunting him, inviting him to come inside in spite of the obvious danger.

Ronan was several steps behind, panting for breath, the thin air making it increasingly difficult to maintain any kind of stamina for long. "Dom, slow down. It could be a trap."

But Dom was of no mind to slow down and think. His lungs scorched with the effort, but what use was breathing if she could no longer do so? He burst into the brightly lit auditorium, shoulders heaving and white teeth bared. The air wasn't nearly as thick inside, and he scanned the room while fighting back the dizziness of anaerobic over-exertion.

The room was empty, save for the slumped form of a woman laying half-prone on the floor.

"Oh God!" Dom cried and took off at full sprint to the centre of the room, collapsing on the ground before her.

Julia lay there, unconscious and covered in blood and vomit.

He barely registered the scent of the iron and acid that surrounded her as he pulled her into his arms, calling to her desperately, "Julia! Love! Can you hear me? Wake up!"

He was shaking so hard himself that he struggled to register if she had breath. She felt warm to the touch though, which was a good sign. Pushing his fingers deep into her carotid artery, he said a prayer as he offered his life to the Gods in exchange for a pulse. It felt momentarily as if the rotation of the world had ceased in its entirety, but at last he found it.

Her pulse was slow, and desperately weak, but she was alive.

"Is she breathing?" Ronan had finally caught up behind Dom's explosive charge to his lover's side.

"She is. But she's badly hurt. I don't . . ." He looked up at Ronan, paralysed with fear. "Can you help her? Please?"

Ronan looked genuinely afraid at what he saw before him, which shook Dom further.

"Lay her back, and I'll have a look."

The two men assessed the situation, Ronan using both medical and Druidic skill to evaluate Julia as Dom held onto her broken body, and her soul, for dear life. He gently wiped away what blood he could to clear her airways and took great care to unstick the individual strands of hair that were plastered to her face, the rest spilling haplessly around her, sticky and wet.

"The bastard broke her nose," Dom said absently as the other man ran his hands over her, searching for any residual binding magic. The break didn't diminish her beauty in any way, and he stared at her in total astonishment for having survived (thus far) what he knew must have been an unfathomably horrific ordeal.

Cassius had once again got to her; but the question remained unanswered, why was she alive? He took small comfort in being able to feel her chest rise and fall now as the Druid leaned close to her face.

Ronan pulled back, obvious concern mounting. "Look at her eyes." They were moving behind their lids, slowly back and forth, almost rhythmically.

"Is she . . . dreaming?" Dom asked.

"Perhaps," Ronan said simply, his unspoken words saying much more.

Had she succumbed to the same fate as Agnes Sweeney? Lost to Dom forever, but still present in this realm in her madness, fully spent and discarded by Cassius like so many others before. More time passed as Ronan continued to inspect the woman in Dom's arms.

Dom noticed that her eyes now danced erratically behind the pale eyelids. It wasn't a peaceful sight. Visions had always been able to torment her even in her weakest state, and this seemed to be no exception. He held her hand then and kissed her gently on the forehead.

He couldn't recall at exactly which point the others had arrived, with Ronan's next words to him registering only as a blur of shapes and sounds.

"Seems to be more of a magical wounding than a physical one. Although she does have two significant entry wounds along her back-right ribcage. Like something was stabbed into her, but whatever it was seems to have cauterized the wounds upon exiting. I'll need to have a closer look for internal bleeding, but not here."

Lennie and Thomas were already working to dismantle the dark web of spells surrounding the building to ease their exit. At Ronan's behest, Thomas ran to retrieve his car and brought it to the back doors so they could move Julia with as little impact as possible.

Someone else would likely stay behind to finish wiping clean any trace of their presence, but Dom didn't care. Cradling Julia close in his arms, he prayed silently to any God that would listen.

Don't take her from me. Please. Not now. I'll give anything.

He turned his thoughts towards her then, willing her to show him some sign that she was still fighting—some sign of life. She seemed so small and hopelessly broken. What had she endured, and why had Cassius left her behind alive?

"Julia. Please. Can you hear me, love? It's your Domhnall. I've found you, like I always do." He cleared his throat, eyes now thick with tears. "I think you managed to get a Send to me. You did it!"

He smiled, pride welling up within him.

Ronan's voice was back in his ear once more. He had no idea how much time had passed. "Dom, you have to let go of her now. We need to move her."

A makeshift gurney was lying beside them, with Ronan directing the others how to safely move Julia to the back seat of his car. Only when they were back at the hotel could he perform the necessary spells and ministrations to hopefully pull her through. He knew what an utter nightmare it would be if she should need to go to an *actual* hospital; the magical and non-magical worlds clashed terribly. But they would do what was necessary.

"I'll be carrying her to the car myself, Ronan."

Dom's voice came out as a low snarl. There was no chance in hell anyone would be handling her but him.

Ronan puffed his cheeks and let out a slow breath.

"Fine. Suit yourself. But don't—"

Dom's responding glare silenced the Druid doctor without a word needed.

Carefully now, Dom raised himself from the ground while tenderly holding Julia against his chest. He had regained his breath and found her weight to be inconsequential as he shifted her body gingerly and strode silently with her towards the car.

She *had to* pull through.

Dom found himself demanding that she survive now. He would give his own life to secure her safe passage if that's what it took. But that had always been his promise to her.

It was bucketing down outside, and unfortunately, they couldn't get the car any closer than about ten metres away. Heavy drops fell onto her blood-spattered face as they walked, and only steps away from the car, he noticed she was wincing from the cool rain.

He stopped in his tracks.

Ronan, who had been following closely in their wake, took her wrist into his hand and immediately checked her pulse.

"Julia, I'm here," Dom said. "You're going to be alright. We've got you now."

A small noise came from her lips then, one that only he could hear, soft as a whisper . . . and then she tried to speak.

"Shh. It's alright now," he said, believing with all his might that this would be true.

Her eyes fluttered open, and he positioned himself so that he was the first thing she saw.

"Domhnall . . ." she said, pearlescent tears forming in the corner of her eyes, beautiful jewels against her abused face. "I'm so sorry."

He placed his forehead on hers, cradling her as he let out a deep sigh of thanks to any of the Gods who were still listening. She was battered, and parts of her were broken, but she was still whole.

And he was going to kill the bastard Cassius if it was the last thing he did.

"You have nothing to be sorry for. Rest now. Ronan's going to fix you up."

She closed her eyes again, and it was only then that Dom allowed for help as they placed her on the back seat, still supported by his strong arms, for the trip towards safety.

CHAPTER 34

Less than a week after the ordeal, we returned to Ireland. I was shocked by the overwhelming sense of homecoming I felt; it would seem that even the short time I had spent here between January and early April had been enough to tie me to this place in more than just my physical, lived experience.

The journey between our hotel-turned-hospital and the manor house had been nothing short of arduous, even though we were able to travel without interruption. We talked little as Ronan maneuvered his slick sedan down the winding roads towards our country home. It was still excruciating to sit or stand for more than a moment at a time, and even laying down, I winced painfully with every sharp turn or abrupt stop. Dom held my head in his lap and stroked back my hair with each shudder of pain, speaking regular soothing words of comfort. Ronan had initially suggested that he induce a magical slumber for our travel, but I shrank at the thought.

"Ronan. I don't think Julia wants to be . . . alone with her thoughts. Not right now," Dom said, relieving me of the explanation.

The last thing I wanted was to be jailed in my mind through sedation, whether magically or medically induced. Intuitively, I knew the worst was yet to come once I was able to rest for longer stretches without pain waking me with each subtle shift in my sleep. *He* had marked me, intentionally or not, and I feared I would be forced to bear witness to his crimes, new and old, anytime I slept. It had not happened yet, but I knew his misdeeds would appear in my dreams. Worst of all, I knew in my heart that he wasn't done with me yet.

"Right. Of course. What about some strong narcotics then?"

I couldn't tell if he was serious or not, but I smiled weakly. "Nothing *too* strong, Ronan."

He was still quite visibly shaken himself from the experience. I felt sorry for him having to do all the driving on the way home on top of everything else. With the internal bleeding being worse than he had initially suspected, it had taken all the medical knowledge, military resilience, and Druidic power he could muster to not only heal me but also keep me out of the hospital.

Seated together in the car now, it was unnerving to see a general of our cause so deeply spent. I wasn't willing to ask anything more from him magically, not for this at least. Not to mention that I was far from ready to sleep anyway and would ultimately only do so when my body was pushed to the point of collapse.

And it had been pushed during our stay at the hotel, several times in fact. I had awoken screaming at the top of my lungs on a few occasions, with Dom frantically trying to calm my fractured mind. This had been the main impetus of our relocation. They moved me perhaps before I was physically ready, but our companions were finding it increasingly difficult to keep me quiet when I did finally sleep.

We also *all* longed to retreat to a place of safety and collaboration.

The relief in the vehicle was palpable as we made the final turn up towards the manor house. I tried to sit up and glance out the window, but the pain was altogether too much. From my viewpoint below, I noticed tears gather in the corners of Dom's eyes as he saw the great lawns and the sprawling lake before the manor house.

He wiped his eyes quickly with his sleeve. "Thank God."

I could also see that Ronan's features were hardened—surely a mask worn frequently to hide the depths of exhaustion that were common in his line of work. He finally placed the Audi in park, rubbing between his eyebrows and squinting, something he had undoubtedly done countless times before.

Lennie and Thomas had gone ahead of us to clear the way, but I could see Lennie's motorcycle still parked near the front door. Evidently, he would be leaving again soon. Peggy and Malcolm must have picked up Thomas at the ferry, and I realized then that I wasn't entirely sure he held a licence.

Peggy came running out to the car, equal parts ecstatic and concerned, fussing immediately with us at the doors. Malcom followed behind her quietly, his cheeks wet with relieved tears. I too would have wept if not for the fact that I was completely empty of any emotion at all. I felt as if I had been stripped to my core and then left in the dirt to shrivel and die in the sun like some ancient victim along the Roman road.

No, there was no source available for tears, but I knew it would all come eventually. I chuckled humourlessly at the thought, trying to think of something clever about a Diviner using divining rods to find a well of tears, but I was too exhausted to entertain any dry, impulsive wit.

Dom looked at me with concern, and I realized I must have been making a strange face.

"Ah . . ." he said, his usually straight brows furrowed into a V.

I gathered my composure, which was currently straddling nausea and hysteria. "I'm okay . . . just glad to be home."

Morgan was still attempting to locate a wheelchair, so in the meantime, Dom lifted me gently out of the vehicle, holding me in his arms as we made our way slowly indoors. Somehow, it hurt less when he carried me than when I was stretched out flat on my back on a stretcher. Apparently, he had known this when he found me. According to Ronan, Dom had turned into a snapping and growling beast if anyone else approached too near or attempted to transport me.

"Liar," Dom had replied to Ronan's retelling, but I had no doubt there was truth to the tale.

Dom had been *fiercely* protective since finding me, flat out refusing to leave my side unless absolutely necessary. I hoped that he would find himself more settled with our homecoming, perhaps even allowing for his own rest and healing; it had been a traumatic event for all of us.

As we passed through the halls of the manor house, the dogs were surprisingly well behaved as they trotted dutifully in tow. I noticed that Peggy had taken it upon herself to suffuse the inner recesses of the home with the healing incense and herbal incantations of her craft. The effect had filled the place beautifully with warm and peaceful energy. I also smelled what

I thought must be roast chicken and perhaps some sort of vegetable soup wafting from the kitchen.

I could only assume that Morgan had taken care of provisions, knowing full well that Dom would eat his weight in meat and potatoes alone just to cope with the stress of the past few days.

And indeed, the days ahead were gruelling in their own right. The effects of Cassius's self-proclaimed "Spear of Destiny" had left lasting effects on both my physical and spiritual body, neither of which were quick to fade even with care and rest. As for my physical body, Dom had been lovingly tender and attentive during the early healing process. He had tried to send the dogs away, but I insisted their presence would be a comfort. Indeed, the great wolfhound had taken up his usual role as protector when Dom wasn't around, vetting anyone who came too near to my recovery bed.

Dom was equally as watchful and the first to suggest that I needed rest when I started to look even moderately tired. He had also taken special consideration for the weakness in my ribs and the discomfort that arose if I sat in any one position for too long, adjusting my pillows any time he entered or exited the room.

In the first few days at home, I had found it difficult to re-arrange myself. I was not struggling as much now, and the fretting felt both excessive and compensatory.

"Dom. Really. I'm alright. Enough fussing," I said one rainy afternoon.

Deaf to my protests, I watched as he deftly readjusted the inner sheet with the outer duvet cover, long arms outstretched as he took great care to line up the corners, all the while humming to himself pleasantly. Despite the tender loving care I had been given daily throughout my recovery, I had my suspicions about how well he was *actually* coping. I could see the intricate lines of exhaustion that had stitched their way across his brow, but so far as I could tell, he had refused to give in to the depths of his fatigue.

"Honestly. Why don't you go out to the pub or something with Ronan, let off some steam? It's been so . . . heavy around here."

He smiled ruefully. "I have plenty of things to do at the house; don't worry about me."

And he left it at that, turning on his heel and leaving the room without another word.

Time seemed to be moving forward at an uncanny rate during my waking hours, largely because my healing had progressed exceptionally well. To the shock of most, exactly one week after the ordeal, I managed to pull myself from the bed without any assistance. Soon, I shakily stood in front of the wardrobe mirror to assess the damage for myself. I had several lengthy bandages wrapped around my ribs and wore one of Dom's large t-shirts over top to keep any extra pressure off the wounds. A bra was completely out of the question at this point, and I felt rather like a poorly wrapped present.

My nose had been painfully re-set back at the hotel by Ronan, done (at my behest) without the use of any magic. Local anesthetic and pain medication would be more than enough, but even if it wasn't, I needed a long break from anyone directing anything remotely magical in my general direction.

Dom had looked like he might implode when Ronan put the speculum into my nostrils and yanked things straight once more, but he'd kept his mouth shut. Once complete, Ronan had assured me the break hadn't been too extensive but that I might be glad that my nose was straight when all of the swelling went down and bruises faded in several weeks.

Surely Dom had witnessed more than his share of facial carnage on the rugby pitch, let alone on the battlefield. When it came to me, however, he had been exceptionally sensitive.

Facing the mirror now, I eyed my overlong hair, which had been kindly pulled back into two easy French braids by Peggy after she'd helped me with a shower earlier in the day. She had been instrumental in supporting me, helping to manage some of the more onerous aspects of my day-to-day life. It wasn't easy to navigate your monthly cycle, for example, when you could barely roll over, let alone take a trip to the washroom without support.

She had offered to blend me some herbs that would stop my bleed for the time being. But I insisted that this too was a necessary process in my healing, in part to know that my womb still carried out its expected functions. As far as I could tell, *he* hadn't altered that potential part of my destiny. It had been a real concern when taking the Prophecy into consideration, whether anyone said it aloud or not.

Perhaps the loudest of the unspoken questions centred on why I had been allowed to live at all, and Ronan at last broached the subject during a physical check on my healing.

"So, he's created himself a new tool, but you've never mentioned it before. You've never seen it in any of your previous visions?" Ronan asked as he gently replaced my bandages for what would apparently be the last time.

I grimaced. "Before, I only saw the bodies after, not when he was . . . in action. But now . . ." As I had expected, the nightmares had been horrific over the past week. I was fairly certain Cassius had gone on a serial-murder streak through the north of England. I also had the distinct sense that he wanted us to know *all* about it.

"Lennie says there have been four or five suspicious deaths reported that he's almost certain are linked," Ronan said. I knew there were far more than that. It was good that my face was obscured as he helped me pull the shirt over my head before I turned around.

While obviously a medical doctor, he had been exceptionally considerate as a friend towards my physical privacy the more my body healed. Personally, I didn't care if Ronan saw me without clothes on in this setting. He had done so during his ministrations at the hotel, but now, he seemed wholly respectful both of me and of his friend's precarious mental state as he looked on.

"It still doesn't explain why he kept you alive this time. That's different, right?" Ronan asked, dropping the bomb at last.

"Honestly, I don't know. And I can't remember very clearly, but he seemed almost . . . weakened by the experience."

Ronan cocked his head. I had his full attention now. "What do you mean?"

"I'm not sure, but then there have been all the murders this week." I shook my head, uncertain how he was managing it all if he'd actually been weakened. "He's certainly been enjoying himself." I thought of the evil laughter I'd heard throughout my visions of him.

Ronan scowled. "He would—"

"Wait! Ronan, do you think his spear, or whatever, is some kind of extraction tool? Using *it* to steal people's power for himself? Not that he found anything to steal inside of me, of course."

I was surprised at my own realisation in the moment, and Ronan's jaw slackened. Dom's shoulders shifted, but he remained silent with pursed lips.

"Julia, you might be onto something . . ." Ronan said, his voice trailing off, and soon he strode from the room, I assumed to consult his research materials.

Dom had sat darkly in the corner during the entire conversation, brooding miserably over the latest reports, and evidently not nearly as excited as Ronan had been about the latest theory.

A week and a half into my recovery, I was joined unexpectedly by Thomas, who—after a short knock—strode into the bedroom carrying a large pot of tea and all of the necessary implements. The day was overcast, and I was feeling sullen, laid out in bed and looking rather dishevelled. I wasn't expecting anyone but Dom or Peggy without notice, but at least I had on a thick t-shirt and sweatpants.

"Took over the delivery from Dom. He said he was going for a run or something." Thomas shrugged as he set down the tea tray with surprising delicacy.

"I'm not surprised. He was *off* this morning."

Dom had been just as tender with me as always when he awoke, but he also hadn't uttered a single word. It had been a rougher night than usual for me, and I had chalked his behaviour up to exhaustion; his stoicism had been growing in the last few days. Thomas was shaking his head, clearly still ruminating, and I grimaced at the look on his face.

"What happened this time?" I asked. He offered me a knowing glance as he poured me a steaming cup of Earl Grey tea in a large pottery mug.

"Lennie said something to him about using his phone differently, or . . . honestly, I don't even know, Julia. You know how Lennie is," he rolled his eyes, "but your brawny Celt just blows up out of nowhere most days. It's—"

"A lot. I hear you. Peggy mentioned it too," I said.

He became increasingly agitated with the others as the days wore on, all the while maintaining the same mustered sweetness with me, even if he was also keeping me at arm's length. It was very unusual behaviour for someone who usually filled any room with energy. Several times already I had attempted to speak to him about what had happened, but he always replied by saying how much time we'd have to discuss it once I was recovered. Or that I should rest.

Worst of all was when he would come up with some random excuse at the drop of a hat and disappear. *That* particular behaviour was fast becoming a source of great frustration, and I felt the need to make a change.

While it was true that I was exhausted—my dreams had been nothing but tumultuous since the ordeal—I wasn't too tired to connect with him again. I found myself missing him desperately in his own house, our house, but he had put his walls up again.

"Hmm," I said, chewing on my bottom lip in thought. "I wonder if maybe everyone shouldn't leave for a few days."

Thomas looked at my torso with mild concern. "Are you feeling well enough though? We're all still so worried about you."

"I really am doing a lot better. Ronan said yesterday that the only useful medicament left to me is time," I said, mimicking Ronan's slight accent. "Just need some 'R & R,' you know? And my visions . . . well, no one can help me with that anyways."

I stared out the window from the high bed in an effort not to make Thomas uncomfortable, but I could see him squirm slightly at the mention of the visions. I knew this was what he'd really meant about me feeling *well enough*.

During the first few nights at the manor, I had apparently screamed so violently in my sleep that I woke up much of the house to full alert. No one had gotten much sleep in those first few days, Dom least of all. There had been a rearrangement of rooms at Dom's request, so we were left completely alone upstairs to battle the night terrors in isolation. I felt deep guilt at this, his lonely nighttime station, alone at my side while my mind waged its own war against our enemies.

"I think Dom and I need some space to reconnect, and I don't think he will be comfortable to do so unless we're alone."

Leaning forward slightly to peer out the window, I could see Dom's distant form running at a full sprint down the driveway towards Morgan's place, Sully and Mags ripping along in his wake, tongues lolling and tails wagging in delight. Naturally, Oisín was still with me, fast asleep by the fire. He was fond of Thomas and comfortable with him being in the room, but I did feel guilty the great beast wasn't out on the run with his pack.

Turning towards Thomas, I chuckled slightly. "I think you could all use a break."

He took his turn to laugh, and then lifted his own teacup to his lips, which looked miniscule in his meaty hands. "Consider it done."

A peaceful smile spread across his face, and we chatted on into the afternoon about considerably more pleasant things.

CHAPTER 35

The others vacated the premises within twenty-four hours of my request without a single question. All of them were evidently grateful for a change of scenery and a break from Dom's brooding and the ever-looming *cause*.

Peggy, Malcolm, and Thomas were planning to take a road trip down to Dingle. The weather was fine, and as was their custom, they had friends they wanted to visit while taking in some of the Atlantic seaside along the way. Meanwhile, Lennie and Ronan were heading north on some unnamed mission, but judging by the weapons and other Druidic implements I watched them load into Ronan's trunk from the window, it had the distinct potential for danger. Still, they looked rather pleased with themselves at the prospect of some adventure, and no doubt Dom was silently disappointed not to be joining them.

For his part, Dom had been outwardly angry towards me at first, which was a direct contrast to his more recent doting sweetness, and I took this to be a good sign.

"Does it look like we have time for a vacation?" he had snapped in my direction when I told him how things were going to be for the next week.

"Does it look like *I'm* going anywhere?" I said, gesturing at my bandages dramatically. I assumed he was embarrassed that I had sent them all away because of his behaviour, but it was fast approaching time for us to have a real discussion about what had happened in England.

"Oh, come on, Dom. You and I both know we need a break from all the company. I am not really *that* much of a people person anyways."

I took his hand into mine and kissed it gently, and he mumbled something from the depth of his chest that I couldn't decipher. I could, however, make an educated guess that it was perhaps not something meant for sensitive ears.

Our friends would be returning in a little over a week, just in time for the Beltane fires on May 1. Following this, we would settle on our next move, hopefully with clear heads and peaceful hearts. And while the reality of both the Prophecy and my own worries about the quilt loomed over us, I felt confident that we needed these seven glorious days to relax, and heal, together. However, in my heart of hearts, I knew it would be an uphill battle for the both of us, at least for the first few days.

I had taken to walking downstairs all the way to the kitchen once each day, but that was about all my internal wounds would handle. Whatever instrument *he* had used had apparently missed my most vital organs; instead, it had done some unspecified damage to my inner fascia, or something, as well as a few scary arterial bleeds that Ronan had managed to magically stem.

It now felt like a permanent stitch in my side, and I was reminded of the pain of elementary school track meets where we would gather in the green field and run as fast as we all possibly could in one direction without any previous training. In the lower grades, I would win purely because of my height and strength advantage over the other girls in my class, but they soon outstripped me in the years approaching puberty, my figure becoming "womanlier" before many of my slighter and more sprightly peers.

We all got there in the end. I reminisced fondly of those days, but I was also truly grateful that they were over. My developing magic at that age had been a whole different source of difficulty; puberty wasn't for the faint of heart, especially for magic Bearers. Today, I felt certain that my inner magical source was fully contained and unscathed. However, it was also completely inaccessible to me once more. Since the ordeal, I could effectively neither Bear nor Wield, and it was beginning to worry me.

I still didn't understand how my magic had shut down so completely while Cassius attempted his extraction, but I was certain that this was the sole reason I was still standing. Had he been able to locate its source, he would likely have consumed me like he had all those other girls, the ones who had been haunting my nightmares since that horrible night. Each day when I awoke, I would only remember fragments, but they were still there, lying in wait for me to re-live their horrific pain during my slumber.

On the first night we were finally alone, Dom had foolishly offered to sleep elsewhere so that I could maybe get some more rest without him disturbing me.

"Are you kidding me?" I said, and punched him on the shoulder, harder than was perhaps reasonable, even if it was in jest.

"Oy, violence!" he said, and feigned blocking any further attack with a pillow.

I winced from my attempted play, and his face fell.

"You're still in so much pain."

"I am. But I feel a little bit better every day." I paused. "I'm going to be fine, Dom. I promise. But . . . I want to know you're going to be alright too."

He froze when confronted with this, and I didn't feel like pushing him yet. He proceeded then to switch off the light, climb under the covers, and roll over, all the while muttering to himself so quietly that I could hardly understand, but I got the gist. Apparently, he was fine and just tired from all the company and would feel better tomorrow.

I stared at his broad back in the low light of the bedroom but remained silent. I was becoming awfully tired of the dual narratives being served to me at present, in that he could care for me in my healing without complaint but fail to care for himself to his own detriment. Martyrdom truly didn't suit his character, and I didn't think he would be able to pull it off much longer.

Two more days passed in much the same rhythm, but I could sense he was slowly softening. While he had continued to hold constant vigil over my tortured dreams, he was also beginning to trust that I was healing. My sleep had become a little more typical, albeit still with a tumultuous rhythm. At this, his own sleep had settled as well.

We'd had no strict schedule to our days thus far, and I could tell he was already bored by the flaky routine. And so, I had convinced him to take the dogs out for a long walk across the lawns, turning his words against him by intimating that I could really use a long nap *without* any disturbance.

"You'll be alright then? Just sleeping?"

"Yes, Dom, just sleeping. I won't re-arrange any of the furniture without you or anything; don't worry!" I said with a grin, and for the first time in weeks, we shared in true laughter. A plan had hatched in my brain over the past several days to bring back some of who we were *before* the incidents in England, and I was feeling hopeful that this would serve to heal more than my physical body.

Watching through the window as his figure shrank in the distance, I collected a set of the softest clothes I had and padded peacefully towards the shower. It was time for action. I was able to lift my arms high enough above my head now so I could wash my hair without too much difficulty, although Dom had been insisting up until recently that he be around to assist, just in case.

In fact, he had been so damn clinical in the matter that I was beginning to worry that he was broken, resisting even when I teased my freshly washed form in his direction.

"Look how slippery I am," I had said, my words dripping with cheeky intent and presenting myself before him like a slithering wet eel. But he'd remained steadfast.

I'd almost heard the gears of resistance grind in his head before he spoke, or maybe that was just his gnashing teeth. "You're not nearly healed enough. I don't want to hurt you."

He was being ridiculous, but that had also been the last time he'd helped me in the shower, suggesting awkwardly that I was probably capable of doing it myself now anyway.

And so, today, I took *great* satisfaction in my solitary shower.

The same scented soap had been stocked in the bath since the very beginning, and soon the fragrant tones of bergamot and lavender were bubbling blissfully around me, with my mind wandering to the first shower we had shared upon our first arrival at the manor house. I took deep personal pleasure in wading into *that* memory, vivid thoughts of his long frame drenched in water, along with the steaming passion that followed.

Sooner than expected, I was rewarded with the knowledge that my own sexual aptitude was still in top working order, body shuddering blissfully as I released much of the held tension from the past few days alone with Dom.

Afterwards, I relished in the slow meditative brushing of my overlong hair. It almost reached past the tips of my breasts now, the longest it had been in years. I would have to see if Peggy would trim it for me when she came back, although Dom would likely dispute this idea, as he lusted almost shamelessly when my hair was long and unbound.

And today, he would be able to do more than simply hunger for me with his eyes.

Having spent the past two weeks wearing nothing but Dom's oversized t-shirts and the same two pairs of worn black stretchy leggings, I felt like the clothes were begging to be tossed or burned in the fire, putting memories of the more difficult days of healing behind us.

I gratefully pulled on a soft pair of forgotten navy-blue jogging pants from the bottom of my suitcase. Loose in the leg, they tapered at the ankle, all the while somehow hugging the curves of my backside quite pleasantly. I wasn't yet ready for any kind of structured bra but no longer needed to wrap my ribs so carefully either. A soft grey bamboo tank-top felt most appealing, if not a bit thin and revealing, but I felt more like myself already in clean clothes that were indeed my own.

Looking into the mirror, I rubbed some tinted moisturiser onto my face, which still bore the yellowing shadows of old bruises, and a touch of mascara. I was thankful for my straight nose and smiled in memory at Ronan's help throughout the ordeal. He had become like family to me now.

Moving along gingerly with my thoughts in tow, I stepped past a pair of Dom's grey sweatpants folded on the bathroom floor before setting my sights on the kitchen, careful all the while not to over-do my movements and sully my plans for the day.

While I didn't have anything specific planned, per se, I wanted to do something nice for Dom. It felt good to move *almost* freely throughout the house all on my own, Oisín still trailing along in silent guard of me as I carefully descended the stairs. I held onto the long, polished railing for additional support but was pleased to discover that it wasn't even as painful as yesterday.

The kitchen was cool and smelled like cold stew and fried onions. It looked like the fire hadn't been lit for several days. Since we were no longer keeping company, I assumed Dom had abandoned the idea of additional heat in the space altogether. The days were steadily growing warmer anyway, and I didn't mind the chill air across my skin following the heat of the shower.

I poked around in the larder and found some nice aged cheddar, along with an unopened jar of pickles. There would be a host of cured meats to choose from, at least if Dom had had anything to say about the most recent grocery list. I added a jar of last year's blueberry jam to the top of my teetering load and eyed a baguette speculatively; I would have to come back for it.

Having collected my elements, I set to work preparing a simple charcuterie board, revelling in the meditative aspect of food prep as I sliced each piece of cheese and pickle with care, laying them out mindfully on the wooden board before me. I couldn't recall with any precision the last time we had simply relaxed with one another, telling stories and snuggling in for the night with a tasty meal or a few drinks. It had been months since we'd even been alone together in the house. I was reminded once more of how hastily we had progressed through the "reunited love" phase of our unusual relationship, digging in heartily to the harsh realities of our existence without delay.

I caught Oisín snuffling around near the stove for scraps and tossed him a slice of cheese off the board. He gratefully consumed it in one gulp. Everything we had been eating this week had been in the form of cold sandwiches or leftover soups or stew. Dom had stuck strictly to milk and water in the evenings, not wishing to hamper his ability to help me through the difficult nights.

I decided then that the evening would call for not just one but two bottles of wine. And perhaps I would also sneak up the special bottle of whisky Peggy had brought for Dom, back when they'd first arrived at the manor, just in case. Hopefully he wouldn't mind.

Since our return, Dom had launched into an increased fitness regimen. If the tire flipping and Olympic lifts outside had been any indication, he was clearly looking to hone his strength to almost inhuman levels. I never did understand cross-fit, but this seemed to be an origin story if I had ever seen one.

Wondering then if he would be extra hungry upon his return, I added a trail of grapes and several extra slices of meat and cheese to the board before calling it complete. I looked around for some kind of basket to haul things upstairs in one trip but had no luck. Two trips it was.

The sun had warmed itself into a late afternoon haze as I began my ascent back to our large corner bedroom, starting first with the food. By the second trip, I was struggling for air, but still ultimately surprised at the stamina I had regained. I was thankful, however, that it wouldn't take a third climb.

By sheer dumb luck, I had made it upstairs just in time. Entering the bedroom, I could see Dom making his way back up the drive with the dogs, whose tongues were lolling out of their heads. Dom had a relaxed smile on his face. He seemed to be having an animated conversation with the beasts, which was a fair sight better than the conflicted and silent brooding I'd observed when he was alone. In fact, he seemed to be singing to himself; my heart leapt.

Laying out the last of my wares thoughtfully on the bedside table, up and away from hungry canines, I climbed back into bed. The wine would have to be warm, as I had entirely neglected any kind of vessel for ice, but beggars can't be choosers.

After several minutes, I heard Dom ascend the stairs, skipping what seemed to be several steps at time, before quietly closing himself into our small en suite bathroom from the hallway and turning on the shower. As usual, he was efficient with his grooming, and soon I heard him hastily drying himself while humming quietly. I took care to slow my breathing, not wanting to indicate the toll my staircase traverse had taken on my still-healing body.

"Oh, Julia! You're up," he scanned the room, noticing the platter of food and the wine glasses, confusion and then intrigue dawning on his face in quick succession. "What's this all about?"

I beamed up at him from the bed.

He was wearing the same grey sweatpants I had noticed folded in the bathroom earlier and nothing else. I was pleased to confirm, at least from the visual data presented, that he had indeed increased his fitness level. His muscles were, if possible, bigger, yet his body was noticeably leaner across his broad frame.

He still gleamed with residual sweat from his trek, despite his shower, and my eyes travelled greedily across his perfected terrain. The tendons that stretched along his Adonis belt flexed deliciously as he closed the bathroom door behind him, the outline of his cock clearly visible through the plush fabric. I thirstily eyed how the waistband sat casually above his muscular ass; yes, that part of my mind was *definitely* still in working order.

"I thought we might have a little date! Nothing fancy . . ." I said, clearing my throat before gesturing keenly towards the small spread of food I had prepared, instantly regretting not preparing more; I could only imagine how famished he was after his excursion.

He smiled, and to my complete surprise, started blushing.

I eased myself off the bed, bare feet landing quietly on the carpeted floor, and turned to grab the two wine glasses from the low bench below the largest window. To my surprise, he was suddenly behind me, breathing into my hair while placing a broad hand firmly on my middle, still careful to avoid any tender regions.

"You smell lovely," he said, and kissed my neck. "I don't know what it is about when you wear your hair down, but . . ."

I decided then and there to leave my hair at its full length.

"Oh, I know," I said, arching my back slightly before reaching to pour each of us a drink.

He stepped around me, an unfamiliar look having clouded his features. Taking and setting down our glasses, he then took both my hands into his and rolled his shoulders back once with a low sigh.

"Julia . . ."

I looked down at his hands, admiring the long bones in each of his fingers, tracing the fine lines thoughtfully with my thumbs while avoiding his heavy gaze. He tilted my chin towards him, and I found his eyes desperately pleading.

"I've been trying to find a way to say this to you, and I keep going over everything in my head . . . but I guess . . . will you forgive me for letting this happen?"

"What?"

He momentarily glanced out the window down the drive, clearly attempting to recall the important points he wished to make. "I keep making the same mistakes. Every fucking time. And you try to tell me otherwise, but I never listen."

"Domhnall—"

"And the cost! Well, this time it almost cost your life. Almost worse. And I don't think . . . I don't think I could have ever forgiven myself if—"

"There's nothing to forgive. Please—"

He was picking up speed. "And then the Wraiths were already following us; Cassius even said we sprang the trap when we visited Agnes. I could have protected you, or at least helped, and I failed. Because I was terrified! Seeing Agnes like that, I thought—Oh God, Julia, you don't remember the last time. What happened before we passed . . ."

The words were spilling out of him now, and my heart pounded aggressively into my throat. He looked to the ceiling and blinked back tears.

"Back in 1968, he tortured you, right in front of me . . . Julia, he made me watch!"

As quickly as the bile rose to the back of my throat, I now fully understood why Dom didn't like to discuss in plain conversation the various ways in which we had been slain over the centuries.

"I'm sure it wasn't your fault," I said, head spinning at the idea.

His entire being heaved in full sobs as he sunk to the floor, frantically attempting to tread the waters of his own grief. I held him then, for as long as it took for him to regain a better grasp on the shore.

Eventually, he cleared his throat. "But this time you survived, my brave, beautiful queen. And *you* protected *yourself!*"

That wasn't entirely true.

"Dom, wait. Something I've been struggling with is that . . . well, I'm not sure I *did* protect myself, not entirely. My magic let me down. I shouldn't have even ended up there in the first place, but I don't know why I couldn't muster it. It just . . . poof."

I waggled my fingers in the air, and he smiled through his tears, a knowing look spreading readily across his face.

"But don't you see? You *did* protect yourself. He wanted to steal your magic, and you didn't let him have it. You hid it from him. That was as much protection as anything else."

"Dom—"

"Julia, listen! Please . . . hear me out."

I snapped my mouth shut, momentarily taken aback. In truth, I hadn't thought of it that way, and wasn't yet entirely convinced of this new perspective.

"You've transformed each time you've come back to me, and I'm always so stuck in the old ways. I keep trying to tell you how it's done, offering you all of my *infinite* knowledge," he said ruefully, "but it's never enough!"

Urging him onward, I cupped his face in my hands, wiping away his tears with my thumbs.

"The thought of losing you this time . . . well, I have never been so afraid in all my *fucking* lives," he continued, pushing his rough beard into my palm. "And I'm so sorry I've doubted you. I really do trust you . . . with all of my heart."

The walls he had so carefully constructed began to crash down, stone by tumbling stone. It would take time to clear the rubble and find one another, but the work had begun, and that was enough for now.

Eyes soft and heart open, he leaned in to kiss me then, slowly, still overly cautious of my wounds. I urged him onward in a different way now, making my consent and comfort plain with every responsive stroke, kiss, and welcoming touch. We had spent enough days in between places of love and life, and I wanted to dive into his soul, anchoring myself securely to this world once more.

Laying back onto the soft sheets, I made my needs clear.

I wanted to push him and fiercely claim him for my own, but my wounds likely wouldn't have allowed it. I also desperately craved his raw power and protection surrounding me, and knew he yearned for the same. I had come to realize over the past several days how truly violated I had been by Cassius's attempted extraction, and Dom's continued physical and emotional distance from me had only emphasised this pain.

Dom gently helped me remove my own clothing before roughly tearing off his own. He was fully aroused then, but paused above me, looking into my eyes for proof of my permission.

"Domhnall . . . I need you to take me back from him. His spear . . . that was the last thing . . ." I coaxed myself towards him, pain suddenly negligible in comparison to my screaming need to have him inside of me. "I need you to drive away the nightmares."

For a split second, he looked like he might say something in protest, but deep passion and urgency overrode any residual sense of caution.

"Don't hold back," I commanded as he pushed inside of me, raking his back with my nails. "I want to feel all of you . . . please . . . bring me home."

He *was* my anchor, and my deep despair at the potential of losing him had obliterated any illusion that we were ever meant to do this apart. Together, we would find the wisdom needed to defeat Cassius. Side by side, in mutual adoration and respect, we would face the oncoming storm. And with any luck, we would survive. After all, knowledge without a heart that was open to growth is hardly what you could call wisdom.

His low moans grew in ferocity with each measured, penetrative thrust, and soon enough, he roared inside of me, a lion prince in his own right, newly found in his own hard-fought homecoming.

The following days were spent consumed with rest and sweet reminiscence.

These blissful moments with Dom quickly became my favourite—the ones where we laughed until we cried, rolling around comfortably in each other's loving embrace. The most surprising aspect of our mutual adoration was how freely my visions and memories came and went once more. My nightmares were still intermittent, but I was feeling distinctly less haunted in my sleep already.

"You're healing well," Dom told me early one morning as he slowly kissed down my back, having recently awoken together from a relatively peaceful slumber. "I'm actually starting to think Ronan broke more than a *few* of his own rules in tending to your wounds . . ."

"Do you think they will ever completely fade?"

He kissed each of the two entry points in turn, giving the most of his love to me.

"Doubtful. And I'm sorry for it."

I knew that I would have some semblance of the scars on the back of my ribs forever. They had already faded from the angry reddish purple to a more faded pink, which I could accept. However, I also sensed that the wounds would always connect me to that time and wondered if there would be an annual ache or seasonal disturbance around them; magical damage had that effect.

Rolling over onto my side, we lay face to face then, smiling at each other, grateful to simply be together. That was the thing about Dom; he made it so easy to live in the moment. I wasn't sure if this was because it was a forced habit on his part because of his regeneration or simply his nature.

He had obviously adapted to the past century with surprising precision. Still, there were certain habits that would arise from time to time that I knew must be shadows of the past. We had recently agreed to keep the memories of the past in the past unless it was important. Yet, with our newfound vulnerabilities together, I was feeling curious.

"What was it like, when we met?"

"You *really* don't remember?" he asked, but he didn't seem to mind.

I shrugged. "I remember feelings and can recall certain events or visions— I remember the necklace now—but I don't remember what it was *like* like."

Thankfully, I'd had the foresight to leave behind the talisman during our trip to visit Agnes Sweeney and was glad to have it now, still in once piece.

Dom smiled, his memories trickling slowly into his thoughts.

"It was a simpler time; that much is obvious. But it was also a lot more frightening. There weren't the same medicaments or technologies, so that made survival considerably more difficult. At the same time, people were just as resourceful."

I actually enjoyed when he spoke about the distant past; it made me feel closer to home—our true home. It was strange to be walking in the modern-most twenty-first century and imagining that your true self had been born well over a thousand years earlier.

"Okay, but . . . what was it like when you met *me?*"

He chuckled. "You were very sought after, even if you were a Witch. All the men noticed you, young and old. So, that's not all that different from now."

He grinned but also reached his hand around my bum possessively for good measure.

"I can't imagine being anything but smitten with you," I said, and it was the truth.

"Oh ho! Absolutely not. It wasn't like that at all! Not at first, anyways. You were very . . . sure of yourself. It's how I knew you were a Witch, actually."

I pushed back slightly, surprise dawning on my face.

"I'd had my fair share of dealings with Druids, sure, but Witches . . . well, they were always a bit off limits for our family, many of them being connected to the Norse and all."

"Hmm, is that so?" I said, pushing a lock of hair back behind my ear before knocking myself against him playfully. "Don't I look like a regular *Irish lass* to you?" My attempt at his accent was terrible.

He groaned deeply. "Well, that was the argument I made to my father."

I laughed. "As if you would have cared."

"I did, unfortunately. We all did. A father like that, you wanted to be in good standing at all times." He looked away wistfully. "Thankfully, I was a late-enough son that I could get away with a bit more . . . leniency. He spent the majority of my childhood away fighting Máel Sechnaill in Leinster anyway, so we weren't close. I felt badly for the expectation placed on some of my brothers, though I wasn't able to *completely* avoid battle altogether either."

I imagined him fighting alongside his father then, the famous Brian Boru, with his triple-lion banner held high. I knew, from the brief history I had listened to on the flight to Ireland, that Dom's half-brother Donnchad had actually gone on to rule for another forty or so years after murdering his full brother Tadc for the succession of the high kingship.

"Tadc was a real miser though; I'm not the least bit surprised young Donnchad had it out for him," Dom had said when I'd brought up the family dirt.

"Looking back, I am glad to have avoided the carnage that followed after the curse struck—you'll recall my father died only two years later. I mean . . . a small part of me would have relished in the chance to battle at Clontarf . . ."

His eyes were dreamy for a moment.

"Hmm. And what about all the other times you have fought for your life in the last centuries?"

He chuckled. "I know; I know. *Definitely* made up for it."

He kissed me hard as he rubbed himself against me; clearly all this talk of ancient battles had him wishing to turn the direction of our discussion to more *current events*.

That's how things continued during the last days before our guests returned, loving, chatting, and peacefully reconnecting. I quickly realized that the real reason I loved Dom so much wasn't that he was a great hero or protector, but rather that he was my best friend. Our conversation was often laced with levity, and the ease with which we transferred from a playful chat to meaningful sex was a marvel. I had never enjoyed loving someone so much and never felt so comfortable in my own skin.

CHAPTER 36

L ennie and Ronan were the first to return, but this time I found myself significantly less annoyed than I had been when they'd descended upon us in January. I had been texting Ronan regular health updates, so he was well abreast of my rapid healing. Nonetheless, I could sense he was grateful to see me in person, as recovered as I had claimed to be. Dom, for his part, was glad to have his workout buddy back, and of course, to receive the news of their findings in the North.

"Well, we ran into a few Wraiths along the way, so I think we can safely assume he's starting to make the moves we predicted," Ronan said, nodding towards Dom.

The four of us had gathered around the dinner table and the massive pot of chicken-noodle soup I had prepared using the bones from the roast chicken Dom had prepared the evening previous. I still couldn't get over how much the man enjoyed his poultry.

My inclusion in the discussions around the impending battle now seemed to be an unspoken expectation among the group, especially after what I had endured. It chafed me somewhat that I'd had to *earn* a position among their ranks but tried to remind myself that, when I'd entered the space, I'd been a stranger to most of them, and now we had become something much more akin to family.

"We've increased surveillance around the North Coast perimeter, as well as the castle ruins, both digitally and with actual manned stations," Lennie said as he dipped the corner of his dinner roll into the broth. I didn't know yet what castle he was talking about but presumed I would be told imminently. "Oh, and I've tapped directly into any available security within thirty miles of the manor house itself. Hope that's alright. I didn't think that, after what happened to Julia, we would want to take any more risks around Wraiths getting too close before we're ready for them."

Lennie had been far less reclusive since the ordeal at the community centre, joining us regularly for meals and helping with any cleanup, though he still had an uncanny knack for grating on Dom's nerves.

"Grand," Dom said, but only I was close enough to hear him say it through gritted teeth. "We can't be sure when he'll make his move . . . but when he does, the more intelligence we have, the better."

Lennie had distinctly left out the part about him making that move *for me*, but I appreciated his discretion nonetheless. We hadn't yet concluded how we would lure Cassius out, but with the increasing rate Witches were disappearing across the UK and Ireland, we could safely assume that Cassius had remained in the area after my abduction. He was making his meaning perfectly clear: The proverbial clock was still ticking.

My dreams had been nothing short of horrendous in the wake of my torture. But then strangely, they'd gradually tapered off to the point where I had essentially stopped dreaming at all, despite the grim reports of bodies piling up almost daily. And while we couldn't, in good conscience, delay much longer—as far too many good people had died already—it was imperative that we make our move when the timing was in our favour.

"We're still quite certain Cassius is in England somewhere. He's got several of his shell corporations operating out of major London offices, which we have been monitoring closely, though we're unsure exactly where he resides while he's there. Ronan thinks he might actually stay in a penthouse above one of the offices," Lennie said. "Which would, of course, be very convenient."

I thought of the wretched stench of decay that had surrounded Cassius once his glamour had come down and couldn't imagine him spending any more time in public than was absolutely necessary. No matter how powerful you were, a glamour like that took immense source power to maintain.

"Then there are his larger industrial firms in the suburbs," Ronan added. "We've detected a significant influx of unmarked vehicles at the loading bay at one of the South Surrey parks—Surrey, England, Julia—but I've got some of my best guys on it, so we should have more intel soon."

I tried to recall what both he and Dom had told me previously about our network of allies, but realized I was still not entirely clear on the intricate network of Druids-turned-spies that were dotted throughout the globe, despite my seemingly *direct role* in the matter.

"Who *are* all these people you have 'on it' exactly?" I asked.

Three pairs of eyes landed on me at once, and I quickly realised I must have struck a nerve.

"I think, Julia, it's important to understand that we keep their identities private not only for their safety but also for the sake of the cause," Ronan said, his tone reticent and resembling the condescension from previous months.

Dom's eyes were now darting between us rapidly, evidently unsure which direction this conversation was about to go.

"It's bigger than all of us," Ronan continued, gesturing to the room at large. "We've put countless years of labour, and lives, into the foundational roots of the cause, all of which has culminated in an understanding that *absolute anonymity* is our best course of action."

With a sharp intake of breath, I paused momentarily to digest his words.

I hated the idea that generations of faceless Druids had met their deaths because of our repeated inability to defeat Cassius. It was a feeling that was now layered on top of the massive guilt I already bore towards the Bearer deaths, being dragged out from hiding one by one. Countless magic users had been horrifically affected by Cassius's dark intent throughout the centuries, but by the sounds of it, in more recent history, most were dying anonymous and alone.

"Okay, I get that, but that's not really what I'm asking. If we're also going to be asking these . . . individuals to be joining us in a massive battle on very short notice, how do we know if they are even going to show up in the first place?"

I knew in my heart that the true strength of humans was their ability to come together in the face of adversity. So, I had the distinct sense that these people, our alleged allies in the cause, might be more inclined to die for something if they *actually* had a sense of the human hearts and souls who were being lost. Otherwise, what were we even fighting for?

Lennie nodded, actually agreeing with me. "And *I'm* still struggling to understand why the Solstice is so important on Cassius's end. And why this all has to be such a bloody rush. Clearly, we don't always have all of the answers." He glared at Dom.

Dom completely ignored Lennie's jab, gazing towards me instead with an expression of mingled pride and ancient grief. "We don't, Julia. We don't know if they will come."

I stared around the room, shocked and angry.

I exploded. *"This?* This is why you've been going in circles behind closed doors all these months? You don't actually *know* if they will come? But you still can't see any other way to destroy him other than to lure him out of hiding by offering me up as *fucking bait?"*

My chest was heaving now with anger, and I placed my hands flat on the table to steady myself. "Let me get this clear. You've been agonizing over planning this battle all this time, in-fighting about the best way forward, when we-don't-even-know-who-is-going-to-be-there?"

"This is precisely what I've been saying from the start," Lennie said, and Dom shot him a scathing look.

Ronan spoke next. "I think, long ago, it would have been easy for our Domhnall here to gather his ranks. But the world just doesn't turn like that any longer."

"There's no honour—"

"Look!" Ronan said, interrupting Dom. "I'm positive the Druids will come, but it's just going to take some convincing that it will be worth coming out of hiding. And if it's any consolation, I think what happened to you in England has convinced a *lot* more of them to join us."

And in that moment, I finally understood why Ronan had been so unsure about me from the beginning. It wasn't me, *per se*, or even Dom and our shared connection to the Prophecy. We were marked by fate and hunted by Cassius; that much was obvious. But the fact remained that he didn't *actually* think the people involved within their vast network would believe that the root cause of all the destruction was so simple: a single man or woman. It also explained why so few had come to the manor house in the first place.

Good against evil, light against dark. What did those sorts of black-and-white conflicts even mean when the ways of the world were so damn grey?

I stared at Dom now, willing him to show me that there had at least been some tiny fraction of human sensibility found within their planning all these months.

"One thing we do all agree on, Julia, is that the only way to defeat Cassius is in the *flesh* and on the field. We have no other choice."

My heart sank, and only Dom's eyes remained on me.

Just then, Thomas's massive frame appeared in the doorway with an equally massive grin on his face. Peggy and Malcom were barely noticeable behind him, but they too were smiling.

"I've got good news!" he beamed, and I slumped back into my chair.

With my crash course on the inner workings of our particular arm of the cause now complete, I had a whole new set of annoyances to process. I had practically felt my body deflate following my flare of frustration. Thankfully, the return of Peggy, Malcolm, and Thomas had indeed brought along glad tidings, and soon we were gathered together, mostly amicably, in the sitting room.

Unbeknownst to Ronan and Lennie, Thomas had been quietly working on a plan to bring together more allies towards our common goal, though he had, in fact, sourced them from outside the greater magical community.

"I've got plenty of friends who might not be magic Wielders, but they can sure as hell wield a sword. Why can't the non-magical folk help us? Why does it always have to be a such a secret? Deep in their cores, these people know magic is real and all around us in the same way evil is. This gives them a chance to actually fight for what they believe in for once," Thomas said, looking around the room at the expected variance in reaction.

Ronan and Lennie both looked extremely skeptical, but conversely, Peggy and Malcom looked positively delighted. Dom, for his part, looked suspiciously smug.

"Ronan, listen," Peggy said, "I know our survival has always been in the protected oral tradition, and that still holds true for the teachings of our own brand of magic. But we aren't *asking* these people to learn our secrets; we are asking them to stand beside us and *fight* . . . for a greater cause!" She was clearly fully on board.

Dom rubbed his hands together. "I like it!"

"Did you know about this then, Domhnall?" Ronan asked, trying his best not to share his friend's bold enthusiasm, though clearly he was excited too.

"Thomas had maybe mentioned it before he left last week, but he wanted to discuss it first with Peg and Mal before bringing it forward to the group."

I smiled widely at Dom then, a tiny seed of hope now wriggling within my belly. Ronan continued to look unsure, but it was also quite evident that he revered Peggy for her deep wisdom and so was trying to take her words to heart.

However, it was Malcolm who spoke then. "It will be dangerous, obviously. But I've still got quite a few tricks up my sleeve that can help bring the fighters up to speed with the Druids, in terms of weaponry anyway."

Thomas grinned broadly, and even Lennie smiled along with him.

The plan was to frame the gathering as a planned LARP games weekend, allowing the non-magical participants safe passage to the North Coast of Ireland. Once there, Peggy, Malcolm, and Thomas would initiate our newest members as quickly as possible. We would have to hope against hope that they would survive the onslaught from the Wraiths long enough for us to defeat Cassius once and for all.

I looked around the room and felt incredible gratitude towards these people. They not only shared a common goal but also the familial values of those who had committed to one another . . . like a work family almost, or better yet, a *chosen* family. We didn't always agree, but in the end, we were all on the same side. I had always known I would be the kind of person to relish a "chosen family," but I'd never felt the depths of this reality until now. The choice brought with it such unexpected joy.

In the spirit of this feeling, I had considered extending an invite to Aisling for our Beltane celebration; however, she had been explicit that her role in the cause was now over. Who was I to command someone else's fate, no matter badly I wished for the presence of another Bearer and more feminine energy within our ranks?

It still wasn't lost on me, or Peggy, the disparity of our grouping being so masculine, and from my perspective, weighted so heavily towards Wielders.

"I don't know how much time we have," Peggy said, "or how easy it would be to invite more Witches into our circle, but I've been saying that to them since the start." She gestured towards the group of five men, who were currently all pouring over their evening game of *Risk* with rapt attention. "This is a significant shortcoming in their strategy." The irony of their boardgame choice was not lost on me.

"You're not wrong," I said, and thought of Aisling. "But I've got the distinct sense that most of the Bearers who know about the cause have deemed it too dangerous to get involved in any sort of combat capacity. And really, who could blame them?"

I absently touched my ribs, which had healed remarkably well thanks to Ronan's deft hand and my own resilience, but the memory of the abuse was still far too fresh to ignore.

The following evening, our chosen family had finally gathered together around the Beltane fires, and it was utterly blissful. We had collectively arranged a great feast with preparations of various meats and vegetables placed across platters of springy seasonal greens. Peggy prepared the most magnificent pound cake, adorned thoughtfully with edible flowers and layered with clotted cream.

She had informed me, during its preparation, that there were distinct ways in which one layers things such as clotted cream onto items such as scones for afternoon tea. Being that she was from Cornwall, it was jam first, then cream; not like those *heathens* from Devon. She had laughed heartily then, but I wasn't quite sure I got the joke. However, when it came to the preparation of this beautifully layered pound cake, such things weren't as important as the presentation itself, and it didn't contain *any* jam, so as not to create a bone of contention.

I'd spent the final day of April looking vastly forward to gathering around the fires on the manor grounds. The weather had been clear and bright for the past several days, and we expected it to hold for our celebrations, allowing the fires to burn fully through the night over May Eve and into the sunset of the following day. It had been a long time since I had properly celebrated Beltane, but I still recalled fondly being a young girl and enjoying the tales my grandma Gertie told me about the Fae, planting flowers and herbs that might attract the little creatures, such as sunflowers, heliotrope, and mint. With age, I began to learn more of the fire and fertility rights, as well as the celebration between the union of the May Queen and the God of the Forest.

Admittedly, the idea had always brought out my more bashful side as a younger woman, but sitting there at last, blissfully gathered together under the stars with our chosen family, I stared longingly over at Dom. He was my very own God of the Forest, his face and hair alight from the brilliant flicker and flame of our assorted fires, and it was then I truly saw the *power* within the ritual.

As we were combining several different beliefs around the ceremonies of the Beltane fires, we opted for a lighthearted celebration, rather than leaning into the specific rituals of more formal circles.

In peak form, Dom had taken to sharing stories of his past, many of which none of the group had heard before. I found myself enjoying them right along with the others, rather than sitting uncomfortably in the disparity of Dom knowing so much of our past and I so little. Even in the group, I was finally feeling like an insider, instead of occupying the all-too-familiar outer fringes. It felt so wonderful to really sit among other magical beings, all of us sharing a common existence in this life.

Dom had insisted that we sleep outside, wild and free under the stars like in the days of old. I had always enjoyed camping in any form, and any season; so, I was delighted to find myself curled up beside the fire with Dom at some unknown time in the middle of the night, warmed heartily with food, drink, and merriment.

Ronan, Lennie, and Thomas were also intending to sleep outside, but had congregated some distance from us around their own fire. From our vantage point, we were only able to hear the occasional rise and fall of their voices, their physical forms completely out of view.

Peggy and Malcolm had left us several hours earlier for more comfortable lodgings indoors, but not before Peggy had placed a delicate flower crown on my head, and Malcolm a stag's pelt across Dom's shoulders with a cheeky wink. It wasn't quite antlers, but evidently, we had been elected May Queen and God of the Forest. The Prophecy continued to ring through the air as I witnessed Dom in his full masculine expression before me. I felt surprising surety around the fact that, if we were ever to conceive a child, it would have been *now* in all our various timelines.

Dom, as usual, read my mind.

"I know you can't get pregnant right now," he said dreamily, stroking my hair back behind my shoulders, eyes alight from the crackling fire, "but if we could, I think it would be tonight . . . and I would relish it." He continued to drink me in as he let his guard fall entirely, and I could sense that he too felt the magic that had been kindled this evening around the fires.

We were at our peak fertility, and our destiny plucked at our heartstrings with urging precision as we gazed into each other's eyes.

As if on cue, a vision arrived as I witnessed Dom in his fully unabashed and complete masculine form beside the fire. The look dawning across his face confirmed what I knew to be true; he too was recalling the same shared imagery from our long history.

Dom stood terrific in form and completely naked in the centre of a ring of several great fires, the long line of his powerful body extending skyward towards his head, now adorned with a crown of stag's antlers. I too was naked, my own crown of flowers perched atop my flowing auburn mane as we danced towards one another in what could only be described as a transcendent ritual of wild sexuality. The images came as a blurred movement, colours of flame mingling with the green of the surrounding forest and the onyx of the night sky. It was then that we truly consummated our destiny, and would ultimately continue to do so, repeatedly, throughout eternity.

Returning to the present and riding the powerful waves of sexual necessity, I noticed Dom's eyes had taken on a distinctive inky shade, as they always did when he was overcome with desire, making it quite clear that the primordial need for our union would no longer be delayed.

Dom leaned me back onto the wool and quilted blankets he had carefully placed down for our bedding, citing the need early for comfort during my continued healing. I knew what his real plans were for this. Then, still within the blur of our shared memory, we were coupled together under the stars, the fire burning ever bright and true through the passage of time. Eventually, he gently rolled me onto all fours, completing the act from behind as he fully enacted his role as true God of the Forest.

Afterward, I lay with Dom's head on my chest, flower crown and stag's pelt long discarded for the more practical cover of quilted blankets. A small surge of embarrassment passed through me as I wondered if the others had noticed our carnal expression; he interrupted my wonderings before I could delve further into my concern.

"I wonder, if when the God and Goddess meet, in that place, time stands still."

He was still traversing placidly between the magic of our dreams and the solidity of our reality, and I smiled peacefully.

"I was more wondering if that was where the saying 'buck naked' came from."

He let out a low, rolling laugh, before pushing himself onto his elbows to kiss me across my brow.

"I don't think so, Julia."

He collapsed beside me then, breathing in the visceral marrying of the green, early summer air, herb and wood smoke, and our own more primitive scents as we lay acquiescent under the stars.

I listened as his breath slowed to the measured rhythm of early deep sleep. The night, which had been as black as a raven's feather, was now beginning to show the early signs of dawn, the sun's light slowly radiating from the east. I closed my eyes at last, savouring the fertility of the earth's womb and the potential for the birth of a future full of promise.

The portents arrived on the aileron of a dream yet were unmistakable when I awoke to the full blaze of the early morning sun. An immense feeling of existential dread washed over me as I sat up and gazed towards the others, who too were beginning to stir around the simmering coals of the Beltane fires.

"Julia? What is it?"

I looked down at my pale, shaking hands, then pulled them into our downy nest of blankets, tugging the covers up close as I mustered the courage to look Dom straight in the eyes.

"He's coming."

"What do you mean he's coming?" Dom asked, still dazed for a moment from his slumber, then he jumped to his feet. Shifting modes, he hastily pulled on his jeans and t-shirt. "Ronan! Wake up!"

"I . . . I saw him," I said, closing my eyes in a failing attempt to dig backwards into the vision, which was quickly becoming a confused mass of shapes and colours.

Dom crouched down beside me. "Are you sure it wasn't just a regular nightmare?"

I nodded. He knew full well that, since the ordeal in the auditorium, I had failed to shake the magical tie between Cassius and myself. Even if things had been quiet as of late, *his* thoughts now walked ominously through my haunted dreamscape with unprecedented regularity. I had hesitated to share with the others the extent of our connection, and Dom had agreed that it was best kept secret, if only for the short term.

Ronan and the others had arrived within seconds, the distance between our two fires seemingly much closer in the daylight.

"Julia has had an ill omen," Dom said.

Unlike Dom, I had pulled my clothing back on several hours earlier when the heat of the fires had begun to die down, and so I remained coiled and clothed on the ground as I took a deep breath of the crisp morning air in an attempt to steady myself.

"What do you mean?" Thomas asked sleepily as he zipped up his black hoodie.

"Julia's nightmares haven't been . . . *usual* since the bastard knifed her," Dom said.

Ronan let out a low whistle. "I had wondered if the injury would have a lasting effect. What was different about this particular dream?"

The four men looked expectantly towards me, which had become a decidedly annoying habit as of late. I fussed with my hair for a few moments, pulling it back off my face into a tight ponytail in an attempt to think more clearly.

"It's like . . . he's decided on a change of course," I said, and then back-tracked momentarily. "Up until now, the nightmares, the visions really, have consistently been scenes of him hunting down various Bearers. Most of them have been Seers, or those who can perform Sight magic. He's been using his spear . . . I think we are right in thinking that he uses it to collect their magic. It's what he tried to do to me, only . . . *they* don't survive the ordeal. Or else he didn't let them."

Dom cracked his knuckles in anger while the others looked at me in astonishment.

"Bit of an important detail, don't you think?" Lennie said.

Ronan shook his head. "We knew he was stealing the magic, Len; this isn't a surprise."

Lennie didn't look pleased. "Sure, but we didn't realise Julia was literally *seeing* his activities with so much clarity, did we? This information might have been a tad helpful!"

Dom shrugged deferentially as the others looked to him for guidance.

"I knew about it. But from what Julia and I could glean from it all, it was never useful information. Not for right now anyways. The murders were always from the past, and it wasn't going to be possible for her to focus on her healing if she had to drag up all of the images each morning like some kind of deranged police radio."

Lennie continued to look annoyed but seemed to drop the issue after Dom shot him a threatening look.

"But what was different about *today?*" Ronan asked once more, getting to the heart of the matter.

"It's like, his motivation has shifted. I could see him, in the nightmare. Now that he's had a bit of . . . of fun," I said, gagging slightly, "it's time to hunt . . . *me*. I can feel him, this push . . . or something."

Silence blanketed our gathering as a flock of sparrows chirped and swooped above us, so peaceful in their flight, so contrary and blissfully unaware of the mounting threat accumulating on the ground below.

"Beltane," Dom said, a painful realization slowly etching across his face.

"What about it?" Peggy asked, as she loped across the lawn, dressed impec-cably, of course, and ready for the day. Malcolm trailed along in her wake, still wearing his night shirt under his tweed jacket, and looking considerably more disgruntled over the early hour chosen for a jaunt.

Ronan caught Peggy and Malcolm up, but I was unable to follow their rapid dialogue. Attempting to sit as still as humanly possible on the ground, I desperately willed myself *not* to be pregnant after the wild magic of the night. Would modern science and destiny agree, or would the foretold child be implanted in my womb regardless of the interventions I had in place to thwart unplanned pregnancy.

Dom knelt down beside me and spoke softly in my ear. "Julia, let's get you inside. You're shaking."

My attempts to still my system had indeed failed, and I was starting to resemble the trembling aspens of my home country as homesickness welled violently within my belly. With Dom's help, I rose slowly to my feet but not before the truth finally travelled the distance from my innermost intuition to my vocal cords, escaping my lungs like an arrow hellbent on veracity.

"I know why he let me live," I said, stopping dead in my tracks.

Dom's face went simultaneously ashen; he had obviously arrived at the same conclusion.

"It's not my role in bringing forth the Prophecy he fears anymore. *That's* what's different this time around. He . . . he wants the baby. And he wants it *alive.*"

"I'm sorry, *what* baby?" Thomas asked, looking towards my flat belly.

"Mine . . . but I'm not having a child," I said, shaking my head. "Not right now anyways."

I gave Dom a half smile, but his face was still as a stone, gears whirring frantically behind his serious façade.

He spoke slowly at first. "In the past, he has always interpreted the Prophecy to mean that Julia is the source of the threat, and in killing her, he would also destroy any possibility of the aforementioned child. Two birds with one stone, if you please. No Julia, no baby . . . no threat. When he tortured Julia *this time,* she hid her magic from him. So, now—"

A loud crash arose as Thomas absently threw several more logs onto the dying fires, visibly discomforted by the danger I was in. Maintaining their flame seemed futile if we were to soon move into action; however, I couldn't blame him for his compulsion.

Ronan and Dom, the two Celtic warriors, exchanged a look of knowing.

"What if . . ." Ronan began.

"We let him *think* she's pregnant," Dom said, completing the thought as Thomas and Lennie began to nod in earnest. "Lure him out *that* way."

"It might just keep her alive long enough . . ." Ronan trailed off, knowing he didn't need to finish his thought.

We had circled back once again to the scenario where I was served up as live bait.

"Great, I'll go get the silver platter!" I said, and as usual, my dry sarcasm under pressure wasn't well received.

Ronan rolled his eyes. "Julia, please. We need to know exactly what gave you the impression that he's changed his tactics. Up until now, all signs have pointed to him waiting for us to make a mistake and expose you, and we were planning to work with that once we had all our resources in place. But from what Dom has told us, Cassius is not exactly the sort to make the first move, not these days anyways."

"Except we *did* fuck up and expose me, and he let me *live*," I said, exasperation mounting. "I don't know exactly *how* I know. I just . . . it's what he's after. It is. And he's going to come for me, soon. Don't forget, he's also got Soothsayers in his midst. He will have his own interpretations of all this, just like the rest of us."

A chill ran down my spine as the winds of the morning began to move with the vigour of a progressing day. Did *he* know something I didn't? Were we wrong?

"So, you're asking us to just trust a vague feeling or random nightmare you had after a night of sex and partying?" Lennie asked, eyebrows raised.

Dom cast a seething look in Lennie's direction and let out a low growl, which I almost mistook for Oisín before remembering that the dogs had spent the night with Morgan.

"I trust Julia entirely. If she says he's making his move, that's what he's doing."

Peggy nodded in rapt approval, and quickly turned on her heel towards the house, Malcolm trotting along behind her with newfound gusto. Thomas glanced at me sympathetically before following his mentors. I could only assume they were heading to the kitchens to prepare more of their mysterious pouches.

"How long will the defences hold at the manor house?" Ronan asked Dom, deferring to his experience with the home and the landscape.

Dom was thoughtful, casting his gaze towards Morgan's gatehouse and the grounds at large, as if he could literally see if our enemy was standing at the gate.

"We will need to move soon. Ronan . . . it's almost time."

The two exchanged a dark look, which was not lost on Lennie, who took off towards the house with Ronan only moments later.

"What does that mean?" I asked.

"It means, it's time to gather our forces. We're going to war."

CHAPTER 37

The location at which I would be served up as live bait turned out to be a remote and dilapidated castle near the northern tip of Ireland. It had been used as a muster point in our past, many regenerations ago, as it was notoriously difficult to access and already magically imbued; modern weaponry and technology would be of little use in such a place.

Lennie and Ronan had spent the week before Beltane at the ruins. They had crafted careful assurances that it was indeed the correct fit for our needs and had set up a handful of pre-fortification and containment spells to keep any wandering Wraiths from beating us to the punch.

"There's nowhere else we could hope to fortify ourselves against the multitude of non-magical threats on such short notice," Ronan said as he triangulated something with a ruler atop of one of the many maps laid out over the kitchen table. "I mean, we could travel to some remote fjord of Norway or inlet in Greenland, but we just don't have the time or the resources."

I had given express instruction that I would not be gathering in the study with them, locked away in the dim light with all that confused magic. I could barely think straight to begin with these days. So, this particular sunny morning found Dom, Ronan, and I sharing a spot of breakfast in the bright kitchen together while discussing logistics.

"Cassius will know exactly the place we're thinking of but will have likely written it off as a weak fortress because of its level of disrepair. It's been hundreds of years since we faced him there," Dom said, barely hiding the pained expression of a man holding onto far too many grievous memories. "So, we should be able to reach the place before he catches up."

I eyed the plate of toast before me, stomach churning at the idea of forcing anything other than water down my throat, and even that was a challenge. It was common for my stomach to turn sour when anxiety reached such great heights, but I was beginning to wonder if it wasn't, indeed, something else. It had been three days since the Beltane fires, and over ten days until I expected my period. Surely, it was still far too early to feel sick from an unplanned pregnancy; it had to be nerves.

"How are we going to get there?" I asked as I moved the plate as far away from me as I could reach, sipping absently on a lukewarm cup of water.

It was all happening so quickly, and my head was spinning. Dom furrowed his brows in my direction momentarily before shoving what must have been his fifth slice of toast into his mouth.

"My motorcycle."

I grinned in response, despite my ill mood. "And the others?"

Ronan piped in. "Well, that's the tricky bit. We need time for all our allies to gather, but that also gives the Wraiths ample time to congregate. It's imperative we move with stealthy precision."

"That means you and I will have to be the last ones to leave, love," Dom said.

I was feeling such a complex array of emotions that it was hard to feel any which way for more than a moment, but I did like the idea of some time alone with Dom, before . . .

I couldn't bring myself to think past that point.

"And Cassius?" I asked, forcing my worries aside for what felt like the hundredth time that morning.

"Lennie's intelligence still has him stationed in London, in what we believe is his penthouse. In fact, it's a little strange, but he's shown absolutely no sign of moving his location at all despite the portents."

After seeing the looks on both my face and Dom's, he added, "But you know, he could be in a helicopter at the drop of a hat. We can't assume his distance or lack of mobility to be any sign of assurance."

There was no room left for doubt in the plan.

With impeccable timing as usual, Thomas, Peggy, and Malcolm waltzed into the room, each of them carrying a massive wicker basket full of various leather pouches, glass vials, enchanted rune stones, and other related implements.

"You've been busy," Ronan said, eyebrows raised.

Malcolm, who was accustomed to playing the peaceful observer in any logistical or planning session around the cause, had begun to demonstrate more of the flavour of the man I'd seen when he'd first driven up to the manor house all the way back in January. And I liked it.

"This isn't even the half of it. I figure we will keep going until we can't," Malcolm said pleasantly, and Peggy beamed. Thomas looked at them both; he was clearly slightly nervous.

It seemed as if it were a culmination of his life's work to prepare as many magical aids for the incumbent battle as possible, but I also had no doubt it was coming at a great spiritual cost. Despite his bright mood, he would have to spend a long time returning what he had taken from the earth's source in their formulation, though that was a price he was clearly all too willing to pay.

Ronan had explained, in one of our strategic meetings, that one of the biggest challenges the Druids, and consequently any Wielders, would face on the battlefield was the need for continued access to magic. In other words, the ability to replenish their magical stores under repeated, violent threat.

"Physical implements such as the pouches have their own strength of course—you've seen that demonstrated with the Wraiths—but they do so with dark magic and no consideration of the cost." He shook his head in disgust. "What sets our side apart is the resiliency born from our connectivity to the earth itself. It allows us to gather a wholly more powerful force, but this also requires greater skill and room for preparation. That's why the castle fortress is the ideal location. It's a thin place, practically teeming with wild magics, and we're going to need plenty of that if we expect to come out the other side alive."

For my part, I still had absolutely no idea how to use my magic offensively as a Bearer, which only bolstered the terrifying plausibility of the bait plan.

And so, it looked like I would be learning to work Wielder's magic alongside the Druids and their counterparts. Following our breakfast meeting, I joined Ronan, Malcolm, and Thomas outside on the front lawns between the house and the lake. Dom would be joining us soon for some weapons training with Thomas, but for now, I had the attention of the three Druids.

I knew that Peggy was working away diligently inside, continuing to reach out to her Druidic connections, advocating doggedly for the cause. Over the past several months, I had gotten the distinct sense that she was *extremely* well known and respected within their community; if anyone was going to convince the more on-the-fence members of their order, it would be her.

Lennie was still deeply engrossed in surveillance and communicating with his network up in his room, and I was yet unsure what his part would be in the battle.

Malcolm, this time, was the one on the lawns to reassure me. "Oh, don't you worry about Lennie, Julia. I've known him since he was a lad. His parents were *great* Wielders. He may have rejected the spiritual elements of Druidry for personal reasons after his parents died, but he's *definitely* one of us."

"It's true," Ronan said. "He's a bit rusty, but he won't let us down. And what he's doing right now is so far beyond any of our expertise anyway. It's critical work."

Glancing briefly towards his dark window, I was filled at last with the proper gratitude around the importance of his role within our cast. However, I still didn't entirely understand why he was here in the first place.

Those of us outside spent the next several hours discussing how to Wield defensively. Using the pre-made spellcasting pouches, which Thomas and Malcolm had been working their fingers to the bone creating over the past few months, I soon learned that Druidic magic was, indeed, rarely offensive.

"I'm sure Ronan's explained this to you before, Julia, but the basis of our magic is to operate without doing any harm," Malcolm said, holding what basically looked like a small green linen pillow in his hand. It was, of course, one of the magical pouches he and Peggy had been working so hard to create. "However, there are ways to . . . get around these sorts of rules." He deliberately coughed at the last words.

With a wink for good measure, he then tossed the item towards Thomas with a distinguished flourish as he silently mouthed an incantation. The pouch exploded in a forceful puff of smoke before ever striking Thomas, who was nonetheless tossed onto his backside.

"That spell," Malcolm said, grinning broadly, "while not *directly* offensive, did the trick, didn't it?"

Eventually, Thomas stood up, breathing heavily but clearly no worse for wear; I *really* liked this side of Malcom.

"You, of course, won't know any of the incantations that go with the spell-casting bags; that takes *years* of study. But they should still work well enough for you, since you're also a Wielder," Ronan said.

I thought of Maureen and how she had managed to control the air around me using her misguided and stolen pouch. It was fascinating to witness magic used beyond the usual practicalities I had always associated with Wielding. I also realized how little I actually knew about my own abilities.

"Honestly, Wielding has always just been practical for me. Lighting fires, boiling a kettle . . . domestic things. Daily Witchcraft."

I felt strangely embarrassed for what now felt like a neglectful misuse of Wielding. They had clearly honed it into an intricate, thoughtful branch of magic, which I had not.

"Oh, that's not fair, Julia," Malcom said. "Don't *belittle* those practical uses. I've known Witches throughout the years who Wielded *very* cleverly."

I thought of Gertie then, and the calm control with which she'd navigated her enchanted world, never using too much but *always* having enough. None of it had felt particularly offensive, however.

"That's the tricky part of how we Druids Wield *our* magic," Ronan said, getting straight to the heart of the matter. "It's both decentralized and knowledge-based. So ultimately, we really *don't* use it the same way that you do. When it comes to the battle, you'll have to let the Druids do their jobs, and you do yours."

But what *was* my job?

Intuitively, and throughout our afternoon discussions, I had come to the realization that what might be considered offensive magic for a Bearer didn't actually come from the outside world at all. The problem was that I still had no idea how to bring forth any of that magic in any practical way, and Gertie sure as hell hadn't done so within her lifetime either.

That said, I still felt heartened that, through the use of the Druidic pouches, I might actually learn a few ways to protect myself. Dom had been silent throughout most of the proceedings, methodically sorting through the small armory that had been brought outside onto the lawns for him to inspect.

"Where did all of this come from?" I asked, during a break in my training.

"Oh, the larder of course. There's an old wine cellar below the manor that I had converted into an armory years ago."

I stared at him then; yet another important detail that had been neglected in my initial orientation to the space.

He blushed sheepishly. "You never asked."

"Indeed."

"It's where the Druids store their tiny pouches too. But you knew that bit, I think."

Despite the proof before me, I was still struggling to believe that it had come to this, a fight to the death, battling for our lives. Before me on the lawns I had witnessed some of the most peaceful people raptly discussing offensive magical tactics and the best way to knife a Wraith, killing them dead.

"But why do we need the weapons if we have the magic?"

"Because the Wraiths *also* Wield magic. Essentially, one of the most important roles of the magic users in the battle is to cancel out their counterparts," Ronan said, a look of loathing spreading across his brow.

"And that's why we need the fighters on the ground," Thomas said, slowly swinging what looked to be an immensely heavy axe before him.

Thomas had been strangely quiet, but I took this as an intense focus on the task at hand, rather than an indication of fear.

"Like this," Dom said in a low voice, adjusting Thomas's stance slightly and re-arranging his hand spacing for him, as he quietly urged him to begin the exercise again.

I recalled what Dom and Ronan had told me so long ago at the cottage, about how Wraiths were essentially already dead, if not for the fact that they'd reaped stolen magic in order to survive. In order to be defeated, they needed to be slain, not injured, and that required force.

I felt such despair around the lengths to which we would need to go in order to draw Cassius out into the open, helpless to the fact that we seemingly had no other choice. My mind would have wandered upstairs towards the quilt, but it was too late for that now. Time had run out, and I resigned myself to the fact that, once more, destiny would have her say, whether we liked it or not.

Peggy, Malcolm, and Thomas were the first to leave our grouping on the sunny morning of May eleventh. They had traded Malcolm's Traveller for a much larger caravan, which of course housed the extensive collection of Druidic battle implements magically encased for transport. The last thing we needed was a catastrophe caused by the more volatile items spilling and setting each other off. Thankfully, it was a wholly believable guise as there were countless holiday goers flocking daily to the coasts all across the country.

"Not exactly the spring holiday I had envisioned, but it will do," Peggy said somewhat ironically as she tossed her purse into the front seat of the van.

To my surprise, after having spent the better part of the last week on the phone educating and encouraging the last of the unsure candidates, she had also managed to entice a small handful of Bearers to join in our fight. It seemed they too had reached their limit for inaction after the most recent events.

In his true mocking nature, Cassius and his Wraiths had upped their ante in England with a series of what were clearly ritual killings, at least to the magical eye. However, my dreams told me that some of the victims weren't even magic users; he had now taken to killing almost indiscriminately, obviously to provoke us.

Enough was enough.

Several days previous, Lennie had carefully set out the initial bait in the form of a faked positive pregnancy test, the results having been faxed to my family doctor back in Canada. He said it was more than plausible they were following all of my personal channels over there by now, as he had apparently done so easily over the last summer. It was perhaps a bit clumsy but would still have the desired effect of building the ruse that we were helpless and unprepared.

In truth, I didn't know if I was actually pregnant and was shocked that I had even suspected it in the first place. Perhaps I too was being sucked into the spirit of the Prophecy, but something about the change in Cassius's plans had shaken me deeply. I couldn't lose the feeling that he knew something I didn't.

Ronan and Lennie would be leaving the day before Dom and I, clearing the road ahead of any potential traps, as well as setting themselves up in the proximity of the battle site to meet the congregating warriors with Peggy, Malcolm, and Thomas.

Thomas had sent his invitation out to the non-magical core, and now his own small league of enthusiastic allies was crossing the waters and moving north, in synchronicity with the rest of us.

At Dom's behest, he and I would be leaving on his motorcycle, completely unencumbered. We would obviously send any necessary items ahead with Ronan, but Dom was strictly adamant that we be able to move freely across the countryside.

"I need to keep you safe, and I can't do that if we're stuck in fucking traffic somewhere," he said. I puzzled at what exactly he thought would be different atop a motorcycle in that circumstance, but then I imagined he also likely wouldn't consider the rules of the road of utmost importance at a time like this either.

The hotel where we would be staying was extremely close to our chosen battle site and was selected specifically to flag our location when the time was right. Lennie was certain they would be using any available means of tracking me by now, including my credit card activity, so when the room was charged the following morning upon check out, the trap would be set. Being that it was a vintage boutique hotel, they apparently didn't pre-authorize.

When Dom and I were finally alone outside of the manor house, standing appreciatively beside his freshly washed and tuned vintage Norton Commando, I suddenly felt very wistful. We had never actually taken the risk of travelling the countryside, always erring on the side of safety by only briefly travelling to the edges of the property line, or at best, the local village.

Our trip to England had unfortunately reinforced the reality that travelling anywhere outside of our enchanted and reclusive bubble posed great threat to my mortality. If we *were* to leave, we would need to be ready for battle.

I had long since given up fantasizing about our life *after,* if not only for fear of invoking some sort of ominous vision of the future that I couldn't make sense of, even if my future divination skills *had* always been shoddy. Aisling's words came back to me then, and I knew she had been right. There was more to all of this than the Prophecy foretold, and my arsenal was woefully empty when it came to defeating Cassius once and for all.

I felt painful regret that we had run out of time before I could attempt to unpack my own magic, or the secret of the quilt. And so, I promised myself that, if we survived the impending battle, I would make it my personal mission to learn how to use my magic with more meaning. Maybe then I could actually feel useful as something other than bait.

More than anything, however, I wished desperately to spend more time with my lover, Domhnall O'Brien. If I could have one true wish in this life, it would be more time by his side. I realized this must have been behind Dom's reasoning for the motorcycle. Fast and efficient, yes, but a part of me suspected he was dying to take me on at least one trip on the bike before we faced destiny.

"I know next to nothing about bikes but . . . wow," I said, whistling through my teeth.

I was very impressed, and I was also feeling particularly frisky at the image of him in his sturdy riding boots standing beside such a sleek, capable machine.

He puffed his chest in pride. "I know. She's a real beauty."

"I wonder why we always personify motorcycles as feminine."

"Probably because they're so powerful," he said, pulling me close before kissing me passionately. His beard tickled me as usual, and I breathed in the woodsy beard oil he saved for special occasions.

"You really are my *ride or die*, Domhnall," I said, stepping back, "and I wouldn't have it any other way."

He gave a bark of laughter and tossed me my helmet before throwing his leg over the bike, patting the seat behind him invitingly. I didn't own any sexy riding boots or a fitted leather jacket like he did and so had opted for my worn leather boots along with the cropped, brown-suede bomber jacket from the bottom of the box of clothes stored under the bed in our old bedroom. As I slid onto the back of the bike, I giggled at the memory of Dom's floral shirt. Admittedly, there wasn't much in the box worth wearing, but there had certainly been a few treasures worth holding onto.

Dom kicked the bike to life, and soon both the beast before me and the one below were roaring loudly with pleasure. Without another look back, we took off down the road headed north.

Surprisingly sore and exhausted, albeit exhilarated from our five-hour journey atop the motorcycle, we at last checked into our hotel room in the late afternoon. Dom had contacted Ronan at both the midway point of our journey, when we'd crossed the border into Northern Ireland, and again upon our arrival. But for now, we were alone.

I supposed this was one of the perks of being the officially designated sitting duck.

We were led to our room by a kindly older woman with mousy grey hair, who had boldly remarked on the state of us upon our arrival, though not in the way I had anticipated.

"Are you two newlyweds? You've got that rosy glow about you," she said sweetly as she handed Dom the keys to our room.

To my surprise, I was blushing, and Dom pulled me into a close embrace, kissing my hair before turning to smile back at the woman, but she had already turned back towards the front desk.

Upon entry to our room, I had opted immediately for a hot shower, wishing desperately to wash off the dust of the road. Dom apparently had logistics to attend to and apologized regretfully that he wouldn't be able to join me.

"Suit yourself," I said with a wink, but he had already put his head down towards his work.

Returning after what was a greedily long shower, I could immediately feel Dom's tension in the room. Its effect was clearly visible as I watched the enormity of our situation ripple across his broad shoulders as he sat strained over the hotel desk, pen in hand. He had changed into a simple white t-shirt and his usual short rugby shorts, which had been stuffed into our small travelling backpack, and was agonizing over the final plans, in hardcopy of course. It was too close to the battle to risk stolen intelligence through technology, and we had already had too many close calls.

Dom's shoulders rolled back characteristically once, twice, and finally three times before he sighed deeply and ran his fingers through his hair. He was reaching his breaking point, and we had only just arrived.

I sat on the edge of the bed, distant in my own confused reveries while acutely aware of the oncoming storm. I was doing my best to still my mind, allowing for clarity around any new information that might possibly come to me in these final hours. Without warning, I suddenly had hot, salty tears streaming down my face as I stared out at the sunset. If this was going to be our end, I really wasn't ready for it.

Ever attuned, Dom startled at my change of state from solid to liquid.

My tears continued in earnest as he approached me at the side of the bed, sitting down beside me as the mattress shifted familiarly with his weight. I wore only a white waffled hotel robe and pre-packaged slippers, leaving nothing else to the imagination underneath. The hot shower upon our arrival had helped soothe my nerves momentarily, but not for long.

"Julia, what is it?" he asked, concern mounting as he took my hands into his own.

I looked at him square on, stifling my sobs. "What's it like to die?"

"Oh. Well, it's not so bad, most of the time. Quick, usually. And it all feels the same on the *other side*, for whatever that's worth. But . . . you can't think about it like that."

"But I don't want to lose you! Or our friends. Or this life. I only just realized it was all mine to have and—"

"Oh, love. Wherever you go, I'll always follow. You *do* know that, right?"

His eyes filled with tears, though they hadn't yet fallen, and he kissed me delicately on my forehead. "It's a lot to swallow. But we have to trust in the Prophecy, and our role in destiny. Why else would they keep sending me back to you?" He rarely spoke about his time spent in the Otherworld, and I took this as a sign that he too was feeling the immense weight of his own mortality.

"We don't know that it will happen again this time. I can't see our destiny anymore. I can't see anything. I don't know anything!"

He held me close for a time, and then unexpectedly, he smiled. "Do you know, Julia, back when I foolishly considered *not* telling you our truth this fall, I had also considered committing a mortal sin."

I was now red-faced, snotty, and utterly perplexed. "What—"

"If you can believe it, I actually thought that if I greeted Cassius alone at the Solstice, perhaps I could die by choice this time. Giving you your life, in exchange for mine. But now I see that my life is *nothing* without you . . . and that there is no way I would have been *remotely* brave enough to face him without you by my side either."

"You . . . wanted to die?" I said, in disbelief.

"There's nothing I've ever wished for more than to give you the gift of a long life, Julia. And to see you age with time, well . . ." He took my face into his palms, his own face strangely serene. "I was starting to doubt if that was even possible, after the last time. But here with you now, I see that's the only thing that's *actually* driving me forward. The promise of a better future, together."

"Oh, Domhnall . . ."

Raw emotion overtook me as I wildly released the pressure of my own tension into him, a tidal wave of fear and unknowing. The final drops of my tears ushered in the pure vulnerability between us that we had both always craved in these final moments in time. He too wept, and we held each other for what felt like an endless moment.

Eventually, I lifted myself from his chest and looked into his beautiful face, his grey-blue eyes red-rimmed with sadness but also bearing a slight glimmer of hope. He was my mirror; our souls spoke fluently to one another in the language of love and of the universe.

As we slowly began to explore each other in our fear and grief, the vastness of our collective pain became apparent as we pushed into one another. He was different tonight. Tender, slow, patient. Savouring each drop of me, and us, together. He wasn't any less intense in his advances, but more focused and intentional than he had ever been.

I felt a deeper desperation to know him than I ever had before. In fact, I was panicking. I was about to be robbed of so many years of exploration and connection with this man who was more than my other half; the term soulmate did no justice when another person was woven so deeply into your destiny. He was the root that tied me to the earth. I was trying desperately to soak what could be years of knowing into a single night.

There truly *was* something different about this time around in the cycle, which we both admitted silently to one another as the sun set beyond our room.

He continued to kiss me, eyes filled with sadness and love, evidence of some past knowledge of how this night had gone so many times before. He seemed determined to linger in togetherness as long as humanly possible, to do it differently, as if it were truly the last time.

He laid me onto my back across the starched hotel sheets and slowly peeled back my house coat, my damp hair spreading around me like the rays of a dying sun in some distant galaxy. He slowly removed his plain white t-shirt to reveal the powerful body beneath. My eyes lingered on his masculine form, golden chest hair standing slightly with the raised flesh of his broad chest as he adjusted to his own nakedness.

It was all too much to possibly bear.

He hastily removed his shorts and boxers as I slipped my arms out of the housecoat, freeing my body at last into complete nakedness with him.

The dimness of the room took on an almost ethereal glow as we explored what could be the last vestiges of our togetherness earth-side. I wasn't sure what I believed when it came to the afterlife but took comfort in the fact that we were inextricably linked, whatever path we walked upon.

"I can't remember life before I met you," he breathed.

"I don't want to live a life without you," I answered, transforming my howling pain into passion as I pulled him towards me and deep inside.

And with this, our bodies met once, twice, and endlessly into eternity as we roared through our grief together, at last arriving in a place of peace and understanding. We would have each other again and again before morning, manifesting the hope for an eternity in this life together, or the ultimate sacrifice of our love for the hope of *our* cause.

CHAPTER 38

We finally slept for a short stint in the early hours of the morning. Dom would make a final attempt at lovemaking as we showered, but then came an abrupt knock on the door.

"Domhnall, it's Ronan!"

Dom's eyes grew large at the unexpected intrusion. He swore under his breath before grabbing a towel and opening the door.

"Christ sakes, what is it, man? You weren't supposed to arrive for another hour."

"Sorry, but it's time to move. I just got off the phone with Lennie; there's been a massive congregation of known Wraiths crossing over into Ireland the last several hours, some on planes and others on the ferries. And that doesn't even include others we don't know about. It sounds like some are already slowly creeping their way north."

"Did they charge the credit card early?" Dom asked.

"I have no idea; perhaps something else tipped them off. Lennie wasn't entirely sure and the signal was absolute shite from where he stood outside the boundaries, so he couldn't offer a whole lot more than to get you two the hell out of here."

The plan remained that we would park the car about three kilometres out from the centre point of the castle, and then arrive by foot to the place where I would be stationed, designated temptress of fate. A guard of spellcasting

Druids along with an assemblage of allied warriors would march alongside us until we could reach the castle. Because of both the naturally occurring and cleverly planted defences, anything that bore electricity or signals would be of no use after that point. Apparently, even the most basic technology would falter; any weaponry that required a form of ignition to work, such as rifles or canons, would be halted by the complex web of spells that surrounded the place. I had to admit, it certainly evened the playing field, and I had no doubt ancient divining magics were at work.

Pulling on my robe from behind the bathroom door, I strode past the two men standing side by side. I silently bid goodbye to this life as we knew it as I collected my dusty jeans and other things. Ronan turned away and faced the door as I dressed, talking animatedly to Dom as he updated him on the latest progressions for our own side.

"How many have come?" Dom asked.

"Not as many as we had hoped but still enough, I figure. And there's still time for a few more to gather. Apparently, there are several cars still attempting to make the trip."

I heard the air escape from Dom's pursed lips as he went over his mental tally once more.

"As long as there's enough to hold the defences until *he* arrives."

Dom had informed me that Cassius never liked to begin any battles out in the open, always preferring to watch from afar like an ancient conqueror. Eventually, he would swoop in like some kind of vanquishing bird of prey to stroke his ego, rescue his usually flailing Wraiths, and attack our allied forces once they were already worn thin and exhausted.

Dom was quintessentially *against* this form of warfare, preferring to fight alongside his kindred, deep within the fray. I'd been hesitant to support his proclivity for being in the centre of the violence, but I knew that our best chance of survival would lie where he was able to harness the most strength *his way*. I could only assume that, if I had that kind of intuition around my own abilities, I would do the same. Suddenly, his dedication to his fitness regime bore a far greater significance.

Crouching down and reaching into the recesses of the backpack, I pulled out the small scrap of linen containing my gifted talisman. It felt wrong to leave such a significant piece behind on a day such as this. Placing it over my head, I tucked it under my t-shirt before standing once more.

"Are you ready to go, Julia?" Dom asked me gently from behind.

Ronan's back was still turned, and Dom walked slowly over towards me, arms outstretched as he took my hands into his own.

"Are you sure you don't just want to run away with me?" I asked, placing both of our hands on the necklace.

For much of my life, I'd felt like I existed in fight-or-flight mode, avoiding anything that felt remotely threatening or would cause any anxiety to arise within me. But today, there was no alternative to bravery. How else do you face what could be your end?

"Would that we could, my love," he said, and squeezed my hands in reassurance, pushing his forehead into my own.

Because of our theory that Cassius wanted to capture me alive, I would be stationed in the highest tower surrounded by Ronan and some of the other most offensively powerful Druids in the order. In this place, I could both be protected and aid in casting helpful Druidic spells from above what was likely to be the formative battlefield. While I hadn't met any of them, Ronan assured me that they would *all* put their life on the line to protect me.

Dom had given the order strict instructions that, should I be removed from the castle alive, they were to track and follow Cassius to the ends of the earth until I was retrieved, whole, no matter what happened to him.

There were no alternative plans. Defeat the enemy, take down Cassius, or die trying.

In fact, I had overheard him hammering this fact into Ronan over the phone only the day previous. While I *was* the bait, I was still the most important aspect of the whole ordeal; everyone else was mere cannon fodder if I were to die or be taken. I got the distinct sense that this had been probably the hundredth time Ronan had received these specific orders in some iteration or another, but Dom's repeated directive didn't diminish my appreciation of it.

Even now, I had no idea how myself, or any potential child I bore, could alone defeat someone so ancient and infinitely powerful as Cassius, especially in this particular regeneration. Furthermore, my period *was* now several days late, and I was beginning to worry that this varied interpretation of the Prophecy might indeed be coming true. And worse, that *this* was the true impetus for the initial movement of the Wraiths. I shuddered to think of how Cassius could have possibly come to such a conclusion.

Regardless, I decided instead to chalk my delayed flow up to the stress of the situation.

"Time to go," Ronan said, breaking me from my reveries as I gazed into Dom's eyes. With that, we picked up our single backpack and left the room without looking back.

I nodded at the front-desk keeper, who was definitely *not* the same kind-faced woman who had welcomed us the night before, but instead a much more grizzled, sinister-looking middle-aged man with an eyepatch. I tried to shake the foolish idea that he was a Wraith simply based on his appearance, but the hotel no longer felt safe, and hadn't since Ronan's early arrival. I was thankful to be leaving, despite our next intended destination.

Time and space bent unexpectedly as we hiked the distance between Ronan's parked car and the border of the castle ruins along the shore. Our displaced ethereal band of heroes carefully traversed the exposed soul of the universe, unsure whether we were travelling towards our intended destination, or into the mists, soon to be carried into whatever lay *beyond*.

The sun didn't shine here as it had several kilometers back. Instead, heavy fog and salty ocean air shamelessly overwhelmed the sky, the sun himself unable to burn off the halo of magic and sea spray, no matter the effort. It was an in-between place, where all too soon the inner and outer worlds would collide violently.

"Are you feeling alright, Julia?" Dom asked as he witnessed my first encounter (in this particular existence) with the *thinnest* place.

"I think so. Is this . . . familiar to you?" I asked, unsure whether I wanted to know the true answer.

He nodded but proffered no explanation of the feeling. Hand in hand, we slipped through the folds of destiny, embodying at last the fateful pilgrimage towards the possibility for a brighter future.

Sooner than anticipated, we were standing at the base of a great, disintegrating stone tower. It held several long ramparts, each of which pointed feebly outwards, their parapets crumbling and notably dilapidated along the majority of their reach. Below, the tide was in, but the coastal dweller in me knew there would be a long white-sand beach when the tide finally receded in several hours' time.

Closing my eyes and feeling rather than seeing, I sensed the familiar maternal magic of the moon, her gentle hand quietly soothing the rise and fall of the waters at the helm of our final stand against Cassius.

I am here, she said.

And I knew in that moment, I was exactly where I was intended to be.

"I don't want to leave you yet," Dom said, eyeing the great stores of weapons, both magical and otherwise, unloaded intentionally along the base of the nearest rampart.

"I know," I replied.

Thomas was there too, alongside Lennie. Both were delegating weapons amongst Thomas' gathered legion of friends-come-warriors, along with the other varied collections of allies garnered through the Druid network.

Lennie wore what appeared to be black military garb, while Thomas was adorned at last in real armour. I felt an unexpected gladness and pride for him, as he had always seemed to be the kind of man born into the wrong generation for his soul's purpose. And now, here he was, living it out in flesh and blood.

"Where are Peggy and Malcolm?" I asked, pausing as Dom continued onward.

"They will be up on the ramparts by now, stashing any additional implements we will need for when the Wraiths arrive. I've convinced them to retreat into one of the small holdings at the base of the tower once the fighting begins," Ronan said, but I had my doubts that either of them would be doing anything of the sort.

Ronan and the other Wielders who didn't bear traditional arms planned to retreat with me into the castle ruins that lined the formidable shoreline. Dom, with the men and women on the beach, would stand their ground for as long as possible to allow us to maintain a magical foothold and hopefully lure Cassius out into the open.

Dom was now standing shoulder-to-shoulder with Lennie and Thomas, the three of them quickly launching into focused discussion about the fighting logistics along the rocky shoreline.

I silently traced Dom's sandy footsteps and approached the trio.

"Your gambeson," I heard Thomas say as he handed Dom some sort of padded garment, which he accepted with a nod. He put it on, and I watched as he pulled on a light chainmail shirt over top, though still wearing his jeans and sturdy riding boots on his bottom half. Dom had expressed that it was his preference *not* to don armour in battle, preferring the ability to move freely in combat, but he had conceded to wearing the mail at my behest.

"Ronan's got several runners placed along the ranks between here and the border," Lennie said. "It's a difficult trek, but the magic knows we're on its side."

Admittedly, I was surprised to hear him speaking of the forces that surrounded us here with such familiarity. Ronan was right though. Lennie wasn't about to let us down; he *was* here, after all.

"Perfect, that should give us the advance notice we need," Dom said as he casually picked up his sword, which I recognized from being mounted on the wall of his study. Now, at long last in his capable hands, the two combined looked wholly transformed.

I watched in awe as he braced his sword firmly before himself, eying it closely for any imperfections before battle. Then he started slowly loosening his wrists, swinging the sword up and back in front of himself. I wondered how many thousands of times he had swung a sword throughout his lifetimes, all of which were now culminating in *this* very moment.

The others stepped back in natural reverence as he began to swing the implement more forcefully, bracing and flexing, slashing silver through the thick air towards an unseen foe. The sword itself almost blurred before us in its speed, whistling keenly in Dom's calm and skillful grasp.

While he wasn't inherently magical, in this moment, it was plain to see the immeasurable strength he *had* imbibed through his countless regenerations— undeniable proof of his time served between lives. And in that rare moment, a beam of sunlight breached the impenetrable surrounding mists, crowing his head in shining, glittering gold. His presence was indeed otherworldly, with his powerful descendance laid bare before the others at long last. *Domhnall Mac Brien*, son of the great lion, had stepped into his rightful place.

No longer a mere man but instead the true stuff of legend, ascending into the mythological and untouchable in his raw grace. In another lifetime, Domhnall may have indeed ushered a great rallying cry, a compelling call to arms hailing each and every willing body to his cause. However, today he knew that our allies needed to truly *see* him in his wildest form.

Gradually gathering in silence around us now, our allies watched as Dom completed the majestic dance between himself, the sword, and his fate, finally witnessing the undeniable proof of the power behind our shared curse and the Prophecy. If this act didn't effectively quell any residual doubts on the matter, nothing would.

With his breath surprisingly calm, Dom quietly handed his sword to a dumbstruck Thomas and then cast his gaze adoringly towards me as I stepped forward into his tender embrace.

"Domhnall—" I said, but he kissed me forcefully before I could utter another word. I could feel the magic that surrounded him then, as it had wrapped itself protectively around me as well.

The spell broke at last when we were cut off by a huffing and puffing Malcolm, followed by what I could only describe as an absolutely *formidable* looking Peggy. She was dressed in emerald-green robes, along with sleek black leather pants and practical low-heeled boots; the woman was a bloody legend. Meanwhile, Malcolm wore a jacket and pants resembling older military garb, his vest's faded khaki pockets and patches demonstrating its well-worn history—that or it was the hackneyed uniform of a well-seasoned detectorist.

Regardless of apparel, they were here to fight, and standing there on the shore, I took great comfort in this brief reconvening of the original members of the manor-house family.

I then cast my gaze out towards our newly gathered comrades, none of whom I recognized, and noticed that the women of our ranks in particular had arrived with the distinct ire of a Goddess scorned. Enough of our kind had been taken, commodified, abused, and discarded; it was time for *his* defeat. A great sense of kinship washed over me then, even though I knew very little of their individual lived experiences. What gathered us here was the need for a unified front against the malice of Cassius and his oppression of magical and non-magical folk alike.

My attention broke as I was jarred by the raw power of Peggy's voice, which was somehow coming at me now from all sides; a monumental ritual in the spiral of Druidic history was about to commence.

"On any other day, and in any other grove, we would call for peace, for without peace, we cannot continue our work." Silence fell on the beach as magical and non-magical folk alike turned their minds towards the force of Peggy's voice. "But today, we must call upon something far greater and infinitely more ancient than anything within our modern reckoning."

Stepping confidently towards the edge of the now gathering circle, she called out to each of the four directions in turn.

Facing foremost to the east, the beginning of it all, she raised her right hand and called out loudly to the air. "May you tread sure and swift with your breath, hearts, and minds open to what may come."

Malcolm and the other Druids raised their right hands in accordance, collectively channeling the element around us. Soon, the scents of sea, land, and the humans gathered together washed through our senses, with each of our bodies intuitively connected, and suddenly I felt light as a feather.

She looked towards the south, where Dom and I stood together locked in a tight embrace, with Dom's kingly magic still surrounding us. "May you channel your inner fire, knowing that your greatest strength is forged together, rather than apart."

Turning to the west, and casting her gaze towards to the sea, she pulled forth the tide somehow higher yet onto the shoreline. "May you find within yourself the resolve to rise yet again, as the tide has so bravely shown us throughout the ages."

When she reached the north, a swirling, circling wind rose around us, drawing the salted sand up from the earth, effectively imbibing the eighty or so members of our gathered force with as much magically forged protection as the land could muster. "May you stand firm upon this land and protect *her* from the darkness that gathers at our gates."

We were wholly connected now, to the land, our ancestors, and each other, for better or for worse.

Following the ritual, I stood back with Dom, eying our force, who were now eerily subdued. I realized then that I had yet to identify the Bearers amongst the masses, but speaking suddenly from behind, Ronan answered my silent question.

"There're seven Witches. The Wielders still far outweigh the Bearers, I'm afraid. But see there, three of the Bearers have actually chosen to fight on the ground."

He pointed towards two middle-aged women and one younger-looking woman, who was clearly their daughter. The trio stood together in a tight circle, holding each other close and speaking quietly. I was struck by their bravery as they gathered their family's collective strength against what would be.

"And rest will be above, with us?" I asked.

"They will, and—"

Suddenly, our attention was forced eastward, where a slight woman no older than nineteen or twenty was toppling forward in a stumbling sprint towards us.

"Ronan!" she said, gasping for breath but determined to deliver her message. "They're at the border . . . only about twenty so far, but . . . there will be more soon."

She collapsed in a heap on the ground as Thomas crouched down to care for her, his great frame overshadowing the runner and her valiant willpower in size only.

Deafening silence fell as we turned our gaze towards the only entrance to the beach besides the sea. There, the tide was slowly receding its lapping tendrils, silently beckoning forth the oncoming storm.

"It's time," Dom said quietly.

The beach warriors swiftly gathered their arms and looked towards Dom, their leader, for direction. I knew then that it was time for us to part, at least for now, somewhere between this life and the next.

He leaned in for a moment and whispered something only for our ears.

But for me, there were no words that could describe how I felt about the man standing before me and the short yet magnificent existence we had spent together during this and all of our lifetimes. Besides, I had spoken goodbyes to him the night before, so now I gave him the next best thing I could muster: a laugh.

"Break a leg," I said awkwardly with a grin, and Dom gave a loud bark of mirth, in spite of it all.

Ronan rolled his eyes as he grabbed me by the arm, his turn now to shoulder the responsibility of delivering the bait.

A silent nod passed between the two men, and we were off, catapulting ourselves up the spiral staircase of the first tower, soon to be sprinting across the conjoined ramparts towards the furthest outpost, where we would ultimately take our final position.

CHAPTER 39

Despite the runner's advanced warning, the Wraiths had arrived with more speed and force than anticipated. Ronan and I were unable to witness the first waves of battle as they crashed along the beach, as we were contending with our own onslaught of formidable enemies before we even reached the top of the stairs.

Somehow, a handful of their ranks had managed to snake their way down the slope and through the magical defences surrounding the castle. They were now attacking with abandon from the lower recesses of the ancient ruins; it was soon clear that they had been given explicit instructions to take down the most powerful Druids as swiftly as possible, and ultimately, gain access to *me*.

"So, looks like the bait theory was correct."

"Julia, come on!" Ronan yelled as I struggled to orient myself to the sudden attack.

Sprinting to keep up, I stumbled briefly over a fallen comrade and was exposed to an attack from a Wraith suddenly approaching me from below.

Before I could register what was happening, Ronan had launched himself backwards off the stonewall before him, throwing himself in a graceful arc through the air towards our foe. He smoothly unsheathed his own dagger and slashed downward forcibly through the Wraith's shoulder and into his chest, killing him dead on the spot. I was reminded boldly of the great Achilles in the way he defied the laws of both the Gods and gravity and knew then that the higher powers Peggy had called into action on the beach only moments before were undoubtedly at work.

"Holy shit!" I said as Ronan righted himself once more.

"Let's go!" he shouted, though he was clearly a little shocked himself.

Behind us, the carnage of our own making continued to char each of our destined footfalls as we forced ourselves onwards. By the grace of the Goddess, we were able to hold our magical fortitudes long enough to reach the final climb before the tallest turret; *this* was the vantage point the Wielders needed to halt the Wraith army as they approached, and the most visible place from which to tempt Cassius out from hiding.

I surveyed the lower beach, where both magical and non-magical battles were unfolding, sure to create considerable carnage. Our allies were easily outnumbered two to one, but to my untrained eye, the lines still looked to be holding mostly in their favour.

Within seconds, the band of Druid-warriors surrounding me set to work, accessing Malcolm's pre-stored magical pouches in a coordinated effort, launching their contents and verbal incantations. Their efforts bolstered the defences across the lower battlefield once more. The sound of shared cheers echoed out from both above and below; evidently our counterattack had indeed been effective. Though I couldn't see it, it was enough to give the warriors on the ground a chance to recalibrate to the next onslaught, which would no doubt arrive with swift force.

Confident that I could safely steal a glance, I turned my attention to the beach in search of my lover amidst the crimson sands.

Dom looked up during the brief reprieve from the oncoming hoard, shoulders heaving and visibly short of breath. He turned his head upwards in vain, searching fruitlessly for me above.

"Can you see him?" Ronan called out, his voice almost lost in the howling wind as we looked out from the degrading castle ruins.

"He's there! Oh fuck, there's so much blood already," I said. Fear seeped into the recesses between my heart and soul, threatening to engulf what minimal powers I currently had access to like a rogue wave. Without warning, the moon and her musings ebbed into my thoughts once more; she continued to pull back the tide to make way for our great battle, blood spatter and bodies already dotting the rough shoreline like shattered stones.

"Fear is your greatest enemy, not death."

The words filled my head like the fast-approaching storm clouds, and I did my best to shake off any more of the self-imposed magical shackles I wore as we contended with the continued darkness attacking us from below.

"Julia, catch!" Ronan said as he tossed me yet another spell bag, this one oddly heavy and smelling strongly of rotten eggs. I quickly released the package towards yet another Wraith who had somehow scaled the walls. Instantly, it fell over the edge in a crumpled black heap, landing soon with a resounding thud on the earth below.

Ronan charged onward, but I paused momentarily to look out once more before pulling back from the rampart.

Even from where I stood, far above the fray, I could see that Dom's face was smeared with sweat and blood. He held his long sword in one hand and a shorter, dagger-like sword in the other. The sand around him was already stained a deep crimson red, tendrils of sea water greedily lapping it up to claim the blood stories of fallen warriors, but never reaching so far as to clear the blood away entirely.

I caught up to Ronan at last on the topmost tower where he was busying himself with more of the thoughtfully planted implements.

"Malcolm will have saved the best for last," Ronan said, smirking grimly.

He fiddled for a time with the complicated lock on a brown and black box, which would have almost resembled a pirate's chest if not for the familiar Druidic symbols painted upon it. I watched nervously as he gingerly lifted the lid, followed by a sharp intake of breath. Inside were a series of carefully stacked pouches and implements that bore a decidedly more sinister aura than anything I had put my hands on yet.

"What *are* those?"

"Looks like Malcolm wasn't entirely telling the truth when he said he had found his way *around* rules," he said, not yet daring to touch the contents within.

I cringed at the thought of what it must have cost him to create what was obviously some *very* dark weaponry, but I knew, especially after hearing Peggy's words, that today we would have to work in a medium well beyond traditional peacekeeping.

I thought then of Dom and the warriors below, fear clouding my expression.

"He's still standing, Julia. I *know* Domhnall; he's got plenty of fight left in him. It's not time to worry yet. We have to focus on the job at hand here and break down their bloody counter-spells," Ronan said, standing now with one of the ominous pouches cupped carefully in his left hand, dagger held firmly once more in his right.

Our eyes locked forcibly, but I said nothing

Squinting fearfully down from the edge of my newly claimed tower, I searched for the piece of my heart who walked so bravely outside of my body. With great relief, I spotted him amongst the gnashing chaos below. He still possessed his simple chainmail shirt, which draped with deceptive lightness across his broad, powerful frame, as well as his short leather riding boots that were currently sunk halfway in the bloodied sand. I could see by the way he rolled his shoulders back and tilted his neck in a slow precise rotational stretch that he *did* still have plenty of fight left in him. But for how long?

I recalled then what he had whispered into my ear only moments before the oncoming storm.

"My love for you never dies, Julia, whether I walk this earthly plane or the next. If this is to be our final battle, then know that I'm *still* honoured to be the one to stand in your protection. Through all of the hurt, the losses, and the pain. It's all been worth it for even a single moment by your side. I'm yours, for eternity."

This had been his rallying cry.

Grief, pride, and utter devotion had filled his eyes as we were torn apart at the shore. Cassius's army had arrived on the backs of their dark magic and brute horror, and I could still sense it now from across and above the battlefield.

I had been given explicit instructions to make myself completely visible once we reached the highest tower, offering myself up to Cassius at last, and hopefully drawing him out into the fight. Standing tall now atop the crumbling tower ruins, I raised my chin in a gesture of strength as my unbound hair whipped about amidst the angry seaside tempest.

Wordlessly, I held my hand out, chilled fingers and open palms reaching towards Dom below, a sign of bereavement for all that had once been. Today, we would face either our impending doom or intended destiny. Regardless, our tomorrow would never be the same.

I love you too. Forever.

I spoke this, screamed it, both from my mind's eye as well as my heart's fire. From my soul's core to everything in between, my inner flames stoked to unprecedented heights in pride for the remarkable Celt who fought so bravely below. It was my heart's song that called out to him then, and at once, he found me, body shifting abruptly as he locked into my presence.

I saw him take a step back, my first *truly* successful Send having reached its intended target at long last. He put his hands to his heart, and then lifted his arms in the air in clear celebration of my success. I laughed, tears now running down my cheeks as I placed my own hands affectionately over the talisman at my neck. But the reprieve was brief.

It would seem my notable presence in the tower had triggered yet another onslaught of Wraiths to descend upon the beach with increasing speed and ferocity. Dom dropped low again, his sword raised as he and the others prepared once more to greet the rising tides of war.

What came next could only be described as butchery in slow motion.

In this second wave, the Wraiths had brought with them a new and unexpected enchantment that descended over the battlefield. It quickly clouded our collective consciousness, pushing every allied member to the brink of a horribly imagined possibility: that they would, indeed, die. For several long moments, it was impossible to discern exactly what was happening as the Druids around me attempted to regain their magical stronghold. The air was thick with both dark and light magic, clashing horribly on every side of us.

As if in response to the Wraiths' complete disregard for the laws of nature, an electrical storm had gathered out at sea, thunder booming ominously as the sky was soon cracked wide open with sheet lightning.

In the flashing light, I could just make out the massive frame of Thomas below. To this point, in a superhuman feat, he had been able to swing his axe repeatedly without tiring against his many enemies. Now, with exhaustion mounting, he was letting it rest heavily on the earth between each solid blow, struggling to gain the upper hand. He had clearly been marked by the wraiths as a mountain to be conquered and faced more enemies than anyone else at once, except perhaps for Dom.

"Julia, can you sense *him* anywhere?" Ronan called towards me in the din, but I knew that this time he was referring to Cassius.

Before I could cast my mind outward to the suspected connection we'd shared since I'd been speared by him, a deafening explosion went off at the end of the lowest rampart. We staggered into one another before bracing ourselves against the sharp, cold stone. Crashing and cascading rocks blew forcibly down the slope from the castle and onto the beach, causing the warriors to only briefly disengage before diving in headlong once more.

This was exactly where Ronan had commanded that Peggy and Malcom be stationed. I looked towards him, terrified.

"Ronan—"

His face went blank momentarily before he stole deeper into Malcolm's wooden chest. He pulled out several more of the volatile leather pouches and handed them carefully to the others keeping guard on the lower steps to the tower.

Eying the fast-depleting contents within, I realized then that we would soon be out of tangible magical defenses, both the common pouches as well as Malcolm's darker implements. And by some gap in the planning, I didn't even have a weapon.

"I don't have any way to protect myself," I said, holding out my empty hands while eying his dagger.

He shook his head darkly. "Let's hope you won't need to."

Suddenly, a lithe figure dressed in black was sprinting towards us at an unprecedented speed along the closest rampart, holding before itself two curved, golden short swords.

"Is that Lennie?" Ronan asked, failing to hide his shock.

My head was positively spinning now with the quick succession of events.

It *was* Lennie. Dressed head to toe in black, he looked like some sort of dark elf who had just walked off the pages of my childhood fantasy novels. Quickly springing like a shadow up the stairs, past the Druids, he landed silently in front of Ronan and myself, his face positively alight with an inhuman grace.

"We're trapped up here," he said, speaking in an unfamiliar tone. "Peggy and Malcolm are on the other side, but they were still alive when I saw them last."

Ronan looked momentarily relieved, but the warring cries carried up from below were instantly sobering. With still no sign of Cassius, and every sign of our forces being rapidly depleted, the magical and elemental storms continued to rage onward with no sign of a hopeful ending. Battle was absolutely nothing like I had imagined; it was lightning fast, endlessly confusing, and immeasurably brutal.

Not including Ronan and Lennie, there were only four left defending my station, which hardly felt like enough to protect against the roiling surge of war being waged below.

I felt panic rising. "There's not going to be anyone left to come after me if—"

"You can't think like that, Julia," Ronan said, cutting me off.

Lennie's voice was still eerily calm. "She's not wrong, Ronan. The Wraiths clearly want the rest of us dead, but her alive. Why do you think we've been trapped up here? You haven't seen up close how many of us have fallen. This is our last stand. She's got no way of protecting herself."

"I have no intention of letting her be taken," Ronan said, and I would have believed him, if not for the aforementioned evidence.

"Give me one of those," I said, pointing shakily at the small pile of dark pouches left at the bottom of the chest.

"Julia, no."

"Why not?" Lennie asked. "She has every right to choose her own ending."

Ronan drew a long breath and looked slowly between the two of us. While he and Lennie both bore arms, along with the skill needed to use them, I was weaponless, surely now resembling an easy meal rather than any cleverly baited trap.

"I *won't* let them take you," he said, taking my hands firmly into his as he pressed the pouch into my palm, making his meaning perfectly plain: He would destroy the pouch with an incantation, and me along with it, before allowing me to be captured, tortured, or worse.

"I'll cover you for as long as I can, Ronan, when the time comes," Lennie said, and raised his dual keening blades before positioning himself at the ready. From above, I could still feel Dom's deep agony within my own body. I knew he was pouring out his soul into Mother Earth beneath him and could only hope she would return his adoration in kind through this continued otherworldly demonstration of power. I had watched with reverence as each and every one of our closest friends stepped admirably into their individual powers. In fact, I had witnessed some of the most incredible magic of all of my lifetimes this day, and yet it *still* didn't seem to be enough.

It was then that the frail bastions of our reality truly came crashing down.

Time bent around us once more, the fragile space between the worlds heaving and shuddering in response to the latest offences by the Wraiths. Another wave of their legion had arrived on the beach, fresh and fully capable of delivering a third round of destruction.

I gripped the edge of the castle in utter terror; the cycle of the Prophecy was disintegrating before my eyes, our collective stories now barreling cata-strophically towards their completion. Searching desperately once more for the sight of my lover amongst the bloodshed, I wished hopelessly that I could at least die beside the one I loved.

At last, I spotted Domhnall in action, surrounded by countless slain bodies, the crushing noise of battle undoubtedly drowning his senses and ability to anticipate anything with apt precision. To my horror, he had fallen to his knees and was crawling forward in an attempt to reach his sword, but it would be in vain; his final attempt to regain his position with three looming Wraiths surrounding him would likely be his last.

Even from where I stood, I could see blood gushing from his left side, his chainmail no longer clean silver but a brilliant ruby red.

It can't end like this.

A new awareness surrounded me. I could see that the tide was now creep-ing its way back up the beach. No. I could feel it. Soon, the battle would draw to a close.

Letting instinct drive my actions, I climbed carefully up onto the edge of the precipice, crouching low, readying myself.

"She's not going to jump, is she?" I heard Lennie say in some distant voice.

I could still feel Ronan moving behind me, anxiously watching and adjusting his stance with each calculated movement I made, but I knew he wouldn't dare intervene.

Raising my hands skyward to the Goddess, I placed my trust in my earthly body to hold fast in perilous balance on the ledge, just as I required it to do. All traces of fear were left behind as I drew myself up, at last, to my full height, standing effortlessly atop the crumbling stone.

It just can't end like this.

Just as Peggy had done, I called to the elements from my soul's core, asking them to fuel my hearth, drawing as deeply from the earth's steadfast roots as I did from the tumultuous ocean depths beyond, willing their aid to my plight. The wind began to whip and swirl in mad furor around me, stoking my inner fire further still, becoming a magnificent inferno.

I called then to my ancestors, Gertie, and my mother, for the lives they had laid down before me so I could have a chance at claiming this one as my own. Forgiveness welled within me as I channeled their extinguished fires at last into my own . . . transcendent, somewhere between our past lives and reaching skyward towards their redemption.

I didn't need the powers of divination to show me, with utmost certainty, that Dom had but moments to live before he met his final demise, and I knew now that my own would follow soon thereafter, if this were to be truly the end of all things.

He would not die today, and neither would I.

High above the battle, I stood posed as the apocalyptic queen at the intersection of death and destruction. I was a gatekeeper between worlds, eyeing the terror below with an unexpected scrutiny—the calm before the final storm.

Dom had abandoned the futile pursuit of his sword, pushing himself up in surrender and slowly turning his head towards the sky, no doubt sensing my mounting presence above the slaughter. Witnessing me now in what he believed were his final moments, peace spread across his face. Serenity. He welcomed death in trade for one last glimpse at love.

At last, I called to the hidden power—the one forged deep within myself.

It was as though a collective breath had been taken by both sides as I drained the darkness that fuelled the bloodshed and took it as my own to feed my flame, bringing life and death interchangeably under my control. The Goddess too would adhere to my will in this moment, whatever the sacrifice she would demand as recompense.

Arms spread wide, I closed my eyes in finality, raising my head to the sky as a primal scream escaped my earthly body, echoing my sovereignty. My power exploded outwards then in an eruptive shockwave across the battlements and distant shore, my feet leaving the precipice simultaneously as I floated towards the heavens high above the halted melee below.

If this were to be my end, what an end it would be.

And for him, I would do it all again.

CHAPTER 40

In the aftermath of the battle, tales would be told and sung of the Great Witch, a spectacular Bearer who'd screamed into the abyss to save her prince. The truth was, though, I had *absolutely* no clue how I had managed it. All I knew was that I had laid all that I was and had been over the centuries on the line for the man I loved, and in that moment, had reshaped our destiny forever.

I couldn't even recall exactly how I had traversed the distance between where I'd stood above the battlements and the theatre of war below. It was likely just another extension of the power I had summoned, but I felt as if I had walked the distance between worlds, and it had brought me to Dom's side. The Wraiths were no more, and nothing would keep us apart.

Our eyes locked as I knelt beside Dom on the sand, gravity suddenly weighing heavily on my shoulders. He looked up at me with a reverence I was certain I had never encountered in any of our lifetimes together, like he had just seen the Goddess herself.

"Are you alright?" I asked.

He was bleeding rather profusely, but so far remained conscious as the tide lapped up softly against him. Ripping off my jacket, I immediately applied pressure against the main wound, but he would need medical attention far beyond my basic first aid, and quickly.

"You did it," Dom said, voice cracking with the effort.

His hair and beard were encrusted with sand, his lips swollen, split, and parted slightly as he breathed deeply with the pain. I tried to return his broken smile, but I was soon filled with a painful awareness that it might have all been in vain.

"Cassius . . . he wasn't even here . . . when I . . ." I let my voice trail off, unsure of what I had even done.

Before Dom could respond, Ronan arrived. Panting from his hasty descent from our location above, he had also evidently seen the need to prioritize Dom's wounds, bringing his military medical kit, which I knew contained more than simple bandages and suturing equipment, despite its simple appearance.

"Julia, what do you mean he wasn't here," Dom forced out, ignoring Ronan entirely.

Eerily quiet now, the wind had died down to less than a whisper, the spectacular thunderstorm conceding to our apparent victory. Around us, our allies began to tend to one another in the resulting calm.

"How could you know that?" Ronan asked, always considering the greater picture, as he looked out at the carnage that surrounded us, mentally counting bodies.

"I just . . . do."

Dom closed his eyes, pain overwhelming him at last.

Ronan worked quickly, using both medical and Druidic skills to shore up the wounds for the time being. I watched him hand Dom a leather thong to put between his teeth, which he did, then empty a vial of black liquid, which singed and bubbled, into the main wound. Dom quickly, and silently, passed out from the pain.

"Wraith blades are often laced with poison," Ronan explained, "and while I can't be sure what did this damage, we can be sure that if it *was* poisoned, he would have been dead within the hour." He studied the darkly oozing wounds. "It's a painful antidote for some nasty magic, but we can't take any chances." He wiped beads of sweat from his brow as he continued to examine his wounded friend. In Dom's weakened state, this brief reprieve from consciousness came as no surprise. After several tense moments, during which Ronan had run his hands back and forth several inches above Dom's body, agonizingly slowly, and whispering some unknown enchantments, he finally spoke again.

"It's not life threatening," he said, relief filling his expression, as he had undoubtedly shared my fear for the worst.

"Thank fuck," I said as I forcefully exhaled a long-held breath.

Ronan chuckled tiredly at the expression. "He will need rest, and a slow and careful recovery, but I expect he's come out of it rather unscathed, all things considered."

As I looked around the bloodstained beach, it was clear that the majority of our allies had fared far worse. He was a great warrior after all, though also the biggest target for the strongest Wraiths.

Frankly, I was fairly certain he was lucky to be alive.

"I've said an incantation to help him sleep for a short while, just to allow time for the antidote to work its way through his system without too much pain." He gave me a strange look then. "Julia, would you walk with me for a moment?"

We travelled quietly through the scattered heaps of Wraith bodies already being arranged into piles to be burnt in great pyres along the shoreline. I could see Lennie and a small handful of the other non-wounded congregating higher up on the beach now, attempting triage as best they could manage under the circumstances, but they would soon need Ronan's guiding hand.

"I need to go help, obviously, but . . . I can't understand how you managed to kill all of *them* and keep the rest of *us* alive," Ronan said, his curiosity overwhelming what (in my opinion) were far more pressing matters.

The area was still enchanted; this much I knew to be true. I could feel the magic pressing in around us as we approached the outer borders of the fortress and grounds, like someone gently squeezing a balloon. It was incredibly claustrophobic—a feeling not high on my list of earthly feelings I could tolerate for long. However, I was comforted that we were still protected from the outside world for now. Soon we would need to deal with the bodies and leave the place just as we found it. I expected the magic would soon lift, its own role in the cycle of the Prophecy complete.

Ronan stopped at the end of the beach, and turning around, he grabbed me firmly by the shoulders, face filled with more vulnerable desperation than I had ever witnessed in him.

"Julia, please. Your power was completely unhindered in that moment! I'm surprised to even be alive after that much force was unleashed."

He rubbed his chest as if it had been deeply bruised, and I turned away from him, continuing to traverse the edge of the rusted beach with him at my heels, considering for a time what he was asking of me. He was interrupted several times by others running up to ask for direction and some semblance of a plan for the aftermath. This was indeed Ronan's time to shine, but he continued to force his attention back towards me, desperate for answers.

After several more minutes, I decided it was safe to share what I knew . . . or was still attempting to understand myself. He had proven his allegiance to me in the battle, holding fast in my defence as I stood above the fray, as well as in our silent pact. He hadn't even wavered an inch. For this, he deserved as much of an explanation as I could offer, but I looked around nervously.

Something about my newly unleashed power felt like it needed protection, particularly because I knew damn well that I had no idea how I had managed it. On the other hand, I had gained an acute sense of *what* had happened, at least in the moment.

"Let's go over there. I don't want anyone to overhear," I said, gesturing towards where Dom was now resting quietly.

Ronan quickly sent a small group of medically gifted Druids to care for Thomas, who had taken an exceptionally bad gash to the face with a sickle. He would be scarred forever but would survive. Lennie was there too; he seemed to be everywhere right now, showing us at last how attuned he really was to his own magic.

At ease by the seaside, we found Dom settled in comfortably with his eyes closed, a gentle smile resting on his noble face. He looked so peaceful lying there in the sunset, now on a makeshift cot made of light-brown linen that looked like it had been stuffed with some sort of wool or cotton. It was best described as very lumpy and medieval, all things considered. I was reminded strongly of the vision with my talisman, which continued to weigh heavily around my neck.

We had been through *so much* together in all of these lifetimes.

He was clearly still in considerable pain, but ever the warrior at heart, he was the picture of grace, riding high on the gratitude of surviving to live yet another day. Magical wounds were harder to heal, however, and even the greatest hero with the cleverest Wielding doctor for a best friend would need ample time to recover.

I felt badly for disturbing him but sat down beside him and took one of his hands into my own, kissing it gently. He jumped briefly, and then smiled at the sight of me before grimacing slightly from the pain. He closed his eyes once more, still managing his physical and mental pain with a concerted effort.

"If you can listen a moment, Dom, Julia was about to enlighten me about what she thinks might have happened up on the ramparts," Ronan said, raising his eyebrows at me, bordering now on a look of accusation.

A striking look from Dom softened his gaze only slightly.

I looked out towards the calm ocean and took a deep breath. "To be honest . . . I don't understand entirely how I did it . . ."

"Well, that much is clear," Ronan said, meeting my gaze with a wry smile. "This wasn't your *usual* style at all."

"I know." I shook my head and pulled my hair instinctively back into a sloppy knot at the back of my neck using the black hair elastic I had placed on my wrist a thousand years ago at the hotel.

Such things felt so trivial after what we had just been through; it was as if we had been transported to another time and place, precariously transcendent on the wings of our own destiny. And now, here we were, chatting casually on the beach.

Dom was staring at me, still mostly speechless from what had unfolded over the past several hours, and no doubt at what had exploded from within me right before his eyes. I had never seen him so pensive, almost reverent.

"It felt as if . . . as if I gathered up all of the magic around us . . . somehow . . . into myself? Or, I don't know . . . it was like I just *knew* what to do. And then I released it all back to where it belonged. Or back where it came from . . . if that makes sense." My brows furrowed, as I was still struggling to make sense of it all.

Ronan considered this. "Cassius's warriors and Wraiths have built so much of their power by taking, commodifying, and defiling magic. It's no surprise that anything you pulled away from them didn't return. If my recent research is correct, it was likely the only thing keeping most of the Wraith's alive, that stolen magic. And the ones you didn't manage to kill fled before we could stop them." He scratched his head. "They must not have been full-fledged Wraiths yet, or had not forsaken enough of their souls."

We sat in silence for a few moments, pondering the new quandary before us.

"Okay, so that explains the *what*, but we still don't know the *how*," Ronan said, impatiently breaking the silence once more.

"Honestly . . . I don't know."

Peggy walked towards us then, shoulders back and her face strangely calm. She was covered in stone dust and her robes were torn, but she was whole.

"Well, the old boy's gone," she said, gesturing with her thumb casually up the beach.

"What? No! Was it the explosion?" Ronan said, jumping to his feet.

She held up her hands, silencing both Dom and my successive outcries.

"Before you panic, I need you to understand. Malcolm knew exactly what he was doing going into this battle *and* in accessing the dark magic," she said, looking directly at Ronan. "We didn't expect him to come out the other side."

I was at a complete loss for words, but thankfully, Dom broke the silence, baritone voice full of gravel. "Malcolm will be sorely missed, but his bravery will never be forgotten."

I could see Thomas at a distance, face heavily bandaged and slumped beside what I now knew to be the shrouded body of Malcolm.

"But . . . how did he fall?" Ronan asked. I knew exactly where his line of questioning was headed.

"It was me," I said, heart dropping like a stone deep into the pit of my stomach. "When I drew in the surrounding force . . . I . . . Malcolm . . ."

I gazed at Peggy then, both of our eyes welling with tears.

She nodded slowly in peaceful understanding as Ronan pulled her into a firm embrace. "As I said, he knew exactly what he was doing. We said our goodbyes long before today."

My hands had started to shake uncontrollably, and feeling it, Dom gently squeezed the one he still held in his own.

"I think that's enough for now," he said protectively. "Julia, you've been through an ordeal. Why don't we sit a while?"

"Hmm," I said, looking out at the shining sea and fighting back heaving sobs.

He wasn't wrong. After recovering from the initial shock, I had felt a surge of adrenaline while getting down to where the fighting had happened and hadn't managed to slow myself down since. Now that I was sitting in the setting sun and leaning on Dom's uninjured side, I suddenly felt utterly and completely spent. This was a grief and exhaustion like I had never experienced before.

"He's right," Ronan said, crouching down in front of me, suddenly concerned. He checked my pulse and assessed my pupils with a pen light pulled from his chest pocket.

Had I fainted? Events seemed to be unfolding in front of me in slow motion.

"I'm just tired," I said, stifling a huge yawn. I was fast losing my grip on consciousness, my body shutting down at long last.

"You two rest. I've still got some work to do, but I'll have someone bring you something sugary to drink. Don't want you going into shock."

With the precision of the military doctor that he was, Ronan took off and regained his command of a makeshift infirmary. Peggy followed along in his wake, attending bravely to the spiritual needs of the small gathering of Druids and friends.

"Ronan's a handy guy to have around," I said, feeling slightly loopy now.

"He's a good man; it's true. I wouldn't have trusted anyone else to be at your side in this battle but him," Dom said, and closed his eyes once more, the pain evidently reaching his psyche and demanding he rest. In time, I would tell him about the pact I had forged with Ronan, with Lennie as our witness. He would understand, of course, but it didn't feel right to bring it up now.

After all, we had *survived*.

I leaned gratefully into his prone and solid body along the margin of shoreline, the familiar scents of sunshine and sea-salt surrounding us. He looked every bit the ancient Celtic prince that he was, a true dynastic son of Ireland's High King.

I watched transfixed as the frothing water of the coastline lapped lazily up onto the shore, the incoming tide still steadily rinsing away the iron-rich blood that had spilled across the sands, gently coaxing the memories of our near demise far out to sea in the same dependable motion.

"Oh—" I said, a soft reply to an all-too-familiar feeling. I was indeed bleeding now, not yet carrying the child of my eternal lover. Looking skyward, I could still sense the power of the moon deep within me, sitting heavily within the bowl of my pelvis. I was surprised to feel real sadness for the now ebbing and changing tide within my womb, a new and unfamiliar dream being washed away along with so many others along the North Coast.

After a time, I spoke. "Domhnall?"

The sun was low now, and soon great pyres for the slain would be alight along the beach.

"Hmm?" he answered, one eyebrow raised, eyes barely open.

He had dosed off once more, or at least moved into a place of peaceful meditation as his body started the all-too-familiar process of healing deep wounds, both physically and mentally.

I felt badly for disturbing him yet again, but I had a new concern growing within me now.

"It's still a little over a month until the summer solstice. Do you think Cassius will attempt to come for us before then?"

This was now the million-dollar question.

His hands were rested upon his chest, still as a slumbering giant, but I could see that his brain was beginning to whir into action once more.

"Well ... I suppose he always could try to find us again before then, but . . ." he paused, considering what we knew now to be true. "I don't think he will, no. Not before the Solstice at any rate. We . . . well, *you've* dealt considerable damage today, and I think he'll need time to lick his wounds."

I looked straight into his eyes, hardly daring to hope. "Does that mean . . . ?"

Neither Dom nor I had ever survived past this fixed point in our story. If he was right, what would it mean for our futures? There had never actually been *next steps*.

"I think that means he'll still hunt us. More so now than ever. But . . . I think we've been given the gift of *time*. For now, at least." His face filled with a tender expression I had never witnessed in him before, and I tucked in beside him on the cot, careful not to disturb his wounds.

This was, indeed, a dream come true.

"Okay, but . . . here's the thing," I said, breaking the enchanted moment.

I had finally found the words I'd been struggling to bring forward for *weeks* leading up to the final battle. It was time to name my truth, long held deep within my soul, right at the centre hearth of my Witch's fire.

"Up until this point, we've relied on our best knowledge to defeat Cassius . . . and so obviously our shared history has dictated how we have approached it all, but . . . despite our efforts to dissuade the urgings of the Prophecy, we've still landed *here.*"

He looked slightly confused as to where I was going with this but continued to listen intently in silence.

"It's two things. First, I can't help but feel like I've been forgetting everything . . . have forgotten our story specifically, for a *reason* . . . like I'm *supposed* to be unhindered by the memories, you know? Not burdened by them. So that I can see things differently than I did before."

I couldn't read the look on his face now. It was pained to be sure, but there was also something else there I didn't recognize. I forged onward despite the growing discomfort.

"And second. I know Cassius seems to be convinced now that the Prophecy speaks of our child—well maybe not anymore, after what happened today— but what I'm saying is . . . okay, it's not that I don't *want* children, it's just that I really don't think the Prophecy is about *our* child at all."

"Oh?" he asked, concern dawning on his face.

Who would father the child if not him? He attempted to raise up to his elbows in response to this notion, but I gently pushed him back down, offering as much reassurance in my expression as I could.

"No, I mean *we* may still have children together—oh, and I'm definitely not pregnant—but that's not it," I said, burying my face in my hands. "Ugh! I'm doing a terrible job explaining myself."

He relaxed a little on the stuffed cot once more, but I could sense confusion still in the wings of his mind.

"It comes back to something Aisling said to me. I'm here now, in this version, to *break* the cycle . . . to create something new," I said, almost pleading now. "*That's* how we defeat him . . . by blowing it all *wide* open."

He nodded slowly. "And it's you that defeats him . . ."

"Yes. It's *me*. Or rather, us, together. But we don't need to put this burden on our child."

Throughout every one of our rebirth cycles, we had never been *completely* sure if it was me, or our child, that the Prophecy had referred to. And frankly, it had never really mattered in the end anyway. Cassius always murdered us by the Solstice, leaving the need for any debate off the table. Now that we could *actually* consider what our future might look like together beyond this moment, I knew the impetus of change did in fact lie with me.

"But the problem is, I have no idea what the hell I'm doing."

"Oh?" he said and stared at me for a long while before closing his eyes and smiling. "Oh."

It was my turn to be confused.

"Domhnall . . . what?"

"Well, I think you're probably right, but . . ." his voice trailed off.

I felt relief wash over me, followed by a renewed sense of dread at all the permutations that would need to be arranged and rearranged to navigate the new direction of our destiny.

"But what?" I said and rubbed the base of my palms into my temples, my head aching with the mounting pressure in response to the obvious mental strain of the day.

To my surprise, he began to chuckle.

It started as a low snicker, but soon he was practically cackling with laughter, tears running down his perfect face and into his beard, at least some (I assumed) brought on by the physical pain his movements caused. As he wiped the tears away from his crinkled eyes, he rearranged his face in attempted seriousness.

"Well . . . it does complicate matters a bit," he said, and then burst out again into snorting laughter, despite the resultant discomfort.

Dazed, and pulling my hands down from massaging my scalp and face, I looked out at the magical fires now being lit before us. Decaying dark-magic bodies would soon be set brilliantly ablaze all along the beach. It was then that I began to tremble, but this time it wasn't from the shock of it all. Instead, I joined Dom in his rolling fits of laughter, earnest tears running down my face as well.

Ronan walked past us in that moment, carrying firewood from the sparse forest just outside the edges of the castle, and shook his head at our ill-timed frivolity.

"Lunatics, the both of you."

Dom howled loudly in his direction, which quickly disintegrated into a wounded moan.

We were positively spent and floating into that fragile place where you either laugh or you cry. In our case, it was both. This was what I loved most about Dom: No matter what, he was always my safest place to land. We gently held onto each other then, averting our eyes momentarily from the blazing fires. Soon we might attempt to join the others, sharing in their stories, but for now, we stayed where we were, in a stolen moment of shocking and joyful survival.

"Julia?"

"Hmm?"

He squeezed my hand tightly. "I'm so proud of you."

"And I, you."

We would soon experience an overwhelming sadness for all the lives lost, and I wondered without an answer whether this anticipated grief would stifle my powers once more, or if my magic had at long last been finally freed. Somehow, I guessed that it would be the latter. I had surrendered my soul to the Goddess, allowing her power to flow freely through me as a conduit; I had gathered in all the magic around me and released it at last to where it rightfully belonged. Even in this moment, I could still feel my Witch's fire burning a glorious inferno within, and though that might have frightened me at one time, now I felt strong.

And while I knew there would be a cost for what I had done, so far, I felt I had come out the other side relatively unscathed.

CHAPTER 41

With the once-roaring beach fires burned down to their last embers, and early dawn fast approaching, we found ourselves arranging at last for our slow return to the manor house. The survivors were surprisingly few, with each small party leaving the battle-grounds in calculated, staggered groups, starting with Thomas, Peggy, and the four other elevated English Druids who had stood as my steadfast guard atop the high tower.

Many of Thomas's brave friends had fallen in battle, but by the same token, equally as many had stood incredibly strong in their conviction and had survived the night. Much like Dom, it would seem that their humanity alone had aided in their ability to withstand the fog of the targeted Wraith attacks. Thomas had once told me about the concept of experiencing an emotional "bleed" after an exceptionally immersive role-play weekend, almost as if grieving the loss of another life lived. I wondered sadly if (on more than one level) this might just have been the bleed to end all bleeds.

Peggy and Thomas would have each other during the difficult times ahead, sharing in their grief together over the coming weeks. After all, Malcolm had become like a father to Thomas over the past several years. I was thankful for their connection, particularly as they would soon face that part of grief during which people begin to forget or move on from their losses and realize they are essentially *on their own*.

Honours had, of course, been spoken to Malcolm's name, along with the many others who were lost along the rocky shoreline. It had been astonishing to hear the tales of some of their journeys throughout this lifetime, at least as recounted by anyone who *might* have known them. I felt a very unsatisfying vindication for my argument against Ronan's call for anonymity among the ranks, the gaps in our knowledge of one another being highlighted all too unfortunately around the fire.

Separate blazes had been built for burning the Wraith corpses, but of course, no one gathered for these fires. After I had pulled the stolen magic from their emaciated frames, there hadn't actually been much left of their *"bodies"* anyway. What had been left burned hot and fast, with far more gusto than the bodies of our fallen comrades.

No stranger to inspecting dead Wraiths, Ronan had struggled to hide his fascination with the unexpected pyrotechnics attached to their burning. Yet he too was soon sobered by the much slower burn emanating from the allied fires. It wouldn't be possible to return the bodies to the outside world; plus, the land likely wouldn't have allowed it even if we'd tried. Indeed, there was an unspoken pact that any bodies that fell here were to remain—payment for the role the ground itself had played in the outcome of the battle. Ronan and Lennie were already working on details for the missing-person reports, a plan they had clearly discussed previously, with Cassius's recent killing sprees unfortunately creating the perfect cover.

"There's not much else that can be done," Dom said, shrugging in clear resignation.

We had just observed the same family of Bearers I had witnessed only hours earlier, now with only two remaining, mourning the loss of a partner and parent as she burned in the great fire. I thought of Gertie and my mother and made a promise to myself that one of my most important missions ahead would be to find more of my "sisters of the moon."

"I wish I could have known her . . ." I said, watching the bereft family and feeling the unsurmountable weight of yet more lost kin.

Dom squeezed my hand tightly then, still unable to offer any sort of embrace, though he was already considerably more mobile than he had been even five or six hours earlier, thanks of course to Ronan's deft mind and hands. However, we would still need to transport him the three-kilometre distance between the castle ruins and Ronan's vehicle.

"Those bastards better not have torched my car," Ronan said as we attempted to get Dom up and walking.

"Hate to break it to you, Ronan, but they probably did," Lennie said in surprisingly good spirits, all things considered. I figured he was probably just glad to not have to haul Dom out from the beach all alone.

Dom had stubbornly insisted that he exit the space on his own two feet, and if it were anyone else, I would have argued the point. However, the idea of carrying Dom's dense muscular frame along the rocky path between worlds sounded like a whole new battle that I wasn't particularly interested in waging this morning. I didn't understand exactly why, but I had the feeling that I was supposed to be the last to leave and metaphorically shut off the lights. I had connected with the earth here in ways I scarcely could have imagined possible in any of my lifetimes, and I felt certain that it was my exit that would knit the magic back together.

Standing on the outskirts of the castle grounds, I raised my hands to the sky once more, but I was met only with bold silence. The moon had indeed gone to her resting place, and so for the time being, I would instead look towards the sun, who spoke serenely.

"Go forth in strength and leave this place behind."

Silent in farewell, I oriented now towards my own waking sun. I had been feeling guilty about not knowing more practical magic skills to aid in Dom's journey back to the car, but thankfully, Ronan still had a few clever tricks up his sleeve. About ten minutes before setting out, Dom had drunk a vial of something that smelled extremely familiar and herbal, and I realized it must have been given to me in the hotel in Leeds as well.

"Just a little booster to carry him through," Ronan had said.

Now, arms braced around Lennie and Ronan like some kind of six-legged race, the three men forged onward up the slope with surprisingly few hiccups, all things considered.

"Come on, you heavy *bastard!*" Ronan had shouted at one point as he was attempting to hoist Dom up a particularly steep embankment, to which Dom released a stream of what I again assumed were rigorous Irish expletives back in his direction. Lennie and I were unaware of what had actually been said; however, Ronan was laughing extremely hard by the end, obviously heartened by his friend's continued fighting spirit.

Because of his wounding, we obviously wouldn't be hopping onto the back of Dom's motorcycle for the ride home. Instead, we opted for a much more comfortable drive in the backseat of Ronan's sleek black Audi, which (thank the Goddess) had *not* been roasted. Much to Dom's consternation, Lennie would be riding his motorcycle back to the manor house for him.

"If you crash that thing, you'll have more to worry about than a bit road rash!" Dom said, only half-threateningly, to Lennie before the Brit climbed onto the collector bike.

"Aye, aye, captain," Lennie said.

"Yeah, Lennie, don't be *squid,*" I said, mocking Dom's concern more so than the actual reality of the matter. Dom had been far less obstinate than usual about the whole thing; Lennie was indeed a very experienced rider, and there was probably no one better suited within a hundred-mile radius to deliver the bike safely.

We had tucked in together in the back of Ronan's sedan. For his part, Ronan was giving us some much-needed privacy, listening to music up front. I was surprised at how quickly Dom was adapting to some of his newfound vulnerabilities in the aftermath of the battle.

"Julia?" he asked after we had been on the road for about an hour.

"Hmm?" I said, almost nodding off from the gentle rocking motion of the car.

He looked at me tentatively. "Sorry to bug you. It's just. Well, I think I'm not . . . I'm going to need time to get settled at home for a bit before we do anything else."

I smiled back at him and noticed that his eyes still bore the grief and exhaustion of a millennium of worry. I wondered silently if that would ever change, with the painful memories from our repeated existence his deepest wounds of all . . . and far from healed.

"Of course," I said, and squeezed his hand reassuringly. They were still *very* swollen and bruised, and he winced. "Shit, sorry!"

The rest of the drive was spent mostly in silence, give or take a few comments about the traffic. I was watching Dom intently for any signs of cracking or breaking down as we made our way towards the manor house, but he held fast. I could sense he was holding in a tidal wave of emotion but hoped for his sake that we would make it safely into a place of renewed fortitude before he had to battle those demons.

I was utterly blown away by the beauty of his smile upon our homecoming.

"Holy Jesus, it's good to be home!" he said with a slight stretch of his spine, giving my thigh a quick squeeze before gingerly hopping out, apparently to collect our luggage.

"Don't even *think* about it, Dom," Ronan said, and the two argued for several moments about whether or not Dom was up for the task. Dom at last conceded, allowing Ronan and I to carry the bags, and I laughed. It was nice to see things already returning to normal, or whatever our new normal might be.

We planned to spend several weeks on the vast estate where we would regroup, and Dom would hopefully relax enough to recover, and then close up the house for a time. As much as I wanted to rest lazily for days on end with Dom, watching movies and preparing scrumptious meals to share, the unfortunate truth was that we had a lot of work to do.

Cassius was obviously still alive somewhere, although according to Lennie, he had dropped completely off the grid without a trace. Dom and I both agreed that the safest place to get any quality rest would likely be back at Gertie's, and so we planned to arrive there in time for the summer solstice; Salt Spring Island would protect me with an extra layer of protective energy that not even the manor house could afford us.

Most importantly, I needed time to ponder the quilt. I felt certain that this was the new map to our destiny, if only I could learn how to interpret it. Its concealed magic was still seemingly just out of my reach. Cassius didn't seem to know about it yet, and I hoped this would give me a distinct advantage, for a time at least. I quietly wondered if my newfound connection to the womb of the earth, and to the Divine Feminine, would impart a clearer understanding of the mysterious fabric. However, I also had the sense that the kind of power I had accessed within myself on that fateful day wasn't exactly an everyday brand of magic.

Ronan would return to Vancouver soon, which gave both Dom and I great comfort. It felt wrong, after all we had been through, to be distanced from such an important friend during this next phase. The roles both he and

Lennie would play in the future of the cause were different from our own, but something changes between people when they stare into the face of death together; we were bonded for life.

The goodbyes (for now) had been swift. Watching the two of them depart down the manor drive, I wasn't surprised in the least by the hot, silent tears running down my cheeks. Dom, propped up carefully in the doorway, gently stroked my hair back behind my shoulders with one hand.

"They'll be alright," he said kindly. "And I'm sure we won't be able to keep Ronan from visiting us at the cottage before the end of the summer. He has a bit of a knack for showing up when you least expect him to."

"I hope so," I said, sniffling.

Alone at last at *Caisleán na Spéirmhná,* I was again staggered by the immense size of the place. With all of our companions gone to their separate corners of the world to refresh themselves and prepare for the next stages of our plans, whatever they might be, it felt slightly eerie not to hear their voices echoing down the halls or see them gathered together in the warmth of the kitchen.

Morgan had restocked the pantry for the duration of our stay, after which he would resume his role of estate keeper until our next return. It had been agreed that, once healed, it would be beneficial for Thomas to foster the dogs for the time being, at least until Dom and I unravelled into a more settled rhythm of life. It wasn't lost on either of us how new and unsure our footing would be for the next while, and the dogs deserved steady companionship. Plus, they adored Thomas.

Exhausted beyond what I even knew to be possible, each night since our homecoming we had collapsed into the luxurious four-poster without more than a few mumbles, giving in groggily to the delicious lure of sleep.

Our first night alone with just the two of us had been no exception. When I awoke, my muscles felt taught and stubborn, stiff, no doubt, from the dreamless, heavy sleep that had overcome me several hours earlier. It had been that way since we returned from the battle—dreamless, dense, and blank—but I wasn't about to complain over settled sleep. I also knew intuitively that it wouldn't last.

With some effort, I rolled onto my back and reached out blindly for Dom. But he wasn't there. Instead, I felt the soft familiar curls of Sully, the Wheaten

Terrier, who had silently migrated from the foot of the bed and curled into a ball atop Dom's pillow. Mags was draped luxuriously at the foot of the bed, her weight trapping my feet under the covers, patently uninterested in play. Noticing that I was finally awake, Sully's tail wagged in utter exuberance, a stark contrast to his body, which would remain perfectly still, waiting, until I acknowledged him. I reached out to scratch him behind the ears, and at once, he began to wiggle all over, batting my hand down with a curly-haired paw and then mouthing my arm softly with his teeth. *Terriers.*

The speed of Dom's recovery had been truly astounding, though perhaps not, considering that he was also incredibly tough and rather hyperactive. He had enjoyed my doting care over the first few days, a bit of a role reversal from only a month past, but soon he was positively antsy to get moving, blatantly ignoring Ronan's recommendation for further rest.

"You should take a few more days at least . . . let your bruises fade," I had said, shaking my head at him as he'd hoisted himself up from bed several mornings previous, proceeding to dress himself with very little help from me.

He had smiled sweetly in reply, adding, "Oh, don't worry too much about me." Then he had slowly descended the steps towards the kitchen in search of breakfast.

And so, today, while I hadn't expected Dom to stick around lounging in bed with me for the better part of the day, I was still disappointed to find him gone from my side so soon. He was anxious to set his affairs in order before we set off for Canada. I knew it would likely take him *weeks* to unwind following the battle, not to mention adjust his mindset around the fact that his life was now moving into a completely new phase altogether.

I sunk down deeper into my pillow, collecting my scattered thoughts on the matter at hand. Moving forward, we would be walking blind unless I figured out the cryptic nature of the quilt, or at least how to decipher whatever messages I had left behind for myself.

I felt a sudden and deep despair about how much I truly *didn't* know about my own magic, a fact made painfully clear during the battle. However, my fire continued to burn on confidently in spite of this; in truth, I had never experienced such a consistent hum of magic through me as I had since the fight on the beach. I took this to be a positive sign. I also reminded myself to have Dom teach me how to use a sword.

I was soon broken from my reveries by a low growl followed by a high bark from a certain fuzzy companion beside me.

"Oh! Do you want to play?" I said and began a little game of what I had dubbed, "Rats Under the Blanket." Much to Dom's amusement, the game had so far consisted of Sully hunting and jumping at my hands under the covers, with lots of petting and scratches mixed in for good measure. Evidently, the happy dog still remembered the game from before, and was egging me on to play now, rather heartily. Maggie took a long stretch and rolled onto her other side, preferring to get some more sleep.

Invisible rats fully accounted for and thoroughly dispatched, I gave Sul a good scratch behind his ear before sliding out of the protective warmth of the bed. I was craving both a strong cup of tea and Dom's steady company. The latter I assumed could be remedied by a visit to his study, where he would likely be fussing over some plan or another.

I stretched tall, body protesting significantly and my mouth dry as sandpaper. *Tea first, then Dom.*

I could almost smell the steeped flowery tips of the broken orange pekoe tea Peggy had left behind in the kitchen. She had assured me this was the best grade for both drinking and the reading of the leaves. I was still such a novice, and arguably a skeptic, around tea-leaf divination, so I just took her word for it.

The house was cool, despite the growing summer heat outside. I padded quietly into the familiar kitchen, Sully and Mags wagging along at my heels. I was unsure where the great wolfhound was but assumed he was at Dom's side once more, reunited at last after yet another great battle. I felt certain that, if Dom would have had it his way, Oisín would have joined him on the rocky beach, dutifully protecting his master's left flank.

Rinsing out the chipped porcelain teapot in the familiar sink, I listened intently for any signs of movement throughout the house but was met only with silence. Reaching out with my senses, however, I noticed that the intense magical noise of the place still remained quite intact. While I was grateful to have the space alone with Dom, I could feel the charged energy emanating from the study even from where I stood in the kitchen. It was something I would have to confront at last.

Taking on one thing at a time, I quickly made myself some tea and buttered toast. It was a hastily cobbled-together snack, but I felt certain it would do the trick, keeping me from attempting the transition into the magic-rich space on an empty stomach.

As predicted, I found Dom sitting in his study, Oisín curled lazily by the unlit hearth. And to my surprise, I immediately noticed that the space bore less of the tumultuous portent energy than usual. Dom had done some redecorating.

Not yet noticing my presence, I watched peacefully as he brushed his hair back from his eyes while busily pouring over some old maps. Ever the strategist, he was clearly already considering our next moves; I felt tired just thinking about it.

"Knock, knock," I said somewhat tentatively and carefully carried the unbalanced tray into the sunken stone-walled room.

He raised his head to meet my gaze with a familiar sweet intensity, and I felt the familiar weakness behind my knees.

"I brought you some toast," I said. The fact there was tea was a given.

He pushed his maps aside and skirted around his desk to join me on the plush couch. His hair was tousled, giving him a look of casual elegance that I couldn't have achieved in a thousand years. Perhaps that was precisely how he had done it: *many* years of practice.

"Thanks, love, I was just thinking about breakfast."

The empty plate on the side of his desk indicated that this was, in fact, actually his second breakfast.

"You've changed a few things around," I said, gesturing around the room with my half-eaten piece of toast.

The look on his face was innocent. "I did. I didn't think you needed all the reminders in here anymore. And neither did I, to be honest," he said, matter-of-factly.

I smiled warmly and shoved the rest of my toast into my mouth.

Dom proceeded to devour several slices himself, followed by a large cup of tea, before settling back onto the couch, contentment spreading across his brow. I eyed the maps across his desk, feeling conflicted about his peaceful demeanour, which stood now in stark contrast to what seemed to be a much more intensely focused project.

"What were you working on?" I asked.

"Oh those?" he said, pushing himself up onto his hands slightly to look back over his shoulder towards the desk. With his impressive physical form stretched before me, my intentions of getting a handle on where he was at, or what would come next, began to melt away.

"I thought I would track all of the places we have ever been together and mark them for you on a map. I thought it might help jog your memory about the quilt. You said you thought that the different scraps were from different regions."

"Oh wow! That's incredibly helpful, actually. Thank you."

It *was* a really good idea, but I wasn't sure it was something that needed to be completed immediately. Suddenly, I desperately wanted to be close to him, unhindered by worry for just a few moments.

"It's somewhere to start, anyways. I know things are going to be different now, but—"

I cut him off with a forceful kiss. I was *so* bloody tired of talking.

"Oh, you woke up in a spritely mood this morning," he said, pulling away momentarily, but it wasn't in protest.

I hopped onto his lap and took his beautiful face my hands. "I just love you."

"I *just* love you too," he said, chuckling merrily.

We decided not to spend our morning talking, after all.

CHAPTER 42

"D om?" I asked as the cabin lights dimmed in the small tin-can of a plane, a significant contrast to our overseas flights between Ireland and Vancouver. The propellers had roared into action only a few minutes earlier, with the rattle and hum of the small vessel's interior making me slightly nervous for take-off.

"Yeah?"

His hands were relaxed on his lap, fiddling with a small, rolled-up piece of paper from a gum wrapper. As always, I was drawn in by the juxtaposition between their elegance and sheer magnitude.

"Have you ever tried a Nanaimo bar?"

He grinned. "I haven't, no. Are they any good?"

"Pretty sweet, but you obviously need to try one. When in Rome and all that," I said.

"When in Nanaimo!" he said, fumbling with the pronunciation of the word.

It felt so wonderful to be light-hearted with him, and I leaned my head comfortably onto his shoulder, relishing the peace. As always, it was a jarringly quick flight from Vancouver, on the mainland, to Nanaimo, located on the east coast of Vancouver Island, not far from Salt Spring. The quick ascent and descent wreaked havoc on my eardrums, but otherwise, we arrived unscathed.

Dom insisted we rent a car for the next several weeks, cost be damned. My truck had been sitting at the cottage, unlicensed and exposed to the elements, for the better part of six months, and I hazarded a guess that it wouldn't be keen on starting. I wished we could travel for a time, hiking and exploring corners of the earth yet unknown to either of us, but we both felt an increasing urgency to return to Salt Spring, especially with tonight being the summer solstice.

Before long, we were in the rental car, waiting in a short ferry line up, which would ultimately connect the final leg of our journey, this time between Vancouver Island and the northwest side of Salt Spring Island. The scent of a nearby pulp mill filled our nostrils, its stench somewhere between the smell of an outhouse and the breath of a hard liquor drinker in the morning.

"Well, that's a smell I won't soon forget," Dom said, scrunching his nose in the passenger seat as the ferry took off.

I laughed. "You get used to it."

It felt incredible to return at long last, and I was suddenly overwhelmed by a feeling of homecoming within my own body. Soon tears were pouring down my face, in gratitude for both the place itself and for the rooted caretakers who stood in bold stewardship over such a spectacular place. Protected and cherished. Home.

There really *was* magic here, wild, free, and earthen. Feminine and womblike, she was a fluid island, yet strong. No doubt there was a reason why Gertie had chosen to stay here all those years ago, and I too felt a draw towards the natural envelopment of the place. Perhaps it was the protective magic she and I had subconsciously woven throughout the years at the cottage. But it felt like there was also something greater at work here, which couldn't possibly be described in simple terms, far beyond anything we had contributed.

"You're glad to be home," Dom said, and I was reminded exactly of our conversation when he had first brought me home to his *castle* in Ireland.

"As long as I'm with you, I'm home," I said, reaching out and squeezing his hand.

Having disembarked from the ferry, we wound our way northeast and quickly broached the more familiar side roads, the very ones we had traversed together so happily back in December. Unsurprisingly, it felt like a lifetime ago, discovering each other once more, but the feeling now bore a remarkable similarity; there was so much unknown ahead, more than ever, in fact. But thankfully, we were surer than ever of our love for one another.

"Hey, Dom?"

"Hmm?" he replied serenely.

"How do you feel about maybe growing a veggie garden? We're a bit late, but we could still get a good harvest!" I said, surprised at how happy the notion made me.

"I think that's a wonderful idea."

I thought then of the quilt hidden in the trunk, tucked away safely and waiting patiently for me to unpack whatever I had somehow hidden within it for myself. We had come full circle now, and at last my intuition told me that it was time. My heart beat excitedly then, and for the first time in many years, I felt legitimately motivated towards a challenge.

Approaching the cottage with our windows open, the air in the car filled with the smell of smoke. However, it was not the soothing and familiar scents of woodstoves and campfires; this was unhealthy smoke, like something was burning that shouldn't be.

Slowing down in caution, we passed in front of Bill's place. It looked empty but for his truck, which was parked in the driveway, door ajar and running lights on. It was facing outward towards the road, which was very unusual.

Turning up the gravel drive to the cottage at last, we understood why.

Gertie's cottage stood fully engulphed in a terrible inferno. Firetrucks had recently arrived, crews attempting to quell the destructive, lapping tendrils of magically charged flame . . . to no avail. The cottage was lost.

Everything seemed to happen in slow motion.

Throwing the rental car into park, I staggered from the driver's seat towards the blaze.

"Stand back!" an authoritative voice called out from nowhere. I saw Bill somewhere in my periphery, but it didn't matter. Nothing mattered.

I felt strong arms wrap around me from behind; Dom's no doubt. We collapsed in a heap onto the earth, watching in shock as my homeplace burned to the ground. This was an all-too-familiar scene from far too long ago, and I was suddenly terrified that I, too, might disappear.

"Don't you dare leave me," Dom spoke into my ear, voice heavy with his own terror as he held me impossibly tight, anchoring me with all his will to this place and time.

Whether by his doing or my own, I stayed firmly in the *now*.

There was no doubt in either of our mind's whose work this was; Cassius had left us a clear message for what we had done, impeccably timed on the summer solstice after all.

He was alive, and he was watching.

The room was clean, but for the crumpled heap of stained, wrinkled cotton and cheap brown khaki fabric scattered disgustingly at his feet. Well, there was also the body inhabiting those clothes.

Desmond was dead; he had discovered too much.

Against his better judgement, Cassius had resisted sending his best Indovino to the battle, erring on the side of caution to keep him close, just in case. This, of course, had been a mistake. The pitiful creature would have surely died there at the hands of the World Ruler and his allied forces, his filthy exit from this life on their hands instead of his own, relieving him of the odorous task. It also would have made leaving England considerably easier.

On the eve of battle, Desmond had come to him with concerns over a recurring vision he was allegedly being plagued with, involving some great power growing *within* the Witch. He had even foolishly gone above his station and suggested that Cassius attend the battle in person so as to secure her capture himself.

"I . . . keep seeing *her*. Stepping off a precipice, but she doesn't fall . . ."

He had glared at Desmond then, falsely assuming that the man was attempting to thwart his plans, or worse, that he knew more than he was letting on about his current situation.

Unbeknownst to his legions of Wraiths, he was no longer strong enough to act in battle. That much had been made painfully clear through the weeks of insatiable hunger leading up to this day, with absolutely no respite to be found from the vast, screaming hollowness within.

He needed *the child*.

And if there was indeed a power growing within the Witch, that must be what it was. His intelligence had discovered a positive pregnancy report faxed to her family doctor. Whether this was accurate or not, she and the Celt seemed inexplicably destined to procreate. After all, the Prophecy demanded it. So, Cassius had stuck with his original plan to send his best generals in to collect her and kill the rest. She had shown no sign of magic upon her capture several weeks earlier, and so the threat was arguably minimal. They would certainly lose many of their ranks in the action, but they were meaningless in comparison to the immortality he sought.

They loved using her as bait, and he welcomed it hungrily.

Standing above Desmond's lifeless form now, he knew that he had indeed been telling the truth all along. *None* of his Wraiths had survived the day, and he had been left with only Desmond's recent and shattered retelling to guide him forward.

"It . . . came true. What I saw. She . . . unleashed . . . *something* . . ." he had said, eyes wide in something that far too closely resembled awe. It was a shame to have to dispatch such a useful servant, but he couldn't have anyone in his league knowing about the Witch's growing strength.

Cassius forced his spear into Desmond, taking any and all stolen magic he might have tucked away inside. He had suspected that the Indovino was siphoning magic for himself through the Soothsaying process, and this confirmed it. The second-hand magic was meagre compared to a Bearer's delicious elixir, but it would hold him over until he could find something stronger. Indeed, what he required now was something far more concentrated than anything he had yet been able to acquire in his long life. He would have to descend into darkness for a time, operating in his most fragile form as he searched for a cure to his mortality.

Had he gone to the battle, he would have surely perished. Now, however, with all of them unchained from the Prophecy, he had been given a distinctly unique opportunity to change his own course. But first, he would leave the Witch and the World Ruler with a parting gift on the eve of the Solstice, as a reminder of what would be at stake upon his return.

He picked up his phone. "Caleb? Yes. I need you to do something for me."

Arrangements made, he hastily cleaned his blades, leaving considerable traces of Desmond's dark blood on the metal before tucking it into the inner recesses of his coat, and stole into the night.

ACKNOWLEDGEMENTS

Thank you to my dear friends and first readers for tolerating this writer's fragmented thoughts and trusting my capacity to pull all the threads together when the timing was right.

Margot, you are the only person in the world I can imagine staying up until three in the morning to read chapters with—thank you for loving Julia and Dom as much as I do. Alecia, Rebecca, and Dalyce, I am eternally grateful for your continued counsel and spiritual guidance throughout. Thanks to Kathleen and James for your help with the details, and to Francine for getting your hands in there for the finishing touches. To Kristy, Becky, Shoshone, and so many other powerful women in my realm, thank you for the individual parts you played in nudging me back towards the lost wells.

My deepest gratitude is to Scott, who so tirelessly journeyed with me (sometimes through rough waters), witnessing my efforts as I practically built the boat around me while pushing off from shore. Your unwavering confidence in my ability to bring this story to life has meant the world; thank you for always believing me (and it) to be seaworthy, even in times when I did not. I'm so sorry for making you re-read the book so many times—even though it *did* fit the theme of repeated life cycles.

Thank you to my sons who tolerated my dominion over our kitchen table, with laptop and books spread out for the better part of a year and a half. Also, for joining me on what must have felt like endless car rides while I worked out new ideas—at least there were (almost) always French fries to be had!

A special thank you to Britt Low who brought my dream cover(s) to life; to Ashley Marston and Matt Gladman who took my crazy idea and ran with it; and Danielle Cunningham and Alex Rakic for jumping in bravely with two feet at the end.

Thank you to Liza Weppenaar, Carly Cumpstone, and everyone else at FriesenPress for your trusted guidance, and without whom this book wouldn't be book shape. And to my dedicated editors, Janet Layberry and Ashley Lee, for handling my book baby with such care.

Lastly, I wish to express my gratitude to my ancestors for their individual voyages, and each of the stories they wove. For without those, I wouldn't have discovered my own path amongst the wilderness.

Author KATE GATELEY holds a B.A. in Linguistics and a B.Sc. in Physiology from the University of Saskatchewan. Her continued areas of personal study include history, Celtic ideology, ancestral memory (and its impact on generational wounding), and the re-emergence of "The Divine Feminine," all of which are significant influences on her writing perspective.

A lifelong fan of this genre, she has always wanted to add another story to its ranks—one with both depth and meaning. After carrying this one around with her for most of her life, when Kate sat down to actually put it all on paper, she relished the way her characters emerged so eagerly onto the page, almost seeming to come alive and dictate exactly what they wanted to say and do next.

Kate currently lives on a small farm in the Cowichan Valley, on beautiful Vancouver Island, with her wonderful husband and two sons, an adorable dog, a few outdoor cats, a number of chickens, and countless bees.

Look for books two and three of the *Lost Wells Trilogy* . . . coming soon.